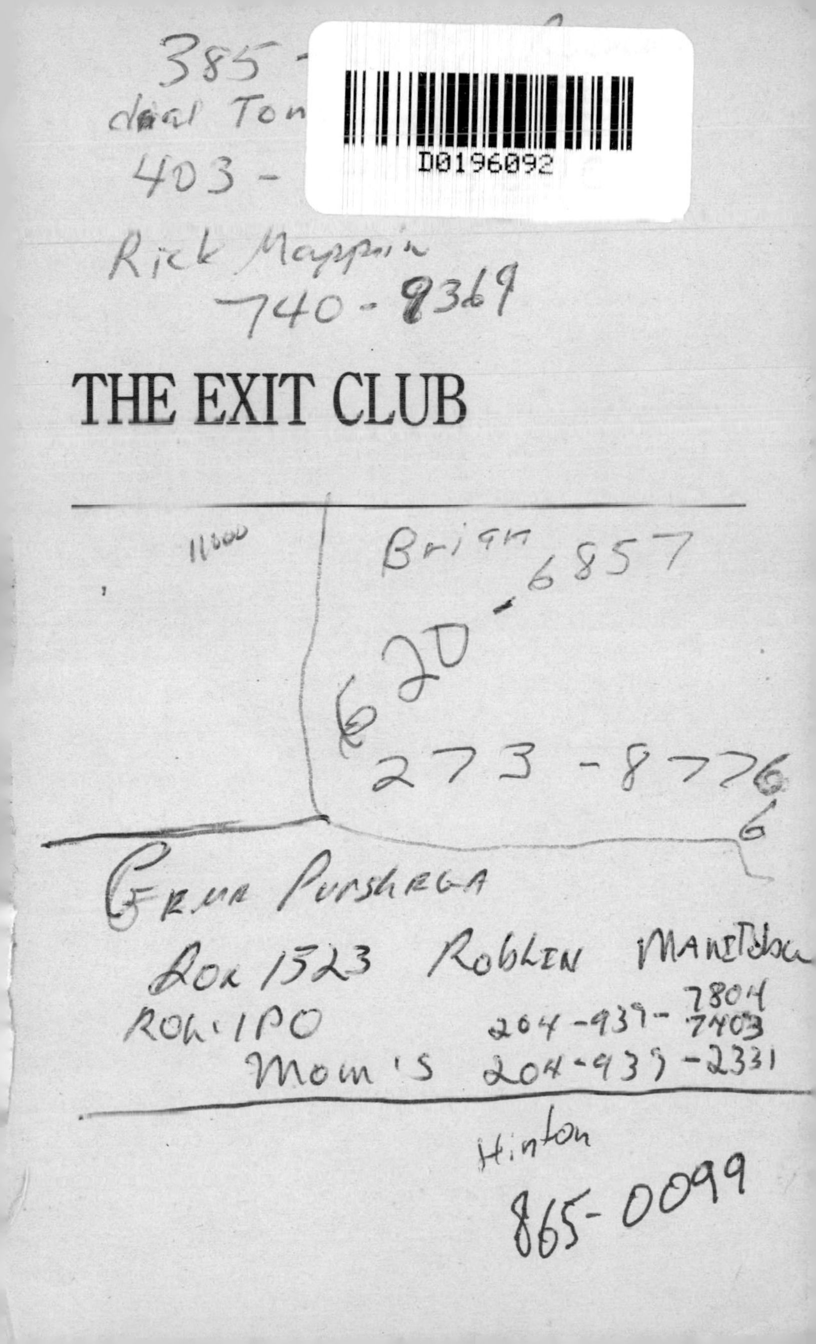

THE EXIT CLUB

THE EXIT CLUB

The Ultimate Novel of the SAS

Shaun Clarke

LONDON · SYDNEY · NEW YORK · TOKYO · SINGAPORE · TORONTO

First published in Great Britain by Simon & Schuster Ltd, 1996
A Viacom Company

Simon & Schuster Ltd
West Garden Place
Kendal Street
London W2 2AQ

Simon & Schuster of Australia Pty Ltd
Sydney

A CIP catalogue record for this book is available from the British Library

ISBN 0-671-85478-X

Typeset in Century Old Style 10/11pt by
Palimpsest Book Production Limited, Polmont, Stirlingshire
Printed and bound in Great Britain by
Caledonian International Book Manufacturing, Glasgow

For David & Beryl Pugh

We are the Pilgrims, master; we shall go
Always a little further; it may be
Beyond that last blue mountain barred with snow
Across that angry or that glimmering sea . . .

from *Hassan* by James Elroy Flecker

BOOK ONE

THE ORIGINALS

31 JANUARY 1991

The Browning nine-millimetre High Power handgun was resting on the table, well oiled and polished, gleaming in the pearly grey light of the early morning. Gazing down upon it, the old man was filled with memories, other times, other places: the sun blazing over the deserts of North Africa; the dark, steaming jungles of Malaya and Borneo; the parched mountains of Oman; the mean streets of Republican Belfast; the frozen seas and rocks of the Falkland Islands; even the Iranian Embassy in London. The well-used weapon on the table reminded him of all that – and of what it was he now had to do, whether or not he liked it.

He was a very old man but looked younger than he felt. Though his face was lined by age and the heat of tropical suns, concealing all manner of horrors and unspeakable brutality, it was surprisingly unscarred and imbued with integrity. Though time had taken its toll, withering once healthy skin, his green eyes remained uncommonly bright and his shoulders were straight.

Sighing, he picked up the weapon, ensured that the fourteen round box magazine was securely in place, checked that the safety catch was on, then slipped it into the badly tattered Len Dixon holster that was positioned slightly to the rear of his waist in the cross-draw position. He then buttoned up the jacket of his pinstripe suit and turned away from the table, instinctively glancing around the lounge of his apartment for what would be the last time.

It was a rectangular room with magnolia-painted walls and french windows overlooking a lush garden in Highgate, North London. The furniture, though contemporary, had been chosen with great care to match the Georgian elegance of the room and give it a countrified appearance. Some silver-framed photographs, browning slightly with age, were propped up on the Welsh dresser near the doorway to the kitchen – family pictures obviously taken before World War Two – but the walls were virtually covered with other photos that covered his life to the present day. It had been an eventful life.

Studying the photos, he saw himself as an impossibly skinny student at Cambridge; then as a nervous young man in a dark suit, arm in arm with an attractive brunette in a white wedding dress. There he was, too, as a broadly grinning subaltern in a British Army uniform, posing with folded arms in front of a Nissen hut somewhere in England. The same young man, now an unshaven lieutenant, wearing a black woollen *agal*, Arab *shemagh*, army shorts and sandals, but with a winged-dagger badge on the shirt, seated in a jeep armed with twin Vickers K machine-guns. Clean-shaven again, though still a lieutenant, shaking hands with an L Detachment trooper (*You looked so young then, Marty*) against a backdrop of British Matilda tanks and featureless desert. Then photographed beaming joyfully outside the walls of Colditz Castle at the end of the war. The really good times had ended then.

(*Why, Marty? Why?*)

Drawn to the photographs, knowing that he was seeing them for the last time, the old man walked closer to them and let his disappointed gaze roam over the years as he watched himself ageing. There he was, back in uniform, this time as a captain in jungle greens, with a machete on his waist and a Bergen rucksack on his back, posing with an Owen submachine-gun beside a tent in a base camp in Malaya in 1957.

Another wedding, not his own. A young man, impishly grinning, embracing a radiantly beautiful, shyly smiling

Anglo-Chinese girl in the days when neither of them could possibly have imagined what would happen to them.

(*Moldering bones in the graveyard of your broken heart. You never recovered from that death.*)

That other young man again, now a sergeant in a woollen hat and Denison smock, with an L4A4 Light Machine Gun strapped across his body, smiling cockily at the camera in the blazing sunlight of the Jebel Akhdar in Oman in 1958.

(*You should have stayed that way, Marty.*)

Virtually the same uniform, but slightly older, a sergeant in the Radfan, no longer smiling. Next, in another photograph, tinted and dressed up to pass as an Arab in the crowded *souks* of Aden. Finally, back in Oman as a sergeant-major with more flesh on his bones, his best years behind him.

(*That was the start of it, Marty: the loss of your youth. That and your growing disillusionment. The rot set in then.*)

More photographs. A large leap across the years. Himself in a pinstripe suit and tie, well fed and prosperous, standing with his hand on Marty's shoulder, the latter not so prosperous, though also well fed, wearing a plain grey suit and rollneck pullover, both at a reunion of the 'Originals' in Bradbury Lines, Hereford. Then Marty and Taff Hughes – the latter blond-haired, blue-eyed, quiet and deadly – at a meeting of the Association in London just a few years ago.

(*Why, Marty? Why? At last I think I know. So now I'll put an end to it. It all ends today, old friend.*)

Nodding, as if speaking to himself, the old man took his final glance around the lounge, reconciling himself to the fact that he would never see it again; then he picked up his morning newspaper and walked out, leaving the apartment by the front door. After locking the door, he dropped the key through the letterbox, then took the elevator down to the ground floor and walked out to the parking space at the back, where the garages were shadowed by the overhanging trees of Highgate Wood.

Parked in his garage was a gleaming Mercedes Benz, which had been rented for this very important day. He opened the front door and placed his newspaper beside the driver's seat. At the back of the garage, he unlocked the toolbox and withdrew a rectangular block of wood fixed to a torpedo-shaped package wrapped in black plastic. Electric wires dangled from it.

It was a simple home-made bomb consisting of Semtex plastic explosive, an electric initiator and a blasting cap with bridge wire.

Resting the bomb on an upturned orange-crate, the old man spread an oil-smeared bedsheet on the ground, dropped to his knees beside it, then carefully fixed the bomb to the underside of the car by attaching the wooden block to clamps put in place the previous evening. Groping blindly with his hand, he found the end of the detonating cord, also inserted the previous evening, running up through the engine and into the glove compartment in the dashboard, where it had been wired to a 'button job' – a remote-control firing device.

When the end of the detonating cord had been connected to the bomb, the old man stood up, took a deep breath and exhaled as he slipped into the driver's seat. Without further ado, he drove the car out of the garage and turned into the road leading to Hampstead.

Once past the customary traffic jam at the Spaniard's Inn, he drove through Hampstead Village, down to Swiss Cottage and then into the rich environs of St John's Wood. He parked the car halfway along one of those leafy streets, near an elegant mansion house that had spy cameras overlooking the dark-suited security guards in its grounds. The driveway contained four gleaming limousines with tinted-glass windows, but, as the old man was parked in a gleaming Mercedes Benz, his presence in the road would not be viewed by the guards as suspicious.

He studied the house carefully, checked his wristwatch, then opened his newspaper and carefully read the front-page feature. Dated 14 January 1991, it was a report of a recent series of mysterious, bizarre 'suicides' of scientists working on highly secret projects.

In fact, as the old man knew full well, all those men had been murdered.

He was, however, particularly interested in the case of a 'signals expert and part-time SAS man' who had died when his BMW went over a cliff in Cornwall shortly after he had taken two men on a fishing trip. According to the man's wife, he had not planned to go fishing, but had been collected by the two men, both of whom were unknown to her. Those two men had not been found at the scene of the accident or suicide.

Another murder. The old man was convinced. They're well beyond the pale now, he thought.

Clipped to the article was another, smaller clipping from a different newspaper, detailing the British government's embarrassment over widespread revelations that it had been using the SAS to train the notorious Khmer Rouge in Cambodia. This training, as the old man knew, had been successfully hidden for a time behind Whitehall's shield of 'total deniability'. Whitehall used that a lot.

Shaking his head in disgust, or possibly despair, the old man put the newspaper down, then slid his right hand around his waist, automatically checking that his Browning nine-millimetre High Power handgun was still in the cross-draw position in its Len Dixon holster. Satisfied, he gazed across the road, studying the front door of the guarded mansion house, realising with grim amusement that the Browning High Power, the Nine-Milly, was the most appropriate weapon to use for this particular job – for more reasons than one.

(*A double tap. It used to be two bullets straight to the heart, but now it's thirteen shots in quick succession. That'll surely be plenty.*)

He then brooded on the fact that he was about to assassinate one of the finest men he had ever known.

That man was his best friend.

CHAPTER ONE

'The Land of the Four S's,' Private Martin ('Marty') Butler, 9th Rifle Brigade, exclaimed as he stepped out of his tent in the Almazur camp, glanced briefly at the desert, then gazed at the lights of nocturnal Cairo, visible beyond the shivering palm trees. Even from here he could discern the sound of distant Arab music borne on the evening breeze, ethereal, exotic, a siren call to his ears, as he inhaled the rich, seductive aroma of jasmine and jackala trees. 'Sun, Sand, Sin and Syphilis!'

'So speaks the newly married man,' his friend, Private Anthony ('Tone') Williams, responded. Tall and rake-thin, his face pock-marked with acne, he was standing beside Marty and gazing out over the star-covered desert with disbelieving, virgin eyes. 'Glad to be back, are you? So soon after your honeymoon and all.'

Reminded by that sardonic remark that he was now a married man and should not be harbouring sinful thoughts, Marty blushed and hid behind jocularity, his standard defence.

'Don't come it with me, sunshine,' he said, grinning and lighting a Player's cigarette, his hands cupped against the wind. 'I'm not saying I didn't enjoy my night of bliss – more than *you're* likely to get! I'm just saying that once you've been here you can never forget it.'

Nevertheless, he felt slightly guilty at the realisation that, though married only four weeks ago, he was undeniably pleased to be back in Egypt.

'It's nothing to do with my missus,' he tried explaining to Tone, breathing in the humid air of the desert. 'It's just that I love being here. I mean, how often do blokes like you and me get to come to a place like this?'

'Not often,' Tone replied affably, blinking dark eyes under jet-black hair. 'But don't try telling that to your missus. I don't think she'd wear it.'

'No, she wouldn't,' Marty agreed. We only had one night for our honeymoon, he thought, and even that wasn't too good.

'Known her long?' Tone asked.

'Off and on since schooldays,' Marty told him, suddenly seeing Lesley's face in his mind and filling up with troubled affection for her. 'We went to the same school in Crouch End.'

'North London.'

'Right. Where I was born.'

'Childhood sweethearts,' Tone said.

'Not really,' Marty replied, clearly recalling the day he had first seen Lesley in the school yard and instantly been stricken by her short-cropped auburn hair, large brown eyes and milky-white, matchstick legs. They had both been thirteen at the time and neither had much to say. 'I always carried a torch for her, but she was sort of middle-class: her dad an accountant, her mum prominent in local church activities, both Tories. My dad, on the other hand, was a local builder with his own construction business and he and my mum both liked to have a good time and didn't care a bugger who knew it. Good people, both, but working-class, which is what Lesley saw me as.'

'Common muck,' Tone said.

'Not quite muck, but common.'

'So how did you get together?'

'Not until after leaving school. We both left at fourteen and went our separate ways, but we met up again a few years later when I was working in my dad's construction business and I went to a Mecca dance hall with some mates and found her there with some girlfriends.' And looking a lot different, he thought, from what she'd been at school. Romantic brown eyes, lips filled out to become luscious, and a figure that is, though slight, almost perfectly formed. I should appreciate that. 'We danced a few times, trying not to touch bellies, then I asked her out and she agreed. That was the start of it.'

'You got engaged.'

'Right. The day I was called up.'

'A *lot* of blokes got engaged when they were called up,' Tone reminded him, gazing at that city of military tents stretched across the barren floor of the desert under a velvet, star-studded sky, illuminated by the light of a great moon. 'That's a fact of life, mate.'

'It sure is,' Marty said. *Only twenty and I'm married already. I should have my bleedin' head examined. Though I love her . . . I'm sure I do.*

He and Lesley had both just turned eighteen when the war began. By then, Marty was working in his father's construction business, learning the practical side of building before going on to become an architectural draughtsman. His parents were known in the locality as a mutually supportive couple whose strong socialist principles were combined with great generosity when it came to entertaining family and friends, which they did a lot. Marty, who loved both of them and took his radical streak from them, had a reputation as a good-natured young man whose restless energy and impulsiveness often landed him in hot water, usually with the local constabulary, invariably for some minor form of drunken mischief. Lesley, on the other hand, had blossomed into a quietly attractive young woman with a steadfast personality and a reticence picked up from her conservative parents. So it was no accident that, when she and Marty met up again, what they felt was the attraction of opposites. Now, in the starlit desert outside Cairo, Marty understood that much.

'Being married is one thing,' he said, 'but being in the Army is another. I love my missus, but being here is something else and she wouldn't understand that. You know what I mean, Tone?'

'I think so,' Tone replied.

'I mean, I know I'm only a conscript,' Marty said, 'but I

feel like a regular soldier, that I *belong* in the Army, that I've found a way of life that suits me a lot more than my work in my dad's construction business. I've felt that from day one.'

This was true. Excited by his rookie training, which had driven others to despair, he had been thrilled beyond measure when posted to the 9th Rifle Brigade and sent in February 1941 to take part in the defence of Tobruk in North Africa. After briefly enjoying the fleshpots of Cairo, he had been transferred to the Allied camp just outside Mersa Brega, in the vast Western Desert of Cyrenaica, and was still there, albeit briefly, when General Rommel's Afrika Korps relentlessly pushed the Allies back to the sea and surrounded Tobruk. In the middle of that violent, spectacular battle, he was concussed by the explosion of a shell from the German big guns and flown back via Alexandria to an army hospital in Anglia. There, as he recuperated, he realised that he wanted to go back to Egypt and rejoin the fight. The realisation startled him.

Discharged from the hospital and given two weeks' leave, he returned to north London, married Lesley (a proper church wedding in Crouch End, attended by both families, one high Tory, the other Labour, each uneasy with the other) and compensated for the lack of a proper honeymoon by booking them into a room in the Savoy hotel. It was a typically extravagant gesture that both thrilled and appalled Lesley, though clearly she was more unnerved than delighted by it, chastising him for the gross waste of money that could, she said, have been better spent setting up home. The following morning, after they had nervously, not too successfully, consummated the marriage to the sound of wailing air-raid sirens, rumbling German aircraft, exploding bombs and chattering ack-ack guns, they had bid each other an emotional farewell at the troop train bound for Liverpool. From there the hundreds of conscript soldiers had been shipped out to Egypt.

After weeks aboard ship, cooped up in the sweltering, stinking hold with its tightly packed tier berths, allowed up on deck only intermittently to breathe the fresh air, moans and groans every night, the smell of spent sperm in the nostrils, fist fights to ease frustration, it had been a great relief when the ships finally arrived at Port Said. Dressed in badly fitting khaki drill that had not been washed since they boarded ship, sweating in the ferocious heat, heavily burdened with their kitbags, Marty and the rest of the regiment had virtually staggered down the gangplank of the ship to spread out and sit, facing the cooling breeze of the sea, on the grass of the Canal Company building, guarded by coal-black Sudanese wearing old-fashioned naval uniforms, with straw hats and blue trousers. After an interminable wait in the baking sun, all the time besieged relentlessly by Arab hawkers, beggars, hideously deformed cripples and children of remarkable beauty, they had been herded onto a convoy of three-ton trucks and driven along the coast road, on the start of the journey to Cairo. The route had taken them through an exotic landscape of domes, minarets, mud huts and palm trees, past white-robed *fellaheen* on donkeys, strings of camels led by Arab traders wearing colourful djellabas, and feluccas sailing along the glittering Nile with sails billowing spectacularly from their forty-foot masts. At the village of Kantara a ferry herded the trucks of the convoy across to the Palestine Railway Station and from there, in the early hours of the morning, they drove on to the army camp at Almazur.

So here he was, back in North Africa, newly married but determined to have a good time in Cairo before being sent on to his unit.

It's all a matter of luck, he thought.

'So how do we get to Cairo?' Tone asked, obviously keen to get going.

'That way,' Marty replied, pointing at the dusty, battered taxis lined up along the Cairo road at the edge of the great sea of tents, their Arab drivers gesticulating frantically at the many soldiers either walking towards them or crouched around open fires, brewing tea under the brilliant stars, shadowed by overhanging palms faintly limned by moonlight. 'Follow me, mate.'

Feeling cool in his khaki shorts, shirt and sandals, still smoking his cigarette, he confidently led Tone over to the line of taxis, where he engaged a lean, gap-toothed Arab driver in an excited discussion about the number of piastres required to take them to Cairo. When the sum was agreed upon the beaming driver, dressed in a comfortable, striped djellaba, opened the rear door of his dilapidated vehicle and ushered them inside with a grandiloquent bow and sweep of his right hand. He then slammed the door shut, took his place behind the wheel, and was soon racing along the Cairo road, between the camp and the open desert, the wheels churning up billowing clouds of sand in the vehicle's wake.

'There it is,' Marty said excitedly, pointing over the driver's shoulder to the illuminated spires and minarets of Cairo, clearly visible beyond a line of palm trees where the road curved away out of sight. 'We'll have no heartaches spending an evening there. I mean, that place has *everything*.'

'And from what I hear,' Tone replied in a droll manner, 'you took advantage of most of it.'

'I did my best,' Marty admitted, recalling his earlier visits to the fabulous oriental city and the fun he'd had in its many bars, restaurants, cabarets, hotels and brothels.

'Now that you're married,' Tone replied, 'you'll have to be a bit more selective in what you get up to.'

'Don't bloody remind me,' Marty said.

'Is that where you fought in March?' Tone asked, indicating with a nod of his head the vast, starlit desert sweeping past on one side of the taxi.

'No,' Marty replied. 'That's the Qattara Depression. Our battle was in Cyrenaica, beyond that desert, about four hundred miles farther west.'

Glancing across the flat, moonlit immensity of the Qattara Depression, Marty recalled his first experience of warfare with a great degree of relish, even given that the battle had been lost and he, with thousands of others, had been forced to retreat. As long as he lived he would never forget his first few days in the great Allied camp located just outside Mersa Brega, in the Western Desert of Cyrenaica: a sprawling collection of tents, lean-tos, makeshift huts and caravans overflowing with the men of the 7th Armoured Division and Selby Force, the 4th Indian Division, the 6th Australian Division, Royal Electrical and Mechanical Engineers (REME), the Royal Army Medical Corps (RAMC), sappers, a Cypriot labour battalion, and the hundreds of ragged Italian Tenth Army soldiers packed into the prisoner-of-war cages near the southern perimeter. Though holding a vast array of artillery and tanks, the camp was also protected with British infantry divisions spread out in a defensive line consisting of a series of 'boxes' (slit trenches for the infantry, gun pits for the artillery) surrounded by barbed wire and minefields – all far away, spread out a good distance, and well out of sight. It also contained what appeared to be hundreds of armoured vehicles, including the M3 Stuart light tanks of the 8th King's Royal Irish Hussars, the Grant tanks of the Royal Gloucester Hussars, the Matildas of the 7th Royal Tank Regiment, the Bren carriers of the 9th Rifle Brigade, and Marmon Herrington armoured cars, all dispersed evenly behind the line.

Since the opening of the British offensive in December 1940, those men had resolutely pushed back the Italian forces in Egypt, stopping their advance at Sidi Barrani, taking Sollum, capturing Bardia with 40,000 Italian prisoners, next Tobruk, and finally, after two months of relentless fighting, cutting off the main body of the Italian Army at Beda Fomm, with approximately 130,000 enemy troops captured. However, in the closing days of March 1941, advance elements of *Generalleutnant* Erwin Rommel's Afrika Korps, including the 15th and 21st Panzer Divisions, arrived in Tripoli. Supported by the Italian mechanised Ariete Division, Rommel's forces advanced relentlessly across Cyrenaica to engage the Allies in the Western Desert, push them back, encircle them and trap them in Tobruk.

Even now, Marty could vividly recollect the beginning of that battle when the first of the German Ju Stukas flew towards the camp – looking primitive and ungainly, the swastikas clearly marked on their fins – and peeled off to begin their dive-bombing. What he would certainly never forget was the appalling noise. In response to the diving German aircraft, the British Bofors guns in the sangars had exploded into action with a deafening roar, jolting dramatically as they belched fire and smoke. Simultaneously, a lot of Tommies had opened up with their .303 rifles and Mark 6 Webley pistols, adding their staccato snapping to the general bedlam. Though slow-moving in flight, the Stukas were extremely fast when diving, which they did through black clouds of flak and criss-crossing tracers. British six-pounders, Bren gun and 0.5-inch Browning machine-gun teams, and even captured Italian 75-millimetre and 79-millimetre calibre guns, had joined in the fight, creating a deafening, head-splitting bedlam that was, in certain ways, even worse than the carnage on the ground.

That carnage was made even more horrific, however, when the Mark IV and Mark III tanks of the Afrika Korps Panzer divisions emerged from a billowing cloud of dust, spread out over half a mile, followed by motorised infantry and six-wheeled armoured cars. When the German tanks opened fire with their 77-millimetre and 55-millimetre guns, creating a dense curtain of smoke and fire, the British Grants moved out between the gun pits and sangars to engage the enemy on the open ground beyond the perimeter. The German tanks then emerged from their own smoke with pennants fluttering from wireless aerials and their treads churning up sand and gravel, as well as billowing clouds of dust.

Marty had felt no fear, only a kind of crazed excitement, as he jumped up and down from behind his sangar wall and fired his .303 rifle at the German troopers advancing behind the tanks of the Panzer divisions. Looking back on it, he realised that he hadn't had *time* for fear, that the speed of the German attack, the sheer noise and pure spectacle, the many explosions on all sides, the dead and the dying, had pushed all thoughts of personal danger aside, leaving only a generalised confusion and senseless excitement.

The latter had rapidly disappeared and the former increased when the Panzer divisions smashed through the Allied lines and Marty found himself marching with hundreds of other British troops through the choking dust left in the wake of Bren carriers, armoured cars, Bedford trucks and jeeps that formed a vast column on the road leading back through the desert to the harbour town of Tobruk, during the retreat from the still-advancing Panzer divisions. Even worse, with too many units on the move at the same time, panic set in, many men abandoning their stalled trucks and running to get on others without bothering to check what had stopped the vehicles. Other vehicles were abandoned when they ran short of petrol – even though there were numerous three-ton trucks loaded with petrol passing them by on either side.

Seeing that panic-stricken behaviour filled Marty with shame, but also taught him a valuable lesson: that panic was no help in such circumstances and must always be fought. It was a lesson he was determined not to forget the next time he saw action.

Luckily, during that particular retreat, the men were not fired upon by the German big guns or dive-bombed by the Stukas that had conducted the 'softening up' before the Panzer attack. Eventually, therefore, they found themselves inside the perimeter of Tobruk, mingling with the Aussies, who directed them to numerous positions along the wired perimeter, between gun pits and boxes of slit trenches, where the tanks and trucks were also lined up behind the wire to afford further protection.

This didn't prevent the German infantry from breaking through the wire a mere hundred yards away from where Marty found himself, grimly and uselessly firing his .303 rifle. As the German infantry opened a path through the Allied lines, letting the tanks and halftracks surge forward through the moonlit darkness, one of the shells from a tank exploded close to Marty, creating a din and hurling him sideways through swirling, hissing sand into a darkness filled with streaming stars and, ultimately, oblivion.

Regaining consciousness on a stretcher laid down on the deck of a destroyer heading back to Alexandria, he found himself surrounded by many other wounded soldiers, also lying on stretchers. After two days in a hospital in Alexandria, he was flown back to England, bitterly aware that his first battle had collapsed into retreat, but excited by having been part of it.

He learned then, if he'd ever had cause to doubt it, that he had been born to be a soldier; that this, right or wrong, good or bad, was the life for him.

It seemed almost preordained.

Right now, however, he was out for an evening of fun and trouble, the latter, for him, invariably being a consequence of the former. Although he had boarded the ship at Liverpool with nothing in his pocket, having spent every last penny on his single night in the Savoy hotel, he had been aboard ship for a month, which meant he now had another months's pay, out of which Lesley's allowance had already been deducted and mailed to her in England. Now, with what was left, he was determined to have the time of his life, despite his misgivings about his new wife.

Knowing Cairo well from his previous visits, he was filled with confidence when he climbed out of the taxi near the Continental Hotel, his feet kicking up dust, and led Tone into the exotic, clamorous sprawl of the city with its brightly lit, packed pavements, open-front cafés, shops and bazaars, its white walls covered in green vines, shaded by palm trees, and strewn with purple bougainvillaea that seemed to glow magically in the moonlight. Here many of the women still wore black robes and kept most of their face covered; the men dressed in djellabas and sandals. Around café tables, the Arabs drank coffee, smoked hashish pipes, played backgammon and talked noisily all evening, ignoring the soldiers swarming up and down the pavements, hotly pursued by filthy, screaming bootblacks. It was also an exceptionally noisy city, with radios blaring out shrill music and high-pitched singing, trams clattering to and fro, horse-drawn carriages, or *gharries*, clattering over loose stones, water gurgling from pipes and splashing onto the streets, and numerous vehicles, including troop trucks, roaring and honking in a never-ending traffic jam. To this deafening cacophony was added the growling and screeching of the many aircraft flying constantly overhead.

'Never heard so much noise in my life,' Tone said as he and Marty made their way along a packed pavement, fighting off gangs of pint-sized bootblacks. 'Except when I was down the coal mines in Wales.'

'It's even worse in the daytime,' Marty informed him.

'And all these bloody smells,' Tone complained.

'Sweat and piss, tobacco and hashish, petrol, the smoke from those charcoal braziers, and exhausts; roasting kebabs, kuftas and ears of corn; jasmine and jackala trees, sarpices and flowers. It's a feast for the senses, mate.'

Already feeling intoxicated, he tugged the overwhelmed Tone through vividly coloured beaded curtains, into the Sweet Melody Cabaret, where, wreathed in cigarette smoke, glamorised by dim lighting, solders, sailors and airmen were watching the sensual gyrations of a scantily clad Turkish belly-dancer. Pushing his way to the bar, half deafened by the Egyptian music, smelling sweat, piss, tobacco and alcohol, feeling crushed by the density of the crowd, Marty ordered two bottles of a deadly brew and handed one to Tone.

'Drink up!' he said, tapping his friend's bottle with his own before taking a mouthful.

'Christ!' Tone exclaimed, almost choking when he tried it. 'What the hell's this?'

'Zebeeb,' Marty told him. 'You'll be high as a kite before long and then this' – he waved his free hand to indicate the packed, smoky cabaret club – 'won't intimidate you.'

Gulping down his Zebeeb, Tone eyed up the many available young ladies of various nationalities, most of them scantily dressed, their skin browned by nature or the oriental sun, their eyes bright with greed, faces flushed with excitement, circulating amongst the men, offering company in return for weak champagne and more intimate favours for money.

'Cherry brandy bints,' Marty exclaimed to the bedazzled, self-conscious Tone. 'They come from all over the place in the hope of making it here in one of the nightclubs, but few of them ever make it out of Cairo and most get fat from the booze, so get 'em while they're still fresh, mate.'

After a couple more bottles of Zebeeb, and increasingly aroused by the suggestive gyrations of the belly-dancer, Tone was drunk enough to start making passes at some of the 'cherry brandy bints'. But he was dragged away by Marty, who, keen to see more of his old haunts, led him back outside and through the teeming streets until they came to another nightclub called Groppi's. Similar to the club they had just left, just as packed, dense with smoke, dimly lit, it offered the customary floor show and more circulating cherry brandy bints. Now drunk, becoming bold, Tone invited a couple of the women to their table for suggestive banter, but Marty, again restless to relive old memories, soon dragged him away and on to another club, the Blue Nile, where they spent more of their dwindling wages on weak champagne for two of the circulating ladies, Rita and Marjorie, self-described as 'exotic dancers' from Lancashire.

'They're ready for it,' Tone whispered drunkenly into Marty's ear when the girls had disappeared into the powder room. 'Where can we take 'em?'

'Did you give Rita some cash for the powder room?'

Tone looked embarrassed. 'As a matter of fact . . .'

Amused, Marty laughed and slapped his hand on the table. 'It's the oldest trick in the book. How much did you give her?'

'Two pounds worth of ackers,' Tone said, referring to Egyptian piastres.

'A quid each!' Marty exclaimed in mock disgust, feeling exhilarated, divorced from the real world, adrift in a swelling sea of light and sound that was sweeping him away from his origins to a new, more exotic world. 'They'll have moved on to another club by now for more pickings from some other cherry boys. You've just dropped a right bloody clanger. Come on, let's get out of here.'

By midnight, when he should have been on his way back to base, Marty found himself even more adrift, raised on high by alcohol, the bright lights of the city shimmering before his dazed eyes, the clamour making him senseless, as he led Tone away from the bar of Shepheard's Hotel, into the infamous Sharia il Berka district. Making his way through that maze of packed, narrow streets, with Tone stumbling behind him, passing through shadow and light, still pursued by jabbering bootblacks, begging cripples, touting pimps, he eventually arrived at the notorious Tiger Lil's brothel. Though a great, gloomy barn of a place outside, it was very lively inside, its many corridors leading off an immensely seedy reception area, stinking of carbolic soap, disinfectant and dried urine, but resounding with the bawling of the many servicemen battling for attention.

Tiger Lil, the obese, good-natured Madame, who was sitting behind the cash desk located near the front door, took the money off Marty in advance and pointed him and Tone in the right direction. As they climbed the creaking stairs, their boots crushing cockroaches and cigarette butts, sometimes slipping in vomit, they came across many young girls, no more than eight or nine, all dressed in rags, most looking like angels, running in and out of the other rooms with towels, cleaning rags and bottles of Condy's disinfectant. Reaching the top of the stairs, Marty and the visibly staggering Tone entered a hallway filled with other drunken soldiers, sailors and airmen queuing up at the doors of the rooms, some peeping through keyholes to see how the first man was getting on and shouting words of obscene encouragement.

'This is a right fucking circus,' Tone slurred.

'It's the best bag shanty in town,' Marty replied. 'That's why there's so many sailors here.'

Joining the queue that snaked down the hallway, Marty and Tone continued to drink Zebeeb from the bottle and traded tall stories about the night's activities while the queue ahead of them inched impatiently forward. Eventually, when it was their turn, Marty, high and mighty, pushed the hysterically giggling Tone into the room. He waited a few moments, then peeped through the keyhole and was gratified to see that his virginal Welsh friend, scared even in his drunkenness, was stretched out on the naked bint on the bed, his pants around his ankles, his pale-skinned spine spangled with the light of an oil lamp, and appeared to be moving awkwardly inside her. Eventually, after what was only a matter of minutes, he staggered out of the room and said smugly, 'Follow *that* if you can.'

'No problem, mate.'

Entering the room, Marty found the Egyptian prostitute, a dark-skinned barrel of lard, her eyes pitch-black and demented, swabbing her bruised thighs with a wet rag. Feeling unreal, the floor shifting beneath his feet, wondering what he was doing here, suddenly thinking of Lesley and then trying to forget her, he obeyed the woman's nod, the mad seductiveness in her gaze, and unbuttoned and stretched out beside her. As she wearily spread her legs, raising knees black with boils, her blistered hands blindly groping, he felt himself falling in and out of consciousness, eyes opening and closing, and realised that he wasn't getting anywhere, being far too drunk. Slipping into a kind of reverie, at once desirous and guilty, he recollected his single night of sex with Lesley in that small room in the Savoy hotel. It was an artful dodge, a born survivor's trick, and he managed a slight erection, wisely slipped on a condom, and felt himself entering the woman as her gaze sucked him in. There was madness in her gaze, something lost, beyond time, and he sensed intimations of a future he did not wish to know. Shuddering, he came too quickly, gaining little satisfaction, and was glad to button himself up again and hurry out of the room, once more hiding behind his jocularity and beaming at Tone.

'Bloody fantastic,' he boasted loudly, though the words tripped his tongue. 'She was so desperate after your pitiful effort, she practically came off the bed.'

'Oh, yeah?' Tone asked sceptically.

'Bloody right, mate. In fact, she told me you'd come too quickly, before you were even in properly, and that I could use up the time you'd paid for. Thanks a million, mate.'

'Pull the other one.'

Giggling hysterically, they left Tiger Lil's, stepping back into the sultry Egyptian night, and made their way unsteadily along the pavement, continually knocking against the outdoor tables of the cafés where Arabs were still drinking coffee, smoking hashish pipes, playing backgammon and talking noisily, drunken soldiers were still entering and leaving the many nightclubs and bars, and the usual swarm of filthy, screaming bootblacks hotly pursued them.

Suddenly feeling hungry, Marty hailed a taxi and had it take them to the Union Jack pension which, though run by a Greek proprietor, specialised in egg and chips for the British. After washing their greasy meal down with beer, which took them over the edge as far as drunkenness was concerned, they decided that it was too late to return to camp and that they had best spend the night here in the pension. Paying for a two-bedded room with the last of their piastres, they fell into their separate beds without removing their clothes.

Marty fell asleep almost instantly, despite the continuing noise outside, and had erotic dreams about Lesley, seeing her large brown eyes floating in darkness as her naked body, sweat-slicked and moonlit, uncoiled to envelop him. In his dream, he was consumed with love for her and felt the pain of his loss. Then sleep's true darkness claimed him.

He was awakened at dawn by a couple of British Army MPs, who drummed their batons on the metal headrests of the beds, creating a shocking din. Jerking upright with a racing heart and splitting head, feeling ill and dazed, he was ordered out of bed, ushered with the dishevelled Tone into a paddy wagon, then driven to the MP barracks at Bab el Hadid. There they were both thrown into a cell, charged with being AWOL.

'Oh, my God!' Tone groaned when the cell door had been slammed shut. 'My first night in Cairo and already I'm up for a court martial!'

'I doubt it,' Marty replied, then lay back on his bed with his hands clasped under his head, his gaze fixed on the ceiling. He tried to ignore his guilt and splitting headache and his stomach's vile rumblings. 'Did you use a condom?' he asked.

'Yes,' Tone replied.

'Wise man,' Marty said, thinking of Lesley waiting patiently for his return, loving him, trusting him, not for one second suspecting that he dallied with diseased whores in Cairo.

I should have more sense, he thought.

Shortly after noon, he was released from the cell and driven back with Tone to the camp at Almazur, arriving there when the sun was still high in the sky and the heat threatened to make them throw up. Escorted to the HQ tent, they were made to stand at attention in the boiling sun until the Commanding Officer, Lieutenant-Colonel Welsh, could see them. Not being a man to take nonsense lightly, he let them cook in the sun for an hour, then had them brought into him by a sergeant-major, one after the other, to a table overloaded with various books, documents and maps. He had a walrus moustache, a sun-scorched, jowly face and eyes as grey and hard as desert stones.

'From a brief perusal of your records, Private Butler,' he said when Marty had snapped to attention, flashed a perfect salute, and recited his name, rank and serial number, 'it would seem to me that you're a soldier rather short on self-discipline.'

'Sorry, sir, but—'

'Be quiet and speak only when spoken to!' the sergeant-major bawled in his ear.

'Yes, Sergeant-Major!' Marty snapped.

The CO stared steadily at him for some time, as if studying some kind of rare zoological specimen, his fingers clasped below his chin and drumming lightly together. Eventually, sucking his breath in and letting it out with a sigh, he said, 'You're a very good soldier – no doubt about that – but you're constantly in trouble, getting drunk or fighting, and you don't even seem to have enough discipline to beat the curfew or get out of bed in the morning. Clearly, Private Butler, you need a more exacting life than you're getting – one that will fill every minute of your day and keep you out of mischief.'

'Yes, sir,' Marty said.

'Shut your mouth, Private!' the sergeant-major bawled. 'And speak only when spoken to!'

'Yes, Sergeant-Major!' Marty snapped.

After another tortuous silence, broken only by the growling and clattering of some passing 7th Royal Tank Regiment Matildas, which filled the tent with swirling sand, the CO cleared his throat and continued: 'It is my belief that you can put your excess energy to good use, and thus hopefully subdue your disorderly habits, by joining the Long Range Desert Group. The LRDG, as it's known, is presently engaged in reconnaissance and intelligence gathering behind enemy lines in the Western Desert. The work is exhausting and dangerous, which should suit you perfectly. Do you have reason to think otherwise, Private Butler?'

'No, sir!' Marty snapped, secretly thrilled at the thought of working with that already legendary group of men. 'When do I leave, sir?'

'The sooner the better,' the CO replied drily. 'Be on the apron at first light tomorrow morning.'

'Yes, sir!' Marty snapped.

'All right, Private, dismissed.'

With the sergeant-major bawling his instructions right

behind him, Marty saluted the CO, performed a sharp about-turn, then marched with singing heart out of the tent, back into the blazing sun. He had just been rewarded for his sins and it made him feel ten feet tall.

CHAPTER TWO

The LRDG camp was located at Siwa Oasis, nearly 300 kilometres to the south-west and across the frontier, at the crossroads of the old caravan routes. With its salt-water lake, fierce dry heat and swarms of black flies, the oasis was a place noted for its ability to tax a man's strength, which is exactly why it suited the Long Range Desert Group: it hardened new men and prepared them for the desert even before they went out on their first patrol.

Disembarking from the RAF Hudson transport that had flown him in with Tone, who had been allotted the same fate, Marty saw that the forward operating base (FOB) was ringed with the 25-pounder gun/howitzers of the Royal Horse Artillery, an equal number of British six-pounders, Bofors anti-aircraft guns, sangars manned by Bren gun and 0.5-inch Browning machine-gun teams, and even some captured Italian 75mm and 79mm calibre guns. Camouflaged Ford F60 cars and 30-hundred weight Chevrolet trucks were lined up along one side of the camp, under a protective canopy of palm leaves. They were, Marty noted, covered in dust, badly battered and peppered with bullet holes.

Beyond the perimeter, on all sides, were the magnificent sand dunes and, beyond them, nothing but the 'Blue' – the common term for the desert – stretching away to the dust-wreathed horizon under an azure sky streaked with silvery-white lines of sunlight.

The men of the LRDG were wearing desert dress: khaki shirt and shorts, regular Army boots with rolled-down socks, and a soft peaked cap instead of a helmet. Each man also had a Sykes Fairburn commando dagger and a holstered Browning High Power handgun strapped to his waist. One of them, a short, broad-shouldered bulldog of a sergeant with windblown tawny hair, a sunburnt face and the fathomless brown eyes and demeanour of a Rottweiler, was waiting for Marty and the others when they stepped out of the Hudson and gathered together around the Bedford trucks lined up by the runway.

'All right, you lot!' he bawled. 'Don't stand there like limp dicks at a wedding. You're with the LRDG now – not with a bunch of regular Army wankers – so hump yourselves up into one of those Bedfords and be quick about it. Are you deaf? *I mean now!*'

Impelled into action by the sergeant's impressive bellowing, Marty and Tone humped their kitbags onto their shoulders and scrambled with the other newcomers up into one of the Bedford trucks. Sitting side by side, they felt the inexorable rise of the desert heat and sweated profusely as other soldiers tumbled in and groped their way along to find a seat.

'Bloody hot, isn't it?' Marty said.

'Hot as hell,' Tone replied. 'We're paying for our sins in Cairo.'

'Too bloody true,' Marty said. 'And coming from the coal mines of Wales, you probably know what hell's like.'

'Damned right,' Tone replied amiably. 'Cold, damp and dark as night. Not like this at all, mate.'

Tone had left school at fourteen and gone straight down into the coal mines, as all the men of his family had done for generations. Two years later, his father died from lung congestion caused by years of inhaling coal dust. About a year after that, the roof of a tunnel collapsed, crushing Tone's only brother under rubble, and Tone had held his hand until he died. Racked by despair, Tone's mother had died eighteen months later, leaving Tone all alone in the world. Deciding that mining wasn't for him, he packed it in and headed for Cardiff, where he became a labourer on a building site and gradually worked his way up through bricklaying to a position as foreman. Hardened by experience and determined to get somewhere, he was just about to start his own construction business when war broke out and he was called up. Though initially angry to have been deprived of his freedom, he was surprised to discover that he actually enjoyed life in the Army. It was a feeling that he shared with Marty and that feeling, combined with their similar backgrounds, had made them firm friends.

'Here we go,' Marty said.

The truck lurched forward, its wheels churning up clouds of fine sand as it headed for the many tents, large and small, that were spread out within a broad, irregular ring of green palms and gleaming white dunes. The journey took only a few minutes, then Marty and the others clambered down to the ground and milled about in front of one of the larger tents. A wooden cross-shaped sign had been hammered into the ground beside the entrance, announcing this tent as the headquarters of the Long Range Desert Group.

'Home sweet home,' Marty said.

He and Tone had to stand there in the burning heat, choking in the sand being churned up by the incoming Bedfords, until the rest of the trucks had arrived from the airstrip. The last was hotly pursued by the Rottweiler sergeant in a jeep being driven by a corporal with a hawklike, freckled face, a mop of dishevelled red hair and bare arms covered in tattoos. When the jeep had screeched to a halt beside the last Bedford, the sergeant and corporal both disembarked and walked up to the waiting men.

The sergeant stared grimly at them, his dark eyes flicking threateningly from one to the other, then he sucked in his breath, let it out with a sigh and said, his voice like gravel, 'Let me introduce myself. Sergeant Ralph Bellamy. It's a name you won't forget as long as you're here, so treat it with respect. You're with the LRDG now and, being a tight, disciplined outfit, we don't stand any nonsense from cowboys. And that's what you men are. You have a bad reputation. You're all basically good soldiers who have too much energy and don't respond properly to discipline. We're going to change all that.

I'll personally see to it. I'll use up your excess energy and the work itself will force you to be disciplined. By the time you've finished with the LRDG, you'll be the finest soldiers in North Africa. Take my word for it.'

'Yes, Sarge,' Marty said with a helpless grin, unable to keep the mockery out of his voice.

Sergeant Bellamy stared steadily at him for some time, as if taking his measure. He grinned tightly, dangerously, then let his gaze roam up and down the rest of the men. 'Right now,' he said, 'you're going in there' – he indicated the entrance to the tent beside the HQ tent with a nod of his head – 'for a briefing from the CO's second-in-command, Captain Alan Kearney, formerly of Number Eight Commando. When that's finished, you'll be allocated accommodations, kitted out, given lunch and then put to work straight away. No peace for the wicked, right? Okay, follow me.'

While the red-headed corporal with the freckled face and tattooed arms – the head of a roaring lion; a heart with an arrow through it and a name embroidered around it; various badges and shields – grinned crookedly and climbed back into the jeep to read *The Strand*, Sergeant Bellamy led the newcomers into the large tent, which had rows of folding metal chairs facing a crudely made wooden platform containing a wooden table, chairs and a blackboard covered with a chalk-drawn map of Siwa Oasis and the surrounding area.

The men had barely settled into the chairs when an army captain entered the tent and walked to the raised platform, taking up a position facing them, his back turned to the blackboard. Immediately, the men stood up and saluted en masse. About six feet tall, with the solid physique of a rugby player, the captain had unusually bright green eyes and dark, mischievous good looks.

'Welcome, gentlemen,' he said, speaking Oxford English with just the slightest trace of his original Irish brogue. 'Captain Alan Kearney at your service. I'm called "Paddy" behind my back, but call me that to my face and you'll be in serious trouble.' When the anticipated laughter had died down, he continued: 'This initial briefing is to familiarise you with the territory in general and the LRDG in particular. You may smoke if you wish.' He waited until the smokers had lit up and were puffing contentedly, then he tapped the blackboard behind him, indicating the marked oasis in the centre of the chalked drawing.

'Siwa Oasis is seven miles long and two miles wide. Beyond the palm groves, to the south, are the great white dunes, running north to south in the Great Sand Sea, known to the Arabs as Devil's Country. An area approximately the same size as Ireland, it can only be crossed two hundred kilometres south of Siwa by a route that passes the artesian well at Ain Dalla, the last watering point in over five hundred kilometres en route for Kufra. To the north-west lies the Qattara Depression, running farther north to stop fifty metres from the sea near El Alamein. Unfortunately, its floor is so far below sea level that it's impassable to ordinary vehicles.'

He paused to let the Hudson transport that had brought the newcomers take off again, heading back to Cairo. When the roaring had died away, he continued.

'It's not a pleasant place, mainly because of the Ghibili: a hot wind filled with dust instead of sand. In fact, as you'll soon find out, true sandstorms are rare in these parts, though dust storms occur frequently and can be bloody hellish, as well as devastating to our vehicles. The Ghibili, however, is even worse. Also, the great variations of temperature inland – fifty degrees by noon, frost in the morning – can cause men to die from exposure. In short, the Great Sand Sea was well named when the Arabs dubbed it Devil's Country. It is, in fact, a murderous terrain for all but the Arabs.'

'And the LRDG, presumably,' Marty said.

The men laughed and Captain Paddy Kearney smiled with a slight trace of mockery, recognising a smart-arse when he saw one. 'Yes,' he said in that same droll manner. '*And* the LRDG. Let us pray you don't let us down, Private, when we take you out there.'

Realising that Kearney was slyly putting him in his place, Marty grinned cockily at the other men but remained silent while Tone asked shyly, 'What does the LRDG consist of, precisely? We're all a bit vague about that, sir.'

'At this point in time we consist of ten patrols,' Kearney

informed him. 'Each patrol has the use of modified four-wheel-drive Ford F60 cars and thirty-hundredweight Chevrolet trucks with a single tank range of eighteen hundred kilometres. We have a survey section, where we make up our own maps. We have our own artillery section with a four-point-five-inch howitzer, an eighty-eight-millimetre, twenty-five-pounder, and a light tank, each mounted on a ten-tonner. We have an air section with two American WACO light aircraft purchased by the War Office. Last but not least, we have a heavy section of three-ton supply trucks, and a Light Aid Detachment for vehicle maintenance. In short, we're a self-sustaining outfit and we're well equipped.'

'For what purpose, sir?' Marty asked.

'Good question,' Kearney replied deadpan. 'The first LRDG patrols spent last summer patrolling from this oasis and Kufra. The work included traffic surveillance on the Axis coast, a good distance away from the main battle area. We also dropped and picked up agents for the Secret Service, recced terrain which the enemy might have to cross, and occasionally raided enemy transport convoys. Though that's still our basic function, we've since split the patrols into fifteen- or eighteen-man teams led by an officer, with five vehicles. Our methods of crossing soft sand and navigating in featureless desert have improved with experience, but they're still based on relatively simple ideas pioneered by Major Bagnold in the nineteen twenties.'

'What ideas?' Tone asked.

'Steel channel strips laid on soft sand, enabling vehicles to cross it. Bagnold first did this in the Sinai Desert in nineteen twenty-six, where he used corrugated iron. By the early forties all vehicles carried such channels in the desert. All our vehicles now carry them and you will, as you'll soon find out, have to use them constantly. It's gruelling, time-consuming work, but it can't be avoided.'

'What about navigation, sir?' Marty asked. 'Do you use normal compasses?'

'Sometimes, not always. It's difficult to set up a prismatic compass in a motorised vehicle, because invariably you'll get magnetic interference from tool boxes and other movable metal parts. To use a prismatic compass in a motorised vehicle, the navigator has to get out and walk far enough away to be clear of the car's magnetic fields. Even then, the compass can be an inaccurate guide.'

'So what did Bagnold use?' Tone asked, becoming bolder and blowing a cloud of smoke from his Woodbine.

'A sun compass with its horizontal disc marked off in degrees and a central needle casting a shadow – rather like a sundial. The graduated disc was mounted in the car, to be rotated as the sun moved across the sky.'

'And you still use this system?' Marty asked, dropping the 'sir'.

'Yes. But we also fix the car's position by taking star bearings or by calculating the longitude and latitude with the aid of a theodolite and astro-navigation tables. It depends on the circumstances, the weather or where we happen to be at any given time.'

'How do the different patrols keep in touch?'

'A sensible question from the feisty private of the Ninth Rifle Brigade,' Kearney replied in a droll manner before turning serious again. 'Each patrol has a radio truck with a number eleven set, which has a range of about thirty-two kilometres, and a separate set to pick up the BBC's time signals.'

'What about communications in general from deep in the desert?'

Kearney nodded, smiling. 'It's not bad. The radio operators are able to pick up morse from a background slush of atmospherics when working at ranges beyond the normal operational limits of the number eleven set. Their radio links from patrols to the group's forward base and from the base to the Eighth Army and MEHQ in Cairo are more tenuous. These operate on ground aerials at frequencies which mean that sometimes a patrol can't contact base until it's about five hundred kilometres along its route. Our radio procedures, however, follow French civilian routines. Invariably, this makes those listening in think they're hearing a commercial station in Turkey communicating with ships in the Levant. Certainly it appears to have deceived the German radio interception services. Because of this, our operators are able to transmit for relatively long periods at night, over great distances, without being identified or interfered with.'

'Water?' Corporal Keyhoe asked sensibly.

'A gallon per man per day for all purposes, including the topping up of the individual's vehicle. No shaving permitted.'

'Are those Chevrolets outside what you use for the patrols?' Marty asked.

'Correct. Modified four-wheel-drive trucks armed with a Boyes anti-tank rifle fixed to the rear and a pintle-mounted Browning M one-nine-one-nine machine-gun operated by the front passenger.'

'And peppered with bullet holes,' Marty noted.

'It's an exciting life in the LRDG,' Kearney replied sardonically. 'If you want to get out, Private, you can get out now.'

'I'm in, sir. No problem.'

Kearney's grin told Marty that he had said the right thing. 'You men have been sent here to gain more extensive experience in desert patrols,' he said, 'but you've also been chosen because all of you are already experienced, to a certain degree, in this kind of warfare. For this reason, we won't be wasting any time on unnecessary training, but will, as it were, throw you in at the deep end by sending you out on patrol as soon as you've been familiarised with LRDG standard operating procedures, known as SOPs. That familiarisation will commence as soon as you've been kitted out and allocated a vehicle, which will happen as soon as you leave this briefing. Are there any questions?'

Many of the newcomers glanced sheepishly at each other, but none of them had any more questions.

'Right, gentlemen,' Kearney said. 'Sergeant Ralph Bellamy here will see you outside the tent, show you to your accommodations, get you kitted out, then introduce you to your respective LRDG team members. Best of luck. Dismissed.'

Even as the men were pushing their chairs back to stand up, 'Bulldog' Bellamy was making his way out of the tent, his shirt stained with sweat around his broad shoulders and chest. Once outside, he snapped at the red-haired, tattooed corporal who was still reading *The Strand*. 'Lester! Get your arse out of that jeep and show these men to their accommodations.

Once they've left their kitbags in the tents, take them to the quartermaster's stores. I'll be waiting there for them.'

Throwing his copy of *The Strand* onto the seat beside him, Corporal Lester hopped out of the jeep, waited until all of the newcomers had gathered around him, then nodded in a westerly direction and said, 'Follow me.'

Being one of the first out of the briefing tent, Marty fell in beside the corporal, studied his bare arms with their many cartoons – there was even one of Jane, the serviceman's favourite cartoon-strip girl – and said, 'Nice collection you've got there, Corp!'

'Tell it to me mum,' Lester replied as he led Marty and the others towards the bell-tents located in the protective shade of regular rows of palm trees. They were also located not far from the motor pool, which was filled with 30-cwt Chevrolet two-wheel-drive trucks, Ford F60 trucks, Bedford QL four-wheel-drive trucks, Series 1 Land Rovers and American Willys jeeps, all framed by a rust-coloured mountain of jerry cans containing petrol, oil and lubricants, or POL.

'If that lot went up,' Tone remarked, 'we'd all be blown sky high.'

'Treat those POL drums as a laxative,' Corporal Lester said sardonically. 'They could help you shit bricks.'

'That Sergeant Bellamy looks like a tough nut,' Marty said. 'Is he as tough as he looks?'

'An iron man,' Corporal Lester replied. 'Hard as nails and knows his business. He's one of the most experienced men in the LRDG and he has very high standards. Meet 'em and you'll find him a fair man; fail to meet 'em and he'll have you for breakfast – and believe me, his teeth are sharp.'

'He looks like a mad dog,' Marty said.

'His bite's worse than his bark.' Corporal Lester grinned crookedly as they arrived at the first line of tents and he turned around to face the men ganging up behind him. 'You lot have been allocated this row of tents. Where you sleep relates to who you're sharing a vehicle with, so those sleeping together will be driving together. You'll find your names on a gummed label fixed to the outside of each tent. When you find your name, remove the label and take any unoccupied camp bed in that tent. When you've done so, leave your kitbag in the tent and meet me over there by the motor pool. Okay, lads, get to it.'

Marty and Tone were pleased to discover that they were sharing a tent, even though it was small, boiling hot and already cluttered with the widely scattered kit of another man. As they were throwing their kitbags on their respective camp beds, Corporal Lester stuck his red head in, gave them a crooked grin, revealing blackened front teeth, and said, 'Sorry 'bout the mess, but I wasn't expecting you so soon. My name's Sammy, but the lads here all call me "Red".'

'We're sharing your jeep?' Marty asked.

'That's my misfortune,' Red said.

When Marty and Tone had introduced themselves, Red, holding a clipboard in his right hand, led them from the tent to where the other newcomers were gathering outside the quartermaster's store, which was one of the few wooden buildings in the camp. There they were kitted out with the clothing favoured by the LRDG for use in the desert: shirt, shorts, Arab headgear and special sandals. The headgear consisted of the black woollen *agal*, a small hat, and a *shemagh*, or shawl with tie thongs, which went around the head, flapped in the wind, kept the face cool, and also protected the nose and mouth in a sandstorm. Normal army boots were useless because they filled up with sand, so they were replaced with a special kind of sandal, the Indian North-West Frontier *chappal*, originally chosen by Bagnold and obtained from the Palestine Police stores. Worn with rolled-down socks, the *chappal* was particularly tough and had a hole in the toe, enabling the wearer to kick out any sand that got in without having to stop when on the march. Also supplied were funnel-shaped leather gauntlets, which stopped sweat from running down the arms and onto the weapons.

Once they had left the clothing in the bell tents, they were marched by Red to another wooden building, the armoury, where each of them was handed the obligatory holstered Browning High Power handgun, Len Dixon leather holster and Sykes Fairburn commando dagger.

'You'll carry these on you at all times,' Red informed them, 'starting right now. You'll pick up the rest of the weapons when you leave on your first patrol.'

When the newcomers had strapped on their holstered handguns and knives, Red led them across to the motor pool. As Marty and Tone would be driving with him, he just pointed out their Chevrolet and told them to have a good look at it while he allocated the others to their respective vehicles, which were, Marty noticed, already being attended to by LRDG NCOs.

Marty passed the time by ghoulishly poking his index finger into the bullet holes in his Chevrolet while studying its many interesting innovations. Before he could work out for himself what those innovations were, Red returned to give him the grand tour.

'Reinforced sand tyres,' he indicated, then reeled off the vehicle's many other innovations, pointing at each in turn. 'Special filters. Larger fans and radiators. Jerry cans and water condensers. For navigation: sun compass and sextants. For use when the vehicle becomes trapped in deep sand, which is often: sand shovels, woven sand mats and steel sand channels. For communications: a number eleven wireless set, an S-phone – which is a radiotelephone, homing beacon and parachute-dropping indicator all in one – and a portable radar responder known as the Eureka beacon. And of course,' he concluded, lovingly patting the weapons that were pintle-mounted front and rear of the vehicle, 'our beloved Boyes anti-tank rifle and Browning M one-nine-one-nine machine-gun.'

Letting his hand slip off the gun, he said, 'I won't bother telling you any more about those beauties because I know you're already familiar with them. However, listen carefully to what I tell you about some tricks peculiar to the LRDG – and ones you'll need to know before you go on your first patrol.'

Marty and Tone were given a quick lesson in the use of the sun compass fixed to the vehicle's bonnet and familiarised with the workings of the sextant. Red then showed them how to improvise a simple compass by stretching a string from the bonnet up to a row of nails on top of the cabin (in the case of a Bedford QL four-wheel-drive truck) or, in the case of the Chevrolets, to another string with hooks stretched taut between the side supports of what had been the windscreen.

'Every hour,' he told them, tugging lightly at the fixed line of cord, 'you switch the string one notch along.' He removed the knotted end of cord from one of the nails hooked, in this case, to the cord strung between the windscreen uprights, and looped it over the hook beside it. 'The driver simply follows the line of the shadow created by the string and that keeps him in the right direction.'

Finally, he showed them how water could be conserved from the car's radiator. In this instance, when the water boiled, it wasn't lost through the overflow pipe, which had been deliberately blocked off to prevent this from happening. Instead, the steam was blown off into a can bolted to the running-board and half filled with water. When the engine cooled, the trapped steam would condense and the topped-up water would be sucked back into the radiator.

'If it works properly, without leaking,' Red told them, 'you can go the whole life of the truck without ever putting water in after the initial top-up. So, that's your vehicle!'

'That's some car,' Tone said.

'I can't wait to get out there and try it,' Marty said with similar enthusiasm. 'When do we start?'

'This afternoon,' Red replied. 'Straight after lunch. Be prepared for some long, hot days and a lot of freezing nights. You'll be gone at least a week.'

'With no preliminary training?' Marty asked, surprised.

'You'll be trained on the job,' Red replied. 'That's the LRDG way.'

CHAPTER THREE

Immediately after a hearty cooked lunch in the fly-filled mess tent, Marty and the other newcomers were told to don their new desert clothing and congregate outside the armoury, where they were forced to wait for some time while a lethargic private sorted out their weapons. They passed the time by joking with each other about how pretty they looked with the *agals* and *shemaghs*, some even acting like flirtatious women by fluttering the veils in front of their eyes like professional strippers. They were interrupted by the abrupt appearance of Sergeant Bellamy, who bawled at them to stop acting like a bunch of bloody pansies and line up for their weapons. When they had done so, looking sheepish, they were given an assortment of heavier weapons, including the Lee-Enfield .303-inch bolt-action rifle, the 9mm Sten submachine-gun, the new M1 Thompson submachine-gun, or tommy-gun, and two machine-guns: the Bren light machine-gun and a Browning 0.5-inch.

'Don't hold them like you're fiddling with your dicks in the dark!' Sergeant Bellamy bellowed. 'Take those weapons back to your vehicles and prepare to move out.'

A few minutes later, when they had placed their weapons on the back seats of their respective Chevrolets and taken the positions given to them by the LRDG drivers, one manning the Browning M1919 machine gun at the front, the other on the Boyes anti-tank rifle at the rear, they were driven out of the palm-fringed oasis into the vast, barren wastes of the desert.

Assailed by the ferocious heat, Marty was grateful for the wind created by the vehicle's forward movement, even though this also created huge clouds of sand that threatened to choke him. Noting that his driver, Red Lester, and Tone, on the Boyes gun in the rear, had both covered their faces with their *shemaghs*, Marty did the same. However, while keeping the sand out of his mouth and nostrils, the *shemagh* in its own way made breathing just as difficult. Within minutes, Marty was sweating profusely and covered in a fine film of sand that stuck like slime to his sweat. Within half an hour he felt as if he was in hell, and he was suffering from intermittent waves of nausea. He was therefore deeply grateful when, after one hour's drive, which had seemed like an eternity, Sergeant Bellamy, up front in the lead vehicle, used a hand signal instructing all the vehicles to stop.

'A break at last,' Tone said, gasping. 'Thank God for that.'

'Break, my arse!' Red exclaimed, halting the vehicle in a cloud of spiralling sand and jumping to the ground. 'Now we check the tyres and let some air out to stop them bursting from heat. We also have to check the carburettors, to ensure that there's no sand in 'em. Last but not least, we check the petrol, oil and water, adjust the compasses, and examine all weapons to ensure that they don't have sand blockage.'

'That's a bloody day's work!' Tone protested.

'We do it every hour,' Red said.

After checking the car, which took a good twenty minutes and was not made any easier by the heat and constantly blowing sand, Marty and Tone, already frustrated and exhausted, checked their weapons and were dismayed to find that most already had sand in them and had to be thoroughly cleaned. Attempting to clean them where they knelt beside the vehicle, cursing vehemently as the sand swirled about them, Marty and Tone soon learned that it was blowing into the weapons as quickly as they were able to remove it.

'Fuck it!' Marty exclaimed. 'This is bloody impossible!'

'No, it's not,' Red replied. 'Here, let me show you.'

Crawling out of the swirling sand, he took a position

between Marty and Tone, sitting upright with his back against the rear wheel of the Chevrolet, and showed them how to do the job with a towel thrown over the weapon resting on the lap and the separate components being cleaned and reassembled sight unseen. This process, though causing more frustrated swearing, was repeated time and again until Marty and Tone got it right and the weapons were cleaned.

They were just about to relax, light a cigarette and have a brew-up when Red glanced to the front of the column and saw Sergeant Bellamy, distorted in shimmering heat waves, using the hand signal for 'Advance'.

'Shit, we're off,' Red said. 'Let's go!'

After the disbelieving Marty and Tone had scrambled urgently back into the Chevrolet and taken up their positions at the guns front and rear, Red followed the other vehicles across the desert, driving recklessly through clouds of boiling sand. Again, though Marty covered his face with his *shemagh*, he felt that he could not breathe properly and a few times was convinced that he was going to throw up. In fact, he managed not to do so until, after precisely one more hour, Sergeant Bellamy stopped the column for another wearying, frustrating check of the vehicles and weapons.

This tedious procedure was maintained every hour on the dot, greatly lengthening the time of the journey and causing a dreadful amount of exhausting work. Eventually, however, when the ferocious heat had started to diminish and the sun was sinking fast, turning into an immense crimson ball that seemed to be dripping blood along the hazed horizon, they stopped in the middle of what seemed like a boundless wasteland covered with breeze-blown, drifting sand. There they were told to make camp for the night.

'Thank God for that,' Marty said as the vehicles spread out and braked to form the loose semi-circular, protective formation known as a laager. 'Another ten minutes of that and I think I'd have died.'

'Damned right,' Tone mournfully agreed. 'Pure hell on earth, that was.'

But they didn't get a rest that easy. First, they had to raise individual shelters by tying the top ends of waterproof ponchos to the protuberances of the vehicles and the bottom ends to small stakes in the ground. A groundsheet was spread out on the desert floor beneath the triangular poncho tent. The sleeping bag was then rolled out on the groundsheet and the bed was completed. Next, with the poncho tents raised, hollows had to be dug out of the ground just beyond the camp, for use as toilets. When these were completed – and enthusiastically used – the men were allowed to have a supper, consisting of sandwiches, known as 'wads', and a cigarette. They could not have a brew-up in case the fires of the portable hexamine stoves were sighted by the enemy; instead, they had to content themselves with cold water from their water bottles.

Absolutely exhausted, burnt by the sun, made even more uncomfortable by the fine layer of sand that had stuck to his skin by his sweat, Marty finished his wads and cigarette, then crawled into his shelter with a great deal of relief, hoping to enjoy a good night's sleep.

He was just about to put his head down when Red Lester kicked his booted foot a couple of times and said, 'Sorry, mate, but you and Private Williams have to take turns on watch – one man at a time on each vehicle – and, as I'm off to consult with Sergeant Bellamy and the other NCOs, I'm designating you to first watch, four hours on, four hours off.'

'You're kidding me!'

'No, I'm not. Now get out of that sleeping bag and get your arse up on the seat behind your Browning machine-gun. Wake Private Williams four hours from now and make him take over, but don't bother me, thanks. As a corporal, I have greater responsibilities and need more sleep than you. Have a good night, mate.'

Grinning wickedly, Red turned away and headed across to Bellamy's Chevrolet, which was parked at the far side of the laager with a soldier already up on watch, surveying the darkening desert from behind his Boyes anti-tank rifle. Groaning in disbelief and despair, Marty wriggled out of his sleeping bag and clambered up onto the Chevrolet, taking his position behind the Browning machine-gun just as the sun sank behind the horizon to plunge the desert into eerily moonlit darkness.

'Cor blimey!' Marty whispered to himself, awed despite his dreadful tiredness by the panorama before him.

Nevertheless, despite the beauty of the nocturnal desert, it was an interminable, sometimes nerve-racking four hours, with his heavy eyes often deceiving him and his thoughts, slipping in and out of near sleep, ranging from the erotic to the fearful. One minute he was recalling his evening in the Savoy with Lesley – her sweat-slicked belly, her hardening nipples, the incredible softness of her thighs as she clamped them around his hips; her closed eyes as she attempted nervously to smile and let him move deep inside her – the next he was staring intently at the moonlit plain, at veils of swirling dust, the shadows of clouds crossing the moon, and imagining that the enemy was coming towards him under cover of darkness. Frequently he heard the faint rumble of heavy bombers high above as Allied planes headed towards the Western Desert. Occasionally, too, he saw flashes of light on the dark horizon where the bombs were exploding.

Naturally, he was convinced that he was always awake. In fact, he often jerked awake after having fallen into a brief, fitful sleep. When, four hours later, his watch period was up and he was able to wake the softly grumbling Tone to take his place, he crept back into his sleeping bag to sleep like a dead man.

Unfortunately, Marty felt that he had hardly slept at all when jerked awake by Sergeant Bellamy's gravelly bellowing at first light. Wriggling back out of his sleeping bag, feeling absolutely shattered, he made his forlorn way to the holes dug in the sand outside the camp, attended to his toilet, then washed as well as he could with a pan of cold water and carbolic soap. Then, since it was daylight, he was at least allowed to light his portable hexamine stove and have a crude fry-up of bacon, sausage and eggs, with bread toasted against the flames of the burning hexamine blocks and, thank God, a brew-up.

When the breakfast was finished and the utensils had been cleaned and packed away in the Bergen rucksack, he and some of the others were detailed to pour petrol over the temporary latrines and light it, burning everything up. This seemed an odd thing to do in the middle of the desert, but none of the newcomers thought to question the necessity as they hurriedly dismantled their shelters, rolled and packed their groundsheets and ponchos, removed all signs of the camp, and loaded their gear into the Chevrolets in preparation for another drive into the desert.

Before that, however, they were ordered by Sergeant Bellamy, bellowing as always, to gather around their LRDG instructors, in the already fierce heat of the morning, for lessons in how to maximise the use of their precious water.

'The first method,' Red Lester cheerfully told Marty and Tone, demonstrating each step with the aid of a toothbrush, strop-razor and metal container, 'is to clean your teeth.' He mimicked cleaning his teeth with the toothbrush. 'Spit the tiny amount of water in your mouth out into the container.' He spat into the metal container, making nauseating gargling sounds. 'Use that to shave with.' He pretended to swish his razor around in the container, supposedly filled with water, though actually holding only his gob of spit. 'Then put it into the radiator of your vehicle.' He pretended to unscrew the top of the radiator, pour the contents of the container into the radiator and screw the top back on.

Beaming with satisfaction while Marty and Tone started sweating in the rising heat, he continued enthusiastically, 'Now! Here's how you make an improvised filtering system out of old food cans.' So saying, he poured a handful of sand into an empty food can, then unbuttoned his short pants, pulled out his cock and urinated on the sand inside the can.

'Aw, Jesus!' Tone groaned in horror.

Acknowledging Tone's disgust only with a broader grin, Red finished urinating, tucked his cock back into his trousers, buttoned up, then turned to the other opened can that he had previously sat upright on the bonnet of the Chevrolet. After punching a series of holes in the bottom with the tip of his commando dagger, he placed the can, bottom downward, on top of the first opened, empty can. He then threw a couple of handfuls of sand and small stones into the top container, until they formed a layer over the punched holes in the bottom. Finally, he poured his sand-filled urine from the metal container into the can, onto the layer of sand and stones, letting it drip through to the lower can.

'*Voila!*' he exclaimed, spreading his hands triumphantly. 'Now the dirty water can be recycled and used again.'

'Fucking wonderful,' Tone murmured, looking disgusted.

'Of course,' Red went on, removing the filter from a captured Italian gas mask and placing it over the opening in the top can of his improvised filtering system, 'you can also use one of these instead of the layer of sand and stones. So, when you've picked up your inadequate water-bottle ration, you clean your teeth, swill your gob out with the water, then spit the water into the filter and let it run back into the can.'

'I could puke at the very thought,' Marty told him.

'If you do,' Red replied, 'just remember to put your puke through the filtering system for a bit of recycling. That's the LRDG way.'

'*Move out!*' Sergeant Bellamy bellowed, signalling the command with a downward wave of his right hand as his own Chevrolet moved out of the laager, its wheels churning up clouds of sand.

'Here we go,' Red said, clambering in behind the steering wheel and revving the engine even as Marty and Tone clambered back on board. 'Another day in paradise.'

They spent that morning learning to drive the Chevrolets across smooth, hard seria, up and down deep wadis and steep sand dunes, and across rocky ground that alternated dangerously with patches of soft sand and gravel. They also learned to fire the weapons fixed to the vehicles while on the move, always aiming slightly ahead of the target and making allowances for the illusions created by brilliant sunlight and the ever-shifting sands. This wasn't as easy as Marty had imagined it would be, since the Chevrolets moved at an erratic speed, sometimes held back by soft sand, other times racing free without warning, and because they were constantly bounced from side to side by loose stones and potholes. Also, he was not only blinded by his own sweat and scorched by the sun's heat, but also found himself burning from the heat that came off his roaring Browning machine-gun. The heatwaves rising off the gun's barrel actually distorted the targets, which invariably were palm trees or dried-out desert plants.

To make life more difficult, when going through soft sand the vehicles were often bogged down and had to be dug out – so the men learned the hard way just what the sand mats and channels fixed to the vehicles were for.

Invariably, the nose of the car would be tipped right forward, the axle buried deep in the sand. Getting it out was harrowing work that would have been impossible without the sand mats and channels. The former were woven mats; the latter were five-foot-long heavy metal channels that had originally been used in the First World War as the roofing for dugouts.

First, the men had to unload all of their gear from the vehicle to make it lighter. After laboriously digging and scraping the sand away from the wheels of the trapped vehicle, they pushed the sand mats, or trays, under the front wheels and the steel sand channels under the rear wheels. When these were firmly in place between the wheels and the soft sand, the vehicle, with its engine running in low gear, could then be pushed forward onto a succession of other sand mats or channels until it was back on firmer ground.

It was a sweaty, back-breaking, exhausting business that had to be done at least every couple of hours and was maintained throughout that long day of relentless desert driving and navigation. Thus, by late afternoon, when Sergeant Bellamy again ordered the men to form a protective laager with their vehicles and make camp for the night, Marty, who prided himself on his endurance, felt physically shattered.

Rest did not come immediately, however. Again, the men had, very carefully, to check, service and clean both the vehicles and their personal weapons. They then had to camouflage the vehicles with hessian nets covered with sand and stones. With those tedious, time-consuming jobs completed, they still had to raise their individual shelters, either on sticks or tied to their vehicles, then roll out their groundsheets and sleeping bags. Finally, as before, they had to dig holes just outside the camp to be used as latrines.

As the stop was taking place about two hours before sunset,

Captain Paddy Kearney, who had repeatedly appeared out of nowhere in his personal Chevrolet truck to check the progress of the exercises, gave permission for fires to be lit, so long as they were extinguished before darkness. Using his portable hexamine stove, Marty was finally able to have a hot meal, consisting of bully beef, tinned M and V (meat and vegetables), dehydrated potatoes and herrings in tomato. By the time he had finished eating, cleaned his utensils and let out his previous meal by squatting over one of the fly-covered holes in the ground, he was so exhausted that he practically staggered back to his shelter, where again he slept the sleep of the dead.

As usual, he and the others were up at first light the following morning to go out on another exercise patrol, this one on foot because they were going to be trained in unusual forms of desert navigation.

It was murder. They hiked for four hours and stopped, about every hour, only to learn one of the various LRDG methods of making their way across hundreds of miles of relatively featureless terrain. After being trained in the proper use of a compass and sextant, they were shown how to make an improvised compass by stroking a sewing needle in one direction against a piece of silk and suspending it in a loop of thread so that it pointed north; by laying the needle on a piece of paper or bark and floating it on water in a cup or mess tin; or by stropping a razor blade against the palm of the hand and, as with the sewing needle, suspending it from a piece of thread to let it point north.

By last light they had learned that, while in the featureless desert maps were fairly useless, they could, nevertheless, get a sense of direction from a combination of marked oases and drawn contour lines. They also learned how to find local magnetic variations, when not recorded on a map, by pointing their compass at the North Star and noting the difference between the pointer and the indicated North. Lastly, while the sun was still up, they were shown how to ascertain direction by planting a three-foot upright in the desert floor, marking the tip of its shadow with a pebble or stick, marking the tip of the moving shadow fifteen minutes later, and joining the two with a line which would run from east to west, thus revealing north and south as well. This was known as the 'shadow stick method.'

Normally when darkness fell, bringing the blessing of cool air, they would have made camp for the night. In this instance, however, even as most of the men were already looking exhausted, the relentless Sergeant Bellamy, after conversing with Captain Kearney, who had again materialised out of nowhere in his personal jeep, made them march even deeper into the desert. There they were taught to navigate by the timing of the rise and fall of the moon, or by the position of certain stars or constellations. Only then, when two of them had collapsed from exhaustion and one from sunburn, were they allowed to commence the long march back to the base camp. They arrived back just before midnight and went to bed without eating.

The fourth, seemingly interminable, day was taken up with more lessons in desert survival, including the avoidance of dehydration, sunstroke and sunburn; the locating and utilising of artesian wells; the hunting of desert gazelles for food; desert camouflage and the digging of shallow 'scrapes' and other laying-up places (LUPs); treatment for the bites of poisonous spiders, scorpions and snakes, or illness caused by lice, mites, flies and mosquitoes; the use of stretched contraceptives to keep dust out of weapons; the construction of a desert still to produce drinkable water from urine; and how to avoid drowning when caught in a wadi during a flash flood.

Marty wouldn't have believed that so much could be crammed into one day, but it was and it left him exhausted. The rigours of training, as he was swiftly learning, were in no way eased by the additional hardships imposed by the desert itself, which affected Marty and the others in strange ways. By night the desert was freezing cold, but during the day the heat was fierce, shimmering up off the sand, hurting the eyes, making sweat flow, and leading to short tempers and fist fights. Tempers were also fused by the constant dust – blowing every second of every day and night, covering everything, filling the throat and nostrils, getting into food and drink, even inside sleeping bags – a constant dust that swirled in moaning clouds and drifted over the plains of rocky ground, soft sand and gravel. The dust also charged the metal parts of vehicles with electricity, shorting out the engines, often stopping the vehicles altogether and giving the men electric shocks.

Worst of all were the flies – thousands of them, all fat and black – attacking eyes and ears, dropping into the tea and food, buzzing noisily, frantically, all day long, and making a visit to the holes used as latrines a veritable endurance test.

Although the nights were freezing, and gave some respite from the flies, a similar torment was offered in the shape of lice, bugs and cockroaches and, if a man became too careless, poisonous scorpions. All of these drove the men crazy and led to frayed tempers.

Then there was the thirst, which was constant and hellish to endure. The drinking water was warm, distilled sea water that just about kept them alive while failing dismally to quench their unrelenting thirst. Foul to drink on its own, it was more satisfying in a brew-up, though even then its high salt content curdled the tinned milk and filled the mugs with soft, disgusting curds. The tea was more refreshing than the water, but even that didn't quench their thirst.

By the afternoon of the fifth day, Marty, like most of the men, was almost mindless with exhaustion and growing stale from too much training. He was therefore relieved when Lieutenant Kearney turned up to announce that the training period was over and they could all return to the base camp.

By last light, the LRDG convoy was back at the FOB at Siwa Oasis and the men were stood down for the night.

'That was the longest fucking week of my life,' Tone complained to Marty.

'The most exciting week of *my* life,' Marty responded. 'Now I want a taste of the real thing. A proper patrol.'

'You must be mad,' Red told him.

CHAPTER FOUR

Marty was filled with excitement when he rose at first light with the other men to attend to his ablutions and get dressed in his special desert clothing, including shirt and shorts, the *shemagh* and black woollen *agal*, leather gauntlets and open-toed Arab sandals. Like the others, he also put on a heavy sheepskin jacket to defeat the icy cold of the desert morning.

After a hearty breakfast in the mess tent, he went with Tone and a bunch of other newcomers – already referred to mockingly by the 'old hands' of the LRDG as 'pale faces' or 'Inglesi' – to the armoury to collect the weapons they had left there the day before. Shortly after, at the motor pool, they found the rest of the LRDG already checking their vehicles.

Shivering with cold even in his sheepskin jacket, Marty glanced about him and saw that practically the whole of the LRDG – ten patrols in all – was moving out with a mixture of 30-cwt Chevrolet trucks, modified four-wheel-drive Ford F60 cars, three-ton supply trucks and a Light Aid Detachment maintenance truck. Also moving out was the LRDG artillery section, consisting of a 4.5-inch howitzer, an 88mm 25-pounder, and a light tank, each mounted on a ten-tonner. He also saw that Captain Kearney was going to lead the expedition and that he was accompanied by the redoubtable Sergeant Bellamy.

'Judging by this lot,' he said to Tone, 'I'd say we're in for a pretty lengthy patrol.'

'You are,' Corporal Red Lester told him before Tone could respond. 'Reconnaissance and intelligence gathering is what it's all about, though you may have some serious fun as well.'

'What kind of fun?' Tone asked.

'Contact with the enemy,' Red replied. 'What the fuck did you think I meant, Inglesi?'

Tone's intended response was cut short when Kearney stood up in his Chevrolet truck and Bellamy bawled that the men should gather around to be briefed. When they had done so, Bellamy folded his thick arms and stared grimly at them, ensuring silence while Kearney talked.

'As you men have probably gathered,' he said, 'we're about to embark on a major reconnaissance patrol that will include cross-country drives to pinpoint enemy bases and positions, road watches to monitor the movement of enemy troops, and harassment attacks against enemy transport convoys. The operation could last as long as a month, which is why we've brought the supply trucks. Our main area of operations will be the Western Desert of Cyrenaica, including enemy positions in the Gazala–Tmimi area. As usual, we'll be making our own maps as we go along and have brought our survey section with us for this purpose. Modest air support can be supplied, if needed, by our two American WACO light aircraft, but apart from those we're on our own. Are there any questions?' There were no questions. 'Right,' Kearney said briskly. 'Let's move out.' When Sergeant Bellamy clambered up into the front of Kearney's Chevrolet, Kearney raised and lowered his right hand, indicating 'Advance'.

'Move out!' Bellamy bawled.

The trucks moved out of the oasis in an irregular column, churning up clouds of sand in their wake. Manning the Browning machine-gun at the front of his Chevrolet, with Tone behind him on the Boyes anti-tank rifle and Red driving, Marty felt a surge of exhilaration as they left the oasis behind and headed into the vast plains of the desert. That exhilaration was short-lived when, the instant the convoy moved out of the shade of the oasis, the sun's blazing heat hit him with the force of a hammer.

'Shit!' Tone exclaimed, removing his sheepskin jacket while still holding his Boyes anti-tank rifle. 'We've only been in the sun for a minute and already I'm sweating.'

'And it's only eight in the morning,' Red reminded him with what sounded like relish, also removing his jacket. 'Just wait till the sun climbs higher in the sky; then you'll know what real heat is.'

'We *already* know what real heat is, Corporal,' Marty responded as the truck bounced roughly across the stony plain, forcing him to cling tightly to the grip of his rattling machine-gun with one hand while removing his sheepskin jacket with the other. 'Apart from those desert runs that only ended last night, Tone and I fought at Mersa Brega – so we know all about heat.'

'Sorry, Inglesi.'

'And you can cut that for a start,' Marty said. 'We might be new to the LRDG, but we're not new to the desert, so don't come it with "pale-face" or "Inglesi". First names or rank only, thanks.'

He saw Red's crooked, black-toothed grin in the rear-view mirror as he nodded assent. 'A soldier who knows his rights,' Red replied. 'Okay, Private, you've got it.'

'Thanks, Corporal,' Marty said.

Already sweating from the heat, he found that even though he was seated behind his weapon, the muscles of his legs were already aching from his constant attempts to keep his balance on the piles of kit beneath his feet.

'You'll get used to it,' Red said when he complained. 'Your legs will only ache for a week or so; after that, you'll have the legs of a wrestler and the girls will go mad for you.'

'What girls?' Tone asked sardonically, squinting into the brilliant light of the vast, flat plain. 'Christ!' he added. 'It's hot!'

The heat increased as the sun climbed higher in the sky and the trucks continued their journey across the hard sand of the seria. Sheer cliffs rose out of the heat haze in the north; sand dunes were visible in the west, so beautiful that they seemed almost unreal. However, as the convoy moved deeper into the Western Desert, to where the conflict had raged a few months before, they came across old battlefields where the debris of war lay everywhere: derelict staff cars and jeeps, scorched, mangled tanks and halftracks, tin hats peppered with bullet holes, empty water cans, derelict vehicles, bits of clothing and the scars of weapon pits. Occasionally they saw protruding from the sand the whithered foot or hand of some rotting corpse.

'Poor bastards,' Tone whispered.

'Rather them than us,' Red replied. 'It's just the luck of the draw, mate.'

By 1000 hours, when the convoy had already stopped twice for the usual tedious checking of the vehicles and weapons, the sun was well up in the sky, over twenty degrees, throwing a sharp shadow from the needle of the sun compass. By noon, with the sun almost directly above them, the vehicles were halted again, but this time in the shadow of a steep wadi side where they would not be seen by enemy aircraft. While the rest of the men lay gratefully under the shade of a tarpaulin stretched between two trucks, the navigator of each vehicle took a fix on the sun through the smoked glass of his theodolite, the radio operator contacted base for any fresh orders – there were none – and Captain Kearney, accompanied by Sergeant Bellamy, wandered from one group of men to another, checking that all of them were okay.

'So, Private Butler,' he said to Marty. 'You're still surviving, I see.'

'Yes, sir,' Marty responded.

'Not letting yourself be run into the ground by the LRDG?'

'No, sir.'

Kearney turned to the granite-faced Sergeant Bellamy. 'Is Butler the private you said was always getting up to mischief?'

'A hard case, sir. Fairly bright, but undisciplined. The kind that needs to be kept busy. He should be all right out here.'

'*Will* you be all right out here, Butler?' Kearney asked.

'Not much option, sir,' Marty replied boldly, 'being stuck here in the middle of nowhere.'

'How wise of you,' Kearney said, then he marched off, still grinning, with Bellamy.

'I think he likes you,' Red said to Marty. 'He's a bit of a wild man himself and likes men with initiative. He's not your regular Army type at all; he doesn't stand on ceremony and he judges a man solely by his work. I think he likes a free spirit.'

'That's me!' Marty retorted.

The column was soon on the move again, heading even deeper into the desert, passing more old battlefields with their sad, sometimes sickening debris, but not coming into contact with the enemy.

'We're still too close to our own lines,' Red explained during another stop. 'We'll make contact tomorrow.'

The heat was truly appalling for most of the afternoon, burning even through the black woollen *agal* and *shemagh* to the skull; but it cooled to more bearable levels in the late afternoon, when Captain Kearney started looking for a place to lay up for the night. Eventually, after another hour's search, he found the ideal spot: on a high ridge overlooking a flat plain divided by an Axis forces' main supply route – or MSR, as such routes were known. Intending to spend most of the following day surveying that MSR, he told the men to form a protective laager and make camp.

The trucks laagered by parking across the wind, then the men covered the vehicles with 'cam' nets of desert-coloured hessian, which blended perfectly with the surrounding shrub, making the trucks hard to see from the air. Each driver then pinned his truck's folded tarpaulin by two wheels on the lee side with the upper half forming a windbreak, the lower a groundsheet. Before resting, however, the drivers had to check their day's petrol consumption and make the usual maintenance checks while the rest of the men checked and cleaned their weapons, then covered the moveable parts with stretched contraceptives.

'It may stretch over *this* weapon,' Red said, carefully drawing a rubber over his 9mm Sten submachine-gun, 'but it's still too small to fit over mine – or so the ladies tell me.'

'I'll bet,' Marty retorted.

'Personally, I don't like rubbers,' Tone chipped in as he wrestled with the contraceptive he was trying to stretch over the ten-round detachable box magazine of his .303 Lee-Enfield bolt-action rifle. 'I can never get the bloody things on and I hate taking them off.'

'How can you hate taking them off?' Red challenged him, recognising a virgin when he saw one, 'when you can never get the bloody things on?'

'He's so big they all burst,' Marty said, trying to help his friend out, 'when he reaches his full length.'

'Pull the other one,' Red said.

Luckily, at that point, the cook – nicknamed Monsieur Verdoux because of his poisonous concoctions – called out that dinner was ready. Though not exactly over the moon to sample Monsieur Verdoux's bully-beef curry, Marty and his friends wolfed it down, rinsed the taste out with a brew-up, relaxed with a smoke, then washed in cold water held in metal containers, trying to get rid of the sweat-slimed sand. Finally, they stretched out under the camouflaged trucks and tried to sleep the best they could, given that the evening was bitterly cold and that the flies and mosquitoes, oblivious of it, whined and buzzed about them.

Those still sleeping were awakened at first light by the soldiers on last watch and found themselves not only shivering with cold, but also bitten black and blue by the mosquitoes that had tormented them without respite. After attending to their ablutions, they put on their warm sheepskin jackets, had a breakfast of wads and hot tea, then settled down to a lengthy reconnaissance of the MSR on the desert plain below the escarpment.

Within an hour, the sun was high in the sky and the heat forced them to remove their jackets. By the end of the second hour, the sun was even higher, the heat was even worse, and the flies and mosquitoes were forming dark clouds around them, driven into a feeding frenzy by the smell of human sweat. Luckily, the MSR was busy, with German and Italian trucks moving constantly along it, clearly heading for Tobruk, where British, Australian and Indian forces were still under siege. This constant activity at least gave the men something to watch, though the only ones who could actually do anything positive were Sergeant Bellamy, who was keeping a log of all enemy troop movements; Captain Kearney, who was in constant radio communication with MEHQ, Cairo, calling up air strikes against the enemy transports; and the NCOs of the survey section, who spent their time making specialised LRDG maps of the vast area stretched out below them, unfolding to the heat-hazed horizon.

'If I have to lie here all day,' Marty whispered to Tone where they lay together on the edge of the escarpment, looking down on the heatwaves shimmering up off the desert plain, 'I'll go bloody mad. Why the hell can't we go down into that desert and drum up a bit of action for ourselves? Better than sitting here roasting our backsides. More productive as well.'

'Hail the hero!' Red exclaimed mockingly. 'He can't wait to get into a fire fight and shit in his pants.'

'The day I shit in my pants,' Marty retorted, 'is the day I have to stand before my maker. It won't happen before that.'

Red laughed and rolled onto his belly to watch the first of the air strikes called in by Captain Kearney. Crawling closer to the edge of the escarpment, Marty watched keenly as a squadron of Hurricane fighter planes swooped on the Italian troop transports snaking across the shimmering plain, along the MSR. As the first of the aircraft swept over the column, guns chattering, the anti-aircraft guns on the Italian transports roared into action, filling the blue sky with criss-crossing tapestries of green tracer and ink-coloured clouds of exploding flak. Simultaneously, the desert around the troop trucks erupted in a series of explosions that hurled columns of swirling sand high into the air to rain back down over the scattering vehicles. Though spreading out to minimise the danger from the attacking aircraft, the Italian vehicles were unable to escape the combined onslaught of machine-gun fire and bombs, many bursting into flames and, in some cases, being hurled onto their sides with burning men spilling out of the rear and black smoke boiling from them.

Feeling safe on the escarpment, though baking in the fierce heat, the men of the LRDG lit cigarettes and watched the attack, cheering each time an Italian truck was either bombed or came to a shuddering, smoking halt in a hail of bullets. Soon that section of the MSR was covered in a pall of boiling sand that temporarily obscured the Italian column. Ten minutes later, the British aircraft, having released all their bombs, fired the last rounds from their machine-guns and headed back to Cairo without causalties. As the spiralling dust settled back on the desert plain the Italian column was seen to be devastated, with many of the trucks burning and pouring smoke. The dead or wounded bodies of those who had tried to escape were scattered widely about them.

Similar attacks took place throughout the rest of the morning as Kearney continued to radio details of passing Axis columns back to MEHQ Cairo. By early afternoon, the Italians, obviously realising that their MSR was under surveillance, sent a couple of CR42s to reconnoitre the area and, if necessary, put the Brits out of business. The aircraft flew over the escarpment twice without seeing the camouflaged LRDG vehicles – but seeing them on the third run, when they flew over at low altitude, they circled around to come back for an attack.

'Move out!' Kearney bawled.

Marty was up and running at the sound of that commanding voice, but Red was already at the truck, ripping the 'cam' net off and throwing it into the front seat as Tone scrambled up to take his position at the Boyes anti-tank rifle. Marty managed to take his position behind the Browning machine-gun just as the first of the Italian CR42's came barrelling out of the azure sky with all guns firing, stitching lines of spitting sand across the rim of the escarpment, right up to where Kearney's Chevrolet was breaking the laager by lurching forward in a cloud of churning sand.

The first of the Italian aircraft had already whined over the LRDG and was ascending again when its two bombs exploded with a mighty roar, accompanied by mushrooms of swirling, hissing sand that erupted from the edge of the escarpment, just short of the first two escaping Chevrolets.

Marty heard the roaring of his Browning machine-gun before realising that he had actually pressed the trigger. As he and Tone opened fire, Red pressed his foot on the accelerator and the Chevrolet shot forward through the swirling sand. Nearly thrown out of the truck, Marty gripped the stock of the Browning tighter, braced his legs, then managed to aim roughly at the next incoming Italian plane and fire a sustained burst as it roared down and up again, its bombs causing two more explosions that made his head ring.

'Bastards!' Tone screamed excitedly, firing at the diving aircraft with his pintle-mounted Boyes anti-tank rifle. 'Take that, you sods!'

The LRDG trucks were now racing down the hill, weaving frantically to avoid the lines of spitting sand being stitched by the machine-guns of the aircraft, bouncing violently over rocks and potholes, their wheels churning up clouds of sand that mingled with that sweeping out and hissing noisily from the explosions created by the bombs. Like Marty, the rest of the LRDG gunners were hammering away at the planes, practically hanging onto the stocks of their weapons and swinging wildly from side to side as they attempted to follow the aircraft that were diving and climbing through a great web of purple tracery and black clouds of flak.

Eventually, one of the Italian planes was hit. Pieces of metal flew off it and flames burst from its fuselage, engulfing the cockpit before the unfortunate pilot could escape. Whining erratically and wobbling, spitting flames and oily smoke, the stricken plane plummeted, spinning, to earth and smashed into the desert plain, exploding as a spectacular ball of fire. The other aircraft, like a flock of frightened birds, turned away and flew off.

As the LRDG drivers eased their feet off the accelerators, slowing down when they reached the bottom of the hill and heading once more across the flat, sunscorched plain, Marty fired a final, defiant burst at the disappearing CR42s, then raised his right fist in the air and whooped in triumph.

Almost immediately, another Chevrolet emerged from the swirling dust and Marty saw the flushed face of Sergeant Bellamy glaring grimly at him.

'What are you celebrating?' Bellamy bawled as his truck kept abreast of Red's. 'We were *pursued*, you stupid prat!

We're not supposed to be bloody pursued. We're supposed to *pursue*! So stop looking so bloody pleased with yourself and act like a real soldier.'

'Yes, Sarge!' Marty shouted back. 'Absolutely, Sarge!'

Bellamy shook his head from side to side, then angrily smacked his hand against the steering wheel and put his foot down again. As his Chevrolet raced away, into the swirling sand, Marty saw, through the murk, another face staring at him, this one grinning in good-humoured mockery. It was Captain Kearney.

For the next few days the LRDG vehicles roamed far and wide across the Western Desert, often crossing their own tracks to ensure that the Axis forces could not easily track them. Once they were off the high plateau and down on the desert floor, Captain Kearney's strategy was to send the Chevrolets off in many different directions, looking for the enemy, with orders to report back at a certain time to the selected rendezvous (RV), when each patrol leader would report on what had been seen.

When previously unknown Axis MSRs were located, the whole patrol would drive there and take up a suitable position from which they could observe the passing traffic. When details of the traffic on the MSR had been ascertained by a single day's observation and the general direction of the MSR calculated by the survey section, Sergeant Bellamy would enter the details in his notebook and Captain Kearney would then relay them to MEHQ, Cairo. From there, the intelligence gathered would be relayed to the British airfield at Geneina where reconnaissance planes would be sent out to track the whole MSR from beginning to end, take aerial photographs of the enemy positions located along it, and arrange for fighter planes and bombers to attack it.

Hiding in their shallow scrapes in the desert floor, or under their camouflaged trucks, the LRDG men were often gratified to hear the distant explosions and see great fans of fire illuminating the horizon where the night raids against the enemy positions located by them were taking place.

Sometimes the enemy MSRs were viewed from far away

through binoculars, with the Chevrolets carefully camouflaged to look like small dunes or rocks and the men lying belly down on the ground, gradually being covered by the ever-shifting sands. At other times, however, Captain Kearney would make them take laying-up positions (LUPs) behind sand dunes that sloped right down to the edge of the road along which the Axis traffic was passing. When this was the case, Marty was simultaneously shocked and thrilled at just how close to the enemy he was – so close he could clearly see the features of the passing Italian or German soldiers – and would study the passing troop trucks, M13 tanks and halftracks with wide-eyed, unblinking fascination, hardly daring to breathe.

The Germans, he was forced to admit, looked like real fighting soldiers – bristling with polished weapons, Zeiss binoculars around their necks and gleaming Beretta pistols or Lugers in their holsters – but the Italians, who did not look like fighters at all, tended to carry their belongings in cardboard boxes and had bottles of Chianti tied to their belts, rather than holsters. With their ill-fitting uniforms and unshaven chins, they looked like peasants who had stepped into this war by accident and did not wish to be here.

Seeing the enemy that close also filled Marty with immense frustration – the circumstances seemed so good for an ambush – and eventually, unable to restrain himself, he raised the subject with Captain Kearney.

'Impatient little devil, aren't you?' Kearney responded.

'Yes, sir, I suppose so. But it seems such a waste to be so close to them and not be able to take advantage of it. A right bloody waste, sir.'

To Marty's horror, Kearney, grinning wickedly, turned to the grim-faced Sergeant Bellamy. 'Did you hear that, Sarge? Young Private Butler here seems to think it's a waste not to attack those Axis forces when we have them under surveillance.'

'Oh, does he now?' Bellamy stared at Marty as if wanting to bite his head off. 'Then perhaps we should send the impatient private out into the desert alone with orders to bring back a few scalps. Perhaps he's seen too many movies about cowboys and Indians and doesn't know what the real world's all about. Maybe thinks he's John Wayne.'

'You may be right, Sarge.'

When Bellamy had stomped off, throwing another fierce glance at Marty, Kearney said, 'He'll ride your back now.'

'Yes, sir, he will. Why did you do that?'

'Because I've read your report, Private Butler, and I've been keeping my eye on you. You're a very good soldier, a natural, but you lack patience and commonsense. When you learn both – and you will if Sergeant Bellamy rides your back – you'll turn into an exceptional soldier.'

'So why don't we attack the enemy when they're so close?' Marty persisted.

'Because we couldn't do so without having personal casualties. Where those casualties are wounded, rather than dead, we'd have to take them with us, which would make our work virtually impossible. As the results of our work do more damage to the enemy than anything we could possibly do alone, we stay under cover and do what we can without endangering ourselves. In other words, we only engage the enemy when it's reasonably safe to do so – or when it's absolutely unavoidable. Any more questions, Private?'

'No, sir,' Marty said.

Kearney led the patrol deeper into the desert, heading straight for the setting sun. As they travelled on across the vast plains, into deepening darkness – featureless desert all around them, a line of mountains in the distance – they passed a caravan of Senussi bedouin: bearded sheiks, women in colourful robes, donkeys and heavily laden camels, all silhouetted by the blood-red, darkening sky.

Though he had seen similar before, Marty could never quite accept that the bedouin were real, that they could remain so unchanged while a war was raging about them with all the might of modern military technology. The bedouin seemed oblivious. Nevertheless, the fact that Captain Kearney was leading the convoy at an exceptionally slow pace, frequently stopping altogether to get out and examine the ground for land mines, was a grim reminder that the war was still engaged and, though presently off stage, was an ever present danger.

Also apt to make the men forget that a war was still raging were the gazelle that often appeared, seemingly out of nowhere, bounding across the desert plain with graceful, almost effeminate, leaps and bounds. Though sublimely beautiful, the gazelle were, particularly in daytime, often shot, cooked and eaten by the LRDG; but as this was night-time, when gunshots could give away the presence of the convoy to the enemy, these particular gazelle escaped unscathed.

When night fell completely, plunging the desert into moonlit darkness, but letting the sky fill up with magnificent tapestries of stars, progress became even slower as the danger of old and new minefields remained. Also, Captain Kearney had to stop even more frequently to navigate by fixing the convoy's position with star bearings and comparing them with his astro-navigation tables with the aid of a flashlight. Last but not least, the usual hourly check of the vehicles and weapons had to be maintained, even given the extreme difficulty of doing so in darkness, aided only by moonlight or torches held downwards to prevent them being seen by enemy patrols or aircraft.

Their daily routine was broken only twice. In the first instance, Kearney received messages from MEHQ, ordering him to use the patrol to transfer important material from one British position to another, which could be done only by passing through enemy territory. In the second instance, they were ordered to pick up a British intelligence agent from a bedouin camp just outside Agedabia, where he had been transported by friendly Egyptians after masquerading as an Arab and living under the very noses of the German forces holding Benghazi.

As the second week ran into a third, Marty felt himself sinking into his environment and becoming more instinctive in everything he did. In fact, for the first time since enlisting, he felt like a proper soldier – a 'natural' as Kearney had put it – and this realisation was, he felt, being silently confirmed by the new respect shown to him by Bellamy.

'That's respect worth having,' Red told him. 'Sergeant Bellamy's a bloody tough bastard, but he's the best there is. If he respects you, you've earned it.'

'What about Captain Kearney?' Marty asked. 'Where does he come from?'

'From Number Eight Commando. Believe it or not, he used to be an Irish rugby international and semi-professional boxer. He's normally good-humoured, as you've probably noticed, but he's got a bloody awful temper that's always getting him into hot water. In fact, he came to the LRDG from a cell at the MP barracks in Bab el Hadid in Cairo, where he was waiting for court-martial proceedings for taking a punch at his CO. But he's an exceptional soldier, already mentioned in despatches for his bravery in action, so instead of a court martial, he was given the option of service with the LRDG. He's a fucking good officer.'

Having also been incarcerated, even if only briefly, in the cells of Bab el Hadid, Marty felt that he had something in common with Kearney and could not help admiring him. In fact, taking the two men together – Kearney and Sergeant Bellamy – Marty thought he was in the company of two men who could take as much as they gave. In short, no matter how hard they pushed him, they were men he respected.

While enemy aircraft had frequently flown overhead and many enemy patrols had been seen, the luck of the LRDG held for nearly three weeks, with no direct confrontations other than that single air attack during the second day of the patrol. During the third week, however, when the Chevrolets were out in the open desert, driving away from yet another road watch in the vicinity of Agheila, a couple of German Ju-87 Stukas barrelled down out of the clear sky to bomb and strafe the convoy.

Before the LRDG drivers had time to disperse, bombs exploded in the middle of the single-file convoy, between two Chevrolets. The powerful blast caught the front of the second car, setting fire to the petrol tank and picking it up off the desert floor to hurl it onto its side in geysering sand and billowing clouds of smoke. Though some of the LRDG drivers had broken away from the column and were racing off across the desert, those nearest to the explosions braked to a halt, with some of the men spilling out to help those trapped in the blazing truck and the others opening up on the diving Stukas with their Boyes anti-tank rifles and Browning machine-guns.

Firing his own Browning while Red and Tone raced across to the blazing Chevrolet, where the men trapped inside could be heard screaming horribly, Marty was conscious only of the snout of the Stuka that appeared to be diving straight at him with its guns stitching twin lines of spitting sand. These raced up to the Chevrolet as if about to cut straight through it, then, miraculously, ran around both sides of it and passed on as the Stuka ascended again.

With the barrel of his Browning almost vertical, Marty kept firing until the Stuka was out of sight, then he lowered the barrel and fired steadily at the next one. He was still firing when two more bombs exploded nearby, this time very close, sending him spinning off the Chevrolet in a roaring wave of sand. He felt the brutal impact of his body hitting the ground, choked in the dense, descending sand, then dropped down through a funnel of darkness, into streaming stars.

Lesley! he cried out in his mind, convinced that he was about to die and welling up with love for her. *Lesley, I . . .*

Regaining consciousness some minutes later, choking and coughing, he instinctively clawed his way out of the impacted sand that could have buried him alive. Crawling back out to the dazzling light of the desert sun, he saw some of the others, including Red and Tone, dragging the scorched blackened bodies of three of the LRDG men out of the still-burning wreckage of their Chevrolet. Clambering to his feet, he staggered over to the others and saw instantly that all three of the horribly burnt men were dead and that one of the charred corpses was minus the lower half of his left leg. The truck in front had also caught part of the blast and was nose-deep in the sand with its reinforced rear bumper hanging off and some of the kit scattered in the sand around it.

Captain Kearney was still sitting upright in the rear seat, but he wasn't moving much and blood was pouring out of his nose and ears, as well as from the many small wounds from imbedded shrapnel. Sergeant Bellamy was easing the wounded officer into a more comfortable position in the seat, prior to the long drive back to base.

Feeling impelled to help, Marty stepped forward and felt his legs giving way beneath him. Again, he dropped down through that funnel of darkness, into streaming stars. This time, when he entered that realm of stars, he travelled on to oblivion.

CHAPTER FIVE

They were called the 'Originals'. The first men to gather together at the ramshackle, ill-equipped camp in the furnace of Kabrit, overlooking the Great Bitter Lake in the Suez Canal zone, had been searched out across the length and breadth of Cairo as soldiers of particular ability and initiative. One of them was Marty, who could scarcely believe that he was here and not actually dead. In fact, only three weeks before, he had regained consciousness in the holding bay of an RAF Hudson transport, relieved to learn that he was still alive, suffering only from mild concussion and bad bruising. When the aircraft had touched down in Cairo, he had been taken by ambulance to the 63rd General Hospital, Helmieh, where he spent a couple of weeks recuperating. Receiving a visit from Tone, he learned that Captain Kearney had also survived the explosion and was recovering in the Scottish Hospital, Cairo.

During his recuperation, Marty slept a lot and had intensely erotic dreams in which Lesley made love to him with an abandon she had not displayed during their single honeymoon night in the Savoy hotel. Nevertheless, the dreams succeeded in resurrecting her almost forgotten image and made him fill up with longing for her. Lying in his bed with little else to do, he thought frequently about the inhibitions she had displayed in bed, blamed it on nervousness caused by her conservative upbringing, and vowed to treat her with care and consideration when next he returned home on leave. He would be a tender lover and understanding husband. He would gradually awaken her to womanhood and enrich both their lives.

By the end of the first week, however, when the headaches and body pains were fading away, he felt fit enough to flirt with the nurses, sit out on the verandah to read, and even secretly drink whisky purchased from some energetic black-marketeering patients. By the end of the second week his low boredom threshold was making him so restless that he talked the British Army doctor into discharging him earlier than planned.

Back in Cairo, at the start of two weeks' convalescence leave, he soon realised that his constant thinking about Lesley had merely increased his sexual hunger. Unable to fight the urge, but determined not to get VD, he had booked himself into a room in Tiger Lil's and hired an eighteen-year-old Egyptian whore, Fatima, for the whole two weeks, on the understanding that she would not fraternise with any other customers during her time with him. He was still there, exploring the city by day and bedding Fatima by night, when he received a written note from Captain Kearney, inviting him to join a new, secret regiment that was being formed by Captain David Stirling, formerly of Number 8 Commando.

Visiting Kearney in the Scottish Hospital, where he was still recovering from a badly wounded leg and temporary deafness, Marty learned that Captain Stirling and another Laycock Number 8 Commando officer, Lieutenant 'Jock' Lewes, had come up with the idea of attacking enemy rear areas with small units instead of hundreds of men. With the support of General Ritchie, the Deputy Chief of General Staff, they were raising a new raiding unit of no more than two hundred men, split into four-man teams, to be inserted by plane behind enemy lines, a long way from their intended destination, to attack several Axis airfields on the same night. Exfiltration would be by a 'taxi service' supplied by the LRDG.

The men selected for this highly dangerous task would be trained personally by Captain Stirling, Captain Kearney, and Lieutenant Lewes. Though Stirling and Kearney held the same rank, the former would be in command of the unit with the latter as his second-in-command. The parent body for the unit was to be a non-existent Special Air Service Brigade, known as L Detachment. Their base would be at Kabrit, in the Suez Canal zone.

'So are you in or out?' Kearney had asked Marty.

'I'm in,' Marty had told him.

Now, mere days after that meeting, Marty was standing in the furnace of Kabrit with Captain Kearney, Sergeant Bellamy, Red Lester, Tone Williams and a whole bunch of other volunteers. The others he did not know, though all of them had already shucked off the badges and uniforms of their former regiments and instead were wearing clothing appropriate to the desert: khaki shirt and shorts, regular Army boots with rolled-down socks, and a soft peaked cap instead of a helmet. Each man also had a Sykes Fairburn commando knife and Browning 9mm High Power handgun strapped to his waist.

The camp itself consisted of no more than three moth-eaten tents for the men, a command tent with a wooden card table and stool, and one badly battered three-ton lorry.

'This is it?' Marty enquired disbelievingly of Red Lester as they stood around the rear of the single three-ton lorry, sweating in the scorching heat, coughing sand from their lungs, and frantically swotting away buzzing clouds of flies, mosquitoes and midges.

Red flexed the muscle of his bared right arm, to make the tattoo of Jane wiggle her hips. 'Seems like it,' he responded with a crooked grin.

'If this is L Detachment, SAS Brigade,' Tone said, 'I want off here and now.'

'Oh, you do, do you?' Sergeant Bellamy bellowed in Tone's ear, having come up unnoticed to stand beside him. 'So why don't you just climb back on that bloody Hudson transport and go back to the brothels of Cairo where you clearly belong? Do us all a favour!'

'Sorry, Sarge!' Tone snapped into that bulldog countenance, glowering only inches away from his face. 'Just a joke, Sarge! No offence meant.'

'I should bloody well think not. Now shut up and listen to what the CO has to tell you.'

Though already informed by Kearney that his new CO was six foot five inches tall, Marty was still impressed when Captain Stirling stood up on the rear of the truck to welcome them to this piss hole in the desert. Captain Stirling looked massive.

'Bloody 'ell,' Red exclaimed softly, 'that bastard's a giant!'

'But he doesn't have his head in the clouds,' Marty quickly responded. 'I hear he's smart and quick on his feet.'

'Let's hope so,' Tone whispered.

With his head practically scraping the top of the truck, Stirling thanked the listening men for volunteering to join L Detachment, apologised for the ramshackle state of the camp, and informed them that there was a 'splendid' Allied camp fifteen miles south of Kabrit, used by British, Australian, Indian and New Zealand troops, with the last, in particular, living in considerable luxury.

'I'm afraid,' Stirling continued – disingenuously, Marty suspected – 'that I have to fly immediately to Cairo to arrange for the shipment of more transport and weapons, so I won't be able to help you improve these awful living conditions. However, bearing in mind what I've just told you about the Kiwis' camp, I trust that by the time I return you'll have managed to sort something out.'

'In other words,' Tone whispered to Marty, 'he wants us to go to that Kiwi camp and pinch all we need.'

'It's L Detachment's first lesson in survival,' Marty responded with a grin. 'We sink or we swim.'

This turned out to be true. Within minutes of Stirling's departure by Hudson transport to Cairo, Sergeant Bellamy, at Captain Kearney's request, was bellowing for 'volunteers' to help him 'requisition' some supplies and equipment from the nearby Allied camp. Before anyone could respond, Bellamy jabbed his finger at a dozen of the men, including Marty, Tone and Red, indicating that they should climb up into the battered three-ton truck. He then personally drove them the fifteen miles to the Allied camp, arriving there just as the sun was going down.

'Tent city,' he said softly to Marty as they both gazed out over the hundreds of tents spread out in neat rows across a dusty plain, with the Mediterranean glittering in moonlight beyond the escarpment. 'There must be thousands of men there.'

'Thousands,' Marty agreed. 'And all living better than us. That isn't right, Sarge.'

'No, it's not,' Sergeant Bellamy replied with a wicked grin. 'New Zealand Division!' he bawled as he drove past the Indian guard. Receiving no more than a weary nod of permission, he continued driving, passing row upon row of tents, tanks, halftracks, jeeps, and the many trucks of the British, Australian and Indian lines, until they arrived at the area used by the New Zealanders. There, with no Kiwis in sight, he supervised the hasty loading of brand-new tents, camouflage netting, proper camp beds, mattresses, sheets, towels, wooden tables and chairs, steel lockers, wash-hand basins, mirrors, kerosene lamps, cooking utensils, portable showers and latrines, and even crates of beer and spirits. At Tone's request, they even stole the piano from the Kiwis' mess tent. Then, without further ado, they drove out of the camp – receiving only another weary nod from the Indian guard on the main gate – and made their way back through the desert to their own, more modest, camp at Kabrit.

By midnight they had raised the tents and filled them with their personal belongings. They had also raised the biggest tent as a mess tent, helped the cook set up his kitchen, carried in the trestle tables and chairs, stacked the crates of beer and spirits beside a refrigerator – which was run off a portable electric generator – and, finally, wheeled in the piano. With Tone playing and leading a singsong, they partied until the early hours of the morning, then collapsed one by one into their beds and slept the sleep of the dead.

When they were woken at first light by the bellowing of Sergeant Bellamy, most of them were exhausted and hung over. Nevertheless, regardless of how they felt, their brutal special training commenced with no mercy given.

The systematic torture of the Originals began with a more

intensive weapons course than any of them had ever undergone before. Assuming that their greatest need would be for a barrage of fire at relatively close range to cover a hasty retreat after acts of sabotage, Sergeant Bellamy gave only cursory attention to the standard bolt-action rifles and instead concentrated on the new 9mm Sten submachine-gun. This was only 762mm long, weighed a mere 3.70kg, was cheap and crude in construction, with a simple metal stock and short barrel, yet could fire 550 rounds per minute from 32-round box magazines and had an effective range of 40m. To cover the same needs, great attention was also given to the M1 Thompson submachine-gun, better known as the tommy-gun and immortalised by the Hollywood gangster movies of the 1930s and early 1940s. Everyone was also retrained in the use of the 0.5-inch Browning heavy machine-gun, the Bren gun, and the lethal Vickers K .303-inch machine-gun, actually an aircraft weapon, which fired a mixture of tracer, armour-piercing incendiary, and ball.

'We've got more weapons than fingers,' Tone noted sardonically. 'What the bloody 'ell do we do with 'em?'

'What you do with them is fire them,' Marty said, 'when Sergeant Bellamy tells you. Don't ask for a reason.'

'The reason,' Sergeant Bellamy told him, materialising like a ghost beside him, 'is that you blind bastards have to learn to protect each other by being able to pick up another man's weapon, no matter what it is. Do you understand that, Private Williams?'

'I understand, Sarge,' said Tone.

'Fucking miracles never cease.'

Firing practice was undertaken on a flat stretch of desert, baked by a fierce sun, often covered in windblown dust, filled with buzzing flies and whining mosquitoes, with crudely painted targets raised on wooden stakes at the far end, overlooking the glittering Great Bitter Lake. This strip of ground was also used for training in the use of 500g and 1kg hand grenades, including the pineapple-shaped '36' grenade and captured German 'potato mashers', which had a screw-on canister at one end, a screw-off cap at the other and a wooden handle.

'Stealing from the bloody enemy,' Tone said. 'That can't be a good sign.'

'It's a good sign in the sense that these potato mashers are better than *our* hand grenades,' Red insisted. 'This handle makes them easier to throw and they're also more reliable in actually going off.'

'Give me a "thirty-six" any day,' Marty said. 'It fits my hand very nicely, thanks.'

'It's long and thin,' Red explained to Tone, 'so he thinks he's holding his own dick.'

'If he could get it that hard and that long,' Tone replied, 'he'd be more of a man than he is now.'

'There speaks the virgin,' Marty retorted, 'about the only married man in this threesome. I'd call that real cheek.'

'Just throw the bloody thing,' Sergeant Bellamy interjected, suddenly materialising over them where they lay belly down on the burning sands. 'If you confuse a potato masher with your prick, you'll be in very bad trouble. Okay, you berks, *throw*!'

'Yes, Sarge!' all three men bawled at once, then they threw their grenades.

'Bloody hopeless,' Sergeant Bellamy complained, when the grenades exploded short of their targets. 'A bunch of wankers I've got here.' After that he worked them relentlessly, throwing one grenade after another, through the blazing afternoon, until the falling of last light, allowing them to go back to camp for a meal and sleep only when they were completely exhausted.

This wasn't unusual. These days, they were all exhausted most of the time. Their nerves were also stretched to breaking point by a combination of relentless training in the vicious heat, constant thirst, the tormenting insects, and a variety of increasingly paranoid fears, including dread of the many venomous snakes and spiders.

They had been training for five days when Hudson transports arrived from Cairo, bringing Captain Stirling in with a horde of Royal Electrical and Mechanical Engineers, who immediately started work on improving the quality of the portable showers and 'thunder boxes'. Other aircraft, following the Hudson transports over the next couple of days, brought in trucks, jeeps and drivers from the Royal Corps of Transport, as well as weapons from the armoury at Geneina.

'I never thought I'd see the day when I'd swop my place with one of *them*,' Tone said as he, Marty and Red Lester watched the REME creating a defensive perimeter of stone-walled sangars containing Bofors anti-aircraft guns. The men were stripped to the waist, burnt by the sun and gleaming with sweat.

'Bloody REME,' Red said disparagingly, swatting flies and mosquitoes away from his flushed face.

'I still don't know what REME stands for,' Tone said, wiping sweat from his forehead.

'Rear Echelon Mother Fuckers,' Marty explained, then he and Red burst out laughing.

They were not laughing the next day when the first lessons in their demolitions training took place on the firing range, under the supervision of a dour Royal Army Ordnance Corps (RAOC) sergeant, Alfred 'Limp Dick' Hardy, an experienced sapper and ammunition technician, formerly with the Royal Engineers. Dramatically scarred by the many accidents of his dangerous profession, Limp Dick was a deadly serious Geordie who demanded their full attention when lecturing them about low explosives such as gunpowder, high explosives such as RDX and PETN, and the intricacies of initiators, time fuses and firing caps. When the lectures and demonstrations were completed, he stopped the men from yawning by putting them through a series of exercises designed to show them how to handle the explosives and set them off in a variety of potential circumstances: the blowing up of aircraft, bridges, roads or buildings, as well as the setting of booby traps. As the men had to complete these exercises themselves, with live explosives, there were many harrowing moments and nerve-racking experiences. Certainly a lot of bullshit flew back and forth, to cover up naked fear.

'You don't have to be so nervous with it,' Limp Dick sneered as Tone attempted nervously to connect a time fuse to a non-electric firing cap. 'It isn't a woman's naked tit you're holding. Just get on with it, lad.'

'He's never held a woman's tit, Sarge,' Marty chipped in

quickly. 'If he got the chance, he wouldn't just be nervous – he'd simply explode.'

'We're *all* going to explode if he doesn't do this bloody job right,' Limp Dick replied. 'That's real explosive he's got there.'

'*What*?' Tone asked, shaking even more and visibly sweating. 'Did you say *real* explosive, Sarge?'

'That's right,' Limp Dick replied. 'You touch one item to the other, make sure they connect, then, if you press the initiator – *voila*! – the whole thing blows you sky high.'

'Oh, Jesus!' Tone groaned.

As it was with the firing range, so it was with explosives: most of the exercises took place in the boiling, blinding heat while flies, mosquitoes and midges buzzed and whined about the struggling men. In combination with the heat, dust and insects, the thirst may have contributed to some of the men's crazier antics. These involved the indiscriminate firing of rifles and pistols, the exploding of Thermos bombs, the collecting of wild dogs as vicious pets, betting at organised scorpion fights and the hunting of gazelles and other desert animals.

Appalled by these antics, Captain Kearney determined to stamp them out. Most hateful of all to him were the vicious scorpion fights in which someone would dig a circular shallow in the sand, pour petrol around the edge, set it alight, then place two scorpions inside the ring of fire. The heat of the flames would drive the scorpions wild and they would viciously fight one another. When Kearney also learned that the men were betting money on the outcome of the games, he resolutely put a stop to them and ruthlessly returned those responsible to their original units. This punishment became known as an 'RTU' and was dreaded by everyone.

Another sport, equally as disgusting to Kearney, was the hunting of the beautiful desert gazelles, which the men would pursue in trucks, firing upon the unfortunate creatures with their rifles. While the animals' carcasses did at least have the merit of supplementing the unit's rations, Kearney viewed it as just another vicious blood sport. He stamped it out with a combination of even more training – now sometimes up to eighteen hours a day – or RTUs for the inveterate troublemakers. This worked, weeding out the last of the undesirables and leaving only the *crème de la crème* of the original volunteers.

As the training continued with radio communications, first aid, nocturnal navigation, and enemy vehicle and aircraft recognition added to the men's growing list of skills, it became apparent to all of them that they were in a combat unit like no other, with no distinctions in rank and everyone, including the officers, compelled to meet the same exacting standards.

The informality went beyond that. The word 'boss', first used, perhaps accidentally, by Sergeant Bellamy, gradually replaced 'sir' and informal meetings, in which decisions were agreed between officers and other ranks after open, often volatile discussion, became commonplace. This in turn increased the mutual trust between the men and greatly enhanced the feasibility of the four-man patrol. Also, as each of the four men had a specialist skill – driver/mechanic, navigator, explosives and first aid – but all had been cross-trained to do the other men's jobs if required, this made them uniquely interdependent.

Their psychological bonding was made even more complete by the harsh fact that anyone who failed at any point in the training, or who bottled out because of fear, exhaustion, thirst or other causes, was RTU'd without mercy. As the numbers were whittled down, those remaining were forming the kernel of an exceptional band of highly skilled, close-knit, fighting men.

Marty was proud to be one of them. Also, he found himself admiring Captain Kearney and Sergeant Bellamy even more than before. With Captain Stirling being compelled to spend an increasing amount of time by himself – either developing the strategies to be used for forthcoming operations or commuting between Kabrit and Cairo to keep MEHQ informed of his progress – Kearney and Bellamy between them were supervising the general training and ensuring that the administrative side of the camp ran smoothly.

Possibly because of his LRDG experience, Bellamy concentrated on exercises in the desert and certainly increased the men's chances of being RTU'd by introducing lengthy hikes by day and by night. Not a man to demand of others what he could not do himself, he turned himself into a human guinea pig by making the first marches entirely alone and gradually increasing the distance he had to cover, the length of time he had to go without water, and the weight he had to carry in his Bergen backpack. Only when he had gauged his own limits in this regard did he demand that the other men follow suit.

Bellamy also set himself precise navigation tests that had to be completed within a certain time. When Marty asked him about them, he responded by inviting Marty to go with him on one of his lengthy marches.

'Pure bloody genius,' Marty related to Tone after the event. 'He told me we were going to hike to an RV twenty miles away and that he'd know when we'd done exactly that. Since the desert's so barren – no landmarks to navigate by – I couldn't figure out how he'd manage it. But the bugger marched across the desert with complete confidence, calculating how far we'd walked every couple of miles and not making a single bloody error. I just couldn't figure out how he was doing it until I noticed that the clever bastard was carrying lots of small stones in a pocket of his trousers and kept transferring them, one at a time, from one pocket to the other. What he was doing, you see, was counting his paces. After each hundred steps, he'd transfer one of the stones to the other pocket. He told me the average pace was thirty inches, so each stone represented about eighty-three yards. That way he knew just how far he'd marched. Pretty smart, right?'

Marty admired Bellamy and Kearney not only because of their many innovations, but because neither man ever asked the others to do anything he had not first tried himself. Indeed, regarding the murderous hikes into the desert, only when Bellamy had personally ascertained what could actually be accomplished did he introduce them as part of the selection course. The desert lessons, or tests, included nights sleeping in laying-up positions, or LUPs, scraped out of the freezing desert floor; signals training, covering Morse code, special codes and call-sign signals; the operation of radios, recognition of radio 'black spots' and the setting up of standard and makeshift antennae; the maintenance of weapons in the windblown, freezing darkness; the procedure for calling in artillery fire and air strikes; and general desert survival by day and by night.

Those who failed to meet the rigorous standards set by Bellamy and Kearney were brutally RTU'd – but, seeing that the sergeant and captain had done all those things themselves, the men at least accepted the harsh justice of it when they were failed and sent back to their original units.

As an NCO, Sergeant Bellamy was close to the other ranks, knowing and speaking their language. Aware of this, Captain Kearney made a special point of taking part in the many arduous physical tests devised by the former LRDG sergeant and, by so doing, succeeded in forging his own close bond with the men. This bond was further strengthened by his willingness to forget his rank and meet the men on a level they understood.

One day, after Kearney had checked the men's canteens to ensure that they hadn't drunk more water than permitted during their latest hike, Red complained that the *officers'* canteens were never checked. Kearney instantly handed Red his own canteen, saying, 'All right, Corporal, finish this off.' When Red greedily opened the canteen, he found it completely full. 'You understand, Corporal?' Kearney asked. 'I made the whole hike without drinking a drop. And if I can, you can.'

'Right,' Red responded, shamefaced as he handed back the full canteen. 'Understood, boss.'

In another instance, during a particularly draining hike along the edge of an escarpment in the blazing heat of midday, when Tone complained that he needed a rest, Captain Kearney grabbed him by the shoulders, picked him bodily off the ground and held him over the edge of the cliff. 'If you don't shut your damned trap,' he bawled, 'I'll drop you into the sea!'

'Yes, boss!' Tone screamed back, hanging upside down over the cliff. 'Christ, boss, pull me up!'

Tone shut up after that and the other men, rather than resent Captain Kearney, respected him even more.

If anything, this respect only increased when Kearney and Bellamy personally demonstrated what they required during parachute training. This began during the final weeks of the selection process with the building of a steel framework ten metres high, which the men had to jump off in order to learn the skills of landing without hurting themselves. While reasonably effective in teaching the men how to land properly, the static frames could not be used to simulate the vertical and lateral movement of a proper parachute drop from an aircraft. Kearney pointed this out to Captain Stirling, who contacted the only parachute school then extant, Ringway in England, and begged for assistance. Rudely ignored – since most officers back in England thought he was merely playing games with a bunch of cowboys – Stirling went back to Kearney and asked him to devise his own methods of training.

Kearney amazed the men by personally standing on the rear of a Bedford truck, burdened with Bergen rucksack and parachute pack, then jumping off as the vehicle raced across the desert. He broke his fall by rolling in the direction of the truck when he hit the ground.

'Rather him than me,' Tone said as he stood a good distance away, watching Kearney repeatedly jump off the racing Bedford into a cloud of churning sand. 'He's going to break his bloody back if he keeps that up.'

'We're next,' Marty replied. 'You can bet your balls on it. If Kearney decides that's a good way to train us, you can bet we'll be doing it.'

This turned out to be true. After personally experimenting with various ways of rolling, Kearney made the rest of the men do the same. The exercise didn't bother Marty at first, because the trucks were travelling at a relatively safe 15 mph; but as the men became more efficient and Kearney gradually upped the speed to 30 mph, Marty realised just how dangerous it was and became much more careful.

There were many accidents during this phase of the training, including severe sprains and fractured bones, but the jumps from racing trucks continued until it was time for the remaining men to make their first jumps from an aeroplane.

MEHQ had finally made a Bombay aircraft available for this purpose. Luckily, unlike the Valentia that had almost killed Captain Stirling during an early jump, the Bombay had a proper overhead suspension for the static-line of the 'chutes, allowing for the use of a snap-link.

Feeling that it was necessary for him to make a showing at this point, Captain Stirling personally made the first two jumps with the men. These were successful and the men were relieved. During the next flight, however, when Stirling remained on the ground to check the landing patterns visually, the snap-links of the two lead parachutists twisted, the rings slipped free, the parachute canopies remained in their packs, and Marty, next in line, heard the two men screaming in dread as they plunged to their deaths. Marty was horrified.

So was Stirling. He cancelled the rest of that day's jumps and gave the men the day off. The jumps, however, were ruthlessly resumed the following morning with Stirling, determined to set a good example, again being the first out of the aircraft. This time the snap-links were carefully checked and there were no further casualties.

Within a matter of weeks, the remaining men were expert, confident paratroopers.

One major problem remained. As the main purpose of the planned raids was to destroy enemy aircraft and other vehicles on the ground, as well as fuel and ammunition dumps, the men, if using orthodox explosives, would be required to hump heavy loads to their chosen targets. As most explosives were too heavy to carry over such distances and the usual constituents – gelignite, thermite, ammonal – took too long to be ignited or exploded, carrying them over such distances did not seem practical.

Faced with this problem, Captain Stirling sought the advice of Lieutenant Jock Lewes, who had been with him when he made his disastrous parachute jump from the Valentia and had since been responsible for many of L Detachment's major innovations. Lewes, a remarkably inventive man, eventually came up with a blend of plastic explosive (PE) and thermite kneaded together with a lubricant into a bomb the size of a tennis ball. This explosive-inflammable mix gave a charge of about 400 grams.

'Placed on the boss of a propeller,' Kearney explained to

the men gathered around him, 'this device, forthwith known as the Lewes bomb, will not only damage the prop but also set alight any petrol or other fuel within range of the blast. In short, it's perfect for the destruction of grounded aircraft and other vehicles, as well as for fuel and ammunition dumps. It's also exceptionally small and light, therefore easy to carry. Last but not least, with the explosive fused in its own right and the incendiary device timed to ignite just *after* the explosion, you won't find anything quicker or more devastating.'

'I'm not sure what all that means, boss,' Marty chipped in.

'What it means,' Kearney replied with a grin, 'is that the bugger will work.'

It did. Tested in the presence of Sergeant Limp Dick Hardy, the device was highly successful, exploding with an ear-splitting roar and creating a mushroom of billowing sand that took a long time to settle.

That same evening, just before standing them down, Captain Stirling made a personal appearance to inform the men that they were to prepare for their first operation the following night. They would be briefed in the morning.

'About time!' Marty whispered.

CHAPTER SIX

Though the unit was not due to move until 1930 hours, reveille was at first light and led to another frantic day. Once the men had attended to their ablutions, they donned their desert clothing, had a good breakfast, then returned to their tents to spend the rest of the morning packing their Bergen rucksacks with everything they would need for desert survival. When fully packed, the Bergen weighed nearly 90lbs.

'A bleedin' beast of burden,' Tone complained. 'Donkeys have it better than we do. You might as well put us in harness and take a whip to us.'

'You might be grateful to have this,' Marty said as he completed packing his own kit belt on the adjacent bed in the sweltering tent, 'when we're back down on the ground.'

'Don't even remind me about that parachute jump,' Tone replied. 'I don't want to know.'

'You'll know soon enough,' Red said, the tattoos on his right arm moving magically as, kneeling over his own bed, he tightened his webbing. 'You'll know when your parachute doesn't open and your arse hits the ground and travels through it until it reaches Australia. You'll know it then, mate.'

'Oh, thanks a lot, Corporal!'

When the Bergens had been carefully packed and repeatedly checked to ensure that they were secure, the men went for lunch, which would be their last real meal for the next few days. Aware of this, they ate as much as they could stomach, then returned to their tents to check thoroughly, clean and oil their weapons. These included 9mm Sten submachine-guns, M1 Thompson submachine-guns (tommy-guns) and Bren light machine-guns. Finally, they attended to their belt kit. When they had finished, their webbing was festooned with 30- and 32-round box magazines, hand grenades, more water bottles with a water filter, survival kits, and, of course, the brand-new Lewes bombs. Strapped to waist belts were the ubiquitous 9mm Browning High Power handgun, a Sykes Fairburn commando dagger, bayonet, compass and binoculars.

'I don't think the parachute's been made to support this lot,' Tone said. 'I see us plummeting straight down like stones and being buried six feet deep.'

'There speaks a true optimist,' Marty responded. 'Now will you please belt up, mate?'

'I *am* belting up,' Tone replied, tightening the buckle of the heavily burdened belt around his waist.

'He means keep your bleedin' trap shut,' Red said as he humped his Bergen rucksack onto his back and adjusted the straps. 'Talk too much about what could go wrong and it might actually happen. All that chat could bring bad luck. Time for the briefing, anyway,' he continued, picking up his weapons. 'So let's go and hear some sensible shit from our sky-high CO.'

Realising that his friends were as tense as he was, Marty was glad to hump his rucksack onto his back and follow Red and Tone out of the tent. Though the afternoon was still bright, with a huge red sun shedding its light on the tents and gun emplacements, the hot air was cooling and a light breeze was blowing clouds of sand over the five Bombay aircraft. Entering the briefing tent and taking one of the wooden chairs, surrounded by other troopers, he saw that Captain Stirling was already standing by the blackboard, towering over Kearney, Jock Lewes and the glowering Sergeant Bellamy.

'Are we all here?' Stirling asked when the men had settled down.

Bellamy cast his baleful gaze over the men seated in front of him, then nodded. 'Yes, boss.'

Stirling began the briefing by informing them that General Auchinleck, the Commander-in-Chief (C-in-C), Middle East, was about to mount his first major offensive to relieve Tobruk and push Rommel's seemingly invincible Afrika Korps out of Cyrenaica. He then told them that, to aid this push, L Detachment, divided into five separate groups of twelve and travelling to the drop zone (DZ) in five different aircraft, would mount attacks against five Axis airfields spread around Gazala and Timini. The five groups would be dropped at different locations, all far away from the targets. They would then march throughout the night to laying-up positions in view of the targets. From the LUPs they would observe the targets and assess their individual situations. Infiltration of the airfields, the placing of the Lewes bombs and detonation would take place in the early hours of the morning with the fuses coordinated, as far as possible, to detonate under cover of darkness. The groups would then make a forced march before first light, back to a preselected RV to join up with the Long Range Desert Group, who would return them to base.

'I feel I should warn you,' Captain Stirling added, 'that there are those in MEHQ, Cairo, and even back in Whitehall, who believe that what we're doing out here is a complete waste of time. Our mission, therefore, is not only to aid the big push but to prove ourselves as a fighting unit. Should we fail to do so, the unit may be disbanded, so let's make sure we don't fail.' He glanced at his wristwatch, then out of the tent at the setting sun. 'Time to move, men. I expect to see you out on the airstrip at nineteen hundred hours sharp. Good luck to all of us.'

After leaving the tent, the men were broken up into five separate raiding parties, with Marty, Red and Tone in the twelve-man group to be led by Paddy Kearney and Bulldog Bellamy. Minutes later, as the sun sank over the horizon, casting long shadows on the vast plain of the desert, they strapped their Irvin X-Type model parachute packs over their packed Bergens and boarded one of the five Bombay bombers parked along the runway.

Knowing that the Bombay was an obsolete aircraft, Marty was not thrilled to be aboard. He was even less thrilled when he went into the hold and saw an enormous long-range fuel tank taking up the middle of the plane, down much of its length.

'I'd rather be cremated,' he remarked, 'than be buried alive like this.'

'The faithful will be resurrected,' Paddy Kearney responded. 'Just say your prayers, Trooper.'

'I would if I could but I can't. It's not in my nature, boss.'

'Then keep your peace,' Bulldog told him.

Those were the last words of unnecessary conversation spoken throughout the flight. When the Bombay took off at 1930 hours, the roar of its twin engines made casual conversation impossible among the twelve men sitting in oppressively cramped conditions on the fuselage floor above the bomb racks and creaking crates of ammunition and supplies.

Glancing to his right, Marty saw that he was third from the door, which meant that he would be jumping out directly after Paddy Kearney and Bulldog Bellamy. This thought made him nervous, but he also felt a stab of excitement even sharper than fear.

The flight seemed interminable, but took less than two hours. Though the Bombay had taken off in a windless night, its engines gradually started labouring against stormy weather and its vibrations became more pronounced. As it was nearing what Marty estimated was the general area of the DZ it entered the heart of the storm and shuddered even more violently. Marty heard a clap of thunder above the labouring engines, then saw bolts of lightning ripping through the patches of sky framed by the windows. Finally, as the aircraft was beginning to buck and shudder, being hammered by the storm outside, the pounding of anti-aircraft guns was added to the bedlam and tracers flickered in eerie green lines past the same windows, adding their phosphorescent glowing to the lightning-streaked dark sky.

The noisy vibrations of the struggling Bombay worsened as Marty methodically checked his kit and prepared himself for the drop. A few minutes later, when the aircraft was flying through a fiery combination of thunder, lightning, snapping tracers and exploding flak, it rocked violently, shuddered, then started going down in a controlled manner.

Though it was impossible to stand upright without holding onto something, Kearney made his way to the pilot's cabin up front and emerged a few seconds later looking grim-faced.

'The aircraft's been hit,' he confirmed, bawling against the noise, 'but it hasn't been badly damaged, so we're continuing on to the DZ. Unfortunately, one of the other Bombays, Lieutenant Pearson's, has taken a worse hit and the pilot's heading back to base. This leaves us short of twelve men.'

The melodramatic moans and groans of the troopers in the hold were cut short by the RAF despatcher. Stepping up to the sliding door where the drop would be made, he bawled, 'Six minutes to zero hour! On your feet, please!'

When the men had done as they were told, the despatcher, a sergeant, checked the static lines that were fixed to 'strong points' in the fuselage and designed to jerk the chutes open as each man fell clear of the aircraft. A man's life could depend on them, but in this obsolete aircraft the fixings looked suspiciously fragile.

'If those strong points twist free,' Marty told Tone, 'the canopies won't open and you really *will* get buried six feet under. Best say your prayers, mate.'

'Fuck off,' Tone responded.

They were secretly relieved, however, to observe that a sharp tug on each line by the RAF despatcher had satisfied him that the new clips would hold firm. He then moved to the door and nodded to the aircraftsman to open it. Suddenly, cold air came rushing in.

With his numbed senses revived by the shock of the roaring, freezing air, Marty lined up behind Kearney and Bulldog Bellamy. Supply packs of weapons and explosives, he noted, all tied to parachutes, were stacked up in the rear of the fuselage, behind the line of men, waiting to be pitched out by the airmen when the last of the paratroopers had gone. Other boxes with parachutes were clipped to the bomb racks, also ready for dropping. Unable to be heard above the roar of wind and engines, the despatcher signalled for the men to get ready, then he pointed to the lamp above his head.

The light was still off.

Glancing behind him, Marty saw that the other paratroopers were wriggling into their 'chute harnesses, fidgeting with their weapons and checking their equipment yet again. Though they were nervous, they obviously wanted to make the jump – to get it over and done with.

The red light came on.

With two minutes to go, Captain Kearney, leading the drop, was first in line at the door, waiting for the green light. When it flashed on, the despatcher slapped his shoulder and he threw himself out.

The second man, Bulldog Bellamy, moved up to the jump position and waited for a similar slap on the shoulder. The first line snaked out and went taut, then it trailed slackly from the door as Kearney fell freely.

'Go!' the despatcher bawled, slapping Bulldog on his shoulder – and he, too, threw himself out, leaving the jump position free for Marty, who took a deep breath.

Feeling nervous, he moved up until he was standing in the doorway, hammered by the howling wind. Looking down, he saw a terrifying black void. Bulldog's line had snaked out, but it suddenly went taut and then just as quickly slackened again.

'Go!' the despatcher bawled.

Marty felt a rough hand slapping his shoulder, then, before realising that he had jumped, he was plummeting through the void with the wind of the slipstream slapping at him. The combined noise was deafening – growling aircraft, roaring wind, snapping parachute and cords – as he held himself upright, heels together, waiting for the slipstream to release him and let him drop vertically. This it did within seconds. There was a sudden, violent tugging, the wind abruptly ceased its roaring, then he dropped through darkness and silence, looking for the ground.

He saw nothing but darkness.

By now he should have felt, or at least seen, the ground, yet the blackness below him seemed bottomless. He continued drifting down. Suddenly, as he gripped the rigging lines, preparing to swing himself clear of potential harm, he was smashed against a rocky stretch of desert. Hitting the ground with a painful jolt, he rolled over and tried to stop, but was dragged a good distance by the fierce wind. Managing to roll again, this time onto his belly, he wrestled to control the rigging lines, collapsing the canopy. Breathless and battered, with sharp pains darting through him, he was snatched away again by another strong gust of wind, then dragged at great speed over a desert floor of abrasive gravel, which cut and burned his skin. Eventually, however, he managed to punch the release box, unravelling his harness and rolling to a stop. Then he passed out.

Regaining consciousness, he found himself lying on his belly. Rolling onto his back, he saw patches of stars between drifting storm clouds and, below them, the pale white flowers of other parachutes descending too far away.

'Bloody 'ell!' he whispered.

Attempting to stand, he was almost knocked off balance by the wind. Hissing granules of rock dust stung his face, made breathing difficult, and finally forced him to turn downwind, into the desert, hoping to find the rest of his party there. Feeling minute and lost in the vastness of the desert, hurting from his many bloody cuts, abrasions and bruises, he walked a long way, for what seemed like ever, through a raging sandstorm that had reduced visibility almost to zero.

When he reached what he thought was the DZ, there was no one in sight. He was all on his own, lost in the desert . . . in a raging sandstorm . . . in the dead of the night. He heard only the howling wind.

Fighting to get his breath back, gritting his teeth against the pain of his cuts and bruises, he checked that his Bergen straps and webbing were in one piece, then switched on his torchlight and headed resolutely into the storm. Eventually, after what seemed like an eternity, he saw another waving torchlight, then a second, a third, and finally he heard voices calling out in English.

Advancing towards the other torchlights, he came face to face with Captain Kearney and Sergeant Bellamy, both smeared in a film of sand and dust, leaning into the howling wind.

'Anyone else with you?' Kearney asked.

'No, boss. What about you?'

Keeping his head low to avoid the howling wind and sweeping sand, Bulldog Bellamy waved his hand, indicating the wadi running east to west. 'Corporal Lester and Private Williams are over there, in the bed of a wadi. We haven't seen any of the others so far. Only those two.'

'What about the weapons and supplies?' Marty asked with a sinking heart.

'Probably dragged halfway across the desert like the rest of the men,' Kearney said, sounding grim. 'A couple of crates landed in the wadi, near Lester and Williams, but they were smashed all to pieces and their contents were strewn all over the place. I don't think we'll find much.'

'Let's go and check,' Bulldog said.

Marty followed the other two across the plain, to where Red and Tone were crouched in the dried-up wadi bed, grateful for its protection from the freezing, howling wind. Sliding down into the wadi, behind Kearney and Bulldog, he came to a rest beside the dispirited Red and Tone.

'What a balls-up,' Tone complained.

'Shut your mouth, Trooper,' Bulldog said, 'and help us check what we have here.'

'Yes, boss!' Tone exclaimed.

They didn't find much. One of the smashed crates contained Lewes bombs without fuses. There were also a few rations, but only enough for one day, and ten litres of drinking water in twelve aluminium bottles.

'Not even a radio or beacon,' Kearney said bitterly. 'So we can't find out how the other teams are faring or where Captain Stirling is.'

'I suggest we find the rest of our own team,' Bulldog said, 'then head back to the RV. With no food or weapons, with no means of communication, we have to assume that the mission's over.'

'No, we don't,' Kearney responded with conviction. 'We can still do *something*, damn it! We can't be too far from that airfield and I'm going to find it. At least, while we're here, we can reconnoitre the area and go back with some information about enemy troop movements. If we can't attack them, we can at least do that. Now let's go find the rest of our men by criss-crossing this area about five miles north and south, east and west. Stick close together and use your flashlights. All right? Let's go!'

Deeply dispirited, but encouraged by the conviction in Kearney's tone of voice, Marty and the others climbed wearily to their feet, clambered up out of the wadi, then advanced into the desert in single-file formation, with Sergeant Bellamy out front on point, acting as scout, and Marty bringing up the rear as Tail-end Charlie.

Following Kearney, they criss-crossed the area, moving first north to south, then east to west, always fighting the howling storm, waving their flashlights up and down while calling out repeatedly, 'Team One! Over here! Team One!' It was an exhausting business, but gradually, one by one, other torchlights waved back, distant voices were heard, and the other men materialised like ghosts in the murk, some alone, others in small groups. Eventually, nearly two hours later, all the men except one had been found. After searching another thirty minutes for the last man, Corporal Barker, they assumed that he had either been killed or was lost in the desert.

'No point looking any more,' Bellamy said pragmatically. 'We're just wasting our time. Either he'll make his own way back or he won't. What say you, boss?'

'I say we send most of these men back to the RV,' Kearney replied, 'while a small group – an officer, an NCO and two privates – try to find that airfield. We can't do much damage, but we may pick up information. We've still got our personal weapons and pistols, so we can at least defend ourselves. What say you, Sarge?'

'I say let's do it.'

Kearney grinned. 'Thought you might.' He glanced at the other men, then settled his steady gaze on Marty. 'What about you, Private Butler? Do you want to go back with the others or try your luck with us?'

'I'm with you, boss.'

'Private Williams?'

'Yes, boss,' Tone replied.

Nodding, Kearney turned to another sergeant, the rake-thin, hard-as-nails Mike Byrne, and said, 'Can you and Corporal Lester manage to get the rest of the men back to the RV? It should be less than fifty kilometres away and the LRDG will be waiting for you there.'

'No sweat,' Byrne replied, standing up from where he had been squatting on the sand and slinging his M1 Thompson submachine-gun over his shoulder. 'You leave it to me, boss.'

'Good man. Get going.' Kearney waited until the seven men had disappeared into the murk, gradually vaporising like ghosts, then he said to Bulldog Bellamy, 'Right, let's head for Gazala. Single file as before. I'll take the first four hours out on point, you and Corporal Williams will cover arcs of fire to the left and right respectively, and Corporal Butler will bring up the rear as Tail-end Charlie. We'll switch around every four hours to ease the tension on all of us. Agreed?' Marty and the others nodded their agreement 'Excellent,' Kearney said. 'Let's move out.'

Turning away, he marched resolutely into the storm, heading in what he had judged from the position of the stars was the direction of Gazala. The others fell into single file, with Bellamy directly behind Kearney, in what would normally be the PC – or patrol commander – position. Tone was between him and Marty, whose position in the rear, as Tail-end Charlie, was the most nerve-racking and exhausting of all.

They marched through the cold, dark morning until the grey light of dawn broke. Only then did they lay up for a short break and a few nibbles of their remaining food, all of them shivering with cold in the freezing wind. Exhausted from hours of having to turn repeatedly backwards to check their rear, as well as constantly keeping an arc of fire to the left and right, Marty was convinced that he would not be able to get to his feet again. He was wrong. In fact, he stood up and marched with the others when Kearney relentlessly led them away again, this time taking his bearings from the Trig el Abd.

'What's that?' Marty asked.

'A track line in the desert,' Kearney explained. 'It was formerly used by the camel trains of the slave trade, then by Axis and Allied vehicles, depending upon which one was holding the area at any given time. If we follow it, we should reach our destination, so start marching, men.'

They marched on in single file. After a hike of about ten miles, with the freezing morning giving way to a fierce, dry heat that lasted until dusk, they reached a featureless desert plateau leading to an escarpment. Creeping carefully along that line of cliffs and lying belly down in the fading light, they were able to see the glittering, pale-blue sheen of the Mediterranean beyond the parched, dusty coast road.

'That road,' Kearney informed them, 'is the main supply route for German and Italian forces loosely holding a line from the sea at Sollum, on the Egyptian border, about a hundred and eighty kilometres east of Gazala. They must use it a lot.'

Seeing the MSR, and the constant flow of Axis traffic heading along it in both directions, they realised that they had been dropped well south of their intended DZ, only fifteen kilometres from the coast.

'There's no airfield here,' Sergeant Bellamy pointed out as he lay belly down beside Kearney on the escarpment and studied the distant MSR through his binoculars. 'We're miles away, boss.'

'But the journey hasn't been wasted,' Kearney replied stubbornly. 'We'll stay here for a bit and gather as much info as we can on the troop movements along that MSR. That'll be something, at least.'

Bulldog sighed with a mixture of weariness and admiration. 'Yes, boss,' he agreed.

They laid up all night and recced the MSR the following morning. Kearney and Bulldog took turns at studying it through the binoculars and entering details of the troop convoys into the logbook. Late that afternoon, however, black clouds formed in the sky, threatening another storm. Hoping to find shelter, they advanced to the very edge of the escarpment, where they resettled themselves in a dried-up wadi bed, which they planned to use as their observation post, or OP. This was a mistake.

When the clouds broke in a deluge of rain, Marty was astonished to hear a roaring sound and, looking along the wadi bed, saw that it was rapidly filling up with water. Flash flood, he thought disbelieving. The rain then poured down with the force of a tropical storm, hitting the sand like bullets and making it spit and splash, becoming spurting mud, as the bed of the wadi gradually filled up with water. With startling speed, this rising water turned into a stream, then became a fast-flowing river that threatened to sweep them away.

'Get out!' Sergeant Bellamy bawled.

Practically submerged and losing most of their personal weapons, they hurriedly clambered up out of the wadi, where they were exposed to the full force of the storm, lashed by a freezing wind and hammered relentlessly by the still-torrential, deafening rainfall, which forced them back down to the ground.

'Jesus!' Marty gasped. 'Christ!'

Even as he lay there with the others, hardly believing what he was seeing, the river in the wadi became a raging torrent that swept baked sand and gravel along with it as it took the line of least resistance and roared along between the high banks. To make matters even worse, the storm and flash floods, which were filling other wadis, had blotted out the landscape and made surveillance of the MSR impossible.

'Damn!' Kearney exclaimed in frustration, wiping rain from his eyes. 'We've lost out again. Even *I'm* willing to call it a day. Let's head back to the RV.'

'If nothing else, we can fill our water bottles,' Bellamy reminded him. 'Let's get *something* out of it.'

'Good thinking,' Kearney said.

After filling their aluminium water bottles from the downpour, they headed back to the Trig el Abd, then turned inland on the start of what they knew would be a 65-kilometre hike. Though completely drenched, they marched throughout the night and eventually managed to leave the torrential downpour behind them.

About three hours before first light, when their soaked clothing was stiffening with frost and all of them were shivering dangerously in the freezing cold, Kearney led them towards where he had judged the RV to be. There, he had been informed, 'A' Patrol of the LRDG would be shining a Tilley lamp from a small hill as a welcoming beacon. When the light did not materialise, Kearney realised that being dropped well away from the original DZ had caused him to miscalculate the distance back and that they still had a long way to go.

'To hell with it,' he said in disgust. 'We've already been thirty-six hours in this bloody desert, so let's at least snatch some sleep.'

It was just before first light when they slumped down in the shade of a hillock and slept the sleep of the dead. Awakening four hours later, when the others were also stirring, Marty noted that his soaked, frozen clothes had mercifully dried out in the morning's fierce heat. Feeling only a little better, he and the others moved off again in the midday haze. By then the heat was murderous, scorching their skin, blistering their lips, and filling them with a relentless thirst that compelled them to finish off the water they had gathered from the rainfall the previous day.

Late that afternoon, just as Marty was starting to feel that he might go mad from thirst, the weather turned yet again, becoming much cooler and, more importantly, bringing back a brief rainfall that enabled them to fill up their water bottles. Replenished and cooled down after their long, thirsty journey, they continued the arduous march across the scorched, barren desert until, like a merciful god, the sun started sinking again.

No sooner had Kearney estimated that they were only twenty kilometres from the RV than he spotted movement far to the south. Raising the field glasses to his eyes, he made out nine figures heading for the Trig el Abd.

'One of the other teams,' he said. 'Come on. We can't give up now, lads. One more night should do it.'

'I can't march another night,' the thoroughly exhausted Tone said. 'I just can't make it, boss.'

'If you don't do it alone,' Sergeant Bellamy responded, 'you'll do it with my boot up your arse. Now keep walking, Trooper.'

Tone kept moving. All of them kept moving. They marched throughout another night, stopping only to observe a sudden, fierce sandstorm that blew up in the distance, just about where the other nine men had been marching.

'Poor bastards,' Marty murmured, knowing that the sandstorm would be hell for men who would already be on their last legs.

'Rather them than us,' Sergeant Bellamy said, pragmatic to the end. 'Now save your breath and keep walking.'

When the sandstorm had abated – its outer edge had swirled across them – they marched on again, finally laying up in the early hours of the morning, dropping off almost immediately, and once more sleeping like dead men.

Awakening just before first light, Marty saw what he thought was a low star in the sky. However, when they continued their march and drew closer to the glowing object, he saw that it was the promised Tilley lamp of 'A' Patrol, LRDG, shining in the south, no more than a few kilometres away.

They had made it back.

Though nearly in a state of collapse when they reached the LRDG camp, they still had to report to a dejected Captain Stirling, who had also made it back by the skin of his teeth. The report was given informally by Kearney while Marty, Tone and Sergeant Bellamy sat on the ground around him and Stirling knelt on one knee in front of them, poking distractedly at the sand with a short stick, as if not really there.

When Kearney had reported the experience of his own group, Stirling, looking even more dejected, confirmed that the rest of Kearney's men had made it back, except for Corporal Barker, who was still missing. He then confirmed that the whole operation had been a disaster from the beginning, mainly because of the storm, with a lot of the men injured as they landed, others lost and the rest marching into the desert as planned, though with most of their weapons and supplies missing. Because the storm hadn't let up, more of the men had been lost. Another had suffered a fatal heart attack during one of the many exhausting hikes through the same storm. Over eighty per cent of the men from one Bombay alone had been lost and not found again, probably captured.

The damaged Bombay, which had turned back for Kabrit,

had been forced to land west of Tobruk, where the crew made emergency repairs and took off again. However, they were then attacked by a German Me 109 and forced to crash-land for a second time, after which communications were cut, probably because they had all been taken prisoner by Axis forces.

The twelve men from another Bombay had also been lost in the storm, then had run into a German patrol, engaged in a brief fire fight, using only their Browning handguns, and only been saved when one of them, Sergeant Tappman, deliberately exposed himself to the enemy, distracting their attention, to let his comrades make their escape along the bed of a wadi. Some of those who were escaping actually saw Sergeant Tappman being captured.

'The truth of the matter,' Stirling said, still poking the stick distractedly into the sand, 'is that this whole operation has been a bloody disaster. Calculating those captured, missing or presumed dead, of our original total of sixty-two men, only twenty-two have made it back. The operation has been a failure of major dimensions and I won't try to deny it.'

'There must be another way,' Kearney said.

'Yes,' Captain Stirling replied. 'We avoid aeroplanes and use the LRDG to insert and extract.'

'Damned right,' Marty said.

CHAPTER SEVEN

This time they weren't bothered by exploding flak, violent storms, unpredictable slipstreams or drop zones lost in darkness; they went in overland, inserted by the Long Range Desert Group, travelling from their FOB to the RV by Chevrolet trucks, dealing only with what the LRDG understood and could expertly deal with. They had to deal with sandstorms, but the LRDG saw them coming. They had to deal with bogged-down trucks, but these the LRDG dug out. They had to deal with the desert's many sly treacheries and traps, but the LRDG knew them all and knew how to avoid them or deal with them. It took longer to reach the RVs – a matter of days instead of hours – but now, when they headed for their targets, they usually managed to reach them.

The first of the overland raids was the attack on Tamit and Marty would not forget it as long as he lived. The LRDG trucks had recently been modified to make them uniquely suitable for the desert but they were still dangerously overloaded with cans of petrol, bottles of water, packed Bergens, blankets, 'cam' nets, pintle-mounted machine-guns and boxes of ammunition. Having already adopted the clothing favoured by the LRDG for use in the desert – shirt, shorts, black woollen *agal* with *shemagh* – the SAS men perched precariously on their piled kit in the trucks were now also wearing the Arab sandal, the *chappali*, and the funnel-shaped leather gauntlets that stopped sweat from running down their arms and onto the weapons.

The journey by LRDG Chevrolet truck from the great white dunes, glittering lake, and cooling palm trees of Siwa Oasis to the sunbleached escarpments of the Sirte coastline took all day and most of the evening, with the usual hourly stops for the checking of vehicles and weapons, but it passed without incident. Instead of having to parachute down in unpredictable winds as they had done the last time, the men were dropped off shortly after last light knowing exactly where they were: close to the Tamit airfield, though in the middle of a flat desert plain that offered no cover other than starlit darkness. The airfield, however, was only a few miles due west and could be seen in the distance, its hangars visible as rectangular blocks darker than the night and framed by the stars. A main supply route ran through the desert, straight to the airfield.

The men advanced in single file, with Sergeant Bellamy out on point as lead scout, Captain Kearney coming second as PC, the rest strung out in a well-spaced, irregular line behind them, and Marty again bringing up the rear as Tail-end Charlie. Kearney was carrying the bag filled with Lewes bombs and fuses, as well as a Thompson M1928 submachine with a 50-round drum magazine; most of the other men were carrying either Sten guns or Lee-Enfield .303-inch bolt-action rifles; and Marty was pleased to have one of the relatively new tommy-guns. Everyone in the group was also carrying a Browning 9mm High Power handgun holstered at the waist, but otherwise they were travelling light, with no cumbersome rucksacks or water bottles to slow them down. The only sound as they hiked across the flat plain was the jangling of weapons.

Reaching the airfield, Marty was surprised to see that there were no sentries in sight and no fencing around the airstrip, even though a mixture of German Ju-87 Stuka diver-bombers and Italian Capronis were lined up along it. About twenty metres from the wooden buildings at the side of the airstrip, Kearney signalled that those behind him should lie belly down on the ground. Doing so, Marty noticed that a faint line of light was escaping from below the door of one of the wooden huts.

He also thought he could hear the murmur of conversation coming from inside.

Handing Sergeant Bellamy his bag of Lewes bombs, Kearney signalled for the men to remain where they were, then he advanced at the crouch, holding his Sten gun at the ready, until his shadow was touching the line of light beaming out from under the door of the long wooden building. The windows were covered in blackout curtains. Kearney stopped at the edge of the line of light, obviously listening to what the Germans inside were doing. After checking that his men were still behind him, he kicked the door open and boldly rushed inside, disappearing in a pillar of yellow light.

The guttural bawling of shocked, disbelieving Germans was followed by the sudden, savage roaring of Kearney's Sten gun.

'Jesus Christ!' Marty exclaimed in helpless admiration. 'He's taking them out on his own!'

The roaring of Kearney's Sten gun was followed by bawling, screaming, the clamour of overturning tables and chairs, smashing plates and glass and, finally, the snapping sound of Luger pistols being fired in desperate defence. Kearney kept firing, obviously covering a wide arc to hit as many men as possible, then the building was plunged into semi-darkness as most of the light bulbs were shot out.

Marty was staring intently at the building, listening to the clamour and trying to visualise what was happening inside, when the remaining light bulbs were shot out and Kearney backed through the doorway, firing his Sten gun on the move. Just as he made it outside, the surviving Germans in the hut fired their weapons and bullets whistled past him, some actually whipping over Marty's head where he still lay on the ground a good distance away.

'Let's go!' Sergeant Bellamy bawled, then he raced at the crouch towards the airstrip, taking advantage of the covering fire still being laid down by Kearney.

Marty jumped to his feet and raced after Bellamy as Kearney and four other troopers aimed a fusillade of fire from a combination of Lee-Enfield rifles and tommy-guns at the Germans attempting to escape from the building or firing from its darkened windows. The Germans outside the building were being cut to pieces as Marty raced across the windblown field towards the Axis aircraft, eventually catching up with Bellamy, who was kneeling beside a German Junkers, distributing Lewes bombs and fuses to the troopers. Some of the men, Marty noticed, were already zigzagging between the aircraft and lobbing the small bombs up onto their wings as if on a cricket pitch. However, before Marty could get his hands on some Lewes bombs, Kearney, who had clearly left the four troopers to keep the Germans in the darkened hut pinned down, raced up beside him, knelt down by Sergeant Bellamy, and said excitedly, 'Give me a couple of those, Sarge. I've waited a long time for this.'

'Haven't we all?' Bulldog replied, handing Kearney three of the unusually small, light bombs. 'The best of luck, boss.'

Kearney grinned. After glancing back over his shoulder to ensure that the four troopers he had left behind were still keeping the Germans pinned down – by now more German troops were firing out of the windows of the other buildings – he ran towards the nearest untouched Italian Caproni to place his first bomb.

'Me, too, Sarge,' Marty said impatiently, holding out his hands.

'Go for broke,' Bellamy responded, handing Marty some Lewes bombs, then jumping up with him and running away in the opposite direction.

Racing towards one of the untouched Capronis, Marty noticed that as the other men planted their supply of bombs – all set to explode in thirty minutes – they were going back to join those still keeping the Germans pinned down in the darkened hut and other buildings. Pleased to see that they were keeping their heads, he lobbed his first Lewes bomb up onto the wing of the Caproni. When he saw it nestling safely, he ran on to the next plane, another Caproni, and did the same, hardly aware that German bullets were whistling dangerously close past his head.

After placing his third bomb, he raced back to Bellamy, who was sitting upright over the collapsed canvas bag, opening and closing both hands to show Kearney that they were empty.

'No bombs left,' he said. 'We only had twenty-three bombs and there are thirty planes. It makes me want to puke, boss.'

Glancing behind him, Marty saw that there were no more troopers in the vicinity of the aircraft – they had all joined Corporal Peterson to pour fire into the German buildings – so he knew that they had disposed of their bombs.

'Twenty-three's better than nothing,' Kearney said, then glanced at his wristwatch. 'Five minutes to zero, Sarge. I think we better hightail it out of here.'

'Right, boss, let's do that.'

As Bellamy and Kearney were climbing to their feet, the Germans in the other buildings poured out through the doors to advance boldly on the SAS troopers. Instantly, Marty joined his fellow troopers in cutting the Germans down, firing his tommy-gun in a broad arc to hit as many as possible. He then backed across the airstrip, firing his weapon from the hip as Kearney, obviously unable to bear the thought of leaving seven planes untouched, suddenly raced towards one of them, weaving to avoid the gunfire, and started clambering up to the cockpit.

'No, boss!' Marty bawled over the roar of his tommy-gun as he backed away from the Germans pouring out of their barracks. 'Those planes are about to blow up!'

Ignoring him, Kearney balanced precariously on the wing of the Caproni, right beside the cockpit, in full view of the Germans heading in his direction. Some of the Germans stopped to take aim and fire at him, but just as they were doing so, the first Lewes bomb exploded, blowing the wing off a Junkers, setting fire to its fuselage, and making it erupt with a deafening roar, spewing jagged yellow flames and billowing black smoke. Kearney was wrenching open the cockpit of the Caproni when another Lewes bomb exploded, setting fire to a second Junkers, followed instantly by a third, which blew a hole in the side of a Caproni. The heat of the fires beat back the advancing Germans, then obscured them in oily smoke, enabling Kearney to reach into the cockpit of the Caproni and, as Marty looked on in amazement, rip the instrument panel out with his bare hands.

Other Lewes bombs were exploding in quick succession,

destroying more planes and filling the night with fire and smoke, as Kearney threw the instrument panel to the ground, then followed it down. He glanced around him, excited, as more aircraft exploded, then followed Marty and the others, now using the pall of smoke to give them cover as they raced away from the airfield.

Knowing that the Germans would continue to pursue them, Kearney set a punishing pace for the hike back to the desert RV, marching resolutely ahead of the single-file column, taking over the position as lead scout, letting Sergeant Bellamy drop back to the second position normally held by the PC. Rising to the challenge, and with little more to carry than their personal weapons and ammunition, Marty and the others kept up the pace and had soon left the airfield far behind. Eventually, when they glanced back over their shoulders, they could make it out only by the crimson glowing in the sky caused by the still-burning fires and by the many fan-shaped, silvery-white flarings of other explosions.

Reaching the general area of the RV, where they had expected to find the Chevrolet trucks, the SAS men were briefly confused by distant, moving lights which they thought were being waved by the LRDG. But, as they soon realised, they were torches being flashed by the German and Italian troops who had come in pursuit of them, lost them in the darkness and were now circling blindly around them, unaware of their presence.

Seeing Kearney's hand signal, Marty lay belly down on the desert floor with the other men and remained there, making no sound, until the lights from the Axis trucks had moved off to the west. When they had disappeared completely, heading away from the SAS men, Kearney signalled that they could stand up again and use the whistling signals they had devised for attracting the LRDG in the desert's deep, starlit darkness.

Eventually, Marty heard the first whistled replies. Heading in that direction, he soon saw the dark outline of the LRDG trucks, their headlights turned off, waiting to take them back to the base camp.

'Home and dry,' Marty whispered.

* * *

The major battle for control of the Western Desert had begun and Captain Stirling's dream of small raiding parties had become a reality. Thus, while his men were flown from Jalo Oasis back to Kabrit, Stirling departed for Cairo to negotiate further with the 'Gaberdine Swine' of MEHQ. Returning as a major, he informed his gathered men that he had been granted permission by the C-in-C, General Auchinleck, to launch a raid against the tankers and dumps in the port of Bouerat, which lay to the west of Sirte and Tamit. For this he planned to enlist the support of Air Reconnaissance Unit (ARU) and the Special Boat Section (SBS).

Also, in open defiance of the Gaberdine Swine, he was giving L Detachment its own badge, designed by Sergeant Bob Tait and consisting of a flaming sword crossed at the base with the scrolled motto 'Who Dares Wins'. The wings, he explained enthusiastically, were based on a pharaonic device of similar shape, such as those depicted in Oxford and Cambridge blues. He had decided, in consultation with some of his officers, that on completion of parachute training an SAS recruit could wear the wings in the conventional manner – on the shoulder – but those who had completed two or three operations could transfer the wings to their chests.

Marty was proud to be one of those who could stitch the new badge onto the breast of his tunic, rather than the shoulder.

The raid against the port of Bouerat was not without its disasters, but Marty was pleased to be part of it. The first disaster came when the raiding party was spotted by an Italian plane as the men made their way along the Wadi Tamit and, after six hours of relentless bombing, the radio truck and operators went missing and were never heard from again. To make matters worse, Stirling had planned to enter the harbour with one of the clumsy, unpredictable foldboats lent to him by the SBS, but the LRDG truck carrying it in total darkness along the wadi struck a boulder and the flimsy craft was smashed beyond repair. Nevertheless, the remaining men continued to the port, where they managed to plant bombs in the many unguarded fuel tankers and warehouses, as well as a radio station, with the fuses set for under an hour. Returning to the RV, the separate teams had the satisfaction of feeling the tremors of the many explosions and seeing the sky turning red from the flames of burning buildings, then black with smoke. Making their way back, however, they ran into a German ambush, though good luck prevailed and they managed to make their escape with no casualties after a vicious fire fight.

From that point on, as the war in the Western Desert raged back and forth, with the opposing forces taking turns at advancing and retreating, at gaining Benghazi then losing it, Major Stirling made it his business to prove to one and all that L Detachment SAS was a unique, invaluable unit, worthy to be a separate regiment.

For Marty, the following months were the most exciting of his life to date and confirmed for him that this kind of life was the only one he desired.

When Major Stirling determined to prove that the SAS could raid waterborne targets in Axis-held harbours, Marty was one of those who trained in foldboats and reconnaissance craft on the Great Salt Bitter Lake, then used them to plant bombs on the boats and in the warehouses of the port of Benghazi.

When Stirling 'liberated' a Ford V8 utility car in Cairo and had it mocked up to resemble a German staff car, naming it his 'Blitz Buggy', Marty was one of the six-man crew who, wearing civilian clothing, braved the heavily mined Trig el Abd to drive right into the heart of enemy-held Benghazi, through German and Italian roadblocks and then, boldly wandering around the harbour area, surreptitiously planted Lewes bombs in boats and petrol dumps, before casually driving back out.

When Stirling decided to commit eight patrols to eight different targets, all airfields, Marty was one of those who planted Lewes bombs in the fuel dump of the satellite airfield of Berka, then fought his way out against vehicle-borne Axis troops to play a deadly game of hide-and-seek all night before escaping by the skin of their teeth.

When Stirling spontaneously decided to return to the scene of a raid to see the after-effects, Marty was one of those who eased the safety catch off his tommy-gun as the truck filled with SAS men was stopped by a German roadblock, managed to get through with one of the SAS men speaking German, and went on to where the men could plant some more Lewes bombs – some in an Axis petrol store, others in German trucks – before striking out across the desert to Wadi Qattara, pursued by German troop trucks for much of the way, again escaping by the skin of their teeth.

Finally, when Tobruk fell to Rommel's Afrika Korps and the British effected a fighting withdrawal towards El Alemain, Marty was one of those who made many daring raids against Rommel's long supply lines, this time without the help of the LRDG, which had evacuated Siwa Oasis and moved 350 miles south to Kufra Oasis.

Left to his own devices, and with over a hundred battle-trained SAS troopers under his command, Major Stirling requisitioned fifteeen new jeeps and eighteen three-ton lorries. The jeeps, which were ideal for the desert, were fitted out with .303-inch twin-Vickers K machine-guns front and rear. As they had been designed for the RAF specifically to shoot down aircraft, Stirling decided to do just that and keep his bombs in reserve. In other words, instead of dropping the men off near their targets and letting them hike in under cover of darkness to plant Lewes bombs, they would just drive straight onto the airfields and shoot the Axis aircraft to pieces with their Vickers machine-guns.

For Marty, this was the most exciting work of all, a dangerous *Boy's Own* adventure that made him feel intensely alive. Nothing in his previous experience could quite match the exhilaration he felt as Corporal Red Lester gunned the engine of his jeep and raced through the floodlit darkness towards an enemy airstrip, the roaring of the jeep's engine drowned out only by the wailing of the enemy's warning siren. As the jeep crossed the desert, with other SAS jeeps spreading out on both sides of it, Marty and Tone – one seated up front beside Red, the other in the rear – would open fire with their Vickers K machine-guns, raking the troops guarding the airstrip, making them scatter and run for cover. As the jeep then bounced off the desert sand and onto the tarmac of the runway, Red would wrench at the steering wheel, turning it towards the parked aircraft, weaving wildly left and right, the reinforced tyres screeching, enabling Marty and Tone to rake the aircraft with a double fusillade of bullets from their pintle-mounted machine-guns.

Expertly avoiding the other SAS drivers doing the same, Red would keep driving, from one aircraft to another, as the planes peppered by the bullets from the machine-guns exploded noisily, filling the air with daggering yellow flames and billowing clouds of black smoke. Obscured by the pall of smoke, and while the Axis forces were still dazed and firing blindly, the SAS jeeps would race back to the desert, the rear gunners laying down a fusillade of fire that ensured they were not pursued by the enemy. They would then drive across the moonlit plains until they were back at the FOB.

During those months of hair-raising adventures, Marty felt more alive than he had ever imagined possible and was seduced by the desert's lunar beauty: the cliffs of the upland plateaux rising out of the heat haze; the golden sand dunes framed by the clear blue of the sky. He was also entranced when, as often happened, the SAS jeeps passed Arab traders, their loose robes fluttering, swaying rhythmically on their camels, distorted by the heatwaves shimmering up from the desert floor, looking archaic and unreal.

To jolt Marty back to the modern world, however, the jeeps also passed the blackened wrecks of Daimler armoured cars, Sherman tanks and Bedford trucks, many with charred corpses still inside them. In such places the desert floor was littered with other gruesome signs of recent battles: tattered clothing, bullet-riddled steel helmets, the odd booted foot or sun-bleached clenched fist thrusting up piteously from the sand. No one ever remarked on these.

Gradually moving deeper into enemy territory, led by the man whom Rommel's Afrika Korps had now labelled 'the Phantom Major', the column of SAS jeeps eventually reached the southernmost tip of the Western Desert, where many even more recent and bloody battles had raged back and forth. Here Marty found himself passing through an eerie landscape of flat white seria littered with the blackened wreckage of bombed tanks, armoured cars, troop trucks and halftracks, Axis and Allied, with whole areas of flatland given over to mass graves covered with hundreds of crude white crosses. Though this was a 'gentleman's war', where the troops of both sides treated each other with respect, the horrors of battle could not be ignored or avoided.

Nevertheless, Marty thrived on it and could have done it for ever had not the hand of God, or the devil, intervened.

Believing that Rommel was going to make his drive for Alexandria and Cairo before October, MEHQ insisted that the SAS, heavily reinforced by regular Army troops, mount an attack against Benghazi. As this would have constituted a total raiding force of 250 men – many of them untrained for this particular kind of warfare – Stirling wanted no part of it, but eventually acceded to it under pressure.

Marty's recollection of the subsequent operation was one of hellish chaos and despair. Sitting up front in the jeep driven by Red Lester, moving in on the garrison of Benghazi during the evening of 13 September, he and his comrades were uncomfortable because this time, instead of being a small group of like-minded individuals, they were accompanied by many other jeeps containing relatively untrained regular Army soldiers. On the approach to Benghazi, the desert's darkness was deep, though a pale moon shone down, and to Marty the silence had an unreal, eerie quality that made him feel even more uneasy. Planes often flew overhead, obviously heading for Benghazi, and occasionally trucks were heard in the distance, taking troops to the front. Lights fanned up far away, illuminating the northern horizon, reminding him that the war was still engaged and that the planes above – Hadley Page Halifax four-engine bombers, judging by the sound of them – were on bombing runs against the beleaguered Axis forces.

Poor bastards, Marty thought.

Suddenly, unexpectedly, the ground erupted with a deafening roar right beside him, pummelling him with its force and filling the air with seething sand and billowing smoke. Even as Red wrenched at the steering wheel, instinctively turning away from the blast, a whole series of mortar explosions tore up the ground between the advancing SAS vehicles.

'Christ, they've seen us!' Red bawled, wrenching the steering wheel in another direction, away from yet another deafening explosion, racing into a cloud of swirling, hissing sand.

Instantly, following on the explosions, the sound of Spandau machine-guns came from the front and the air was filled with the whipping sound of many bullets, which ricocheted noisily off the wildly weaving, screeching SAS jeeps.

'Open fire!' Red bawled at Marty and Tone as more mortar shells exploded and he was forced to keep driving straight into the furious clouds of sand and smoke.

Shocked to have been taken by surprise this way – yet aware enough to realise with burning anger that Major Stirling's doubts about this attack had been correct – Marty opened fire with his twin Vickers K machine-gun. He aimed desperately at the only thing he could see ahead – the flashing of enemy guns in the murk – as the jeep raced into the swirling, choking sand, between the violently erupting soil of more explosions. Behind him, Tone did the same, the roaring of his machine-guns hammering at Marty's head and adding dreadfully to the general bedlam as the jeep bounced over potholes and rocked wildly from side to side, pummelled relentlessly by the many explosions, deluged in swirling sand and boiling smoke.

Even as Marty was firing at the silvery flashes in the murk ahead, having nothing else to aim at, the ground erupted beneath the front of a jeep right beside him, throwing it up and over onto its side, with men screaming as they hurtled through the air and were slammed to the ground. Other men, desperately firing their machine-guns from the sitting position, screamed and shuddered violently as they were riddled with a murderous fusillade of bullets. Two more jeeps, swerving wildly to avoid the mortar explosions, crashed into each other. One toppled over in an immense fountain of sand; the other exploded into flames that engulfed the unfortunate men, turning them into quivering, blackening shapes that emitted dreadful, inhuman screams before they collapsed, still burning and smoking, over the melting barrels of their machine-guns.

Marty was still firing his own machine-gun at the silvery flashes straight ahead when he saw the jeep driven by Sergeant Bellamy cutting across the front of the advancing column. Ignoring the hail of enemy gunfire, Captain Kearney stood upright beside Bulldog, his body rocking from side to side with the swerving of the jeep, holding onto the frame of the windscreen with one hand and frantically signalling with the other that the SAS drivers should turn their jeeps around and retreat.

Releasing his finger from the trigger, Marty braced himself where he sat as Red careened in a wide turn, narrowly avoiding collision with another jeep that emerged suddenly from a murk of raging smoke and sand. Even as Red completed his turn, a mortar shell exploded just behind the other jeep, picking it up from the rear and spinning it over, throwing the men out like so many rag dolls. Marty saw the men sailing through the air and disappearing into clouds of sand as the jeep smashed upside down on the desert floor and burst into flames.

Seated behind him and now facing the rear, Tone opened fire with his machine-gun, pouring a fusillade into the unseen enemy, venting his frustration.

Most of the jeeps not damaged or destroyed were racing back the way they had come, through dense clouds of spiralling sand and drifting, black smoke. Just as Marty swung his machine-gun around to pour a hail of gunfire at the enemy positions behind him, he was deafened by a mighty roaring, blinding by a jagged, expanding sheet of white light, seared by a wave of fierce heat, then sucked up into a funnel of swirling darkness and noise. Almost instantly he was spat out again, sent flying through the air, turning over, in a roaring vacuum, then slammed brutally back onto the ground, his head filled with streaming stars.

Turning onto his back, he saw the jeep tipping over, throwing Red and Tone out. Rolling away frantically, he just managed to avoid the spinning vehicle when it crashed upside down onto the ground where he had lain, causing clouds of sand to billow up around it.

Clambering to his feet, feeling dazed, spitting sand from his mouth, Marty heard the whipping of bullets on both sides of him, followed by a harsh, metallic cacophony as they ricocheted off Red's overturned jeep. Two of the tyres were melting in yellow flames, giving off an acrid smell; the other two exploded when they were peppered with more enemy bullets. As he was hauling himself back to his feet, Red suddenly went into convulsions, becoming a patchwork of blood, torn clothing and gleaming bone. He was slammed back against the side of the jeep, from which more bullets were ricocheting noisily, then he shuddered even more violently and collapsed.

Horrified, Tone lurched forward to help his dead friend, but Marty, just as shocked, bawled '*No!*' and grabbed him by the shoulders to push him to the ground, falling on top of him as the jeep's petrol tank exploded, engulfing the vehicle and the dead Red in flames. Crawling away from the searing heat and tugging at Tone to make him follow, Marty raised his head when he felt that he was safe and saw the last of the retreating SAS jeeps disappearing into the murk. Seeing Red's charred body not far away, he was badly shaken by an unfamiliar combination of horror and grief.

Suddenly, the mortar shells stopped falling and the firing of the German guns tapered off. Spitting sand from his mouth and rubbing it from his eyes, Marty squinted into the dense, lazily drifting clouds of sand and saw two shadowy figures, both crouching behind their overturned jeep. When eventually they stood up, facing the enemy positions, he recognised them as Captain Kearney and Sergeant Bellamy.

Shocked and still not quite believing what he was seeing, Marty was about to call out when the silence was broken by the soft jangling of weapons and spare magazines as many men advanced from the direction of Benghazi. Before he could turn in that direction, he saw Kearney and Bellamy reluctantly raising their hands above their heads, signifying surrender. Looking in the other direction, he saw a great number of shadowy figures, all carrying their weapons at the ready, emerging ghostlike from drifting sand and smoke. As they came closer, spreading out, taking on shape and detail, he realised, with a sinking heart, that they were German soldiers.

Clambering slowly, carefully to his feet, with a nervous Tone beside him, Marty raised his hands above his head, understanding that for him and the others this war was over.

BOOK TWO

BAD BOYS

31 JANUARY 1991

In the rented Mercedes Benz in the leafy street in St John's Wood the old man picked up his newspaper. Scanning the article already practically memorised, he was shocked once more by the list of so-called 'suicides' and appalled by their bizarre and cruel nature.

(*You've surely gone beyond the pale, you and your friends – but you know what you're doing. All the victims worked on national defence projects that you disapproved of, so you did what you thought was right. How wrong can you be?*)

Eventually he put the paper down and glanced across the road, studied the security guards in the grounds of the mansion house and noted that the front door was still closed. Checking his wristwatch, he saw that he was early, so he leaned his head back against the seat, closed his eyes, relaxed, and tried to work out just how they had gone about it.

(*It's perfectly natural. That first they turned on their own. They turned on their own to protect themselves and then it got worse. It's a natural progression.*)

No accident, then, that the first victim was a former SAS signals expert who had gone to work for Plessey on the System X digital communications project. That project, the old man knew, had defence connections; and the signals expert, upon retirement from the SAS, had obtained his place on the project through the Association. They would have wanted something in return. By this time they had turned that way. They would have wanted feedback, some kind of covert monitoring, and knowledge of where the project was heading, for good or for ill. Should it have taken off in a direction they disapproved of, they would have asked their former SAS colleague to take remedial action, no matter how drastic, perhaps even sabotage. Maybe that's what happened. They had asked and been refused. Their former SAS colleague, feeling secure in his new job, might have stuck by Plessey and rejected the demands of the Association. He would then have become an enemy, working for the other side, and the Association would have been compelled to neutralise him and make it look like suicide.

(*You would have known how to do that, you and your friends.*)

The former SAS man was collected from his house in Cornwall by two men. According to his wife, the men seemed to know him and certainly he went willingly with them, saying he was going fishing and driving them off in his own BMW. He died when his vehicle ran off the edge of a cliff and plunged into the sea. The two men who had gone with him were not found at the scene of the accident. The cause of the accident was unknown, though it was thought to be suicide.

(*I can see you now. You'd been friends for a long time. Two honourable men blinded by obsession, convinced that the end justifies the means and that the Association is always right. Well, damn it, you're wrong.*)

They help their SAS colleague land the job with Plessey shortly after his retirement, but he decides not to do what he's told and so they pay him a visit. They say they want to have a talk and, when he attempts to reject them, they offer veiled threats against his family and that does the trick. He agrees to go with them, tells his wife he's going fishing, and then they force him to drive them away in his own car to their prearranged RV on that Cornish clifftop. There, still in his car, he's rendered unconscious with chloroform, which will leave no trace in water, and then propped up behind the steering wheel. The ignition is turned on, the accelerator is jammed down, and the vehicle goes over the cliff and he dies in the sea. The two men then walk back to the Association car that has been waiting for them at the RV. They are driven away.

(*Yes, that's how you would have done it. You learned tricks like that in Northern Ireland and never forgot them.*)

Opening his eyes, the old man glanced across the road and saw that the security guards beneath the swivelling spy cameras were leaning lethargically against the bonnet of the Rolls Royce, signifying that they weren't yet expecting their boss to materialise. Aware that the man inside the house was running a little late, simultaneously annoyed and relieved to be delayed, the old man lowered his gaze to the newspaper and saw, in the article, that the former SAS man was not the only victim working for Plessey.

Indeed, no. Another scientist, employed by the Plessey Naval Systems at Addlestone, had been found electrocuted in a shed at his home near Esher, apparently after locking himself in. That scientist, the old man knew, had been working in weapons intelligence on a project requiring digital communications like those of the highly secret System X. The linked projects, it was rumoured, were being developed for sale to Iran and other equally repressive regimes, to be used for illegal surveillance and other dubious purposes. The Association would not have liked that and might have moved to prevent it.

Thus the two 'suicides' at Plessey and the others elsewhere. All the dead men had worked on secret defence projects and all of those projects were interlinked. The pattern was clear now.

He was determined to stamp out all aid to repressive regimes, the old man thought as he gazed through the window of his Mercedes Benz at the big, guarded house across the road. The rumour that the work at Plessey would benefit such regimes was enough to make him try to stop those projects with neutralisation, a euphemism for killing.

(*It had to be the work of the Association and you're still its head. For this reason, I must neutralise you, my friend, and put an end to it.*)

The second killing was clear-cut. They would have had covert intelligence operating around the house and ascertained the second victim's working habits. They would have learned, as his wife later confirmed, that he often worked in the evening in the shed at the back of his home. Trained in silent killing techniques, they would have gone there in the evening, sneaked up behind him and, instead of slitting his throat, covered his mouth with a rag soaked in chloroform, exactly as they had done with the first one. In those jungles of the Far East where they had learned their silent killing techniques, in the mean streets of Belfast where the law of the jungle reigned, they may, they surely must, have seen how men were broken when electric wires were tied around their teeth and charged with short bursts of current. This hurt but did not kill. Only a full charge could do that. So to make it look like suicide, like the scientist's own work, they rendered him unconscious, then tied electric wires around his teeth and plugged him into the mains. As their victim was dying, they locked the door from inside, clambered out through the side window, closed the window from outside and made their silent escape without being seen or heard.

His wife said the door was locked. But no one checked the window. Almost certainly, although the window was closed, the lock wasn't on. It was as simple as that.

He stared across the road, feeling grief and rage at once, waiting for his best friend, a fine man, to emerge from the house.

(*Please come out. Let it end today. Pay your dues and be done with it.*)

He had come a long way for this.

CHAPTER EIGHT

'Yes,' Marty said impatiently as he buttoned up the tunic of his Territorial Army uniform, before going out for another weekend. 'I'll admit it. I detest bloody peacetime. That's why I joined the TA. That's why a lot of us joined it. What's wrong with that?'

Lesley sighed, not wanting another argument. She was sitting by the blazing coal fire in the spacious lounge of their large, detached house with garden in Weybridge, Surrey, where they had moved last year when Marty realised he had made a lot of money. The flickering light fell on her pale face and made her brown eyes shine. 'I'm not saying there's anything wrong with it. I just wish you were home more.'

'I'm home enough,' Marty said, though he knew it was a lie. 'I only attend a couple of nights each week and one weekend each month. I don't think that's too much.'

'It wouldn't be,' Lesley insisted, 'if you weren't working so much as well. But when you're not with the TA, you're running all over the place for your work. The fact is, you're hardly ever here. Don't try denying it, Marty. At this rate you're not even going to see your own children growing up. I don't think that's right.'

'Most men don't see their kids growing up,' Marty said, though he felt guilty about not seeing John and Kay enough. 'They're too busy working.'

'Says you!' Leslie retorted. She was in an armchair, knitting, still slim and curvaceous in a woollen cardigan and grey skirt, her short auburn hair framing delicate, soft features and those troubled brown eyes. The domestic kind, she had knitted her own cardigans and Marty's pullovers; but, instead of being grateful for this particular economy, Marty viewed it as something that revealed another difference between them.

She's rooted to home and hearth, he thought, *while I yearn to be fancy-free. That's it in a nutshell.*

Gazing down at her, he could scarcely believe that it was now 1951 and that the marriage was already a decade old. It had not been an easy marriage. For a start, they'd had only that one night together in the Savoy hotel before being parted for four years. Marty had spent that time either in North Africa, fighting with L Detachment, or in a prisoner-of-war camp in Germany, where he had ended up with Tone after their capture outside Benghazi. Released at the end of the war, they had been returned to their original unit, the 9th Rifle Brigade, then demobbed in September 1945.

Six years ago, Marty thought, *but I keep thinking it was just yesterday. I'm growing old already.*

Returning to the wife with whom he had shared only one night of marriage, he had felt that he was facing a stranger. Lesley had spent most of the war working in a munitions factory in north London while wondering if Marty was alive or dead. Eventually informed by the War Office that he was still alive and about to be released from a German POW camp, she had written that she was looking forward to seeing him again; but in fact, when he turned up on her doorstep, she was as nervous as he was. Marty knew that this was because they'd spent only that one night together in bed, that it had been fraught with sexual uncertainty, and that being forced to start all over again would be far from easy. This turned out to be true.

'Can I ask you something?' Lesley had put down her knitting and was gazed steadily at him as he adjusted the army beret on his head and prepared to leave. Disconcerted by the tone of her voice, he nervously lit a cigarette.

'Obviously you're going to,' he said. 'What is it, Lesley?'

She took a deep breath. 'Do you still love me, Marty?'

'Of course,' he said automatically, though the question had taken him by surprise, particularly since Lesley wasn't the type to discuss such matters. 'You know I do. Why ask?'

'Because I don't think it's true,' she replied in her quietly direct, often devastating manner. 'I don't *feel* your love, Marty. I don't think I ever did.'

'Never?'

'No.'

'That's bloody rubbish, Lesley.'

'It's true,' she replied. 'We've never been really all that close. We liked each other and had respect for each other, but I've never felt love. At least not after you returned from the war. Only when we were young – before we were married – not after that. It all changed after that. Was it my fault, Marty?'

He thought carefully before replying, not wanting to blame her wrongly, aware that he may have been as much at fault for the distance between them. It was possible, he thought, that neither of them was responsible. Like the hundreds of couples who had married when the war began, he and Lesley had married on impulse, then found out, when reunited, that neither was as the other had imagined. Though he couldn't bring himself to tell her that, he made a stab at the truth.

'No,' he said, 'it wasn't your fault, luv. It wasn't anyone's fault. I mean, I loved you when we married, but we were a lot younger then and young people need to live together and adjust to each other. We didn't have that opportunity and that was the rub. We were married, had one honeymoon night, then were parted for four years – nearly five. When we saw each other again all that time later we were strangers to each other and should have had more privacy than we got. In the event, when I got back, we had to stay on in Crouch Hill with my mum and dad. I think that put an even greater strain on our relationship and drove us farther apart. It was nothing to do with whether or not I loved you. We simply never had a chance to get really close and maybe now it's too late. That's the truth of it, Lesley.'

At least *part* of it, he thought. Certainly, it was true that when the war ended they had been obliged to stay in his parents' house in Crouch Hill, sharing his old bedroom right beside his parents' room. That had made Lesley, in particular, extremely self-conscious when attempting to make love, fearful of being overheard. To complicate this situation, Marty's promiscuity with the whores of Cairo had given him sexual urges that Lesley, with her middle-class moral values, was unable to accommodate. Lesley was, in his view, a fundamentally loving, maternal woman, easily shocked in bed, shying away from anything too uninhibited, and more concerned with the emotional than the physical. This had often frustrated Marty and led to diminishing returns with regards to their sex life. That problem, combined with their lack of privacy, had increased the distance between them.

'Is that what you really think, Marty?' she asked. 'That it might be too late for us?'

He glanced at her through the smoke from his cigarette, feeling love and pain. They had lost each other somewhere along the way, but the love was still there. It was just different, less romantic, not blind – and it was hurting them both.

'I don't know,' he said. 'I only know that we're both different and that we can't go back to being what we were. You're a fine woman, Lesley, a good mother, and I respect you for that; but, though I try to be a decent husband and father, I need other things.'

'To get away. To live in a man's world. Your work, the pub and the TA. Is that what you mean, Marty?'

'Yes, I suppose so. I'm too easily bored with routine and I have to get out. That's why I do all the things I do.'

'Dangerous things.'

'Yes.'

'You enjoyed the war too much for your own good.'

'I can't deny that.'

It was true that he believed the best time of his life had been in North Africa with L Detachment and the Long Range Desert Group. The contrast between his recollection of those days and his present life here in Surrey kept him awake at nights, increased his boredom during the day, and too often drove him out to the pub where he could talk to other demobbed soldiers about common experiences. Those conversations always reminded him of the sheer excitement he had felt during the SAS raids against Axis airfields and the enormous respect he had gained for men like Paddy Kearney and Bulldog Bellamy. Even his incarceration in a German POW camp had been infinitely more exciting than what he was doing right now. If nothing else, his three years as a POW had strengthened his feelings of camaraderie with his fellow prisoners and made him more addicted to a man's world of danger and endurance. For this reason, when the war ended, he and his best friend, Tone, after going into business together, had restlessly started trying out different sports, particularly boating and mounting-climbing, before enlisting in the TA. Neither had found in marriage or fatherhood what it was they most needed: the excitement of danger. Lesley knew this and feared it.

'I wouldn't mind if I felt closer to you,' she said, studying her clasped hands and trying to keep her emotions in check as she had done for so long. 'But you're never quite here, your thoughts are always somewhere else, and I feel that I'm being cut out of your life, that I no longer exist for you. That's hard to take, Marty.'

He stubbed his cigarette out in the ashtray on the mantlepiece, then sighed, exhaling the last of the smoke as he glanced at the front door of the house, wanting to leave. 'It's not that bad,' he lied. 'You're exaggerating the situation. We're not all that different from other couples. Our problems aren't that uncommon.'

'I know,' Lesley replied. 'But that doesn't make them any better. Hundreds of couples who got married during the war are queuing up for divorce. I don't want that to happen to us, Marty. I'm frightened of that.'

'It won't happen,' Marty said. 'We're just going through a bad patch. 'We have a good home, two healthy children and a pretty nice life in general. I like to get out of the house. I like to do things. You like to look after the house and kids, which means our problems are minor. Things will gradually work themselves out. Don't worry about it.'

Lesley sighed. 'I'll try not to. I just don't want our different interests to drive us apart.'

'They won't,' Marty said.

He leaned down to kiss the top of her head, filling up with guilt and concern when he saw her wet eyes. She still loved him, he realised as he left the house, and that made it more difficult. The sun was shining over the green hills of Surrey and that made him feel better.

Having a pint in the pleasantly crowded pub in the West End of London, waiting for Tone to arrive, Marty thought of Lesley and the kids back in the big house in Weybridge and realised that he had come a long way in a short time.

Mere weeks after his demob, when he had been back in his father's construction business feeling distinctly bored, he had read that many local councils were seeking state aid to ease the chronic housing shortage caused by German bombing. One such plan was for the purchasing of prefabricated homes for demobilised servicemen and bombed-out families. The 'prefabs' were steel-built, single-storey dwellings that could be erected in a few hours by a small number of workmen and half a million of them were to be built by the motor industry. Within weeks, he had obtained contracts with various manufacturers and was constructing prefabs all over the London area. Delighted to have a challenge, he threw himself into the work with all the enthusiasm he had lost since being demobbed. He was also enthusiastic because the work, which was plentiful, kept him away from home a lot and entailed travels to many areas outside London.

Pregnant with their first child, Lesley sometimes complained about his constant working, but as the money was finally pouring in, enabling her to buy luxuries she could not afford before and, as she put it, prepare properly for the baby, she was more often pleased than displeased.

Within a year, Marty had a healthy bank account and was able to purchase a proper home for Lesley and the expected child. Familiar with the property market, he soon found the detached house in Weybridge. Lesley, with her middle-class pretensions, was thrilled to move into it. A few weeks after the move, their first child, John, was born and Marty was almost as pleased as Lesley.

Almost, but not quite. Thrilled to hold his newly born son in his arms, he behaved at first like many fathers, showering affection on the baby, watching his every move intently and subconsciously mapping out his future. That, however, did not last too long. Within weeks, the baby's constant crying had encouraged him to take an even greater interest in his work and, as Leslie settled to being a devoted mother, he began spending more time at work, running the business side of it while Tone, whom he had hired in the first flush of his success, supervised the actual construction of the prefabs.

The money kept rolling in and Marty enjoyed himself, not least because he was back in a man's world, dealing with level-headed businessmen, builders, plumbers, electricians and hard-drinking, mainly Irish, labourers. Realising that he felt more comfortable with these men than he did at home, he frequently socialised with them, often joining them for drinks after work and even meeting them at weekends to go to the dogs or the racetrack. This did not thrill Lesley.

During that time of growing unease, she gave birth to their second child, Kay, and, though Marty was again delighted, he still found himself looking for any excuse to get out of the house. He realised, then, that he enjoyed his work because it took him from one location to the other and led to many evenings and weekends of rough-and-ready fun. To his surprise, shortly after Kay was born, when Lesley was even more involved in being a mother, he had found himself thinking increasingly about his days with the SAS and yearning to do something just as exciting.

By this time Tone was having the same problem. Married himself and the father of three children, he confessed to Marty that he had never recovered from the excitements of the war and was desperately bored in Civvy Street. Coming from Wales and knowing the territory, he suggested that he and Marty take up some challenging sports, including sailing and mountain-climbing. This they both did for the next couple of years, sailing around most of the English coast and climbing the soaring, freezing mountains of the Brecon Beacons, an imposing and dangerous mountain range in South Wales.

But when even that became too routine Tone suggested the Territorial Army.

'I've just heard that a TA group's been raised at Aldershot,' he told Marty as they sat together near the summit of the Pen-y-far, the highest mountain in the Brecon Beacons, having a lunch of 'wads' and hot tea. 'I think we should join it. What do you say, mate?'

'I agree,' Marty said.

Already seeing so little of him, Lesley had been outraged when she learned what he was planning. Nevertheless, he and Tone enlisted in the TA and were childishly thrilled to be back in uniform. The company had a drill night every Thursday, weekend exercises every three weeks and a two-week camp once a year. Though all of this made life with Lesley more difficult, Marty could not resist it, feeling that it filled a gap and only surprised that he still wasn't content, that he still missed the Army. Leslie knew that as well.

Looking up from his pint, Marty watched Tone enter the pub, also wearing his TA uniform, to make his way through the other smoke-wreathed customers until he reached the table.

'Your glass in nearly empty,' he said. 'I suppose you want another one?'

'Bloody right,' Marty replied.

Grinning, Tone made his way to the bar to order the drinks. Lean and fit, with a face scarred from the coal pits and a hazel-eyed, cynical gaze, he now had the confidence that comes from success and the restlessness of a man who needs adventure. The former came from his work in the once-thriving prefab business; the latter had been picked up in North Africa. He and Marty had that in common and were bonded by it.

'So what's new?' Marty asked when his friend had brought the drinks and was facing him across the brass-topped table.

Tone shrugged, had a good swallow of his beer, then put the glass down. 'Not much since I saw you yesterday,' he said. 'I picked up my paycheck, went home to the wife and kids, had a pint, went to bed and spent all of today, this being Saturday, trying to be a good daddy. I'm bloody bored, I can tell you. I can't take Civvy Street.'

'Neither can I, mate.'

'I'm so bored I've actually thought of re-enlisting. I really have, Marty. The thought crosses my mind a lot. I mean, it's 1951, six years since we were demobbed, and yet I feel even less settled now than I was way back then. I keep thinking about L Detachment and I know what I'm missing.'

'You could go back to the coal mines,' Marty kidded him.

'No way,' Tone responded indignantly. 'I fought like shit to get out of the coal mines and I'm not going back. I'd rather work in your dad's business that do that, but it's just not enough. When I think of the times we had with the SAS, I know why I'm bored now.'

'A hell of a regiment,' Marty said, 'but it no longer exists.'

'Right,' Tone said. 'Those bastards.'

He was referring to the fact that, regardless of the tremendous work the SAS had done during the war, it had been disbanded in 1945. Indeed, after the war Marty had learned from former comrades just how much his fellow SAS men, officers and other ranks, had done in his absence, even when some of them were also prisoners-of-war. Captured with Marty and Tone, Bulldog Bellamy had been incarcerated in a POW camp deep in Italy from where he had made many escape attempts, none of which were successful, though all had given the Italians a lot to think about. Captured at the same time, Captain Kearney, after repeated attempts to escape from the officers' POW camp in Gavi, Italy, was transferred to the 'escape proof' Colditz Castle, Saxony, deep in the very heart of Nazi Germany. Even there, the Allied officers, termed 'bad boys' by the Germans because of their repeated attempts to escape, continued with their activities, showing remarkable ingenuity by forging German identification papers and other documents, making German uniforms and other clothing out of stolen rags, digging tunnels under the very noses of the German guards in a remarkable number of different ways, abseiling down the walls with ropes made from knotted bedsheets and pieces of cord stolen over many months, even constructing a piloted glider in secret in an attempt to fly over the walls. This plan had been stopped by the ending of the war. Major Stirling was captured in 1943, during Operation Torch in

Tunisia, and after escaping four times from Gavi prison camp had also been transferred to Colditz Castle. There, with the support of Paddy Kearney, he spent the rest of the war years coordinating the black-market activities of the other prisoners as part of an ingenious intelligence-gathering operation.

Meanwhile, his brother, Lieutenant-Colonel William Stirling, then with the British First Army, had formed 2 SAS and, with the Special Raiding Squadron (SRS) – which was 1 SAS temporarily renamed – performed invaluable work in the Allied capture of Sicily. The SAS then went on to aid the Allied advance in Europe by conducting a series of daring night raids in France, often working with the Maquis: Frenchmen who lived in the forests and conducted sabotage missions behind enemy lines. The brigade was also used extensively in Sicily, Holland, Belgium and Germany. During the closing months of the war those particular SAS raids were so successful that Hitler personally ordered that all SAS men captured should be tortured and then summarily executed. Nevertheless, regardless of this great work, the regiment was officially disbanded at the end of the war.

'The thing about being with L Detachment,' Marty said, feeling his anger stirring, 'is that we really believed in what we were fighting for, we took pride in doing a good job, and we were willing to risk our bloody lives for what we thought was a just cause. Those values don't exist in Civvy Street. No values at all, really. They just go on from one bloody day to the next, hoping to make a bob or two and concerned that they've got a decent pension plan. In L Detachment, every day was a brand-new day in the sense that it was always unpredictable. Now everything's bloody predictable; we're just drifting along. No wonder you feel like re-enlisting. I've thought about it myself.'

'So why don't we do it?' Tone asked.

'It wouldn't be the same. There's no real war to fight. That Suez Canal business will be over in no time, so we'd just end up helping the Yanks in Korea or standing guard duty in Berlin. Bloody boring, mate. No, thanks.'

'So why are we in the TA?' Tone asked him.

Marty shrugged. 'Why are you?'

'If I wasn't in the TA,' Tone explained without irony, 'I'd probably be out robbing banks. That or something just as bad and dangerous. You know what I mean, mate?'

'Yes, I know what you mean. I'm beginning to feel that way myself. No matter how much I might care for Lesley and the kids, when I'm at home with them I often feel that I'm about to explode. *That's* why I'm in the TA.'

'It has its own rewards,' Tone responded with a grin, 'and you're going to get one this evening.'

'Oh?' Marty said. 'What's that?'

Tone's grin became wicked. 'Finish off your pint and let's get to Aldershot. There's a commando officer coming this evening to give us a lecture on standard operating procedures. We can't afford to miss it.'

'Why are you so excited about commando SOPs?' Marty asked when he had finished his pint and was getting to his feet. 'It sounds boring to me.'

'You won't be bored when you hear who's giving the lecture,' Tone said, still grinning wickedly.

'Oh? Who's that?' Marty asked.

'Captain Paddy Kearney,' Tone told him. 'Are you still bored, my friend?'

'Hell, no!' Marty exclaimed.

CHAPTER NINE

'Well, well, what a pleasant surprise!' Paddy Kearney said chirpily when he had completed his lecture and joined Marty and Tone at the crowded, noisy TA bar. Kearney had lost neither his rugby player's physique nor his dark Irish good looks. His green eyes, Marty noticed, were as bright as ever when he flashed them his wicked grin. 'I recognised you immediately, of course,' he continued, 'when I scanned all the eager faces seated before me. Nice to know you survived. So which one of you is going to buy me a drink? A large whisky on ice, thanks.'

Marty did the honours and was pleased to hand the drink to the man he admired more than any other. 'Real good to see you, boss. I often wondered what had happened to you after the war and it's nice to see that you're still in the service.'

'Cheers!' Kearney said, raising his glass, then swallowing a good mouthful. 'Oh, yes,' he said, lowering his glass again and smiling at each of them in turn. 'Still in. RTU'd to Number Eight Commando the minute I got out of Colditz. Not that it made any difference, since L Detachment was already being disbanded.'

'I thought that was a bloody disgrace, sir.'

'So did I. Damned shame, if you ask me. Naturally it was a decision taken by the Gaberdine Swine of the British General Staff, who seemed to think that with the ending of the war there was no proper role for us. Of course, Major Stirling, the minute he returned from Colditz, was all for using the regiment in the Far East. Wanted to use us in northern China and make attacks on Manchurian railways, cutting off supplies to the Japs. Then the bombs fell on Hiroshima and Nagasaki and that was the end of it. When the regiments returned from Norway, where they'd disarmed about three hundred thousand Germans, they were deemed to be of no further use and quickly disbanded. Pretty rotten, yes?'

'Too bloody true,' Tone responded, nodding affirmatively, then drinking from his fresh pint of bitter.

Kearney chuckled, shaking his head from side to side in rueful recollection. 'The last I recall of you two, you were like ghosts in the swirling dust of that plain outside Benghazi, raising your hands above your heads and being led off by Jerry. Ended up in a POW camp, did you?'

Marty nodded. 'Yep. In Augsburg, Germany. It wasn't all that bad, though. The worst things, as I recall, were the cold, the general shortage of food and the bloody boredom. But all in all, Jerry treated us decently.'

'The war in North Africa was a gentlemen's war,' Kearney said. 'Maybe the last of its kind. Each side treated the other with respect. When you think of what the Krauts were up to elsewhere in Europe, you realise just how lucky we were to be captured by Rommel's Afrika Korps. Every time I think of how those bastards in the Gestapo cold-bloodedly massacred thirty-two SAS prisoners outside the camp at Gaggenau . . . Well . . .' He shook his head sadly from side to side. 'What can one say?'

Neither Marty nor Tone said anything, both still rendered uncomfortable by the thought of that notorious incident.

Kearney put his glass down and lit a Player's cigarette. He inhaled, glanced along the crowded bar, then exhaled a thin stream of smoke. 'So,' he said, smiling brightly again, 'you had it okay in your POW camp?'

'We were treated fairly,' Marty said. 'Even when we tried to escape and were recaptured, the worst punishment was a month in solitary.'

'That seems fair enough,' Kearney said. 'And did you try that on often?'

'Not as often as you lot at Colditz,' Tone replied. 'But we had a good go. Have you heard anything more about Major Stirling?' he asked, not wishing to recall the many unsuccessful escape attempts he also had made. 'I hear he's left the service altogether. Living overseas now. Any truth in that?'

Kearney nodded. 'Yep. Once back in England, he was all set to pick up the reins of the SAS, but by that time the regiment was under the overall command of Brigadier Mike Calvert – who'd formerly headed the Chindits, operating deep behind Japanese lines in Burma—'

'Mad Mike,' Marty interjected, using the nickname for the legendary officer and guerrilla fighter.

'Correct,' Kearney said. 'Anyway, by this time the SAS had been scattered all over the place, with some operating in small raiding parties in France, others conducting mopping-up operations in Germany, and First and Second regiments in Norway to disarm over three hundred thousand Germans. And, of course, by that time there were also two French SAS regiments and a Belgian regiment that was almost the same size as two normal ones. But even worse than this scattering of the SAS was the fact that Stirling's brother, Lieutenant-Colonel William Stirling, who had raised Two SAS, refused to let his men be used in ways which he thought were improper. For this reason, he was constantly fighting with his superiors. He finally exploded on the eve of the Allied invasion of Europe, when Supreme Headquarters, Allied Expeditionary Force, insisted on using the SAS behind the beaches, instead of letting them attack strategic targets behind enemy lines.

'Bill Stirling resigned and Two SAS was taken over by Lieutenant-Colonel Brian Franks, who proved to be an admirable commander. Naturally, our very own David Stirling, the legendary Phantom Major, by now a lieutenant-colonel, was thoroughly disgusted by all this, but still planned to use the regiments against the Japs. Then the bombs fell on Hiroshima and Nagasaki and that was the end of it. The War Office, in its misguided wisdom, decided to disband the SAS as no longer relevant and the regiments were paraded for the last time, under Mad Mike, in October of forty-five. Even more disgusted, Colonel Stirling retired to his home in Scotland.'

'Still up there, is he?' Tone asked. 'Doing a spot of fishing?'

Kearney chuckled at the thought. 'Not likely. He felt deprived of his beloved SAS, but he still wanted new adventures. He'd moved by the end of that year to Salisbury in Rhodesia, as the manager-director of a London-based financial development company. His job was to check out the business potential of the mineral deposits and agriculture of the country, but once he got over there he soon met a lot of old friends from the SAS and the LRDG – Mike Sadler and other Rhodesians – and, as is his way, became more involved than he'd originally planned. First thing he did was resign from the company that had hired him and set up his own to invest in mining, road construction and agriculture. He's dead against apartheid, and he's now the head of something called the Capricorn Africa Society. It's reportedly dedicated to the creation of a true multi-racial society, based on the notion that a policy for Africa must come from within Africa and be acceptable to all races on the continent. Quite the idealist, really.'

'I'm not at all sure that I'd want all them Sambos running themselves,' Marty said. 'I'm not so sure that they could.'

'That's a racist remark,' Kearney told him without rancour.

'It's not racist,' Tone noted. 'It's plain to see. Those blackies are so busy fighting amongst themselves, they can hardly light their own bloody camp fires.'

'That's not true,' Kearney responded. 'Also, as former SAS men, you should have learned to judge other men only as individuals, not by racial stereotypes.'

'What's a stereotype?' Tone asked.

'Never mind,' Marty said, flashing him a quick grin before turning back to Kearney. 'Do you ever see Stirling?'

'Yes, occasionally. He comes to Britain three or four times a year, not only to visit his family home in Scotland, but also to spread the gospel of his Capricorn Africa Society and attract investments for his companies. I think he does cross-over business with his brother, Bill, who's involved in road-building, quarrying and ore concessions. Certainly, Stirling tends to use the offices of the family company in Upper Grosvenor Street as his London HQ; so I see him there occasionally. Naturally, he also keeps in touch as much as possible with his old SAS chums, the Originals, through informal gatherings and, of course, the Regimental Association. So, yes, I've kept in touch. He's as feisty as ever.'

'But not officially involved with the SAS any more,' Marty said.

'Alas, no. You sound almost regretful, Private Butler.'

Marty knew that there was no point in denying what he felt. Just talking about the SAS had filled him with a real feeling of loss, reminding him of all that he, too, had done before he returned to Civvy Street and became just like other men. Now, despite being successful, a husband and father, he was bored, merely living out his life, yearning for the thrills that had made him feel keenly alive.

'Yes, sir,' he admitted, 'I feel regretful. I miss the life a lot. What do men who had the experiences *we* shared do when it's all over?'

Kearney shrugged, a secret smile on his lips. 'They do everything from becoming Members of Parliament to teaching school or labouring in the docks. Some compensate for the lack of thrills by becoming policemen, mercenaries, military advisors to foreign powers, even poachers and, possibly, bank-robbers. Others, like you and Tone, join the TA; yet others simply can't live without it and return to the Army.'

'But not to the SAS,' Tone informed him. 'And there *is* a big difference, sir.'

'Right,' Marty said. 'A hell of a difference. I enjoy the TA, but I'm not sure I'd like to join the regular Army – not if it wasn't some kind of special forces. Tone and I, we've both been tempted to enlist again, but we still have our doubts.'

Kearney was still wearing his slight, secret smile. 'And have you been keeping in touch with your old mates from the regiment?'

'We did for a year or so,' Marty said, 'but gradually we all scattered in different directions – just like the old regiments.'

'So you aren't aware of what's been happening recently with regard to the SAS?'

'No,' Tone said. 'What do you mean, what's been happening to it? It's still disbanded, isn't it?'

Kearney's secret smile broke into a wide grin. 'No,' he said. 'It isn't. And I'm scouting for new recruits.'

Marty and Tone glanced at each other in astonishment, then, with a quickening heart, Marty returned his gaze to the still-grinning Lieutenant Kearney.

'Just what are you talking about, boss?'

Kearney stubbed his cigarette out in the ashtray and waved at the barman to fetch them another round of drinks. Then he turned back to Marty and Tone, this time looking more serious.

'Mad Mike Calvert and Lieutenant-Colonel Franks didn't give up the idea of a special force. In fact, in nineteen forty-six, with other senior officers who'd served with the regiment, they persuaded the War Office to set up an inquiry by the Technical Investigation Committee, to look into possible roles for the SAS, or a similar unit, in the future. The committee's conclusion was that there *was* a place for a similar unit, but at that time – when the War Office was actually *reducing* their military forces – it was politically impossible to raise a new regiment. To get around this, a TA unit of reservists was formed by amalgamating the SAS with the Artists' Rifles.'

'The *what*?' Tone asked.

'The Artists' Rifles,' said Kearney. 'It's a volunteer regiment first raised in eighteen sixty and always headed by a CO who was a professional artist, painter or sculptor. It had a distinguished fighting record in the First World War and served as an officer training unit in World War Two. It was deactivated briefly after the war, and then made part of the Territorial Army and affiliated to the Rifle Brigade.'

'Right,' Tone said. 'With you, sir.'

'So,' Marty asked impatiently, 'what happened then?'

'As I said, in September forty-seven, a TA unit of reservists was formed by amalgamating the SAS with the Artists' Rifles. The new unit was called Twenty-one (Artists) – that's in parentheses – SAS. A total of one hundred and eighty former SAS officers and men joined as reservists. Because the Artists' Rifles had always been officered by men who'd first served in the ranks, many of the officers enlisting in Twenty-one (Artists) SAS joined in the ranks – and this stood for *all* of the officers who've since gained commissions in the regiment.'

'I like the idea of *that!*' Tone commented.

Kearney flashed him a grin. 'Anyway, Twenty-one (Artists) SAS was placed under the command of Lieutenant-Colonel Franks, the former commander of Two SAS during the liberation of Europe, and the selection and training of its recruits was as rigorous as it had been for L Detachment in the early days in North Africa. Incidentally, one of those who enlisted was your old friend, Bulldog Bellamy. Remember him?'

'God, yes!' Marty exclaimed, elated to know that his old tormenter, then friend, had survived the war and was serving with the new regiment.

'RTU'd to the Dorset Regiment after the war and was bounced back to buck private when he volunteered for the new unit. Of course, he's already made it back up to corporal and still bawls like a sergeant, which he will be quite soon.'

Marty grinned at the thought of it. 'So what's this new unit up to?'

'Earlier this year, the regiment was about to fly off to Korea – at the specific request of General McArthur – but instead it was diverted to Malaya, where it's been operating against the twelve hundred communist Chinese who fled into the jungle in forty-eight and only emerged to murder the Malayan villagers, local political leaders and, of course, white rubber plantationers. While Twenty-one (Artists) SAS was operating along with the so-called Ferret Force in Malaya – a paramilitary group composed of army volunteers, former members of the Special Operations Executive Force One Three Six and other civilians – General Sir John Harding, the Commander-in-Chief of Far East Land Forces, ordered Mad Mike to fly to Malaya and study the situation.

'When he'd done so – after having toured the country for six months and personally joined infantry patrols and made long hikes into enemy territory, as befits his adventurous nature – he returned with the recommendation that a special force be formed to harass the communists in their jungle hide-outs.

He named that force the Malayan Scouts, SAS. Apart from twenty-one (Artists) SAS it's composed of volunteers who served with the SOE in Malaya in nineteen forty-five, in the Ferret Force, and, of course, in the SAS during the war.'

'And you're involved?' Marty asked, becoming excited.

'Yes. I'm being transferred to the Malayan Scouts next week and I'm already looking for suitable new recruits. As former SAS members and still serving members of the TA, you pair could enlist if you wished. You'll be trained for eight weeks in Johore in southern Malaya and operate out of Ipoh, in the north. What do you say?'

As the busy barman set fresh drinks on the counter, Marty and Tone glanced at each other, both clearly thinking along the same lines. Certainly, Marty was thinking that he wanted to do it. He was also thinking that Lesley, who had been reduced willy-nilly to a mere shadow in his life and was becoming ever more irate about his increasing absences from home, would positively explode if he told her that he was re-enlisting in the SAS. On the other hand, the thought of missing this golden opportunity just because of her anger was something he simply couldn't wear. Nor could he bear the thought of spending the rest of his life in his present circumstances, merely passing the time, constantly filled with recollections of his thrilling days in North Africa and unable to drag himself out of bed with enthusiasm except on the days when he was going to the TA. Knowing this, he picked up his pint knowing what he would do.

'I'm in,' he said.

Also picking up his pint, Tone said, 'So am I.'

Kearney grinned and picked up his glass of whisky. The three men touched glasses.

'To the Malayan Scouts, SAS,' Kearney said.

They all drank to that.

CHAPTER TEN

Sitting in a draughty, freezing hall in the Malayan Scouts (SAS) base, located in the Airborne Forces HQ and Parachute Regiment's Depot in Aldershot, Surrey, waiting to begin his training and selection course, surrounded by forty other candidates, all still in their civvies, Marty found it hard to believe that his marriage was over. But that seemed to be the case. When he had told her that he was re-enlisting, Lesley, normally reticent, had exploded with rage, then collapsed into shocked disbelief and tearful entreaty. Eventually, managing to regain control of herself, she said, 'If you do this – if you walk out that door – you'll be choosing the SAS over me and I won't forgive that. So you better think about it very carefully before making your choice.' Marty made his choice. Though he didn't find it easy, though his pain was real enough, he packed his suitcase, kissed his kids goodbye, then resolutely turned away from Lesley's tears to walk out of the house.

'Don't come back,' she said to him.

Now, sitting in this bleak, draughty hall, waiting for his new CO's introductory briefing, he finally faced up to the fact that although he still loved Lesley in his fashion, and certainly adored the kids, he had increasingly, cruelly, neglected them in order to pursue his own interests. In truth, his married life had made him feel trapped in a world that was too commonplace to maintain his interest. He needed the thrill of fresh adventures to keep him alive. He now had to accept this harsh truth and learn to live with it.

'I don't believe it!' Tone exclaimed in disgust beside him. 'A twelve-week training and selection course. We've been through the bloody war, we've done our TA training, and we're *still* not getting in automatically. Bloody cheek, if you ask me!'

Marty was amused. 'You can bet that Paddy Kearney knew this all along and didn't mention it in case we said, "No, thanks." Clever bastard, he is.'

'I hear it's a tough one,' Trooper Roy Weatherby said from where he was seated at Marty's other side. Though a former Royal Signals sergeant, like the others present he had accepted a reduction in rank in order to get into the Malayan Scouts. 'Even tougher than selection for the Commandos. There's even something so bad it's called a "Sickener", which I'm told really cuts down the numbers. It's supposed to be bloody murderous. In fact, I've heard that they only expect about a quarter of us to make it through to the end. The RTU rate's high.'

The CO, Lieutenant-Colonel Phillip Mackie, entered the hall, flanked by Paddy Kearney and a regimental sergeant-major. As the three men stepped up to the blackboard, Marty was reminded by the new insignia on Kearney's uniform that he had automatically dropped back in rank to lieutenant when entering the SAS.

'Attention!' the RSM bawled.

Every man in the room jumped out of his chair, snapped to attention and saluted the CO. The latter returned the salute, then indicated that the men could sit down again.

'Welcome to the Malayan Scouts,' he said when they were seated. 'You men have volunteered for a regiment that's like no other in the British Army. As some of you have previously served with us during the war, you'll know the principles upon which we operate. For the benefit of the rest of you, our philosophy is that small groups of exceptionally well-trained, self-reliant and highly motivated men can perform certain tasks much better than large groups or regiments. Given this, we're not looking for undisciplined cowboys, but for men who can work alone or in small groups, rather than as part of big battalions. Such men have to be superbly fit, capable of enduring isolation and other forms of stress for long periods, and always ready at a moment's notice to take over the duties of any other man in their team. For this reason, the training and selection you're about to undergo will be both psychologically and physically demanding – indeed, rigorous in the extreme – and little mercy will be shown to those who fail at any point along the way. Be prepared for what will undoubtedly turn out to be the most brutal experience of your life.'

Satisfied that he had put the fear of God into them, the CO nodded at the burly regimental sergeant-major standing beside him, holding a clipboard. 'RSM Neil Farrell will now take you to your accommodations, then on to the quartermaster's store to be kitted out. Once that's done, you'll have an hour to make up your beds, then you'll line up outside your barracks to immediately commence training and selection. Good luck. Dismissed.'

When the CO and Lieutenant Kearney had left the hall, the latter throwing Marty a grin, the RSM bawled that the candidates were to gather outside. They were then marched across the wet, windswept quadrangle, around administration buildings, hangars, NAAFI canteen and corrugated iron hangars until they arrived at the bleak wooden barracks designated for them. There they each claimed a steel-framed bed by placing suitcases and other personal baggage on it. Then they rushed back outside and lined up as before, in order of size and still wearing their civvies, to be marched by the RSM to the quartermaster's store, where they were each kitted out with an olive-green uniform known as OGs, boots, beret, underclothing, a Bergen backpack, sleeping bag, wet-weather poncho, webbed belts, water bottles, brew kit, three twenty-four-hour ration packs, a heavy prismatic compass and, more ominously, Ordnance Survey maps of the Brecon Beacons and Elan Valley.

'At least we know that bloody mountain,' Tone muttered to Marty.

'We sure do,' Marty replied. 'If that's where they intend making us march, at least we'll have a head start.'

'Bloody right,' Tone whispered.

After being marched from the quartermaster's store to the

armoury, where each man was equipped with a primitive .303 Lee Enfield rifle, they were practically run from the armoury back to the barracks. There they were given the promised hour to make up their steel-framed beds, put on their OGs, berets and boots, sling their empty Bergen backpacks over their shoulders, pick up their Lee Enfields and assemble outside the barracks where, while they waited for the arrival of RSM Farrell, they were whipped by a freezing November wind that gave hints of the snow to come.

In fact, RSM Farrell did not return. Instead, the new candidates were faced with an even more stony-faced sergeant, a barrel-chested six-footer with sandy-red hair, piercing blue eyes and a face flushed from fresh air and sunshine.

'The name is Sergeant Doyle. I'm a member of the Directing Staff, or DS, and your main drill instructor, in charge of your training and selection from this moment on. If you have any complaints about our methods of training, I don't want to hear them. If, at any time, you think you can't go on, you either try to go on despite yourself or you drop out and get RTU'd with your tail between your legs. You can also be RTU'd at any stage in the training and selection process at the recommendation of myself or any other member of the DS. There are no means of redress or complaint. Before you think to whinge, please be reminded that you won't be asked to do anything that your DS and officers haven't already done themselves. If we can do it, so can you. If you can't, you'll be RTU'd. I really don't want to hear any questions, but I'm obliged to ask: are there any questions?'

Since the huge sergeant Doyle seemed set to explode, none of the candidates had the nerve to raise their hands.

'I love the sound of silence,' Doyle said. 'Your training commences right now.'

Marty soon learned that even the tough training in the North African desert could not compare to the rigours of this new SAS selection course. For the first few days, beginning at 0400 hours and not ending until at least 2200 hours, he and the other candidates alternated between weapons training in the freezing cold of an open firing range and brutal route marches over the hills of the surrounding countryside, each one longer and tougher than the one before, all leading to a final slog up an ever-steeper gradient that mercilessly tortured lungs and muscles. These dreadful hikes, or 'tabs', through rain, sleet, hail and snow were rendered even more murderous when the formerly empty Bergen backpacks were loaded with bricks, the load being increased every day.

Even with the minimum load, which was eleven kilos, the weight, combined with the difficult terrain and vile weather, was enough to make some candidates drop out. Each time someone did so – to be labelled a 'crap-hat' and returned to his original unit, often in tears – the DS would add more bricks to the Bergens of the others. They kept doing so until the total weight was a back-breaking twenty-five kilos.

To make matters worse, the route marches also took place at night, sometimes after the men had already endured a long day of the same thing. A dangerously high degree of stress was deliberately introduced by forcing them to hike to a given RV manned by merciless DS. Only when the candidate had reached the first RV would he be told the location of the next one – and so on until the course was completed. He would not know, until the very end, just when that would be. This lack of knowledge about just how much longer he would have to go, added to the stress of nocturnal navigation, made many a candidate drop out, either exhausted, in a state of complete despair, or just plain bloody angry.

'I tell you, mate,' Tone fervently told Marty as they sank gratefully onto their uncomfortable steel-framed beds during the second week, 'I'm sometimes not too sure of what I'm doing out there. I mean, sometimes, on those hikes, when the going gets really rough, I get dizzy, disorientated, careless. I hardly know what's east or west, north or south, and I lose control of my limbs. It's bleedin' scary, I tell you.'

'I know,' Marty replied, closing his eyes and longing for sleep, drained by physical exhaustion of the kind he had never experienced before. 'I often feel the same way. I see and hear things. Ghostly voices. Hallucinations. And that's always when the DS spring out of the bushes, bawling a stream of questions and all set to slap an RTU on you if you're too dazed to reply. If there's any way I'm going to fail this course, I think that'll be it.'

'Just don't let it happen, mate.'

Though Marty survived the first three weeks, as did Tone, he soon noticed that he and his fellow candidates were all talking constantly, fearfully about the forthcoming 'Sickener 1'. More alarmingly, they were visibly drawing into themselves, not wanting to become too friendly with any other candidate, lest that friend suffer the same humiliating fate as the other RTU'd crap-heads.

'All I know,' Marty said to Tone as they shared a rare beer in the NAAFI canteen, 'is that I want that bleedin' Sickener One to be over and done with – not least because I don't know what it is.'

'That's part of it,' Tone replied, wiping his wet lips with his hand. 'Not knowing what it is. It's another form of DS psychological warfare, designed to make you shitless before it even begins. Don't let it get to you, mate.'

'I won't,' Marty said.

In fact, Sickener 1 came at the end of the third and toughest week, known as Test Week, when the pressure was really piled on the candidates, with the distances of cross-country marches increased and the time to complete them decreased proportionately. Though Marty still hadn't found out what Sickener 1 was, he started guessing when, in the early hours of the dreaded day, he and the other candidates, now greatly reduced in number, picked up their Lee Enfield rifles and brick-filled Bergens to be run to the four-ton Bedford trucks that were waiting for them in the early-morning darkness. As they had just spent a couple of days studying their Ordnance Survey maps of the Elan Valley, Marty wasn't too surprised when the Bedfords dropped them off at that very location, in the Cambrian Mountains of Mid Wales. Gazing around him at frighteningly steep hills and towering ridges, all wreathed in a hellish mixture of rain, snow and mist, he had his first intimation of what Sickener 1 was.

'This course is known as the "Long Drag",' Sergeant Doyle informed him and the others when they had gathered around the lead Bedford truck in what was still cloudy darkness. 'You have twenty hours to complete it. You won't know where or when the hike will end until you actually reach the end. You must do so by making your way to the first RV shown on your map. If you make it that far, the DS will give you another RV, and so on until the course has been completed. Those who fail to reach any of the RVs, even the final one, will be RTU'd. Those who drop out for any other reason, including physical injury, will also be RTU'd. Those who stop, or even turn back, to help other candidates, will be RTU'd with the man they were helping. You can take it from me that a lot less will finish the course than are starting right now.' Doyle checked his wristwatch and raised his eyes again. 'All right, commence marching.'

Marty had never been on a tougher tab in his life. During the first day he noticed that the journey to the RV took him up progressively steeper, increasingly higher hills. In some places the gradients were so steep that he felt he was climbing a sheer cliff face; in other places the gravel rolled beneath his boots and frequently made him slide backwards. Nor was he helped by the fact that even when dawn broke the mist, rain and snow not only reduced visibility, but also soaked him and turned him numb with cold. The wind howled constantly, hammering brutally at him, often threatening to throw him off balance and send him rolling back down. Nevertheless, he kept going and was not surprised, though he *was* embarrassed, when he passed the first of the crap-hats, sitting with his head in his hands, quietly sobbing, as the other men, not daring to acknowledge him, scrambled on up the windblown hill.

To add to the natural stress of the arduous hike, the DS often popped out from behind rock formations, either to bawl abuse at those lagging behind or to suggest that they might find it more sensible to return to the waiting trucks. Some candidates, looking grateful, actually did so.

'Don't do it,' Trooper Roy Weatherby, the former Royal Signals man, whispered to Marty and Tone as he wiped sweat from his gaunt face before it could freeze on his skin. 'If you turn back, even at their suggestion, you get RTU'd. It's known as "beasting". First they scream abuse at you, then they're nice to you. Another one of their psychological tricks and an absolute bastard.'

Grateful for the advice, Marty kept hiking up the ever higher hills, eventually managing to make it past the first two RVs and on to the third where, since it was after last light, he was compelled to rest up for the night. Frozen and wet, his feet badly swollen, shoulders blistered from carrying the brick-filled Bergen, he spent the night in appalling weather, eating twenty-four-hour rations heated on his portable hexamine stove and then bedding down in his sleeping bag, protected from the lashing rain only by his wind-whipped, noisily snapping poncho. For this very reason, he didn't sleep much at all and clambered back to his feet feeling more tired than he had been the night before.

'Their very intention,' Roy Weatherby whispered to him, indicating the rainsoaked DS who were checking their wristwatches and entering the time on their clipboards.

'Right!' one of the SNCOs bawled. 'Up and out, Troopers!'

Again, the hike commenced in foul weather and took them up a series of increasingly steeper, higher hills. This time, however, they were faced with the 'entrail ditch' – a long trench filled with stagnant water, mud, rotting sheep's innards and animal excrement. In order to get to the next RV, they had to crawl through the ditch on their bellies, face down, holding their rifles horizontally, well clear of the mess. They had to ignore the stench, try not to swallow any of the mess, and either avoid throwing up or swallow their own vomit if they did so. Failure to get to the other side would cop them an RTU. So would throwing up.

When Marty slid, belly down, into that nauseous mess, the stench nearly made him retch and the cold made him shudder. Crawling along on his belly, he was compelled to bend his neck back as far as possible to keep his mouth and nose out of the slimy, stinking mess. Also, he had to prop himself up on his elbows and hold his Lee Enfield horizontally in both hands. This forced him to curve his spine to a degree that sent savage pains stabbing through him and made him fear that his back was going to break.

Even as he reached the halfway mark, he heard the retching

of someone being sick, followed by a choked sob of despair. Not daring to look sideways, he kept crawling forward, trying to hold his breath, keeping his lips closed, but eventually the slime got up his nose, forcing him to open his mouth to breathe. Instantly, that vile mess dribbled into his mouth. Thinking of rotting sheep's innards and animal excrement, he almost threw up, but managed to control himself and swallow it.

With his stomach heaving, his body shuddering, and his muscles twitching from the darting pains, he made it the rest of the way and crawled out the other side, smelling his own stench. He cleaned himself of mud and slime the best the could, then hiked on to the next RV.

'You're a filthy bastard, aren't you?' the Irish DS said when Marty reported in at the sangar. 'Sure I ought to RTU you for not washin', but I'm the soft-hearted kind.' He handed Marty a folded piece of paper. 'That's your next RV. Have a brew-up before you move on, but don't take too long. You're running out of time, boyo.'

'Christ,' Tone muttered to Marty as they had a brew-up out of earshot of the DS, 'I thought I was going to die in that fucking ditch. My stomach was churning.'

'Mine, too,' Marty replied. 'And two more poor bastards are being RTU'd. We're being whittled down all right.'

'We'll stick it out,' Tone insisted. 'You and me, we'll survive it.'

'Damned right, we will,' Marty said.

Nevertheless, late the following morning, after the remaining candidates had spent another sleepless night on the summit of a frozen, windswept hill, their soaked outfits freezing over and still stinking from the entrail ditch, they had to wade the dangerous rapids of a flooding rock-strewn river. Too frightened to cross, one man turned back, preferring to be RTU'd than risk his life. Another, though managing to get halfway across, slipped on a rock, plunged into the river and was swept away, bounced brutally from one rock to the other until he had disappeared. He, too, when eventually he was found, would be RTU'd.

Reaching the other side and the penultimate RV, Marty, Tone and the other twenty-four remaining candidates – sixteen of the original forty had been RTU'd already – were surprised to find all the DS they had encountered along the route waiting there for them. After being congratulated on making it across the rushing river, they were further gladdened to hear that the final RV was only a mile away and that, once there, they would travel by Bedford truck the remaining ten miles back to base.

Their joy at this news was quickly, brutally crushed when the SNCO in charge of the other DS, pointing to twelve stretchers laid out on the ground, informed them that they were to divide into twelve two-man teams and that each team would carry one of the twelve SNCOs, complete with his brick-filled Bergen, personal weapons and other kit, on a stretcher for the last mile of the hike.

Already exhausted to the point of imminent collapse, two of the men refused this final task, one almost in tears, the other loudly cursing out the SNCOs. Those remaining divided into two-man teams and each pair picked up a stretcher between them. When each of the stretchers had been occupied by a grinning SNCO, the already exhausted teams fell into single file and humped their heavy burdens up and down the hilly, windswept last mile of the hike, still deluged by sweeping, freezing rain.

Another two of the candidates gave up during that last mile, too exhausted to carry their SNCO any farther. Marty and Tone carried the rock-solid Sergeant Doyle, who bawled abuse at them for most of the hike, accusing them of not moving fast enough, of rocking him too much, of almost turning the stretcher over and tipping him out. However, despite Doyle's relentless psychological warfare, they managed to complete the final mile and stagger up to the last RV.

There were no Bedford trucks waiting for them.

'Sorry about that,' RSM Neil Farrell said as they placed the stretchers on the ground and let the SNCOs roll off. 'Bit of a blunder, lads. The RCT drivers thought you were never coming, so they decided to piss off back to base. I'm afraid you'll have to hike the last ten miles. As you've only got two hours and twenty minutes to make it, you better get moving.'

'That's not fair!' Trooper Tom Crowley exploded, throwing his rifle into the mud and then kicking it towards RSM Farrell in uncontrollable frustration and fury. 'You promised that that was the last mile. You lied! That's not fair! I'm not doing it! Go fuck yourselves!'

'Anyone else feel this way?' RSM Farrell asked, looking calmly from one man to the next. When no one replied, he checked his wristwatch and said, 'Your time's running out. You now have two hours, *nineteen* minutes, so you better get moving.'

As the raging Trooper Crowley slumped down against a rain-drenched rock, pulled his poncho sheet over his head and defiantly lit a cigarette, two of the remaining men, unable to face that final, unexpected ten-mile hike, sighed and joined him, preferring to be RTU'd than attempt to go on.

Glancing at Tone, who nodded grimly at him, Marty held his rifle at the ready, as demanded by the rules of the Long Drag, and proceeded to hike the last ten miles, praying to God that it really *was* the final stretch. The following couple of hours were like an eternity, but the ground was reasonably level and although he stopped twice to throw up, as did Tone, he made it back with his friend close behind him.

Slumping against the wheel of one of the waiting Bedfords and gratefully dragging on cigarettes, they learned from those still struggling in that another two unfortunates had dropped out during the last mile or so. To do so at that final stage was beyond Marty's imagining.

After Sickener 1, the remaining fifteen candidates were given the weekend off. Feeling that he had just awakened from a bad dream, though also exultant at still being in the running, Marty made his way back home, hoping to have a reconciliation with Lesley.

She spoke to him on the doorstep but refused to let him in, instead informing him that she had since been in contact with a solicitor, with a view to divorce proceedings, and that he had warned her not to let her husband into the house until the matter had been legally resolved.

'You've got to be kidding me,' Marty said.

'No, I'm not,' Lesley told him, brushing locks of hair from her brown eyes and refusing to meet his gaze.

Shocked that the situation had gone this far, still finding it hard to accept, Marty pleaded with her to let him in, at least for a few minutes, just enough to let him see the kids. Still helplessly attached to him, Lesley relented and he was allowed to spend the next hour inside, chatting and playing with Johnny, now five years old, and Kay, who had just turned four. When the time came to leave, he felt a lot better and, on the doorstep, between the rose bushes, begged Lesley to reconsider.

'Not as long as you're in the SAS,' she told him, still avoiding his gaze. 'I won't live with that any more.'

'I can't give it up,' Marty said. 'It's what I have to do, Lesley. I miss you and the kids, but I can't return to Civvy Street for you. I can't bear the thought of it.'

'Then we're finished. Goodbye, Marty.'

Homeless, he spent the weekend with Tone and his family in Croydon. Like Lesley, Tone's wife, Maggie, was angry that Tone had re-enlisted and convinced that he simply hated home life. Though she hadn't threatened divorce, she was certainly not amused, repeatedly criticised him for it, filled the house with the smoke from her nervous chain-smoking, and screamed far too much at the kids, two girls and a boy. For this reason, Marty and Tone were both glad, despite the horrors of Sickener 1, to return to Aldershot and face up to more weeks of intensive training, followed by Sickener 2.

The second phase in the recently developed SAS selection process consisted of another six gruelling weeks of training in patrol tactics, combat survival, demolitions, signals, psychological testing and more weapons practice. The last of these was conducted this time with a wider variety of weapons including the standard-issue Browning nine-millimetre High Power handgun, the M1 0.3-inch carbine with 30-round detachable magazine; the Owen nine-millimetre submachine-gun, and the relatively new 7.62-millimetre semi-automatic SLR (self-loading rifle) with twenty-round box magazine. While this part of the training was also tough and relentless, most of the men, when they talked to each other, confessed that they were now living in horror of Sickener 2.

It began at 0400 hours with a drive in the Bedfords to the gently rolling fields of Llanfihangel, Wales, followed by a murderous climb to the very summit, 1,640 feet, which was, as the DS helpfully informed them, an ideal trig point for map-reading. Four of the fifteen men had dropped out in the previous five weeks and the remaining eleven had to make the climb by foot with the usual heavy load. This time, to ensure that the climb was as difficult as possible, the DS had carefully avoided the gentler slopes on one side of the mountain and pointed the candidates up the nearly vertical side. As part of the test, each man had to take his turn at leading the others up the sheer face to the summit, using his heavy-duty Silvas compass, then guide them back down without a mistake. This procedure was repeated many times throughout the first day until each man had taken his turn as leader. This also ensured that the climb and equally rigorous descent were made eleven times in one day, causing unbearable agonies of body and mind.

Broken, another candidate was escorted back to the waiting Bedford, shuddering with physical fatigue and muttering to himself in his state of shock. Yet another man got himself lost, probably through being dazed, and a third simply dropped out in despair, finally accepting that he simply couldn't make it.

During the second day, the teams were split up and each man was tested alone, with the hikes becoming longer, the time permitted shorter, the mountain routes steeper and the Bergens packed even more heavily. By this time, the 'beasting' by the DS had become more frequent and ruthless, including last-minute changes of plan and awakenings at unexpected times, by day or by night.

Determined not to let it beat him, Marty just rode with it, though often he felt himself tugged between rage and despair.

The climax of Sickener 2 came at the end of the week with a 'cross-graining' of the peaks of Pen-y-fan, the highest mountain in the Brecon Beacons: 2,906 feet. 'Cross-graining' means going from one summit, or trig point, to another by hiking up and down the steep, sometimes sheer, hills instead of taking the easy route around them. As part of Sickener 2, it was deliberately planned at the last moment for the worst possible weather – in this case, sleet and snow – thereby doubling the difficulties for the few remaining candidates.

The DS were in hiding all along the route, ready to jump out from behind rocks either to bawl abuse at the men or to cajole them into taking the easy way out by going back down to the Bedford trucks. Given the state of disorientation and spiritual anguish of some of the men, this final trick by the DS was the feather than made more candidates collapse and be dropped from the course. The DS even materialised on the very highest, snow-covered peaks, where they had been waiting for the hardiest, to hurl a volley of tactical questions at them. When the candidate was too dazed or weak to give a coherent answer, he, too, was sent back down to the waiting Bedfords and the inevitable RTU.

On the final day of the last week, Marty, Tone and the remaining few men – a total of only nine out of the original forty – were made to do what the DS referred to as the 'fan dance': an especially cruel, lonely, forty-mile solo cross-graining of the Pen-y-fan. Following a course deliberately mapped to turn the hike into hell on earth, Marty found himself crossing icy rivers, peat bogs, pools of stagnant water, fields of dense fern and overgrown grass. He also found himself scrambling up loose gravel paths and climbing sheer, almost vertical, ridges, hanging on by his fingers. Last but not least, he found himself doing all of this in blinding fog, freezing wind, driving rain and gusts of snow, carrying the usual Bergen filled with 25 kilograms of bricks, as well as his heavy personal kit.

Even for him, who had been through so much already, this final hike nearly broke his spirit and he found himself, when eventually on the summit of Pen-y-fan, shivering with cold, ravenous, in a state of complete exhaustion, slipping in and out of consciousness. He endured his long dark night of the soul in the snow-filled late afternoon, feeling more alone, more confused and indecisive, than he had ever felt in his life, fighting the urge to scream out his protest, give up and go back down. It was a singular moment – one he would never forget – but in the end he recovered, shook himself out of his gloomy reverie and shakily moved on to the next trig point, then the next . . . and the next. It seemed to take him for ever.

Early that winter's evening, but just after last light, he staggered down to the final RV, nodded dumbly at the waiting DS, including RSM Farrell and Sergeant Doyle, and was surprised to see them all grinning at him and breaking out in applause.

'You've just won your badge,' the RSM told him. 'Congratulations, Trooper.'

CHAPTER ELEVEN

At the end of January, 1952, Marty, Tone and the other seven newly badged troopers were on their way to RAF Butterworth in Malaya as part of A Squadron, 21 SAS (Malayan Scouts). As he sat beside Tone in the RAF C-130 Hercules transport, in the shadow of piled-up, dangerously shaking crates of supplies, he realised that he was glad to be going overseas, certainly for the adventure, but also to be well away from Lesley, who was, as she had recently informed him, proceeding as planned with the divorce. He wanted a distraction from all that and was glad to be gone.

'Feels like we're going down,' Tone said. 'That's why she's shuddering so much.'

Twisting round in his seat to glance through the window, Marty was thrilled to see the dense canopy of the Malayan jungle, known to the natives as the *ulu*. Silvery rivers and streams snaked through that vast, undulating green sea, glittering in brilliant sunlight, pouring down the sides of mountains, curving around rocky promontories, disappearing temporarily into dark secondary forest before reappearing. Here and there were streaks of brown – the thatched roofs of *kampong* (or village) shacks – and he also saw roads and tracks winding through lowland forests.

The Hercules was indeed descending, roaring and shuddering as its flaps were lowered, then Marty saw the densely packed brick buildings of George Town, Penang Island, followed instantly by the sampan-cluttered waters of the Malacca Straits, then the paddy-fields, forests, and *kampongs* of the mainland as the aircraft descended over RAF Butterworth and raced towards the airstrip. The trees suddenly rushed at him, the paddy-fields broadening out, and then he saw the aircraft hangars and brick buildings of the camp as the Hercules bounced heavily on the runway, shuddering and shrieking as its brakes were applied and it gradually slowed down. It seemed to take a long time, but eventually the transport trundled noisily, shakily, to a halt. The doors were soon opened, shafts of sunlight poured in, and then Marty followed the other SAS troopers out. He stepped into dazzling brightness, fierce heat and a suffocating humidity.

After blinking repeatedly, letting his eyes adjust to the brilliant sunlight, he gazed across the airstrip, past the hangars and the paddy-fields beyond, to see a green line of jungle, a tangle of raintrees and banyans, cutting through the silver-streaked blue of a vast azure sky. When he looked in the other direction he saw the thatched shacks of a nearby *kampong*, smoke billowing up from a couple of open fires to coil around shivering papaya trees. He then accepted that he was in another world and that he was thrilled to be here. It made up for his marriage.

RAF Butterworth, run jointly by the Royal Air Force (RAF) and Royal Australian Air Force (RAAF), was merely a transit stop on the journey to Johore in the south, where, as the recently badged SAS troopers were informed, they would be undergoing special jungle training. Nevertheless, once ensconced in one of the plain brick buildings of Minden Barracks, surrounded by grassy fields lined with papaya trees, they were given the rest of the day off while Lieutenant Kearney, industrious as always, made the complex arrangements for the trip to Johore.

Recalling the wonderful time he'd had in Cairo, Marty, freshly showered and wearing civilian clothing of shirt, shorts and sandals, led Tone to the main gate of the sprawling base, where they took one of the waiting taxis, telling the Malay driver to take them to the Butterworth–Penang ferry. Pleased to oblige in return for some Malayan dollars, the driver shot off like a maniac along the Butterworth Road, weaving through a bedlam of trishaws, bicycles, motor-scooters and cars, passing broad, flat paddy-fields lined with raintrees, papaya and banyans; dilapidated shacks on stilts, many with thatched roofs; shops constructed from old floorboards, pieces of corrugated iron, lumps of cardboard and newspapers, but visually enhanced with gaudily painted signs; markets with steaming *makan* stalls and crowded bars; ancient temples draped in overhanging foliage; and *kampongs* filled with smoking fires, barking dogs, squawking chickens and happily shrieking children. Wearing bright *sarongs*, the women carried baskets of food and live chickens on their heads; the men squatted in the dirt, smoking hashish pipes and talking the day away – all under a darkening sky smudged with distant rain clouds.

The drive ended at the Butterworth–Penang ferry, where Marty enjoyed haggling with the wily driver before queuing up with the jostling locals – Malay, Indian, Chinese, Tamil and European – at the turnstile leading to the ferry platforms. Out on the water, sampans and other boats were silhouetted by the sinking sun; overhead, in the blue sky turning pink, some silvery Sabre jets were performing spectacular aerial manoeuvres. Even now, in the descending darkness of twilight, the air remained hot and clammy.

'This is just like a movie,' Marty said. 'If this is Malaya, I love it. I'm going to stay here for ever.'

'I'm losing pounds in this heat,' Tone complained, 'and it's almost dark already.'

'We'll lose a lot more when we get to the jungle,' Marty reminded him, 'so let's enjoy this one night.'

'I'm game for anything,' Tone said.

Once through the gate, they lit up cigarettes and watched the ferry crossing the dark surface of the water, approaching from Penang, packed with as many vehicles and people as were waiting to board it. When eventually they boarded the docked boat with the many other passengers, they walked down the steps to the lower deck. Leaning on the railing as the ferry headed for the dark breast of Penang Hill, trying not to ogle the beautifully shaped Eurasian girls in their brightly coloured, figure-hugging *cheongsams* and *saris* and *sarongs*, they watched the sun go down, casting pink light on the sluggish grey water, silhouetting the sampans and small boats against Penang Hill. The lights of the boats were winking on one by one, as were the lights of the island, gradually turning the bubbling white of the ship's wake into darting, faintly phosphorescent green lines. The lights of George Town formed a glittering necklace in the gathering darkness.

'There she blows,' Marty whispered.

When the boat docked at the other side, he led Tone to a taxi and asked the Chinese driver to take them to the Eastern and Oriental Hotel, which had been recommended by Paddy Kearney as a good place to pick up decent women who would not have VD. Grateful that his Squadron Commander was still looking after him, even *in absentia*, Marty lit another Player's cigarette and sat up straight in the back seat of the taxi, all the better to see the sights en route. The cab took them along the docks, now surrendering to crimson twilight, past travel and shipping offices, a post office and bank, more steaming *makan* carts, old men playing *majong* on the cracked, packed pavements, a temple with candles burning inside, fitfully illuminating the darkness within. Marty heard the distant wailing of the imam calling the faithful to prayer.

Arriving at the imposing entrance to the Eastern and Oriental Hotel, he paid the driver in Malay dollars, then hurried inside with Tone hot on his heels. Still following Paddy Kearney's recommendation, he crossed a lobby crowded with white rubber plantationers and their elegantly dressed though rarely attractive wives, as well as Eurasian women of stunning beauty. He entered the Board Room Bar with Tone still behind him. The bar had cushioned seats along the walls, dim lighting, paintings of London Bridge and Regent Street on the walls and a clientele consisting of RAF and RAAF officers, mostly pilots, and ravishing ladies wearing glittering *cheongsams*, split up the side to expose golden thighs, figure-hugging *saris* or *sarongs*, or the breast-hugging short coats known as *bajus* – all worn, of course, with leg-enhancing high-heels. Most of the ladies looked delectable and friendly, sipping cocktails through straws.

'I've got a hard-on already,' Tone boasted. 'It's almost busting my pants.'

'Cool it down with a drink, mate.'

They began with Haig's Dimple whisky, chased it with Carlsburg beer, then decided to try the local beers, Tiger and Anchor. Marty was on his fourth drink, the Anchor beer, when he saw one of the Asian beauties on the stools studying him in the mirror above the bar, an inviting smile on her delicate, heart shaped face, framed by jet-black hair that fell down her shimmering dark green *cheongsam* to her delectable rump. Aware of the fact that, apart from his days in Cairo, he had not betrayed Lesley, he realised that, if he wanted to do so now, he could do it without guilt. He had Lesley to thank for that.

Again glancing in the mirror and catching the smile of the gorgeous Malayan woman, he was briefly embarrassed and turned his eyes in the opposite direction. When he did so, he caught another smile, which surprised him even more, because this one was being offered by Paddy Kearney, who had obviously just arrived, ordered himself a drink, and then noticed his two hard-drinking troopers at the other end of the bar. Casually sophisticated in a light tropical suit with shirt and tie, he sauntered up to join Marty and Tone where they were perched on their high stools.

'Cheers, gentlemen,' he said, grinning wickedly and holding up his glass of whisky. After sipping at his drink, he lowered the glass, glanced over Marty's shoulder at the women farther along the bar, then grinned again. 'I see you took my advice and came to the best place in town. For that reason I'm glad to note that it's not empty and that the view on all sides is wonderful.'

'It sure is,' Marty responded. 'But if I may say so, boss, these ladies look a little bit on the expensive side for the underpaid other ranks.'

'A good point well taken.' Kearney was amused. 'However, I should make it clear to you that most of these young ladies aren't professional prostitutes. Indeed, they're more likely to be the highly respectable, well educated daughters of well-off families, here to find themselves a decent white man and potential husband.'

'Do they . . .?' Tone tried asking. 'Would they . . .?'

Kearney chuckled. 'Some do and some don't, though mostly they need a reason. A declaration of love might do it; an offer of marriage certainly would. Occasionally a scarlet lady manages to slip in, but they're usually frowned upon.'

Marty glanced in the mirror and caught a glimpse of the beauties farther along the bar, that particular inviting smile, before becoming embarrassed again and lowering his eyes. 'A bit classy for the likes of us, boss. I think we're out of our depth here.'

Kearney feigned dismay. 'What's this I hear? I thought you were SAS men, full of initiative and courage. I'm disappointed in you. I truly am. I should slap an RTU on the pair of you for letting the side down.'

Marty shrugged and Tone puffed on his fag, obviously trying to hide his discomfort behind the screen of dense smoke. 'Thing is,' Tone said, trying to find an excuse, 'we haven't really done the town yet, so we'll be heading off soon.'

'You'd best be careful of the girls you meet in George Town,' Kearney warned him. 'VD is rife in that place and we don't want *that*, do we?'

'No, sir!' Tone snapped.

Grinning, Kearney returned his gaze to Marty. 'Are you sure you wouldn't rather stay here?'

'No, thanks.' Marty finished his Anchor beer. 'I think we should explore George Town. But you have my word, boss, that we'll both be careful. No hanky-panky, like.'

Kearney shook his head from side to side as if sorry for them. 'Pity,' he murmured. Then he glanced up again, looking over Marty's shoulder, and waved as if recognising someone. 'Mas!' he called out, offering a dazzling smile, his gaze obviously focused on the gorgeous Malayan woman whom Marty had thought was smiling at him. 'I didn't see you there in this dim light. *Do* let me join you, Mas!' He returned his gaze to Marty and Tone. 'See you tomorrow, lads.' Grinning again, he made his way along the bar to join the beauty called Mas.

Looking over his shoulder, Marty saw his dashing troop commander kissing the luscious creature full on the lips.

'Well, I'll be buggered!' Tone exclaimed softly, his eyes as wide as two spoons.

'To hell with it,' Marty said in disgust. 'Finish off your drink and let's go. The night is still young, mate.'

'Let's hope so,' Tone said.

Leaving the bar, they went back across the lobby and left the hotel, stepping into the lamplit night, its darkness illuminated by great clusters of brilliant stars and a fantastic, magically glowing moon. A light breeze had cooled the air, lowering the humidity, so they decided to walk. Soon they were in Penang Road, packed and noisy, all its shops still open, traffic honking and snarling, the pavements strewn with bootblacks, beggars, hawkers and the occasional prostitute. Passing the busy Oasis Restaurant, they were surrounded by trishaw drivers, wearing floppy hats, shirts and shorts and flip-flops, waving frantically and shouting, offering to drive them around the town, show them the sights, find them good, clean girls or, should they not be so inclined, young boys just as good and clean.

Not yet in the mood for food, clean girls or nice young boys, they embarked on a pub crawl through the alien heart of George Town, disorientated by constant noise, dazzled by frenetic activity, and sensually aroused by the aromas of grilling meat, frying fish, a wide variety of exotic spices, gasoline and urine. First they tried the Sydney Bar, filled with lovely Malayan girls dressed in *cheongsams*, slim legs crossed to expose luscious thighs. Next, the Broadway Bar, farther along, filled with more of the same. Then the Boston Bar, just beside the Capital Cinema, where the queues were a riot of conversation.

Walking from one bar to the other, they passed coffee shops, restaurants, *makan* carts and many open-front hovels. They then passed a garage where Chinese coolies were cutting the throats of yelping dogs, letting the blood drip down into the monsoon drains by the roadside, before selling them to the local chefs to be used, so Marty was informed when he boldly asked, for that locally renowned delicacy, dog soup.

'Christ, I'm going to puke!' Tone exclaimed, making vomiting sounds.

'Just remember the entrail ditch,' Marty said, 'and you'll think nothing of this.'

'Bloody right,' Tone agreed.

Drinking more beer in the Boston Bar, they gave serious consideration to the possibility of picking up two of the gorgeous Malayan girls in figure-hugging *cheongsams* without running the risk of gonorrhoea or syphilis, but wisdom prevailed over lust and they decided to leave it.

'I can't bear the thought of missing out on going into the jungle with the squadron,' Marty explained, 'for being dumb enough to pick up a dose of the clap. So thanks, but no thanks, mate.'

Perhaps because of the heat, he was still fairly sober when he and Tone left the Boston Bar, then headed back to the Eastern and Oriental Hotel and, so they hoped, its much safer, more sophisticated ladies. Entering the Board Room Bar, feeling drawn to its subdued lighting and soft furnishings, they were initially disappointed to find that Paddy Kearney had gone – as, indeed, had Mas and most of the other customers. The only customers remaining were three young Asian ladies dressed in Western clothing – loose blouses and slacks, flat shoes, silk scarves – and sitting at a table in the far corner. They all glanced up when Marty and Tone walked in, then coyly lowered their eyes again.

Taking the same stools, Marty and Tone ordered Tiger beers and drank them slowly while surreptitiously studying the reflection of the girls in the big mirror on the wall behind the bar. From where they sat, they had a dim, distant view of the girls, but they saw enough to note that all three of them were Chinese, were very attractive, and seemed to be as Westernised as their clothing. Marty assumed this Westernisation from the way they were dressed and because all three of them were sipping cocktails and smoking cigarettes. He also knew that they knew they were being looked at in the mirror; they were responding by whispering to each other and giggling a lot.

'What do you think?' Tone whispered.

'I think,' Marty replied, feeling only slightly drunk but certainly very confident, 'that we should go over there and introduce ourselves. What can we lose?'

'Right on,' Tone said.

Carrying their drinks, they crossed the room and stopped in front of the corner table. The girls looked up, smiling nervously. This close, Marty saw that they slightly resembled each other, that all three of them were slim and shapely, that two of them were very attractive and that the third, the one sitting closest to him, was stunningly beautiful.

At least, she was to him. She had jet-black hair framing a flawless, oval shaped face, with a fringe cutting a straight line above big eyes the colour of chocolate. Innately graceful, she was wearing an open-neck white shirt that revealed a delicate, swan-like neck and was belted tightly at the waist, emphasising surprisingly full breasts and a slim, shapely body. Her gleaming hair fell all the way down her spine to spread out on the seat around her broad hips like a dark, sensual flower.

When she stared up at Marty, her brown gaze shyly curious, he was instantly confused, hot and bothered, embarrassed, and had to work hard to keep his voice steady when making his first move.

'Good evening, ladies,' he said, sounding bolder than he felt. 'We're two lonely soldiers desperate for company. Do you mind if we join you?'

Two of the girls giggled, lowering their eyes coyly, but the third one, the one that Marty fancied, asked, 'Are you drunk?'

Surprised to hear her speaking perfect English, thrilled by the liquid sensuality in her voice, he did a double-take, trying to keep his wits together, then responded, 'Absolutely not. We've just had a couple of beers so far and are perfectly harmless. So, can we join you?'

The same two giggled again, then glanced at the serious one. She studied Marty with a steady, brown gaze, then finally nodded assent. The girls were sitting on the soft seats with their backs to the wall, and when Marty and Tone sat opposite them, at the other side of the table, Marty was careful to place himself directly in front of the girl with big brown eyes. His heart raced when she smiled at him.

'I'm Tone,' Tone said while Marty was still trying to pull himself together. 'Malayan Scouts, SAS.'

'You're an officer?' the girl in the middle asked, also speaking perfect English, puffing a cloud of smoke to hide her shyness.

'No,' Tone said. 'A private.'

'Ah,' the girl responded, disappointed.

'Marty Butler,' Marty said, glancing briefly at the other two girls, then letting his gaze rest on the one directly facing him, hoping he sounded calmer than he felt. 'Same regiment. Also only a private.'

'Nothing wrong with that,' the girl opposite said while the other two giggled. 'I'm Ann – Ann Lim. And this,' she continued, pointing to the tiny girl beside her, 'is Mary. And that's Kathy,' she added, indicating the short-haired girl at the other end, sitting opposite Tone. The other two girls giggled softly, nervously at the mere mention of Kathy's name. 'We're sisters,' Ann Lim explained.

'Ah,' Marty said. 'That's why you all look a bit alike.' He nodded as if deep in thought. 'Sisters,' he echoed.

'Yes,' Ann Lim confirmed.

'Chinese?' Marty asked.

'Of course,' Ann replied, looking mildly affronted. 'Can't you tell the difference between us and the Malays?'

Embarrassed, Marty said, 'I can tell the difference. I'm just a little surprised at your names. Those are English names.'

'My father's a fanatical Anglophile. We were brought up in a Malayan convent and taught only English. We can't even speak Chinese.'

'That must feel strange.'

'Not really.' She shrugged. 'One language is good enough.'

'You live here in Penang?'

'Of course. Near Tanjong Tokong.'

Having read up on the area on the recommendation of Paddy Kearney, Marty knew that Tanjong Tokong was a suburb largely populated by well-off Chinese and Europeans and, to a lesser extent, Indians and Malays. He could safely assume from this that these girls were exactly the kind that Kearney had said frequented this bar. They were not professional prostitutes but merely well-brought-up girls looking for male company, preferably white and with potential as future husbands. Instead of being put off by this, Marty was relieved and, whether or not he qualified as a potential husband in Ann Lim's eyes, knew that he found her wildly attractive.

Not surprised to feel this way after the break-up with Lesley, he bought a round of drinks, then settled down to an easy conversation with Tone and the girls. While a slight awkwardness arose from the fact that he was giving most of his attention to Ann Lim while Tone was gradually focusing on Kathy, which left Mary slightly out of it, the next two hours passed easily enough, with the conversation ranging from the latest movies and popular records to what Marty and Tone did in the SAS. Unable to discuss this, Marty changed the conversation by asking how the girls passed their time, since none of them worked. Living in a good home with servants, Ann Lim explained, they were not allowed to take on work, but instead were learning French with a private teacher in Penang before being sent to finishing school in Paris.

'Yes,' she agreed calmly when Marty said that they appeared to be well off. 'I suppose we live a privileged life. We're all lucky that way.'

'You seem to be the most serious,' Marty said, noting that Tone was talking to the other two. 'Is that because you're the eldest?'

'Yes,' Ann Lim said.

'What age are you?' Marty asked boldly.

'Twenty,' she told him.

Feeling like an old man, though he was still only thirty, he ordered another round of drinks and let the presence of Ann Lim flow around him. During the rest of that evening, his only real problem was in hiding his growing feelings for Ann Lim: a combination of sexual attraction and emotional need. He was certain, however, that she had sensed his reaction to her and was responding in kind. That made him feel damned good.

The evening came to an abrupt end when Ann Lim glanced at her wristwatch, looked shocked by the time, and said that she and her sisters were going to be late if they didn't hurry on home. Realising that they, too, had to be back at the camp to prepare for the next day, Marty and Tone left the bar with the girls, walked them across the lobby and escorted them to the taxi rank just outside the hotel. The stars were still bright and the moon looked enormous. A cool breeze was blowing across the lawns and moaning through the papaya trees.

'Do you come here often?' Marty asked of Ann Lim when she was gazing up at him through the open front window of the taxi and her sisters were giggling in the rear seats.

'Most Fridays,' she replied, almost whispering.

'Maybe we'll see you in the bar when we get back,' Marty suggested, having to fight the urge to lean down and kiss her, feeling sensual and unreal.

'That would be nice,' she replied. 'When will that be?'

'I don't know,' he said.

'Too bad,' Ann Lim said. 'We might be gone by the time you get back, but it was nice to meet you.'

'Same here,' Marty said.

Ann Lim smiled and the other two giggled as the taxi drove them away.

'Bloody hell!' Marty exclaimed softly, hardly aware of where he was walking, trusting Tone to lead him back to the ferry, across the water to the mainland, then on to the air force base at Butterworth. 'I must be losing my mind.'

'You are,' Tone informed him.

At first light the following morning he and his fellow troopers, most with bad hangovers, boarded Sikorski S–55 Whirlwind helicopters and were flown to Johore.

CHAPTER TWELVE

Hastily thrown together in a clearing in the jungle, the camp in Johore consisted of little more than a few rows of wood-and-thatch barracks, open latrines and showers, a corrugated-iron mess hut that was always like a furnace, a NAAFI store, an armoury and quartermaster's store, both in rotting wooden huts, and a large administrative building. West of the camp was a short airstrip for the regiment's three Valetta twin-engined aircraft, a Hercules C-130 transport and four Sikorski S-55 Whirlwind helicopters. To the east, but inside the mined perimeter, was a centrally located sports ground with an obstacle course at one end because the so-called 'sports' usually took the form of close-quarters battle (CQB) training and unarmed combat practice. This uninviting piss-hole was surrounded by coconut palms, papaya trees and deep monsoon drains. Though protected from direct sunlight by the high jungle canopy, it was always as hot as hell and dreadfully humid.

Nominally the training camp for the Malayan Scouts (SAS), it also included a support contingent of Gurkhas, Royal Marines, RAF flight and ground-crew personnel, British REME, Kampong Guards from the Federation of Malaya Police, Mad Mike Calvert's SAS intelligence section – known as the 'Int' section and manned by Hong Kong Chinese interpreters and men who had worked with Calvert in Burma

– and, finally, the SAS Regiment, including A and C Squadrons, the latter composed mainly of Rhodesian volunteers. Contrary to what the new arrivals of B Squadron (formerly M Squadron of 21 SAS) had expected, it was a crude but extremely crowded, active base camp.

'I thought it was going to be only a couple of tents,' Tone said, 'but it looks like Piccadilly bloody Circus.'

'It's all go,' Marty agreed.

Once settled into their wood-and-thatch barracks, the new arrivals, now wearing their OGs, were allowed to go to the mess hut for lunch. There they were nearly asphyxiated by the clammy heat and driven mad by fat black flies, mosquitoes and midges that whined and buzzed about them throughout the meal. Thus forewarned about the hell they were about to find when they entered the jungle, or *ulu*, they gathered outside the mess and were marched to the administration hut, including the HQ, where they were crammed into a small briefing room.

When their Troop Commander, Paddy Kearney, now back in uniform, entered the room to take up a position directly in front of the large map of Malaya pinned to the blackboard, Marty was first taken aback, then absolutely delighted, to see his old North African NCO, Sergeant Bulldog Bellamy, marching in behind him. Bulldog, he noted, was wearing corporal's stripes, indicating that he, too, had been reduced to Trooper when transferring back to the SAS but had since been promoted again. Seeing Marty and Tone in the audience, he gave them a nod of recognition and the slightest of grins.

'The fucking terror of North Africa,' Tone whispered to Marty. 'I think we're in trouble, mate.'

'I'd say we're in good hands.'

When the newcomers had settled down, Lieutenant Kearney said, 'You men are here to undergo special training and a rather unique parachute course, prior to going into the jungle from our forward operating base at Ipoh.' The newcomers shot startled glances at one another at the ominous mention of 'a rather unique parachute course' but then soon returned their attention to their Troop Commander. 'However, it was thought advisable that before training commences you be briefed on what's going on over here and precisely what kind of war we're waging.'

Looking up at the officer he most admired, Marty, while certainly trying to concentrate on the briefing, found himself wondering if Kearney had spent a profitable night with the delicious Malayan woman he'd kissed so intimately in the Eastern and Oriental Hotel. This in turn made him recall the equally beautiful Ann Lim, the well-educated Chinese girl who spoke only English and now haunted his thoughts. Feeling a fierce stab of desire for her, he had to force himself to concentrate on the briefing.

'The basic situation,' Kearney continued, 'is that when we British set up the Federation of Malaya in nineteen forty-eight, the Chinese minority resented the dominance of the Malayans within the Federation. That same year, certain Chinese communists expressed their resentment by fleeing into the jungle, forming the so-called Malayan Races Liberation Army, or MRLA, and then emerged to attack, and often murder, estate owners and rubber planters, be they white or Asian. The British proclaimed a state of emergency and organised an immediate military response.

'The communist terrorists, hereafter referred to as the CT, then retreated into the jungle interior where they grew their own food, rice and maize in the clearings. Pursued by British Army and Commonwealth forces, assisted by Iban trackers brought in from Borneo, they retreated even deeper into the jungle. As British military thinking had it that three weeks was the maximum time possible for regular troops to remain in the jungle, it was decided to create a deep-penetration unit that could remain in the jungle for much longer than that. This is where the SAS enter the picture.'

At this point, Kearney stopped, as if deep in deep thought but actually taking a pause to let his words sink in. He then looked up and said, 'Since nineteen fifty, when the SAS first came here as part of the Malayan Scouts, Lieutenant "Mad Mike" Calvert evolved and acted upon the theory that victory in this war will not come about by military action alone, but by winning over the hearts and minds of the jungle aborigines – the Sakai. In order to do this, he developed the concept of the three- or four-man patrol and sent them into the jungle not only to ambush the CT, but to give medical and other aid to the aborigines, thus winning them over to our side – in other words, winning their hearts and minds. At the same time, he was testing the absolute limits of those patrols, asking them to remain in the jungle for periods of much longer than three weeks. That one patrol actually managed to remain there for a hundred and three days without a break was confirmation that the SAS could do what other soldiers could not.

'Your special training, therefore, will be in jungle survival: how to contend with enemy ambushes, booby traps, an exceptionally hostile environment, including swamps and dangerous rivers; and, of course, the equally hostile wildlife, including wild boar, water buffalo, elephants, tigers, snakes, hornets, mosquitoes and even blood-sucking leeches. You will also learn how to communicate and, in many instances, actually live with the jungle's indigenous, still relatively primitive, population.

'Last but not least, you'll be the first to rehearse and then put into practice a new method of insertion known as "tree-jumping", which means parachuting into the jungle canopy and then descending by rope to the jungle floor, which is sometimes a hundred and fifty feet below. Though this is dangerous, we think it might work and you men will help us find out if it does or not.'

Kearney smiled when he saw the newcomers glancing nervously at one another. 'The CT live by Mao Tse-tung's philosophy of moving through the peasant population like fish in a sea and then using them as a source of food, shelter and potential recruits. What we have to do, therefore, is dry up the sea and leave the CT without adequate supplies or men. To this end, we're engaged in relocating as many aborigines as possible to *kampongs* and forts defended by British and Federation of Malaya forces. In this way, we often win the hearts and minds of the indigenous peoples while simultaneously depriving the CT of food, other supplies and new recruits. Your job, therefore, apart from reconnaissance patrols and setting up ambushes, will be to live for long periods of time in the jungle, often in aboriginal hamlets and *kampongs*, in order to win them over to our side by giving them free food, medical aid and protection. The ambushes will be a combination of jungle-edge patrols and deep-penetration raids, depending upon the circumstances and terrain.

'As part of the so called "hearts-and-minds" programme, you'll construct primitive medical clinics and personally administer basic treatment, aided by RAMC NCOs attached to the regiment. As you'll be in the jungle or *kampongs* a long time, you'll be resupplied by river patrols in inflatable craft supplied by US Special Forces or by fixed-wing aircraft. We're also hoping that eventually we'll be able to arrange resup flights using our own choppers.'

Kearney stopped talking while a Sikorski S-55 roared into life and then took off, heading, by the diminishing sound of it, back to RAF Butterworth. When the roaring had faded away in the distance, he looked up again.

'I know you're feeling frustrated that you've just completed your training and selection back in England and now have to start all over again. However, your special jungle training is vitally necessary for this particular kind of conflict, so please try to give it everything you have. It includes a daily two-hour lesson in the native language. If you fail to complete any part of the training, you will of course be RTU'd.'

That comment encouraged a lot of shocked eye contact and some muffled grumblings, which were blandly ignored by Lieutenant Kearney.

'The training will commence immediately with the first of your lessons in the native language. After that, you'll be marched to the quartermaster's store to be kitted out. This will be taken care of by Corporal Bellamy here, whom some of you will have met before when he was a sergeant with L Detachment in North Africa. He has, as a matter of interest, been promoted again and will be back to sergeant by tomorrow morning. I now place you in his expert hands and wish you the best of luck. Corporal Bellamy?'

When Kearney nodded in Bulldog's direction, Bellamy, looking as rock-solid and ferocious as ever, bawled for the men to stand at attention. Kearney then touched two of his fingers to his badged beret and walked out of the briefing room.

Bulldog immediately ordered the men outside, met them there, and marched them across the clammily humid sports ground to another administration building, where he made them file into a large room containing a blackboard and desks with notebooks and pencils on them. Once they were seated, pouring sweat, suffocated by the humidity, still tormented by the buzzing or whining insects, Bellamy left them and an Army lieutenant entered. He introduced himself as their language teacher, Lieutenant Alan Bourne, and proceeded with their first lesson in the native language.

It was not an easy lesson. Explaining to the class that their time was limited and that he would have to cram a five-day week's lessons into each two hours, Bourne proceeded to do just that. By the end of the two hours, most of the men were feeling brain-dead and could hardly wait to get back out into the fresh air.

Alas, Bulldog Bellamy was waiting outside. He bellowed for them to line up in formation, then marched them, practically running, to the quartermaster's store, where they had to queue up in the rising heat to be kitted out, all the while trying unsuccessfully, with a lot of angry swearing, to swat away the relentless flies, mosquitoes and midges that hovered in dark clouds about them and repeatedly dived at them.

'Bloody 'ell!' Trooper Roy Weatherby, Royal Signals, complained, frantically swatting flies and mosquitoes away from his morbid brown eyes. 'These bastard insects could give a man malaria before he has his first lesson.'

'Oh, I don't mind them,' said the blond-haired, mild-mannered Trooper Dennis 'Taff' Hughes, Welsh Guards, not blinking at all. 'They never seem to come near me.'

This was true, as the others noticed.

'Lucky bastard,' said the quick-tempered Trooper Rod O'Connor, Irish Guards, swatting flies and mosquitoes away from his darkly flashing eyes. 'Sure some bastards are born with that kind of blood. These fuckin' insects can't smell it. That wee Welsh shite is lucky.'

'They don't bother me neither,' said the unconcerned Trooper 'Rob Roy' Burns, Royal Highland Fusiliers, his flaming red hair blowing in the wind when he briefly removed his badged beret to wipe sweat from his forehead. 'It's just the heat that gets to me. It's always cold in Glasgow, so I'm not used to this effin heat. Makes m' blood boil, it does.'

As the moans and groans continued and the queue inched forward, Bellamy, standing in the doorway of the store, ticked off the name of each man as he entered to collect his kit. He had not yet approached Marty or Tone, but, when they were second in line from the door, he lowered the clipboard and stared at them with a mocking grin on his sunburned, deeply lined face.

'I never respected the Germans much,' he said by way of a greeting, 'and when I heard that they'd let you two survive, I understood why.'

'Gee, thanks, Sarge,' Marty replied automatically, then instantly corrected himself. 'Sorry, *Corporal*.'

'That still makes me senior to you, Private Butler, and don't you forget it.'

'Good to see you, *Corporal Bellamy*,' Tone said. 'We were pleased to hear you'd survived that POW camp and got back into the SAS.'

'Were you, indeed, Private Williams?'

'Absolutely, Corp'.'

'You won't be so pleased, Private, when I get my sergeant's stripes back and start running you layabouts fucking ragged.'

'You'll just be doing your job, Sarge – I mean, Corporal.'

Clearly Tone was confused.

Bulldog shook his head from side to side, as if weary already. 'How *you* two managed to get back into the regiment, I'll just never know. Though we *were* desperately short of men for a while, so I suppose that explains it.' He ticked off their names on the clipboard, then jerked his head towards the door of the quartermaster's store. 'Okay, Butler, get in there. You too, Private Williams.'

Entering the building, Marty and Tone were kitted out with a set of rubber-and-canvas boots, soft green bush hat to be worn instead of the badged beret, and a new kind of OG shirt and trousers, the former with long sleeves and manufactured from cellular-weave cotton.

'The full-length tails of the shirt and high waist of the trousers have been designed,' the quartermaster explained rather portentously when queried by Marty about the change, 'specially to protect you dumb bastards from the *ulu*'s many disease-carrying insects and leeches. Also from the sharp spikes and edges of rattan, bamboo and palms, which can cut to the bone and leave festering wounds. Nice place, the *ulu*.'

In addition to the standard kit, they were also supplied with special waterproof jungle bergens, cosmetic camouflage ('cam') cream, dulling paint and strips of 'cam' cloth, lengths of para-cord to replace their weapons' standard-issue sling swivels, a plentiful supply of Paludrine, salt tablets, sterilisation tablets and a Millbank bag. This was a canvas container used to filter collected water, which was then sterilised with the tablets.

'We're in for a healthy time,' Marty said sardonically. 'I can tell that by the number of different tablets piled up on the counter there.'

'*I* should take those sterilisation tablets,' the enormous quartermaster said wearily. 'I've got seven kids.'

'You won't have any more kids if you take the tablets you're giving to us,' Tone told him. 'I hear those bloody things have bromide in them – not to stop the shits or sterilise water, but to keep us from getting hard-ons and being distracted. A diabolical liberty, that is. A man could be ruined for life.'

'You've been a ruin since the day you were born,' Marty told him, humping his kit up between his arms and turning towards the door. 'Come on, mate, let's move it.'

Outside again, burdened by their kit, they grinned at Corporal, soon to be Sergeant, Bellamy and were told to carry their kit to their barracks, leave it on their bed, and then join the others back here. When they had done so, they were marched the few yards to the armoury, where they were given a selection of weapons, including those fired on the range of Minden Barracks. They were also given a Sykes Fairburn commando dagger and a *parang*, or Malay jungle knife, which looked rather like a curved machete.

'From now on,' Bulldog Bellamy told them when they were

kneeling on the parade ground in the noonday sun, sweating, burning and furiously swatting away flies, mosquitoes and midges, 'you'll keep your weapons with you at all times, either on your person or in your lockers. If any man loses a weapon or ammunition he'll be RTU'd instantly. Although you'll all be training together, you'll be split into four-man teams that'll sometimes operate alone, other times with the other teams. This system, we believe, combines minimum manpower with maximum surprise. We also believe it to be the most effective because members can pair up and look after each other, both tactically and domestically, sharing duties such as brewing up, cooking meals, erecting shelters, or camouflaging their position. Finally, each four-man team can divide into pairs to tackle most of those tasks.'

'Man and wife,' Tone whispered to Marty. 'Pass me my apron.'

'*What* was that, Trooper?' Bulldog bawled.

'Nothing, Corp'!' Tone bawled back. 'Didn't say a word, Corp'!'

Bulldog stared grimly at him, sucked in his breath, then continued: 'All of you men have been trained in signals, demolitions and medicine, and you've now started your lessons in the local lingo. However, although you have this cross-over training, within each four-man group each individual will have his speciality. Those of you who've been trained to Regimental Signaller standard in morse code and ciphers – Trooper Weatherby, for instance – will be used as your team's specialist signaller and be responsible for calling in aerial resup missions, casualty evacuations and keeping contact with base. Likewise, though you've all been trained in demolitions, those with advanced skills in this area will be made responsible for either supervising, or carrying out, major sabotage operations.

'Those who pick up the local lingo quickest will specialise in conversing with the Sakai for two distinct purposes: to gain their trust as part of the hearts-and-minds campaign and to gather any information that can be gleaned from them. Last but not least, the specialist in medicine won't only look after the other members of his patrol, but will also attempt to win the hearts and minds of the natives by treating them for any illnesses, real or imagined, that they might complain of.'

'I feel ill myself,' Roy Weatherby whispered to the mild-mannered, seemingly distracted Taff Hughes, who was smiling beatifically as he squinted up at the high jungle canopy and languidly scratched his blond hair. 'If we have to stand here much longer in this heat, I'm going to throw up.'

'The heat's never affected me much,' Taff replied mildly, still looking distracted, his baby-blue eyes brightened by sunlight. 'Not the cold either. I just seem to adjust.'

'Sure the Welsh git must have ice in his veins,' Rod O'Connor whispered out of the corner of his mouth, his dark eyes flashing with disgust. 'He doesn't feel the heat, he doesn't feel the cold, and even the flies and mosquitoes ignore him. That wee fucker's from outer space.'

'*What* was that, Trooper O'Connor?' Bulldog bawled.

'Nothing, Corp!' Rod bawled back.

'Any more of that bloody whispering,' Bulldog said, 'and the perpetrator will be circling this parade ground – in full kit and with his personal weapon held above his head – for the rest of the day. Is that understood?'

He glanced left and right, along the rows of kneeling men, then, not really expecting a response, he went on with his lecture.

'Though the basic unit will be the four-man team, we have three different kinds of patrol here. First is the reconnaissance patrol. This is tasked with observation and intelligence gathering, including topographical info; the selecting of sites for RVs, helicopter landings and good ambush positions; location of the enemy; and the checking of friendly defences, such as minefields. Second is the standing patrol, which can be anything from a four-man team to a troop or more. The standing patrol provides a warning of enemy advance and details of its composition, prevents enemy infiltration, and directs artillery fire or ground-attack aircraft on to enemy positions. Finally, we have the fighting patrol, composed of either two four-man teams or an entire troop, depending on the nature of the mission. The job of the fighting patrol is to harass the enemy; conduct raids to gain intelligence or capture prisoners; carry out attacks against specific targets; and prevent the enemy from obtaining info about friendly forces in a given area.

'Sooner or later, you'll take part in all three types of patrol. Right now, however, you're going to undergo a weapons training programme more rigorous than anything you've imagined in your worst nightmares. Now stand up and let's shake out.'

Already exhausted just from kneeling on the ground in the draining heat of noon, the men stood up and fell in behind Bulldog, who marched them off for a couple of hours of practice on the firing range before they had even had lunch. The heat continued to rise.

Sergeant Bellamy (for he did, indeed, have his new sergeant's stripes sewn on by the next morning) had not been exaggerating. While the training that the new arrivals had recently undergone in order to get badged was already the most demanding they had ever experienced, even that hadn't prepared them for the relentless demands that were placed upon their physical stamina and skill, from dawn to dusk over the next two weeks. Every day was a relentless routine of early Reveille, hurried breakfast, the two-hour language lesson, ten-minute tea break, two hours on the firing range, a one-hour lunch break, two hours of battle tactics, both theoretical and physical, a second tea break, another two hours of close-quarter battle (CQB) and hand-to-hand combat, an hour for dinner, then an evening filled with map-reading, medical training, signals training and demolitions. Second best wasn't good enough. They had to be perfect at everything and were pushed relentlessly hard until they were.

They were called upon not only to have target practice in the scorching heat while being assailed by bloated flies, dive-bombing mosquitoes and a host of other insects made ravenous by the smell of human sweat, but also to practise numerous tactical movements relating to the special requirements of jungle warfare.

When Sergeant Bellamy was satisfied that each man had proven himself a crack shot at target practice, he moved on to lessons in the standard operating procedures (SOPs) to be carried out in case of contact with the enemy: the proper order of march when in the jungle, the silent signals required when changing formation, and the various drills for encounters with natural and man-made obstacles.

As they were worked into the ground by Bulldog, repeating the tedious, exhausting exercises over and over again, they gradually learned that he had nominal interest in drill and uniform, but loathed sloppiness when it came to battle discipline. His punishments for such sloppiness were salutary.

'Ach, he's fucking ruthless, I tell you,' a shocked and still trembling Rob Roy Burns informed the others as they kicked off their boots in the barracks and prepared to shower and change for yet another drill. 'I accidentally fired a shot from my rifle out there and that mad bastard took the rifle off me, removed the safety pin from a hand grenade, gave me the grenade, then told me to carry it for the rest of the day, sayin' that by last light I should know how to handle my weapon. I shat bricks for the rest of the day, I'm tellin' you. I've learnt my lesson all right.'

'He was the same in North Africa,' Marty told those not too exhausted to listen. 'He has his own way of doing things.'

'Bloody right,' Tone added. 'He even imposes discipline in what he calls the good-old fashioned way: with his fists instead of with the rule book.'

This was true enough. More than once, Bulldog, instead of placing insolent or rebellious troopers on a charge, had told them to 'step outside' to settle the matter with fisticuffs. The hot-tempered Rob Roy Burns and the volatile, sometimes violent, Rod O'Connor were only two of those who had been asked to 'step outside'; but so far no one had managed to beat Bulldog and all of them, even when making fun of him, respected him for it.

In Marty's view, the fisticuffs were merely an extension of Bulldog's obsession with 'realistic' training and certainly most of the training was realistic to a dangerous degree. Bulldog even had them throwing unpinned hand grenades and then diving for cover in the deep monsoon drains running through the camp area. In fact, this was only one of his many dangerous drills with live ammunition – drills that disregarded the normal safety rules for field firing ranges. They were also dangerous to innocent passers-by – REME, Ghurkas, Royal Marines, RAF – because the camp lacked proper facilities for such routines and so they had to take place on the sports ground and other clear spaces.

The working day usually ended at ten in the evening, leaving the men a couple of hours free. As there was nowhere to go – they were surrounded by the jungle – they drank a lot of beer, became drunk too quickly, and often got up to boyish pranks or engaged in fist fights. Rob Roy Burns and Rod O'Connor, both highly volatile, were particularly prone to the latter and caused lots of aggro.

'I wouldn't trust those two fuckers as far as I could throw them,' Tone confided in Marty. 'A pair of troublemakers. From what I hear, they caused so much shit in their old regiments that their NCOs made them apply for the SAS just to get rid of 'em.'

'See no evil, hear no evil,' Marty replied. 'The less we know, the better, mate.'

It was true, however, as Bulldog confided to Marty over beers in the NAAFI canteen, that a drastic shortage of manpower in the early days of the regiment's re-formation had led to many men being selected without proper regard to their past history – men who had transferred to the SAS simply because they were persistent troublemakers whose original units had been happy to see them go elsewhere. To make matters worse, owing to the speed with which the Malayan Emergency had built up there had been little time to select or train them properly.

'For Christ's sake,' a frustrated Bulldog told Marty, 'we even picked up a bunch of deserters from the French Foreign Legion. They'd escaped by swimming ashore from the troop ship that was taking them to the war in Indo-China. So here we are, lumbered with the bastards – and believe me, they're trouble. Right now, they're on patrol in the *ulu*, hopefully getting their balls shot off. I'm actually praying that they don't make it back, which I suppose says it all.'

Indeed, it was perfectly clear to Marty that even his own

recently badged squadron was not without its troublemakers: men such as Rob Roy Burns and Rod O'Connor who, though good soldiers, were undisciplined, insolent and often unco-operative with the other members of their patrol or the squadron in general. Another problem was the heavy drinking that often followed the long, murderous days of relentless training in the jungle's draining humidity. It was this that led to many fist fights and dangerous pranks, such as the setting off of minor explosions in the canteen, the barracks, the latrines, or the 'spiking' of food and drink with laxatives and other dangerous substances.

Lieutenant Kearney gradually solved this problem by slapping RTUs on the more persistent troublemakers. Bulldog mostly did it by asking them to 'step outside' or by making them perform arduous drills. Within a matter of weeks, between Kearney's ruthless RTUs and Bulldog's expert fisticuffs and other nerve-racking punishments, the bad boys had been weeded out and the good, albeit troublesome, troopers, such as Rob Roy and Rod O'Connor, had been pulled into line and, though sometimes still a nuisance, had proved themselves to be worth the trouble. When that stage had been reached, the men were deemed ready to be moved out of the base camp and into the jungle.

At first they were only driven to a nearby *kampong* to live in primitive conditions and acquire new skills from the Sakai villagers and Iban trackers brought to Malaya from Sarawak. They did not actually live with the Sakai, but instead raised their poncho tents beside the Sakai's thatched huts and otherwise shared in village life as well as they could, eating coconuts and pineapples brought down from the soaring trees, catching fish in the rivers and cooking them on open fires, pissing and shitting in the undergrowth, and being particularly careful, as they had been warned by Lieutenant Kearney, not to ogle or exploit the often bare-breasted Sakai women. They also constructed a crude medical hut of thatch and wood, and dispensed basic medicinal treatment from it. In return, the grateful Sakai taught them their primitive, highly effective jungle survival skills.

Their first lessons were in the use of the *parang*, or Malay jungle knife, needed for hacking through dense undergrowth. This was not as easy as it looked and was, indeed, brutally hard work, making them sweat profusely, causing sharp pains to stab through arms and between shoulder-blades, even leading to sprained bones and muscular cramps. It also required a high degree of skill and in the course of learning it a lot of the men cut themselves.

Wounded or not, bandaged or not, they were given no respite when it came to learning the vitally necessary skills of tracking in the jungle and swamps. This was another exhausting business, requiring constant observation and concentration. While a top speed of approximately 1.5 kilometres an hour could be attained in a jungle environment, going that quickly was discouraged as it could mean missing vital clues regarding the passage and location of the enemy. Instead, a slow, cautious, ever-vigilant advance in single-file formation was encouraged, with the lead scout taking the 'point' out front, followed by the Patrol Commander, or PC, and the signaller, with the second-in-command, or 21C, bringing up the rear as 'Tail-end Charlie'. The scout had the Owen submachine-gun, the PC had an SLR, and the other two men carried M1 carbines or Browning twelve-gauge autoloader shotguns.

For the purposes of training, one four-man team would head into the jungle and make camp at a preselected RV. The second group then had to track down the first. This they did with the aid of an experienced Iban tracker, who showed them what to look for by way of telltale signs, such as broken twigs, faded footprints, or threads and cotton from drill fatigues that had been caught on branches when the first group, the 'enemy', passed by. The Iban tracker also taught them how to magnetise a needle to act as a compass by rubbing it across a piece of silk and dangling it from a string, how to do the same with a razor blade by stropping it against the palm of the hand, and in general how to navigate in the jungle using the minimum of natural and artificial aids.

Finally, though the men had already been trained in map-reading and the use of the standard-issue prismatic compass, they were taught how to judge distance in the jungle, how to use maps in relation to dense, impenetrable forest, how to use compass bearings and 'pacing' (counting the number of footsteps required) to reach a given destination, and how to take bearings and triangulate by means of the prismatic compass in daylight or darkness.

The Iban trackers came into their own with silent killing techniques and makeshift weapons. The SAS troopers had already been trained in various methods of the former, including martial-arts blows to the heart, lungs, liver, larynx, subclavian artery and spinal column, and the cutting of the jugular vein with a knife. The Iban trackers, however, showed them how to make spears by binding a knife to a 90-centimetre staff, shape a spear-thrower from a tree limb, make a compound bow, and improvise weapons such as a sharpened wooden stake, a bone knife, a sock filled with soil, and a garrotte made with two short wooden handles, each attached to one end of a length of razor wire.

'Slice your bleedin' head clean off, that would,' Tone said.

'They say a severed head remains conscious for up to twenty seconds after being lopped off,' Taff Hughes dreamily informed them, his baby-blue eyes distracted, his blond hair windblown.

'My worst nightmare scenario,' Rod O'Connor said, 'is the twenty seconds of conversation I'd get from Rob Roy after I'd garrotted him. One second is bad enough.'

'Very funny,' Rob Roy retorted. 'Why don't you go and fuck yourself with this improvised spear? All ninety centimetres of it right up your arse-hole.'

'Don't offer him that,' Roy Weatherby said, trying to join in the good-humoured bullshit, but sounding as though he was at someone's funeral. 'He might actually enjoy it.'

'Watch your mouth,' Rod said threateningly.

Although they had already learned special jungle preventive medicine from RAMC medics back in the base camp, out here in the *ulu* the Sakai showed them many primitive, though highly effective, skills that were not dependent upon modern medicine. One was the cleaning of wounds where hot water was not available: the Sakai used urine instead because it was, in fact, an extremely sterile liquid. Another was the packing of infected wounds with maggots, which will eat only the 'dead' tissue. Yet another was the removing of worms from the system by swallowing a small amount of kerosene or gasoline. The Sakai even showed them how to suture severe cuts with needle and thread, making each suture individually.

Other jungle skills, handed down through generations of aboriginals, were the improvising of a splint with sticks rolled in cloth, a stretcher from tree branches rolled in blankets, or a jungle 'litter', or dangling stretcher, from bamboo or saplings bound together with creepers and suspended beneath a long pole. Finally, the repeatedly amazed SAS men were shown how to improvise a tourniquet by wrapping a cloth three times around the limb, tying it with a half knot, placing a stick over the knot and securing it with a double knot, then twisting the stick until the cloth tightens enough to stop the bleeding.

'Got to hand it to 'em,' Tone said to Marty. 'These bleedin' natives are smart cunts.'

'Now we're smart as well,' Marty said.

Even when they had mastered their jungle survival skills, the troopers were kept in the *ulu* to learn special fighting tactics, such as ambush fire control procedures, contact drills, fire and movement when breaking contact (known as 'shoot and scoot') and firing at close range or in darkness. When they finally emerged from the jungle, all of them had lost a lot of weight but gained considerable knowledge.

'I feel like bleedin' Tarzan,' Tone said. 'Now I *belong* in this jungle.'

'I guess that was the point,' Marty replied.

Tone's comment about feeling like Tarzan was not too far off the mark when, returning to base, they were presented with the most frightening part of their training: tree-jumping. While this did not mean jumping from tree to tree – like Tarzan – what it *did* mean was something just as dangerous: parachuting into the dense jungle, which was sometimes as high as 150 feet high, then lowering oneself to the ground by abseiling down a knotted rope.

'Though this technique hasn't actually been tried before,' Bulldog informed them, smiling tightly while Paddy Kearney, standing behind him, offered a sly grin, 'we *have* anticipated three specific dangers.' He held his right hand up and counted the dangers off one by one, raising a finger for each possible catastrophe. 'When a man crashes into the treetops: one, his parachute could snag; two, he could be smashed into thick branches; and, three, he could plummet all the way through dense scrub to the ground, smashing every damned bone in his body before he gets that far.'

While the men stared at him in silence, not heartened by these pronouncements, Kearney took up the briefing: 'I think it's only fair to tell you that even our Parachute Regiment instructors have had no experience in this particular exercise, so they could only help us with the reminder that those trying it out should attempt to stay calm and use common sense if things don't work out. I trust you will do so.'

'I admire his aplomb,' Marty said to his mates after the briefing. 'I'm not sure of the sentiments.'

In fact, he had little time to worry about Kearney's sentiments as the training began that very afternoon with what Sergeant Doyle, 1st Parachute Regiment, described sardonically as a 'static-line course' which would, he explained, 'focus on the ground work'. By this he meant that they would be taught to deal with any problems that may arise during freefall and landing. These included what to do if the trooper's 60 kilograms of equipment sent him into an uncontrollable spin or if his parachute caught in branches and had to be disentangled while he was dangling 150 feet above the ground.

Having been told what to do by the esteemed Sergeant Doyle, the troopers were made to put the lessons into practice. First, they climbed up to the jungle canopy while carrying 30 metres of rope, knotted every 450 millimetres. Then they tied one end of the rope to the nearest treetop, let the other end fall to the ground, sometimes as much as 150 feet below, and finally lowered themselves by abseiling down the knotted rope. Two troopers didn't make it down because they lost their nerve; one didn't make it because his parachute became entangled in the treetops and he couldn't shake it free; and a fourth fell most of the way, smashing through the branches, and had to be choppered out with his broken bones wrapped in swaddling clothes. 'Casevac', they called that operation: casualty evacuation.

'I'm beginning to think he was luckier than us,' Tone said to Marty. 'At least he's managed to avoid what we've got coming – and it isn't good, mate.'

'Who dares wins,' Marty said.

In fact, Marty loved it. He even loved it when the stomach-churning abseiling was followed by a series of experimental freefall jumps, carrying a rifle and a 25-kilo Bergen strapped below the parachute, from a variety of aircraft into thinly wooded areas, leaving the aircraft at an altitude of 10,000 metres and opening the chute at a dangerously low 760 metres.

'As high-altitude, low-opening – or HALO – jumps into densely wooded areas have never been done before,' Bulldog helpfully explained, 'the Parachute Regiment instructors can't give us any advice, so we're just going to try it and be damned. If any of you don't want to try it, you can back out now and take an RTU.'

No one backed out and finally, after 50 freefall jumps, some from high altitudes, others from dangerously low altitudes, the men were as prepared as they were ever likely to be.

'Congratulations,' Lieutenant Kearney said after the last HALO exercise had been completed without casualties. 'I think you've all proved that you can do it. This being so, you can now do it for real. We leave for Ipoh at first light.'

Marty had no complaints.

CHAPTER THIRTEEN

Having learned it, they did it. Inserted by Vickers Valetta twin-engined aircraft, they dropped over the vast green canopy of the jungle north of Ipoh, their parachutes billowing like white flowers in the dawn's pearly light. Marty would never forget it as long as he lived: the fierce roaring of the slipstream as he jumped out of the aircraft, then the jerk of the rip-cord, the sudden, startling silence as he floated down, looking down, seeing only that great sea of greenery slowly rising towards him. Slowly at first, but gaining speed, then rushing at him, suddenly becoming a solid mass spreading out to envelop him. He hit the top of the trees, smashed through branches and giant leaves, became entangled in the cords of the parachute, was spun around and swept sideways. His head seemed to explode, pains jolted through every limb, then he recovered and found himself dangling from the straps of the parachute.

Glancing down, he went dizzy. He saw a vertical tunnel of darkness. Down there, over a hundred feet below him, was the floor of the forest. Breathing deeply, he relaxed, let his racing heart settle, hung there for at least another minute until he knew what to do. He reached out and grabbed a branch, praying to God that there were no snakes, then pulled himself onto another branch and pressed himself to the tree trunk. Feeling secure, he thought more clearly, looked up and saw the sky, other paratroopers floating down from the Valettas, first in slow motion, then coming down fast, smashing brutally through the trees all around him.

He was not the only one trapped. Other men were cursing and wriggling. One man screamed as he kept plunging down, smashing though branches, bouncing repeatedly off the tree trunk and hitting the ground with a sickening thud.

'Jesus Christ,' Marty muttered.

He took another deep breath, tried not down to look down again, then removed his commando dagger from its sheath and slashed through the tangled cords of the parachute, cutting himself loose. When he was free, clinging carefully to the branch, he removed the knotted abseiling rope from his webbing, tied it around the thickest branch, tugged hard to check that it was secure, then began his descent. He went down carefully, trying not to burn his hands, planting his feet on any branch he could find, using the tree as a ladder. It took a very long time, filling his body with aches and pains, but eventually, just as his lungs started burning, he dropped to the forest floor, landing on hands and knees. He remained there, taking deep, even breaths until he knew he was all right.

Eventually satisfied that he hadn't damaged himself, he adjusted the heavy Bergen on his shoulders, stood up, looked around him. Other troopers were doing the same, wiping foliage off their OGs and checking their personal weapons, looking unreal in the gloom of the forest floor. But they were real for all that.

Bulldog Bellamy was there. So were Tone and Roy Weatherby. Taff Hughes, blond-haired and blue-eyed, was smiling beatifically as Lieutenant Kearney who, after abseiling down a tree, was wriggling out of his harness. Rob Roy and Rod O'Connor emerged from the jungle, looking pleased with themselves. Marty sighed with relief.

The supplies were still falling on the ends of parachutes, though some of the parachutes were entangled in the treetops with the crates dangling just beneath the canopy. Some troopers, including Marty and Tone, were assigned the dangerous, arduous task of climbing back up the trees, over a hundred feet up, to cut the supply crates loose and let them drop to the ground. Most of them smashed open on impact, spilling the heavier weapons – general-purpose machines guns and two-inch mortars – and extra supplies over the forest floor. When these had been gathered together and distributed among the men, the patrol was ready to march into the *ulu*.

Even as the first of the troopers were moving out behind Sergeant Bellamy, out on point as lead scout, Lieutenant Kearney was on the Clansman High-Frequency radio (also called the PRC 320), calling in a casevac chopper to lift out the man who had crashed all the way down through the trees. The hurt man was on a stretcher, unconscious, covered in blood, and someone whispered that he'd broken both legs and most of his ribs. He was left there in the care of his three other patrol members while the rest of the men began their long hike into the *ulu*.

Their single file was well spaced apart and Marty felt acutely isolated. Holding his SLR across his chest, he comforted himself by remembering that B Squadron was not alone: that other branches of the Security Forces (SF) were closing in on the same target from different directions and by different means.

According to Kearney's briefing of the previous day, the CT had recently been attacking *kampongs*, isolated police stations, telecommunications posts, railways, buses, rubber estates, tin mines and the British SF. British infantry, with the help of Gurkha and police patrols, had responded by cutting off food supplies going to the CT in the jungle and also booby-trapping supplies of rice, fish and other foods prepared for collection by the terrorists. With the subsequent removal of 400 Chinese squatters' villages from the edge of the jungle to wire-fenced enclosures defended by the SF, the terrorists were deprived of another source of food, supplies and manpower. For this reason, they had moved even deeper into the jungle, to the Belum Valley, where they were attempting to grow their own maize, rice and vegetables. In order to do this, they'd had to make an immense cleared space in the *ulu* – and that space had been spotted by Auster light observation aircraft flown by the Army Air Corps. The SAS mission, therefore, was to advance on that clearing and take out the guerrillas.

They were not alone in this. Gurkhas, Royal Marine

Commandos, Malayan Police and other SAS patrols were already approaching the site on foot from a mountain valley that ran along the Thai border. That advance was actually under way when B Squadron, acting as a 'stop' or 'blocking' party, parachuted into their confined DZ near the area and began their advance. How long this would take could not be accurately ascertained since, as Kearney had warned them, the terrain could not be gauged precisely from aerial photos. Kearney's estimate of anything from a few days to a fortnight was based on the knowledge that they would have to hack their way through the undergrowth, might find their way blocked by swamps, and would almost certainly run into rains so heavy that they could practically wash a man away.

Marty was already becoming uncomfortably aware of something else he had been warned about during the briefing: that even in good weather the *ulu* canopy was so thick that little light reached the jungle floor and visibility was rarely more than fifty metres. Right now, it was less than that. Also, he and the others had been warned that no matter how tough they felt themselves to be, they might have to overcome a natural fear of the jungle environment, which was claustrophobic in the extreme and could cause severe lethargy owing to stress. While not quite lethargic yet, Marty was certainly feeling claustrophobic in the *ulu*'s gloom and humidity.

Here, far inland, the forest was dense and dark, with the trees as high as 150 feet, where they formed a solid canopy of green, with patches of sky visible only occasionally. Little sunlight penetrated to the marshy forest floor, which was covered with a thick carpet of dead leaves and seedling trees, though no grass or flowers were to be seen. A dense undergrowth of young trees and palms of all kinds climbed to a height of about twelve feet, obscuring the giant roots of the trees. The tree trunks, though similar in that they were all of a uniform thickness and straining up towards the dim light, were of every colour and texture: smooth and black, scaly and ochre, pale grey or green with moss, some as finely dappled as a moth's wing.

Also, the trucks were often hidden by jungle vines, the *rotan*, which had creepers with sharp thorns and in places broke out into enormous, equally sharp leaves. Elsewhere, the *rotan* hung straight down from the branches to the ground, where they had taken root again, looping themselves from tree to tree like the strands of a gigantic spider's web. Up in the treetops, where the great trunks suddenly burst into branches, were hanging gardens of moss and ferns covered in tangled webs of liana and creepers. This canopy of dense foliage provided few windows through which the sky could be glimpsed and certainly kept the sunlight out, though the air remained hot and dreadfully humid.

Marty had started sweating profusely within minutes of starting the hike. Even worse, the dreaded whining of flies and buzzing of mosquitoes were soon filling his ears, the insects made ravenous by the smell of human sweat and the blood that now seeped from the many small cuts caused by thorns and sharp leaves. After a couple of hours of this, Marty, feeling dazed with exhaustion, his clothes soaked in sweat, his every muscle aching, thought that the hike couldn't possibly get worse – but it did. Shortly after they had crossed a relatively less dense patch of forest, which made them heave a collective sigh of relief, they moved back into forest that was worse than the one they had just left. Known as *belukar*, it was land that had once been cleared but gone back to secondary jungle, with swampy thickets of thorn, bracken and bamboo and, of course, the trailing creepers of the *rotan*. Even more dense and impenetrable than the original growth, it contained vast stretches of swampy ground covered with *mengkuang*, a gargantuan leathery grass with sharp blades, about twenty feet long and four or five inches wide, with a row of curved thorns along each edge. In one hour of back-breaking work, only a hundred yards would be covered. Another obstacle was the sharp-edged *lalang*, which were grass clumps nearly twice the size of a man, with sharp edges that could, like the *mengkuang*, slice the skin open.

Nevertheless, though exhausted, sweating, sometimes bleeding and constantly attacked by vicious red ants as well as the flying insects, the patrol kept inching forward, with the tension increasing, every man aware that this agonisingly slow progress made him a good target to the enemy and that the easiest, quickest routes through the *ulu* would have to be avoided for fear of ambush.

This particular fear had encouraged Kearney to order the hike to be made in single file, with Bellamy out front as lead scout, Kearney just behind him as patrol commander (PC) and the steam-breathing Sergeant Doyle bringing up the rear as Tail-end Charlie. While Bulldog had to cover an arc of fire to the front and Doyle an arc to the rear, the men in between, the rest of the squadron, were compelled to cover arcs of fire to both sides. This necessitated a constant turning from left to right, adding more stress to that already being caused by the hostile elements.

Though trying to give his attention to the immediate task, which was making his way through the jungle, Marty frequently found himself thinking about what might happen when they reached the CT base camp in the Belum Valley. Asked at the briefing if the SAS troopers were to kill or capture the communists, Kearney had replied that he would rather have them alive than dead – as the 'green slime' (the officers of SAS intelligence) could probably extract valuable information from them. On the other hand, the main purpose of the mission was to take them out and destroy their crops. How they did that, Kearney had said, would be decided by him at the time.

Not fearful, but certainly feeling a distinct tension in the pit of his stomach at the thought of that still distant encounter, Marty tried concentrating even harder on the immediate task: searching the undergrowth not only for enemy snipers or ambush parties, but also taking care that poisonous snakes, centipedes and scorpions did not crawl over his booted feet or, even worse, though just as likely, fall upon him from the overhanging foliage.

Wiping sweat from his eyes, he noticed that as he moved deeper into the *ulu* it became more colourless and, indeed, almost alien. Here, the forest floor was covered in a thick carpet of dead leaves and seedlings, which lay around the giant roots and thick creepers of the soaring trees, entwined with tangled vines and liana. Ferns, mosses and herbaceous plants were pushing through the fungi that had formed a thick covering on leaves and fallen tree trunks. This made Marty feel even more suffocated as he followed the men up front on their still agonisingly slow advance into the *ulu*.

Not allowed to talk or trade bullshit while on the march, forced to communicate only with hand signals, the troopers could not ignore the sounds of the jungle and therefore were prone to imagine things, which made for even more jagged nerves.

The men had already been warned that the patrol would be on the move ten hours a day with only occasional breaks and brief halts, and this turned out to be the case that first day. Their advance took them alternately from the humid swamp of the jungle to open river beds, where the harsh sun temporarily dried their sweat-soaked fatigues, but then baked their bodies and feet in fierce dry heat, which in some ways was even worse. Also, weapons, radios and other items of equipment were a source of considerable frustration, leading to a lot of whispered obscenities. The weapons, however they were carried, scraped and bruised the hip bone, dug into the ribs, and caught on the creepers, branches and twigs of the undergrowth, sometimes tugging the unwary trooper practically off his feet. Humping the other equipment and supplies, mostly in the Bergen rucksacks, became a back-breaking task.

Towards the late afternoon of the first day, Lieutenant Kearney, using a map in combination with aerial photographs of the terrain, managed to locate a stream that he hoped would provide an easier route to a friendly Sakai village, where he intended picking up some guides. Unfortunately, when the patrol reached the stream, it was more like a river: too deep and rough to follow easily, with sides so steep, so covered with bamboo thickets and *lalang*, that their progress was actually slower than it had been in the jungle. Slowing them down even more was the muddy bank of the stream, which made them slip repeatedly, clutching at branches to prevent themselves from falling. A lot of them ended up with torn, bloody hands.

They camped that first evening on a sandbank several feet above the rushing water. Before doing anything else, they had to remove the fat, blood-sucking leeches that were stuck to the skin of arms, legs, bodies and even faces. Some of them did this by simply pulling the leeches off, which often tore the skin and made the wounds bleed more profusely; others had their own particular methods.

'Jesus, this is disgusting!' Tone exclaimed as he stubbed the burning end of his cigarette onto one of the many leeches on his left arm, making it sizzle, smoke and shrivel up. 'I can't stand these things.'

'Bloody revolting,' Marty said, 'but we'll have to learn to live with them.'

Removing his shirt and trousers, he found that he was completely covered in bloated leeches and dripping blood. Knowing that if he simply pulled the leeches off, as some of the men were doing, their minute teeth could stay in the skin and fester, he used the same method as Tone: burned them off with his cigarette, feeling queasy as they sizzled and shrivelled up. Other troopers were removing them by covering them with salt, tobacco or a solution of the local areca nut.

'Fucking vampires, these little bastards are,' Rob Roy said, pouring salt on his leeches and looking attentively as they shrivelled up and fell off him. 'They'll drain us dry before we get out of here,' he said. 'We'll all be bloodless and end up at half our present weight.'

'I don't give a shit about that,' Rod O'Connor responded, burning his leeches off with his cigarette and watching them sizzle. 'I just can't stand the sight of 'em.'

'I don't mind them,' Taff Hughes said softly, pulling the leeches off with his thumb and forefinger, then studying them with his blue-eyed, beatific gaze. 'They're just nature's creatures.'

'So why don't you fucking cook 'em and eat 'em?' Roy Weatherby said. 'Or try 'em with a little salt and vinegar. They might go down a treat.'

'You never know,' Taff said mildly.

When they had managed to remove the leeches, which took a long time and was often painful, they made their laying-up positions by gouging shallow 'scrapes' out of the soil with their small spades and then covering them with hollow-fill sleeping bags, unrolled and laid down on plastic sheeting. Above the scrapes they raised a shelter made with a waterproof poncho draped over wiring stretched taut between two Y-shaped sticks, forming a triangular shape with the apex facing the wind. Then, with the camp guarded by the troopers out on all four points, Kearney gave them permission to cook some hot food on their portable hexamine stoves, followed by a much appreciated brew-up and, for many, a smoke.

As clothes saturated with sweat would quickly rot, Kearney also ordered some of the men to make a community 'trench fire'. The men assigned to this task dug a trench of about 30 by 90 centimetres and 30 centimetres deep, lined the bottom with rocks and stones from the river, then lit a fire of sticks and hexamine blocks on top of the rocks. The flames of this sunken fire were protected from the wind and could not set the surrounding foliage alight; the fire was therefore also ideal for drying out their soaked fatigues.

As they could not raise their LUPs off the ground to escape the spiders, scorpions, centipedes and snakes that were drawn to dry clothing and footwear, they solved the problem by constructing a simple raised platform of elephant grass and palm leaves woven through branch cross-pieces supported on four pieces of split bamboo. Their dried clothing and jungle boots were then placed on the raised platform, which had also been constructed, for additional protection, near the all-night-burning trench fire.

Just before bedding down for the night, Marty asked Bellamy how he and the others could protect themselves from the creepy-crawlies. Bulldog responded by telling him and the others to smear themselves with mud from the river, then cover their sleeping bags with sapling and leaves. That would, he told them, keep the creepy-crawlies at bay.

Marty did as he had been advised, smearing his face, hands and arms in mud before slithering into his sleeping bag. He then scooped the leaves up over the sleeping bag. This, however, meant that he would have to try to sleep without moving too much. This became one bar to sleeping. Another was the fact that, as darkness closed in, the jungle chorus, which had been hushed during the day, came to life and reached an almost deafening crescendo, with every imaginable species of grasshopper, cicada and tree-frog competing in a discordant, cacophonous medley, accompanied by a generalised humming that sounded like millions of insects trapped in glass jars. Those insects attacked Marty all night and nearly drove him mad.

The final bar to sleeping was, of course, the restless mind, recollection and yearning, the fevered erotic imagination, thoughts that ranged from his children to golden-coloured pints of bitter to visions of himself and Ann Lim in carnal embrace. Marty slept very badly, woke, slept again and was torn between the torments imposed by the jungle and the demons of love, lust and yearning created by his mind.

'No question about it,' he told Tone at first light. 'That was, absolutely, beyond any shadow of doubt, the worst fucking night of my whole life.'

'No argument,' Tone replied.

The men's faces in the morning were so swollen and distorted by insect bites that they were, in many cases, almost unrecognisable. Some had cheeks so swollen that their eyes were closed and they couldn't see until they bathed them in cold water. And when they moved out they found it to be even worse than the first day.

In the depths of the *ulu*, visibility was reduced to even less than the previous fifty yards. Even when clambering up a steep hill, where a small window in the trees enabled them to catch a glimpse of another tree-covered hillside surmounted by sheer blue sky, they hadn't a clue to their whereabouts, one hill being exactly like another. Also, they were continually forced off their course by swamps, thickets, precipices, outcrops of rock, and rivers. Sometimes they clambered up hills so steep that they had to hold onto the vegetation with both hands to pull themselves up, then lower themselves carefully from branch to branch as they made their way down. On such arduous climbs and descents they met every kind of thicket, including coarse shrubs so dense that a man could clamber over the summit of a hill without actually touching the ground.

Worst of all, however, were the valleys full of huge granite boulders half covered with a treacherous layer of slippery moss and roots so entangled that a single false step could send a man tumbling down to the stream below. Also, their Bergens seemed to get heavier and heavier, while their weapons, still snagging on everything around them, became close to unbearable.

Frustrated, Kearney called a halt to the advance and made the men gather around him. 'We're having a bit of a problem,' he told them. 'When the lead men can't see the sun or any landmarks, they lead us in circles. From now on, then, the man out on point won't carry his Owen submachine-gun; instead, he'll use his *parang* to cut a path that he can pass through. A second man will then widen the track and mark the route more clearly by bending saplings down or marking tree-trunks. The third man will follow through and check the course with a compass.'

'That sounds like hell for the first man,' Marty said, always ready, willing and able to dissent.

'It will be,' Kearney replied, actually pleased with the remark because he liked input from his troopers. 'But we'll change the man on point every half hour, which should make it easier for all concerned. What are you like with a *parang*, Trooper Butler?'

'Game enough,' Marty told him.

'Exactly as you are with your tongue. Okay, you go first.'

The system worked well, though Marty and the men who followed him every half-hour were soon exhausted by hacking their way through the undergrowth. Most of them also suffered minor wounds because of their inexperience with the razor-sharp *parang*, despite their training by the Iban in Johore. Nevertheless, the system gradually hastened their advance and eventually, after another four days on the march, they reached a Sakai village, where a couple of the aboriginals, known to Captain Kearney, agreed to act as their guides to the RV. They moved out shortly after, this time with the Sakai guides out front instead of SAS point men, but the hike through the jungle was no easier and, at times, even worse than before.

The rain came. It was a torrential downpour that almost washed them away. Even worse, it was merely the prelude to a brutally violent gale – one that began as a loud roaring in the distance, but gradually increased in volume until it sounded like a squadron of fighter aircraft flying overhead.

In fact, thinking it *was* an air-raid, most of the men, including Marty and Tone, instinctively dived for cover. Face down in the mud, Marty soon realised that he'd been wrong – that he wasn't hearing aircraft but something much worse. Sitting up again, he squinted into the rain and saw, through a narrow window in the rain-lashed, windblown trees, a boiling mass of black clouds streaked by jagged fingers of lightning. The roaring sound was a combination of thunder and wind.

'Shit,' Tone whispered, sitting upright beside him and wiping the mud from his face 'that bloody wind is a nightmare!'

'*Sumatras!*' the Sakai guide nearby exclaimed in a hoarse, frightened whisper.

'Take cover!' Bulldog Bellamy suddenly bawled, then he threw himself down behind a tree trunk.

The storm exploded over them with awesome force, tearing the trees to shreds, filling the air with flying debris, picking some of the men up and flinging them back down like rag dolls. The noise was terrifying – a combination of thunder and the wind's demented roaring – and bolts of lightning daggered down into the forest like crooked fingers of silvery fire. The wind hurled the rain before it, turning it into a deluge, creating a whirlpool filled with flying foliage – sharp-edged palms slashed like razors. Men were screaming with pain even as a couple of trees toppled over, crashing through the other trees, tearing shrubbery off, creating a deluge of branches, vines, liana, creepers and giant leaves, which rained down to add their own noise to the bedlam. The trees smashed through the other trees and crashed into the forest floor, right across the path of the patrol.

As quickly as it had arrived, the storm passed on, leaving a sudden, eerie silence that was gradually broken by the sound of men crawling from the widely strewn debris, many badly cut and covered in blood. Others, not so lucky, had been crushed to death under falling trees and could not be moved. They were left there to rot as the rest of the men, most horrified and disbelieving, some sobbing with grief, others shaking with exhaustion or shock, picked themselves out of the mud and continued the march. Marty was one of them.

Hearing over the PRC 320 that the foot patrols consisting of Gurkhas, Royal Marine Commandos, Malayan Police and two squadrons of SAS were nearing the RV, Lieutenant Kearney was merciless in pushing his dispirited men even harder. Their damaged morale was not boosted when Roy Weatherby complained of a terrible pain behind his eyes, aching in all his joints, and alternating spasms of fever and freezing cold. Diagnosed by the squadron medic as suffering from benign tertiary, a form of malaria, Weatherby was given a fistful of quinine and ordered back into line. However, a few hours later the march was halted again to let the medic attend to Trooper Neil Gardner, who was suffering relentless vomiting and dysentery, accompanied by agonising pains in the small of his back and across his pelvis. Diagnosed as having contracted blackwater fever, Gardner rapidly became worse and finally had to be held down by two other troopers as he went into violent spasms. Though eventually the spasms subsided, he was too weak to walk and had to be rolled onto a make-shift stretcher and carried the rest of the way.

Moving on, the patrol soon arrived at a series of parallel rivers. These they crossed on bamboo rafts constructed with the help of the Sakai. Four feet wide and thirty feet long, the rafts were made by lashing together a double layer of four-inch bamboos. A central area twelve feet long was raised above the deck by lashing on an additional deck of shorter poles. The supplies were placed there, amidships, where they remained comparatively dry. As soon as it was light enough to see the feathery bamboo groves overhanging the bank, the men started poling the raft downriver to the RV, now only a few miles away.

While still poling down the river, they learned over the PRC 320 that the foot patrols, which had been marching for seven days, had finally reached the CT's jungle hideout and were taking up positions around its northern perimeter, waiting for the arrival of B Squadron to take up positions along the southern river flank and form an effective block.

Thirty minutes later, Kearney's men reached the RV, tied their boats to the trunks of the trees by the riverbank, and then moved at a half-crouch through the forest, darting carefully, quietly from one tree to another, until they saw the CT's jungle hide spread out in the clearing before them.

The guerrilla camp was a collection of lean-tos with *atap* palm roofs constructed around a roughly levelled parade ground, open latrines covered with clouds of black flies, and fields of maize and rice to the east and west. Smoke was billowing up from open fires, which were surrounded by kneeling guerrillas, male and female, few over twenty years old, many hardly more than adolescents. Some of the males wore khaki shorts, shirts and military caps, but most wore no uniform and were either dressed like coolies or wearing white shirts, grey trousers and felt hats. Most of them were barefoot, though some wore *terumpas* – wooden clogs held on by rubber straps. Almost without exception, the women were in long-sleeved, high-necked white smocks and wide black trousers, either with wide straw hats on their heads or with their hair bobbed up.

'Jesus Christ!' Marty whispered involuntarily as he knelt beside Tone. To his immediate right, Rob Roy Burns and Rod O'Connor were placing the GPMG onto its tripod. Beyond them, Bulldog Bellamy was kneeling with Kearney by the PRC 320 Clansman radio being operated by the solemn Trooper Weatherby. At the other side of Tone, to the left, Taff Hughes had removed his jungle hat to scratch his blond hair and was smiling dreamily to himself as he studied the guerrillas crouched around their camp fires. The rest of the Troop were fanning out in a long line on both sides, taking up firing positions and preparing the GPMGs and two-inch mortars.

'Those are women over there,' Marty whispered. 'I can't fire at a woman.'

'You better learn,' Rod O'Connor said. 'Those pretty little things all carry knives and know how to use them. They describe bastards like you as "white devils" and who's to blame them? They'd chop your head off as soon as look at you, mate, so you better fire when you have to.'

'It's not right,' Marty said.

By this time, Kearney had made contact with the SF forces in position north of the CT camp, using an encoded short-burst transmission, and received details of the attack plan before the CT could work out exactly where the messages were coming from. Having received the information he needed – basically, the precise timing of the first mortar attack by the SF units at the other side of the base – he raised and lowered his right hand, indicating that his men should open fire.

Marty heard the distant *thump-thump* of the SF mortars to the north. A few seconds later, the first mortar shells exploded almost dead centre of the CT parade ground, which erupted with a roar into columns of swirling soil and smoke. Instantly, as the mortar shells fell and the SAS on both sides of the camp opened fire with their personal weapons, the guerrillas either dived for cover or grabbed their own weapons and started firing blindly in all directions, still not sure where the enemy was. When more mortar shells fell, with the ground erupting and roaring and spewing soil towards the sky, the smoke from the exploding shells swirled darkly across the clearing, fitfully obscuring the guerrillas as they either fell belly-down on the ground, firing from that position, or ran for the shelter of the thatched huts or fly-covered latrines.

Close beside Marty, as he took aim at a running guerrilla with his SLR, Rob Roy and Rod O'Connor were hammering away with the GPMG, Rob Roy feeding in the belt, Rod firing in sustained, deafening bursts which, with the other SAS machine guns, caused the ground between the guerrillas to turn into a convulsion of spitting dust. Bullets stitched the open fires, making hot ash and flaming sticks explode in showers of sparks, sending iron pots flying in all directions. Some guerrillas, also stitched by the hail of bullets, shuddered wildly where they lay or, if they were running for cover, spasmed dementedly, staggered drunkenly backwards, spun away to the side as if punched by an invisible fist, or collapsed face down in the spitting dust.

Feeling oddly remote from what he was observing, Marty

fired his SLR in short, careful bursts at a group of guerrillas running for the protection of the latrines. One threw both his hands up, letting his rifle fly away, and shuddered wildly as if having a fit, then collapsed to the ground. Another was punched forward, also dropping his weapon, and staggered forward a short distance until he fell, disappearing, into the monsoon drain that encircled the clearing.

Even as Marty was taking aim at the other two running men, he saw a female CT coming into his line of vision, raising what looked like a British tommy-gun to the firing position and aiming along the sights. Startled, Marty released his finger from the trigger, unable to fire at her – but then a short, savage burst from Tone's Owen submachine-gun – he was lying beside Marty – peppered her midriff, punching her backwards, tearing her white tunic to shreds and soaking what was left of it in blood. She went into what seemed like an epileptic fit in a circle of exploding dust, then dropped her weapon and collapsed, not moving again.

Simultaneously shocked by that sight, relieved that he had not killed the woman himself and feeling guilty that he had failed to do so, Marty took aim at another group of kneeling CT, all male, and cut them down with a series of short, sharp bursts. As they fell in all directions like skittles, the ground beside them erupted from more mortar explosions, obscuring their final, anguished writhing in clouds of smoke and showering soil.

Marty kept firing, aiming only at the male guerrillas, torn between excitement and horror, triumph and shame. A series of mortar explosions tore across the clearing from east to west, blowing one of the thatched huts apart, setting fire to a couple of others. Though partially deafened by the roaring of the GPMG to his right, his head being hammered by the two-inch mortar firing behind him, he was aware of the enemy bullets whipping past and above him, thudding into the trees, tearing the foliage to shreds, and showering him with smoking leaves and smashed branches.

By now the flames from the burning thatched huts had set fire to the branches of the trees above them, with tendrils of yellow, blue-tipped flame licking through the black smoke.

As more huts exploded, spewing debris in all directions, the guerrillas attempting to hide behind them were either bowled over by the blasts or left without adequate protection. Desperate, the survivors charged the SAS positions, firing on the run, weaving left and right to avoid the continuing mortar explosions. Those not killed by the mortars were brutally cut down by the combined firepower of the SAS machine-guns and automatic weapons, their bodies littering the ground under a deepening pall of drifting black smoke. Others, managing to escape the murderous hail of fire, disappeared into the remaining thatched huts, latrines and monsoon drains, from where they continued to fire on the advancing SF troops.

Marty saw those troops – a combination of Royal Marine Commandos, Gurkhas, Malayan Police and two SAS squadrons – advancing over a broad front down the shallow slope at the other side of the clearing, looking like ghosts in the murk as they emerged from the *ulu*, their weapons spitting licks of yellow flame. Briefly exhilarated, he was already standing up when Kearney, crouched by the radio operator, Roy Weatherby, about fifteen metres away, raised and lowered his right hand, indicating, 'Advance.'

'Let's go!' Bulldog bawled.

Together, the men of B Squadron advanced into the CT clearing, crouched low, weaving left and right, firing at anything they saw moving in the smoke now surrounding them. The SAS mortar teams were no longer firing, leaving the ground clear for the advance, but the guerrillas were continuing to fight back, firing from the inadequate protection of the thatched huts, latrines and monsoon ditches. With no choice but to despatch them, the security forces moving in from the north and the SAS troopers advancing from the south did the only thing possible: they spread out to encircle the clearing and moved in by methodically attacking the remaining guerrillas with a combination of hand-held GPMGs, Browning 12-gauge autoloader shotguns, M1 carbines, Owen submachine-guns, SLRs, and white phosphorous incendiary grenades.

Practically deafened by the noise, shocked by the sheer number of dead in the clearing, and disorientated in the dense smoke that was drifting from the burning huts and trees, Marty advanced with the others, seeing Tone to his left, Rob Roy to his right and Rod O'Connor just in front holding his GPMG like a rifle and firing from the hip, the hail of bullets peppering the thatched huts and decimating the guerrillas attempting to fire back from the windows. As some of the troopers were taking care of the guerrillas in the monsoon drains by throwing incendiary grenades in upon them, others tore the latrines to shreds in repeated fusillades of semi-automatic weapons fire, killing those inside, and the rest moved methodically from one thatched hut to the next, throwing in grenades, then carefully entering the huts to despatch the survivors with short bursts from their submachine-guns and rifles.

Marty was just stepping up onto the porch of a burning thatched hut, intending to enter, when a female guerrilla burst out of the smoke, swinging a *parang* over her head. Startled and shocked to be confronted by a woman for the second time, Marty stepped back and ducked as the *parang* whipped through the air just above him. Wearing a high-necked white smock and wide black trousers, hardly more than eighteen and exceptionally pretty, the woman screamed a stream of abuse in Mandarin, then advanced again, slashing viciously at him with the *parang*. Still unable to shoot a woman, Marty kept backing away, ducking the *parang*, until he stepped on a small log and it rolled beneath his boot, tipping him over. Landing on his belly, he quickly turned over until he was lying on his back, looking up at the girl. She was spreading her legs to stand over him, raising the *parang* above her head to swing it down and cut him in two. Marty thought he was finished.

At that moment Taff Hughes advanced from the swirling smoke, his baby-blue gaze steady, a dreamy smile on his lips, and stopped just behind the Chinese girl. Raising his Browning High Power handgun until it was practically touching the back of the girl's head, he took aim and calmly squeezed the trigger.

The girl's head exploded in spewing blood and flying bone. She staggered forward, dropping the *parang*, then shuddered violently and collapsed in a quivering heap right beside Marty. Shocked, he rolled away and clambered back to his feet, still holding his SLR, to see Taff smiling dreamily at him.

'She almost had you,' Taff said, then, still smiling in that other-worldly manner, he turned away and disappeared into the swirling smoke and drifting dust, firing his Browning High Power on the move, despatching more guerrillas. Feeling humiliated, shocked by Taff's cold-blooded efficiency, Marty followed him into the murk as the mopping up continued.

Within an hour, the last of the guerrillas had been either killed or taken prisoner. The camp was secured.

Having been informed by Lieutenant Kearney that they were to remain in the camp and turn it into a forward operating base (FOB), the SF soldiers were pleased to relax, most stretching out on thatched mats in the shade of the remaining CT lean-tos, eating, having a brew-up, or washing and shaving with the aid of hand-mirrors.

Though the Sakai and Iban scouts had not been changed by their two-week hike through the *ulu*, Marty and most of his mates were shocked by what they saw in those mirrors. In fact, they were astonished to discover just how much weight they had lost – their bones stuck out everywhere. Even more disturbing was the discovery that their skin had turned a sickly yellow and was mottled with the purple spots of hundreds of leech bites. Their hands, knees and faces were covered with a network of cuts. Their clothes were in tatters.

'We look like the walking dead,' Marty said.

'We're alive and we're still walking,' Tone replied, 'so let's count our blessings.'

'Who dares wins,' Marty told him.

CHAPTER FOURTEEN

The capture and utilisation of the CT jungle hide set the pattern for all subsequent SAS operations in the *ulu*. Once the camp had been secured and the prisoners handed over to the green slime for interrogation, the camp was taken over by the security forces and turned into an FOB filled with Gurkhas, Royal Marine Commandos, Malayan Police, Sakai and Iban scouts, and the SAS. Fresh supplies, weapons and equipment were dropped by parachute from a Blackburn Beverley. By the following morning, with all the resups on the ground, the construction of the FOB began.

The guerrillas' camp had consisted of not much more than a few thatched lean-tos scattered around the clearing near open trenches filled with human excrement, urine, thousands of seething, stinking maggots and, even worse, the decomposing bodies of the guerrillas who had boldly dived in among the maggots to avoid detection, only to be cut down by SAS hand grenades and bullets.

'What I want,' Lieutenant Kearney explained to the men gathered around him above one of the stinking trenches, now covered by clouds of buzzing flies, 'is to construct a fully circular base camp surrounded by a cleared track, hemmed in with wire, and protected by Claymore mines and sentry posts. However,' he continued, gazing down at the hideous mess below him, 'the first task is to clean out those trenches.

Please attend to it, gentlemen.'

'Attend to it?' Tone asked, holding his nose and trying not to look down into the hellish trenches as Kearney, throwing Marty a quick grin, sauntered away. 'How the fuck do we do that?'

'Kerosene,' Taff Hughes informed him, taking in the seething maggots and corpses with his blue-eyed, unblinking gaze. 'Just pour kerosine in and set it alight. Burn the whole mess away.'

Mindful of how the seemingly mild Taff had ruthlessly despatched the *parang*-wielding female guerrilla with a bullet to the back of the head, Marty was not unduly surprised at how calm he was now.

'Good thinking,' he said. 'So let's go and get some kerosene and have us some bonfires.'

Though even the 'bad boys' of the unit, such as Rob Roy Burns and Rod O'Connor, looked slightly ill as they got on with this unsavoury task, they poured the kerosene into the various trenches as instructed, set it alight, and jumped well away as the flames leaped up out of the trenches and the stench of roasting flesh filled the air, accompanied by the sizzling sound of burning maggots. The bonfires burned for a long time, while the rest of the work proceeded in earnest.

'It's vital,' Kearney explained, 'that the FOB can be defended by only a handful of us while the rest of us are out on patrol. For this reason, the camp has to be designed within a circular cleared track that divides it from the surrounding jungle. It will in effect form an open area that will have to be crossed by anyone, enemy or friendly, wanting to enter the camp. Go to it, gentlemen.'

The surrounding track was dug out of the ground over a period of days by SAS troopers with shovels and spades. While this job was under way, other troopers were put to work digging a series of defensive slit trenches at regular intervals around the camp, on the inner side of the circle, to be used as permanent sentry positions that would face out in every direction. The defensive trenches were similar to rectangular observation posts in that they had room for at least four men and shallow 'resting-up' scrapes. However, unlike long-term OPs, though rather like sangars, they lacked roofing and were exposed to the open air.

More trenches were dug out in a smaller circle near the centre of the compound where the Sakai were constructing a large headquarters. This would be surrounded by similar constructions to be used as accommodations, cook house and mess hall, stores, armour, and even a small sports ground for football and general exercise. As the camp would have no vehicles, there was no need for a motor pool, but a helicopter landing pad was levelled in the south-east corner of the circular compound.

The Sakai were expert at constructing such buildings out of local foliage and did so with the aid of fascinated SAS men. The framework of each building was made from five- or six-inch poles of green timber. The stronger timber from standing trees was used to support the main beam of the roof. As most of the Sakai were expert axe-men, they felled and trimmed the poles while the SAS troopers went out collecting the rattan required to bind the joints. When rattan of suitable thickness was found, two or three troopers hauled it in, pulling it out of the ground or down from the trees. Using a small, sharp knife, the Sakai craftsman split each rattan into two separate parts or, for finer lashings, into strips, then he cut away and discarded the inner part.

While some of the Sakai were splitting the rattan or building the framework of the huts, others were teaching the SAS troopers to plait *atap* for the roofing material. Large clumps of *atap* palms were to be found nearby, with drooping fronds twenty or thirty feet long. The fronds were pulled down with a crook and the top eight feet of the pithy stalk cut off, stacked in special racks to prevent the leaves being damaged, then carried back to the camp in bundles. To plait the *atap*, the leaves on one side of the central stem had to be bent back sharply, then threaded under and over the leaves on the other side, giving a plaited surface six or eight inches wide. The *atap* was placed horizontally on the framework of the roof, starting at the bottom, then lashed in two places with fine rattan. At the apex of the roof a number of plaited *atap* were laid along the join of the two sides and pegged beneath the roof beam. The gables of the huts were filled in with *atap* placed just near enough together to form an unbroken surface, with the sides and ends left entirely open.

Initially, some of the SAS men, particularly Rob Roy Burns and Rod O'Connor, resented having to take instructions from the aboriginals, but Kearney soon put them right.

'The word "Sakai" means "slave",' he told them, 'but call them that, or try treating them like that, and you'll get a spear in your belly. Treat them with respect.'

Having already noted that the Sakai always carried their spears with them and looked as if they would be quick to use them, the men took note of what they had been told and treated the aboriginals with respect, if not great affection.

'I don't think I'd look good,' Rob Roy explained, 'with one of those spears sticking out of me arse – so, you know, I'll be careful.'

'Bloody right,' Rod O'Connor said.

For the SAS sleeping accommodations, now nicknamed 'bashas', an aisle about six feet wide was left down the centre of each hut, with the timber-framed beds, or sleeping benches, on either side raised about two feet off the ground. The beds themselves consisted of elephant grass and palm leaves woven through branch cross-pieces supported on pieces of split bamboo. Some of the troopers were able to sleep comfortably on these; others rolled their sleeping bag out and used it as a mattress. All the buildings were raised off the ground on stilts to lessen the chance of invasion by poisonous snakes, centipedes, scorpions and giant jungle rats.

'We've got every creepy-crawlie known to man,' Tone complained to Marty. 'Anything you can find in your worst nightmares, you can find in this piss-hole.'

'They don't bother me,' Taff Hughes said, dreamily checking the sharpness of his commando dagger by running his finger along the gleaming blade. 'They're just nature's creatures, after all. They don't give *me* bad dreams.'

'Does anything give you bad dreams?' Marty asked, now convinced that the normally mild, baby-faced Taff was a natural killer.

'No,' Taff replied.

'He's fucking inhuman,' Tone said. 'Those big blue eyes are quietly mad.'

When the fires in the latrine trenches had stopped burning,

which took a few days, thatched lean-tos were raised over the separate trenches, with bamboo walls between them affording a modicum of privacy to the users. The trenches were then filled with a mixture of quicklime and kerosene to prevent the return of the hideous maggots.

'Not that they'd bother Taff,' Tone told Marty as he studied the blond-haired, blue-eyed, baby-faced killer. 'He'd probably eat 'em for breakfast.'

'I don't doubt it,' Marty said.

By this time the cleared path around the compound had been completed and was lined with a barbed-wire fence in which there were two openings, one as a patrol route entry, the other as a patrol route exit. The defensive trenches spaced at regular intervals around the inner side of the fence were manned permanently by SAS teams with tripod-mounted Bren guns and three-inch mortars. Claymore mines were laid around the camp, just outside the perimeter, on the other side of the cleared path, except for the areas directly facing the patrol route entrance and exit. Set to be activated manually, or when someone stepped on them, they were shaped like concave plates which, when exploding, would fire about 350 metal balls over a fan-shaped area, shredding anyone within their range of 100 metres.

The circular compound was now a well-defended combination of base camp and forward operating base.

The policy of food denial and political isolation had been successful in driving the CT deeper into the jungle. The SF were therefore obliged to pursue the enemy there, which gave the SAS a second chance to prove their value and, at the same time, enabled Kearney to burn off some of the excess energy of his more troublesome men.

While more orthodox units, such as the Gurkha, Malay, African and Fijian battalions, concentrated on harrying the guerrillas of Johore, Kearney's men were making their first serious contact with the aboriginal tribes of the interior. Their main task was the protection of the Sakai jungle-dwellers who, being completely at the mercy of the guerrillas, had been forced deeper into their service as a source of food and reluctant manpower. Now Kearney's men, moving out from the FOB, began to win over the Sakai, essentially nomad tribesmen, often staying with them for long periods, sometimes as long as thirteen weeks, before being relieved by other men from the camp.

One of their main tasks was to build landing strips or helicopter landing pads to enable the aboriginals to market their supplies. They also brought them medical and engineering aid. In particularly dangerous situations, where the CT were terrorising a village, the SAS simply moved the whole village and helped the natives build new homes elsewhere. These 'new' villages became known as just that: 'new villages'.

'Just like being back in England,' Tone joked. 'Remember that, Marty? The new towns we were going to build when the craze for prefabs died out?'

'Right,' Marty responded. 'And here we are, building "new villages" in the jungle instead. Same difference, right, mate?'

Generally speaking, the new villages needed a remote part of the jungle, well away from any paths that might be used by prying Malays, yet not too far from the *kampongs*, which would supply them with food. A good defensive position was needed for the guard post, if possible on the only route into the camp. Water and *atap* for thatching also had to be near at hand.

Most of these new villages, actually camps or *kampongs*, took the same form: a small piece of ground capable of being levelled for a parade ground and sports ground, two long huts nearby for the men, a smaller headquarters housed a little way back from the others, a cookhouse, preferably beside a stream, and community latrines, or 'thunder boxes'. The villages were then turned into fortresses, in which police posts and even artillery were established.

Much of the success of these new villages depended on the few lone SAS troopers who lived in them for long periods to sell the Sakai the idea of self-defence. This was part of the battle for hearts and minds.

For a couple of months Lieutenant Kearney engaged his SF in a special operation designed to saturate a known CT area with troops so that the guerrillas' mode of life would be disrupted. A concentrated programme of police checks on roads and new villages was put into action, forcing the guerrillas to retreat and use up their invaluable food reserves, always hidden deep in the *ulu*. When this was under way, more military units moved in to specific areas where it was hoped, by intensive ambushes and patrols, to force the terrorists out into the open or into the many 'stop' positions (points of ambush) established on tracks in the *ulu*.

Helping the SAS were Gurkhas, Royal Marine Commandos, 22 Jungle Companies of the Malayan Field Police Force, and Iban trackers from Sarawak, Borneo – former headhunters who, though fierce fighters, had to be trained by the SAS in the fundamentals of modern soldiering. Now formally recognised as a locally raised unit of the British Army and named the Sarawak Rangers, they were issued with rifles, which they used with more enthusiasm than skill, often firing them by mistake and, just as often, in the wrong direction. Nevertheless, they were invaluable as trackers and guides.

'You've got to hand it to 'em,' Rod O'Connor said, his dark eyes flashing dangerously as he studied the Iban trackers. 'They mightn't know one end of a rifle from the other, but they sure know the jungle.'

'Just keep them in front of you,' Rob Roy replied, 'and you should be okay when they fire those bloody rifles by accident. That way, they'll only shoot themselves and we should be safe.'

'Amen to that,' Rod said.

As the SAS troopers continued to learn from the Sakai and Iban trackers, they began to live in the jungle for longer periods of time, engaging in a series of arduous, usually dangerous, CT 'cleansing' operations that certainly burned off the excess energy of potential troublemakers such as Rob Roy Burns and Rod O'Connor, both of whom, when not getting drunk, picking fights or playing dangerous pranks, were very good soldiers.

A typical CT cleansing operation was a joint effort between the RAF and the SF. When the enemy was identified as being concentrated in a particular area, the RAF would mount a heavy bombing raid of the jungle location by Lincolns. A couple of SAS squadrons would then parachute into the area cleared – or, more accurately, devastated – by the bombing.

They would then either take out the surviving CT or, if the survivors had fled, take command of the area, ensuring that any remaining crops were destroyed, to deprive the CT of even more food.

By now the SAS had made frequent parachute jumps into the *ulu* and suffered many casualties in their dangerous attempts to perfect tree-jumping. These casualties had occurred mainly because of the unpredictable behaviour of the parachutes as they were 'bounced' by the thermal effect of air above the trees. However, in the view of many officers, including Captain Kearney, the technique of abseiling out of the trees was proving to be more dangerous than it was worth.

In theory, the soldier detached himself from his parachute, lashed a long webbing strap to a branch, and descended safely to the ground. In fact, the webbing often bulged at intervals, where it had been stitched, and therefore snagged at high speed as it travelled through the D rings on the paratrooper's harness. All too often this would jerk him to a violent halt, sometimes smashing him against the tree, resulting in broken bones or even death, which usually happened when the paratrooper, badly hurt and unable to stand the pain, cut himself loose from his snagged harness and fell 150 feet to the forest floor. Nevertheless, as tree-jumping was the only way to get into the areas cleared by the RAF bombing raids, it remained the standard operating procedure of the campaign.

Paddy Kearney was an officer who liked to try things himself before asking his men to do the same. This was a sentiment he shared with Bulldog Bellamy and both men, subconsciously adopting Marty, whom they viewed as a natural soldier, often took him with them into the *ulu* when they went on their exploratory hikes. Invariably, they ended up in a Sakai village where they would settle in for a few days, using it as a base camp for even deeper patrols into the jungle, these led by a Sakai guide.

To Marty, being in such villages was particularly fascinating: almost like returning to the Stone Age. The youths and older men carried eight-foot-long blowpipes with bamboo quivers for poisoned arrows ornamented with strange designs.

Dressed only in a scanty loincloth, each carried on his back a small bag closely woven with fine rattan to hold his tobacco, flint, steel and tinder. The older men also carried an apparatus for preparing betel nut for chewing. Many of them wore strings of coloured beads looped over their shoulders, crossing front and behind, with more beads or an amulet of some kind around their necks. Some of them also wore a circle of woven and patterned bark to keep their hair in place, invariably with bright flowers tucked into it.

The women were bare-breasted, wearing only a *sarong* of cloth or bark. Some had red, white or ochre paint smeared on their faces, and a few were ornamented with a matchstalk thrust through the piece of flesh below and between the nostrils. All were smoke-stained and unwashed, but a few were beautiful, with luxuriant black hair tied in a bun held up with a bamboo comb.

'I like a little piece of Asian occasionally,' Tone said, ignoring the fact that Marty was obsessed with Ann Lim in Penang, 'but this lot I can do without, big tits or not.'

'You should have more respect,' Marty said. 'That's just the way they live. They think nothing of bare tits.'

'The Sakai men must be blind,' Tone informed him. 'Only that could explain the way they hardly take any notice of those knockers.'

'You're pig ignorant,' Marty said.

Realising that the only way to win the hearts and minds of the aboriginals was to share all things with them, Kearney made sure that the members of his patrol ate with them, suppressing their natural tendency to queasiness when they partook of turtle soup, pig, *kijang* (barking deer), monkey and snake meat, sweet potatoes, lizard eggs, mixed vegetables with spices and ginger, and fried rice – all of it washed down with *samsu*, a strong spirit distilled from rice. Invariably, the *samsu* made them drunk, which at least helped the food go down more easily.

'If it wasn't for the *samsu* I couldn't digest that stuff,' Marty confessed.

'One gets used to it after a while,' Kearney replied. 'Don't you think so, Sergeant?'

'It goes down a treat with me,' said Bulldog. 'I got used to it months ago.'

'There you are, Trooper Butler,' Kearney addressed Marty in his sardonic manner. 'All good things come to him who waits. Keep eating! Keep drinking!'

'I hear you loud and clear, boss.'

On their deep-penetration patrols they usually stowed their unwanted kit in covered trenches beneath the Sakai houses, then moved out at first light with their guide. Even after ditching the kit, invariably they would still be carrying 25-pound loads each, including an Owen submachine-gun, one Browning twelve-gauge autoloader shotgun, full magazines for both weapons, six '80' white phosphorus incendiary hand grenades, Browning High Power handguns, a week's food, water bottles, one change of clothes, ground sheets without blankets, a pair of field-glasses, button compass and small-scale maps, *parangs*, commando knives, fishing line and hooks, and a basic medical kit that included antibiotics, antihistamine, water-sterilising tablets, anti-malaria tablets, painkillers, and a good supply of waterproof plasters and bandages.

'But no rubbers,' Bulldog joked with Marty. 'That means we're in for some real work. No play at all, lad.'

It did not take long for Marty to understand why they needed an aboriginal guide, no matter how well they had been trained at Johore. Born and bred in the *ulu*, the Sakai had a keen eye for the most minute traces of human movement through the forest, including dislodged pieces of bark, broken branches, twisted leaves, threads of clothing caught on twigs, and even broken spider-webs. Sometimes the terrorists would deliberately go without shoes in the hopes of making the SF think the footprints were those of the Sakai, but the Sakai guides showed Marty the difference. If the toes of the footprints were cramped it was because they belonged to feet that normally wore shoes or boots, the feet of guerrillas, not of the barefoot Sakai.

Marty was also shown when a guerrilla had attempted to obscure his tracks by treading lightly in the footmarks of an elephant or a *seladang* – the wild ox or bison of Malaya. He had to look very carefully to discern the human footprint within the larger, deeper print of the animals. The guerrillas were clever.

During such patrols, the three men would spend the night in a hide in some particularly dense part of the *ulu*. Soon, with the help of their guide, they became experts at constructing relatively luxurious accommodations. Using a *changkol* – the large hoe which replaces the spade in Malaya – each of them dug himself a shallow scrape to lie in. A large tent was then raised over the three scrapes. The *changkol* was also used to level a platform outside the tent, where they put a crude table and chairs made from the packing crates. Over this they placed bamboo split in half and laid alternate ways up to make a covering against the rain.

'Home sweet home,' Kearney invariably said when they had settled into a new hide. 'What have we to eat?'

In fact, food was no problem. A staple diet was edible tapioca, which they soon learned was plentiful in the *ulu*. They also learned to catch fish by dropping small charges of gelignite into the pools. When the minute explosions dazed the fish, they could be lifted out of the water by hand. Their Sakai guides also showed them how to find pig, *kijang* and even monkeys.

Though the pig were scarce, Bulldog managed to bring down a few barking deer with his twelve-gauge. The guides showed them how to attract the deer by hiding in the jungle and giving out a piercing scream with the aid of a small section of bamboo split in a traditional Sakai manner. If there were any *kijang* within earshot, they would reply with their harsh bark and come closer, doing so each time the SAS men used the split bamboo, until finally the deer were in range of the shotgun.

Marty began using his standard-issue M1 carbine for anything larger than monkeys, though in the jungle, as he soon noticed, he rarely got a good shot in at anything over fifty yards. Nevertheless, he soon became as good as Bulldog, and between them they shot, cooked and ate a wide variety of wild creatures, including pigs, deer and monkeys, though the monkeys were low on their list of culinary favourites.

'Neither tender nor tasty,' Kearney said. 'To be recommended only if we're desperate. I pass on monkey.'

Much tastier were the many mud turtles to be found in the swamps. The Sakai guides taught the SAS men how to look for a slight cloudiness in the mud, which was an indication of the movement of a turtle just below the surface. When they saw the movement, they simply scooped the turtle up with their hands. The resulting soup, which was delicious, included lichens and mosses soaked overnight in clean water; and the meat, when served on its own, was, according to Kearney, 'quite tender and tasty.'

Snakes also made excellent food, being similar in taste and texture to a mixture of chicken and lobster. After getting rid of the poisonous secretions on the skin or the venom glands from the head (which they did by removing the entire head), the snakes were gutted, then cooked in their skins on hot embers. When the heat caused the skin to split, the meat was removed and boiled. Cooked in a similar manner was the monitor lizard – a reptile six or seven feet long – whose eggs were also very tasty and could be used in mixed vegetable salads. Frogs, which had poisonous skins, were first skinned, then gutted and roasted on sticks.

'I've never even had frogs' legs before,' Marty said, 'and always thought that only a Frog – meaning a Frenchman – would have the stomach to eat them. Now here I am, not only having the legs, but the whole bleedin' frog. I'm a gourmet at last.'

On the ground of the jungle were snakes, centipedes, scorpions and giant spiders, all of which were dangerous. Just as dangerous, however, was the *seladang*, which would attack humans on sight. Nevertheless, when Bulldog managed to shoot one, the meat went down well with rice, sweet potato and vegetables, particularly when followed by sweet coffee, strong *samsu* and a good cheroot.

Finally, on the correct assumption that meat would not always be available, the Sakai taught them how to pick out edible fungi, leaves, nuts, roots, berries, and fruit from the *ulu*'s wide variety of produce, much of which was poisonous. The more edible fruits and plants had to be brought down from the jungle canopy, which entailed an arduous, dangerous climb and descent, though the SAS men eventually mastered this without the aid of abseiling ropes.

It gradually became clear to Marty that Kearney and Bulldog

were, between them, using the jungle as a laboratory where they could constantly experiment and devise new jungle survival skills and operational procedures. As part of this, before setting out on patrols in search of the CT, Kearney made them practise walking and running past each other in a way that ensured that no bit of metal caught the light and nothing could betray them by its rattle, such as ammunition, metallic kit or half-used boxes of matches. They even wrapped their weapons in adhesive tape to stop them shining in the moonlight. Kearney also discovered that if they walked heel first on hard ground and toe first on softer ground, they could pass absolutely silently and would be, with their camouflaged clothes and darkened faces, virtually invisible.

Nevertheless, to follow a jungle path, even on a moonlit night, it was necessary to use light of some sort. This problem was solved by putting a green leaf inside the glass, not only to make the torch less bright, but to accustom their eyes to a dim light. If the battery ran out, a few fireflies or luminous centipedes in the reflector of the torch gave just enough light to read a map, lay a charge, or even follow a path through the *ulu*.

The three of them temporarily gave up smoking because of the effect on their sense of smell – and that was often the first means they had of detecting a nearby enemy. Also, they evolved a special system of signals that made talk unnecessary. One was a clicking noise between the upper teeth and side of the tongue – the sound used to encourage a horse. This signal carried a great distance on a still night, and, even if heard by the enemy, would be mistaken for a bird, an insect or a rubber nut falling off a tree. A single click meant *stop* or *danger*.

The only other signal they needed was a rallying cry – the signal used being the hunting cry of the British tawny owl. This piercing cry carries a great distance, even in thick woodland. It cannot be confused with any other cry heard in the Malayan jungle, yet to the uninitiated it passes without notice in the wide variety of weird nocturnal sounds.

Occasionally they would catch a brief glimpse of a jungle tiger, a few leaf-eating monkeys or some noisy gibbons. There were abundant signs of pig in the deep muddy puddles that were their wallows, and where the rivers were bordered by meadows of green grass, kept short by water buffalo, or Chinese vegetable gardens.

The leeches were everywhere. By now, however, the three SAS men took them for granted (the Sakai guides hardly noticed them) and got rid of them by using the Chinese method: removing the leeches by hand, then putting a pinch of their fine-cut tobacco on each bite. This congealed the blood and stopped it flowing, but before long their legs, particularly the shins and ankles, were covered in suppurating, stinking sores about the size of a shilling and a quarter of an inch deep. Pus poured out of them and, as a result of infection, the lymphatic glands in their groins became so painful and swollen that at times they could hardly walk, much less go hunting or on recce patrols. When suphathiazole powder had also failed to cure them, they managed to draw the pus from the wounds by smearing the tar-like Chinese substance, *kow-yok*, on a piece of cloth and covering the wounds with it. This treatment also protected the wounds from the water.

'We all look like lepers,' Marty noted wearily one morning as they prepared to move out again. 'And I don't feel much better.'

'We must learn to endure,' Kearney responded, grinning from a face which, through still handsome, had grown gaunt and dreadfully pale, almost yellow. 'That's why we're here, Trooper.'

'I'm not about to give up,' Marty told him. 'Where you lead, boss, I'll follow.'

'That's what I like to hear.'

Once on patrol, they were surprised by the number of rivers they had to cross. The jungle sometimes rose to hundreds of feet, from where, through windows in the jungle wall, they could see the sheer extent of the forest, as well as the many rubber estates further west. Those steep hills, however, also turned some of the many rivers into foaming torrents that rushed, roaring, between boulders, slabs of granite, and high mud banks.

Sometimes they took boats, less than ten feet long and pointed at each end. With the Bergens in the stern, the three men could fit in, one behind the other, if they stretched out their legs on either side of the man in front. The Sakai also taught them to build various kinds of jungle raft. Though primitive, the rafts were perfectly adequate for travel on all but the most violent of rivers.

Often, after coming in off the cooling river or emerging soaked in sweat from the *ulu*'s dreadful humidity, they would spend the night in a deserted Sakai village, where all the houses were made of bamboo and raised on stilts. Their aboriginal guide explained that the villages were deserted either because the Sakai were up on high ground, clearing the jungle to grow tapioca and maize, or because they had fled from the guerrillas. Ah Hoi, the present leader of the guerrillas, had recently been committing dreadful atrocities to terrorise the whole *ulu*.

The most dangerous activity ordered by Kearney was when he and his men passed themselves off as Malays or Chinese to pick up intelligence at close hand. The least dangerous way was to disguise themselves as Indians and dress like Tamils, wearing the standard white shirt, a *dhoti* or *sarong* around the waist, and a white cloth, deliberately dirtied, around the head and hanging down behind. Their complexions were darkened with a mixture of coffee, lamp-black, iodine and potassium permanganate. When going on such missions, they always kept a pistol and grenade tucked into the tops of their *sarongs* in case of emergency.

Often, they saw Malay cyclists or Tamil bullock-carts moving along the muddy, narrow paths by the river. Following the tracks of these people invariably brought them to a Sakai village or Malay *kampong* where they would pick up more intelligence on the movements of Ah Hoi's guerrillas. Though Ah Hoi's main force seemed to be truly invisible, the SAS men often came across isolated bands of roving guerrillas or, possibly, bandits who had to be 'neutralised', 'taken out' or 'despatched' with ruthless efficiency. This Kearney, Bulldog and Marty did with the shotgun, the M1 carbine, the incendiary hand grenades, home-made bombs and even, on occasions when silent killing was necessary, with their commando daggers. Luckily, Marty never had to use this, though otherwise he had been toughened up and was able to kill the CT using more impersonal weapons without revulsion or conscience.

When engaged in their murderous activities, the team adopted a routine of leaving the hide-out at last light, with their faces and hands darkened, wearing battledress carefully camouflaged with patches of mud. Each of them carried a main weapon, plus a Browning High Power handgun and a couple of grenades or home-made bombs. These were made by putting a stick of gelignite, with detonator and fuse attached, inside a tin or a section of bamboo, then filling it up with several pounds of road metal. The fuse was lit by pressing a small igniter in a copper tube, thus obviating the use of matches. One great advantage of making their own was that they could vary the length of the fuses, so that the explosions would continue for some time after they left the scene. This would keep the guerrillas from answering their fire or following them until they were well away from the scene.

Once they followed the tracks of four guerrillas for five days until they spotted their hut. Settling down a good distance away, they waited for an impending rainstorm to arrive. When, as they had anticipated, the sentries took shelter from the rain, Kearney and Marty, covered carefully by Bulldog, crept up to within five yards of the soaked, still-smouldering camp fire. Kearney then pressed the igniter on a home-made bomb and lobbed it straight through the open entrance of the thatched hut. The guerrillas bawled in panic just before the bomb exploded, destroying most of the hut and setting what was left of it on fire. When two of the four guerrillas staggered screaming from the swirling smoke and flames, both of them on fire, they were cut down by Bulldog, who used his shotgun with methodical, fearsome efficiency.

Occasionally the team separated to pursue guerrillas who had deliberately split up to elude them. Kearney would not normally have allowed this, but he made an exception in their case, confident that Marty and Bulldog could do what was required and come back in one piece.

He was correct in this assumption. Sent in pursuit of a guerrilla who had escaped one of their ambushes, Marty, armed with his carbine and employing the aboriginal tracking knowledge he had gleaned from the Sakai, pursued his quarry relentlessly through the jungle, from the early afternoon to last light. Finally, realising that he could not elude him any longer, the guerrilla turned around to face him in a jungle clearing. The two men were barely twenty yards apart. Marty fired six rapid repeat shots with his M1, so fast they were like a single shot, and the guerrilla was picked up and slammed back to the forest floor, his hand frozen around his unfired weapon.

Marty didn't even bother to check that the man was dead. He just turned away and retraced his own route back through the forest, feeling that he had done his job, no more and no less.

When, many weeks later, Lieutenant Kearney finally emerged from the *ulu* with Bulldog and Marty, the three men had learned all it was possible to know about counter-insurgency warfare in a highly hostile environment. Those lessons were passed on to the rest of the SAS in the old CT camp, now an FOB, and the men were duly sent into the jungle, one patrol after the other, to put their lessons into hard practice.

When the time finally came for the SAS to leave the FOB and repeat the whole experience elsewhere, continuing to win the hearts and minds of the indigenous peoples, building more *kampongs* and protected fortresses, cutting off the flow of supplies and weapons to the CT, they could correctly judge themselves to be among the most highly trained, professional soldiers in the world.

That same year, the Malayan Scouts became officially 22 SAS and Marty, one of the regiment's most experienced men, was promoted to corporal.

CHAPTER FIFTEEN

On his first trip back to Penang, three months after entering the *ulu*, Marty rushed immediately on a Friday evening to the Eastern and Oriental Hotel, desperately hoping to find Ann Lim in the Board Room Bar with its RAF pilots, drunken rubber planters, and nostalgic paintings of London Bridge and Regent Street. He was disappointed. Crushed, he spent the rest of the evening grimly clinging to his bar stool, side by side with Tone, insisting ever more drunkenly that Ann Lim would show up eventually.

When this didn't happen, he continued to drink relentlessly until he and Tone, now practically legless, were politely asked to leave. Marty responded by threatening to punch the barman out, but he was reminded by Tone that, if he carried out his threat, he would not be allowed into the bar again. Mindful that this was the only place he was likely to see Ann Lim, Marty took Tone's advice and left the hotel.

He went back to the bar every evening during the following week but Ann Lim did not materialise. The next Friday, however, she was there with her two sisters, sitting at the same table, and her face lit up when she saw him.

Joining them at the table with Tone by his side, he was struck once more by the beauty of Ann Lim's deep-golden, oval-shaped face, large chocolate-coloured eyes and waist-length, jet-black hair. She and her sisters were, as they had been three months before, looking slim, fine boned and curvaceous in Western clothing: Kathy and Mary in tightly belted shirts and slacks, with patterned scarves and flat shoes, Ann Lim in a simple cotton dress buttoned down the front and low at the neck, leaving her shoulders bare and clinging to the curves of her slim body. She was also wearing a pair of high-heel shoes and her long legs were crossed.

As usual, all three girls were smoking filtered cigarettes and drinking cocktails. While Tone immediately gave his attention to Kathy, Marty couldn't take his eyes off Ann Lim, whose quiet, rather hesitant smile he still found irresistible.

'We just got back last week,' he explained when he had bought a round of drinks, 'and I came here first thing. You told me you came here every Friday, so I was disappointed.'

'I didn't mean *every* Friday,' Ann Lim replied, reminding him that she spoke perfect English. 'I meant *most* Fridays. We don't actually *live* in this bar . . . And you've been gone a long time.'

Marty nodded. 'Three months.'

'You look a lot thinner.'

'We *all* looked a lot thinner when we came out of the jungle, believe me. But Tone and I have already put some weight back on. It's amazing what a few beers can do.'

'And a decent night's sleep,' Tone replied. 'Not to mention some decent grub. It all helps in the end.'

'What did you do there?' Kathy asked him.

'Can't say,' Tone replied. 'Soldier's business. All rubbish and bullshit.'

'You meet any nice girls?' Mary asked, then giggled softly at her own impertinence.

Marty caught Ann Lim's glance, which was steady and searching. 'No,' he said. 'No girls where we were. Well, there *were* some bare-breasted ladies, but we weren't allowed near them.'

'I didn't know we still allowed bare-breasted women in Malaya,' Ann Lim said.

'Yes, you do.'

'You must have been very far from here.'

'We were.'

Ann Lim smiled. 'Did the sight of them embarrass you?'

'Embarrass him?' Tone laughed at that one. 'He couldn't keep his eyes off 'em!'

'Not true,' Marty retorted, abashed; then he grinned and shrugged. 'Well, I have to confess, it was hard not to look, but when I did I did it discreetly.'

'You looked but didn't touch,' Ann Lim said.

'I didn't touch.'

'That's nice.'

Trying not to stare too intently, which he felt he might do, Marty realised yet again that this girl was no casual pickup to him. He was attracted to her, sexually aroused by the sight of her, but her hesitant smile and shy, steady gaze touched something deep inside him. He wasn't a man for casual encounters, needing time to approach a woman, serious about romantic attachments; but, for the first time since leaving England and Lesley, he felt the need for involvement. He wanted to be involved with Ann Lim and he had no doubts about it.

'Was it dangerous?' she asked him.

'Pardon?'

'Where you were. What you were doing. Was it dangerous?'

Marty shrugged. 'Not really.'

'I don't believe that.'

'Why?'

'I think you're being modest – that's so English. I suspect it was dangerous.'

'We're so brave,' Tone declared. He was clearly pleased to be facing Kathy. 'We're professionals, so we don't like to talk about it, but by God, we were brave.' He burst out laughing, enjoying the drink and the company, then stood up and asked if anyone wanted another drink. When Mary and Kathy, giggling, nodded to say yes, he made his way unsteadily to the bar, his face flushed and happy.

Slightly embarrassed at being left alone with the girls, Marty was silent for a moment, contenting himself with studying Ann Lim's face. Eventually, realising that the silence was becoming obvious, he said, 'So what have you three been up to since we saw you last? Still taking French lessons?'

'Yes,' Ann Lim confirmed.

'When do you go to the finishing school in Paris?'

'Next year.'

'How often do you go to the language school?' Marty asked. He was looking at all the girls in turn, trying not to make his feelings for Ann Lim obvious. But, judging by the way Mary and Kathy giggled and nudged each other every time they looked at him, he was not succeeding.

'Five days a week,' Ann Lim told him.

'Sort of like a full-time job.'

'Yes. That's why we don't work. My father thinks education is more important. Besides, there aren't many good jobs around here for educated women. Most of the women here work as coolies, as labourers in the paddy-fields, as poorly paid secretaries, or as barmaids and—'

'I know what you mean,' Marty interjected, thinking of the many whores in George Town. 'Not too many opportunities around here. It's a tough life for some.'

'Education is better,' Ann Lim said. 'It's not much help in finding decent work here, but it helps overseas and, perhaps, in finding a husband. My father thinks about that a lot.'

'Do you?'

Ann Lim smiled and the other two girls giggled. 'You disapprove?'

'Not necessarily.'

'Naturally it's what we want eventually. A good husband and children. What else is there in the end for a woman? Especially here.'

Marty appreciated her honesty and was about to tell her so when Tone, still flushed and happy, squinting through the smoke of the cigarette between his lips, returned with a tray of drinks. After passing them around he sat facing Kathy again, raised his glass in the air and said, 'Cheers!'

They raised their glasses and drank. Glancing at the English paintings on the walls, the soft furnishings, the well-dressed clientele at other tables, Tone said artlessly, 'Back in England I wouldn't be seen dead in a place like this. In fact, I doubt that they'd let me in in the first place. But here I feel right at home.'

'You *seem* right at home,' Kathy said, smiling, stroking her short-cropped hair with delicate fingers. 'So why wouldn't you feel the same way in a similar place in England?'

Mary, a shapely schoolgirl, giggled again, fully aware that her sister fancied Tone.

'Because he's working-class riff-raff,' Marty explained, 'and usually frequents noisy, smoky pubs. We both do, as a matter of fact. We normally don't drink in hotels.'

'We can *only* drink in hotels,' Ann Lim informed him. 'At least when we're alone. If we went anywhere else unescorted, we'd gain a bad reputation.'

'Boring, boring, boring,' Tone intoned. 'No wonder you come here every Friday evening. That must be boring as well.'

'Why?' Kathy asked him. 'We're not bored with you. If we hadn't come here, we wouldn't have met you. Now we're having a good time.'

'Really?'

'Yes.'

Tone was pleased to hear that. 'Well, if it's okay to go somewhere else with company, why not take us somewhere right now? We're just tourists here, after all, and don't know the place. You could show us around.'

'I think we should eat,' Marty said. 'Maybe in some other hotel. Somewhere out of George Town. That would be a real change for all of us. What do you think, girls?'

'You haven't been out of George Town before?' Ann Lim asked him.

'No.'

'Then I think you'd really enjoy it.' She glanced at her sisters. When they nodded, both smiling enthusiastically, she turned back to Marty. 'If we get a taxi, we can go out to the beaches. There's an hotel with a good restaurant out there. Would that be all right?'

'Sounds wonderful,' Marty replied. 'Let's drink up and go.'

'I'm with you all the way,' Tone said.

Outside, Marty was disconcerted to find Tone cramming into the back of the taxi with the three sisters, leaving him to sit up front with the Malayan driver. Glancing back over his shoulder and seeing Tone's broad grin, he realised that this arrangement had been deliberate, designed to wind him up.

'All right up front, are you?' Tone asked.

'Fine,' Marty replied. 'I get to see all the sights.'

Leaning forward and brushing the back of Marty's shoulder with her fingers, Ann Lim told the driver to take them to the Golden Sands beach. Pulling away from the palm-fringed hotel, in the evening's starlit darkness, they drove out of town and were soon going along the winding coast road.

Glancing out, Marty saw the darkly glittering surface of the Malacca Straits, the sails of the sampans silhouetted against a star-filled sky. The taxi took them through shanty towns, past widely scattered *kampongs*, while Tone chattered excitedly to Kathy and Mary, laughing wickedly and making the two sisters giggle. Ann Lim, on the other hand, remained silent throughout the journey, only occasionally leaning forward, practically breathing into the back of Marty's neck, to check the road ahead. That warm breath on Marty's neck was like a benediction to him. When Ann Lim leaned forward again, her fingers brushing his right shoulder, a tremor of sensual pleasure rippled through him and made his cheeks burn.

I don't believe this, he thought.

Ann Lim had seen the hotel and was telling the driver to pull in. As Marty stepped out of the car he saw the large, Colonial-styled hotel standing in its own grounds and lush gardens. Made from bamboo and thatch, with broad balconies and balustrades, it overlooked a vast beach of white sand, fringed with palms and papaya trees. The stars were remarkably large and moonlight brightened the rippling sea.

'It's beautiful,' Marty whispered without thinking.

'Yes, it is,' Ann Lim said.

Tone and Kathy had clambered out of the taxi behind Ann Lim, but, when Marty went to pay the driver, Mary, still in the back seat, slammed the door shut, told the driver to take her to Tanjong Tokong, then waved and flashed a mischievous smile as the vehicle moved off.

'What . . .?' Marty began to ask.

'Five is an awkward number,' Ann Lim explained, smiling, 'and Mary felt superfluous. She doesn't mind. She understands.

Kathy and I would do the same in her place. So come on. Let's go inside.'

The hotel's restaurant was surprisingly elegant, with bamboo tables, dimly lit wicker lamps in shades of many colours, a profusion of exotic plants, and Malayan waitresses wearing *sarongs* and flat slippers. The food, chosen jointly by Ann Lim and Kathy, was a delicious combination of Chinese and Malay. With the wine flowing freely, Tone was engrossed in winning Kathy's affections and seemed to be succeeding, leaving Marty free to concentrate on Ann Lim. The conversation rambled, moving back and forth, first among the four of them, then between each couple. Gradually, however, as Tone became more engrossed in Kathy, Marty found himself leaning ever closer to Ann Lim, entranced by the delicacy of her features, her brown eyes and quietly radiant smile. Though hesitant, the smile was lovely, at once sensual and mysterious, drawing him towards her inner light, making him want to possess her and be possessed by her.

Eventually leaving the restaurant, they went into the bar, ostensibly for more drinks, but really just to let the evening continue. Midnight came and went. Tone and Kathy were drunk, constantly laughing together, embracing each other, gradually becoming less inhibited and more intimate. Marty was feeling drunk, too, though in a milder way, lit up with an inner luminescence that had heightened his senses. He wanted to be as free with Ann Lim as Tone was with Kathy, but, though she was warm and good-humoured with him, she was also still subdued, a little distant, held in check by her reticence. He loved her all the more for it.

'Let's go outside and get some fresh air,' Ann Lim said. 'I think those two could do with it.' She nodded at Tone and Kathy, now smiling drunkenly at each other, touching their foreheads together. 'Let's walk on the beach.'

'Yes, let's do that,' Marty said. He turned to Tone and Kathy. 'Hey, you two! We're going for a walk on the beach and think you should come, too. It might sober you up.'

'Not too sure that I want that,' Tone replied, slurring, his arm around the giggling Kathy's shoulders, his grin decidedly wicked. 'Might do me some damage.'

'It'll do you good,' Marty said, though in truth he wanted to be alone with Ann Lim. 'So come on, let's go. You can bring your drinks with you.'

'Wouldn't dream of going without 'em,' Tone responded, slipping his arm around Kathy's waist. 'Come on, luv, let's go. We'll play follow the leader.'

Marty and Ann Lim walked out first, with the other two following. It was dark outside, though moonlight fell through the palm trees. Marty reached out for Ann Lim's hand and met no resistance. Taking the steps that led down through the trees, they soon emerged to the beach; in the moonlight, under a vast umbrella of stars, it was white and magnificent. Ann Lim kicked off her high-heeled shoes and held them in her free hand. A light breeze slapped at them as they started along the beach, still hand-in-hand, with Tone and Kathy trailing a good way behind, laughing and giggling. Ann Lim, on the other hand, remained quiet and thoughtful, her gaze fixed on the sand that she was kicking up distractedly with her bare feet.

'Are you married?' she finally asked him.

'I was,' he replied.

She glanced at him, then looked away again. 'You're divorced?' she asked.

'Not quite,' he confessed. 'But I'm separated from my wife and the divorce proceedings are under way. I won't be married much longer.' They walked on in silence for some time, still holding hands but otherwise not touching, until Marty said, 'Why do you ask? Does it bother you to be with a married man?'

'Yes,' Ann Lim replied emphatically.

'You've never been involved with one?'

'Not intentionally – no. And always, when I've been told that they were married, I've immediately stopped seeing them.'

'You've never been in love with a married man?'

'I've never been in love.'

Marty was surprised to hear that, but he kept holding her hand. 'I don't even know about your parents,' he said eventually. 'You've only mentioned your father. What about your mother?'

'I didn't think to mention her,' Ann Lim replied in a low, even voice. 'My mother is dead.'

Shocked by this statement, Marty glanced at her and saw that she was kicking up the sand, looking down at her own feet. Her long black hair was blowing across her face where it lay like a dark veil.

'You don't know?' he asked, feeling embarrassed.

Ann Lim shook her head. 'No. When the Japanese came here during the war, they took many of the women away to be used in their brothels. Mostly they only took the single girls, but for some reason – maybe because she was still young and attractive and, I think, because she sacrificed herself for her children – they took my mother. My father wasn't there at the time. Then, as now, he worked as an exporter for the rubber planters, but he'd heard that the Japanese were searching out his kind for execution. So he went into hiding at my mother's request and was away when the Japs came looking for him. We lived on the mainland then. The Japs came at night. When they couldn't find my father, they became very angry and started to make threats about us children. We were all so young at the time – I was only twelve; Kathy and Mary were ten and nine – that we didn't really know what was going on; but I think they wanted to rape us. I think that's why they took my mother.

'I still clearly remember my mother pleading with them – she had learned a little Japanese to ingratiate herself – and even as we huddled together on the bed, all frightened and crying, the officer in charge felt my mother up and down, probing her with his fingers as if inspecting a farm animal. Then he nodded and barked his agreement and dragged her out of the house. I heard the soldiers laughing outside, making loud remarks. I heard my mother sobbing as they heaved her up into the truck. Then they drove her away. She offered herself in exchange for us. I think that's what she did.'

Marty continued walking along the beach with her, holding her hand, not knowing what to say, feeling ashamed of being a man. He hadn't felt that before, but when he looked sideways at her, she glanced at him and gave him a tender smile, absolving him instantly.

'We never saw her again until after the war,' she told him.

'We stayed in that house alone for about a week – until the food ran out. Only then did we go and see relatives, to tell them that our mother had been taken away and had not yet returned. Our relatives took care of us and contacted our father where he was hiding in the house of a friend, on his rubber plantation. When he heard what had happened, my father instantly returned, ignoring the danger to himself, and collected us and took us back home. Luckily, the Japs never bothered us again and my father managed to scratch a meagre living until the war ended. Then my mother was found in a military brothel deserted by the fleeing Japanese. The British sent her back to us.'

Ann Lim stopped walking, kicked up more sand, watched it fall over her bare foot, then she glanced back to where Tone and Kathy were following, pausing every now and then to embrace, both still holding their drinks. Smiling, Ann Lim turned away and started walking again, her hand still held by Marty.

'My mother had changed terribly. She was out of her mind. By then I was three years older, fifteen, and her condition frightened me. She never told us what had happened to her, refused to talk about it, just stayed in her room and sobbed a lot and talked to the walls – real talk, not whispering. Often she had very bad nightmares that led to much screaming.

'She never talked about the brothel, but one of her friends did: a younger woman, single, who'd been taken when she was only seventeen and just about survived it. She told us that the women had been used from dawn to dusk. The Japanese soldiers queued up to have them. The women had to do anything asked of them. If they refused or if they failed to satisfy someone, if even a common soldier complained about them, they'd be tortured and killed, or killed in terrible ways – breasts cut off, eyes gouged out with knifes, bayonets put up inside them – dreadful, nightmarish punishments that were often carried out in full view of the other captured women, to let them see exactly what would happen to them if they failed to satisfy. So not only were they raped from dawn to dusk every day, but they had to live each day with the knowledge of what would happen to them should someone, any one of the hundreds of soldiers, decide to complain.

'That, as much as anything else, drove a lot of them mad. My mother was one of those driven mad and that's how she came back to us.'

She shuddered briefly, as if slapped by a freezing wind, and Marty, touched only by the warm breeze, felt his heart go out to her. The breeze was gentle, crooning softly through the papaya trees, blowing the sand in languid clouds towards the glittering, moonlit sea, whipping Ann Lim's long hair around her face. Her head was bowed as she studied her own feet, but her profile was exquisite, the black hair falling past it.

'War is vile, isn't it?'

'Yes,' Marty said.

'Did you ever do anything that awful?'

'No,' Marty said, though he knew that he was probably capable of it, as most men were.

'A few months after being brought back home,' Ann Lim continued, speaking softly, hypnotically, 'my mother killed herself.' She stopped walking and nodded towards the sea. 'She walked in there in the middle of the night and was found three days later, washed up on a beach miles away.' She started walking again, still holding Marty's hand. 'The family was devastated. My father nearly had a breakdown. Then he pulled himself together, went back to exporting rubber, and soon had put enough money aside to send us to private school.

'Three years later, just as we were beginning to feel safe again, the Chinese communists went into hiding in the *ulu* and only emerged to torture and murder the rubber planters, even their own kind. Remembering the Japanese, not seeing too much difference between them and the CT, my father moved us off the mainland, found us the house in Tanjong Tokong and then put us into a convent.

'He greatly admired the English but feared his own kind, the Chinese. He wanted to keep us out of harm's way and make us as English as possible. So that's why we have English names and will soon be going off to Paris to become fine young ladies. Also, at least so my father hopes, to find husbands in Europe. Now you know it all, Marty.'

'I don't want you to go to Europe,' Marty said, choked by what he had heard. He squeezed her hand, then lightly tugged at it, to make her stop walking and turn towards him. 'Not unless it's with me.'

She stood facing him, close to him, her brown eyes reflecting moonlight, strands of black hair lying like shadows on the gold of her flawless skin. The breeze, he saw with pleasure, was pressing the dress against her body, outlining every curve and hollow: breasts and hips, the flat belly and long legs. He burned up with wanting her.

'What do you mean by that, Marty?'

'I think you know what I mean.'

'But we hardly know each other.'

'I know all I need to know,' Marty told her, his voice sounding hoarse. 'I know what I want.'

Ann Lim smiled gently. 'Even knowing that I might be a woman searching for a white husband?'

'Is that all this is to you?' Marty asked.

'Is that what you feel?'

'What I feel is the opposite.'

'Always trust your feelings,' she told him.

'I do,' Marty said.

Ann Lim smiled again, brushing black hair from brown eyes. She glanced back over her shoulder, along the moonlit beach, to where Tone and Kathy had been following them. But they had disappeared, melting into the trees. Ann Lim smiled again, facing Marty, her gaze steady; then she tugged him closer, retreating into the trees, stopping only when she was leaning against a tree trunk, in the shadow of the large papaya leaves that cast their shadows upon her.

She tugged Marty against her, pulling him gently by one hand. She dropped the shoes from her other hand, then placed both her hands on his shoulders and pressed her body against him. He felt her lips on his mouth. His hardness beat against her. When he parted his lips, she slipped her tongue in and used it to render him senseless. Her breasts flattened against his chest as her belly rubbed against him, her hip bones grinding against his, her long legs radiating the heat that made him erect. He kissed her lips and neck. She put her tongue into his ear. He undid the top buttons of her dress and slid his hand down her silken skin until it cupped her bare breast. She was wearing no brassiere and her heat filled his hand.

He slid his other hand down her spine, to her rump, and explored it dementedly. She moaned and kept kissing him – his mouth, eyes and ears – and he felt the warmth and softness of her belly inflaming his cock. He undid more of her buttons, all the way down to her waist, then slid the dress off her bronzed shoulders and down to below her breasts. She placed her hands behind his head, pulled him low, bending back for him, letting him cover her bare breasts in kisses and suck on her nipples. They were as brown and as hard as nuts – surprisingly hard on the soft breasts. He licked them and sucked them in a delirium that held no thought of stopping.

'God, I want you!' he whispered.

She sighed and bit his neck. He groaned and undid more buttons. When the last button was undone, the dress fell off to lie around her bare feet. Almost naked, she was breathtaking, a vision in light golden brown, bare breasts firm above a tapering waist, a flat belly, long legs. He dropped to his knees, kissing her breasts and then her belly, tugging her white knickers down around her hips to kiss her right there. She moaned and held his head, slightly parting her thighs, then, before he could pull her knickers down farther, she lowered herself to the sand. He lay down beside her, twisting towards her, tugging her knickers along her smooth, golden thighs, then down her legs to her ankles. She kicked the knickers off and he took her in his arms.

She unbuttoned his shirt and kissed his chest, then tugged his shirt off. This aroused him even more. He felt his hardness pulsating against her. He reached down to start unbuttoning himself, but then she did the work for him. Pulling his cock out, she groaned. Her squeezing fingers drove him mad. He groaned, also, without shame, and rolled over to press himself onto her. She opened her legs to him, breathing harshly, needing air, and he saw the light of total distraction in the brown of her wide eyes.

He entered her and both of them gasped. He moved deep inside her, trying to sunder her, as her legs curled about him. She drew him in even deeper, as if wanting to be sundered, and they melted together, becoming one, moving their bodies as one. It did not last too long, but it was at least intense. She soon shuddered and cried out, holding him tighter, writhing against him; and when she did so, when he felt her and heard her, he too lost control, coming in a series of spasms that made his head reel.

He groaned in helpless release, spending himself deep inside her, and she held him in the soft vice of her limbs until his shaking had ceased. When he was spent, gazing down into her eyes, she smiled dreamily and stroked his fevered brow.

'I love you, *tuan*,' she said, using the Malay word deliberately, slightly teasing him while letting him know she meant it. 'I will *always* love you.'

He knew then, without any shadow of doubt, regardless of Lesley and the kids, his parents or friends, that he was going to marry her.

CHAPTER SIXTEEN

Marty had been back in Johore for just over a month, engaging in regular jungle patrols and thinking a lot about Ann Lim, when B Squadron was summoned to an unexpected briefing in the HQ building. Arriving there in OGs, jungle boots and soft green bush hats, as instructed, he and the others were informed by Lieutenant Kearney that they were about to embark on what would surely be their most difficult task to date.

'In our first six months here,' Kearney explained, 'we've managed to drastically reduce the number of CT in this area, but a hard-core group remains and has to be eradicated before we can move on elsewhere. This particular group, led by one Ah Chan, has tried to put itself out of our reach by entering a swamp near Selangor. Getting them out won't be easy. Though not exactly impenetrable – the guerrillas are in there, after all – the swamp's very large. It consists of exceptionally dense forest, including *belukar*, and it's flooded with rust-brown water, mangroves and glutinous mud. It's also home to every kind of bug, insect and creepy-crawlie known to man, including blood-sucking leeches. Last but not least, from what intelligence has picked up, Ah Chan's guerrillas, who know the swamp back to front, are also experts at every kind of booby trap. So when I say that this is going to be a difficult task, I really mean it will be hell and that we could be in there for a very long time, sometimes eating and even sleeping in the water. Please be prepared for that.'

Realising that he was not going to see Ann Lim for another few weeks, maybe months, if indeed he survived, Marty felt a stab of helpless pain. He was, however, also filled with excitement at the thought of the operation to come. This realisation slightly shocked him, making him face the hard fact that, no matter how much he might love someone, his love for the SAS, a man's world, was even greater.

'Insertion,' Kearney continued, 'will be by means of a secret parachute drop from a Beverley to the jungle canopy five kilometres west of the swamp, followed by a march into the swamp itself. Once there, we'll be waist deep in water all day and sleeping by night in hammocks or on improvised rafts. If absolutely necessary, resups will be dropped by RASC Valettas, but you'll be supplied with a seven-to-fourteen-day patrol ration, allowing you to operate for up to two weeks without needing new supplies. This operation commences immediately, following the usual routine: quartermaster's store, armoury and personal preparation in that order. You're expected out on the airstrip at ten hundred hours. I'll see you all out there. Okay, men, dismissed.'

Leaving the briefing room, knowing that this was serious, Marty marched with the others to the quartermaster's stores where, in his group of ten, he picked up, along with the usual kit, special waterproof jungle Bergens, cosmetic 'cam' cream, dulling paint and strips of camouflage cloth for the weapons, lengths of para-cord to replace the standard-issue sling swivels for the rifles, a plentiful supply of Paludrine, salt tablets, sterilisation tablets and a Millbank bag for filtering water. At the armoury, next door, he collected his personal weapons, including an SLR, and other members of the squadron picked up a couple of L4A4 .303-inch Bren guns with curved 300-round box magazines. The Originals, including Marty, were especially fond of this weapon as all of them had used it in North Africa and knew it to be simple, old-fashioned and highly reliable. The squadron also took possession of two- and three-inch mortars, fragmentation and smoke grenades, magazines of tracer bullets and flares.

The most unusual weapon picked up, however, and the most recent to be used, was the crossbow with twenty-four lightweight, slim, alloy bolts and arrows, used for silent killing, and an air rifle that fired poison darts which could kill or stun.

The blue-eyed, gently smiling and, as Marty had come to realise, deadly Taff Hughes was the one who had been chosen for special training with the crossbow and had proved himself to be a natural at it, having already killed enemy sentries by putting the bolt and arrow into his victim's heart, or through the back or side of his neck, with unerring accuracy. For this reason, Taff had also been given the air rifle and poisonous darts, his special job now being the silent killing of enemy sentries or point men.

'You have the eyes of a fucking hawk,' Bulldog had told him, 'and you're just as fucking deadly. It's all yours, Geronimo.'

When the weapons had been collected, the men moved along to the radio store where they signed for their Clansmans, one for each of the four-man teams. The radio sets operated on compact batteries, though each patrol also carried a lightweight hand-powered generator to recharge the batteries. Finally, each man collected his relatively simple World War Two parachute, an Irvin X-type, which he had to strap immediately to his back, enabling him to carry his packed Bergen and weapons by hand.

Returning to their barracks, the men went to their respective bashas, where they proceeded to pack their kit properly. When this was done, they painted their weapons with quick-drying green camouflage paint, then wrapped them in the strips of cloth specially dyed to match the jungle background. In both instances, they were particularly careful not to let the paint or strips of cloth interfere with the weapons' working parts or sights. After wrapping masking tape around the butts, pistol grips and top covers, they replaced the noisy sling swivels with para-cord, which made no sound at all.

With the weapons camouflaged, their last job was to camouflage themselves, applying the 'cam' cream and black 'stick' camouflage to the exposed areas of their skin, including the backs of their hands, wrists, ears and neck.

Camouflaged and heavily burdened, the thirty-seven men left the gloom of the barracks and marched into the rising heat of the early morning. A couple of Bedford three-tonners had been driven across from the motor pool and were waiting outside, but before the men could board they were inspected personally by Lieutenant Kearney before he gave them persmission to board the Bedfords. The trucks then transported them the short distance to the airstrip, where a Blackburn Beverley, which could carry seventy parachutists at a time, was waiting to fly them into the interior. When the men and their equipment had been transferred to the Beverley, the aircraft lost no time in taking off.

For half an hour after take-off, Marty and Tone, wedged tightly together and hemmed in by their kit and weapons, swopped the customary bullshit, but eventually they fell silent, each preparing himself in his own way for what was to come. Luckily, as the aircraft was suffocatingly hot and humid, the flight to the DZ took only thirty minutes and soon they were lining up to jump, their eyes fixed on the warning light.

Kearney went out first as the drifter – the one whose angle and speed of drop enables the pilot to check wind strength and velocity. The others went out after him, on the command of Bulldog Bellamy, in sticks of four from the port and starboard bows, left and right of the boom door.

By now parachuting had become almost routine for Marty, though he never failed to catch his breath and feel his heart racing when he was swept away on the roaring slipstream, only to escape suddenly and drop like a stone, before jerking the parachute cord and drifting down through a silence broken only by the wind whipping under the chute. This time, when the treetops suddenly raced up towards him, he calmly noted the exact location of the DZ – a fairly clear area of stunted grass and bush – and used the lines of his chute to steer himself in that direction.

Suddenly, the jungle canopy was racing up towards him, faster and faster, then he was plunging down a deep well of blurred greenery, smashing noisily through branches and foliage, until he landed in a shower of raining leaves on the grass-covered earth, letting his legs buckle and rolling over with the parachute tugging at him. He reined the lines in, 'popped' the chute free, then rolled away and clambered to his feet, still in one piece.

After wrapping up his chute and then burying it in the undergrowth, he unslung his SLR and saw Kearney doing the same with his Owen submachine-gun. Bulldog had his Browning twelve-gauge slung across his back and Taff Hughes, surveying the jungle with his mild blue gaze, looked oddly anachronistic with his crossbow strapped to his Bergen rucksack. The rest of the men were hiding their parachutes in the undergrowth, breaking open the crates of supplies that had already fallen to the forest floor, or clambering back up the trees to disentangle the supply parachutes that had become entangled high up in the canopy. Surprisingly, there had been no casualties during the tree-jumping and all of the men were accounted for.

When the spare weapons, ammunition and supplies had been distributed as evenly as possible among the men, they marched, as heavily burdened as pack mules, in the direction of the guerrilla-infested swamp, which was twelve miles away. No one made a sound.

The first hour was easy, a casual stroll in single file through the forest, kicking up the loose leaves, feeling grateful for the shade. However, when they reached the edge of the swamp, the trees closed in upon them, forming an almost impenetrable wall that had to be hacked away with the *parangs*. The ground became more marshy, squelching underfoot, making walking more laborious and exhausting. After they had been only thirty minutes in the swamp, the normal forest had disappeared, the sky was blocked out, and the air had become suffocatingly humid. Even worse, it was filled with whining flies, mosquitoes, midges, flying beetles, the occasional hornet and other equally ravenous insects, which attacked noisily, viciously and constantly, further distracting the men from what they were doing. Unlike the jungle, the swamp offered a constant chorus of croaking, squawking, clicking, drumming and sudden, startling rustling in the undergrowth. This in particular made the men jumpy, even causing them to raise their weapons suddenly, preparing to fire.

Gradually the wet ground became even more marshlike, turning to mud, slopping over their boots, soaking their trouser legs, and giving every impression of turning into dangerous quicksands. Walking became ever more difficult and soon rendered most of them breathless. Within an hour, the mud had turned to rust-brown water that became deeper with every step they took. Three hours later, when every man in the squadron was soaked with sweat, he was also wading hip-deep in water and forced to hold his personal weapon either across his chest or above his head. Both positions placed tremendous strain on the arms, causing sharp pains to dart along them, from shoulder to wrist.

Already the trek was leading them along river banks and through more muddy water, the depths of which varied from shin to neck height. Those parts of the body that were submerged were the prey of fat swamp leeches which, as Marty knew, could consume as much as half a pint of blood before being detected. Also, when the men came to high ground that brought them out of the water, they became the target for the malarial mosquito and similar insects. Before long, even Marty, who prided himself on being tough, was beginning to think that he was in hell on earth.

Their trials were made no easier by the fact that they were not allowed to speak on the march for fear that lurking guerrillas might overhear them or that their voices would hide the sounds of an approaching enemy. Using only sign language, they were forced in upon themselves, thus distracted even more by the sounds all around them, particularly the sudden, sharp rustling which indicated movement in the undergrowth, caused by snakes, jungle pigs, monkeys and rats as big as squirrels.

By mid-afternoon the humidity was appalling, making the men pour more sweat and feel suffocated or nauseous, less capable of coherent thought and quick reactions. This only made many of them more anxious about the unseen CTs and suspicious of every sound in the teeming undergrowth.

Before last light they looked for somewhere to lay up, but even where there wasn't waist-deep, muddy water, the ground was too marshy to be used. So they were compelled to lie in hammocks slung from the trees, mere feet above the water, kept awake by the jungle's nocturnal racket, by the countless insects that buzzed and whined about them all night, and by the fear that snakes, venomous spiders or other creepy-crawlies would drop onto them from the dense foliage above.

When, at first light, Marty rolled off his hammock to commence the new day, he felt even more exhausted and bruised than he had before resting.

'I feel a hundred years old,' he said.

'You're not alone,' Tone informed him.

The deeper into the swamp they went, the worse it became. Each day, from the steamy mists of dawn to the damp, chilling sunset, they had to force their way through stinking mud, rotting vegetation and thorny branches, sometimes wading neck deep in the marsh channels, other times practically swimming across open water, under drooping coils of vine, rattan and giant, razor-sharp leaves which cut arms and faces, driving the insects into a frenzy and giving the growing number of fat leeches even more blood to feed upon.

Within a couple of days, Marty could smell the bog on himself, his rotting clothes adding to the general stench and hanging ever more loosely on his shrinking physique. Tone looked the same. In fact, everyone was losing weight – not only because of the heat and humidity, the relentless grind of hacking away the foliage and wading through debris-filled, mud-thickened water, but also because they were unable to use their portable stoves to cook decent food and instead had to rely on high-calorie rations, which were dry and tasteless.

Adding to their increasing frustration was the continuing lack of contact with the enemy. Frequently they came across jungle hides recently vacated by the CT, but the guerrillas themselves were not to be seen. Finally, realising that the guerrillas knew they were being followed and were keeping ahead by continuing on across the swamp, Lieutenant Kearney decided to block their escape by asking for another SAS squadron, backed up with SF men, to be dropped north of the swamp, where they could form a cordon and then move in on the CT as B squadron advanced from the south.

'We'll box them in,' he explained.

Contacting HQ Johore, he was informed that, while his plan was approved, the required SAS and SF were presently on patrol in the jungles around Johore, so would not be available for another couple of days. In the meantime, B Squadron was to continue its pursuit of the CT as well as it could.

Satisfied that the blocking party would be forthcoming, Kearney ordered the march to continue. This time, the route brought them to a river where Marty, now an expert tracker trained by the Sakai, noticed small piles of broken branches and loose leaves sprinkled over human footsteps, indicating that some men in bare feet had hiked north, trying to cover their tracks as they retreated towards the centre of the swamp.

Immensely frustrated by this endless marching, some of the men wanted to follow the CT's footprints. However, pointing out that it would soon be last light and that this was a relatively dry area, Kearney suggested that it would be safer to basha down for the night. While they were doing so, a three-man patrol consisting of men especially skilled in jungle tracking would follow the camouflaged footprints to check if the CT were still in the vicinity.

'That means me and Private Butler,' Bulldog said, pleasing Marty immensely. 'And I think we should take Taff along – him and his crossbow. That weapon could come in handy.'

'Right,' Kearney replied. 'You three it is.'

Thrilled to have something more challenging to do than the endless hiking, Marty held his SLR at the ready and followed the other two into the jungle, bringing up the rear as Tail-end Charlie, with Bulldog out front on point. Leaving the relative space and dry ground near the riverbank, they ran almost immediately into a stretch of *belukar*, where the thickets of thorn, bracken and bamboo, almost impenetrable in themselves, were covered with the leathery *mengkuang*. The pointed blades of this dense undergrowth slashed Marty's face and hands, drawing blood and attracting even more mosquitoes. About half an hour later, just as the blood was congealing, he sank, chest deep, into muddy water and felt the leeches sticking to his legs and hands.

Continuing to wade through the water, holding his SLR above his head, he temporarily froze when a geometrically patterned snake, the venomous Malay pit viper, emerged from the vegetation by his right elbow, slithered across the branch floating directly in front of him, then disappeared into the dense foliage to his left. He was seriously relieved when, after continuing to wade through the swamp, behind the other two, the ground started sloping upward, letting him rise gradually out of the water.

Back on marshy land, he followed the others deeper into the swamp, tormented by the many leeches still sucking on his blood. With no time to stop and remove them, he just kept advancing, checking every leaf and branch, detouring only when faced with something hideous in the undergrowth: another snake, a venomous spider, sleeping vampire bats, ten-inch centipedes, and nests of hornets whose sting, when not actually fatal, could be horribly painful.

Suddenly, he was stopped by a silent hand signal from Taff up front, who in turn had received it from Bulldog out on point, indicating that they should stop advancing and drop to the kneeling position. When Marty did so, he saw Taff signalling that he should advance silently at the crouch. Even as he was signalling, Taff was doing the same: making his way up to the kneeling Bulldog and dropping beside him. When Marty also reached them, going down on one knee, he saw the back of a man kneeling at the other side of a short stretch of swamp water, examining the ground around his bare feet. Though dressed like a Chinese coolie, but with a military cap on his head, he was carrying a British M1 rifle – a sure sign that he was one of the guerrillas.

Not wanting to fire his twelve-gauge, which would have alerted the other CT in the area, Bulldog indicated with a nod of his head that Taff should dispatch the guerrilla with his crossbow. Smiling dreamily, Taff removed the crossbow as quietly as possible from where it was strapped across his Bergen. Still kneeling, he cocked the weapon, inserted a lightweight alloy bolt and arrow, then prepared to fire.

At that moment, a large spider, about the size of an outspread human hand, materialised eerily from under the leaves and climbed onto Taff's boot. Though Marty felt his skin crawling with helpless dread, Taff merely glanced down and watched with academic curiosity as the enormous spider crossed over the toe of his boot, moved up the laces and onto his leg, to just above the ankle, then changed its mind and turned back down to crawl off the other side of the boot and disappear under the carpet of leaves.

Marty let his breath out while Taff, looking unconcerned, quietly raised the crossbow. The guerrilla was still kneeling, studying the ground around him. Taff took aim along the sights of the crossbow, then squeezed the trigger, sending the alloy bolt and arrow racing through the air and straight into the back of the man's neck.

The man quivered violently as if whipped, then stood up and turned around to face the river, looking surprised. He gripped the bolt in his right hand, tried to tug it out, winced and stopped, then shuddered violently and sank unsteadily to his knees, where he convulsed and fell face down in the mud. He shook for a few seconds like an epileptic, then he was still.

At that moment, Marty heard a rustling noise in the undergrowth behind him. Looking back over his shoulder, he was relieved to see the mournful Roy Weatherby emerging from the *ulu*, along the overgrown trail that Marty and the others had avoided. Assuming that Weatherby had been sent forward to give the team a message, Marty was just about to wave him down when, to his horror, he saw that an enormous log, impregnated with six-inch nails and sharpened hardwood spikes, had been suspended above the trail on a rope that formed a trip-wire.

Unable to call a warning, knowing it was too late anyway, Marty and the others could only look on in horror as Weatherby tripped over the rope. He stumbled as the rest of the rope rapidly unravelled and the heavy, spiked log fell upon him, instantly crushing him, giving him multiple stab wounds, and pinning his mangled body to the ground. He hadn't even had time to scream.

'Shit!' Marty whispered, then advanced, crouched low, his

heart racing and his throat dry, now checking his surroundings even more carefully, until he reached Weatherby's body. The unfortunate man had been flattened beneath the log and pressed deeply into the mud. Blood was squirting out of his numerous wounds and soaking him thoroughly.

Marty didn't have to check that Weatherby was dead, but as Bulldog and Taff approached he looked for the dead man's weapon, failed to find it, and realised that it must have been buried under him.

Even Bulldog winced when he saw Weatherby's crushed body and multiple stab wounds, but Taff, looking down with unblinking curiosity, merely said, 'That was stupid of him. He should have known better.'

'So should that poor fucker who's just had your steel bolt and arrow through his neck,' Bulldog responded. 'Now get over there and check out the area, then report back to me.'

Taff smiled dreamily and waded through the short stretch of swamp. He frisked the dead guerrilla, withdrew some papers from his tunic, then disappeared into the *ulu* to reconnoitre the area.

'The Chinese Chopper,' Bulldog explained to Marty, describing the booby trap, deliberately keeping his voice even to disguise his revulsion.

'Can we move it off him?' Marty asked, still feeling shocked and unwilling to look back down upon that awful sight.

'I doubt it,' Bulldog replied. 'But we can certainly try.'

They tried but failed – the spiked log was just too heavy – so instead they simply checked out both sides of the track, then waited for Taff to return. By the time he did so, a mass of black flies and mosquitoes were already buzzing frenziedly over Weatherby's bloody face. Red ants were crawling in and out of his open mouth, up his nose, into his eyes and ears.

'Well?' Bulldog asked. 'Anything out there?'

Taff shook his head. 'Nope,' he said, glancing down at the insects swarming all over Weatherby's face, but registering only mild curiosity. Looking up again, he smiled and handed Bulldog the personal papers he had found on the dead CT. 'Not a single CT. I guess the others moved on.'

'Then let's head back to the hide. There's nothing we can do here for Weatherby, so we might as well leave him.'

Treading carefully around the dreadful mess on the forest floor, they made their way back to the hide by the river. There, they found most of the men asleep in a wide variety of jungle bashas, with Lieutenant Kearney resting on a bamboo raft that was floating in the middle of the river and tied to a tree on the bank. While Bulldog waded out into the river to give his report to Kearney, Marty and Taff each made themselves a triangular shelter with groundsheets and stick supports, fixing the ends of the sheets with string and short wooden stakes. Then, absolutely exhausted and, at least in Marty's case, shocked, they lay down and slept.

Moving out the next morning, the patrol had to make their way across the hellish swamp to where the dead Roy Weatherby was still pinned beneath the spiked log, his crushed body now rendered even more hideous by being covered in congealed blood, bloated flies and red ants, his face half eaten away by the ants. No one really wanted to touch him, but some of the men, at Kearney's insistence, rolled the log off him and buried him in a shallow grave, forced to beat the flies off as they did so. Once the body was covered up, the patrol moved on across the short stretch of swamp to where the CT was still lying face down in the mud with Taff's alloy bolt and arrow through his neck, protruding front and rear, the congealed blood around it also attracting swarms of flies and an army of ants. Even more revolting was the fact that some animal from the *ulu* had fed off the corpse, tearing an arm from the shoulder and carrying it off to its lair. The bloody stump of the arm had become an ants' nest, but was being attacked by many different kinds of insect. As no one would volunteer to bury him, he was left there to rot.

'What's left of him will disappear soon enough,' Bulldog rationalised to those within earshot, possibly because he felt guilty. 'There won't even be bones left.'

'More efficient than cremation,' Rod O'Connor retorted, his dark eyes flashing with grim mirth.

'Very funny,' Tone said.

After that they were silent, marching deeper into the swamp, leaving the dead men well behind and keeping their eyes peeled for other booby traps. In fact, they had only marched another hour when Bulldog, still on point, saw another Chinese Chopper across the trail. Stepping aside, he let Rod O'Connor put it out of action by shooting the rope to shreds with a couple of sustained bursts from his Owen submachine-gun, enabling the viciously spiked log to crash to the ground, crushing only leaves and red ants.

'That could have been you, Sarge,' Rob Roy said with a wide, cheeky grin.

'You bastards should be so lucky,' Bulldog replied. 'All right, let's keep moving.'

An hour later they came across a thatch-and-palm lean-to once used by some guerrillas, as could be seen from a pile of ant-covered chicken bones, turtle shells covered in swarms of flies, decaying vegetables, and a couple of line drawings showing various routes through the swamp. Excited, Corporal Len Baxter bent down to snatch up the maps.

'*Don't touch them!*' Bulldog bellowed, then threw himself out of the lean-to as a hidden fragmentation grenade, unpinned by a trip-wire fixed to the phoney maps, exploded with a deafening roar, hurling Baxter backwards in a fountain of loose soil, his flesh shredded by razor-sharp, red-hot shrapnel that set fire to the few parts of the lean-to not blown apart.

The scorched, shredded Baxter was lying on his back, shuddering spasmodically and screaming like an animal as Bulldog picked himself up and wiped soil from his face.

'Damn!' he exclaimed, then turned to the other men. 'Don't ever touch anything!' he bawled. 'Check everything first!' He knelt beside the screaming man, saw the scorched, shredded flesh, and was still deciding what to do about him when the man coughed up a mess of blood and phlegm, then shuddered and died, evacuating his bowels with his last breath.

'Jesus!' Rob Roy whispered, licking his lips, glancing down at the dead man and looking as white as a sheet. 'Jesus Christ! What kind of war is this?'

'The kind that'll become more commonplace in the future,' Kearney wearily told him. 'All right, men, keep marching.'

The patrol moved on. Forced to follow the river, they encountered a lot of snakes where they were sheltering in the relative cool of the muddy banks. As it was now clear that the CT knew the British were here, the men were no longer concerned with maintaining silence and either despatched the aggressive snakes with a short burst from their semi-automatic weapons or sliced through them with the *parangs*.

Lieutenant Kearney had no compunction about breaking the silence when he had to pass under a branch on which was resting an enormous, hairy spider. He despatched it – and the branch – with a sustained burst from his Owen submachine-gun. Likewise, when an enormous wild ox charged out of the undergrowth – probably goaded into doing so by one or a number of guerrillas – it was brought down by a burst from Bulldog's powerful twelve-gauge.

Trooper Mark Beacham was the first man to see the next Chinese Choppper. After calling out a warning, he skirted around it – and tripped over another string stretched along both sides of the narrow track. His scream was dreadful to hear as he staggered back from the impact of the wooden spear that slammed into his chest – fired from a bow concealed in the earth, operated by a trigger mechanism set off by the trip-cord. He kept screaming as he dropped his M1, staggering as if punch-drunk, and instinctively tried to jerk the spear out of his smashed chest and pierced heart. He was dead by the time he fell backwards into a pool of mud.

Marty activated the spiked log of the Chinese Chopper by shredding the supporting cords with bullets, then, just to be sure, he also peppered the area on both sides of the track. When it was clear that the ground was safe, he and the others moved on, leaving a couple of men behind to dig a shallow grave for Trooper Beacham, as they had done for the other casualties en route.

About an hour later, when they had managed to hack their way through another exhausting stretch of secondary jungle, Marty, Tone and Bulldog, now acting as a team, all out on point, spotted three guerrillas about seventy yards away across a stretch of open, rust-brown water.

After using a hand signal to tell the rest of the squadron to drop to the ground, Bulldog indicated that Marty and Tone should follow him. Discarding their Bergens and other kit, the three of them slipped into the water, holding their weapons above their heads, until they could grab hold of a floating log. With the log in front of them, they inched through the water, resting their weapons near the top of the log, though slightly behind it, so that only the log would be seen if the guerrillas turned around. When they neared the other side, all still hidden by the log and about fifty yards from the bank, they saw that the guerrillas were two men and a woman. As they were quietly bringing their weapons up into the firing positions, resting the barrels on the floating log, they heard the distant rumble of aircraft and saw the guerrillas pointing at the sky.

A couple of Beverley aircraft were flying overhead with parachutes billowing out beneath them. The men on the ends of the parachutes were the other SAS and SF men, falling towards their DZ north of the swamp, where they could cordon off the CT.

Bulldog nodded at Marty, then aimed along the upraised sights of his twelve-gauge. Marty did the same with his SLR, as did Tone with his carbine. They opened fire simultaneously, taking out the two men, who convulsed in a dramatic explosion of spitting soil and foliage. The woman, however, jumped to her feet and fled into the jungle.

'Damn!' Bulldog exclaimed. 'Now the bitch'll go and tell the others. No point in stopping now.' Pushing the log aside, he waded to the bank with Marty and Tone behind him. After they had scrambled out and were standing over the two dead CT, dripping wet, Bulldog waved to the rest of the squadron, still carefully hidden in the jungle, to advance. Like ghosts, but led by Lieutenant Kearney, the men emerged from the trees and waded across the river.

Kearney, even in the middle of the river, was talking into the handset of the radio, obviously keeping in contact with the SAS and SF men advancing on the guerrillas from the north. When he saw Bulldog and Marty looking at him, waiting for further instructions, he hand-signalled that they and the other troopers should keep going. Pleased, they turned away from the river, skirting the dead bodies of the two dead CT, and continued advancing.

As they neared the centre of the swamp, they had to watch out for an increasing number of booby traps as well as guerrillas, who suddenly started appearing in the undergrowth just long enough to fire quick bursts from their M1 rifles and British tommy-guns before disappearing again. When this happened, the SAS troopers broke from their lengthy single file and fanned out across the *ulu* to form a broad cordon of two or four-man teams, from which the CT could not escape.

Aware that they were now boxed in on all sides, the CT responded by attempting a suicidal last-ditch stand. When the first of them jumped up from behind some foliage just ahead, firing his tommy-gun and wounding one SAS trooper, Kearney sent up a flare, indicating to the SAS and SF to the north exactly where the guerrillas were.

The CT sniper disappeared as quickly as he had materialised, but Tone switched to the M203 grenade-launcher on his M1 carbine and fired a 40-millimetre shell where the sniper had been, blowing the foliage to pieces and setting fire to the bark of a tree.

When the smoke cleared, the sniper's scorched, shredded body was revealed, broken and sprawled over a fallen tree trunk.

'Advance!' Kearney bawled, then he jumped up and ran, leaping over the dead guerrilla and racing on into the jungle, though safely at the half-crouch, with Bulldog, Marty and Tone close behind him. When another guerrilla appeared, taking aim with an M1 rifle, Bulldog fired his autoloader from the hip, three shots in quick succession, and the guerrilla was picked up and punched back into the shrubbery with half of his chin gone, his throat a bloody mess, and the bones of his chest exposed through the tears in his tunic.

He had hardly hit the ground when two more guerrillas jumped up to be despatched by a fusillade from Marty's SLR and Tone's M1 carbine. Tone then switched again to the grenade-launcher, firing on a trajectory that landed the grenade just beyond the men he had killed. The explosion was catastrophic, filling the air with flying foliage and setting fire to the trees, and Marty realised, even before the smoke had dispersed, that Tone had inadvertently set off another booby trap, probably some kind of landmine.

'Landmines!' Marty bawled. 'Booby traps!'

His warning was, however, too late for Trooper Gordon McPherson, who dived for the cover of a small sapling, shaking it enough to dislodge the mortar shell lodged loosely in its branches. Marty saw it falling and threw himself to the ground just in time to avoid the explosion. When the showering debris had settled down, he looked to the side and saw a severed leg pumping blood onto the green grass a dozen feet away. Jumping back to his feet, he saw the rest of Trooper McPherson – a leg here, an arm there. Realising that nothing could be done, resisting the urge to vomit, he raced on, attempting to catch up with Bulldog, almost directly ahead with Kearney and Tone close behind him.

By now the forest was filled with smoke and reeking of cordite, reverberating with the sounds of explosions and the screams of wounded or dying men. Dropping to one knee to replace his empty magazine, Marty almost choked in the smoke. Wiping tears from his eyes, he saw an SAS trooper tripping over a hidden rope, releasing a springing shaft with a wooden spear lashed to its tip. Impaled through the stomach, the soldier was punched violently backwards. He stared down in shock at the spear and almost collapsed, but was held up by the springing shaft. Screaming in agony, he died there on his feet, remaining that way, held upright even in death, as Marty jumped up and advanced again into the smouldering, smoke-obscured *ulu*.

Bulldog and Tone were advancing together at the half-crouch just ahead of Lieutenant Kearney when another guerrilla popped up from behind some undergrowth to take a shot at them. They dropped to the ground and the bullets whistled over their heads, but a second burst kicked up a line of spitting soil between them, making them roll apart.

The ground caved in under Tone and he disappeared from view, then burst out with a dreadful, anguished screaming.

Shocked, Marty released the pin on a fragmentation grenade and hurled it towards the guerrillas. He covered his ears while it exploded, sending foliage and loose soil spewing skyward, then he wriggled across to where Tone had disappeared and was still screaming dreadfully. Finding a hole in the ground – previously covered in a false surface raised on breakable supports – he looked down to see his friend writhing on a bed of wooden stakes that had been sharpened and then smeared with excrement to cause maximum damage.

'Punji pit!' Marty bawled like a madman, hardly recognising his own voice. 'Help! For God's sake!'

Kearney and Bulldog appeared out of swirling smoke to kneel beside Marty and look into the pit.

'Dear God!' Kearney exclaimed in horror.

Tone was still screaming at the bottom of the pit, shuddering helplessly as blood squirted around the spikes that had pierced his back and legs. A couple had gone all the way through, their tips protruding slightly from his chest and belly.

'Jesus Christ!' Bulldog whispered.

'We've got to get him out of there!' Marty shouted above the din of the continuing battle, feeling hysterical and unreal, having to fight to control himself. 'We can't let him—'

Rob Roy Burns and Rod O'Connor emerged from the swirling smoke and dropped to their knees beside Kearney and Bulldog.

'Cover us,' Kearney said. 'We've got to get Trooper Williams out of this pit, so I'm going down into it. Make sure no one gets near us.'

'Right, boss,' Bulldog replied, then pointed his index finger at Rob Roy Burns and the dark-eyed Rod O'Connor. 'Lay down covering fire with that Bren gun,' he said, 'and keep firing until we tell you to stop.'

'Will do,' O'Connor said. He unstrapped the L4A4 Bren gun from his Bergen, released the swivel-down bipod located under the barrel, mounted the weapon, slotted in the curved 300-round box magazine of .303 bullets, held the pistol grip just behind the trigger and aimed along the raised sights at the enemy positions in the undergrowth. When O'Connor saw the foliage shifting, he opened fire and kept firing, the gun making a sustained roaring sound. Bulldog then did the same with his autoloader, blasting the foliage to shreds, and Rob Roy joined in with his carbine.

'No,' Marty said to Kearney as the others were firing. 'Please, boss, let me do it. That's my best friend down there.'

Kearney stared thoughtfully at him for a second, then said, 'Right. I understand. But be careful down there.'

'Thanks, boss,' Marty said.

As Kearney turned away and joined the others, firing his Owen submachine-gun at any movement in the undergrowth, Marty put his SLR down, wriggled out of his webbing, then lowered his heavy Bergen to the ground. Freed of all encumbrances, he lay belly down on the grass, slithered backwards, and very carefully lowered himself into the punji pit, where Tone was still pinioned on the excrement-smeared wooden stakes. Tone had, however, stopped moving to prevent further physical damage. Now he was breathing heavily while staring up at Marty with anguished, terrified eyes.

With extreme care, Marty placed his feet between the stakes, steadied himself, then leaned over his sobbing friend. Pain and fear had made Tone almost unrecognisable. Blood was pouring profusely from the many wounds in his back and legs, from his chest and stomach, where some of the stakes had gone all the way through him. Seeing those wounds, Marty knew that his friend was doomed, but he still had to rescue him.

'This is going to hurt terribly,' Marty told him, 'but you'll just have to bear it.'

'Yes, mate. Oh, God!'

A mortar shell exploded near the men above, causing loose soil and foliage to rain down over Marty's head and fall on Tone's sweat-slicked, frightened face. When it finally settled, Marty checked that the men above were still firing their weapons – obviously unhurt, they were – then he took a deep breath, leaned over Tone and said, 'Okay, bite your lower lip. This'll hurt like hell.'

He took hold of Tone's shoulders and eased him up off the sharpened stakes. When Tone started screaming, Marty stopped being gentle and hauled him upright as fast as he could. Tone screamed even louder, his body quivering like a bowstring. When he was free of the stakes, he collapsed into Marty's embrace and clung, sobbing, to him.

'It's not over yet,' Marty said, 'and you can't let me down. Scream as much as you want, mate, but do what I tell you.' He glanced directly above him. Bulldog Bellamy was looking down. The others continued pouring gunfire into the forest where the guerrillas were lurking. 'Okay, Sarge,' Marty said to Bulldog. 'You've got to haul him up. It doesn't matter how much it hurts him, nor how much he screams – you've just got to do it.' Still holding Tone in his arms, he whispered, 'You scream as much as you want, mate, but try to climb out of here. Okay, let's do it.'

Marty released Tone and patted him on the cheek. Tone just stood there, swaying, his feet between the punji stakes, his back and legs pouring blood, a dazed look in his eyes.

'Yes, mate,' he croaked.

'Raise your hands as high as you can,' Marty told him. Tone did as he was told. Bulldog grabbed his hands, glanced at Marty, received his nod and started pulling Tone up. Tone screamed like an animal, being torn apart by pain, but Marty pushed as Bulldog pulled, and eventually Tone was out of the pit, face down on the ground.

Though no longer screaming, he was sobbing like a child, helplessly, shamelessly, hardly aware of himself. Turning towards him, Kearney gently stroked the back of his head and said, 'We've got to leave you now, Trooper. We can't casevac you yet. We'll call in a chopper the minute this is over, but in the meantime you'll just have to endure it. There's no more we can do.'

'The pain!' Tone groaned and started sobbing again. 'Ah, God, the pain!'

'I'm going to give you some morphine,' Marty told him, reaching into his Bergen for his medical kit. 'That's all we can do for now.'

'Yes, Marty.' Tone screamed again. 'Oh, Jesus! Please God!'

The number and depth of the wounds, combined with the excrement left in them from the stakes, had already convinced Marty that his friend could not survive. Nevertheless, he put him out of his pain by injecting him with morphine, smeared the areas between the wounds with river mud, which would help to keep away the insects, and finally covered him with a waterproof poncho.

'Right,' he said, speaking loudly against the roaring of the combined weapons of the other men. 'Sorry, Tone, but we have to go on now. We'll be back for you soon.'

'No, Marty,' Tone begged him, still face down in the grass because he couldn't possibly lie on his damaged back. 'The guerrillas might pass through here. Please God, Marty, you know what they might do if they . . .'

He didn't have to say more. Marty removed his own nine-millimetre Browning High Power handgun from its holster and laid it on the grass by Tone's fingers, so he could shoot himself – join the 'Exit Club' – should the guerrillas find him still alive.

'Okay, Tone, good luck.'

Rod O'Connor stopped firing the Bren gun and turned around to glance first at the sobbing Tone, then at Marty. 'We just leave him?' he asked, his dark eyes flashing with outrage.

'We've no choice,' Kearney told him. 'Now get up and advance to the north and don't look back, Trooper.'

'Yes, boss,' O'Connor replied. He turned away, clearly fighting to control himself, and said, 'Okay, Rob Roy. Let's pick up this fucker and go get the rest of those bastards. Are you set?'

'Yes,' Rob Roy said. 'Let's put an end to this shit.'

As O'Connor picked up the Bren gun and slid it under his right arm, holding it like a rifle and firing from the waist, Rob Roy stood up, switched his M1 to the grenade-launcher, inserted a 40-millimetre shell, then fired it at the undergrowth straight ahead. When the shell exploded, tearing the foliage apart, setting some of it on fire and filling the area with smoke, he and the others raced on at the half-crouch, leaving Tone to his fate.

Determined not to show his tears, Marty raced on ahead with Bulldog coming up just behind him. Now that his radio operator, Roy Weatherby, was dead, Kearney was stumbling along in the rear with the heavy PRC 320 radio set. When a flare exploded over the *ulu* to the north, indicating that the other SAS and SF troops had made contact with the enemy, the men knew that they were close to the CT camp.

As if magically protected by the anger and grief caused by what had happened to his best friend, Marty raced on ahead, taking point but, suicidally, crashing through the undergrowth, firing his SLR from the hip, lobbing hand grenades at anything that moved, and running into the blinding smoke like a man both invisible and untouchable. He managed to kill a lot of guerrillas – but no one touched him.

Eventually arriving at a narrow track that sloped downhill into a low, sheltered area, he suspected that the CT might be down there, preparing to make their last stand. Even as he was thinking this, a guerrilla stepped out from behind a tree below and took aim with a British tommy-gun. Without stopping his advance, Marty opened fire with his SLR, swinging it in an arc, cutting across the guerrilla, throwing him into convulsions, practically lifting him off his feet and slamming him backwards into the undergrowth.

'Good man,' Kearney said breathlessly behind him. 'Now, are the rest of them down there or not?'

'I think they're down there,' Marty replied.

'Then let's go and get them.'

They advanced down the hill and through the trees at the bottom as the other SF advanced from the north, boxing the terrorists in. Filled with cold rage as he advanced on the guerrillas, Marty marched boldly through the smoke, firing at anything moving in front of him, while Bulldog, right beside him, used his twelve-gauge to shoot snipers out of the trees, blowing branches and leaves apart, and Kearney alternated between talking into the radio and firing short, killing bursts from his Owen submachine-gun.

When a female guerrilla suddenly appeared in front of Marty, swinging a *parang* that was, he noticed, still dripping blood, he ducked and weaved, backing away, instinctively trying not to fire at her. Then, while ducking, he caught a nightmarish glimpse of a man's head sitting upright on the ground, the eyes flicking frantically from left to right, fresh blood gushing out around its neck – the severed head of Rob Roy Burns.

Rage suddenly flared through Marty, obliterating all reason, making him stand upright to fire his SLR at close range into the woman's frail body – repeated bursts of semi-automatic fire that nearly cut her in two. She screamed and staggered backwards, dropping the *parang*, then collapsed to her knees, appeared to be bowing, then coughed blood and fell face down in the mud.

Marty didn't bother checking that she was dead: he just walked right over her and kept firing his SLR until someone, Bulldog, grabbed his arm and jerked him back, bawling, 'Stop it, Butler! It's all over! We've done it! The rest of the CT are surrendering. Go back and check on your friend!'

Jerked back to reality, though still feeling feverish, Marty glanced in disbelief at the dead bodies, male and female, Chinese and SAS, that were littering the muddy ground. Then he saw the last of the guerrillas raising their hands in surrender as smoke swirled across the jungle clearing and SF men closed in on them from both sides. Not wanting to see more, with only one thought in mind, he turned away and raced back up the hill, then back through the *ulu*, not stopping until he reached the place where he and the others had left Tone, lying on his belly, sobbing, with the Browning High Power handgun in his right hand.

Marty stopped when he came to that spot, then he turned cold all over.

Tone was still there, face down on the ground, exactly as Marty had left him. But he had placed the Browning High Power to his temple and blown his own brains out.

Marty knelt in the grass, held his dead friend in his arms, and closed his eyes to stop himself from crying as grief convulsed him. He remained that way, devastated and disbelieving, until Paddy Kearney and Bulldog Bellamy arrived to offer what comfort they could. They were with him when Tone was carried away and they stayed with him a long time.

Marty wanted to cry, but no tears fell as he marched out of the swamp.

Big boys don't cry, he thought.

BOOK THREE

THE PROFESSIONALS

31 JANUARY 1991

He checked his wristwatch, annoyed that his friend was late, then he smiled at his awareness of his own impatience, putting it down to his old age. You could never prepare for ageing, the acceleration of passing time, the sudden, dramatic shrinking of your horizons as the body destroyed itself. Why was he doing this? They were both too old for it. Why did he not simply sit back and let time do the job for him? His friend's time was running short as well, so why all the urgency? Why kill him today?

(*It's a matter of principles between two men who once had them. That's what this is about, my friend.*)

His friend, still in that big house, preparing for the new day, was a man whose principles could not accommodate compromise and had finally led him over the edge, into the abyss. He was a man of honour, of strongly held beliefs, who had not been able to deal with a world that was not of his making. An imperfect world. A vale of tears and vice. He had seen the rising tide of all that he loathed and feared and then taken it upon himself to hold the tide back. In doing so he had gone beyond the pale and marched into the dark lands, his principles still extant but perverted, his vision distorted.

You went too far, the old man thought as he gazed across the road, trying to see through the walls of the big house and look into his friend's eyes.

(*You used your finely honed, deadly skills without just cause or sanction. You thought you had a cause, a moral right, but you were terribly wrong. What you did, what you are doing, is criminal and it has to be stopped. That's why I am here.*)

Why had he done it? The old man thought he knew. The first victim was a signals expert, a former SAS sergeant, who had gone to work for Plessey on the System X digital communications system. The second victim had been employed at the Plessey Naval Systems at Addlestone on another digital communications project. Seven more victims had also worked for Plessey and the remaining two had been working at the Royal Military College of Science at Shrivenham in Oxfordshire. There had to be a connection. That connection was the fact that all of those scientists were working on top-secret defence-related projects that he believed would ultimately be sold to repressive regimes. In the end, he couldn't tolerate that and decided to put a stop to it. Because of that, eleven decent men died – and they did not commit suicide.

(*It had to be you – you and your quietly spoken friend. You would have done it together.*)

He closed his eyes and visualised them arriving in Oxfordshire, driving on to Shrivenham, then using their old identity cards to get them into the grounds of the Royal Military College of Science. Once in, they drove to the parking lot and parked the car in a position that gave them good surveillance of the building's entrance. They had a photo of the senior metallurgist who was working on the electronic warfare system and they identified him from it when he emerged from the establishment at the end of a routine working day. When he drove home, they followed him. Then, to ensure that they had the right man, they checked his address against his name in the local telephone directory. Satisfied from this and the photo that they had the right man, they spent the next few days in a surveillance of the house, ascertaining the routine of its occupants and working out the best way of neutralising their victim and making his death look like suicide.

It would have been relatively simple, though exactly how it was done would never be known. The metallurgist was found dead under his car in his closed garage, his mouth aligned with the car's exhaust pipe. He was known as a man who liked to maintain his own car, so they had either waited until he entered his garage and followed him in or had actually taken him in against his will. They had forced him to lie under his car, as if working on it, with his mouth against the exhaust pipe; then they had turned the ignition on and remained there, well away from the vehicle, until he slipped into unconsciousness. Either way, they would have had little trouble in neutralising their victim and making it look like a suicide.

The old man found it hard to accept, but he knew that that's what had happened, one way or the other.

(*How could you have gone that far? And even that wasn't far enough. You took it farther*. Too *far*.)

Ignoring that first warning by the Association, the Military College of Science continued with its electronic warfare defence project. Another victim was called for. This time the Association went higher up, targeting the head of the work-study group that was part of the programme. This man, a mature man, was given a pistol for self-defence, but he may have been uncomfortable with it, as he kept it in the boot of the car, not the glove department.

They would have watched him and waited. The pistol wouldn't have bothered them. They would have seen, from their patient surveillance, that the man had a yacht and that he often took it out at weekends, driving to the harbour in Folkstone in his MG sports car. Knowing that made it easy.

Though the old man could only speculate, he thought he knew what had happened.

The victim left his house and got into his MG sports car, intending to go to work as usual. As he was driving along an empty side road, another car, expertly driven, harassed him so much that he must have known it was deliberate. He tried to elude the other car, but it deliberately hit him broadside, damaging his sports car, and in the end he was forced to pull into the roadside, just in front of the other car.

A man climbed out of the other car, approached the sports car and ordered the frightened scientist, at gunpoint, to do what he was told. He then slipped into the passenger seat, resting the handgun on his lap, and told the scientist to follow the other car all the way to Folkstone.

The scientist did as he was told. The two cars arrived at Folkstone. They parked at the harbour and the scientist, at gunpoint, was ordered out of his car and onto his yacht. The yacht was taken out to sea, to where another boat was waiting, almost certainly a large inflatable, and the scientist was despatched with a double-tap and left where he was lying. His executioners placed a remote-controlled HE bomb on the yacht and then quickly transferred to the inflatable, which immediately took them out to where they could safely use the button job. The yacht was blown up, its debris widely scattered, and then the executioners were spirited away in the inflatable, leaving no trace behind them.

(*The same inflatables that were used in the Falklands. Your friends could have arranged that.*)

He gazed across the road, at that wealthy man's home, and wondered at the distance the man in that house had travelled to get where he was now. He had travelled a straight road for a very long time and detoured onto a crooked highway only at the very last moment. The problem being that once he had made that detour he could never turn back.

(*Since you can't turn back, you have to be stopped . . . and I have to do it.*)

He sat patiently, staring across the road with his failing eyesight, waiting for his best friend to emerge and end it for both of them.

He had lots to think about.

CHAPTER SEVENTEEN

'Welcome to the crumbling estate,' Paddy Kearney said, grinning, stepping aside to let Marty and Ann Lim enter the darkly varnished hallway of his house near Peterchurch in Hereford. It was a rather grand house with oak panelling, tinted-glass windows, a variety of carpets on the floors, old paintings on all the walls, and rooms of a size that Marty had never seen before.

'It's not as posh as it looks,' Paddy added, obviously sensing Marty's discomfiture. 'It really is falling to pieces and we can't afford to maintain it. Some family inheritances a man can do without, but we must shoulder tradition.'

'It's beautiful,' Ann Lim said, meaning it.

'So are you,' Paddy replied. 'Fortunately, you're a lot younger than the house – and, if I may say so, much better maintained. Your husband's a lucky man.' Marty glanced at his wife and saw her hesitant smile. 'So,' Paddy continued, turning towards the broad staircase, 'let me show you to your room, then you can have a bath and come down for a couple of drinks before we have dinner. Angela's doing some last-minute shopping, but she'll be back fairly soon. Did you have any problem getting here?'

'No,' Marty replied. 'Malvern's practically next door, after all. We got here in no time.'

'Well, you won't be at Malvern much longer.'

'So I've heard,' Marty said.

The Sabre Squadrons of 22 SAS had come to Britain from Malaya earlier in the year, but to Merebrook Camp at Malvern in Worcestershire, instead of the Parachute Regiment's Depot in Aldershot in Surrey. However, early next year they would move into their own base at Bradbury Lines in Hereford.

'Living here,' Marty said as they reached the top of the stairs and he and Ann Lim followed Paddy along the landing, 'I suppose it's handy for getting to the new base.'

'Lucky me.' Paddy opened a door and ushered Marty and Ann Lim into what was, to Marty, an exceptionally large bedroom with a double bed, Victorian furnishings, heavy curtains and tall windows overlooking the expansive gardens at the rear. 'All right?' he asked.

'It's wonderful,' Ann Lim said with an admiring smile as her eyes took in the room. 'So this is how the English live!'

'The English aristocracy,' Marty corrected her.

'Irish aristocracy,' Paddy reminded him. 'We just happen to live in England, that's all. Our roots go back to the bogs. Anyway, why don't you both freshen up and come down for a drink?'

'Do we have to dress formally for dinner?' Marty asked, feeling self-conscious.

Paddy grinned. 'No.' He spread his hands in the air and glanced down the length of his own body, indicating his informal clothes. 'We dress like this,' he said. 'We only dress up for proper dinners and tonight there's no one coming but you. Now tomorrow evening – that's different. Slightly more formal.'

'What's slightly more formal?' Marty asked, feeling even more nervous.

'Stop worrying, Marty. No need for a bow-tie or dinner jacket. Just a normal suit and tie. Even when being formal, we're not *that* formal, so stop looking terrified.' He turned to Ann Lim. 'Your husband's faced dangers you can't possibly imagine and done so without batting an eyelid. But, when it comes to the trivialities of daily life, he starts falling to pieces. I trust you're not the same.'

'No,' Ann Lim said. 'I'm not.'

'Good. Glad to hear it. I'm sure you'll take care of him.' He grinned again at Marty. 'So get cleaned up and then come on down, wearing your glad rags. I'll be there with a glass in my hand. See you soon. *Au revoir*.'

He bowed slightly and left the room, closing the door behind him. Ann Lim sat on the bed, bounced up and down, then smiled like a satisfied cat. 'Mmmm,' she said. 'Wonderful.'

'The bed?'

'Yes, the bed. Did you think I meant your friend?'

'He's a good friend.'

'Your superior officer, Marty.'

'My superior officer *and* a good friend. It works that way in the regiment.'

'Yet you don't seem comfortable with him.'

'It's his place,' Marty confessed. 'I knew that Paddy came from an upper-class background, but I tended to forget it when with the regiment. I mean, we seemed the same somehow. He was an officer and I was an other ranker, but both of us wore the same uniform and had the same aims. Now, seeing him in civilian clothes, in this place, makes it different somehow. I'm reminded that we come from different backgrounds and that makes me uncomfortable.'

'Why? You come from a good background as well. Just poorer, that's all.'

Marty smiled at her, pleased by what she had said. She had met his parents and liked them a lot and they had liked her. Now he understood why. 'Yes,' he said. 'That's true, but I still feel out of place. I'm not ashamed of being working-class and I'm really fond of Paddy, but I can't help being reminded by this place that we come from different worlds.'

'That's an English vice, Marty.'

'Yes, I guess so.' She was still sitting on the bed, wearing a short woollen coat over a knee-length dress buttoned down the front – like the dress she had worn when he first walked with her, then possessed her, on that beach in Penang. Her superb legs, in nylon stockings, were crossed and, as usual, enthralled him. He walked to the bed and sat beside her, then bent down to kiss her knees. He worshipped her knees. 'I love you,' he said.

'Yes, darling, I know. I love you, too.' She stroked the back of his head while he kept his lips on her knee, sucking it, licking it, kissing it, his manner at once playful and sensual, rooted deeply in yearning. 'Paddy Kearney really likes you. There's no doubt about it. The differences in your backgrounds don't matter. That man is your friend.' She tightened her fingers in his hair, then gently tugged it, making him raise his head until he was looking up at her warm smile. 'Now I have to freshen up with a bath, so please get away from me. Please let me stand up. Either that or come and have the bath with me.'

'I just might do that,' Marty said, grinning, raising himself from his knees, then standing upright and starting to take off his clothes. 'Yes, darlin', why not?'

They had it together, enjoying themselves, facing each other from opposite ends of the bath, their legs intertwined. Naked, Ann Lim was perfection, at least to Marty's eyes, her skin golden instead of white, her breasts small but firm, her waist tapering down to round hips and long, shapely legs. Even her hands and feet had a delicacy that greatly appealed to him.

'What's it like to be pregnant?' he asked her.

'It's exciting,' she said.

Marty smiled again. Though Ann Lim knew that he had two children by his previous marriage, she had insisted that they have their own child as soon as possible. 'To bond our love,' as she put it. Recalling those words, Marty realised that the baby due to be born five months from now, after a very long wait – indeed they had thought they might not have one – was not only a child of love but of singular passion. The love-making between him and Ann Lim had been uninhibited in ways that would have seemed inconceivable to Lesley. Indeed, in marrying Ann Lim, he felt that he had opened the door to another way of life, one in which certain English constraints had little place. Though Ann Lim's father had tried to turn his daughters into English women, he had failed, at least with Ann Lim. She was proud to be Chinese, still wore colourful *cheongsams*, was not at all thrilled by the British weather, and often admitted that she missed Malaya, now Malaysia, a lot. He wasn't upset by this confession, understanding perfectly. He missed Malaysia as well.

When they had finished bathing, they dried each other down and started dressing for dinner.

'You really like him?' Marty asked, meaning Paddy Kearney.

'Yes,' Ann Lim assured him. 'I like him and I think he's your friend, so stop worrying about him.'

'He warned me about marrying you.'

'I know. You told me. But he only warned you because he knew it would be difficult – and that's what friends are for.'

Not as difficult as it might have been, Marty thought as he dressed himself. A few problems here and there, a few embarrassments, but here we are, still married. Love conquers all.

After coming out of that hellish swamp near Selangor, in 1952, nearly seven years ago, he had alternated between more patrols into the *ulu* with short breaks back in Penang, usually staying in a hotel where he and Ann Lim could make love, though often visiting her house in Tanjong Tokong, attempting to win over her father.

He didn't have to work at it. Ann Lim's father, Lee Kong, had started life in Singapore as little more than a coolie, without the benefit of formal education, but he had worked like hell to educate himself and rise above his station. A successful exporter for the British rubber planters, even after what he had suffered during the war, he was, though lacking in arrogance, quietly proud of himself and admiring of other men of initiative. When he learned about Marty's background – working for his father, starting his own business, fighting in North Africa and Malaya – he viewed him as one of his own kind. More importantly, because he was without a male heir, he had subconsciously adopted Marty as his own, bringing him into the fold.

Subsequently, when Ann Lim's two sisters had flown off to Paris to attend finishing school, Ann Lim was allowed to remain in Penang and become engaged to Marty. A few months later, Marty went to see Paddy Kearney – recently promoted back to his original rank of Captain to get official permission for the marriage.

'You must be mad,' Captain Kearney bluntly told him. 'These mixed marriages rarely work. You've just been promoted to corporal; let that be your reward. Go back to England alone,

Corporal Butler, and find yourself a nice English girl. You'll be better off that way.'

'I want to marry her, sir.'

'It's ill-advised and the Army officially disapproves of it, which is no help at all. Believe me, I have nothing against the woman – I have met her, as you know, and found her charming – but the odds against the marriage working are considerable. Racism is a fact of life. It also exists in the services, and careers can be blunted by mixed marriages. Don't do it, Corporal.'

'I want to marry her, sir.'

'I strongly disapprove.'

'I'm not here for approval, sir. I'm here for your permission.'

'You've always been a hard-head, Butler, and you know you don't need my permission when push comes to shove.'

'Your informal permission, sir, would be a great help when it comes to push-and-shove with officialdom.'

'I'm surprised you can pronounce that word, Corporal, but you *can* state that you have my permission and I'll arrange all the relevant paperback *vis-à-vis* the Army. Good luck to both of you.'

Marty had wanted to have Captain Kearney as his best man, but service protocol dictated otherwise. Instead, the former 'bad boy', Rod O'Connor, now an excellent SAS corporal, though one still prone to troublemaking, was best man in a ceremony that took place in an English church in Penang, attended by a beaming Lee Kong, his two daughters, Mary and Kathy, who had flown in from Paris just for the occasion, a few of Ann Lim's friends, both English and Chinese Malays, and a lot of Marty's grinning SAS mates. The wedding ceremony was followed by a noisy, drunken reception in George Town's Broadway Bar, which Marty had taken over for the day. The honeymoon was two weeks in Kuala Lumpur, then Ann Lim moved into an army house on the mainland and Marty went back into the *ulu* for more dangerous patrols. A few months later, when he was shipped back to Aldershot, Ann Lim went with him.

The following years had been divided between tours in Malaysia and boring periods back in Aldershot, doing practically nothing. Ann Lim had endured his many absences with stoicism and surrounded him with love when he returned. They had a good, strong relationship.

'Are you ready to go down?' Ann Lim asked as Marty slipped his jacket on over an open-necked shirt, suddenly realising, from what he saw in the mirror, that he would soon be thirty-eight years old: no longer a young man.

'As ready as I'll ever be,' he replied as he turned to face her. She was wearing a simple cotton dress that exposed her throat and shoulders, clung to her curves, fell to just below the knees and was buttoned down the front. She was also wearing high-heeled shoes and had her long black hair hanging loose. Though dressed informally, she looked like a dream and brought a lump to Marty's throat. He slipped his arms around her waist, kissed her, then stepped back and smiled at her, still holding her hand. 'Let's go,' he said.

They left the room and went down the broad stairs to begin their weekend.

The following evening, just after midnight, when the rest of the guests had left and the two wives had retired to their separate bedrooms, the two soldiers sat in Paddy's dimly lit study, drinking brandy and puffing on cigars. Marty didn't normally smoke cigars, but he was enjoying this one.

Despite his initial nervousness, the weekend had been almost perfect, beginning with the introduction to Paddy's wife, Angela, whom neither Marty nor Ann Lim had ever met before. Always thinking of Paddy as being a dashing man, Marty had assumed that his wife would be some kind of sophisticated beauty. In fact, she had turned out to be a plump and homely woman who looked older than her thirty-nine years, the same age as her husband. She did, however, have a warm and ebullient personality that made Marty and Ann Lim like her instantly.

The children, two boys and a girl, had turned out to be as pleasant as their parents. Any other doubts Marty might have been harbouring about the weekend, mostly based on his unease with people not of the working classes, had been put to rest when Paddy proved to be a generous host with the drink, pouring it almost non-stop from the minute his guests came down the stairs to join him in the kitchen, which was, he said, his favourite place in the house.

'Kitchens and booze go together,' he said. 'You can put a lot of bottles on a kitchen table and not feel guilty about it.'

Angela Kearney had arrived home a couple of drinks later, flushed and pleasantly flustered because her shopping had taken longer than expected and she felt bad about not greeting her guests.

'At least it gave Paddy a head start on the drinking,' she pointed out, 'so I bet *he* was pleased!'

After that it was plain sailing. The first afternoon was spent in the kitchen, where Angela prepared the dinner with Ann Lim's help, both of them drinking wine as they worked and as the men, also drinking with relish, sat at the table. Dinner was served after they had all gone for a brief, brisk walk in the surrounding Hereford countryside.

The dinner, just for the four of them, took up the rest of the evening and ended in the enormous living room, where brandy was poured and the air soon thickened with cigar and cigarette smoke. Some time after midnight, back in their guest bedroom, Marty and Ann Lim had made love in a drunken haze that may have diminished Marty's capabilities but did not dim the pleasure for either of them.

The following morning, after a leisurely breakfast of eggs, bacon, fried mushrooms and toast, all washed down with cups of hot tea, the four of them went for another long walk, this time ending up at Paddy's local pub, where clearly he and Angela were well known. Two more hours were passed in the pub, then, pleasantly drunk, the four of them walked back to the house where they had a light snack, went to their separate bedrooms for an afternoon snooze, then awakened to bath and dress more formally for dinner that evening.

At the dinner Marty and Ann Lim met some of the people they had met earlier in the pub. As Paddy had promised, dress was not formal, though most of the women were dressed up for the occasion and all of the men at least wore shirts with ties. The dinner made for Marty's only uncomfortable time because although the other guests were friendly enough – and were, indeed, soon drunk and rumbustious, which seemed natural in this house – they struck Marty as being well educated, sophisticated, and certainly middle-class.

They also reminded him once more that Paddy, though now his esteemed friend, had been born in this grand house, educated at Cambridge, and moved in society with the kind of ease that Marty would never attain. This in turn reminded him that, even though Paddy had adopted him in North Africa, helped him become a first-rate soldier, and now treated him as a personal friend, officers and the lower ranks did not usually mix socially and were not normally encouraged to do so. There were, as Marty knew, sound reasons for this, most notably the need for pragmatic judgement on the part of an officer giving orders to those under his command; so Marty, a soldier to his fingertips, though enjoying his midnight brandy and cigar, still felt a little uneasy.

'Well,' Paddy said, exhaling a cloud of cigar smoke and looking quite mellow, 'Ann Lim certainly seems like a happy woman. The marriage must be working out.'

'It is,' Marty replied.

'Despite my grim warnings.'

'Offered with the best of intentions. Ann Lim told me so herself, so it must be true.'

'You told her I tried to talk you out of it?'

'Yes. Just yesterday, in fact. She said you were concerned for both of us and spoke as a friend.'

'Sensible woman.'

'She is that.'

'Did you, in fact, have any problems?'

Marty sighed. 'It would probably have been worse if she'd been black, but being Chinese . . . Well, it wasn't so bad. The odd shitty remark here and there, a few friends lost, but nothing too difficult to handle. The friends we now have are the friends we're going to keep, so that makes up for all of it.'

Paddy was silent for a moment, studying the ceiling, exhaling cigar smoke. 'What about the SAS?' he asked eventually. 'Any problems there?'

'Not really. Again, the odd remark, usually from a resentful crap-hat; rarely from one of the Originals. Also, the occasional veiled threat from some Rupert – usually about the hindrance my Chinese wife could be when it came to promotion. But invariably it was a Rupert doing his first three years and not about to qualify for another. *That* kind of officer. Apart from that, no real problems. The English are starting to eat Chinese food, so maybe that helps.'

Paddy chuckled. 'Who knows? Food, like music, doesn't require a common language and can certainly cross a lot of frontiers. So maybe you're right.'

'Let's hope so,' Marty said. 'They could do with it in Civvy Street. At least in the SAS we know what winning hearts and minds means. We're taught to understand foreign cultures and find the value in them. That's why being married to Ann Lim has caused few SAS heads to turn: they're more inclined to respect her for what she is. They see her purely as a beautiful bint, which makes them envy me instead of resenting me. If you learn to live with Malays and Chinese and the Sakai, you're not likely to stay a racist for long. That's one of the strengths of the SAS and it's one that I'm proud of.'

Paddy shook his head from side to side, smiling as if at a private joke. 'What an honourable man you are, Marty.'

'You think so?'

'Yes. In some ways I think you're the most honourable man I've ever met. You don't think about it, you haven't reasoned it out; you'd probably even deny that you're that way – but believe me, you are. You're a man of strong principles, my friend, and you don't even know it.'

'I don't think I'm like that at all.'

'There you are – you're denying it.'

'I'm not denying it – I'm just saying I'm not like that. I mean, I'm not all that honourable. I'm just a working-class lad, for Christ's sake, who loves the regiment and wants to stay in it, so I do what I have to do.'

'No, you do more. You operate by strict principles. You're almost puritanical in your attitude to the regiment. You demand and expect a lot.'

'I think a man should give his best.'

'And you despise men who don't.'

'I think that's pretty normal,' Marty said.

'It's bloody unusual,' Paddy said. He inhaled on his cigar, held the smoke in for a moment, savouring it, then blew it out in a series of smoke rings, which he watched dissolving slowly in the air. 'Someday,' he said quietly, 'your principles are going to get you into trouble.'

'Oh? How come?'

'We must always weigh our principles against expediency,' Paddy said, 'and that's something you still haven't learned.'

'I don't know what you mean, boss.'

Paddy chuckled. '"Crap-hats" for RTUs or members of the Regular Army, "Ruperts" for officers, and "boss" instead of "sir". The SAS is creating its own language as well as new ways of waging war.'

'It sure is,' Marty said. 'I mean, take the word "basha". At first it meant a waterproof shelter made from a poncho, but now it can also be a barrack room, a house, a bed – in fact, anywhere you can lay your head down. Of course, the best place to lay your head down is in the spider, which is the name recently given to the barracks because most barracks have eight legs – the dormitory areas – running off their central section. So, you know, you can now basha down in your spider and go to sleep muttering insults about crap-hats, the greens – that's regular Army soldiers, of course – Ruperts and even the Head Sheds.'

'What on earth's a Head Shed?' Paddy asked.

'A senior officer, not just a common Rupert,' Marty told him with glee. 'You want to hear more, boss?'

Paddy chuckled. 'No, thanks.'

'So since I'm drunkenly talking to a bloody Rupert and Head Shed, what did you mean when you said that I have to learn to weigh my principles against expediency? I'm confused, boss. I really am.'

Paddy remained silent for some time, as if deciding whether or not to reply

'Well?' Marty asked eventually, now requiring an answer.

Paddy sighed. 'Remember that swamp in Malaya? Not the Telok Anson swamp of last year. The first one – the one near Selangor – nearly six years ago?'

'Yes,' Marty said. 'Hell on earth. I still have bloody awful dreams about it. But what about principles against expediency? I had no principles then.'

'Yes, you did,' Paddy said. 'And they almost got you killed. A female guerrilla came at you with a *parang* and you couldn't bring yourself to shoot her, even though she was hell bent on killing you.'

'I killed her,' Marty said, not wanting to remember. 'I emptied my SLR into her. Damned near chopped her in two.'

'That was the second time,' Paddy reminded him. 'The attack that took place after your friend Tone Williams fell into a punji pit and Rob Roy had his head sliced off by the same *parang* that woman was swinging at you. You were mad by that time. You were practically out of your mind. But even then you hesitated – I saw you: you backed off – and it was only when you saw Rob Roy's severed head that you went over the edge. You killed that particular woman in a blind fury. In other words, you lost control.'

'That's true,' Marty admitted. 'I lost control and I've never forgotten it. It won't happen again. So what about the first time?'

'The first time you were attacked by a woman swinging a *parang*, you didn't defend yourself at all. If Taff Hughes hadn't shot her in the head, you would have been dead.'

'True enough,' Marty said. 'That cold-blooded little bastard saved my life. But I'm still not sure what point you're trying to make.'

'The point I'm making, Marty, is that when the first woman attacked you, your damned principles about not hurting a woman nearly cost you your life. More importantly, your inability to sacrifice your principles to do what was necessary could have cost the lives of some of your friends. The point I'm also making, Marty, is that when the second woman attacked you, your principles made you back away – which was wrong – and then you only did what you had to do when you lost your head, which also was wrong. In both cases, then, you failed to weigh your principles against expediency and instead, in both cases, behaved irrationally.'

'I accept that,' Marty said.

'Principles, my friend, are all well and good – but not when they become a danger to yourself and your friends. The final arbiter for the soldier is pragmatism. Don't ever forget that. You're too emotional, Marty. Maybe too puritanical. Those are virtues that could turn into vices and make you destructive. I hope that never happens.'

'It won't,' Marty said.

Paddy was silent for a moment, then he asked in a hesitant manner, 'You still have nightmares about that operation?'

'Yes,' Marty said. 'Even years after the event. The Telok Anson swamp was even worse, but the Selangor swamp was the first. It was also where we lost Tone and Rob Roy, so that's the one that I dream about.'

'It was a nightmarish operation,' Paddy conceded. 'No doubt about it. It was there that I first realised that the nature of war was going to change and that a civilised war, the kind we mostly fought in North Africa, was a thing of the past. Wars are going to be much dirtier in the future and we'll have to adapt to that.'

Marty knew what he meant. Even seven years after that patrol into the Selangor swamp, he found himself having nightmares about it and often pondered, during the day, on the difference between it and the war in North Africa. There, the war had indeed been a gentleman's war, with each side respecting the other, even on an individual basis such as the treatment of POWs. It was a war that took place out in the open, in the vast desert plains, usually in brilliant sunshine, and this may have helped the men on both sides to remain civilised.

Unfortunately, the same could not be said for the Malayan jungle where, in water and mud, in gloom and humidity, with an extraordinary variety of venomous wildlife, in scenery suggestive of man's primordial origins, the human soul may have been driven back in upon itself, to its most primitive and ignorantly cruel nature. Certainly the war in Malaya, particularly in the swamps, had been one of the most ingenious cruelties and unremitting squalor. It haunted Marty even now and would not let him go.

Tone's death had not helped. Nor had having to tell his wife. She had, of course, been informed officially, but Marty, when he returned to England, had felt obliged as Tone's best friend to go and see her. He had lied through his teeth, saying that Tone had died quickly, but he believed that what she saw in his eyes had told her all she needed to know.

'Thanks,' she had said. 'It was kind of you to try. But it's all in the past now. Goodbye, Marty. Good luck.'

Though Marty never talked about the hideous death of his best friend – the dreadful agony of the punji pit, followed by the Exit Club, or suicide – nor about the wide, seemingly terrified eyes of the severed head of Rob Roy Burns, those recollections were never far from his thoughts and they had, he knew, changed him for all time.

'Well,' Marty said thoughtfully, licking brandy off his lips and studying the glowing tip of his cigar, 'at least we learned a lot in those bloody swamps. Those lessons will be put to good use in the future, so we have that to thank them for.'

'True enough,' Paddy said, puffing another cloud of smoke. 'And that particular kind of conflict – counter-insurgency – will become more common in the future. In fact, the future of the SAS was clearly mapped out in Malaya. We mustn't forget that.'

'I won't,' Marty said. 'And I won't forget to weigh my principles against expediency. You have my word on it.'

Paddy smiled, finished his brandy and placed his empty glass on the low table between them. He also stubbed his cigar out in the ashtray and stood up to stretch himself.

'Did you have a nice weekend?' he asked.

'Terrific,' Marty said.

'I knew you were a bit nervous at first, wondering what you'd let yourself in for. That's due to your working-class background, but you'll have to learn to get over that.'

'So Ann Lim told me. I suppose I was also worried about her and your middle-class friends. My lack of breeding *and* my Chinese wife. Yes, I think I was nervous. But it was great. It really was.'

Paddy grinned, yawned, glanced at his wristwatch, then looked into the middle distance as if his thoughts were far away. 'Ann Lim's separated from the British by race,' he said. 'You and I, no matter how deep our friendship, are helplessly separated by class. And I, Marty, with all of my inherited wealth, am separated from the England I love by the fact that, although I'm a bit of an aristocrat, I'm also Irish. The world's a bloody mess, right?'

'It's all bullshit,' Marty replied, using that word now so popular with the SAS. 'Which is why I love the lack of distinction between rank or class in the regiment. There's no bullshit there.'

'Amen to that,' Paddy said.

CHAPTER EIGHTEEN

The following year Marty, promoted to sergeant, attended the opening of Bradbury Lines in Hereford as the official SAS training and administrative base. Wearing his full uniform, his badged beret, and the decorations he had received for service in North Africa and Malaya, he was proud to take part in the formal opening ceremony, but also felt regret that he would now be spending most of his time, at least for the foreseeable future, training new recruits instead of taking part in active service.

Later, when the ceremony was over, he joined the others in the informal celebrations in the bar, to which friends and relatives had also been invited and where the officers mixed freely with the NCOs and other ranks.

As Ann Lim had given birth a week ago to a son, Ian, delighting Marty, she was compelled to remain at home and look after him. Marty was, however, pleased that his parents had come down from London and was amused by the excitement his ageing father, in particular, showed when introduced to some of the SAS men he had heard so much about. Marty's mother, on the other hand, though not interested in soldiering, could not resist what she clearly viewed as a glamorous event and was particularly charmed when Captain Kearney said, 'Just call me Paddy', and talked to her for a good part of the evening.

Even having alternated for years between Malaya and England, Taff Hughes, now also a sergeant, had remained blue-eyed, blond-haired and impossibly young for his age, retaining a kind of distracted innocence that belied his ferocious killer's instincts. However, even Marty, who could never forget just how ruthless Taff was in battle, was surprised at how attentive he was to his parents when introducing them to his superior officers and fellow SAS troopers. He was also surprised to find that Taff's parents were almost as quiet as their son – rather shy, in fact – and it made him wonder just where Taff, clearly a much-loved only child, had picked up his cold-blooded, deadly nature.

'Meet me mum and dad,' he said to Marty, offering his beatific smile and flicking the blond hair out of his distracted blue eyes with an airy wave of his hand. 'Mum and Dad, this is Marty, who was badged when I was. I think I've told you about him.'

'He has that, boy,' his father confirmed to Marty, smiling happily, his jowly cheeks flushed, his bald head gleaming with sweat between tufts of greying hair. 'Nothing but good to say of you. Said you were a really good soldier and he was proud to work with you.'

Marty couldn't help grinning. 'I think just as highly of your son,' he replied. 'He's a bloody good soldier, Mr Hughes, and I'm pleased to have him on our side.'

'He always *was* a good boy,' Mrs Hughes chipped in, flushed and happy when she beamed at her darling son, who smiled lovingly back at her. 'Always quiet as a mouse and so gentle. A real little saint, 'e was.'

'I'm sure he was,' Marty responded, glancing at Taff, seeing his gentle smile, and recalling his calm, brutal despatch of the female terrorist with a familiar feeling of disbelief.

'Excuse me, Marty,' Taff said, glancing distractedly around the room, 'but I want to introduce m'folks to some of the others before they drive back.'

'You do that,' Marty said.

Later, when the visitors had departed and the new base was settling into darkness, Marty sat down to a bout of heavy drinking with Bulldog Bellamy, now a staff sergeant, and the dark-eyed, still volatile Rod O'Connor, who had made it to sergeant but been demoted to corporal after one of his many drunken brawls. Though O'Connor could be a dangerous man to know, Marty would never forget his outrage when forced to leave the mortally wounded Tone behind as the patrol advanced deeper into the swamp near Selangor. He had respected O'Connor ever since.

'You didn't bring any guests,' he said to O'Connor as the Irishman drank some more beer. 'Why was that, mate?'

'Who the fuck should I have brought?' O'Connor replied, wiping his thin, mean lips with the back of his hand.

'Your mum and dad?'

'Dead and buried.'

'Sorry to hear that.'

'No, you're not. How the fuck could you be sorry to hear that when you never even knew 'em?'

'It was a rhetorical statement,' Bulldog explained.

'What the fuck does "rhetorical" mean?' O'Connor asked. 'Is he tryin' to be funny?'

'It means he was trying to be polite,' offered Bulldog.

'That's right,' Marty said. 'Don't take offence, mate. I mean, when someone says their parents are dead, you automatically say these things.'

'Dead and buried,' O'Connor repeated. 'A fucking good thing, too. They both drank like fish and fought like cats and dogs and beat me up when they weren't beatin' up each other. Good riddance, I say.'

'Where was that, then?'

'In Bandon, West Cork. I remember that it had this one long street and not too much else. Lots of pubs, nat'rally. My fucking parents knew 'em all. They used to take me shopping, hand me the shopping bags, then make me wait outside some fuckin' pub while they went in for a quick one. They'd be in there for hours and come out pissed as newts. They'd argue all the way home, sometimes hittin' each other, an' when they got inside the house they'd hit me instead and then uncork some more bottles. Unemployed, the fuckin' pair of 'em. Too much time on their hands. When they beat me once too often, I left home and never went back. I was seventeen then. Caught the first boat to England. Spent a few months in Liverpool, sweeping the fuckin' streets, then went to London and lived in Shepherd's Bush and got into the buildin' trade. Labourin', of course. That's all we Paddies were worth. But at least it was honest work an' I was paid and kept m'self to m'self. A few bints here and there. Mostly picked up in pubs. I started drinkin' with one and she drank me under the table and we were pissed as two newts when we got married in a registry office.

'The marriage lasted a month. We were pissed the whole time. When she started fuckin' around with a mate, I started beatin' her up. She left me soon after. Took all my savin's. I took my temper out on m'mate on the building site an' they sacked me on the spot an' I was broke and didn't know what to do. So I joined the fuckin' Army. Just walked in and signed up. The psychologist told me I was borderline mad, a proper head case, but the Army was pretty desp'rate at the time, so they let me in anyway. How the fuck I got accepted by the SAS, I'll just never know.'

'You have to be borderline mad to *want* to join the SAS,' Bulldog told him. 'We're *all* borderline mad.'

'No, we're not,' Marty said. 'We're just different, that's all. We're men who can't settle for a normal life, but we're nowhere near mad. If we were, we wouldn't get into the SAS. We got in 'cause we're special.'

'And modest,' Bulldog said.

'I'm just stating a fact,' Marty told him. 'I'm not boasting, but I'm saying that we're special – and, damn it, we've proved it. In North Africa. Certainly in Malaya. What we did in those swamps was something special. Come on, Bulldog, admit it.'

Bulldog nodded. 'Okay, I admit it. But I still don't think we're special enough yet. We have to go farther.'

'Exactly my sentiments,' Paddy Kearney said, having come up to stand at their table and listen attentively. 'May I join you, gentlemen?'

'Sure, boss,' Bulldog said.

Paddy pulled up a chair and sat between Bulldog and Rod O'Connor. He sniffed delicately at his fresh glass of whisky, had a sip, then put his glass back on the table and lit a cigar.

'I agree with your sentiments,' he said to Bulldog, 'but what, precisely, are your proposals?'

'Well, boss,' Bulldog said, 'I've been thinking about what you said – about how the war in Malaya was a counter-insurgency job and that's the direction most will take in the future.'

'I stick by that,' Paddy said.

Bulldog inhaled on his Marlboro cigarette, let the smoke out in a leisurely sigh, then cleared his throat with a cough. 'Well, boss, it seems to me that until another real war comes along, we're all going to be stuck here in Hereford, just playing war games.'

'We must keep in practice, Staff Sergeant. That's what we *do* in peacetime.'

'Exactly. We keep in practice. But we learned an awful lot in those swamps in Malaya and it's changed our whole perception of how to do things. So what I'm saying is that we've not only got to keep in practice – keep going over the old ways – we've also got to build on what we learned in Malaya and create a whole new method of training to meet future requirements.'

'With special regard to counter-insurgency operations.'

'Right,' Bulldog said. 'In hostile environments.'

'Pardon?' Marty asked.

Bulldog stared steadily at him. 'We work best in hostile environments,' he said. 'We started in the desert with the LRDG, then we worked with the Sakai in the jungle, another hostile environment. We already insert by parachute. We've learned the art of tree-jumping. We've poled down rivers on makeshift rafts. We've learned to live off the land, to sleep waist-deep in leech-filled water, to win the hearts and minds of the natives and then train them to fight for us. What I'm saying, then, is that we've got to include all that, and even expand on it, in the future. We've got to be prepared to go anywhere and tackle any task. It's the only way we'll survive.'

'You're talking politics,' Paddy said.

'That's right, boss – politics. We all know what happened after World War Two: the SAS was disbanded. They didn't need us any more. At least, they *thought* they didn't need us. And the minute they thought they didn't need us, the bastards ruthlessly axed us. If they did it once, they'll do it again. They'll say we're surplus to requirements. And the only way we'll stop them from doing that is to make ourselves indispensable.'

'So we turn ourselves into a unit that can do what other soldiers can't do.'

'Right, Marty, exactly.'

Paddy blew another cloud of cigar smoke, watched it spiralling in the air directly in front of him, then squinted through the purple haze at Bulldog.

'What kind of programme?' Paddy asked.

'Something a damned sight more extensive than standard military training. I call it cross-training. As I see it, what we need are men who're particularly good at most kinds of military activity – weapons, battle strategy, teamwork, endurance – but who also have specialist training in other areas that ensure we're ready for just about any kind of environment: heat, cold, jungle, mountain, rivers, the sea, the air.'

'But we already do that,' Marty said. 'I mean, basically we work on a system of four-man teams, with each man in each team being trained – cross-trained, as you put it – in signals, demolitions, medicine and basic languages.'

'Correct, but that only evolved gradually out of our needs in Malaya and it still isn't a regular part of our training. What I'm saying is that we have to make such training the *modus operandi* of the regiment and, more importantly, extend it to include specialist techniques relating to survival not only in jungles and deserts and in the air, which we've already done, but also at sea and on snow-covered mountains. In other words, in the future we should be prepared for all contingencies even before we leave the base – not learn as we go along, which is what we did in Malaya. I also think there should be an even more rigorous selection course.'

'That's a fucking joke,' Rod O'Connor said. 'An even more rigorous selection course than the one we've already got would break even me.'

'Like breaking a bleedin' matchstick,' Marty joked. 'I'd ignore *that* complaint!'

'Very funny,' Rod retorted, his dark eyes flashing belligerently.

'You have some specific ideas?' Paddy asked, treating the matter more seriously.

'Yes, boss.' Bulldog stubbed his cigarette out in the ashtray, then immediately lit another one and exhaled a cloud of smoke into the cloud already created by Paddy's cigar. 'I think we should break it down into a three-part selection and training course. First is selection. We only consider men with at least two years' service in another regiment and who, while being self-sufficient, will have no record of troublemaking and can still work well in a team.'

'That gets rid of O'Connor here,' Marty said.

'Up yours!' Rod retorted.

'The selection,' Bulldog continued, ignoring the pair of them, 'will be based on a three-week training period tougher than any so far devised, concentrating on physical stamina and endurance, determination, map-reading skills, which would have to be exceptional, and, of course, cross-country navigation.'

'All already on the agenda,' Paddy reminded him.

'The initial three-week training period,' Bulldog continued doggedly, 'will be followed by a week of particularly demanding mental and physical testing. Those who fail, even by injury, will be returned to their original units without recourse to appeal.'

'Same as we're doing now,' Marty said, 'only even tougher. Right, Staff Sergeant?'

'Right,' Bulldog said. 'Being twice as tough to pass, it'll rid us at an early stage of the those who're psychologically and physically unsuitable, leaving us with only the *crème de la crème*.'

'What's that mean?' O'Connor asked suspiciously. 'Why speak fuckin' French?'

'It means the very best,' Marty said. 'You know? The cream always rises to the top.'

'Does it?' O'Connor asked, looking puzzled.

'In coffee,' Marty clarified.

'I always have milk with my coffee,' O'Connor told him. 'I keep cream for dessert.'

'You're so common,' Marty said.

'Okay, what's next?' Paddy asked.

'Those passing basic training and selection,' Bulldog continued, casting a baleful look at Marty and O'Connor, 'then go on to a few months of further training. I've called this continuation training. It consists of patrol tactics for every conceivable situation and environment, including jungle, desert, mountain and sea; advanced signalling; demolition; first-aid and combat survival. Anyone failing at any point is RTU'd instantly.'

'Aye, aye, aye!' Marty whimpered melodramatically, shaking his right hand as if in agony. 'It hurts just to think of it.'

'So what happens next?' Paddy asked, ignoring Marty's histrionics.

'The survivors—'

'Good word!' O'Connor interjected.

' go on to special, extensive jungle training, learning what we picked up in Malaya, preferably in a real jungle environment. If they manage to survive that, they'll be given a static-line parachute course and a set number of actual jumps.'

'Still being RTU'd at any point if they don't come up to scratch.'

'Right, Marty. Exactly.'

'And those passing,' O'Connor speculated, 'are finally allowed to wear the beige beret and Winged Dagger badge.'

'Yes. But their training isn't over yet.'

'I always knew you liked tormenting troopers,' Marty said, 'but this is beginning to sound like pure sadism. As the virgin said to the whore when she pulled out her chains, whips and gags: "Excuse me, but is all this really necessary?"'

O'Connor laughed at that one, but Bulldog glared at him, shutting him up. Paddy Kearney rested his chin in his hands like a man deep in thought. 'Continue,' he said.

Bulldog nodded, grateful for the encouragement. 'Once badged, they go on to cross-training proper. This will include escape-and-evasion, or EandE, and resistance-to-interrogation, or R and I, exercises. It'll also include high altitude, low opening, or HALO, insertion techniques; special boat skills for amphibious warfare and insertions by sea and river; extensive training in mountain climbing, preferably in arctic conditions, including snow; lessons in the driving and maintenance of every kind of military vehicle, including motorbikes; and close-quarter battle, or CQB, skills in a special building designed to simulate indoor fire fights against subversives or terrorists, with pop-up targets and false decoys. I've tentatively named the envisaged building the Killing House.'

'Fucking beautiful!' O'Connor murmured, throwing Marty a sneaky grin.

'Honesty is all,' Marty told him. 'Best to know what it's there for.'

'Anything else?' Paddy asked, smiling slightly, dangerously, the way he used to smile at Marty in the North African desert when he was about to spring a surprise.

'Yes,' Bulldog said. 'Last but not least, they're given comprehensive lessons in advanced medicine and languages relevant to anywhere the regiment might be sent in the next decade. By the time they finish that lot, your SAS troopers will be the finest and most versatile in the world. No question about it.'

Paddy stared at Bulldog for some time, that small smile still playing at his lips; then he stubbed his cigar out and leaned back in the chair with his hands folded behind his head.

'Now isn't that interesting?' he asked rhetorically. 'Great minds truly think alike.' The others looked at him questioningly. He watched their expressions as he told them that their commander, Lieutenant-Colonel Phillip Mackie, had already been talking about a similar kind of cross-training, with each man trained in all of the required skills while specialising in one particular task.

'Really?' Bulldog said.

'Really. In fact, he's already discussed the possibility of dividing the Sabre Squadrons of the regiment into four sixteen-man troops. Each of them, while manned by men with cross-over skills, will have its specialist role. So far, he's decided on a Mobility Troop, specialising in operations in Land Rovers, fast-attack vehicles and motorbikes; a Boat Troop, specialising in amphibious warfare and insertions; a Mountain Troop, specialising in mountain and arctic warfare; and an Air Troop to be used for free-fall parachuting, tree-jumping and HALO insertions. Naturally all of the men will be interchangeable as the need arises – so your ideas for a special SAS selection-and-training course should go down nicely with him. Congratulations, Bulldog. You've anticipated all of it.'

'Thanks, boss.' Bulldog grinned laconically at Marty and Rod O'Connor, then finished off his pint of bitter and smacked his lips with self-satisfaction.

'Nice one, Bulldog,' Marty said. 'You're not only going to run the new candidates into the ground but also work their directing staff to death – and that's going to be us, right?'

'Right,' Bulldog said. 'What else can you limp dicks do when there's no wedding to go to and no new war to fight? You either recycle your old training or instruct the new candidates and help shape the new selection-and-training course at the same time. As for being worked to death, it's up to you to set a good example, like the DS in Aldershot set for you. You only demand of the candidates what you've already done yourself. So everything that they're going to do, you lot'll do first. At least it'll keep you from wanking.'

'Thanks a lot,' Marty said.

'For nothing,' O'Connor added.

'We have to be cruel to be kind,' Bulldog replied. 'Believe me, you'll thank me for it later.'

'I'm sure we will,' Marty said.

Removing his hands from the back of his head, Paddy finished off his whisky, then sighed, shook his head from side to side, and said, sounding regretful, 'It all sounds wonderful to me. What a pity I won't be taking part in it.' The others stared at him in silence for a moment, wondering what he was saying. He toyed distractedly with his empty glass, then continued: 'The rules and regulations of the regiment have now been firmly established. As you know, one of the rules is that no officer can remain with the regiment for more than three years, though he may occasionally return for another three-year stint. As you also know, this is why I'm being RTU'd to Number Eight Commando.'

'You'll be back, boss,' Marty said.

'No,' Paddy replied. 'I don't think so. This was my last stint with the regiment.'

This time the silence around the table was almost palpable, lying heavily upon each of them as they glanced uneasily at one another, their eyes troubled and questioning.

'What does that mean, boss?' Bulldog asked eventually.

'Why your last stint? You can come back to the regiment in three years, so what's the big problem?'

Paddy's green gaze was regretful and his slight smile was sad. 'I'll soon be retiring from the service,' he said. 'It's bad enough that I can't spend longer than three years at one stretch with the regiment; worse is the fact that I'm reaching the age where, even if I returned, I could only be used in an administrative capacity – and that, I'm afraid, isn't for me. In Civvy Street – yes – it has a much wider range of exciting opportunities for men such as me. It's not ideal, but it's better than what I'd find if I stayed on in the regiment without the chance of further active service. I couldn't bear to be stuck behind a desk here in Hereford while you men went off to fight the wars. I just couldn't stand it. Not in the SAS and not even in the commandos. In fact, nowhere in the Army. So I'm planning to retire altogether and set myself up in my own business in Civvy Street. I want to be my own man.'

Marty felt a dreadful sense of loss as those words sank in. To hide this, he lit another cigarette and exhaled a cloud of smoke. He couldn't imagine the regiment without Paddy Kearney. It just didn't seem right somehow.

No one said anything for a long time, until Bulldog, clearly agitated as well, shook his head disbelievingly. 'I can't believe . . .' he began. But Paddy dropped his hand lightly on Bulldog's shoulder to shake him gently, affectionately. Then he pushed his chair back and stood up.

'Before I leave, gentlemen, please let me say this. You were talking earlier about how the SAS is a special regiment and how we must ensure that it remains this way. This is your responsibility. Though SAS officers can only serve three years at a stretch, NCOs can make the regiment a career. This gives them an authority unique to the military forces. So, given that only the NCOs have lasting authority within the regiment, it's up to you to ensure that its moral precepts and unique skills aren't degenerated or lost altogether. I trust that in my absence you will do this. Now good night to you all.'

He turned away and walked hurriedly across the smoky room, skirting around the crowded tables and the many groups standing between them to leave by the front door. When he was gone, the others stared silently at one another, none of them knowing what to say, all slightly choked up.

'Well, here we are,' Bulldog finally managed, 'celebrating the opening of Bradbury Linco and being told that our favourite officer won't be sharing it with us. It's the end of an era.'

'Fuck it,' Marty said, feeling close to tears, but pushing his chair back and standing upright. 'I'm going to get another round of drinks. Let's all get blotto.'

No one argued with that.

CHAPTER NINETEEN

When Marty stepped down from the train that had brought him to London from Hereford, he was in a state of shock because he had come to attend the funeral of his father, who had died unexpectedly of a heart attack two days before. Deeply upset that he had not been present when his father passed away, had not been able to speak any final words to him, he felt that he had lost a whole world and been finally, brutally wrenched from the last hold on his childhood. He had aged overnight.

Not wishing to go home immediately, still trying to prepare himself, he wandered the streets of the West End for an hour or two, popping in and out of a couple of pubs, fortifying himself, distracting himself with the changes he saw all around him. London was, he noticed quickly, a city given over to youth culture. The Soho streets of 1961 were filled with a mixture of teddy boys in long, velvet-collared jackets, drainpipe trousers and string ties, who lounged in threatening gangs outside the pubs and coffee bars, and other youngsters, variously dressed, all listening to the rock 'n' roll music that thundered out of jukeboxes. Marty still liked Vera Lynn, Glenn Miller and Frank Sinatra. He did not like rock 'n' roll and was deeply suspicious of a youth 'culture' that included in its philosophy a contempt for authority and personal discipline. Also, these young people despised soldiers, and he found that offensive.

Having imbibed enough alcohol to help him face what was

to come, he took a taxi to Golders Green crematorium where he found his distraught family and relatives gathered for the ceremony. Sitting beside his weeping mother, he slipped into a protective trance as the minister conducted the last rites and the coffin moved into the furnace. Eventually he found himself outside again, breathing gratefully of the crisp autumnal air, dazedly shaking hands with old friends and relatives.

So distraught was he that he hardly noticed half of these people, not really focusing upon them. He did not even see that Lesley was present until he was at the wake, held back at home in Crouch End. There, as he sat in the kitchen, staying close to the drinks table, Lesley appeared out of the crowd. Leaning forward, she kissed the top of his head, then stepped back to study him.

'You look good,' she said.

Though she had put on some weight, her hair was still dark and she was as attractive as ever in a black skirt, matching jacket and white blouse. Though she was clearly upset by the funeral, her smile held no malice.

'So do you,' Marty replied, meaning it.

Lesley glanced about her, then waved her right hand, indicating those milling about in the kitchen, drinking, smoking and making polite conversation – most of it, as Marty had overheard, filled with fond reminiscences about his father. 'I'm sorry about this,' she said. 'He was a very fine man.'

'I know,' Marty said. 'He also thought a lot of you. He was hurt when we parted.'

Lesley smiled. 'It was only us who were mismatched, Marty. Not me and your parents.'

'That's true enough.' Marty managed to pour himself another beer without moving out of his chair. 'Where are the kids?' he asked, glancing about him and hoping to see them.

'I didn't think this was appropriate.'

Though disappointed, he said, 'I agree. So how are they?' In fact, he saw them about once a month and was pleased at how well they were turning out. Johnny was fifteen and Kay was a shy fourteen-year-old. Allowed to visit them when he wanted, which was at least once a month unless he was overseas, Marty had remained close to them and noted that they were close to each other. He had Lesley to thank for that.

'They're fine,' Lesley said. 'Johnny's preparing for the future by aping Elvis Presley and begging me to buy him some drainpipe trousers for his birthday. Kay thinks she's Brenda Lee, the little lady with the big voice, and I often catch her experimenting with my make-up, pursing her lips in the mirror.'

'Two normal, healthy kids,' Marty said.

'Yes. They both send you their love.'

'Tell them I'll come and see them later this month.'

'They'd like that,' Lesley said.

She was still living in their old house in Weybridge, which was where Marty went to visit the kids at times when Lesley had conveniently arranged to be out. While entering his former home never failed to give him a brief feeling of loss (it was a larger and much nicer house than the one he shared with Ann Lim in Redhill) he was deeply grateful to Lesley for letting him visit when he wished and for taking pains, as she had done, to ensure that their parting remained amicable. Clearly, she had done this mainly for the children, to avoid upsetting them, but she had also done it because, as she had told him, animosity between her and him would bring little happiness to either of them.

That decision, Marty thought, had shown remarkable commonsense and it had indeed made life a lot easier for both of them. Now, aided by his generous alimony payments, which came out of income still accruing from his old construction company (he was still a sleeping partner), and with additional income from her own work as a legal secretary, she was financially comfortable and happy with the life she was leading. This included a frantic social life, including charity work. Certainly, she still looked pretty good and seemed fairly happy.

'So what about you?' he asked her, glancing across the crowded kitchen, to see his clearly distraught but bravely composed mother sipping tea and chatting to friends. 'Any man in your life at the moment?'

'Yes, as a matter of fact. Charles Pugh. A lawyer I met

through the company I work for. He works for another, smaller legal company and took over the business of some of the charities I'm involved with. A nice man. Marched for CND. Votes Labour, naturally. Not your type at all.'

'I've nothing against anyone who votes Labour. I just don't happen to vote for them myself.'

'You should. You're working-class, Marty.'

'Like you used to be. Now you live in bloody Weybridge, Surrey. An area more Tory than Weybridge I just can't imagine.'

Lesley smiled at that, but refused to give in. 'I don't vote on behalf of my neighbours, Marty. I vote for myself. And how you can support the Tories beats me. You *used* to vote Labour.'

'That's when they were more liberal. I stopped supporting those bastards the day they sang "The Red Flag" in the House of Commons. Socialism's one thing; communism's another. The Tories represent certain values that I happen to share, including the defence of the realm. I'm not sure that I approve of leftie groups like CND; I think the country needs defending and nuclear weapons are a deterrent, just like the armed forces are. Of course, an awful lot these days sneer at the armed forces, saying we're just a bunch of sanctioned killers. That's the kind of liberal, woolly-headed thinking that probably fills the ranks of the CND. Thanks, but no, thanks, luv.'

'You haven't lost your fighting spirit, I see.'

He glanced up and saw that she was smiling. 'No, Lesley, I haven't.'

'Still in love with your precious Army.'

'The SAS,' he corrected her.

'Same thing,' she said.

'No, it's not,' he insisted. 'We're a separate entity altogether. We have our own rules and regulations, our own methods of training, our own ways of doing things, our own base. We're exceptionally well trained and highly motivated, and we have a lot of pride in what we do. We're not just an offshoot of the greens. We're very much our own men.'

'Greens?' Lesley asked, puzzled.

'Regular Army,' Marty explained. 'We're not like the regular Army, believe me. We're something very different.'

'You're still soldiers, Marty.'

'I'm not ashamed of that. I've never been a pacifist. Pacifism wouldn't have stopped Hitler; only soldiers could do that. Some wars are worth fighting.'

Lesley sighed. 'I suppose so.'

'Anyway, why the hell are we talking about this? You never *did* like me being in the Army. Not even the TA.'

'That's because you were never at home,' she reminded him.

He shrugged. 'That's true enough.'

'How does your present wife take it?'

'A lot better than you did,' he said.

'Is she a devoted little creature? Are Chinese women like that? Is that why you married her? For total obedience?'

'No, Lesley, I didn't marry her for that and she isn't like that, though being an Anglified Chinese-Malay certainly gives her a different attitude to the Army. They suffered a lot under the Japs in Malaya; then later, when the war was over, they suffered under the CT.'

'Pardon?'

'Communist terrorists. They caused bloody mayhem over there. Because of them and the Japs, people of Ann Lim's age, men *and* women, know at first hand what it's like to be abused and terrorised. So they believe in the need for national defence. They want soldiers who'll go out there and fight for 'em. They don't believe in your bloody pacifism. They've suffered too much for that.'

'This is Britain, Marty. It isn't Malaya.'

'If we hadn't fought Hitler, we'd all be in concentration camps right now – or maybe in our graves. Now we have the USSR to worry about and don't you forget it. A free country will only stay free if it's ready, willing and able to defend itself. My wife knows that. I know it, too. Ann Lim's proud of me being a soldier and that makes me feel good.'

Lesley smiled and nodded. 'You and your principles. Even when we first met, when you were just a wild teenager, you always had your principles. Your dad was the same. He was quieter about it, but he had his principles and would argue his case. You're a chip off the old block.'

'Dad was a good man.'

'You're not bad yourself, Marty If the kids grow up to be like you, I won't complain much.'

'Thanks, Lesley I mean that.'

She smiled again, then glanced across the crowded kitchen at Marty's mother. 'She was pretty broken up,' she told Marty, 'but she's handling it well.'

'She won't handle it so well when we all leave, but no one can help with that.'

'And you – are you all right?'

'Yes, I'm fine. I have to confess, I've felt better, but I'll manage okay. I'll be okay when I get back to Hereford. It's being here that hurts most.'

Lesley sighed and placed her hand on his right shoulder to squeeze him affectionately. 'Well, I think I'd better be going. Get back to the kids. I'll pass on your love.'

'You do that,' Marty said.

She kissed him on the cheek, turned away and walked off. It had been the longest conversation he had had with her since they had split up. Usually it was just a phone call to tell her when he would be visiting the children. He watched her as she stopped to kneel beside his mother, smiling at her, stroking her cheek, offering words of comfort. His mother responded with a smile, then Lesley stood up and left the room, turning back to give him a wave before disappearing around the doorframe.

Marty gazed at that empty space for some time, as if Lesley was imprinted on it. He suddenly swelled up with emotion – for his dead father, his grieving mother, for the pain that all failed marriages leave in their wake – then he poured himself another stiff drink and lit up a cigarette.

He saw the people crowded around him, his relatives and old friends, and suddenly realised that they, too, belonged to his past and that now he was a fatherless child with a world of his own. That world was the SAS base, Bradbury Lines, Hereford, and the wife and child who lived together near the base and waited for his return. That world was all he required now

He stayed for another couple of days in his childhood home in Crouch End, helping his mother with the complex paperwork that invariably follows a death. It was an extremely painful time, both for him and for her, and though he was pleased to help out, loving her as he had his father, he was secretly relieved when it was over and he could return to his own home in Redhill.

Sitting on the train taking him back to Surrey, he felt that he had left London behind him for good and could no longer cling to old memories. The passing away of his father had lobotomised him from his past, aged him overnight, and made him feel even more protective of those who were left: his grieving mother, Ann Lim and Ian, his other two kids, Johnny and Kay, even Lesley. He also felt that the values he had lived by were more important than ever; and that the regiment, as it was presently evolving, upheld those values. He was proud to be part of it.

Ann Lim was waiting for him at Redhill Station in her Mini car, in the gathering gloom of the early evening, with Ian, two years old, gurgling contentedly in his baby-chair. After placing his travelling bag on the rear seat, Marty kissed the baby on the cheek, then sat beside Ann Lim.

'Hi,' she said, smiling, leaning sideways to kiss him on the lips. 'How did it go?'

Giving birth to Ian had not changed her much and now, in a loose sweater and slacks, she looked as slim and perfectly formed as she had always been. With her jet-black hair hanging all the way down to her waist, framing her oval-shaped face and big brown eyes, she still looked like a dream.

'As good as can be expected,' he replied. 'Things okay here?'

'Nothing's changed,' she told him, then started the Mini and drove away from the station. 'Are you feeling okay?'

'Yes, I'm fine. I've got over the worst of it.'

'How did your mother take it?'

'I think worse than she's showing. She was okay during the funeral and at the wake; not so good when everyone had left and we were there alone. She was trying to be philosophical about it, but I think she's finding it tough. She's not young herself and I don't know how she'll take being alone. When I think of what it'll be like for her, it makes me appreciate what I've got, meaning you and Ian. These are the best days we'll have.'

'Not necessarily the best, Marty. We have lots of good days left. We have a son to look after and maybe more to come, so we should have a fairly full life before we grow old. But it's too early to think about that. Let it come in its own time.'

Marty smiled. 'Yeah, you're right.'

The drive home took only a matter of minutes and soon they were inside their modest bungalow-styled house, which was all they could afford on Marty's income. It was, however, very pleasant, with fine gardens front and rear and a grand view of the gently rolling green hills of the Hereford countryside. Once inside, Ann Lim placed Ian, still in his baby-chair, on the floor by her feet. Then she embraced Marty, clinging warmly to him, kissing his neck and lips. Eventually stepping back, she said, 'Let me put Ian to bed, then we'll have something to eat.'

'Great. I'll have a quick bath while you're doing it. That should freshen me up.'

'Good idea, Marty.'

He soaked himself in the hot bath for about twenty minutes, listening with pleasure to Ann Lim's loving baby-talk and Ian's excited gibberish. He was out of the bath and putting on fresh clothing when Ann Lim entered the bedroom to prepare Ian for his cot. Slapping her affectionately on the rump as he passed by, he went into the living room where he settled down in front of the television set with a glass of whisky.

According to the TV, a nuclear war had been averted when Mr Khrushchev promised to dismantle Russian missiles based in Cuba and ship them back to the Soviet Union. In return, President Kennedy had promised that the United States would not invade Cuba and would lift the blockade it had imposed on it. Marty was cynically entertained by the news that the British Foreign Secretary warmly welcomed Mr Khrushchev's decision, the Chinese were furious about it, Fidel Castro was displeased because he had not been consulted, and the CND was embarrassed because some of its leaders, believing that nuclear war was imminent, had fled from the demonstrations outside the American Embassy in London and gone to Ireland where they thought they would be safe.

Maybe Lesley's boyfriend is one of them, Marty thought with sour amusement. She's probably blushing with shame right now.

Turning off the TV, he poured himself another whisky, then put on his favourite Frank Sinatra LP, *Songs For Swinging Lovers*, which he now had in stereo. He sipped his whisky and hummed along, warming his feet on the gas fire, while Ann Lim stayed in the kitchen, making dinner. It was a Chinese meal, which Marty loved, and eventually they had it on the table in the living room with the lights dimmed, a candle burning between them, and a bottle of red wine to enhance the food and complete the romantic ambience.

'You're so nice to come home to,' he told Ann Lim, paraphrasing from one of his favourite songs.

'That's nice to hear.'

'This food is terrific – like the cook. It's something worth savouring.'

'I'm savouring the compliments.'

'You look beautiful in candlelight.'

'Keep it coming.'

'That's all I have to say.'

'That's more than enough for now, Marty. I'm a satisfied woman.'

They ate in silence for a moment, then he sat back in his chair and sipped some wine. 'Are you really happy here in England?' he finally asked her.

'Yes, Marty, you know I am. You must feel it, even when I don't say it. I miss Malaya, as you know, but so do you. It doesn't mean I'm not happy here. We have a nice house, nice friends and a nice life in general. I can't ask for more than that.'

'Does it bother you that I go away a lot?'

'Like it bothered Lesley?'

Marty nodded. 'I suppose that's what I mean.'

She shook her head. 'It bothers me, of course – I feel lonely when you're gone – but I knew you were a soldier when I married you, so I can't complain now.' She reached across the table to hold his hand, and squeezed it tenderly. 'Are you sure you're all right?' she asked.

'Yes, I'm fine. Even better now I'm back in my own cozy world.'

'But you're hurting, aren't you?'

'That won't go away too quickly.'

'I can see it in your eyes. You can't disguise it. You're thinking of your father right now and it hurts you a lot.'

'When someone dies, you start thinking about the living,' he said, 'and right now I'm also thinking about my mum. She's completely alone now. It's all over for her.'

'It's never over until you're dead,' Ann Lim said, perhaps thinking about the tragedy of her own mother in Malaya, knowing what it was like. 'Your mother may be resilient.'

'Let's hope so,' he said.

Ann Lim wiped her lips with the napkin, then stood up and came around the table to slip her hands behind his head and press his face to her stomach. 'You know what I'm going to do for you?' she asked rhetorically, neither expecting nor waiting for a reply. 'I'm going to make love to you like I've never done before. I'm going to do it all myself. I'm going to make you stretch out naked, just lying there, my victim, and I'm going to do exactly what I want to you, which will be what you need. You'll forget yourself, Marty. I promise, you'll lose yourself. For a while you'll be aware of only me and what I'm making you feel. For this one night – at least for this night – you'll forget pain and grief. You'll come back to the land of the living and want to remain there. Now let's go to bed, Marty.'

It was a night to remember.

The following morning, feeling like a new man, he put on his SAS uniform, and drove to Bradbury Lines in his second car, a rattling 1953 Ford Popular. As he drove into the base, feeling secure again, he realised that he had now been here for two years as a member of the Directing Staff (DS), conducting selection and training courses instead of being overseas on active service, which he would have preferred.

The new, much tougher selection and training programme, as initially suggested by Bulldog Bellamy, had been put into practice by Lieutenant-Colonel Mackie and was progressing healthily. Now, only men who had served at least two years with another regiment would be considered for possible transfer to the SAS. Having applied, they were put through a three-week basic training and selection course much more rigorous than any so far devised. That period, if survived, was followed by a week of particularly demanding mental and physical testing, which invariably led to an even greater number of failures, or crap-hats. Those who got through that went on to a few months of continuation training, consisting of patrol tactics for every conceivable situation and environment, including jungle, desert, mountain and sea. The few that were left went on to special jungle training, most of it based on the lessons learned by the old hands in Malaya. Finally, if they managed to get through that, they were sent to the RAF's prestige parachute training school at RAF Brize Norton in Oxfordshire for a static-line parachute course, followed by a set number of actual jumps. The few who managed to complete that course were finally allowed to wear the beige beret and Winged Dagger badge.

After parking his car, Marty walked to the training wing, thinking of how frustrated he and men like Bulldog were because so much was yet to be accomplished. Though special jungle training still took place in densely forested areas of England, it was hoped that eventually it would take place in a real jungle environment. Also, a cross-training programme had been implemented to include escape-and-evasion (E and E) and resistance-to-interrogation (R and I) exercises; high altitude, low opening (HALO) insertion techniques; special boat skills for amphibious warfare; extensive training in mountain-climbing; and lessons in the driving and maintenance of every kind of military vehicle, including motorbikes.

Though most of this still took place at Bradbury Lines, Brize Norton or on the mountains of Wales, it was not ideal and the commander of the regiment was still exploring the possibility of extending the cross training to overseas, with particular regard to mountain-climbing in genuine arctic conditions, hopefully Norway. Last but not least, while the need for close-quarter battle (CQB) skills was becoming more urgent, the so-called Killing House envisaged by Bulldog was still under construction and until it was completed the outdoor simulation of counter-terrorist operations was unsatisfactory.

On the other hand, Marty thought as he entered the training wing and saw his fellow NCOs gathered together outside the briefing room, much progress had been made in other areas. The Sabre Squadrons of the regiment had been split up into four sixteen-man troops, each with its specialist role. Now, there was indeed a Mobility Troop, specialising in fast-strike vehicles, a Boat Troop, specialising in amphibious warfare and insertions, a Mountain Troop, specialising in mountain warfare, and an Air Troop to be used for freefall parachuting, tree-jumping and HALO insertions. The training for all four troops was still extremely demanding, but what was needed was more training overseas in proper hostile environments. Hopefully that would come soon.

Having been called back to base specifically for this briefing, Marty joined the other men where they were milling about in front of the briefing room, having tea and a smoke. Seeing that they were unusually excited, he approached the eternally youthful Sergeant Taff Hughes to asked what was happening.

'Borneo,' Taff told him.

CHAPTER TWENTY

Marty was still depressed by the death of his father when he arrived in Borneo with the rest of D Squadron early in 1963. After settling into his basha in the Chinese merchant's house taken over by the SAS as their spider and located near the converted warehouses being used by the Army, Marine Commandos and Gurkhas, he joined the other men in the 'Haunted House', the SAS HQ, for their introductory briefing to the area. Actually a large building lent to the SAS by the Sultan of Brunei, the Haunted House was so-called because during the days of the Japanese occupation it had been used as a Tokyo Gestapo interrogation centre and the ghost of a young British woman tortured to death there was said to haunt the building. Given that many times since his father's death Marty had imagined seeing him – usually when he saw another man of roughly the same age – he was not thrilled to be entering a building so named. He did, however, feel a lot better when he actually explored it and found that it contained a communications centre (COMMCEN), sleeping quarters, showers, thunder boxes, recreation room and admin offices, including the briefing room. The Haunted House seemed marginally less haunted when he saw what was in it.

The briefing was conducted by an SAS intelligence officer, or green-slime Head Shed, who informed them that the so-called 'confrontation' between Britain and Indonesia was being fought in an area as intractable as Malaya. The main problem facing the British commander was that he had only five battalions to cover over 1,500 kilometres of jungle-covered border. Also, in addition to Sukarno's Indonesian insurgents, he had to contend with an internal threat in the shape of the Clandestine Communist Organisation, or CCO, composed mainly of Chinese settlers from Sarawak. The SAS would therefore be operating along the border, not engaging with the enemy unless absolutely necessary, but providing early warning of any Indonesian or CCO incursions.

'*Not* engaging with the enemy?' Taff whispered into Marty's other ear. 'What does that mean?'

'Reconnaissance patrols,' Marty told him.

'Bloody waste of our skills,' Taff replied, sounding affronted.

In order to accomplish this, the green-slime Head Shed droned on, the SAS would live almost entirely in the jungle, relying on the Border Scouts for local information. Once they had ingratiated themselves with the indigenous population, their function would be to patrol the areas where the Indonesians were most likely to cross the border. Their main zone of operations, however, would be the unexplored stretch of jungle known as 'the Gap', lying east of the Pensiangan valleys of Sabah, where small Indonesian patrols were known to infiltrate by less visible routes. Largely unexplored, the *ulu* of the Gap was populated with Land and Sea Dyaks, Muruts and Punans, some of whom were headhunters.

'In other words,' the Head Shed dryly summarised, 'the Gap will be the ultimate challenge to SAS ingenuity and endurance. The best of luck to you.'

'Condescending bastard!' Rod O'Connor whispered.

The rest of that first day was entirely taken up with preparations for the lengthy patrol. For jungle clothing, they were given OGs similar to those worn in Malaya, but the soft peaked hat with its sweat band had a yellow marker inside for identification and the rubber-and-canvas jungle boots had a special 'riveter's cleat' metal plate inserted in the sole to prevent sharp objects, such as punji stakes, going through the sole and into the foot. This reminded Marty of Tone's death in Malaya and did not make him feel good. In this he was not alone.

'Fucking punji pits,' Rod O'Connor said. 'I could take just about anything they threw at us in Malaya, but those punji pits gave me bad dreams. What a way to go!' He stopped and glanced at Marty, recalling that he and Tone had been close friends. 'Sorry, mate. Me and my big mouth.'

'No sweat,' Marty said.

Their kit consisted of ammunition pouches; two external water bottles; and the usual Bergen rucksack packed in this instance with a useful bamboo carrier, two spare water bottles, rolled-up sleeping bag, canvas sheeting and camouflaged hessian for temporary bashas, and an escape belt with high-calorie rations, hexamine fuel blocks, fishing line and hooks, a small knife, a button-compass and a small-scale map.

'I always feel like a Boy Scout,' Taff Hughes mildly informed them as he was carefully packing his kit into his steadily expanding Bergen rucksack, 'when I'm sorting out this stuff. Bit of an adventure holiday, really. That's what it feels like.'

'Were you ever in the Boy Scouts?' Marty asked him, realising once more that he knew practically nothing about the seemingly mild, absolutely deadly Welsh lad.

'Yes,' Taff said. 'Joined the minute I was old enough – on my birthday – and stayed in it as long as I could. Loved it – the uniform, the drills, the camping out – it was right up my street. That's why I ended up in the SAS. When I heard about them, they seemed just like the Boy Scouts for grown-ups. I still feel that way.'

'Wonderful!' Rod O'Connor exclaimed in disgust. 'Suddenly I'm in the fucking Boy Scouts. And I thought I was special.'

'The only person who might have thought *you* were special,' Bulldog said, 'is your mother. Now shut up and let's move it.'

The weapons chosen as most suitable for the task were the standard-issue M16 5.56-millimetre assault rifle with 20-round box magazine, the less popular 7.62-millimetre SLR, and the Armalite 7.62-millimetre assault rifle, which was light and compact. Each man was also given a supply of '36' hand grenades and '80' white phosphorous incendiary grenades, which were clipped to the webbed belts around the chest and waist. All of them were given a standard issue Browning nine-millimetre Double-Action High Power handgun with thirteen-round magazines and Len Dixon holster. They were also given a Sykes Fairburn commando dagger and a *parang* of the kind they had become familiar with in Malaya.

'I see that *parang*,' Rod O'Connor said, 'and I know it means work. Fucking back-breaking work. We're in for a hard hike.'

'I don't mind,' Taff said mildly.

'You never mind anything,' Marty said. 'You're inhuman that way.'

'Nothing wrong with me,' Taff said mildly.

'If there's nothing wrong with you,' O'Connor told him, 'there was nothing wrong with Jack the Ripper either. Christ, this Bergen is heavy!'

The unusual heaviness of the Bergens, Marty realised, was due to the fact that in support of the signaller – heavily burdened with his A41 British Army tactical radio set as well as personal kit and weapons – each of the other men carried spare radio batteries and a SARBE lightweight radio beacon to enable them to link up with casevac choppers should the need arise. Also, in support of the team's demolition specialist, each man was issued with his share of mixed explosives, mostly plastic such as RDX and PETN, electrical and non-electrical initiators and the relevant firing caps and time fuses. Finally, as every man in the patrol had been trained in first-aid and basic medicine, he was obliged to carry his individual medical pack, which included codeine tablets and syrettes of morphine; mild and strong antiseptics (gentian violet and neomycin sulphate); chalk and opium for diarrhoea and other intestinal disorders; the antibiotic tetracycline; and an assortment of dressings and plasters.

In short, they were much better equipped, though more heavily burdened, than they had been in Malaya.

At dawn the next morning, after a hurried breakfast, they were driven in a Bedford truck to the airfield, where they transferred to a stripped-out Wessex Mark I helicopter piloted by an Army Air Corps lieutenant. After taking off, buffeted violently by the wind, the chopper rose vertically until it was well above the treetops, then it headed west, flying over a vast panorama of densely forested hills and mountain peaks, winding rivers, waterfalls, swamps, shadowy, winding pathways through the *ulu* and aerial walkways stretched across the gorges, hundreds of feet above boiling rapids.

'My stomach heaves just to *think* of those things,' Rod O'Connor confessed. 'I just don't want to know.'

'I don't mind them,' Taff said.

Eventually, after a relatively short journey, the chopper descended to the LZ, chosen because it was in a jungle clearing located within 'yomping', or marching, distance of the RV. Jumping out of the chopper, one after another, into the whirlwind of swirling dust, stones and foliage whipped up by the still-spinning rotors, the men, half deafened by the noise, ran at the crouch into the surrounding trees and had melted into the *ulu* even before the chopper took off again. By the time it had ascended, the jungle clearing was empty.

From the LZ, in appalling heat and humidity, the troopers hiked the rest of the way, hacking through the dense jungle undergrowth with their *parangs* while being attacked relentlessly by fat black flies, ravenous mosquitoes and midges. Thirty minutes later, though it seemed longer, they reached the RV – another clearing on the bank of a narrow river snaking through the *ulu*. There they found Sergeant Will Pankhurst waiting for them in a shelter consisting of two Y-sticks hammered into the ground about six feet apart, with a length of rope running tightly between them and a waterproof poncho draped over the rope, its ends pegged down to form a tent. Pankhurst had been in the jungle for a couple of months now, gaining the trust of the aboriginals in the first of the Iban *kampongs* selected as a base for the troop. Though pale and undernourished, he looked pretty cosy in his triangular shelter.

'Welcome to Paradise,' he said, waving languidly to indicate the babbling river and surrounding jungle. 'It isn't exactly hearth and home, but it *does* sustain a man.'

Judging by the emaciated appearance of the speaker, Marty wasn't too sure of that. Nevertheless, while he and his mates had a rest and brewed up on their portable hexamine stoves, Pankhurst gave a short briefing, explaining that, once at their selected *kampong*, they would break into small groups and spend the next couple of weeks ingratiating themselves with the Iban, adopting a hearts-and-mind approach as they had done in Malaya. Finally, when the trust of the natives had been gained, the SAS commander would persuade the village headman to let him bring more troops in by helicopter – the regular Army, Royal Marine Commandos and Gurkhas – to turn the *kampong* into a fortified camp.

'Once that's established,' Pankhurst said, 'we'll use it as an FOB and commence reconnaissance patrols into the surrounding *ulu* – either with or without the help of the Iban trackers, who may or may not be agreeable.'

Finally, before leading the men on through the *ulu* proper to the *kampong*, Pankhurst informed them that, though the natives were physically small, generally cheerful and lazy, they could be murderous when offended, so the men had to be particularly careful not to do that.

'I'm telling you this,' he said, 'because the Iban don't dress above the waist – not even the women – so you have to be careful about how you behave with all those bare tits around you. No fancy remarks and no ogling,' he added when some of the men sniggered helplessly. 'The Iban men carry spears and will use them if you get up their noses. Okay, let's move out.'

Even though experienced from his years in Malaya, Marty could not help feeling oppressed as he hiked through the *ulu*, into a vast silence that made his own breathing seem too loud. Here, instead of a riot of birds, flowers and brightly coloured foliage, there was only a sunless gloom deepened by the dark green and brown of vines, tree-ferns, snakelike coils of rattan, large and small palms, long and narrow spiked leaves, knotted branches and mud. Though the hike took only five minutes, it seemed much longer, and Marty was not alone in sighing with relief when the group emerged to the relative brightness – grey light filled with motes of dust – that fell down through a window in the canopy of the trees upon the thatched longhouses of the *kampong* spread out around the muddy banks of the river.

Raised on stilts, the longhouses were piled up one behind the other, each slightly above the one in front, on the forested slopes that ran uphill from the river. Some did indeed, as Marty noticed with a shivery feeling, have shrunken human skulls strung over their doorways. The spaces below and between the houses, where the ground had been cleared for cultivation, were crowded with Iban villagers – also known as Sea Dyaks because they had once been pirates – who were stripped to the waist, male and female, and engaged in a variety of tasks, such as cooking, fishing, laundering, picking jungle fruit – figs, durians, bananas and mangoes – or working in a small dry *padi* where their basic food, rice and tapioca, was grown. This they did with no great display of energy, except when playing odd games and giggling. Their longboats were tied up to a long, rickety jetty which bobbed and creaked noisily in the water. Buffalo and pigs also congregated there, drinking the water or eating the long grass as chickens squawked noisily about them.

'They fish in that river,' Sergeant Pankhurst explained. 'They also hunt wild pig, deer, birds, monkeys and other animals, using traps and the odd shotgun, but mostly blow-pipes that fire poisoned arrows. Annoy them and they'll fire one of those bloody things at you or stick a spear up your arse. They're not as mild as they seem.'

Within a few days the SAS troopers had got used to the bare breasts of the women and were involving themselves in the diplomatic task of ingratiating themselves with the natives in general. This they did by living in various kinds of temporary shelters in a jungle hide just outside the *kampong*, within walking distance of it, and spending most of their days in the *kampong* itself, interacting with the Iban, or Sea Dyaks, to create goodwill.

So gentle and good-natured were the Dyaks, Marty thought, you couldn't imagine them as pirates, let alone headhunters. Yet they were, or had been, headhunters at least, as could be seen by the blackened, shrunken heads above the doors of their longhouses. Certainly they lived a primitive, relatively casual life, fishing in the rivers, hunting animals with blowpipes, tilling the *kampong*'s one small dry rice-and-tapioca *padi*, and constantly maintaining their longhouses with products from the forest. They also engaged in amiable barter, trading jungle products in return for clothes, boots, rifles, tins of baked beans, chewing gum and cigarettes. Trading seemed the easiest way of gaining the affections of the Dyaks, leading to much giggling and mutual back-slapping.

'It's better than Petticoat Lane,' Marty said, 'and much more entertaining.'

'It's a pain in the arse,' Rod O'Connor responded, 'and takes all fucking day.'

Once the bartering had become commonplace, the SAS started winning the Dyaks' hearts and minds in other ways: showing them how to use explosives for various small tasks, such as blowing fish out of the water; running an open-air clinic to deal with their real and imagined illnesses on a daily basis; entertaining them by tuning the short-wave radio into various stations, which invariably reduced them to excited giggles; training certain of them in the selective use of weapons; and teaching the more important men of the village to speak English.

'If that's English they're speaking,' Rod O'Connor complained, 'then *I* must be speaking fucking Swahili. But I suppose we'll get used to it.'

'I'm used to it already,' Taff informed him. 'I understand what they're saying.'

'That's because you're Welsh,' Rod said.

Spending most of their waking hours with the Dyaks made for a long and exhausting day for the SAS. Invariably, it began at first light when, just after breakfast, they would make the short hike through the *ulu* from their hidden camp to the *kampong*. After about twelve hours in the *kampong*, taking their lunch with the Dyaks, they would make their way back to the camp, usually at last light, concealing their tracks as they went, to have a brew-up and feed gratefully off compo rations.

Unfortunately, the Dyaks were very sociable, and often, in the interests of good manners and better relationships, the troopers would be obliged to stay in one of the longhouses to partake of native hospitality. For all of them, this was pure torture, particularly since the Dyaks' favoured meal was a stinking mess called *jarit* – a length of thick bamboo filled with raw pork, salt and rice, then buried for a month until it had putrefied. Indeed, while Marty, Bulldog Bellamy and the imperturbable Taff Hughes were able to digest this stinking mess without too much bother, others could do so without throwing up only when drowning it in mouthfuls of the fierce rice wine, *tapai*, which looked like unfermented cider, scalded the throat, and led to monumental hangovers. Nevertheless, when taken through straws from large Chinese 'dragon jars', the *tapai* was potent enough to drown the stench and foul taste of the *jarit*.

'I could drink my own piss easier,' O'Connor said, 'and my piss doesn't burn like hell.'

'You've tried, then?' Marty asked him with a grin. 'When you were desperate some bleak night?'

'Piss off, Marty. Go drown in it.'

Social life with the Dyaks was made no easier by the fact that many aboriginal families shared a single longhouse and the air was fetid, not only from heat and sweat, but from the fact that they used the floor as a communal toilet, pissing and shitting through the slatted floorboards onto the ground below. The fetid air was therefore filled at all times with swarms of flies and mosquitoes.

'You'd smell less if you stuck your head down a toilet bowl,' Marty told Bulldog. 'Even *I* find the stench hard to take – and I've been to Malaya.'

'Malaya was bloody civilised compared to this,' Bulldog replied. 'I'd rather spend a year in a swamp in Malaya than a day in this longhouse. There's no comparison, Marty.'

'Too true, Bulldog. Too bloody true.'

Luckily, the men were also called upon to explore the surrounding area and fill in the blank spaces on their maps, showing waterways suitable for boat navigation, tracks that could be classified as main and secondary, distances both in linear measurements and marching hours, contours and accessability of specific areas, primary and secondary jungle (*belukar*), and swamps, and areas under cultivation (*ladang*). They also filled their logbooks with important details about the locals' habits and customs, including the variety of their weapons and each man's individual measure of importance within the community. Finally, they marked down potential ambush positions, border crossing points and suitable locations for parachute droppings and helicopter landings.

While this invaluable work was conducted in the suffocating humidity of the *ulu*, it was, in Marty's view, infinitely preferable to socialising in the stinking longhouses.

'I'm beginning to *like* the *ulu*,' Marty said, 'and that must mean I'm mad.'

'No argument,' Bulldog said.

By the end of the first two weeks, close relationships had been formed between the villagers and the SAS troopers, with the former willing to listen to the latter and do favours for them. Sensing by this that the time was right to step up the campaign, the squadron commander, Major Adam Parsons, in consultation with the more experienced Sergeant Pankhurst, decided to ask the village headman if they could bring in regular troops – a 'step-up party' – and fortify the *kampong*. After lengthy negotiations, which included Major Parsons's promise to let the SAS helicopters be used to transport the Iban's livestock to local markets, the headman agreed. He also offered his villagers as labourers to help clear a part of the jungle for a landing zone.

The following day, Iban tribesmen expertly felled a large number of trees with small axes, dragged them away with ropes, then flattened the cleared area to make a helicopter LZ. A couple of hours later, Army Air Corps Wessex Mark I helicopters appeared above the treetops, creating a tremendous din and a whirlwind of swirling foliage, before descending vertically into the cleared area and disgorging many small, brown-faced Gurkhas, all armed with sharpened *kukris*, or machetes, as well as modern weapons. When the next wave of helicopters arrived, they brought Royal Marine Commandos, the regular Army and the remainder of D Squadron, SAS, all of whom were armed to the teeth.

With the arrival of this Security Forces step-up party, the fortification of the *kampong* was soon accomplished and it became, in effect, a forward operating base complete with landing pads for the resup helicopters, riverside sangars manned with Brens and Gurkhas armed with LSRs, and defensive pits, or 'hedgehogs', encircled by thatch-and-bamboo-covered 40-gallon drums, bristling with mortars and machine-guns.

The bartering of portable radios, simple medical aid and

other items beloved by the villagers rapidly ensured that the SF troops became a welcome body of men within the community – so much so that eventually the natives were making endless requests for helicopter trips to outlying *kampongs* and help with the transportation, also by helicopter, of their rice and tapioca, timber, children, old people and even pigs and chickens to market. In short, they came to rely more on the soldiers and airmen than on their own civilian administration.

By now the SAS team had its own quarters in a separate longhouse on the edge of the village, from where they broadcast daily reports to the SAS HQ, the Haunted House, in Brunei, on a more powerful PRC 320 Clansman radio that had been flown in with the other supplies of the step-up party. By this time, also, most of the first batch of SAS men, including Marty, had lost a lot of weight from either living in the longhouse for weeks at a time or venturing into the *ulu* to watch, listen, patrol and report. In either environment they were constantly dripping sweat and gasping for air.

Even when making the shortest hikes through the jungle, they often found themselves dragging their booted feet laboriously through mud as thick and clinging as quicksand, or wading, chest deep, through swamp water covered with sharp, heavy palm leaves and broken branches. These physical demands were in no way eased by the constant strain of trying to look and listen for signs of the enemy, who was known to be able to blend with the *ulu* as well as the animals. Their first two months, then, living with the Dyaks, placed an enervating physical and mental strain on them, which led to an even greater loss of weight.

'Now we all look as pale and emaciated as Will Pankhurst,' Marty said to Bulldog as he was shaving with the aid of a small mirror pinned to a tree trunk.

'My wife would kill for our diet,' Bulldog replied, 'so I think you should count your blessings, mate.'

'I stand corrected, Bulldog.'

Once the Gurkhas, Royal Marine Commandos, British Army and other SAS personnel had moved into the *kampong* and completed its fortification, the smaller SAS patrols were able to move deeper into the *ulu* on reconnaissance missions, which never brought them into contact with the enemy but enabled them to collect a great deal of intelligence about the environment and terrain – some of it in the form of photos taken by Marty. Eventually, however, when four Dyaks who were clearing another LZ for the SF helicopters were found dead – obviously shot by a passing Indonesian or CCO patrol – Major Parsons decided to send patrols even deeper into the *ulu* to seek out the enemy and, if necessary, engage with them.

The hearts-and-minds campaign had ended. The real war was beginning.

CHAPTER TWENTY-ONE

Operating through his new FOB in the *ulu* and with SF men dug in over a broad defensive arc around it, Major Parsons began sending out more ambitious patrols, trying to track down the infiltrators and put a stop to them. Because they knew each other well and had worked well together before, Bulldog Bellamy, Marty, Taff Hughes and Rod O'Connor were put together in one patrol, along with an inexperienced newcomer, Trooper Tommy Taylor and three Dyak trackers. The patrol was to hike into the high jungle hills of the Pueh range and back down to the lowlands in the hope of locating a CCO forward base used by the terrorists somewhere in the region of Batu Hitam, or Black Rock.

Before moving out, the men painted their weapons with quick-drying green camouflage paint, then wrapped them in the strips of cloth specially dyed to match the jungle background and disguise their distinctive shape. After wrapping masking tape around the butts, pistol grips and top covers, they replaced the noisy sling swivels with para-cord, which made no sound at all. They also camouflaged themselves, applying 'cam' cream to the exposed areas of their skin, including the backs of their hands, wrists, ears and neck.

The patrol was escorted by five Police Field Force scouts as far as the border, which ran north-south along the mountain ridge. There the men moved out on their own, striking west from the border, heading into Indonesian jungle where they could as easily be ambushed as ambush an Indo patrol, which made it dangerous country.

Within minutes of hiking into the dense jungle of the mountain range, Marty again had that oppressive awareness of vast silence, combined with a chilling absence of colour and light. The newly badged trooper, Tommy Taylor, medium-sized, slim and with the lean and hungry look of a poor lad from the Midlands, was marching right behind him and Marty knew, from the expression on his face, that he had the same feeling. Mercifully, as they were already high in the hills, there were no swamps to brave, but almost as frightening, even to the experienced Marty, were the many aerial walkways that swayed in the wind high above the roaring rapids in the gorges, sometimes over a hundred feet below.

The first walkway they came to was a challenge for all concerned, as none of them had ever crossed one before. Even though they had all undergone parachute training and were therefore used to heights, the constant swaying and creaking of the walkways, their openness to the beating wind, the roaring of the rapids far below, and, worst of all, the illusion that there was really nothing below one's feet – the walkway being no wider than the three lengths of bamboo laid down side by side – made for a stomach-churning, nerve-racking crossing that, even worse, had to be taken at a snail's pace and seemed to take for ever.

The first time they came to a walkway, they spent a lot of time staring down at the roaring water in the gorge then goaded each other, with a lot of bullshit, into volunteering to be the first to cross. As the patrol leader, Bulldog made a point of going first, insisting that Marty go last, directly following the inexperienced Tommy Taylor, who might suffer most. In the event, though Tommy was clearly nervous, he seemed no more so than the others and managed to reach the other side without Marty's help.

Marty, when it came to his turn, understood why the other men had been nervous, particularly when he was halfway across and the fragile, narrow walkway creaked dramatically and sank visibly in the middle, under his weight, while swaying even more widely from side to side, buffeted by the wind that rushed howling through the narrow gorge. Indeed, more than once he was convinced that his feet had missed the narrow walkway, or perhaps plunged down between two of the bamboos, but this proved to be a mere illusion caused by glancing down and seeing only the boiling, roaring rapids. A final moment of gut-wrenching tension was then caused when he reached the end of the walkway and had to let go of the hand grips in order to leap back onto solid ground. When he did so, landing safely on the edge of the gorge, Rod O'Connor and Taff grabbed him by the shoulders and hauled him into the trees, away from the gorge. He was immensely relieved.

'Nearly shit your pants, did you?' Bulldog whispered.

'Yes,' Marty confessed.

'I didn't mind it,' Taff Hughes said, smiling beatifically. 'It was pretty exciting, really.'

'Jesus Christ!' Rod O'Connor exclaimed, then hurried into the forest.

That, however, was only the first of the many walkways they would have to cross as they made their way over the forest-covered, mountainous terrain. For all of them, except Taff, the walkways, no matter how many they crossed, were a constant source of nervous tension and few of them managed to get used to them. The aerial walkways were a nightmare.

Nevertheless, though feeling immensely relieved each time they stepped off one, the men were then faced with yet another steep climb through the dense, often impenetrable undergrowth on the face of the steep hills. Their aching, forward advance often involved hacking away the undergrowth with their *parangs*, a task rendered even more difficult and dangerous by the steep fall of the hills, the loose soil underfoot, and the lack of something to cling to. Indeed they often slipped back, even falling and rolling down, while desperately trying to keep the blade of the *parang* away from their face and hands as they reached desperately for a hold on something.

All of this was made even more frustrating by the almost suffocating humidity, the sweat dripping constantly into their eyes, and the usual swarms of fat flies, mosquitoes and midges. As it had been in Malaya, here, too, they were faced with a disturbing number of snakes, some venomous, which slept coiled around branches or slithered across the forest paths. Also, spiders and stinging ants often fell upon them when the branches of trees were shaken accidentally.

Even after the draining heat and humidity of the day, the high mountain ranges could be very cold at night. The patrol's LUPs consisted mainly of uncovered shallow 'scrapes' in which they unrolled their hollow-fill sleeping bags, laid down on plastic sheeting. Above these simple bedding arrangements they raised a shelter consisting of a waterproof poncho draped over wiring stretched taut between two Y-shaped sticks, making a triangular tent with the apex pointing into the wind.

For Marty, the nights were the hardest to take, and he suspected this was true for the others. Often too tired to sleep, tormented constantly by buzzing flies, whining mosquitoes and midges, unable to move freely or stretch cramped limbs on his narrow bed, he would drift in and out of semiconsciousness, neither fully awake nor properly sleeping, and be tormented by thoughts of Ann Lim and by his unfulfilled sexual needs. With eyes closed, he would see her, imagine her naked, recall the sublime softness and warmth of her body and limbs, the sensual touch of her moist lips. The torment was exquisite, diabolical in its refinement, and engorged, he would secretly touch himself and bring release by his own hand. He wasn't proud of this and never would be, but it was all he could do.

Before moving on the next morning, just before first light, he and the others meticulously removed all signs of their overnight bivvies. Even tree branches and leaves that had been disturbed were pushed back into their natural positions – a tedious, but vitally necessary, routine.

As they moved further west, cresting the summit of the mountain range, exploring along it, then circling back down to lower ground, the need to be alert to a chance meeting with a Land Dyak became more pronounced. The Land Dyaks were not familiar with white men and tended to be suspicious of all strangers, including the Sea Dyaks from the coastal areas, such as the three travelling with the SAS patrol. As they were skilled at jungle warfare and still prone to headhunting, they were certainly a breed of native best avoided.

At one point Bulldog helpfully informed the rest of the group that the Land Dyaks were likely to come out of the wilder forests heading towards the settlements along the Sempayang River, where there were many wet paddy-fields (as distinct from dry *padis*) for the growing of rice. The men saw these paddy-fields soon enough when they reached the lower slopes and began their sweaty hike along the river. The crops of seedlings, which would not be harvested until April, gave no cover, so the patrol kept mainly to a jungle-covered spur, which kept them within view of the river.

Heading upriver, sticking close to the riverbank, they made it to Batu Hitam in two hours. There, from where they were hiding at the edge of the forest, they saw a Dyak settlement, clearly filled with headhunters, judging from the number of shrunken skulls strung over the doors of the thatched longhouses. They saw no trace of the Indonesians, however.

Circling around the settlement, crouched low, weapons at the ready, taking note of the fact that the male Land Dyaks were armed with spears and blowpipes, they carefully checked every aspect of the village, but still saw no signs of either Indo soldiers or the CCO.

Bitterly disappointed that they had not made contact with the enemy, let alone made a sighting of them, they had to turn around and make the same lengthy, exhausting hike back to the FOB.

Luckily, their frustration didn't last long. A few days later, just as they were becoming bored, they were moved back to the unmapped mountain border of Sarawak – the so-called Gap – known officially as the Third Division. There they were to concentrate their efforts on the shorter frontier between Indonesia and Brunei. Their task was to engage in aggressive raids into enemy territory.

'The object,' Major Parsons informed them, 'is to pre-empt any likely Indonesian build-up or attack; to harass the Indos on patrol and in their camps; and to gradually compel them to move their forces away from the border.'

Nevertheless, as this was still an unofficial war, the rules of engagement were strict. Because the major purpose of the SAS patrols was to deter or thwart aggression by the Indonesians, no attack was to be mounted in retribution or with the sole aim of damaging the enemy. Indeed, the enemy was only to be engaged as a last defensive resort and, even when such was the case, minimum force was to be used rather than large-scale attacks, to avoid escalation.

'How the fuck we use minimum force,' the volatile Rod O'Connor complained, 'I'd really like to know.'

'It means you fire only when fired upon,' Marty explained.

'By which time we'll be dead and buried,' Taff said mildly. 'I don't think I approve of this.'

As if these restrictions were not enough, they were then informed that initial penetration distance into Indonesian territory would be a mere 5,000 yards. The penetration would include the river routes used by the Indos as MSRs, or main supply routes, to move men and equipment up to the border. Where possible, the SAS were to count the boats and the men in them, and map suitable areas from which they could be ambushed from the riverbank. Then they were to locate the *kampongs* and bases from which the boats were coming and, if possible, enter them without alerting the sentries or dogs, reconnoitre them, then slip back into the jungle. Should it be necessary, they would engage in fire fights to make their escape. The raids would be known as 'Claret' operations and classified top secret.

Those first cross-border patrols were made by two five-man teams *not* accompanied by local guides. The teams carried exactly the same equipment and weapons they had used in Sarawak, with the main small arm being the Armalite assault rifle, which was now being viewed as the perfect jungle weapon, being portable and powerful.

'It's also being used,' Bulldog told his men, 'because it's *not* standard issue to the British Army, so if any of us are wounded or taken prisoner, we can claim that our presence in Indonesian territory was due to a map-reading error. HQ believes that this will, in the present circumstances, sound reasonably plausible.'

'HQ doesn't know shite from shinola,' O'Connor said bluntly. 'If those fucking Indos find us on their territory, they'll just slit our throats.'

'True enough,' Bulldog replied, since this was a so-called 'Chinese parliament' with all opinions welcomed. 'Therefore let it be known that word's come down from the Head Sheds that if an individual trooper gets lost or is captured, no rescue will be attempted by the other men in his patrol. Also, nothing's to be left in enemy territory that could betray our presence there.'

'Just what does that mean, Staff-Sergeant?' the newcomer, Tommy Taylor asked, nervously scratching the acne spots on his pale, increasingly gaunt face.

'What it means, Trooper, is that no casualties, dead or wounded, are to be left behind. No identity discs, photos or letters from home. No ciggie stubs. No spent cartridge cases. Not even the prints of our fucking boots. In fact we're being given special footwear, with sacking or hessian placed outside the boots to blur any marks indicating their origin. Also, when yomping through the *ulu*, we're going to check every leaf and spider's web, leaving absolutely no trace of our movements. In short, we try to become invisible. *That's* what it means.'

Under Bulldog's command, Marty and the others were given the specific task of reaching the headwaters of the Koemba River to cause as much disruption as possible. Their main problem, as they had been warned by Major Parsons, was that previous SAS patrols to that area, though managing to reach the edge of the Sentimo marshes, had been unable to penetrate the marshes north of the river.

'You might have the same problem', Major Parsons warned them.

Navigating by a wide variety of means, they spent over a week trying to reach the upper part of the river and the mountain plateau separating it from Sentimo. This involved hiking through dense *belukar*, where the jungle had been cleared and was growing back again, thicker than ever, to form an often impenetrable tangle of palms, seedling trees, rattans and other sharp thorns. Also, the moss-covered tree trunks often soared over a hundred feet high, wrapped in another tangle of huge leaves, thick creepers and liana, forming an almost solid canopy above, blotting out the sunlight. Because of this the ground was wet and often slippery with mud, making progress slow and dirty; it also reminded the already struggling men that the feared swamps could not be far away.

This turned out to be true. Finally emerging from an epic struggle through a stretch of *belukar*, they found themselves faced with primary jungle filled with expansive swamps. These were hell to cross. The water often came up to the waist – sometimes the chest. It was covered with drifting debris, including large, razor-sharp leaves, thorny brambles, broken branches, seedlings and spiders' webs surrendering to mud-slime. This debris was in turn covered with dark swarms of flies and mosquitoes that buzzed and whined frantically around the men, covering their unprotected eyes, lips and nose. The men were further tormented by this because they could do nothing to prevent it, being forced to hold their weapons above their heads while trying to feel their way with their booted feet over an underwater bed rendered treacherous by shifting mud, tangled weeds, sharp or rolling stones that moved when stepped upon, and unexpected holes that could trap the feet. Nor could they prevent themselves from being covered by the slimy, wormlike leeches that crawled onto them from wet vegetation and sucked their blood as they waded through the swamp.

Even more tormenting was the fact that in many areas of the swamps, the lower branches of the trees stretched out across the water, often practically touching it, forcing the men either to work their way around them, which could double the distance travelled, or to duck under them. This latter course of action presented the risk of being cut by thorns and sharp palm leaves or, even worse, could cause them to shake more leeches, snakes or venomous spiders off the wet leaves, branches or glistening webs filled with trapped insects.

In fact, one of the main dangers of wading through the water was the possibility of an encounter with venomous sea snakes, which had flattened, paddle-shaped tails and, being the same brownish colour as the broken branches, could easily be mistaken for them until it was too late.

Luckily, no one was attacked. Nevertheless, it took a few more days to make it through the swamps and marshes, which meant that they had to sleep there as well. Sometimes, if they were lucky, they could sling hammocks between tree trunks; but when this was not possible they were forced to sleep standing upright, often waist deep in water, usually tying themselves to a tree trunk to prevent themselves falling over. While acutely uncomfortable, this afforded a little sleep, though it was rarely deep or for very long.

Marty knew damned well why he couldn't sleep. Normally he could have slept even when tied upright to a tree, but in this particular swamp, which was oppressively silent during the day, the night was filled with an eerie cacophony of croaking, hissing, flapping, snapping, rustling, squawking, buzzing and whining that penetrated the senses and repeatedly jerked him out of whatever restless sleep he was having. To this kind of disruption he could add his own helpless fear of slipping out of his ropes and sinking into the water, too tired to realise what was happening before he drowned; or of being bitten by venomous snakes or eels while his body sagged in the water. The fact that the leeches fed off his blood all night no longer even concerned him. There were worse things than leeches.

Finally, after five days of such horrors, already exhausted and only halfway through the patrol, they reached the upper part of the river – only to find that the sheer cliffs of the plateau separating it from Sentimo offered no possible route to the jungle 250 metres below, on the other side of the mountain range.

They had to turn back again.

Frustrated by the failure of his men to get beyond the Sentimo marshes and still constrained by not being permitted to use them for overtly aggressive actions, Major Parsons revised his strategy and, instead, mounted cross-border operations by the Gurkha battalions with the SAS acting as scouts. Though small and cheerful, the brown-faced Gurkhas were fearless fighters for whom no task was too dangerous. Marty was not alone among the SAS in having great admiration for them, but he was as frustrated as the others by the fact that the SAS were only permitted to act as scouts for the Gurkhas and then had to let them mount the actual attack, while the SAS could only give covering fire.

Surrounded by thick undergrowth, the Indo camps usually consisted of no more than a few thatched huts on stilts, some open latrines covered with clouds of flies, and a protective ring of sunken gun emplacements and defensive trenches. Invariably, when the Gurkhas arrived and spread out in a great circle around the camp, remaining well hidden in the forest, the Indo soldiers would be seated in large groups around open fires, breakfasting on roast pig and fried rice. In that same thick undergrowth, the Gurkhas and SAS would then quietly bring British three-inch mortars, Soviet RPG-7 rocket launchers, M79 single shot, breech-loading grenade-launchers, and general-purpose machine-guns (or GPMGs) and Bren light machine-guns into position. The gun and mortar teams would keep in touch with one another through their small, backpacked A41 radio sets and, at the command from the Gurkha CO, would fire simultaneously, tearing the camp to shreds with mortar shells, missiles, fin-stabilised grenades and tracer bullets, which flared across the clearing and disappeared into the daggering flames and boiling smoke from the mortar explosions. Within seconds, the camp would be obscured in a grim pall of smoke through which shadowy figures and brighter flames could just about be discerned, with the screams of the wounded and dying rising dreadfully above the bedlam of the roaring guns and explosions. With the SAS continuing to give covering fire, the Gurkhas would then move in to clear the camp, advancing at the crouch, firing on the move, and not stopping to take prisoners or ask questions. When the smoke eventually cleared, the camp would be a mess of dead and wounded men, the smouldering or still-burning remains of thatched huts, black shell holes, spent shells, buckled weapons, shreds of clothing, dismembered limbs and spreading pools of blood. It would not be a pretty sight.

Nevertheless, the SAS remained frustrated at their lack of more positive involvement – those raids were essentially Gurkha operations. They were therefore overjoyed when, a few weeks later, with the Indo incursions increasing, they finally received official approval to do more than 'watch and count', or act as scouts for the Gurkhas.

Immediately, Major Parsons broadened the scope of the

'Claret' raids to include attacks on enemy approach routes and MSRs, either by road or on water, ambushing tracks and rivers, and setting booby traps where it was known that the Indo or CCO raiders would pass. The range of penetration across the border was also greatly increased and the pre-emptive actions undertaken by the SAS increased in both frequency and ferocity.

Basing most of their attack methods on the 'shoot-and-scoot' procedure developed by Paddy Kearney in Malaya, the SAS groups made the essence of their ambushes speed of movement and reaction: hitting the enemy from close range with a brief, savage fusillade of small-arms firepower, including hand grenades, then vanishing speedily, leaving the counter-attackers to find nothing but empty jungle. These tactics were highly successful, causing a lot of damage, and soon the SAS were getting tales back from the Dyaks and other aboriginals about how the Indonesians and CCO were whispering fearful stories about their 'invisible' attackers.

'The Tiptoe Boys,' Marty said exultantly after a particular, highly successful raid. 'That's us. That's what we should call ourselves.'

'Why not?' Bulldog responded. 'Sounds good to me.'

The title took on and soon most of the SAS in the *ulu* were calling themselves just that, both in jest and with a certain amount of pride. Perhaps emboldened by the name they had adopted for themselves, in the weeks that followed, the attacks of the Tiptoe Boys became lengthier, more sophisticated affairs, even using electronically detonated Claymore mines to catch the enemy column's front and rear while the automatic fire of the SAS weapons raked the centre.

Invariably, the Claymore ambushes of the SAS followed the same routine. While Bulldog, Marty, Taff and Tommy Taylor, who was fast gaining confidence, knelt in the firing position in the shadow of the trees by the side of the road, spaced well apart to give a broad arc of fire, their demolitions expert, Rod O'Connor, would quickly and expertly lay his four Claymore mines approximately equidistant along the centre of a 100-metre stretch of road, placed so as to catch the front and rear of the Indo column, as well as the middle. The mines would be buried in the ground face up, resting on their spiked base, with earth and leaves thrown back over them to make them invisible. O'Connor would wire them to be detonated by remote control, then melt back into the trees at the side of the track, taking up a firing position beside some of the others.

Eventually, the first troops of the Indo patrol would approach around the bend in the path, emerging slowly from the trees, wearing jungle-green fatigues, soft-peaked caps and jungle boots. Armed with bolt-action rifles and Soviet submachine-guns, they also had hand grenades clipped to the belts around their waists and ammunition bandoliers criss-crossing their chests. O'Connor would wait until the first soldier in the column had passed over the row of mines and the last soldier was just stepping onto the last mine, then he would detonate the mines by remote control. When the mines exploded, four deafening roarings as one, they would blow the soil up and outwards in great fan shapes that spewed smoke and fire. Also blown apart, the Indonesian troops would be picked up and slammed back down, or slashed to ribbons by the hundreds of razor-sharp slugs that flew with the speed of bullets in all directions.

That the SAS men should open fire simultaneously with their Armalites and SLRs was almost an act of mercy, since many of the Indonesians not instantly killed would be staggering about in the swirling smoke, or writhing on the dust-choked ground, their skin either scorched and blistered or slashed to the bone and, in many cases, stripped right off the ribcage or limbs, exposing bloody intestines and naked bone.

The hail of SAS bullets would stitch through these unfortunates, cutting off their demented screams, then move left and right in a broad arc, taking in those who had escaped the blasts of the Claymores and were now retreating into the forest, firing on the move. Then, before the remaining Indonesians could get their senses back together and retaliate, Bulldog would bawl for the SAS to 'bug out' and they would, as the Tiptoe Boys, beat a hasty retreat, melting back into the *ulu* and leaving no trace of themselves behind.

After many more such raids, the Indonesians became convinced that the SAS Tiptoe Boys were indeed invisible. When the Dyaks brought that news back to the SAS FOB, it made the whole bloody business seem worthwhile to Marty and his mates.

But the worst was yet to come.

CHAPTER TWENTY-TWO

After three months in the *ulu*, with occasional short breaks back in the FOB, Marty and the other members of Bulldog's raiding party were flown to Kuching, Brunei, for a well-earned leave. They had been back only four days, however, when they were called to a briefing in the Haunted House, where Major Parsons, also back temporarily from the FOB to receive his instructions from the Head Sheds, informed them that they were to return to the Koemba River, north-west of Poeri, where the Indos had a staging post for men and supplies going eastward to Seluas. The patrol's task was to disrupt or completely stop the river traffic.

'Why us?' Bulldog asked.

'Six other patrols have attempted to reach specific points on the river near Poeri, but they all failed because the marshes are too deep. You lot actually made it as far as the headwater. This time, when you get there, we want you to choose a good location for an OP – we need as much intelligence as you can garner – and also cause a little mayhem near the town. Just one decent assault on passing traffic could scare the Indos into avoiding that river. So that's what you're tasked with.'

'Lucky us,' Marty said.

They left the following morning. Inserted by helicopter to an LZ near the frontier with Kalimantan, due north of Achan, they melted into the *ulu* and headed roughly south, following

Bulldog's compass bearings, intending to turn due west seven days later. By noon of the second day, or the first full day of hiking, they had crossed the border north of Achan and started circling around it, heading through a combination of primary jungle and *belukar* for the swamps that lay between it and the River Koemba. By noon the third day they had reached a broad track running north-west from Poeri and almost certainly used regularly by soldiers going to Achan. Satisfied that the track was clear, they crossed it swiftly and vanished again into the *ulu*, now heading on a direct line for the swamps that led east to the Koemba.

That afternoon they came to a recently cleared track running compass-true parallel to the river. Realising that the track would make a good Indo ambush point, Bulldog silently indicated that Marty, the team's cameraman, should photograph it from a few different angles. When Marty had done so, writing details of the location into his notebook, they crossed the track unnoticed. They were, however, uncomfortably aware of the fact that in such a clearing they might have been spotted by an unseen Indo OP. In the event, no enemy patrols appeared and soon they saw, just beyond some bamboo screens and a tangle of *belukar*, stretching away for as far as the eye could see, the swamp they all dreaded.

'Here we go,' Rod O'Connor said with a despairing sigh while Tommy Taylor, staring at each of the others in turn, registered understandable trepidation.

'Let's go,' Bulldog said.

Moving into the swamp from north-east of the river bend, they soon found themselves knee deep in slimy, debris-covered water and assailed by madly buzzing and whining insects. Though the bed of the swamp was soft and yielding – a combination of mud and small stones, dangerously cluttered with larger stones, felled logs and other debris – they were able to push onward until, in the early afternoon, the water became too deep to cross and the mud too soft to walk on, made more so by the weight of the men's weapons and packed Bergens.

In this area gigantic bright green palm leaves floated on the swamp and lay on small islands of firm ground, covered with seedlings and brown leaves. Surprisingly hard, they split if stepped upon, giving off a loud cracking sound. For this reason, the men tried to avoid them, but, even when they were pushed gently aside in the water, they often split with what seemed in the stillness a noise like a pistol shot.

'I keep thinking we're being attacked,' Marty whispered.

'That should keep you on your toes,' Bulldog replied.

That night, making themselves as comfortable as they could on a small island in the swamp, the five men held a 'Chinese parliament' to pool suggestions. Their shared decision was that they should continue south-east, following the line of the River Sentimo until they reached the River Koemba. They could then track the Koemba due east until it took them to Seluas.

As agreed, they moved out the next morning, heading south, wading waist deep in the water for what seemed like an eternity, though it actually took them only three miles, to the confluence of the Poeteh and Sentimo rivers. As Bulldog had predicted, the water here was deeper, the foliage more obstructive, but when they tried to follow the river, wading through even worse swamps, they soon lost it in impenetrable jungle. Doggedly wading on, they found themselves emerging to relatively clear, swampy land which Bulldog calculated was due north of the Koemba.

Continuing onward, they came to a series of slow-flowing tributaries that wound their way between a maze of dry banks and curtains of bamboo. They were trying to cross this maze, waist deep in river water, when a large boat swished by on the other side of a high bamboo curtain. Its wash lifted the flotsam of leaves so high that O'Connor and Taylor were practically submerged and surfaced, thrashing wildly and choking, completely drenched.

No one laughed at them. No one dared speak. Unable to see through the curtain of bamboo, beyond which was the channel that the boat had passed along, Bulldog decided to change direction and head back into the swamp to avoid accidentally breaking out into the river just as another Indo boat was passing.

This turned out to be their first lucky break, since after wading for another four hours, hidden in the swamp but following the line of the river, they came up onto firm ground which was, Bulldog was convinced from its appearance, the fingertip of the spur he had been seeking.

'No doubt about it,' he said, checking his map against a compass reading. 'This is what we've been looking for.'

Pleased, he put the map and compass away, then took in the scene as they knelt on the edge of the narrow strip of dry jungle, hidden by tall grass, looking at the broad sweep of the River Koebma where it curved around the well-spaced trees of a rubber plantation, glittering in the early afternoon sunlight. On his left the strip of jungle continued right up to the mud-brown, irregular riverbank.

Bulldog pointed to it with his forefinger. 'That could make a good OP,' he said.

He was right. In the centre of the strip of dry jungle a large tree spread its branches above dense scrub and a shallow ditch, but with open ground surrounding both – as open as it was to his right, where the plantation's rows of rubber trees were spread along the riverbank. The trees were being 'rested', with no sign of recent tappings, though Bulldog saw that there were some well-used paths through the plantation.

'That means the plantation's still being worked,' he told them. 'So we better be careful.'

As a site for their observation point (OP), Bulldog plumped for the lone tree and its scrub-covered, shallow ditch. Feeling exposed where he was kneeling, and having made sure that there were no Indo troops in the immediate vicinity, he ordered the patrol into the scrub surrounding the ditch.

'Make the OP simple,' he said. 'Four scrapes under the scrub. And be quick about it.'

They made a rectangular OP with four shallow scrapes for their bashas, two overlooking the river for the purposes of observation, the others facing the jungle behind: one for the watch, the second for sleeping in. The scrapes were filled with a bed of leaves, then sleeping bags were rolled out on the leaves. Another shallow scrape, placed in the centre of the four large ones, was used as a well for weapons and kit. To help keep out the rain, ponchos were raised on forked sticks above the scrapes and pegged to the ground. The scrub was pulled closely over the ponchos and in turn covered with local foliage. Narrow 'windows' were made to the front and rear of the foliage to give broad views of the river and jungle.

When the OP was completed, they settled down to a long day of observation and recording of what was seen, updating logbooks and redrawing maps in the light of their recent explorations. Marty photographed the river and any traffic on it, taking notes on what he was shooting, while Rod O'Connor, acting as sentry facing the jungle behind the OP, but also the team's signaller, checked through the various wavebands in the hope of picking up enemy transmissions and encoded news of other SAS patrols. While they were thus engaged, Bulldog checked the traffic on the river, noting its frequency and exact details in his logbook, and informing Marty of its coming to enable him to take more photographs. Meanwhile, Taff and Tommy kept their eyes on the river, weapons at the ready.

The river was busy, with a little local traffic in the morning followed by a greater number of military supply boats flying the Indonesian flag and manned by armed troops. Obviously they were cruising to and from the trading settlement at Seluas, which Bulldog estimated was about five miles downriver. He was even more convinced of this when Indo helicopters flew overhead, patently on reconnaissance.

'Sooner or later they're going to see us,' Bulldog said, 'so I recommend we cause a stir as soon as possible and then bug out of this place.'

'I agree,' Marty said.

Their chance came soon enough. First thing next morning, shortly after they had competed a cold breakfast, a longboat containing three uniformed Indonesian soldiers came along the river, heading upstream. Taken by surprise, Bulldog plunged into the shelter of the trees by the riverbank and was followed immediately by Marty and the others. Kneeling there in the firing position, Marty watched the longboat approaching. Meanwhile, Rod O'Connor was unclipping an '80' white phosphorous incendiary grenade from his webbed belt.

'Let's not take any chances,' he said grimly.

After unpinning the grenade, he stepped forward for a better view, though still protected by the trees. He waited until the longboat was abreast of his position, then hurled the grenade.

Marty saw the Indonesians in the boat glance up, startled, as O'Connor stepped back into the trees. Raising their eyes even higher, the Indos saw the grenade, then, shouting frantically, threw themselves face down in the boat as the grenade fell towards them. Bouncing off the stern off the boat, it exploded with a thunderous clap, creating a great fountain of rushing, roaring water and smoke streaked by silvery phosphorous. The stern of the boat was thrown high into the air, forcing the prow down into the water and throwing the soldiers forward, one into the other, with the third one – the one nearest the explosion – bursting into flames and catapulting over his tangled friends to splash into the river.

Even as the remaining two Indos were struggling to right themselves, one reaching for his rifle, Marty and the others opened fire, peppering the boat from front to rear, making the soldiers spasm epileptically as hundreds of chips of wood were torn from the hull, exploding upwards and raining back down. In a matter of seconds the two soldiers were dead and the hull of the boat was disintegrating, sinking even as Marty and the others continued firing to ensure that it would sink.

Less than a minute later, when the SAS men had finally stopped firing, the boat was practically in pieces, taking in water, and sinking as the water turned crimson with the blood of the dead men.

The boat broke apart, the dead men drifted with the debris in swirling blood-red currents, then all evidence of the attack – the wooden flotsam, the dead men, the bloody water – was carried away downstream and eventually disappeared.

'Clear the area and let's bug out,' Bulldog snapped. 'I want no trace of us left here. *Move it!*'

Within minutes they had demolished the OP, filled in the shallow scrapes, and strewn local foliage over the area to make it look almost exactly as it had been. Then, packing up their kit, they turned away from the river and embarked on the short, difficult hike back over the maze of watery channels, dry banks and curtains of bamboo until they reached the southern tip of the swamp, bordered by a dense tangle of *belukar*. Forced to stoop under the lower branches and palm leaves, they had an arduous trek for the next hour, their backs breaking and every muscle aching. It was therefore a relief when they could straighten up again and advance like human beings, though each step was taking them ever deeper into the scum-covered water.

Nevertheless, they waded farther into the swamp, forced as usual to endure the swarms of flies, mosquitoes and midges, constantly alert for sea snakes, concentrating at all times on not breaking an ankle on one of the many large stones on the bed of the lake, or losing balance by treading on an underwater log, or sinking or slipping in the thickening mud. Also forced as usual to carry their personal weapons above their heads to keep them from the water, they soon had badly aching muscles and sharp, stabbing pains between their shoulder-blades.

'Fuck!' Bulldog suddenly exclaimed. 'The bastards are on our tail!'

Even as Bulldog was speaking, Marty saw an Indonesian Army helicopter flying low overhead, obviously searching the swamp. Instantly, he and others froze where they stood, hoping that their camouflaged clothes would make them merge into the swamp and that their lack of movement would leave no rippling wake on the water, to be seen from above. When the helicopter finally disappeared, they moved on again.

'They won't give up that easily,' Bulldog said.

He was right. Twenty minutes later a second helicopter appeared, this time roaring out of the southern sky and hovering right above where they were wading through a stretch of swamp covered in tangled vegetation. Holding their rifles up with one hand and hacking at the dense foliage with the *parang* held in the other, they were taken by surprise and had no time to freeze before the helicopter pilot saw them and brought the chopper down to hover above them.

An Indo soldier was kneeling behind a machine-gun fixed to the floor at the open side door of the chopper. When he saw the men struggling through the swamp, he opened fire on them.

With the helicopter hovering dangerously close to the trees and swaying slightly from side to side, the gunner had difficulty in keeping his aim steady. His first burst went wide, making the water boil violently very close to the men. This gave them time to wade behind the nearest tree trunks, from where they were able to fire back with Armalites and SLRs switched to automatic. But instead of ascending, the helicopter dropped lower to give the gunner a better view of his targets.

Having the more powerful SLR, rather than the lighter Armalite, Marty was able to put some bullets into the helicopter, stitching a line just above the door and hitting something inside that burst into flames. Sucked out on the helicopter's slipstream, the flames roared through the open door to engulf the unfortunate gunner whose screams were like nothing remotely human. As the helicopter ascended, still on fire and pouring smoke, a crewman inside, attempting to put out the flames, kicked the blazing, screaming gunner out. The man fell like a burning projectile, kicking and screaming, leaving a vertical stream of smoke to mark his downward course, and was silenced only when he plunged into the swamp a good distance away. The helicopter turned around and headed back the way it had come, still pouring smoke.

'Good one, Marty,' the imperturbable Taff said.

They continued wading through the swamp, passing the dead Indo pilot whose charred, smouldering body was sinking slowly, heading deeper into an area covered with overhanging *belukar*. When another helicopter flew overhead the *belukar* hid them from view, but half an hour later they saw a fourth chopper behind them, this one a larger transport, hovering low enough to enable a good dozen Indo troopers to climb down a rope ladder into the swamp where the first pilot had seen them.

'Shit!' Bulldog said. 'They know this swamp like the back of their hands. They'll catch up in no time.'

'What do we do now?' Tommy Taylor asked, looking nervous but controlling himself.

'We keep going,' Marty said.

This they did, wading laboriously through the muddy water, often having to clamber over drifting logs and chop their way through overhanging branches and spiky leaves. Then, to their dismay, another Indo helicopter appeared to drop another group of troops about a mile directly ahead of them.

'Shit!' Bulldog said again. 'The bastards are going to put a cordon around the swamp and then close in on us.'

'So what do we do now?' Tommy Taylor asked, still nervous, but looking determined for all that.

'We *still* keep going,' Marty said. 'We either ambush those bastards before they see us or we fight our way through.'

In fact, they had been wading only another twenty minutes when a rustling of reeds and swishing of water straight ahead indicated that someone was coming. Melting into the undergrowth at both sides of an imaginary track, they waited until the advance scout of the inserted Indo patrol emerged, waist deep in water, holding a Lee-Enfield bolt-action rifle across his chest. Like the others, Marty was just about to raise his SLR and fire at the Indo when he saw Taff slipping around behind the trees and coming up out of the water behind him. Before the scout knew what was happening, Taff had thrown one arm around his face, smothering his nose and mouth, then jerked his head back to draw the blade of his Sykes Fairburn commando dagger across his windpipe. The scout shuddered with his throat spurting blood, held upright by Taff, and kept shuddering for what seemed like a long time before he was still. Only when his frantic, dying movements had stopped did Taff lower him quietly into the swamp. The dead man's blood flowed out in a large circle that turned the muddy-brown water red.

'We can ambush that patrol coming towards us,' Taff suggested, pushing the floating Indo body aside as if it were no more than an obstructing log, 'then mine our wake to disrupt the ones coming up behind us. Could you do that, Rod?'

'You mean the Claymores?'

'Right.'

'I could tie them to the trees,' O'Connor said, getting the picture. 'Fucking right, I could, mate.'

'Okay, Bulldog?' Taff asked.

Bulldog nodded. 'Okay.'

Stunned once more by the cold-blooded killer instincts of the blue-eyed, mild-mannered Taff, Marty hid with the others behind the shivering foliage at the side of the imaginary passage through the water while O'Connor clambered up to the lower branches of the nearest tree, checking carefully that there were no snakes sleeping there. Sitting on the thickest branch, which was just above the surface of the plant-covered, scummy water, he tied one of the Claymores to its underside with the cord from his Bergen, then attached a lengthy piece of trip-wire to it. Climbing down again, he let the trip-wire run out through his fingers as he waded across the route taken by the Indo patrol, which he treated as an imaginary 'path' about ten foot wide. He stopped at a tree growing well to the other side of this 'path'. After tying the trip-wire to the tangled roots of the tree, he tugged until it was tight enough to trip the mine if moved by the passage of a human body or leg. As the trip-wire was just under the surface of the water it would not be seen by its potential victims.

'Have you got any more?' Bulldog asked him.

'Three or four.'

'Good. Let's keep advancing until we hear the approach of that Indo patrol up front, then we just let them pass. They'll be the first to trip that wire. Then lay the others about a quarter-mile apart to take out the patrol that's following us. That might just about give us time to get clear of this swamp.'

'Understood,' O'Connor said.

'Right, lads, let's move out.'

They advanced carefully through the swamp until, about thirty minutes later, they heard the sound of swishing water and rustling foliage not too far ahead. Spreading well out and melting into the trees on either side of what they assessed to be the path of the oncoming troops, they were rewarded when the five-man Indo patrol emerged from the foliage ahead, wading with extreme care, and passed by without noticing their presence.

Up close, Marty noticed, the Indos looked like adolescents – slim, short, with handsome, decent features – not at all like a bunch of seasoned jungle troops, which is what they were. It was always harder, Marty knew, to kill men whose faces you had seen. He was therefore glad when the five Indos had passed on, disappearing into the foliage behind him as if they had never been.

Bulldog waited for a good five minutes, until he was sure that they were out of earshot of the retreating Indo patrol, before silently waving the others on. Again, they made their laborious way through the swamp, pushing the foliage and drifting branches aside, ignoring the many fat leeches now sticking to them, stopping only when O'Connor had to climb a tree and attach another Claymore to it, which he did three more times.

Eventually, when they were nearing the end of the swamp, they heard the first Claymore exploding well behind them. Even from this distance the noise was shocking, a mighty clap of thunder, and when they glanced back they saw a cloud of black smoke boiling up from the swamp. They even heard men screaming from this distance, but those sounds were much fainter.

O'Connor grinned at Taff, who stuck his thumb up in the air. Then the patrol advanced once more.

Another Claymore exploded about fifteen minutes later, then two more at fifteen-minute intervals, with the screams of men heard in the distance and more black smoke billowing up where the Indos were being cut to shreds by the hundreds of sharp-edged, red-hot, flying metal slugs of the Claymore mines.

It would be pure hell back there, Marty knew, as he continued to wade forward, finally emerging, with an immense feeling of relief, from the putrid swamp.

He did not get a rest, however. Convinced that the Indonesians would not give up the chase until their quarry reached the border, Bulldog made his men keep marching. The hike took them into the relative ease of primary jungle, which led to a series of high ridges and forested hills, criss-crossed with rushing streams and deep, dangerous gorges, only some of which had aerial walkways spanning them.

Just after noon, when the *ulu* was like a steam bath, they saw an Indo soldier in the branches high up a tree, looking directly at them, then signalling frantically with both hands, clearly telling his friends he had seen them. Taff picked the soldier off with a single shot from his Armalite, making him spin backwards off the tree and plunge screaming to the ground, smashing through many branches as he fell.

'They've seen what those Claymores did to their friends,' Bulldog said, 'and now they're not going to stop until they get their revenge. We better move out of here fast and get across that border.'

They started running, weaving through the trees, but within minutes an Indo helicopter was rising out of the jungle nearby. Heading straight for the SAS men, it was soon roaring overhead. Descending vertically, it created a storm and then hovered directly above them, dangerously close to the trees. A gunner was kneeling at the side door, taking aim with a Chinese gas-operated machine-gun, and when it roared into action it tore the clearing all to hell, with lumps of bark and leaves flying in all directions, the ground convulsing and spitting soil.

Marty was still running, weaving frantically through the trees, when he saw Rod O'Connor, obviously outraged, raking the Indo helicopter with his SLR. Whether the hail of bullets actually damaged the chopper or merely panicked the pilot, it tilted sideways and its rotors struck the treetops, slicing off branches, before buckling with a harsh metallic screeching. Crippled, the chopper shuddered, leaned farther to the side, then plunged to earth, smashing through the branches, bringing whole trees down with it and exploding into a fierce ball of yellow-and-blue fire that engulfed the surrounding trees and foliage, creating an even bigger blaze.

'Keep running!' Bulldog bawled.

Yet even as they did so, leaving the smoking *ulu* behind them, the distant crump-crump of firing Indo mortars was followed by a series of violent explosions that tore up the ground around them. Sucked up in a roaring vacuum and hurled back to earth, Marty rolled through boiling smoke and swirling soil, then clambered back to his feet. Shaking his head, trying to clear it, he glanced back through the trees and saw a great number of Indo troops advancing. Grabbing his SLR from where it was lying on the scorched grass, he followed his comrades into the protective shadows of the forest, lost them temporarily, then emerged into light again and saw Tommy Taylor standing nervously at an aerial walkway that spanned a deep gorge.

Looking down, momentarily dizzy, Marty saw a river squeezing through a bottleneck of large rocks and emerging at the other side, directly below the aerial walkway, as a raging torrent.

'Oh, shit!' he whispered.

Hearing a noise to his right, he glanced up and saw Bulldog emerging from the forest and also stopping at the edge of the deep gorge, which he studied with undisguised dismay. Within seconds, Taff and Rod O'Connor had also appeared, the latter emerging backwards from the trees, firing on the move at the advancing Indos.

'They're coming close!' O'Connor bawled.

'We have to cross and then blow the other side of this walkway to hell,' Bulldog said, 'to ensure that the Indos can't follow us. Taff, you first. You go next, Marty. When you get to the other side, give us covering fire. Trooper Taylor goes third and I'll come up behind him to ensure that he makes it across. O'Connor covers us and then comes across when we can all cover him. Get going, Taff.'

Cool as a cucumber, Taff stepped onto the aerial walkway, took hold of the vertical length of bamboo, and then started walking carefully across the three parallel lengths of narrow bamboo that formed the floor of the walkway. As soon as he advanced, the whole walkway shook and Tommy Taylor visibly winced. As Taff continued across, seeming almost to be walking in thin air, a hundred-odd feet above the roaring rapids, Bulldog ordered Marty and Tommy to join Rod O'Connor in keeping the advancing Indos pinned down. This wasn't easy. The Indos were advancing by darting from tree to tree, two or three at a time, while the others poured a fusillade of fire at the SAS, causing branches and leaves to fly wildly about them.

'Next man!' Taff bawled from the other side of the gorge, having made it safely across.

Turning away from the advancing Indos and taking a deep breath, Marty stepped carefully onto the narrow walkway. Though trying not to look, he found it impossible to avoid the wide spaces between the uprights, the bits-and-pieces nature of the fragile bamboo walkway, and the raging torrent that wound between the rocky walls of the gorge over a hundred feet below him. As soon as he had both feet on the walkway and had started gingerly across, it moved perceptibly, swaying from left to right. It was also being shaken constantly by the wind sweeping through the gorge, but it moved more with each step that Marty took, almost making his heart stop.

To steady himself, he grabbed the bamboo support on his right. Looking down, he felt dizzy. The actual floor of the walkway was only the width of its three lengths of thick bamboo, laid down side by side and strapped together with rattan, which did not look too strong. In fact, it was hardly much wider than Marty's two booted feet placed close together.

The uprights angled out and in again overhead, bending where they were strapped with rattan to the horizontal holds. Because of this, Marty could slide his hand along the holds only as far as the next upright. Once there, he had to remove his hand for a moment and lift it over the upright before grabbing the horizontal hold again. This meant that every few steps there came a moment when he couldn't hold onto anything and had to use only his body to keep his balance.

He judged the walkway to be about 150 feet across, though it was so narrow it looked a lot longer. Its swaying was visible, its creaking constant, and the wind blowing along the gorge had the force of a hammer blow. Given the wide spaces between the uprights, he realised that he could be blown off with nothing to stop him from falling through those wide spaces to his doom. His stomach churned at the thought of it.

He inched forward, a step at a time, balancing precariously each time he had to release his grip on the horizontal hold and lift it over an upright to grab the next hold. As he did so, his stomach churning, his heart beating too fast, he saw the foliage exploding around the kneeling figure of Taff, where the Indo bullets were spraying the forest about him as he gave covering fire. Realising that the Indos were rapidly coming closer, Marty forced himself to move more quickly and finally, reaching the end of the walkway, virtually threw himself off, landing on hands and knees, then rolling over and clambering to his knees to kneel beside Taff. Even as he opened fire on the forest at the other side, he saw Tommy Taylor crossing the bridge, followed closely by Bulldog.

By now the forest around Rod O'Connor was being torn to

shreds by a hail of bullets from the advancing Indo troops. Mortar shells were also exploding around him as, still giving covering fire, he inched ever closer to the aerial walkway. In fact, just as Tommy and Bulldog reached the middle of the walkway, a mortar explosion tore up the earth dangerously close to the supports on the far side. When the whole walkway shook more violently, battered by the blast, Tommy hurried across and was soon jumping off. Instantly, with an excited gleam in his brown eyes, he joined Marty and Taff on the edge of the gorge, giving covering fire to Bulldog and O'Connor.

O'Connor was backing towards the walkway, firing on the move, as Bulldog jumped off the other side. He turned around beside Marty and dropped to one knee to give covering fire also, as O'Connor backed right up to the bridge, still firing his SLR from the hip, this time at the first of the Indo troops to charge out from behind the trees. Some of the Indos went down, but others were still advancing when O'Connor jumped onto the walkway and started across.

He didn't get very far. Just as he was beginning the 150-foot walk, an Indo machine-gun roared from just inside the cover of the trees, raking the aerial walkway, sending lumps of bamboo and pieces of rattan flying off in all directions, then finally finding him. Convulsing in a noisy explosion of bullet-torn bamboo and rattan, he dropped his SLR, which fell over a hundred feet to splash into the rapids. He screamed in agony, his body shuddering, doubling up, pieces of clothing flying off him as more bullets stitched him and blood began soaking his shredded OGs. Gripping the side of the walkway, he tried to haul himself forward, but then fell to his knees, nearly slipped off the edge, and managed to straighten himself up, though still screaming and shuddering.

Suddenly, even as more Indo troops burst out from the trees, firing at O'Connor as well as across the gorge, Bulldog jumped back onto the walkway and started towards him, determined to rescue him.

'No, Bulldog!' Marty bawled without thinking. 'It's too late! Come back!'

But Bulldog didn't come back. He was hurrying across the

walkway, holding on with one hand and firing his Armalite with the other, the stock tucked into his waist, when more bullets stitched O'Connor and he screamed even louder and was punched violently forward, hitting the narrow floor of the walkway, then rolling off the side and plunging, still screaming, to his doom in the roaring rapids far below.

Bulldog stopped advancing then. Trapped on the walkway, unable to turn around, he attempted to inch backwards while still firing his Armalite with one hand. As he was doing so, the Indo soldiers poured a fusillade of fire at him, tearing the bridge immediately around him to shreds and eventually tearing him to shreds as well. Slammed backwards by the bullets, he dropped his Armalite, which fell to the roaring rapids far below, but he managed to keep his grip on the horizontal hold and attempted to pull himself backwards. Somehow, even while still being peppered with bullets, he managed to twist himself around until he could grab the hold with both hands, holding on for dear life.

At that very moment, a final Indo mortar shell exploded on the edge of the gorge, where the end of the walkway was attached to it, tearing the supports out of the earth and making the walkway buckle and then collapse. As Marty and the others looked on in horror, even while still firing their weapons, the far end of the aerial walkway dropped towards the rapids, with Bulldog still clinging to it. Amazingly, Bulldog managed to hang on as the remains of the walkway, the narrow floor, fell down and swung in towards the other side of the gorge, right beneath the shocked SAS men. Bulldog was smashed against the hard-mud wall, hammered to hell just like the walkway, and plunged in a shower of splintered bamboo and torn rattan to the boiling rapids below. Marty saw his broken body splashing into the rushing water, smashing onto the sharp rocks, then bouncing off and being swept away until he was out of sight.

'Shake out!' Marty bawled with tears in his eyes, then he and the others raced away into the trees, into safety, leaving the Indos to fire furiously, frustratedly, without further effect, from the other side of the gorge. As the aerial walkway was no longer there, they could not get across.

The SAS survivors were safe, though they were all devastated by what had happened – Marty most of all.

He never really recovered.

CHAPTER TWENTY-THREE

'You're past forty,' Ann Lim told Marty as she dressed young Ian, preparing to take him to the nursery school in Hereford. Dark and handsome at five years old, he was wriggling and giggling where he sat on the cluttered kitchen table, framed by the window that overlooked the rear garden and the rolling green hills of the countryside. 'You're going to be forty-four this year – a bad time for a man.'

Marty had just confessed that he had lost something in Borneo and, whatever it was, it hadn't come back. The bloody death of Bulldog had cut as deeply as the loss of Tone years before in Malaya; the equally horrible death of Rod O'Connor, though not as seriously wounding, was also hard to take. With the departure of these good friends, Marty felt that a hole had been cut deep inside him and that nothing could ever replace it.

'Don't mention my age,' he said. 'You'll just give me more sleepless nights.'

'That's childish.'

'That's me.'

'I married a man and you're still that.'

'Well, thank God for that, at least.'

His feelings of loss were only compounded by the fact that the man he admired most of all, Paddy Kearney, was no longer with the SAS, having been RTU'd to a desk job in Number 8

Commando, and was soon to retire from the Army altogether and return to Civvy Street. This loss, to Marty, was like a death in itself, making him feel that his best days were behind him and could never be replaced.

'Come on, Marty, let's be honest,' Ann Lim persisted. 'The problem's your age. You're really trying to face the fact that you're not a young man any more and that there's no turning back of the clock. Sooner or later, all men have to deal with that dilemma and now it's your turn.'

There was a certain amount of truth in that, Marty knew, but it wasn't the whole of it. While he could not deny that turning forty had been troublesome, filling him with fears that he despised in himself, his ageing could not completely explain the deeper changes within him. The brutal deaths of his closest friends had given him many nightmares and caused him to build a wall around himself, not encouraging close friendships within the regiment in case those friends, too, came to a bloody end. He wanted to be detached, objective, prepared for any possible future loss, treating even the deaths of comrades as the natural outcome of his dangerous profession. Yes, he thought of it as a profession and wished to be the ultimate professional. He could take his pride from that.

'You're restless,' Ann Lim suggested, still trying to dress the wriggling Ian who was, Marty noted, beginning to look more Chinese every day. 'You want to be back in Borneo. You're always restless when your squadron's returned to base and you've nothing to do. You hate being back here.'

'I don't hate being at home,' he told her, anxious to avoid a repetition of Lesley's resentment at his constant absences when on overseas tours of duty. Ann Lim had not shown a similar resentment so far and he didn't want her to start.

'Good.' She brushed the black hair from her brown eyes. 'You can love your work when you're doing it, so long as you still like coming home. I still expect your attention.'

'You always get it.'

'I spoil you in order to be spoilt. I'm a clever woman that way.'

'No argument. I'm yours until Doomsday.'

'That's my man,' she said.

Now thirty-three years old, she had cut her long hair to shoulder length which, she insisted, suited her more at that age. Marty still missed the long hair, which he had thought looked very sensual, but he'd had the sense not to complain. *Nothing lasts for ever*, he thought, studying her new hairstyle with undeniable regret. He was grateful, however, for the fact that she had kept her figure and now, in a tight, black dress and white jumper belted at the waist, emphasising her full breasts and slim waist, she was looking more attractive than any of his friends' wives could manage.

'Do you really think I'm having a male menopausal problem?' he asked her.

She nodded, smiling, still trying to dress the giggling Ian as he tickled her and lightly kicked his legs. 'I think you haven't been the same since you first came back from Borneo. We both know why. Probably what happened there also made you start thinking about mortality in general and your age in particular.'

'True enough,' he agreed.

'On top of that, you've had these problems with your mother, which must have been draining for you and probably still is.'

'That, too, is true, darlin'.'

'It's not been a good time for you, Marty, but unfortunately that's also part of being over forty. You're at the age where things start going wrong with a lot of people you love. That makes you feel that things are going wrong with you as well – but in fact, they're not. You're still okay. *We're* okay. We have our lives to get on with.'

What she was saying was true enough. During the past couple of years, as he had alternated between tours of duty in Borneo and acting as an instructor in the training wing at Hereford, his life had seemed to be falling in pieces all around him. This had really started with the death of his father, which had happened shortly before the first Borneo tour. But his feelings had certainly not been helped by the violent deaths of Bulldog and Rod O'Connor. That aerial walkway, he knew, would haunt him for the rest of his days.

'You're right,' he confessed. 'I haven't been the same since I returned from that first bloody tour of Borneo. I'm also depressed at the realisation that the only old friend I have left in the regiment is Taff.'

'The one you call the mild-mannered, cold-blooded killer.'

'Right, that's him. The only old friend left – and he doesn't even go back as far as the Originals, the old gang from North Africa. On top of that, he's absolutely unknowable.'

'A friend who can never be a real friend.'

'Well, not quite. I mean, he still goes back a long way with me, so, even though there's no way of really knowing him, I feel warm towards him. I wouldn't like to see anything happen to him; that would hurt me as well.'

'But he's still unknowable, Marty. Finally, he's out of reach. That's why you've taken young Tommy Taylor under your wing. You need someone more human.'

'Yes, I think so.' He'd taken Tommy under his wing after that first tour of duty in Borneo and treated him as a protégé ever since. Tommy was now an experienced corporal with extensive experience gained in Borneo. Marty was proud of him. 'I have to admit, though, that every time I return to England I'm faced with the undeniable fact that my world's changing rapidly and will never be the same again.'

The death of my father, he thought. The deaths of friends. The death of John F. Kennedy. The death of Sir Winston Churchill. Now astronauts are walking in space and a New Age is dawning. My past's growing longer every day and my future's shrinking.

'Not helped by your mother,' Ann Lim said, breaking his reverie as she lifted Ian off the table and planted him on the floor. She sipped at her coffee while the boy put his jacket on. 'That's been hard to take, too.'

Marty sighed. 'I suppose so.'

Even while trying bravely to cope with the death of her husband, his mother had been broken up inside and was visibly ageing, with increasing lapses of memory and a general loss of interest in most things. Though once houseproud, she rarely cleaned up any more and Marty, when he managed to visit her in London, was usually shocked by the neglected state of his old home. Also, as he was gradually finding out, she rarely saw her friends any more, drank a lot in private, and was receiving a wide variety of sedatives from her doctor. She often rang Marty here at Redhill, usually in the early hours of the morning, sobbing drunkenly and saying she was frightened for her future. Though Ann Lim had invited her to come and live here, she had always refused. The desperate phone calls still came though.

'I don't think she's going to get better,' he admitted. 'She'll just get worse and worse. I don't want to think about what might happen then – particularly if she still refuses to come out here. I mean, even thinking about a nursing home . . . I can't bear the thought of it.'

'We'll face it when we come to it, Marty. Don't let it get you down now.'

She was standing with her rump pressed to the sink, her back to the window that framed the green hills of Hereford, her brown eyes focused lovingly on young Ian.

'It's great talking to you like this,' Marty told her. 'You're always so calm. How do you manage it?'

'It's my background. Don't ever forget that, Marty. When my mother was taken away by the Japanese, to be used as a soldiers' whore, my sisters and I had to fend for ourselves, until we were rescued eventually by relatives. Then, when Mother returned, we had to suffer her madness and, finally, we had to survive her suicide. It was a pretty tough childhood.'

'That's true,' he acknowledged. 'But that should have made all of you pessimistic or even paranoid. Instead, you all turned out psychologically sound – more so than most.'

Ann Lim smiled. 'We were helped all the way by my father,' she reminded him. 'He loved us and always made sure we knew it and that helped a lot. So I think the combination of harsh experience and fatherly love was what did the trick. It gave us all inner toughness, optimism and, I guess, faith in life. It made us accept the bad.'

'Which I'm not doing,' Marty said.

'You're doing okay. You could be worse. Other men get it much worse. You could be drinking too much, fouling up with the regiment, or even playing around with other women. You're doing none of those things. At least, I *think* not!' she added, meaning the other women. 'You're not, are you, Marty?'

He grinned. 'No, I'm not.'

She stared steadily at him over the rim of her coffee cup. 'You ever think about it?'

He hesitated before answering. 'I think about it,' he confessed. 'Every man thinks about it now and then. We're all pretty dumb that way.'

'So why don't you do anything about it?'

'I don't want it *that* much. I just fancy them because they're *there*, they're available, and I haven't had them. Like most men, I'm basically Neanderthal and want all I can get. But it remains wishful thinking. In the end, I don't want another involvement. I don't want the guilt.'

'Any other reasons?'

'Yes. My wife's more attractive than most of the women I fancy, so in the end, I suppose, I don't want to run the risk of losing her. That loss would be too great.'

Her smile was radiant. 'A combination of honest answer and sly compliment. Very good, Marty. Nice one.' She placed her empty coffee cup beside the sink and walked around the serving counter until she was standing right in front of him. 'So, I guess I'd better be on my way. Are you going to work today?'

Marty liked the way she called the SAS 'work', as if it was just another job, which in a sense it was. 'Yep. I actually have the day off, but since I've nothing better to do, I thought I'd drop into the Sports and Social for a bit of a yarn. See what the lads are up to.'

Knowing that by 'Sports and Social' he meant the SAS barracks, Ann Lim smiled and kissed him on the lips. 'Always doing more than you should,' she said. 'But if it keeps you from chasing after other women that's okay by me. Hey, you!' she exclaimed, turning to young Ian. 'Let's get going! Time we left for school!'

Seeing her making a grab for him, Ian giggled and tried to race away, around the the kitchen table, but after pretending to chase him, deliberately losing him a couple of times, Ann Lim grabbed him by the hand and addressed Marty over his shoulder.

'Say goodbye to your son,' she said.

He kissed Ian on the forehead, then planted one on Ann Lim's golden cheek. 'Enjoy school,' he said.

'We will. See you later.'

She left the house, holding Ian by the hand, letting the front door slam closed behind her. Deciding to check the news before leaving for the Sports and Social, Marty went into the front lounge, where the radio was still on, blaring out the Beatles' 'Ticket To Ride'. Though he still preferred singers like Frank Sinatra and Peggy Lee, now, like most of the rest of the population, he was addicted to the four mop-heads – so he waited until the song was finished, tapping his foot to the rhythm and mouthing the words, before turning on the TV. The main news items were about Edward Heath, elected this very day as the Tory Party leader, and President Lyndon B. Johnson, about to commit another 50,000 American troops to the war in Vietnam. Pleased that a former grammar school boy had made it to the top in England, though not thrilled with what the Yanks were getting up to in Vietnam, he turned the volume down, left the picture on and looked through the front window as Ann Lim strapped Ian into the rear of her Mini, then slid in behind the driver's wheel, closed the door and drove off.

Watching the car disappearing around the end of the street, in the shadow of the trees in the summer's morning light, he realised that, in spite of his present doubts about himself, he and Ann Lim shared a better life than most. Many men, he knew, would have envied him the life he was leading with his still-slim, beautiful Chinese wife and healthy young son.

Sighing, turning away from the window, he turned the TV off and went up the stairs to the bedroom where, while bathing and putting on his clothes, he silently counted his blessings.

He was just about to leave the house for the Sports and Social when the telephone rang.

One phone call can devastate a life, and that's what happened to him. He had tried to cry many times in the past and never succeeded; now he cried like a lost child. Though he refused to believe what had happened, he still couldn't stop crying, which meant it was true. There could be no worse nightmare.

'*No!*' he screamed like the damned.

CHAPTER TWENTY-FOUR

The party was already in full swing when Marty arrived. He was not really in the mood for it, as he had not been for months. He was only attending because he knew that Paddy would be hurt if he didn't show up. This was, after all, a special occasion: a celebration of Paddy's resignation from the Army and imminent return to Civvy Street. He was, as expected, leaving in grand style, throwing the party in his grand house in Peterchurch, Hereford, where the celebrations could go on all night.

Greeted at the front door by Paddy's two teenage sons, both flushed with forbidden drink and teasing their fifteen-year-old sister, Marty crossed the hallway to the door where the noise was coming from. Taking a deep breath, he inched into the spacious, packed lounge and saw Paddy, his wife Angela, a lot of their friends and some familiar faces from the SAS: officers, NCOs and other ranks, many in uniform.

Still in a state of shock, feeling unreal, he avoided the familiar faces and went straight to the bar where he asked for a double Scotch. He retreated with it to a corner of the room, hoping to watch all that was happening without actually taking part. Sitting in a chair to make himself less visible, he sipped his Scotch and fought the urge to get up and leave. This was a manifestation of the panic that had seized him so much in the past few months. When he thought of the accident, he almost lost control again, but the drink kept him level.

As he sat there, the odd SAS man who knew him came up to get another drink and stopped for a chat. Knowing what he had been through recently, they didn't stop long, invariably hurrying away to leave him to his grief.

Marty sat on, not knowing what else to do. He saw Paddy talking cheerfully to a small group that included Angela and another woman. Glancing sideways, Paddy saw him and waved him over, but Marty just raised his glass, indicating that he was happy with his drink. Grinning, Paddy went back to his conversation, but every so often he would turn and wave again, always receiving the same response. Eventually, noticing Marty's reluctance to join the group, the other woman stared curiously at him. Tall, bone-thin, with shoulder-length blonde hair, she was wearing a snow-white Mary Quant miniskirt and high heels that emphasised her fine legs. When she saw Marty raise his glass another time, she smiled and turned back to Paddy.

Marty sat on, drinking alone and talking only to SAS friends approaching the bar to replenish their drinks. Eventually, however, Paddy broke away from the group and came towards him. As he did so, Marty stood up to refill his glass. He badly needed another drink.

'Marty!' Paddy held out his hand. 'I'm so glad to see you. I wasn't sure you'd come. What with the . . .' He shrugged as he shook Marty's hand. 'How do you feel?'

'I don't know.'

But he did know. He felt like hell. He had felt this way for the past four months, ever since the phone call that devastated his life, informing him that his wife and child had been killed in a motor accident en route to Hereford. It was as simple and as brutal as that. The details were now irrelevant. All he knew – all he needed to know – was that a truck had emerged from a side-road, too quickly for Ann Lim to avoid it, and she had crashed into it and died instantly, as did baby Ian. It was over in seconds.

'I know what you mean,' Paddy said. 'There's no way to gauge precisely how you're feeling at a time like this. I still can't quite believe it really happened. It doesn't seem possible.'

'No, Paddy, it doesn't.'

Paddy had gone to the funeral. Everyone had gone. Marty's ailing mother. Ann Lim's terminally ill father. Her two sisters, Mary from France, Kathy all the way from Malaya with their father. Marty's friends and Ann Lim's friends. Even Lesley, who had brought Johnny and Kay – Johnny now nineteen, a handsome young man looking distraught, Kay eighteen and lovely, but with eyes streaming tears. No, it didn't seem real. Not now and not then. One phone call had devastated his life and now he felt broken up inside.

Recalling it, he shivered and had another sip of Scotch, trying to kill the pain that had not gone away in four months. The pain had swooped down to envelop him when the news came and he still couldn't shake it off. Thank God he was leaving.

'How are you dealing with it?' Paddy asked him. 'Are you managing, Marty?'

'I'm being posted to Aden,' Marty told him, 'and I can't wait to go. I can't deal with it here.'

'Yes, I understand that.'

'I'm selling the house and moving back into the Sports and Social. I don't want any memories. I think that's best, don't you?'

'It's sound thinking, Marty. You'll be better off with your men. Bury yourself in work, in what you do best, and let time do the healing. For your kind it's the only way.'

Paddy asked the barman for two more Scotches. While he was waiting to be served, Marty emptied his glass, thinking of the house he was leaving and of what had died there. He sometimes felt that *he* had died there. It had been a sudden death. One minute he was watching his wife climb into her Mini and the next, or what had seemed like the next, his wife and child were no more. He had been in shock for days, crying helplessly, drinking constantly, not turning on the lights when darkness came, wanting only oblivion. Then the horrors of the morgue. Identifying the smashed remains. Looking down, holding his breath, choking back a flood of nausea, trying to identify the barely recognisable features and filling up with revulsion. That and rage – a pure hatred for God and mankind – before stumbling back out to the light of day and surrendering to disbelief. More tears and more drinking. More dark nights of the soul. Then a different kind of nightmare: the funeral service at the crematorium, before the flames took his wife and child away, once and for all. He'd known then, if he had never known before, just what hell on earth was.

'Here,' Paddy said, handing him another Scotch. 'Drink up, old son.' They both drank. Marty felt a little better. It was good, after all, to be out of the house and back in the presence of people having a good time. Life went on regardless. 'Are you back at the base now?' Paddy asked him. 'Or still staying at home?'

Marty sighed, catching his breath. 'I'm still nominally in the house, but I'm practically living on the base. I've accepted an offer for the house and the sale should be finalised next week. I deliberately timed it for a week before I leave. I'm being flown out to Aden.'

'Yes, Marty, you said.'

'I can't wait to get going. I need something to do. Something more than just training new recruits. I'll be okay out there.'

'I agree. The timing's perfect. You'll have your hands full over there and that's just what you need. Constant distraction.'

'That's what I'm hoping. It's what I was praying for. I felt better as soon as I heard the news. I feel better right now.' He raised his glass of Scotch and managed his first smile in months, though it felt slightly unnatural. 'And this is helping as well.'

Paddy grinned in response. 'Good. I'm glad to hear it. That's why I invited you. So what's going on over in Aden with regard to the regiment?'

'They said it was something special,' Marty replied. 'That we'd be going into the Radfan mountains first, then back to Aden. Why there, I don't know.'

'Counter-insurgency work. It's a whole different ball game. There's no hearts-and-minds campaign over there: it's all shoot-and-scoot. A bloody mess, frankly. You're going to fight a war that's already been lost – propping up the last remnants of the British Empire – but at least you'll be fighting.'

Marty knew what he meant. Located at the southern entrance to the Red Sea, between Arabia and eastern Africa, Aden was a commercial centre for neighbouring states and a vital refuelling stop for ships. It was also of great political importance because of the Suez Canal and the rich oilfields of Arabia and the Persian Gulf. In 1963 it was incorporated into the Federation of South Arabia, the FSA, but steadily mounting antagonism towards the British presence there, which began with the abortive Suez operation of 1956, had led to an undeclared war between the two colonial powers in the area: a British-backed Aden Federation against a Soviet-backed Egypt. Most of that war was taking place in the barren, mountainous territory of the Radfan, lying between the Gulf of Eden and Saudia Arabia. Right now, operating out of secret bases in the Aden Federation, the SAS were fighting two campaigns simultaneously: on the one hand they were engaged in putting down a tribal uprising in the Radfan, adjoining the Russian-backed republic of Yemen; on the other, they were faced with their first battle against highly organised terrorism in Aden itself. The latter engagement was what Paddy meant by counter-insurgency work. That would take place in the streets and *souks* of Aden. Marty hoped to be part of it.

'The Radfan,' Paddy said, 'is pure desert of the kind you haven't worked in since nineteen forty-one. Desert as hot as North Africa, but reportedly even more difficult because it's mountainous and criss-crossed with deep wadis. For the time being, then, you can forget what you learned in Malaya and Borneo. This is something quite different.'

'So what *did* he learn in Malaya and Borneo?' a distinctly sensual female voice asked. 'A woman likes to know such things.'

Turning his head, Marty saw the moisturised full lips and steady green gaze of the blonde woman who had been talking to Paddy and Angela at the other side of the room. This close, it was clear that she was no longer young, probably in her late thirties. Bone-thin, as he had already noted, and almost flat-chested, but certainly exceptionally attractive and seemingly self-contained.

'Ah, Diane!' Paddy grinned at her. 'You've come to meet my favourite SAS man.' He turned back to Marty. 'Watch what you say about the regiment. This lady is a freelance journalist of right-wing persuasion, specialising in matters political. I've just been telling her all about you – how we met in North Africa and so forth – and it was clear that she was dying to meet you. Marty Butler' – he waved his hand at the smiling woman – 'meet Diane Lavery.'

'Hi,' Marty said, holding out his free hand.

'Pleased to meet you,' she replied, shaking his hand. 'Paddy *has* been telling me all about you, so I *did* want to meet you. I gather you go back a long way together.'

'A *long* way,' Marty emphasised, uncomfortable because he found her attractive and that made him feel guilty.

'So what did you do in Malaya and Borneo?' she asked.

Marty shrugged. 'Soldiering.'

'He can't talk about it,' Paddy explained. 'Tongue-tied by secrecy, but also a naturally modest man. That's what makes him so special.'

'*Are* you a modest man?' Diane asked him.

'I wouldn't know.'

'That war in Borneo's pretty awful,' Paddy said, 'and Marty's been in the thick of it for the last two or three years. He's seen all there is to see.'

'*Was* it that bad?' Diane Lavery asked, studying him with unusual intensity, though slightly mocking and teasing.

Marty felt embarrassed. 'It's a real war,' he said, recalling the aerial walkway, the Indo gunfire, the deaths of Bulldog and Rod O'Connor, then his race with the other survivors back to the border. Though he had been back to Borneo many times since, that was the day he always remembered and, he guessed, always would. The memory of it still pained him.

'Are you going back there?' Diane asked.

'Pardon?'

'To Borneo.'

'No.'

'So where are you going next?'

'I don't know,' Marty lied.

'Just hanging around the SAS base at Hereford, waiting for a posting?'

'That's right,' Marty said.

Diane glanced at the grinning Paddy. 'Then perhaps we'll meet again,' she said, turning back to Marty.

'I can't imagine where.'

'Paddy says you're a very dear friend, so we might meet right here, sometime in the future.'

'That won't be for a long time, Miss Lavery. Not until I come back from—'

He stopped himself short, but she noticed the slip. 'Ah! So you *are* going away. Now where might that be?'

'A regular little bloodhound,' Paddy said. 'Never trust a reporter! Marty's lips are sealed tight, my dear.'

Diane smiled. 'I'm not as bad as he makes out, Marty. Naturally, I can't help asking questions, but I'm sure you can deal with that.'

'I'm sure I can,' he said, attracted to, and disconcerted by, that steady green gaze and slightly teasing smile, her combination of shrewd intelligence and girlish flirtatiousness. Clearly, she was a woman of broad experience, both in and out of bed. 'So who do you write for?'

'I freelance for *The Times* and the *Telegraph*. Plus some work for various European papers. As Paddy said, it's mostly politics. Profiles and interviews. The deepening immorality of our political parties, right and left. Increasing government repression. The growing links between politics and big business – that kind of shit.'

'Which is why she's interested in the SAS,' Paddy said. 'So don't tell her a damned thing.'

'Why the SAS?' Marty asked. 'We're not political. We're just a bunch of highly trained soldiers, doing what we're told.'

'You're a quasi-secret regiment,' Diane corrected him.

'Secrecy's vital to national defence, Miss Lavery, and not used just to cover up corruption. There's nothing corrupt about the SAS. We're an honourable regiment.'

'It's *Mrs* Lavery, actually.'

'Sorry.'

'My husband and I have been separated for years, but we never divorced.'

'Oh, I see.'

She smiled at him, not concerned. 'Anyway, I'm not at all sure that there's such a thing as an honourable regiment. Mind you, Paddy did tell me that you're one of the most moral men he's met. So I thought, since you're a moral man loyal to the SAS, that you'd be particularly interesting to talk to . . . My, my, Marty, you're blushing!'

Indeed, he was: his cheeks were burning. 'I'm not all that moral,' he insisted. 'I'm just a working-class git who's been treated well by the regiment and I believe I should do my best in return. That's all there is to it.'

'That sounds terribly moral to *me*,' Diane said.

'And bloody boring,' Marty said.

'Not boring,' Paddy said. 'I never said boring. I just said that you were a highly principled man and an exceptional soldier.'

'A moral man and highly principled,' Marty said, embarrassed but also starting to enjoy himself. 'You make me sound like Jesus Christ.'

'Not Jesus Christ and not boring,' Paddy said. 'You have a flamboyant streak tied to old-fashioned moral values, which means there's a lot of inner conflict, which means you're not boring.'

'Me flamboyant? You've got to be joking! I'm really pretty conservative.'

'Bullshit. I knew you were flamboyant the moment you told me about taking your first wife on a single night's honeymoon at the Savoy. Then, of course, in Cairo, you were often seen in the gambling casinos, which was another notable display of flamboyance for someone picking up private's wages. And dare I remind you of Tiger Lil's?' He turned to Diane Lavery. 'The most popular soldiers' brothel in Cairo. Not content with spending his money there like the other humble soldiers, he rented his own room *and* girl for his whole fortnight in Cairo. I thought that showed remarkable initiative as well as flamboyance and—'

'It also shows a certain wickedness,' Diane interjected, staring boldly, teasingly, at Marty.

'He said he didn't want VD,' Paddy explained, 'though in fact he simply didn't want a girl who was on the conveyor belt. He needed a woman all to himself, a regular girlfriend, to convince himself that she wasn't really a whore.' He turned back to face Marty. 'And you're still like that, my friend – even all these years later. Why, you even married a Chinese Malay, despite official disapproval, which just shows that . . .' He tapered off, embarrassed. 'Damn it, Marty, I'm sorry. I truly am. I didn't mean to remind you . . .'

'It's okay,' Marty said, though the pain had rushed back in, reminding him that Ann Lim and Ian were gone and would never be coming back. Reminding him, also, that he had seen very little of his wife and child because he was always away. Though Ann Lim had never expressed resentment, he had always felt guilty. He felt that guilt now.

'Anyway,' Paddy continued, trying to lighten the conversation. 'Flamboyant, puritanical, daring and full of initiative. Not boring at all, my friend. Indeed, if you weren't in the SAS, I'd surely hire you myself.'

'Hire me for what?' Marty asked, keen to change the subject. 'Just what *are* you planning to do in Civvy Street?'

'TV,' Paddy replied. 'Television's the coming thing. It's big already, but it's going to be even bigger and used for much greater things.'

'Such as?'

'TV's going to become the quickest and most powerful medium for swaying public opinion and educating the masses. This is as true for the Third World as it is for the West. So, to capitalise on it, I'm forming a film production company to make propaganda documentaries that can be sold to Third World and Middle East governments. Naturally, we'll offer our services only to democratic rulers who'll use the movies to combat growing communist influence in their countries. I think that's worthwhile, don't you?'

'I didn't know you cared,' Diane said dryly.

'I do,' Paddy replied. 'I believe in my country, I believe in democracy, and I believe that those are the values the SAS fights for. So I'll continue the fight in the private sector by producing those films.'

'You'll also get to travel a lot,' Marty said.

'Exactly,' Paddy replied.

After a brief silence, Diane gave Marty a warm smile and then turned back to Paddy. 'Propaganda can be dangerous and easily bent. If you're going to make those kind of films, *you're* the one who'll need principles.'

'He has them,' Marty responded without hesitation. 'He has them in spades. Much more than me, in fact. *He's* your moral man, Diane.'

'He better be,' Diane replied without irony.

'Anyway,' Paddy said, grinning cockily, 'that's what I'm planning; so if you decide to retire early, Marty, I'll give you some kind of job. Right now, however, I'd best be getting back to my other guests. I'll see you both later.'

'Right,' Marty said.

When Paddy had left them to return to the main party, which was increasingly noisy, Diane turned back to Marty. 'Propaganda, no matter how it starts, invariably turns out crooked in the end. I think Paddy's going to have to watch his step.'

'Paddy's the most moral man *I* know. If he does it, he'll do it right.'

'You really do respect him, don't you, Marty?'

'Yes. He taught me everything I know.'

'And of course he's a moral man.'

'Yes, he is.'

'And do you really think the SAS is a moral regiment?' she asked with a steady gaze.

'I think it's evolved along moral lines and operates on strict principles. I think it tries to instil those principles in its men, which makes it something special.'

She stared thoughtfully at him for some time, then nodded and smiled.

'Yes,' she said. 'You're a moral man.'

Marty placed his glass on the cluttered table behind him. 'Anyway,' he said, 'I have to go now. I'm not really up to parties these days and—'

'Yes, I know. Paddy told me about your wife and child. I'm really sorry, Marty. It must be terribly hard for you.'

Shocked that Paddy had told her that, but oddly touched by her comment, Marty nodded and sighed. 'It's okay. I get by.'

'Here.' She reached into her handbag and withdrew a calling card. 'Take it. I know I'm being bold, but I'd really like to see you again, when you get back from wherever it is you're going. Please, Marty, take it.'

He took the card and glanced at it, not really seeing it, then slipped it carefully into his wallet.

'Right,' he said. 'Thanks. Now I've got to be off.'

'You take care.'

'You, too.' He crossed the crowded room to say goodbye to Paddy and Angela. After wishing them good luck for the future, he started leaving the room, but glanced back before he left and saw Diane Lavery's steady green gaze following his progress. He waved at her and then walked out, still filled with grief and the pain of his dreadful loss, but surprised that she was there in his thoughts. He felt oddly renewed.

CHAPTER TWENTY-FIVE

Dressed like an Arab and with his skin tinted dark, Marty almost *felt* like an Arab. Having driven up to Crater in his deliberately battered and cluttered Volkswagen Beetle Q, he and Taff Hughes had made their way through the packed, noisy rabbit warren of the *souk*, or market-place, in this particular quarter of Aden and were now sitting in an equally crowded square, sipping mint tea and waiting for their target to emerge from the restaurant across the road. Both men were wearing the flowing Arab *futah*, a robe with long sleeves that fell loosely over the head to hang from the shoulders, all the way to their feet, which, like other exposed skin, had been darkened with a mixture of coffee, lamp-black, iodine and potassium permanganate to make a colouring similar to that of the local Arabs. This had then been applied carefully to their faces, hands, wrists and all the way up to their arms, to ensure that no white skin would be glimpsed should the loose sleeves of the *futah* rise too high up the arm. As they were wearing Arab sandals instead of shoes, they had also dyed their feet, ankles and legs up as far as the knees. Finally, even though they were wearing the Arab head-dress, or *shemagh*, they had dyed their hair black to ensure that their 'whiteness' would not be exposed by loose strands.

Strapped in the cross-draw position under their *futahs* was a holstered Browning Nine-Milly, which would be used for this 'double tap' assassination when their target emerged. They had no other weapons.

Sitting with Taff at a table deliberately picked because it was against a wall, though close to the restaurant he was watching, Marty was aware of the fact that to get out of here he would have to retrace his steps back through a rabbit warren of narrow streets and *souks*, all packed with shops, bazaars, coffee houses, cafés, Arabs and animals. Here in the square, many of the Arabs were playing draughts or other games at tables placed outside the coffee houses and cafés. Others were smoking from opium pipes. Nearly all were drinking mint tea. However, the many alleys that surrounded the square were filled with burning braziers and pots of cooking food or boiling tea, outdoor tables and chairs, and a veritable flood of Arabs. More importantly, men often herded cattle through the narrow, packed *souks*, letting them ease their way through the tide of people, including many children and their veiled mothers. That would make getting out in a hurry dangerous and difficult.

Nevertheless, as he sat there sipping his mint tea and mumbling monosyllabic greetings in Arabic to the Arabs greeting him as they passed by, Marty felt almost regretful that this would be his final 'double tap' before returning to Bradbury Lines. He had been here for many months now, first up in the Radfan mountains, then in Aden, and now he wiled away the time by thinking back to how he had come to be here, in the middle of this packed square in the highly dangerous Crater area, dressed up and made up like an Arab.

It was a long way from Borneo.

Even as he sat there, the war in Borneo was drawing to its close. After A Squadron's cross-border operations with the Gurkhas, plans had been drawn up for even more ambitious 'Claret' raids. However, in March 1966, less than a year ago, a military government had replaced the aggressive President Sukarno and the war eased a little. A treaty was concluded between Indonesia and Malaya the following August, bringing to a definite end an 'undeclared' war that had lasted nearly four years, killing over a hundred Commonwealth soldiers, including members of the SAS. The

Indonesians, however, had suffered five times that number of casualties.

The so-called 'Confrontation' in Borneo had shown the necessity of having troops who could solve the unique problems raised by an 'undeclared' war where British forces could not overtly take the fight into enemy territory. It had also confirmed once and for all that the kind of hearts-and-minds campaign devised by the SAS in Malaya could work wonders where direct military action was not a viable option.

That option, however, was not viable here in Aden where, though the war was likewise 'undeclared', it was fought in circumstances that did not allow for hearts-and-minds, being engaged either in the sun-scorched mountains of the Radfan or right here in the packed *souks* of the port town of Aden as a very dangerous close-quarter-battle conflict.

Marty had spent the previous couple of months either in the SAS forward operating base in Thumier, located in the Radfan area, fifty kilometres from the border with North Yemen, or up in the sun-scorched Radfan mountains of the interior. Flown from RAF Lyneham in Wiltshire, to the RAF base at Khormaksar, Aden, in a Hercules C-130 transport, he and the other members of D Squadron were packed into four three-ton Bedford trucks, in a column guarded front and rear by British Army six-by-six-drive Saladin armoured cars, each equipped with a 76-millimetre QF (quick-firing) gun and Browning .30-inch machine-gun. They were then driven sixty miles through the hellish heat of midday, over relatively flat plains of sun-baked limestone, sandstone and lava fields, to the FOB at Thumier.

The base was little more than a haphazard collection of tents pitched in a sandy area surrounded by high ridges, swept constantly by dust. It was protected by sandbagged gun emplacements nicknamed 'hedgehogs' because they were bristling with 25-pound guns, three-inch mortars and Browning 0.5-inch heavy machine-guns. Though the area was inaccessible to fixed-wing aircraft, it contained a flattened area of desert that was being used as a landing zone (LZ) for two helicopters: a Wessex S-58 Mark 1 and a Sikorski S-55 Whirlwind. There was also a motor pool containing Bedford trucks, a couple of Saladin armoured cars of the kind that had escorted the convoy, and some modified four-by-four Willys jeeps with armoured Perspex screens and Browning 0.5-inch heavy machine-guns mounted on the front. The larger tents were being used as a quartermaster's store, armoury, NAAFI and surgery; the smaller tents were for make-do bashas, or sleeping quarters, located near portable showers and boxed-in, roofless chemical latrines, naturally called 'thunder boxes'. Beyond the tents lay the flat, scorched desert and the purple-hazed mountains.

'A typical FOB,' Tommy Taylor said, spitting languidly into the dust around his feet, still proud of his corporal status and now pretty confident as a medical specialist. 'A right bloody piss-hole.'

'I don't mind it,' Taff Hughes responded. 'It looks okay to me.'

'You like anywhere that isn't remotely normal,' Marty told him. 'So this place seems like home.'

'I've known worse,' Taff said.

Other SAS squadrons had already been and gone, having put down a tribal uprising in the Radfan and also protected military traffic on the Dhala road, which linked Yemen to Aden and was the MSR for the Federal Regular Army (FRA). Replacing those earlier SAS squadrons, Marty and his fellow squadron members, commanded by Captain Michael Keating of the Somerset and Cornwall Light Infantry, were initially tasked with giving back-up to A Squadron in the Radfan, beginning with a series of Reconnaissance patrols.

Moving out at first light in four-by-four Bedford three-tonners driven by men from the Royal Corps of Transport (RCT) and escorted by Saladin armoured cars equipped with 5.56-inch Bren guns, they had passed through an area scattered with coconut and doum palms, acacias, tall ariatas and tamarisks, then bounced and rattled over parched ground strewn with potholes and stones until, about thirty minutes later, they arrived at the lower slopes of the purple-hazed Radfan mountain range. From there, wearing DPM (disruptive-pattern material) cotton shirt and trousers, ankle-length rubber-soled desert boots and an Arab *shemagh* to protect the nose, mouth and eyes from the sun, sand and insects, they had marched into the mountains, as heavily burdened as donkies with sixty-pound Bergen rucksacks, water bottles, ammunition belts, '80' hand grenades, spare batteries for the A41 tactical radio, the ubiquitous Browning High Power handgun, a wide variety of assault rifles and dismantled heavier support weapons, including various machine-guns and mortars.

The Radfan could sometimes be as hot as 150 degrees Fahrenheit, was constantly windblown and covered with drifting dust filled with flies and mosquitoes. Some of the men vomited from nausea and exhaustion during that first climb up the wind-smoothed rocks of the slopes, often slipping back on loose gravel or tripping in dips and holes covered by sand, soil or shrubs. Eventually, however, they reached the summit, 1,500 feet high, where they rested from the blazing sun under triangular bashas, made from Y-shaped sticks and poncho sheets, quenching their thirst with the juice from euphorbia, the bulbous plant that hangs from the branches of a tree resembling a cactus, and from the plum-like jujube fruit, which could also be eaten.

After resting, eating and cleaning and oiling their weapons, which were filled with dust and sand, they were given firing practice under extremely arduous conditions: forced to crawl over sharp, hot rocks that could, as they had been warned, be concealing snakes, scorpions and other poisonous insects, and which certainly burned them and cut their skin. They were also taught how to time their shots for when the swirling dust and sand had blown away long enough for them to see their targets clearly and to fire accurately into the sunlight by estimating the position of the target by its shadow, rather than trying to look directly at it.

Thoroughly exhausted and, in many cases, bloody and bruised from the rocks, they marched on in diamond formation – preferred by the SAS in open country and on 'tabs' by night – throughout the boiling heat of the afternoon, from one summit, or trig point, to another: across windswept plains of lava remains, soft sand and silt, along dried-up wadis, and up sheer slopes of limestone, sandstone and igneous rocks. Moving from the relentless heat of day to the numbing cold of night – so cold they were breathing steam – they saw little on the mountains other than the occasional ibex or oryx, the flickering fires, candles or paraffin lamps of lonely stone tower houses or mud-brick hovels, and the odd walled hamlet by small patches of cultivated land.

Eventually, close to midnight, they arrived at the selected RV, on a high ridge overlooking an Arab village known to be held by Yemeni guerrillas. There, with moonlight glinting off patches of frost and ice, they constructed two temporary OPs, both star-shaped, with four legs shaped like a cross: one for the sentry, another for the observer and the remaining two as rest bays, where the men could lie on their waterproof ponchos. Throughout that night, operating in two-hour shifts and aided by PNGs (passive night-vision goggles), which showed the dark landscape in an eerie green glow, Marty and the others observed the Arab village on the lower slopes of the ridge.

By first light, when the sun was rising as an enormous crimson ball over the Radfan mountains, they were able to view the village without the aid of the PNGs and saw only a few Arab men going out to till their single, sparse field, veiled women washing clothes around a desert spring, and children running playfully about between barking dogs, squawking chickens and a few braying goats. There was no sign of Yemeni guerrillas or any kind of weapons.

'That's just a normal Arab village,' Tommy Taylor said. 'There are no guerrillas down there.'

'Another wild goose chase,' Taff replied. 'Just like this whole damned war.'

Nevertheless, the patrol remained there throughout the long day, as the rising sun melted the frost on the rocks, the flies and mosquitoes returned, the sun became fierce, and waves of heat rose shimmering from the parched ground.

When not on watch or otherwise engaged, Marty felt his mind filling up with thoughts of his past year – the death of his father by natural causes; the deaths by violence of Bulldog and Rod O'Connor in Borneo; then the brutally accidental deaths of Ann Lim and Ian. Life, he now realised, was brutal by nature, a series of random events that either broke or renewed those taking part, but could neither be anticipated nor prepared for.

Yet people survived the worst and were often strengthened by it. Certainly, the past few years, beginning with his father's death, had been the worst in his life to date; yet, though he still felt pain, he also felt the light of hope, the flickering flame of renewal, and sensed that he was over the worst of it and starting to mend. Now, in these foreign mountains, a real soldier once more, he felt the steady quickening of his pulse, the building charge of excitement. He was coming alive again.

By nightfall, when it was clear that Tommy was right and there were no guerrillas in the hamlet, Captain Keating ordered the OPs dismantled, prior to moving out. When the men had completed this task, they covered all traces of their presence in the area, then began the long hike back to the RV. Once there, they found the Bedford trucks still waiting to return them to base.

Nearly three months later, sitting beside Taff Hughes in the busy square in Crater, the commercial centre of Aden, waiting for his target – a local businessman and double agent – to emerge from the restaurant, Marty thought of that first trip through the Radfan mountains and smiled bitterly behind the veil of his *shemagh*. It had been a proving trip – a way of learning the terrain and the specialist skills required to master it – and, although it had served its purpose well, it had been a relatively uneventful affair. The second patrol, however, as well as being the complete opposite, turned out to be a cruel, lost battle in a war that had already been lost and was being fought only to save face for the politicians.

Marty's squadron had gone into the Radfan for the second time in order to lend support to a major offensive against the Yemeni guerrillas, launched by two battalions of FRA infantry, 45 Royal Marine Company, the Parachute Regiment, a troop of Royal Engineers, a battery of Royal Horse Artillery armed with 105-millimetre howitzers, and a Royal Tank Regiment supported by Saladin armoured cars. The object was to seize back from the Yemeni rebels two vitally important hills that dominated the camel routes from the Yemen and the only two fertile areas in the region. The 45 Royal Marine Company was to march seven miles from the Dhala road and then climb and seize the northern hill, known as Rice Bowl. At the same time, the Parachute Regiment was to be dropped by parachute near the foot of the other hill, Cap Badge, then climb the hill and take it by force. It was the job of the SAS to go in first and establish, mark and protect the chosen LZ for the Paras, nicknamed the 'maroon machine'.

For this particular job the SAS added to their usually heavy load more detailed maps, navigational equipment, a spare short-range radio, SARBEs (surface-to-air rescue beacons) for emergency communication with support or extraction aircraft, special equipment for dealing with land-mines and booby traps, 200 rounds each of .303-inch for the patrol's Bren gun, wire-cutters and hessian for clearing barbed-wire entanglements, various explosives, including RDX and PETN, and M23 grenade-launchers, which could be fixed to the barrels of the L42A1 bolt-action sniper rifles. They also darkened the exposed parts of their skin with stick camouflage and the shinier parts of their weapons with 'cam' cream.

Moving out at dusk, they travelled in specially reinforced, heavily armed Saladin armoured cars north along the Dhala road. Turning off the road at Wadi Rabwa, the Saladins descended into the eerily moonlit wadi and then began making their cumbersome way along it, gears grinding noisily and engines shrieking in protest as they skidded in loose gravel and bounced over large, sharp rocks. Just as they reached a point where the moonlight was cut off completely by the high banks on either side, forcing them to advance through almost total darkness, some of the armoured cars became stuck in deep sand and had to be rescued with the aid of woven sand mats and steel sand channels, reminding Marty of his early days in North Africa with the LRDG.

Unfortunately, they were forced to do this job with the aid of hand-held torches, which exposed their position to the enemy. As they were attempting to roll one Saladin out of deep sand, gunfire erupted from the hills beyond the wadi, green tracers laced the night, and a hail of bullets kicked up dust from the wadi floor and ricocheted off nearby rocks, causing pieces of stone to fly in every direction in dazzling showers of sparks.

As the green tracers looped down languidly from the dark hills, gaining speed as they approached, then exploded in phosphorescent streams around the Saladins, Marty and the others, who had just managed to free the trapped vehicle, jumped back in and the column continued its advance along the wadi without the benefit of lights.

Luckily, it moved out just in time to avoid a series of mortar explosions that erupted in mushrooms of boiling smoke and soil seared by jagged, silvery flashes. Within yards, however, the lead Saladin became trapped in another bed of soft sand, forcing the whole column to grind to a halt again, with the mortar explosions, though obviously fired blind, making the ground erupt in spiralling, roaring columns that were gradually coming towards them.

Knowing that they could not rescue the trapped Saladin with the aid of hand torches – which again would have given their position away to the enemy – Captain Keating sent Marty back along the line to order the men out of the Saladins and up into the dark hills, heading away from the enemy fire. As the men moved out, the 76-millimetre QF guns and Browning machine-guns of the Saladins opened fire, raking the dark hills in the general direction of the enemy gunfire, hoping to keep the rebel gunners pinned down until the SAS men were safely away.

They must have succeeded, because Marty and the others made it unharmed up the moonlit slopes and were soon out of the wadi and heading east, away from the flickering lights of the guerrilla gunfire. Falling into the diamond formation more suitable to open country, with Marty out front on point, Keating second in line as PC and Taff Hughes as Tail-end Charlie, they marched through the night in silence, until, just before first light, they saw the 3,900-foot Jebel Ashqab soaring up before them.

Their objective lay on the other side of the mountain and they would have to climb the mountain to reach it. Even on the lower slopes, they found the climb punishingly arduous, with loose gravel sliding underfoot, patches of smooth, slippery lava giving way abruptly to sinking sand that could not be seen in the darkness, and sharp rocks constantly tripping them and threatening to sprain or break ankles.

To make the climb even more difficult, one of the men, Trooper Albert ('Al') Reid, in charge of the company's A41 radio, developed fever, started vomiting repeatedly, and was soon falling regularly behind the others. As medical specialist, Tommy Taylor diagnosed food poisoning and gave Reid a brew of tea, powdered charcoal and milk of magnesia, plus a couple of aspirins. The radio was then passed on to another soldier, Trooper Les Smythe, and Reid was ordered back into the middle of the column where he could be watched.

By now they were halfway up the mountain. When the climb began again, the slopes became even steeper and more treacherous, with the men constantly tripping or slipping, then rolling back downhill in a noisy tide of gravel, stopped only by the hand of a comrade or, less gently, by a large boulder or dusty rock outcropping. Even those not so frustrated were soaked in their own sweat and fighting for breath because of a combination of sheer exertion and the night's stifling heat.

The men were forced to halt because of Al Reid's illness, and rested by two ancient stone sangars that had obviously been constructed as firing positions by local tribesmen and were located just below the summit of the mountain. Though aware that they were only three miles from their objective and that the rest of the hike would be downhill, Captain Keating did not want to expose the patrol to enemy snipers by completing the hike during the day; instead, he ordered the men to basha down in the two sangars, which would not draw attention from the locals, having been there a long time.

Divided into two groups, with Marty, Taff and Tommy Taylor looking after Al Reid, the men set up their respective sangars like regular OPs: rubber groundsheets rolled out in shallow scrapes for sleeping, ponchos raised over the sangars and covered with loose gravel and vegetation, and a well for weapons dug out in the middle between the groundsheets. Then, while some slept, the others kept watch until, when dawn broke, they saw that the sangars were overlooking an Arab hamlet filled with guerrillas and, directly above it, hardly more than fifty yards from the SAS positions, a guerrilla OP and machine-gun post.

By now Al Reid had stopped sweating and vomiting, but was suffering from severe stomach pains. Though sympathetic, Marty realised that the unfortunate trooper could not be casevacked or even carried on a stretcher back down the mountainside, so he had to let him suffer, breathing harshly, in a shallow scrape in the small sangar which was, in the rising heat of the day, becoming hot, suffocatingly humid, and filled with buzzing flies and whining mosquitoes. In fact, Tommy was sick from the heat alone and threw up into a paper bag while Marty and Taff, seated right beside him, had their cold rations of dried biscuits and cheese.

'You're sick because you're not eating,' Marty told Tommy even as he was heaving noisily into his paper bag. 'It's empty stomachs that the heat always gets to. You should know that, Tommy.'

'Ah, God!' Tommy groaned in response, which was all he could manage.

'Nothing like cheese and biscuits,' Taff said, 'to keep the stomach in order. Why not try some, Tommy?'

'Ah, God!' Tommy groaned again.

By noon, when the sun was high in the sky and the heat was truly ferocious, more armed guerrillas had climbed the hills to take up positions above the hamlet where the Arabs were getting on with their daily business: feeding the goats and chickens, tending their pitifully small area of cultivated ground, drawing water from a well, and, judging from the smoke coming from the chimneys, lighting fires and cooking. Veiled women emerged from the mud-and-stone huts to wash clothes in tubs placed in the middle of the village, children played noisily in the dirt, and the older men, sitting outside their houses, talked to each other, smoked hookahs, or just gazed distractedly at the mountains and the desert beyond them.

Captain Keating was hoping that, because these were old guerrilla sangars, attention would not be drawn to them. However, in the late afternoon a goatherd from the hamlet, feeding his animals on the lower slope below the sangars, caught a glimpse of movement and bawled a warning to the others. Even as he was shouting his warning, he was cut down by a fusillade of gunfire from the SAS's combination of bolt-action sniper rifles, SLRs and M16 assault rifles.

Instantly, the guerrillas opened fire from the OPs located on the hills directly opposite, adding to the bedlam. Within seconds, the battle was fully engaged, with guerrillas bursting out of the huts in the hamlet, their *djellabas* and *shemaghs* fluttering in the breeze, and advancing up the slower slopes of the hill, firing their Lee-Enfield rifles while on the move. The SAS's single Bren gun and light machine-gun roared into action simultaneously, adding their roarings to the general clamour, the bullets tearing up sand and soil in a line that zigzagged across the ranks of advancing guerrillas, making many of them shudder, jerk sideways and collapse.

Bullets from the rifles and machine-guns of the guerrilla positions on the high ridge ricocheted off the walls of the sangars, fragmenting the rock and filling the space inside with dust and flying pieces of sharp stone that cut the men's faces and hands like razors. As the ridge was only fifty yards away and twenty feet higher than the SAS sangars, that gunfire was devastatingly accurate and becoming even more so by the minute.

Realising that they were in a bad position and almost certain to be overrun eventually, Captain Keating told Trooper Les Smythe to contact HQ Thumier on the radio and call in air support. Meanwhile, the Bren-gun team, leaving the light-machine-gun team to hold back the guerrillas trying to advance up the slope from the hamlet, was trying to keep the snipers on the ridge pinned down with a relentless fusillade, aided by the SLRs from the other sangar.

Braving the SAS gunfire, the guerrillas on the lower slopes were still advancing by darting boldly from one boulder to another while their comrades covered them with fire from their Lee-Enfield rifles. Ignoring the guerrillas behind the boulders, the SAS concentrated on those advancing uphill from one boulder to another and had the satisfaction of seeing quite a few throw up their arms, drop their weapons and then collapse, often to roll all the way back down the hill in billowing clouds of dust.

Thirty minutes later a pair of RAF Hawker Hunter single-seat fighters from the Khormaksar airstrip appeared over the southern horizon, then roared down with guns snapping savagely, turning the hills opposite into a convulsion of geysering soil, boiling dust, flying gravel and stones, eventually covering the ridge completely in a pall of dark smoke out of which emerged the terrible screaming of wounded and dying guerrillas. By the time the Hunters had flown in low over the sangars, saluting the SAS before flying back to base, the survivors from the devastated guerrilla OPs on the ridge had made their way downhill to join their fellow fighters on the lower slopes in front of the hamlet.

Realising that the greatly increased number of guerrillas were preparing to advance up the hill and take the two sangars – knowing, also, that marking a DZ for the maroon machine was now out of the question – Keating decided to bug out under cover of darkness and head back to Thumier, no matter how great the odds seemed against the SAS.

In fact, by last night, the odds against the SAS had increased dramatically, with repeated assaults on the sangars leading to the death of Trooper Reid, who was peppered by a hail of Arab machine-gun fire while groaning in delirium in his shallow scrape in the small sangar while Marty, Taff and Tommy looked on helplessly. Two other men were wounded: Sergeant Barry Chambers, with two bullets in his left thigh, and Corporal Graham Moore, shot in the right thigh with a single bullet. Another trooper had bullet marks across his back; most of the others were bloody from flying pieces of rock and stone; and all of them were choking in the dust that now filled both sangars.

With no choice but to leave the dead behind, Captain Keating ordered the evacuation of the two sangars even as the guerrillas, still darting from one boulder to another, were coming dangerously close. Some of them had, in fact, been clambering over the wall of the largest sangar before being cut down by a burst from Marty's SLR. Now, with the fall of darkness, there would be no air support and they would also be handicapped by the slow progress of their own wounded.

Nevertheless, Keating arranged for Thumier to lay down an artillery barrage on the southern hill, covering the slopes between the sangars and the hamlet below. That barrage would commence at precisely 1932 hours, two minutes after the SAS emerged from the sangars to make their escape. While it was assumed that the guerrillas would pursue them all the way back to Thumier, the barrage might at least give them a head start.

Knowing that they would have to travel light, the men smashed everything that was no longer needed, including the A41 radio and separate Morse set; then they moved out at 1930 hours precisely, carrying only their personal weapons, water bottle, ammunition pouches and emergency rations. Instantly, the guns of the guerrillas on the lower slopes opened up, filling the air with whipping, ricocheting bullets, spewing stones and erupting dust as the sangar walls were torn to pieces.

While Marty, Taff and Tommy, all in the smaller sangar, gave covering fire, the group in the large sangar, including Sergeant Chambers and Corporal Moore, both limping from their leg wounds, made their escape under cover of darkness, heading for the northern hill.

At that moment an enemy machine-gun roared into action and streams of green tracer looped up the hill, whipped between the running men, and converged on Captain Keating, who was punched violently sideways, then spun around and fell to the ground, hitting the stones with a sickening thud and flopping onto his spine. Even as some of the men were about to turn back and help him, more tracers stitched him, as did the combined firepower of many .303 Lee-Enfields, and his body was punched sideways across the slope until stopped by a rock. There he spasmed repeatedly under the impact of more bullets, gradually turning into what looked like a tattered pile of rags and stopping his quivering only when the guerrillas, realising that he was dead, transferred their fire back to the sangars.

'Oh, Jesus!' Tommy Taylor whispered.

'So it goes,' Taff told him.

Suddenly, peals of thunder were heard from the dark horizon, accompanied by jagged flashes of what even Marty thought was lightning. Within seconds, however, the first shells from the 25-pounders in Thumier were exploding across the southern hill, tearing up soil, sand, gravel and rocks between the advancing guerrillas, many of whom were swept up and smashed back down in the swirling dust and billowing smoke.

While the barrage was devastating the hillside, Marty, Taff and Tommy made their escape from the small sangar, with no choice but to leave the dead body of Trooper Reid behind, and headed rapidly down the northern hill to join the first group, including the two wounded men, where they were lying on their bellies, giving cover with the combined firepower of their assault rifles. Once joined by the others, the group on the ground stopped firing, climbed back to their feet – though the two wounded men were wobbling unsteadily – and hurried away from the southern hill, leaving Marty, Taff and Tommy to keep an eye on the guerrillas surrounding the sangars and, if necessary, hold them off.

The barrage from Thumier ceased temporarily, leaving an eerie silence and a pall of black smoke that deepened the darkness over the southern hill.

'They're advancing on the sangars,' Taff said, speaking with no tremor of emotion. 'They think we're still in there.'

'Thank God we're not,' Tommy said.

Using a pair of binoculars and his PNGs, Marty watched as the guerrillas, recovering from the barrage, fired a ferocious fusillade at the large sangar, mistook the showers of sparks flying off the stone walls for enemy gunfire, and broke into two separate groups in order to charge the sangar from both directions. Encircling the sangar, they lost each other in the darkness, fired from both directions, mistook each other's fire for an SAS reaction and commenced to slaughter each other.

'Bloody beautiful!' Marty whispered with satisfaction.

His satisfaction was short-lived. While the two groups of guerrillas were thus engaged, a third group entered the small sangar and emerged with the lifeless body of Al Reid, which they carried awkwardly down the hill, making their way between the scorched, blackened craters torn from the earth by the 25-pound shells from the Thumier barrage. Even as that sight filled Marty with bitterness, another group picked up the body of Captain Keating and likewise carried it down the hill, eventually disappearing in the darkness.

Knowing that they could not recover the two SAS bodies, Marty, Taff and Tommy picked themselves off the ground and hurried away to catch up with the main group. Together, the men headed back towards the Dhala road and, ultimately, Thumier, pursued all the way by the vengeful guerrillas.

Sitting three months later in that square in Crater, Marty realised that the war in the hills had been lost because it was already a lost cause created by politicians intent on getting Britain out of the colony while leaving a token British presence there. That remaining presence, of which the SAS was a part, had the uneviable task of defending a people who did not want to be defended and increasingly supported the so-called enemy. Marty had thought of this with bitterness when he'd come down out of the hills of the Radfan after that aborted, bloody operation and he thought of it now, even more bitterly, as he sat in this square, waiting to cut down a man known to be spying for the guerrillas.

Naturally, he thought, as he peered over the veil of his *shemagh* at the packed outdoor tables of the restaurant from which his target would emerge, he would not be here now if the squadron had not made it back to Thumier after that bloody, aborted operation. They had, however, made it back only after a night of hell on earth, pursued across rocky slopes, along dried up, pitch-black wadi beds and across flat, windblown plains by a swarm of guerrillas intent on avenging the havoc created by them. The Arabs had been as thick as flies on the dark hills, popping up from behind rocks, darting out from behind parched bushes, *djellabas* and *shemaghs* fluttering, to snipe relentlessly at the hiking enemy. More than one SAS man died that night, others were wounded, and a couple hallucinated from loss of blood and exhaustion as they made their slow progress with the two wounded men acting as back markers. Nevertheless, by inching forward, from the protection of one rock outcropping to another, given covering fire by their comrades, they finally managed to reach the main Wadi Rabwa and, beyond it, the flat, dangerously exposed plain that led to Thumier. There, even as the Arabs were swarming down off the hills to annihilate them, they were rescued by four Saladin armoured cars that raced out of the FRA base at Thumier, firing their 76-millimetre QF and 0.30-inch machine-guns. Eventually, even as the firepower of the Saladins was forcing the Arabs back up into the hills, two Hawker Hunters flew out from the Habilayn airstrip and roared in over the ridge, pouring a murderous hail of gunfire into the Arabs even as they were trying to make their escape back to the Radfan. The SAS survivors were then picked up in the Saladins and transported, exhausted and bloody, back to the safety of Thumier.

Now, made up and dressed like an Arab, feeling almost like one, Marty realised just how lucky he was to have made it this far. That failed operation in the Radfan, which, for him, symbolised this whole damned war, marked the end of his time in the mountains and already it seemed like a distant dream.

Shortly after his return to Thumier, when he had enjoyed a brief rest period, he and Taff had been chosen for a special, secret assignment in Aden and subsequently flown in a Sikorski Whirlwind from the parched lava rock and desert of Thumier to the industrialised clutter of Aden, then driven in a British Army jeep to the military complex at Khormaksar. There, at a briefing conducted by a green slime officer, Captain Alan Saunders, they were informed that they were about to engage in a clandestine plain-clothes operation of the kind first devised by Major Frank Kitson during Kenya's Mau Mau campaign, which the SAS was briefly involved in during the 1950s.

According to Saunders, the campaign in Kenya had led to the formation of a few so-called 'counter gangs', or anti-terrorist teams, composed of former terrorists and loyal tribesmen led by British officers disguised as natives. The same type of operation had also been used in Cyprus as the basis of the undercover Q units. However, when the SAS first set up a CQB course in Khormaksar for a carefully selected group of men, they knew that there was no hope of 'turning round' Arab terrorists and so decided, instead, to function more like the Q squads of the Palestine police as started by Roy Farran, a veteran of the wartime SAS.

The work in Aden, Saunders informed them, in some instances involved driving around in Q cars, or unmarked cars, searching out possible Yemeni agents; in others the job was to pick up terrorists alive and bring them in to Khormaksar for questioning; and in others still it simply meant shooting them before they had a chance to do the shooting. In all three cases, it was a highly dangerous, face-to-face business that required lots of nerve and the ability to go into the alleyways and *souks* of Aden, made up and dressed like an Arab. And when it came to shooting, it required special skills in a killing method known as the 'double tap' This dangerous work was carried out by the 'Keeni-Meeni' teams of the SAS.

'Keeni-Meeni', they were informed, was a Swahili term used to describe the movement of a snake in the long grass: sinuous and unseen. The word had become a synonym in Africa – and with the slave trade in the Arabian Gulf – for undercover work. The British Army picked it up during the Mau Mau campaign in Kenya and from there it travelled to the SAS in Aden, where it was related specifically to operations involving a relatively new SOP (standard operating procedure) known as the 'double tap', which they would be learning in Khormaksar as part of a special CQB course.

The Keeni-Meeni squad was located and trained in Ballycastle House, a block of flats formerly used as married quarters. When Marty and Taff first arrived, they were taken straight to the quartermaster's store where they were kitted out with an Arab *futah*, then given a Nine-Milly with a Len Dixon holster and told to belt it into the cross-draw position, slightly to the rear of the waist at the left side, making it easy to withdraw, or 'cross draw', with the right hand. Then they were led to a large gymnasium converted into a combined firing range and CQB training area. This was crowded with Fijian SAS troops who were, they soon learned, among the deadliest of the Keeni-Meeni teams. There, side by side with the Fijians, some of whom were enormous, they were repeatedly put through the SOP known as the 'double tap' – a way of very quickly drawing the Browning from under the folds of the *futah* and firing with perfect accuracy at close range.

Though the original 'double tap' had been so named because it meant firing two shots in quick succession from the handgun, their counter-terrorist experiences had shown the Keeni-Meeni teams that a determined terrorist often carried remote-control detonation devices or a second weapon, which could be fired even when the terrorist was seriously wounded. For this reason, the Keen-Meeni teams now used sustained firepower to 'neutralise' the terrorist, which meant firing at least six rounds in under three seconds.

Marty and Taff repeatedly practised whipping the Nine-Milly out from under the *futah* and bringing it into the firing position quickly enough, and accurately enough, to down the enemy before he could react. As this was made no easier by the complicated folds of the *futah*, they had to rehearse for hours before getting as far as the actual firing range. Once there, however, they were taught to follow the quick withdrawal of the handgun with the equally quick 'neutralising' of the target with the double tap.

This method of firing had begun with the unorthodox triangular posture devised by Major Roy Farran during World War Two and evolved into the so-called Grant-Taylor Method: legs spread, pistol raised and held two-handed in the triangular firing position, then six shots fired in quick succession. For the purposes of training, the shots were fired at a target at the end of a firing alley and the men were trained repeatedly until they could put six rounds through a playing card at fifteen yards. When they could do this, they were ready to have their faces tinted dark, put on their proper Arab clothing and go into the streets of Aden to hunt down the enemy.

'I like dressing up,' Taff calmly told Marty as he carefully tinted his blond hair dark and slipped brown contact lenses over his blue eyes. 'Remember how we used to do it in Malaya and Borneo? I always thought that was great.'

'This isn't a game,' Marty responded, feeling like an assassin.

'It is to me,' Taff assured him.

Before leaving, they were informed that the Keeni-Meeni teams did not carry identification, did not pick up wounded team members, and did not go back for those who got lost. If a man was wounded or became lost in the *souks*, he was all on his own.

Initially, Marty and Taff were placed under the wing of the highly experienced Sergeant Pete Hopper, who gave them a guided tour of the port of Aden, including the business section, at-Tawahi, the harbour area, Mal'alah, and the 'high-risk' areas of Crater and Sheikh Othman. This introductory tour was taken in a Q car, or unmarked car: a deliberately battered and soiled Volkswagen Beetle that had been packed with cardboard boxes, Arabic wrapping paper and merchandise such as cigarettes, binoculars, cameras and boxes of ballpens, to make it look like a local trader's vehicle.

'It smells like a toilet bowl,' Marty noted.

'It's not bad,' Taff said.

In the Mal'alah, or harbour area, they drove through densely crowded narrow streets, past the many duty-free shops and food stalls, and parked on the Tawahi main road, close to the fenced-off harbour, but a good distance away from the armed British soldiers guarding the entrance to the Aden Port Authority Trust. A newly painted P & O passenger liner was anchored in the bay, looming large beyond the iron railings, concrete municipal buildings and warehouses of the docks, with passengers coming ashore from the transit craft and emerging from the Aden Port Authority Trust gateway to be greeted by importuning taxi drivers. The Tawahi main road itself was packed with shops, smoking and steaming food stalls, Sunni and Saydi Muslims, Hindus, Yemeni Jews, holy men and traders, beggars and thieves, veiled women and dirty children, as well as mangy dogs, cats, and even cows – all watched carefully by British Army soldiers armed with Sten guns and SLR rifles.

The harbour area, Marty and Taff were informed by Sergeant Hopper, was difficult to work in because Aden was a free port used constantly by shipping-line passengers, despite the presence of the armed 'greens' in the streets. Because of this, tourists often crammed the packed alleyways, doing their shopping, and either blocked the planned line of fire of the Keeni-Meeni teams or went into a panic and got in the road when the SAS men were trying to make their escape. It was also a hard fact of life that often, after an SAS assassination, the locals would take their revenge on the nearest available white person – invariably an innocent tourist.

The side-streets of the main town were not much easier to work in, being filled with shops, most with British names – the London Store, the New Era – but all run by Arabs who sat outside on wooden chairs to sip tea and haggle with the tourists, mere feet away from the tense British soldiers standing guard at nearly every corner.

Worst of all, however, was the 'high-risk' area, Crater, on the lower slopes of the volcanic mountain, with its teeming narrow streets, traders and animals. It was also cluttered with burning braziers and pots of cooking food or boiling tea. So when they were in the Crater area the SAS men would be hemmed in on all sides, at all times, and almost nose-to-nose with their targets. It was not a comforting thought.

Once Marty and Tommy had been familiarised with the area, Hopper acted as team leader in a series of attacks on local double agents who had to be shot down as they went about their business in the port of Aden. The first one was 'neutralised' while stepping out of a taxi in a crowded part of the business area, at-Tawahi, the second in the harbour area where he was about to pick up some tourists in his taxi, and the third in a packed *souk*, gunned down as he was dining on *couscous* at an outdoor table.

In each case, the team operated the same way. Once out of the Q car, the three men did not speak to each other, kept well apart, and made sure that they were always in sight of one-another. If any Arab spoke to them, they tried to avoid replying, though in a manner that would not offend, usually by just nodding in response and walking on. If that was not possible, they replied in basic Arabic, learned at the Hereford and Army School of Languages, though they spoke as briefly as possible and always acted as if they were in a hurry. Finally, when they reached the RV, the first man to see the target would be the one to neutralise him. If, on the other hand, they all saw him at once, they all fired simultaneously. They would then make their escape under cover of the confusion created by the shooting, often pushing shocked bystanders aside, hopping over café tables, or knocking over footstalls, to run back through the maze of alleyways until they had reached the Q car parked some distance away. Once in the car, they would drive out of the area as quickly as possible, not stopping until they were back in the safety of the military complex of Khormaksar.

The first three shootings, led by Sergeant Hopper, were the worst for Marty, as he wasn't used to shooting people in such a close-up, calculated way, outside the heat of battle, and doing so filled him with reservations. He was, of course, as usual, taken aback by the ease with which Taff did the same thing. By the third shooting, however, he had managed to distance himself from the act by concentrating almost solely on the details of the operation: the environment, the people in it, and anything that might impede the shooting itself or his route of escape. He also forced himself to remember that the men he was shooting down, most acting as double agents, had caused the deaths of British operatives, members of the SAS Keeni-Meeni teams and Arab friends of the British. This justified what he was doing and made it easier to deal with.

Once Marty and Taff started going out on their own, working as a two-man team, they became highly proficient and even addicted to the excitement of it. Now, as Marty sat beside Taff at a café table in a crowded square in Crater, he realised that the Keeni-Meeni operations had been therapeutic for him, heightening his awareness of mortality, giving him back the lust for life, and helping him to place the last few years into perspective. He now accepted that his world, if irrevocably changed by personal tragedy and the natural fears of middle age, had not been completely shattered and still held out the hope of a decent future.

He realised, also, with a great deal of regret, that this would be his final operation in Aden before he returned to the relatively normal world of Bradbury Lines. To offset this regret, he had already planned to get in touch with Diane

Lavery. This, too, was a sign of the emotional renewal that had been wrought through his work in the harsh mountains of the Radfan and the crowded, highly dangerously streets of Aden. In truth, perhaps *because* of the danger, he had gained a new lease of life here.

Taff nodded silently towards the door of the restaurant they were watching from their outside table. Looking in that direction, Marty saw his target emerging from the building. He was an Arab, a big man, wearing an English suit with striped shirt and tie – an 'old-school' tie, no doubt – and he was grinning as he stepped from the shadows of the doorway into the sunshine, talking over his shoulder to the man coming out behind him. Though he looked good-natured and civilised, Marty knew that he was a Yemeni-trained double agent, alternating between giving false information to the British and passing on to the enemy information about British activities in the area. Either way, his activities had led to many failed missions and casualties, including some dead Keeni-Meeni operatives. He had to be neutralised – assassinated – before he could do further damage.

Still sitting at their table in the outdoor part of the restaurant, mere metres from the Arab, Marty and Taff waited until he had stepped well away from the door and the man directly behind him, possibly a bodyguard, could also be seen. Only then did they push their chairs back, stand upright, and reach under their *futahs* to whip the Browning High Power handguns out of their holsters and adopt the double-tap position.

Locking their arms and bending their legs slightly as they had been taught, aiming squarely at the advancing Arab from a distance of less than five metres, holding the pistol firmly and applying pressure equally between the thumb and fingers of the firing hand, they simultaneously fired six rounds in quick succession.

The big Arab in the English suit was punched violently backwards, blood spurting from his chest, to crash over the table directly behind him. The customers cried out and scattered as the table collapsed beneath the falling man and he fell to the ground with bottles and glasses smashing under him. Even as the mortally wounded man was hitting the ground, the Arab behind him, also wearing an English suit, was dropping low and reaching into his jacket. Not waiting to see if he was reaching for a gun or not, Marty and Taff swung simultaneously in that direction, still holding their Browning High Powers in the double-tap position, and each fired another six rounds, which punched the man back into the wall, where he shuddered violently, his jacket drenched in blood, and then flopped face down on the hard ground.

Not taking the time to check that the men were dead, Marty and Taff turned away and raced across the square, pushing shocked passers-by aside, knocking over at least one food stall, ignoring the screaming of women and the bellowing of men behind them as they plunged into the nearest alleyway. Holstering their handguns while still on the run, they made their way through the narrow, packed thoroughfare, again pushing the jostling Arabs aside and often knocking over pots and pans, until they emerged to the dazzling sunlight at the far end, where they crossed another, much quieter square and eventually, breathlessly, reached their parked, dusty Volkswagen Beetle.

Taff took the passenger seat, Marty sat behind the steering wheel, and then they burned out of the square on shrieking tyres. Once outside Crater, taking the road back down to the town centre, Marty slowed down and drove more normally, not wishing to attract attention, and kept driving until he and Taff were back in the safety of the military compound at Khormaksar.

The next day, after a good night's sleep, both men were flown back to England.

CHAPTER TWENTY-SIX

'Well, now we know where you went, don't we?' Diane Lavery said, smiling at Marty through the cloud of her own cigarette smoke across a candle-lit table in a modestly priced Italian restaurant in London's Notting Hill Gate.

'I don't know what you're talking about,' Marty said, grinning back at her, pleased with himself for having worked up the courage to take her business card out of his wallet and actually call her, which he had debated doing for a fortnight, ever since his return from Aden to Hareford. He had been as nervous as a schoolboy when making the call, thinking she might have forgotten him; but she had remembered him instantly, said she was delighted to hear from him, and arranged to meet him in a pub right beside the restaurant, near to where she lived.

'Read your newspapers,' Diane replied, brushing strands of blonde hair from green eyes and still smiling with that appealing mixture of mockery and girlish coquetry. 'The usual lies and retractions which, when the wheat's separated from the chaff, show the real picture.'

'Give me the picture,' Marty said. He had come up for the weekend, arriving only this morning and staying with his mother in Crouch End, nervously awaiting his reunion with Diane in the evening. However, delighted to find that his mother was no longer grieving and had, in fact, created a lively new life for herself – frequent visits to Lesley and the kids, church every Sunday, bingo with friends in the evenings, even holidays in Spain – he had arrived at the pub feeling more relaxed than he'd thought he would be. Though the pub was filled mostly with young people, the girls resembling Julie Christie or Jean Shrimpton, the boys either into the mop-haired Beatles or the long-haired Rolling Stones, he had relaxed even more when Diane arrived, wearing a svelte figure-hugging dress under a tightly buckled overcoat and high heels that showed off her long legs, and turned out to be as easy to talk to as he'd remembered. The evening had progressed pleasantly since then and now, having moved from the pub to the restaurant, where they had shared a good Italian meal with red wine, he was feeling deeply satisfied and more romantic than he had a right to be at his age.

'First,' Diane said, 'a Radio Taiz Yemeni propaganda report claims that the severed heads of two dead British soldiers were put on public display in the Yemen. Next, the GOC confirms at a press conference – which of course I attended – that he'd received reliable information on the decapitation of two British soldiers and the public exhibition of their heads on stakes in Yemen.'

'I read that,' Marty said blandly. 'But I've also read that the republican government in Yemen has denied its own propaganda broadcast and denounced the decapitation story as a British lie. And don't forget that the US Embassy in Taiz is handling British interests in the absence of UK diplomatic recognition of the republicans, and it's investigated the matter and says there's no truth to it.'

'Don't hold your breath for the next instalment,' Diane told him. '*The Times* will be running a story in tomorrow's edition, under my byline, confirming that a patrol of the Federal Regular Army *did* in fact find two headless bodies in a shallow grave in the Radfan, near to where the SAS was engaged in a battle a few months ago – exactly the same time as you were out of the country on SAS business. You were in Aden, weren't you?'

As the decapitation story of two British soldiers known to be SAS had overnight made the regiment a subject of intense speculation in the press, Marty saw little point in denying it any longer. 'Yes,' he confessed. 'It was Aden.'

'And you were in that battle?'

'Yes.'

'So you know the identity of those unfortunate soldiers.'

'I can guess,' Marty said.

'Do you care to tell me?'

'No.'

Diane smiled and nodded. 'Okay. I understand.'

The decapitated heads, Marty knew, were those of Captain Keating and Trooper Al Reid, whose bodies he recalled being carried away by the Yemeni guerrillas shortly after he and the rest of the patrol had evacuated the besieged sangars. Even now he could recall his anger as the bodies were carried away and the bitterness he had felt at the war in general. A war staged for the benefit of politicians. No more and no less. Marty burned just to think of it.

'Were the two men close friends of yours?' Diane asked.

'Not really close,' Marty admitted. 'But naturally I knew them and respected them.'

'Does this conversation bother you?'

'No.'

Diane looked relieved. 'I just can't help behaving like a journalist. I have to talk about these things.'

'It's no problem,' Marty said.

In fact, he was grateful for something to talk about as he had been quite nervous about calling her and still wasn't sure why he had done so. Certainly, there could be no denying that he had found her attractive from the first moment of meeting her at Paddy Kearney's resignation party in Hereford. Also, he could not deny that he had thought often about her during his enforced celibacy in Aden and the Radfan – more so as the dangerous excitements of the Keeni-Meeni operations had burned away the grief he had been carrying over the past few years. By the time he returned to England, as he now realised, he was ready to take on life again and Diane was the start of that healing process. He needed to lose himself in a woman and he sensed that she wanted him. That was enough for now.

'From what I gather,' Diane said, 'the news about two

headless bodies being found in the Radfan and the severed heads being put on public exhibition in Yemen has led to singular embarrassment for the security forces.'

'I can't speak for the SF in general, but it certainly embarrassed the SAS.'

'Why?'

'The next of kin had been unaware of the deaths and, even worse, had been informed that the men were on a routine exercise on Salisbury Plain.'

'I think that's disgusting,' Diane said.

'Maybe,' Marty replied. 'But it was necessary at the time. We were operating under strict secrecy, so we couldn't tell the relatives where those men were. We couldn't even tell them where they died. A necessary evil, you might say. Sooner or later, in fighting for your country, you get dirt as well as blood on your hands. Unfortunately, regarding that particular war, the sacrifice wasn't worth it.'

'Well,' Diane said, stubbing her cigarette out in an overflowing ashtray and sipping the last of her Chianti, 'the incident has certainly made the press interested in the SAS. Do you like that or not?'

'I don't,' Marty confessed. 'I think a regiment like the SAS works best when it's anonymous. I'd hate for it to become an item of public speculation, which too often is fanciful. Anyway, let's hope this business will soon be forgotten and the press think of something else to write about. Then we can go back to what we do best – quietly, behind the scenes. Are you ready to leave?'

Diane glanced at her wristwatch and nodded agreement. 'Yes.' She raised her eyes again as Marty called for the bill. 'I'm not at all sure I agree with that,' she said, continuing the conversation. 'Any organisation that favours anonymity is open to corruption.'

'Not the SAS,' Marty said. 'For a start, it doesn't work for its own good, but for the good of the country, which means that it doesn't necessarily make its own choices – it only chooses *how* it should do its work. Secondly, it encourages personal initiative and shared responsibility, which is very different from the regular Army and, I think, safeguards it from becoming too rigidified. The anonymity is purely for reasons of security in what's usually very specialised, highly dangerous work. In our case, the anonymity is a necessity, not a vice, and I think we work best with it.'

'Let's hope it lasts,' Diane said.

'Sorry,' Marty said as he was paying the bill, laying the five-pound notes out carefully in the saucer presented by the cheerful Italian waiter. 'Would you like a brandy?'

'In my place,' Diane said.

Glancing at her, noting the steady gaze and slightly teasing smile, Marty left a generous tip, then pushed back his chair and stood up. 'Great,' he said. 'That sounds wonderful.'

'Just like the meal,' she responded, also standing. 'Did you like it?'

'I loved it,' he replied sincerely, walking her to the door. '*And* I liked the restaurant. Cheap, unpretentious and easy-going. My kind of place.'

'What about smarter, grander places?'

'I don't like them at all.'

'You must still be a working-class lad at heart.'

'No question about it.'

Leaving the restaurant, they stepped into the bright lights and noisy traffic of the Bayswater Road, wet from the rain and swept with a cold November wind. After buttoning up her overcoat and putting on a headscarf, Diane took Marty's hand and walked him along the glistening pavement, then turned right into Kensington Church Street. As they walked downhill, passing elegant antique shops and a couple of old pubs with lights beaming invitingly over the drenched, lamplit pavements, he felt the return of his former nervousness at the thought of entering her flat. He wanted to make love to her and thought she might want it, too, but it had been an awfully long time for him – he hadn't touched a woman since the death of Ann Lim – and now he wasn't too sure how to start. He felt like a schoolboy on his first date. It was a very strange feeling.

'What age are you, Marty?' Diane asked him, as if reading his thoughts.

'Hold on,' he replied jokingly. 'Let me think about that. It's been so long, I can't . . .'

She tugged at his hand and said, 'Come on! Stop fooling around. Just tell me, Marty.'

'Forty-five,' he said truthfully. 'Going on for forty-six.'

'My God, you don't look it!'

'Are you disappointed that I'm older than I look?'

'No. Why should I be? I'm not that young myself. Thirty-eight this year. Are *you* disappointed?'

'No. I like what I see.'

'So do I, Marty.'

They walked farther downhill where the wind was less strong, then turned right into a street of elegant Georgian houses where, presumably, Diane lived. 'So what happens to you now? Will they still send you overseas?'

'It depends when they next have to go,' he told her. 'As a matter of fact, I *do* still go overseas on training exercises with other special service units in Bavaria, Germany, Norway, Finland, Greece, Italy, France and even the United States. So travel's certainly still on the agenda.'

'I meant on *active* service,' she clarified. 'Will you ever get to fight another war?'

'Unfortunately for me, in my advancing years – ho, ho! – that'll depend entirely on when the next war starts and on exactly what kind of activity's required. I've probably got until I'm about fifty or, depending on how fit I remain, a few years after that for major assaults requiring great physical stamina. But I may still be allowed to take part in other operations even when I'm slightly older, particularly the counter-terrorist or counter-insurgency type.'

'And right now?'

'I'll probably alternate between return trips to Aden and acting as a DS at the training wing at Bradbury Lines. When the war in Aden finally ends, which it will soon, I'll be condemned to the latter.'

'What does "DS" mean?'

'A member of the Directing Staff. Something like a drill instructor, but much more wide-ranging. Running the training and selection courses. Supervising the actual training – the rifle range, route marches, parachuting, navigation . . . That kind of thing.'

'Sounds interesting.'

'It's not as interesting as fighting, I'm afraid. That's the beast in the man.'

'So how can a nice man like you enjoying fighting in wars?'

'I don't know. At least, I'm not sure. I've certainly thought a great deal about it, but I can't find an answer. Of course, I believe in the necessity of it – the need to defend your country – but on a personal level I can only offer the fact that danger has its attractions. You never really know how precious life is until you come close to losing it. That's a sad fact of life.'

'What about sex?' she asked him.

'Pardon?'

'Doesn't sex do the same? You never really know what life is until you're having good sex. That moment just before the orgasm, when you're right on the edge. Isn't that the same feeling?'

'Sex and war have certain similarities,' he agreed, though he felt uncomfortable talking about it. 'They both offer danger, excitement, a heightened awareness of the moment. So in that sense, yes, I guess you're right. They're very similar that way.'

'We'll soon find out,' she said, surprising him, even shocking him a little. Before he could respond, however, she stopped walking, turned into him, kissed him lightly on the lips, then pushed open the gate they were at and walked up the garden path. Confused and pleased at once, he followed to stand behind her as she opened the front door of the Georgian house and motion him inside.

The house had been converted into flats and Diane's was on the third floor. As they went up in the lift, facing each other, close to each other, she smiled at him in that slightly mocking, coquettish way, then reached out with her hand and lightly stroked the side of his face without saying a word. When the lift stopped at the third floor, she led him into her flat, which was just along the corridor. The flat was spacious and airy, with Habitat furniture, lots of potted plants, Oriental carpets, mock-Picasso curtains, packed bookshelves and original paintings on the walls – the kind of place you saw advertised in women's magazines selling fashionable living.

While still at the closed flat door, Diane kicked off her high-heeled shoes, then removed her soaked overcoat and hung it up on a coat hanger. Marty did the same. Then Diane, still wearing the scarf on her head, went to the drinks cabinet in the lounge, which was, he noted, centrally heated and comfortably warm.

'A brandy?'

'Great,' he said.

As Diane poured them each a cognac, he noticed, as he had done when first seeing her, that, in the Mary Quant white dress that fell to just above the knees and left her arms and shoulders bare, she was bone-thin, almost flat-chested, yet undoubtedly, inexplicably sensual. She did, in fact, look a bit like Jean Shrimpton, but with a fuller figure and a more mature, lived-in face and, of course, those searching green eyes. In fact, to him she was not merely attractive, but damned near irresistible.

Turning away from the drinks cabinet, she handed him one of the two large brandies, then motioned to the white-leather sofa that faced the TV set and what looked like expensive hi-fi equipment and a cabinet filled with long-playing records.

'Over here,' she said with no trace of shyness, leading him to the sofa, letting him sit first, then settling down beside him, so close her thigh was pressing against his. 'Cheers, Marty,' she said, raising her glass of brandy in the air.

They touched glasses and drank. When Diane lowered the glass from her lips, she glanced at the table in front of her, at the empty ashtray, and asked, 'Do you have a ciggie?'

'Yep.' He reached into his pocket and withdrew a packet of Benson and Hedges. When they were both alight, Diane leaned back on the sofa, crossed her long legs, which, with the high hemline, were exposed for most of their length, then blew a thin stream of smoke and said, 'God, I'm glad you called. I confess, I wanted you to call. I wanted to see you again. I knew I'd want to see you again the minute we met. That's why I gave you my business card. I'm not always that free with it.'

'No?'

'No.' She stared steadily at him from behind a veil of smoke. 'Why do you ask? Do you think I give it out to every Tom, Dick and Harry? Do you think—?'

'No,' he interjected. 'I simply meant, you being a journalist and all . . . You know? Giving it out all the time for business purposes. I didn't think it meant anything.'

'But you still called me.'

'Yes.'

'So you must have known I wanted to see you.'

'I didn't *know*. I was hoping.'

She smiled. 'Well, that's nice.'

They were both silent for a moment, enjoying the brandy and cigarettes. Then Marty, perhaps emboldened by the drink but still not wanting to ask directly about her husband, said, 'So what about you? Where did you come from to finally end up here in London as a freelance journalist? Were you born in London, like me?'

She shook her head. 'Nope. In Buckingham in Oxfordshire. My father was a solicitor, my mother kept house, and I grew up with two younger sisters and an older brother in a happy, healthy environment. We were quite well off. Even had a couple of horses. It was a terribly middle-class upbringing, actually, which might have spoiled us for life. I loved my dad. He was a real crusading solicitor, dividing his time between local business and another practice in London, taking on all sorts of lost causes and fighting the good fight. It was he who told me that most of society was corrupt from top to bottom, that the law was no better, and that there was one set of laws for the rich, another for the poor. He detested that and fought it all his life and I loved him for doing it.'

'Damned right,' Marty said.

Diane smiled and nodded, her green eyes hazed in the cigarette smoke drifting out of pinched nostrils. 'Anyway, that's why I decided to become a solicitor as well and went to Oxford with that in mind.' She smiled ruefully and shook her head, brushing strands of hair from her eyes and blowing smoke from moisturised, pink lips. 'But it was too tough for me. I just couldn't hack it. Instead, I studied history and then, when I came down, went to London and wangled my way into journalism. Dad helped, of course. He knew a lot of people. He pushed me in the direction of politics, but then, just as I was starting out on my new career, he contracted a brain tumour, practically overnight it seemed, and was rushed into hospital and died.' She snapped her fingers and shook her head again. 'Just like that. One minute he was there, the rock of my life, and the next he was gone. I was twenty-three years of age and devastated. I thought my whole life had ended.'

Finishing off her brandy, she held the glass out to Marty and said, with a wicked smile, 'Can I have another, thanks?'

Nodding, he took the glass and went to the drinks cabinet, where he poured himself another as well. Returning to the settee, he sat beside her again, their hips practically touching, his gaze drawn to the sheer length of her leg, which was curled up against him. He felt breathless and dizzy, slightly out of control. She held her drink up and they clinked glasses together.

'Cheers!' she said.

'Cheers.' Each had another sip of brandy, then Marty asked, 'So what happened next?'

Diane sighed. 'The usual disasters that befall a young woman who loses the father she depended upon so much. Of course, I'd been overly protected. I never knew it, but I was. Then, when my father died so suddenly, I started trying to find him again, to get him back, as it were, through a succession of affairs with older men – usually men about his age. Naturally, I was used. I was fair game for most of them. Being older, they were experienced, knowing how dependent I was, and they used it and took what they could get from me before finally dropping me. Mostly married, of course. I was their little bit on the side. They liked it until it threatened their marriages, then they always wanted out. I drifted on like that for years, from one affair to another, drinking too much, rarely happy, but somehow managing to get my work done and gradually becoming a good journalist. I had my father to thank for that. I inherited his crusading zeal. He'd told me that society was corrupt from top to bottom and that's what I was always looking for, particularly in politics. I became the scourge of politicians, left and right, with my profiles and interviews, and that made me successful in public, if not quite in private. So by the time I was thirty, I was pretty well established in Fleet Street. It was as simple as that.'

She moved her legs to lean towards the coffee table and stub her cigarette out in the ashtray. Marty did the same, then settled back beside her as she curled her long legs up again, letting the dress ride up her stockinged thighs to just below the hips. That sight took his breath away.

'So what about your husband?' he finally felt compelled to ask, sipping more cognac to cover his uneasiness.

'He's my second,' she said. 'I married the first when I was twenty-eight – already pretty late – and it turned out to be an absolute disaster. He was the same age as me, the first I'd had that young, and he worked as a broker in the City and was rarely at home. I'd met him in a wine bar. We were both drunk and randy with it. We tumbled into his bed, had great sex together without using contraception, and I got pregnant and we decided to tie the knot. But it wasn't for either of us. He was a natural bachelor and I was too critical, castigating him for being a greedy bastard who made money simply by buying and selling assets while contributing nothing of value to society. We fought a lot about that. Then I lost the child and was told I could have no more. The marriage broke up within weeks of that and the divorce was finalised two years later. We never kept in touch.'

She was drunk, Marty knew, on too much wine and brandy, but still in control for all that. Though her normally pale, almost gaunt cheeks were flushed, her green eyes were certainly not bloodshot and her gaze was still steady, if presently a little introspective. Her legs, still curled beneath her, were silky smooth and seductive in the sheer stockings, exposed most of the way up the thighs, making him feel sensual and unreal. He wanted to lean forward and kiss those legs, but this wasn't the right time.

'As for my second husband . . .' She sighed again. 'He really wasn't bad at all, but he wanted children and I couldn't have them, so he went to another woman and had them with her. Donald Wakefield. A fellow journalist in Fleet Street. A very bright man, very decent, very controlled, he taught me a lot of the tricks of the trade, always gave me good advice, was a considerate, expert lover and easy-going husband . . . but he wanted children. Our marriage floundered on that and he was honest enough to say so when he left to move in with the other woman, ten years younger than me and him. Now they live in sin in Richmond in a nice house on the hill. They have two kids, a boy and a girl, and are a golden, if unorthodox, couple, still not legally married. Sometimes I resent them, but mostly not, mainly because Donald's always kept in touch and is there when I need him. So mostly I'm happy if they are. It's a good arrangement.'

'Anyone at present?' Marty asked.

'Yes,' she said. 'You.'

He stared at her, startled, not used to such boldness, simultaneously amused and slightly shocked, feeling even more unreal. She leaned towards the table, put her brandy glass down, then took the glass out of his hand and put that down as well. Hands free, she smiled at him, mischievous and challenging, compelling him to turn sideways, place his hands on her shoulders, then cup them around her thin face and pull her in to him.

He kissed her on the lips and she instantly responded, sliding her tongue into his mouth as she pressed her body against him. He responded in kind, pushing her back, leaning upon her, kissing her lips, the side of her neck, her throat, the breasts beneath the white dress. She was crushed beneath him, with no room to move her legs, though she had managed to bend the left leg up beside him and let him run his hand over it. The hem of the dress was stretched tight now, cutting a line across her hips, and he found himself groping between her thighs in a trance of desire. She moaned softly and writhed beneath him, arching her back, pushing her stomach up, letting him feel the softness and warmth beneath the cloth of the dress. Marty groped between her thighs, touched her panties, felt the warm damp; further excited, he pressed his body upon her, crushing her breasts with his chest.

Their lips mangled together. She tugged his jacket off, then ran her hands up under his thick, rollneck pullover to massage his bare back and spine. He shuddered and hardened further, wanting desperately to enter her, and she helped him by arching her body to let him tug the dress up. He drew it over her flat stomach, over her small, bare breasts, was thrilled by the fact that she wore no brassiere, then tugged it over her head. Her headscarf came off as well, letting her blonde hair tumble free, and he let the dress fall to the floor as he kissed her neck, throat and ears.

She unbuttoned his shirt. He couldn't work out how she had managed it. She stripped the shirt off him and kissed his bare shoulders, then sank her teeth gently into his arm. He pushed her back down again, his hand crushing her breast, then with her help he managed to undress her and stretch out beside her. She had very long legs, beautifully shaped, cradling his hips, and he felt her fingers unbuckling his belt as he pressed down between them. She gasped and chuckled again, unsnapping his buckle, reaching down to unzip him. She had managed to get his trousers open when they both rolled off the small settee.

'Oh, Christ!' she groaned as his thrusting repeatedly jolted her frail body, pushing it back, until she was half off the settee, her bare shoulders in mid-air, her blonde hair hanging down to the floor. He didn't know how they were managing it. They seemed, for a brief moment, to be suspended in space. Then she twisted back farther, her legs still clamped around his hips, and he followed her down as her shoulders touched the floor and she twisted slowly, sinuously sideways. He went with her, on top of her, still between her sweat-slicked thighs, and felt her fingers tugging at his unbelted, opened trousers as he stretched out on the carpeted floor, first beside her, then on top of her again, as he kicked his trousers off and prepared to enter her. She guided him in, holding him, raising her groin to receive him, and he touched the soft warmth, the veil of hairs, then pierced the opening and slipped in.

'Oh, God!' she exclaimed as he heard his own muffled groaning and began to thrust in and out, penetrating her deeply, moving with an urgency born of too many months of deprivation. 'Not too fast,' she admonished him. He slowed down and took more care. She moaned softly and he picked up her rhythm and moved more naturally with her.

They flowed together like grains of windblown sand, each scorched by the other's heat, and drove each other to that point beyond reason, where mind and body became one. They lost themselves there, obliterated by lust, and then spasmed in uncontrollable waves of feeling, one piled on the other. They shuddered and groaned together, collapsed one on top of the other, and then lay there, breathing harshly, recovering, until the real world returned.

It was, Marty realised as he rolled off Diane's body and reached for her hand, a much brighter world. It was the land of the living.

He was committed again.

CHAPTER TWENTY-SEVEN

'How have you spent your last year or so?' Paddy asked when they had settled comfortably into his local pub in Peterchurch in Hereford, sitting over two pints of Yorkshire bitter.

'Between Aden and the Sports and Social,' Marty said.

'So how was Aden?'

'Bloody awful. We divided our time between the war in the Radfan mountains and the Keeni-Meeni actions in Aden. Mind you, since few of us had any interest in what we thought was a pointless conflict, we spent most of our time trying to kill our boredom by talking endlessly about the good time our mates, the so-called urbanites – the Keeni-Meeni teams – were having in the fleshpots of Aden. Then, when we were back in Aden, doing the Keeni-Meeni stuff ourselves, we vented our frustration by complaining about the overcrowded *souks*, the treachery of the Arabs, and the fuck-ups of the greens guarding the streets. In short, we were just passing time to save face for the bloody politicians. It was a sickening business.'

Paddy sighed. 'Well, at least it's all over at last.' He was referring to the fact that the Radfan had been handed over to the Federal Regular Army – now the South Arabian Army – on 26 June 1967, at the end of the Six Day War between Israel and Egypt. This had led to the singular humiliation of Arab nationalists and riots in the streets of many Muslim cities. The British presence in Aden –

and that of the SAS – formally ended in the November of that year.

'Yes, thank Christ for that, though it *did* mean that for the past couple of years I've been condemned to the training wing at Bradbury Lines. It's enjoyable enough, if not wildly exciting. But I've been compensated with a lot of trips overseas to other special service units for some more training and the exchange of ideas. A lot of booze and back-breaking work. That breaks the monotony.'

He sipped his beer and glanced at Paddy, pleased to note that he looked as young as ever, if slightly fuller in the face from rich living in the upmarket bars and bistros of Civvy Street. It had taken Marty a while to get used to the sight of his old friend in suits with shirt and tie, but now it seemed normal; and Paddy was, he had to admit, as rakishly appealing in the attire of a businessman as he had been in his SAS uniform. He still had his charisma.

'So what happens now?' Paddy asked.

'Oman. You should remember it from nineteen fifty-nine, when we launched an assault on the Jebel Akhdar in the north.'

'Of course,' Paddy replied. 'The Green Mountain, nicknamed "Sabrina". We did a hell of a job there.'

The British had treaty obligations to the Sultan of Muscat and Oman, located on the southeast corner of the Arabian peninsula and strategically important because a hostile regime in Oman could interrupt or stop completely the flow of oil to the West. In 1957 the Sultan's rule was challenged by Sulaiman bin Hamyar, chief of the Bani Riyam tribe, supported by the rebel forces of the imam, Ghalib bin Ali, and his brother Talib. Drawn into this conflict, the British dispatched an infantry brigade from Kenya to aid the Sultan, but by 1958 the rebels of Talib bin Ali were controlling the Jebel Akhdar, the highest point in the northern region of the country, surrounded by mountain peaks and accessible only by narrow passes, which were ideal for ambushes.

In an attempt to win back the mountain, D Squadron SAS was flown from Malaya to Oman in November 1958, managed to reach the summit of the mountain by climbing the northern side, and established sangars only 2,000 metres from rebel positions. Those sangars were held against repeated attacks by the rebels, with heavy enemy losses. Meanwhile, on the southern side of the mountain, a rebel cave containing weapons and ammunition was assaulted by an SAS group led by Captain Peter de la Billière, but after a bloody battle he was forced to conduct a fighting withdrawal. Finally, in January 1959, a determined push was made against the rebels with A Squadron assaulting Sabrina from the north, then linking up with D Squadron in Tanuf. A few hours later, while a diversionary attack was made from Tanuf by some of the SAS, the majority of A and D squadrons, heavily burdened, made the gruelling climb up the massive jebel, flushing out the rebels as they went and gradually clearing them off the summit, allowing soldiers from the British Life Guards and the Sultan's Armed Forces to be brought in to secure the whole mountain. The SAS then moved into the surrounding villages to disarm the rebels. Shortly after, the rebel leaders fled into Saudi Arabia, leaving the way clear for the SAS, over the next few months, to mount a successful hearts-and-minds campaign that gradually turned the local inhabitants into supporters of the Sultan.

'That assault,' Paddy said after a thoughtful pause, 'was a prime example of just what a small number of men can do against a strongly entrenched enemy position. We won the summit with boldness and imagination, not with brute force. And the climb to the top of the mountain was a definitive test of SAS fitness and tenacity. We passed with flying colours. So what's happening there now?'

'The usual shit,' Marty said. 'The problem's in Dhofar, in the south-west of the province. It's dominated by another mountain, the Jebel Dhofar. Desert to the west; a narrow coastal strip to the east. A few years back a bunch of rebels formed the Dhofar Liberation Front and turned against the Sultan. The Sultan's Armed Forces put down the rebellion, but the DLF gradually merged with a communist group, the PFLOAG, backed by the People's Democratic Republic of Yemen, the Soviet Union and China. This strengthened the arm of the rebels, known as the *adoo*, and the Sultan's regime started falling apart. The old bastard was saved by his son, Qaboos, who mounted a bloodless coup to remove his dad. With the Sultan out of the picture, the way was clear for a counter-insurgency operation, designed to defeat the communist hardliners and win the hearts and minds of the people.'

'So the SAS stepped into the picture.'

'Yes,' Marty said. 'Within hours of the coup, an SAS team arrived secretly in Dhofar. It was listed officially as a British Army training team and gradually, as more SAS squadrons arrived, more BATT teams were formed. Right now, under the command of Lieutenant-Colonel John Watts, we're waging a five-pronged counter-insurgency war. Meanwhile, back at Hereford, the Head Sheds of the Kremlin are talking about the possibility of forming *firqat* – companies of Dhofari troops and turncoat rebels – to fight for the new Sultan. We'll train them and provide radio communications in the field. If the Sultan agrees to the plan, that's what I'll be doing in Dhofar, alongside the ongoing hearts-and-minds campaign.'

'Direct action?'

'Ultimately we'll have to launch an assault against the rebels commanding the heights of the Jebel Dhofar. I want to be part of that.'

'Christ, Marty,' Paddy said, wiping his wet lips with the back of his hand and placing his mug on the table, 'if the Jebel Dhofar is anything like Sabrina, that's going to be a killing climb, with or without enemy sniper fire. You're going to be forty-seven this year. Do you think you can hack it?'

'That's a bloody brutal question,' Marty replied, feeling mildly insulted.

'It's a bloody brutal business,' Paddy replied as he lit a cigarette, 'and you have to face up to certain facts. Let's face it, you're not young any more and that jebel's a big one. Are you sure you can climb it?'

'I can climb it,' Marty insisted, though he secretly had his doubts. He had seen himself in the mirror and did not like what he saw: thinning, greying hair, lines of age in the face, a body not as slim and as muscular as it had been some years back. Also, he suffered mild aches and pains that he forced himself to ignore. Time was taking its toll all right.

Paddy grinned. 'Grabbing at your last opportunity for some real action, are you? Before they retire you to the training wing or the Kremlin.'

'You've hit the nail on the head, mate.'

'Well, I don't blame you. Bloody dreadful how quickly it comes, isn't it? The years pass so quickly.'

'That's the truth of it,' Marty said.

Leaning back in his chair, he glanced around the pub, all black-tarred beams and brass pots, with an open fire burning in the grate and strands of smoke spiralling up from the flickering yellow flames. It was lunchtime, and the pub was crowded with people eating, mostly country-squire types in tweed jackets with patched elbows, accompanied by horsey wives in 'sensible' clothes that made them seem almost masculine. Luckily, there were also some sleek-faced local businessmen with their leggy, attractive secretaries, leaning on the bar beside local farmers and tradesmen, some in overalls, and some SAS men from Bradbury Lines, now wearing their civvies. It was a congenial, traditional, cosy pub and Marty felt at home in it.

'So what's it like being married again?' Paddy asked sardonically, 'And living at home with your new wife instead of in the spider?'

'Diane and I aren't married,' Marty responded, 'and damned well you know it. Nor do we live together all the time. She works in London, after all. So we only live together off and on, either when I'm on leave and can go to London or when she comes down here.'

'Living in sin, my old son. It all sounds very cosy.'

'It's not bad.'

'No plans for marriage?'

'She's still married.'

'Ah, yes, I remember. She told me when you brought her here on your last visit. Have you met her husband?'

'No, thanks.'

Paddy grinned. 'Don't want to see the competition, eh?'

'He's not competition,' Marty insisted. 'They're just good

friends. He's happily living in sin with *his* girlfriend and they have a couple of kids.'

'Try to avoid that yourself, old son. You're too old to start all over again. Either have kids when you're young or don't have them at all, I say. And, since you've already got two perfectly nice kids, you don't need any more.'

'Diane can't have kids,' Marty told him, 'so there's no problem there. What did you think of her?'

'I wasn't sure,' Paddy replied frankly. 'I thought she was attractive and she seemed nice enough, but she *did* have a certain amount of inner tension that I found disconcerting. Is she easy to live with?'

'Yes,' Marty replied, though it wasn't quite true. In fact, his relationship with Diane was based on mutual sexual attraction and worked very well on that level: they were a hot couple in bed, completely uninhibited, endlessly inventive, and usually well satisfied when it was over. Nevertheless, out of bed, Diane *was* filled with tension and could be disconcertingly single-minded. Her belief in the baseness of politicians bordered on the obsessional and made her argumentative over the most seemingly trivial issues. In truth, they fought a lot and were still living together only because they were so strongly attracted sexually to each other and could heal the most savage wounds in bed. The relationship was more physical than emotional and it had its dark sides. Nevertheless, he needed it.

'I also thought she was rather serious,' Paddy said. 'Good-humoured at times, a little mischievous as well, but beneath it all . . . *very* serious. Particularly, as I recall, when it comes to politics. She *is* political, isn't she?'

'Yes.'

'Leaning to the left as I remember.'

'More or less. She despises the establishment, which she insists is corrupt – but she's also suspicious of the trade unions and what she calls creeping communism.'

'So am I,' Paddy confessed, 'though not with Diane's passion. To be truthful, by and large I don't get involved much. Angela, of course, takes it all very seriously – she's Tory to her fingertips – and complains because, although I vote as she does, I never involve myself more than that.'

'But you believe in the establishment. I know you do.'

'In the end, I support it, but I'm not obsessed with it. I rarely worry about reds under the beds and I believe that the British people, with their innate common sense, will always act properly – taking the middle ground, as it were – when it comes to politics. Nevertheless, I *do* believe in democracy, not in socialism, and sometimes find myself worrying about communist expansionism in the Third World and the Middle East. You must do as well, having been to so many of those damned countries with the regiment.'

'That's true enough,' Marty said. 'Those trips always made me appreciate where I come from. I mean, we whinge about our own country no matter who's in charge, Labour or the Tories, but just about every country I've been to with the regiment has been brought to its knees because of communism. The commies are always in there somewhere, stirring the bloody pot. Socialism's one thing – I'm working-class, so I understand it – but communism's something else again and it's spreading everywhere. But what the fuck are we talking about this for? I take it from what you said about Angela that she's still okay. Things all right with you, are they?'

'Fine,' Paddy replied. 'No major problems health-wise, thank God' – he crossed his fingers – 'and otherwise things are running smoothly. Angela keeps herself busy as always with her local charities and Conservative Party meetings; and the kids are all at university and appear to be doing well. Apart from being a bit lonely with the kids away from home, we still manage to have a decent life – lots of dinner parties and so fourth. And of course, my own work keeps me busy and, I must confess, entertained.'

'It's nice to enjoy yourself while making money. It makes life worth the living, mate.'

'Thank you, my friend, for those kind words.'

'Still making those propaganda TV documentaries and flogging them off to Third World countries?'

Paddy grinned impishly. 'Naturally, dear boy. And very successfully, I might add.'

'I've never worked out if you're sincere about those documentaries or just plain bloody cynical.'

'Definitely not cynical, Marty. As I've just said, I *am* concerned about worldwide communist expansionism – I think that comes from the regiment – and, though I'm not obsessive about it, I believe that my propaganda films serve a valuable function. Pictures speak louder than words where illiteracy reigns. And of course, I'm very selective in who I work for. I don't make propaganda films for despots; nor do I let my clients dictate what goes into the films. I select and shape the material after consultation with them. They then buy the finished product or not.'

'*After consultation with them*,' Marty emphasised. 'That's the dodgy issue.'

'No, Marty, it's not. I'm not a mouthpiece for views I don't approve of, but only for values that I personally hold, which are those of democracy. Should they want propaganda contrary to that, I refuse to deal with them.'

'I still think it's a dodgy business. You don't know the long-term ambitions of the governments you work for. You don't know how they'll use those films, how they'll interpret them.'

'Yes, I do,' Paddy insisted. 'I carefully research all my potential clients. I do my homework.'

'There's still the possibility that slowly but surely you'll let yourself be swayed in certain ways – and let your standards drop. We're all open to that kind of corruption. It's bloody easy to fall for.'

Paddy grinned. 'Still the moralist, I see. Well, old son, I accept what you're saying and I *have* thought about it, and believe me, I won't let myself be bent. I'm too self-aware for that. I also happen to believe that all those years with the SAS have left their mark on me. The regiment instils certain values and I've never forgotten them.'

'Oh, yeah? What values would they be?'

'Democratic values. Freedom of speech and thought; the encouragement of personal initiative; loyalty to one's country whilst avoiding xenophobia; a belief in, and the practice of, moral choice. The regiment's been run on those principles and I still abide by them.'

Marty sighed and glanced around the busy pub, his gaze drawn instinctively to the fashionably blonde, leggy girls in miniskirts. Their youth and beauty, while attractive to him, also reminded him of how quickly he was ageing. He found that hard to take.

'It's too bad,' he said to Paddy, 'that nothing lasts for ever. Even the original ideals of the regiment aren't what they used to be.'

'How come?'

Marty had a sip of his bitter, then put the glass back on the table. 'Increasingly, when not on active service overseas, the regiment's being asked to do work that strikes me as being pretty dubious.'

'Such as?'

'In the past couple of years, we've been asked to test supposedly escape-proof prisons by breaking out or sneaking in. We've been asked to perform tasks more suitable to riot-control police. We've been asked to act as bodyguards for VIPs. In a few instances, we've even been asked to train the troops and police of countries with dubious political track records. That kind of arse-hole work.'

'You say the SAS has been *asked* to do such work. Has it actually done it?'

'Some of it. Reportedly, when he's really been against the proposal, the CO's refused; but at other times he hasn't been able to wriggle out of it. It depends, I suppose, on who's making the demand and how much damage to the regiment the CO thinks a refusal could cause. That's the short-term problem. The long-term problem is that too many men in high places want to place the regiment under their own control and use it for their own purposes. The pressure piled on by those bastards increases each month.'

'I don't think you're alone with that anxiety,' Paddy told him. 'In fact, the subject's been raised at every regimental reunion I've attended over the past few years. Your fellow NCOs, in particular, serving the longest and being the backbone of the regiment, seem to be aware of what's going on and are clearly concerned by it. One of them even suggested forming an association of older, or even retired, SAS men whose function would be to quietly stop such activities. It might not be a bad idea.'

'Sounds like a good idea to me,' Marty said. 'I might give it some thought.'

'You do that,' Paddy said. He glanced at his wristwatch. 'Time for me to be going. I have an appointment at three o'clock with an oil-rich Arab and potential client. Are you ready to leave?'

Marty nodded at his unfinished pint of bitter. 'I'll finish that first. I've plenty of time to spare. Meeting Diane at Redhill Station at four o'clock – she's coming up from London – so I might as well hang on here.'

Grinning, Paddy pushed his chair back and stood up. 'Okay, old son. I'll see you when you get back from Oman. Until then, you take care.'

'You, too,' Marty said.

They shook hands, then Paddy hurried out, buttoning his pinstripe jacket as he left. Marty sat on, distractedly studying the younger girls in the smoke-wreathed bar. His thoughts, however, were not focused on sexual matters, but on the possibility of forming a clandestine association of SAS men dedicated to the protection of the regiment. He thought about it a lot. Eventually deciding to do it when he returned from Oman, he finished his beer, left the pub, and drove the short distance to Redhill Station to pick up Diane.

CHAPTER TWENTY-EIGHT

As the four-engined Hercules C-130 transport landed at RAF Salalah in Dhofar, after a flight from RAF Lyneham with a refuelling stop at Akroterion in Cyprus, Marty, recently promoted to staff-sargeant, felt the exultation of a man about to have his last fling. Marching down the tailgate from the gloom of the aircraft, he stepped into the burning furnace of the Arabian sun and was pleased to feel it on his skin. Adjusting his eyes to the fierce glare, he saw large defensive trenches, or hedgehogs, encircled by forty-gallon drums and bristling with 25-pound guns and 5.5-inch Howitzers. He then saw Strikemaster jets and Skyvan cargo planes in sandbagged emplacements covered by camouflage nets. The Strikemasters were armed with Sura rockets, 500-pound bombs and machine-guns; the Skyvan cargo planes would be used to resupply the SAF (Sultan's Armed Forces) and SAS when they were up on the plateau of the mighty jebel. There were also Bedford trucks lined along the runway, with the drivers lounging about them, most wearing shorts, boots with rolled-down socks and a loose, flapping shirt, each with a Browning High Power handgun holstered at the waist.

Beyond the airstrip was an immense, sunbleached mountain, its sheer sides rising spectacularly to a plateau from the flat desert plain. That was, Marty knew without asking, the Jebel Dhofar, which right now was crawling with *adoo* and was soon to be assaulted by the SAS. *Adoo* is an Arabic word for 'enemy' and judging from the appearance of that mountain, the enemy would not be easy to dislodge.

The Hercules was unloaded with the aid of Omani helpers, all wearing *shemaghs* and *djellabas*. When this task was completed, the newcomers boarded the waiting Bedfords and were driven to the Sultan of Oman's Air Force Headquarters (SOAF HQ), a single-storey building guarded by local soldiers wearing red berets. After being cleared by security to enter the country, the convoy moved out of the camp, through gates guarded by RAF policemen armed with submachine-guns, then rumbled along the rough terrain adjoining the dusty, rocky road. When Marty asked why they were not on the road, he was informed by Corporal Alf Biggins of the Royal Corps of Transport that, because the *adoo* often mined the roads, the only safe way to travel was to stay off them by driving alongside them and following the tracks of previous vehicles.

'On the other hand,' Alf added, 'the *adoo* are smart little buggers who sometimes roll an old tyre over a newly placed land-mine to make it look like the tracks of a previous vehicle. Then, boom! Up you go!'

'Is it true that the *adoo* are crack shots?' Taff asked, blinking his radiant blue eyes against the flashing sunlight.

'Damned right. You won't find better snipers anywhere. They're also good at keeping out of sight, even managing to hide in what seems to be flat desert. Finally, they're bold as brass when it comes to infiltrating our territory, so you can never feel safe at any time. Those bastards are *everywhere*.'

Marty glanced automatically at the land they were passing through, but saw only clouds of dust billowing up behind the trucks, obscuring the sun-scorched flat plain and the soaring, parched sides of the Jebel Dhofar. The sky was a white sheet.

'Paradise on earth,' Corporal Tommy Taylor said, shaking his mop of dark hair in a vain attempt to get the dust out of it. 'It's sure nice to go travelling.'

After turning off the road to Salalah, the truck bounced

and rattled along the ground beside a dirt track skirting the airfield, reducing the risk of being blown up by *adoo* landmines. About ten minutes later it arrived at a large camp surrounded by barbed-wire fencing, with watchtowers placed at regular intervals around its perimeter, each holding a couple of armed SAF soldiers, a machine-gun and a searchlight. There were sangars manned by RAF guards on both sides of the main gate.

'Um al Gwarif,' Corporal Biggins explained when he halted his truck at the main gate. 'HQ of the SAF.'

A local soldier wearing a green *shemagh* and armed with a rifle checked Biggins's papers and then waved the convoy through. The trucks passed under another watchtower as they entered the camp where the sole object of interest was an exotic old whitewashed fort, complete with ramparts and slitted windows. It was the centre of the enclosure and was flying the triangular red-and-green Omani flag from its highest turret.

'The fort of the Wali,' Corporal Biggins explained. 'The Governor of the province. Right now, though, it's being used as the camp's command post.'

Beyond the Wali's house, Marty could see an old pump house and water well, which he assumed supplied the camp's water. Beyond that again, beside a line of silhouetted palm trees, was what looked like the officers' mess and accommodations. Otherwise, the main camp area seemed to be little more than a dusty clearing the size of a football pitch, with only two other stone buildings and some prefabricated huts near the Wali's fort. Everything else was in tents shaded by palm trees and separated by defensive slit trenches.

'The prefabricated huts,' Corporal Biggins explained as the Bedfords ground to a halt near the tents, 'are the barracks of the SAF forces. But you lot have been assigned that big British Army marquee, used as the basha, and those bivouac tents right beside it. No luxuries for you, lads.'

'Bloody typical!' Tommy Taylor complained, wearily picking up his dusty Bergen rucksack and inching towards the tail end of the truck.

Climbing down from the Bedfords with his Bergen and kit

belts, Marty stepped into fierce heat, drifting dust and buzzing clouds of flies and mosquitoes. He selected one of the large bivouac tents and entered with Taff and Tommy, finding only rows of camp beds covered in mosquito netting and resting on the hard desert floor.

'Shit!' Tommy exclaimed.

'Home sweet home,' Marty said grinning.

After picking a basha, each man unrolled his sleeping bag and placed his kit belt down as a rough pillow. Already bitten repeatedly by mosquitoes, Marty was now also covered in a film of dust, which would prove to be permanent. When he looked at the others, he noticed that they were the same.

'Just like North Africa,' he said.

'I wouldn't know,' Tommy replied. 'That was before my time, boss, when I was just a nipper.'

'You make me feel so old,' Marty replied. 'Let's go for a beer.'

Given the rest of the day to explore the camp, they headed straight for the large NAAFI tent, which had a front wall of polyurethane cartons, originally the packing for weapons. Inside were a lot of six-foot trestle tables and benches, at which some men were drinking beer, either straight from the bottle or from pint mugs. Surprisingly, a lot of frogs were jumping about on the dusty ground between the tables, completely ignored by the drinking men. The barman, young, shirtless, smoking a pipe and sitting beside a graffiti-covered refrigerator, told them to help themselves to whatever they wanted and then write their names and details of what they'd had on the piece of paper lying on top of the fridge.

'The system works on trust,' he explained, 'and you'll be billed at the end of each month, so help yourselves and enjoy.'

Sitting at one of the tables beside Taff and Tommy, relaxing with a couple of Tiger beers, Marty engaged the barman, Private Paul Redfield, in conversation.

'So what do you do here for fun in the evenings?' he asked.

'Not much,' Private Paul Redfield replied. 'It's hardly Piccadilly Circus and you don't get much free time anyway.

The evenings always begin with "prayers", a meeting of personnel where the ops captain reads out the day's news about Dhofar, followed by a summary of world news. If you don't attend without good cause you get a fine. "Prayers" is followed by dinner in the mess tent, then the evening's actually free. You either spend it right here, running up a tab, or at the outdoor cinema where you can see the latest English or Yank movies. Of course, during the fucking movies those hedgehogs outside are picking up readings of ground movement on their Battlefield Surveillance radar and so they let rip with mortars and GPMGs. They make a hell of a noise, as you know. Naturally, the *adoo* on the jebel return the fire and all hell's let loose. Not that that stops anyone watching the movies. Most of the men just sit through the noise. They just have to strain to hear and try to ignore all the bloody gunfire. Afterwards, they usually come in here for another few beers.'

'Anything else interesting?' Tommy asked him.

Redfield grinned sardonically. 'Oh, yeah,' he said. 'We call it "shaking out" and it's a fucking nightly ritual. You have to shake out your bedclothes before climbing into your basha – because apart from all the frogs this camp's a fucking haven for giant crickets and flying beetles. Then there's bloody hornets, red and black ants, centipedes and camel spiders. Oh, and venomous scorpions. Those buggers are particularly fond of taking shelter in your boots, socks and clothes.'

'We'll shake out,' Tommy said.

Finishing their beers, Marty and his two friends went exploring and soon saw that the only two solid buildings, apart from the Wali's fort, were being used as an armoury and a radio operations room. They also saw that the camp contained an unusual mixture of Batmen (members of the British Army Training Teams, or BATT), spooks (intelligence officers, or green slime), Signals, Ordnance, REME (Royal Electrical and Mechanical Engineers, or Rear Echolon Mother Fuckers), Catering Corps, the RCT (Royal Corps of Transport), and the four different regiments of the SAF: the Muscat Regiment, the Northern Frontier Regiment, the Desert

Regiment, and the Jebel Regiment. The men of the different Omani regiments were distinguishable from one another by their different berets: red, green, grey and sand-coloured. However, when in the field, the berets would be traded for black-and-maroon-patterned *shemaghs*, which the SAS would also wear, as protection against the dust, when the time came for them to tackle the plateau of the Jebel Dhofar. A few Arab SAF officers could be seen here and there, but most were British – either seconded officers on loan from the British Army or contract officers, whom Marty viewed cynically as mercenaries.

Periodically, the 25-pounder guns roared from inside their protective rings of forty-gallon drums, about a hundred yards from the camp's wired perimeter. The noise was tremendous, with smoke and flame belching out of the long barrels and the backblast making dust billow up around the Omani gunners, who were covering their ears with their hands to block out the clamour. When Marty saw the shells exploding in spiralling columns of dust and smoke on the slopes of the Jebel Dhofar, he realised that the SAF gunners were firing on the mountain to deter the *adoo* hiding in the wadis from coming closer to the camp. The SAF guns fired with monotonous regularity throughout the day.

Early that evening, just before last light, the newcomers were called to a briefing that took place in a corner of the marquee tent known as the 'Hotel'. There they found the CO, Lieutenant Phillip Barkwell, waiting for them with an officer, presumably green slime, though this could not be ascertained immediately because, like the CO, he was wearing only a plain shirt, shorts and sandals. After introducing himself and confirming that the other officer, Captain Mark Yarrow, was indeed green slime, the CO explained that while they were in this camp the SAS men would not wear identification discs, badges of rank, cap badges or formation signs because, though they were in the country at the Sultan's invitation, there were those, both in Oman and in Great Britain, who would disapprove of their presence here.

Marty knew what he meant. Not everyone considered the SAS's aims in Oman to be laudable. In fact, Britain had been accused of supporting a cruel, reactionary regime merely to protect its oil interests. Though Marty happened to think this was true, he also believed it was justified. Britain could not survive without the oil, so it had to be protected. It was as simple as that.

'The war is well engaged here,' the CO informed them, 'and is starting to turn in our favour. Between September nineteen seventy and March the following year, two hundred *adoo* surrendered to the government. We then formed them into *firqat* units whose first action was the assault on Sudh, thirty kilometres east of Mirbat. When that turned out successfully, we decided to launch an offensive on the Jebel Dhofar itself, and the following month, with the help of the *firqat*, we managed to take Eagle's Nest, a position of caves and ridges on the edge of the plateau, despite heavy enemy attacks, which lasted for a week. Now, in order to bring civil aid to the people and the hearts-and-minds campaign to full fruition, we have to establish firm bases on the jebel. For this reason, we're about to launch an assault on the mountain. It's codenamed Operation Jaguar, and it'll be a force of one hundred SAS, two hundred and fifty SAF, a few Baluch Askars and five *firqat* units, totalling three hundred men, making eight hundred men in all. Two positions, Jibjat and White City, will be secured in addition to the creation of the Leopard Line, a barrier consisting of barbed wire, booby traps, mines and ground sensors designed to cut off guerrilla supplies coming into Dhofar. That assault will take place approximately two weeks from now, preferably during a night when there's a full moon. In the meantime, please note—'

He was cut short when the 25-pounders, roared from the SAF emplacements near the camp's perimeter. Waiting until the noise had died away, he continued: 'Please note that in all matters relating to Oman, the SAF and *firquats* must be seen to be their own men and the SAS are officially engaged only in a support role. Please note, also, that the *firqats* are volatile by nature and also bound by Islamic restrictions, such as the holy month of Ramadan, when they require special dispensation to fight. When they fight, they can be ferocious, but they'll stop at any time for the most trivial reasons – usually arguments over who does what or gets what, perhaps some imagined insult. This makes them highly unreliable and that's something you'll just have to learn to live with. As for the enemy, the *adoo*, they're fierce, committed fighters and legendary marksmen who can pick a target off at four hundred yards and virtually melt back into the mountainside or desert. As for the Jebel Dhofar itself, it's approximately three thousand feet high and scorched by the desert sun, so the climb, even apart from the problems of *adoo* snipers, will be considerable. Please don't underestimate the difficulties and be prepared for anything.'

He was interrupted again by the roaring of some Saladin armoured cars moving out of the base. After waiting until the noise had faded away, he finalised: 'In the meantime, while you wait for the assault to begin, you'll be given a thorough indoctrination and educational course. This will include a tour of the whole area with particular emphasis on the increasingly successful hearts-and-minds campaign. The SAS civil aid programme has been in full swing since February nineteen seventy-one, with the BATT teams establishing clinics for the people and their animals, as well as bringing in advanced drilling equipment to bore new wells or open up old ones that were sealed on the orders of the now deposed Sultan Sin bin Taimur. In order to familiarise you with this, you'll be broken up into three-man groups, with each assigned an experienced Batman to act as a guide. Given the dangers extant outside this camp, you will, even if of greater rank, do exactly what your Batman says. You'll now find your chosen Batman waiting for you outside this tent. Thank you, gentlemen. Dismissed.'

Marty, Taff and Tommy wangled themselves into the same team under the supervision of John Crowley, a laconic, broad-shouldered sergeant, formerly 3rd Battalion, Queen's Regiment. For the next two weeks they were driven around the area in Crowley's dusty, battered Land Rover, taking turns at driving, with Crowley in the front passenger seat, pointing out the sights, and the other two men in the rear, all keeping their eyes peeled for *adoo* snipers. The heat was fierce, burning out of a blue sky that often seemed white, so, to ensure that they didn't dehydrate, they took along a plentiful supply of water bottles and *chajugles* – small canvas sacks, rather like goat skins, that could be filled with water and hung outside the vehicle to stay cool. Just as the RCT drivers had done on their day of arrival, Marty and his two friends always drove alongside the roads, rather than on them, to minimise the risk from land-mines laid down by the *adoo*.

Sometimes, to escape the heat, Sergeant Crowley instructed them to drive along the beaches, covered with crabs, lined with windblown palm trees, running parallel to rushing surf and the white waves of a turquoise sea. Yet no matter where they went, inland or by the sea, the view was dominated by the towering gravel plateau of the Jebel Dhofar, reminding them that soon they would have to climb it and that they might die while doing so.

Marty, though thinking about this a lot, was looking forward to it. This might be his last tour of active service and he wanted to make the most of it.

As he drove through the main gates that first morning, with Crowley beside him and Taff and Tommy in the rear, the 25-pounders in the hedgehogs just outside the perimeter fired on the Jebel, creating an almighty row, streams of grey smoke and billowing clouds of dust, reminding him that the *adoo* often mounted small raids against the camp, coming down from the Jebel during the night to plant mines around the base or dig themselves in for a bit of sniping during the day. He was also reminded of this when a Saladin armoured car moved out across the dusty plain ahead, through clouds of windblown dust, to sweep the surrounding tracks, clear any mines left, and search for hidden *adoo* snipers.

After driving for three miles, following Crowley's instructions, the Land Rover bouncing constantly over the rough gravel-and-sand terrain beside the dirt track, they arrived at the guarded perimeter of RAF Salalah, passed the main gate by the single-storey SOAF HQ, then kept driving until they came to where the Strikemaster jets and Skyvan cargo planes were being serviced in dispersal bays encircled by empty forty-gallon drums. There they were introduced to the semi-naked, sweating Corporal Arthur 'Art' Wellman of 55 Air Despatch Squadron, Royal Corps of Transport, normally based on Thorney Island, recently on a three-month tour of detachment to the army camp in Muharraq, Bahrain, but now here to supervise the resup support.

When the introductions had been completed, Wellman pointed inside the cargo hold, where other semi-naked men, all RCT loadmasters, were lashing bundles to the floor by web freight straps and 1,200-pound breaking cords.

'This is what we drop to our lads in the FOBs at places like Simba, Akoot and Jibjat,' he explained. 'Eighty-one-millimetre mortar bombs, HE phosphorous and smoke grenades, seven-point-six-two-millimetre ball and belt ammo, compo rations and water in jerry cans, four to a bundle. We also dropped food resups to the *firqats* out in the field, since those bastards are quick to go on strike if they think they're being ignored. Fierce fighters, but also a bunch of fucking children, always having tantrums.' Moving to the other side of the cargo hold, he pointed to some bundles wrapped in plastic parachute bags for extra protection. 'Scran for the *firqats*,' he explained. 'Tins of curried mutton or fish, rice, flour, spices, dates, and the oil they use for cooking. And those' – he pointed at bundles of papers wrapped in string – 'are propaganda leaflets to be dropped on the locals *and* the *adoo* as part of our hearts-and-minds campaign. Give 'em something to read, right?' Finally, he pointed to some forty-gallon drums lined up on the peri track by the runway. 'Our home-made incendiary bombs,' he explained. 'We call 'em Burmail bombs. The drums are filled with aviation oil, or Avtur, with polyurethane dissolved in it to thicken it. The drums are sealed, six Shemolly flares are fixed to each side of them, they're fitted with cruciform harnesses, and then they're rolled out the back of the Skyvan to cause fan-fucking-tastic explosions. Mostly, we use 'em for burning fields cultivated by the *adoo* for food, but we also use 'em as support for ground troops when the Strikemaster jets aren't available.'

'Why call them "Burmail bombs"?' Taff asked in his thoughtful manner.

Wellman shrugged. 'I say it's because "Burmail" is an Arabic word for oil drums, but others insist it's a derivation from "Burmah Oil" or the Burmah Oil Company. Who the fuck cares? The buggers work a treat, believe me, and that's all that matters.'

'Damned right,' Marty said.

Leaving the SOAF base, they drove back out onto the sunscorched desert plain where they saw Jebelis taking care of small herds of cattle or carrying their wares, mostly firewood, on camels en route to Salalah. Later, they were compelled to wait for ages at the main gate of the old town while the Sultan's armed guards, the Askouris, searched through the bundles of firewood on the camels of other traders to ensure that they weren't smuggling arms for *adoo* supporters. Eventually, when the camels had passed through and their own papers had been checked by the same Askouris, the SAS team were allowed to drive into the town, passing through a cluster of mud huts to an oasis of palm trees and lush green grass. Circling around the large jail building near the oasis, they arrived at the white-painted, fortified Sultan's palace, guarded by gendarmes armed with .303 Short-Magazine Lee-Enfield, or SMLE, rifles.

Once he had shown them the palace, explaining that it was now used by Qaboos as an administrative centre, Crowley guided Marty back out through the walled town's main gates and down to the shore, where he made him head for Taqa, located halfway between Salalah and Mirbat. The drive took them along the shore, with the ravishing turquoise sea on one side and rows of palm and date trees on the other. As the surf of the sea carried a cool breeze towards them, the journey was quite pleasant, though Marty had to be careful of not getting stuck in the fine sand. Also, as he had noticed before, there were a great many crabs, sometimes in their hundreds, scuttling in both directions across the beach like monstrous ants and being crushed noisily under the wheels of the bouncing Land Rover.

On the approach to Taqa, Marty found himself driving into the shallow water of a small bay. Engaging the four-wheel drive, he got them across to dry land, then drove on past high cliffs and sand dunes, until they arrived at a second beach. There, flocks of seagulls were winging repeatedly over piles of rotten, stinking fish that were scattered between the fishing boats. Passing the boats and the Arab fishermen sitting in them, repairing the nets, they arrived at a small village of mud huts. At the end of its single, dusty street were two buildings taller than the others, one with the Omani flag flying from it.

'The building with the flag,' Sergeant Crowley explained, 'is the Wali's house. The other's the BATT house.'

On the first floor of the BATT house they found three of the Batmen, all stripped to the waist and pouring sweat, brewing tea. After shaking hands with Marty and the other newcomers, they offered steaming tea in tin mugs, sitting around a six-foot trestle table. As one of the Batmen explained what was happening in the general area, Marty glanced around the room and noticed that the shelves were stacked with tins of compo rations and cooking utensils, indicating that this area was used as a combined kitchen and mess room. SLR and M16 rifles were stacked up in a corner, along with boxes of grenades, webbing, phosphorous flares and other ammunition.

'You want to see what we do here?' the Batman in charge, Sergeant Harry Smithers, asked.

'That's why we're here,' Crowley replied.

'Then let's go,' Smithers said, leading them out of the BATT house. Once outside, back in the scorching heat, he took them around the dusty village and showed them the various enterprises of the Batmen, including new irrigation methods for the fields, improvements in animal husbandry, and a medical clinic consisting of a makeshift, corrugated-iron shed and a single trestle table, where a lot of Omanis in *shemaghs* and *djellabas* were waiting excitedly to be treated.

Sweating in the afternoon heat as he got on with his business, the medical Batman, trained at the US Army's special forces medical school at Fort Sam Houston, in Texas, and at Fort Bragg in North Carolina, told them what he was up to as he continued working: cleaning and bandaging cuts, lancing boils, treating bad burns and dispensing a wide variety of tablets. The most common problems, he explained, were boils, burns, ruptures, messed-up circumcisions, conjunctivitis, dysentery, malaria, yellow fever, sand-fly fever, dengue from mosquitoes, trench fever from lice, spotted fever from ticks, every kind of typhus, even leprosy and the bloody lacerations caused by floggings ordered as punishments by the Wali.

The major problems were the fight against the primitive practices of local witch doctors and working out which of the villagers were really sick and which were merely becoming pill addicts.

'However, more and more of the villagers are coming to depend on us while rejecting the advances of the *adoo*, so the hearts-and-minds campaign is undoubtedly working. We're pretty proud of ourselves.'

'So you should be,' Marty said, taking his leave with the others.

The following day, Crowley guided them to Mirbat on the south coast of Dhofar. This was little more than a collection of dusty mud huts and clay buildings, with the sea on one side, a barbed-wire fence running north and east. The settlement consisted of a cluster of houses to the south and a market by the sea. About thirty Omani armed guards, or Askouris, were housed in an ancient Wali's fort to the west. Another small fort, about 500 metres further west, held 25 men of the Dhofar Gendarmerie, or DF; and another Gendarmerie outpost was 800 metres north of the northern perimeter, on the slopes of Jebel Ali. Near the market, in the middle of the compound, a mud-built BATT house held nine Batmen under the command of the 23-year Captain Mike Kealy.

'The *adoo* have publicly sworn to capture this town at any cost,' Captain Kealy told them. 'Unfortunately for us, our only heavy weapons are a twenty-five-pounder in a gun-pit next to the DG fort, a single seven-point-six-two-milimetre GPMG on the BATT house roof, an eighty-one-millimetre mortar placed beside the building, and a point-five-inch-calibre heavy machine-gun. In other words, practically nothing – but when the time comes, we'll defend this town, no matter the cost. And that time will come soon.'

Leaving the BATT house, they were introduced to three Fijian members of B Squadron, including the immense Labalala, whom they knew from the Keeni-Meeni operations in Aden. After shaking hands all round and trading a few jokes about Aden, they left the sandbagged gun-pit, where the three Fijians had been cleaning the 25-pounder, and then saw their first *firqats*. Just down from the hills, they were returning their FN rifles and other weapons to the armoury in the Wali's fort. Though they all had similar *shemaghs*, the rest of their clothing was widely varied, from the *djellabas* worn by most locals to khaki drill (KD), or light tropical uniforms. Festooned with webbing, ponchos, bandoliers of ammunition and, in particular, with the large Omani knives, called *kunjias*, tied around their waists, they looked like a particularly fierce band of brigands.

'I wouldn't like to cross swords with *those* bastards,' Tommy said. 'They all look bloody murderous.'

'Only when they're aroused,' Taff replied.

'And from what I've been told,' Marty said, 'it's easy to do that. One word out of place, one sidelong glance, and they'll slit your throat open.'

'At least they're on our side,' Sergeant Crowley said. 'Thank God for small mercies.'

The grand tour continued. At Rayzut they found British Army engineers constructing a new harbour from large blocks raised around the bay. In the same place, an SAS BATT team was inoculating the local labour force, many of whom, Marty noticed, were so intrigued by modern medicine that they were queuing up eagerly to have their jabs. At Arzat, little more than a random collection of mud huts with a small garrison of Dhofar Gendarmerie, they found an SAS BATT team showing the locals how to purify the water tanks with fluoride and transform their rubbish into fuel. SAS veterinary surgeons were showing them how to improve the breeding of their cattle and training them in basic veterinary medicine. In other small town, Janook, Marty and his friends were given an enthusiastic lecture by a four-man BATT psyops team, formerly of the Northern Ireland regiments and now responsible for psychological operations in Oman. These included, apart from the writing of the propaganda leaflets dropped from the Skyvans, the showing of English and Hollywood movies to the locals. In a similar propaganda exercise, they found at Suda, another windblown, dusty village scattered around a lovely bay on the Arabian Sea, a BATT team teaching the local children English with the aid of carefully selected, illustrated books that showed them the wealth and wonders of the West – none of which, as the Batmen repeatedly emphasised to their impressionable pupils, would be supplied by the communists.

Finally, during the late afternoon of their fourth day, Crowley guided Tommy Taylor, who had replaced Marty as driver, to a desolate village of clay huts in scorched flatland west of the Jebel Dhofar, in a region once patrolled by the rebels, but now back in the hands of the SAF. There they found a group of SAS sappers gathered around the village well with explosive charges, detonating cords, primers and other demolition equipment. They were being watched attentively by many villagers, including excited children.

When they stopped to watch what the sappers were up to, Sergeant Crowley explained that the *adoo* were fanatical communists, backed by the Soviet Union and China. Often removed from their parents to be schooled in the PDRY – the People's Democratic Republic of Yemen, formerly Aden – or sent to guerrilla warfare schools in Russia and China, they were returned to their mountain villages as fanatics who would establish communist cells, break down former loyalties, and then organise their equally fanatical converts into village militias or battle units who showed absolutely no mercy to the Moslems. They also banned all religious practices, tortured village elders into denying their god, and routinely raped Moslem women. In other words, they were engaged in a campaign of terror designed to wipe out Islam altogether and establish communism in Oman – and they were ruthless in doing it.

About sixteen months before, just before the old Sultan had been deposed by his son, Qaboos, he was informed that this village was sympathetic to the *adoo*. Reacting as the always did, the Sultan sent his SAF troops in to hang the suspected *adoo* and seal the wells, the lifeblood of the village, by pouring in gallons of wet cement direct from mixers. This didn't stop the *adoo* from carrying out their customary brutalities against the same unfortunate Moslems. Indeed, the *adoo* came into the village that very afternoon, while some of the Sultan's victims were still dangling from ropes – deliberately kept up there as grim reminders to the villagers and guarded by SAF troops. The *adoo* shot the troops, then engaged in their usual practice of trying to persuade the village elders to renounce their Islamic faith publicly. As is one of the *adoo* customs, when the elders refused, their eyes were gouged out and their daughters repeatedly raped. When the *adoo* then melted back into the wadis of the Jebel, the villagers were left without their life-giving water and, even worse, with many of their menfolk dead or blinded. In short, the village was doomed.

Now that this area was back in Sultan Qaboos's hands, it was the job of the SAS to right the wrongs of the previous Sultan and remind the Moslems of what would happen to them should they let the *adoo* return. In the case of this particular village, their first task was to unseal the well and give water, therefore life, back to the villagers. Once that had been accomplished, they would bring in BATT teams, including medics and veterinary surgeons, to restore the sick to health and help the rest get the most out of the water, the crops it would help to grow, and the livestock it would help to increase. After that, they would bring in English teachers, radio sets, comics, books and other seductive Western luxuries. This, Marty realised, was a hearts-and-minds campaign at its very finest.

To seal the well, the former Sultan's men had poured wet concrete in from mechanical mixers and let it harden at the bottom. That hardened concrete was now six foot deep. What the sappers were trying to do right now, Crowley explained, was blow the concrete apart without also destroying the walls of the well, which would only top the concrete with more debris and make the sealing even more permanent. If they were successful, the pieces of broken concrete could be hauled up from the bottom of the well in buckets, giving access to the water still below.

While Marty and the others watched, the SAS demolition team, led by a former Royal Engineers sapper, then ammunition technician with the RAOC (Royal Army Ordnance Corps), drilled about halfway through the hardened concrete, filled the narrow hole with C3 plastic explosive, then fixed a time fuse, blasting cap and detonating cord to the explosive, with the cord running up out of the well and across the village clearing where its other end was fixed to a detonating plunger.

In this case, when the plunger was pressed, the explosion at the bottom of the well was just enough to break up the concrete and leave the water beneath exposed. With the water back, the village was saved. The Arabs cheered and applauded.

Finally, near the end of the two weeks, Marty and the other newcomers were driven out of the base for three days of weapons training in the baking heat and dust of the Arzat ranges. Regardless of the heat, they were kept at it all day, every day, practising on the firing range and learning to clean and reassemble their weapons in the desert's harsh environment.

It was hell on the firing range, the heat relentless, the light too bright, with the dust getting up their nostrils and filling their mouths, the sand clogging the chambers and barrels of weapons, jamming the works. Also, the ground was the habitat of poisonous scorpions, centipedes and hideous camel spiders, and the buzzing flies, whining mosquitoes and stinging hornets assailed the men constantly as they tried to take aim and fire their weapons.

As the *adoo* were renowned marksmen, the troopers were issued, apart from their customary M16s, with a range of sniper rifles, including the L42A1 7.62-millimetre Lee-Enfield bolt-action and the L1A1 SLR semi-automatic which, in the furnace of the firing range, they were required to disassemble repeatedly, clean of dust and sand, oil, and reassemble repeatedly – sometimes blindfolded. However, as close contact with the *adoo* was likely, they were also issued with Heckler & Koch MP5 nine-millimetre submachine-guns, or SMGs, and practised firing them from the sitting, kneeling and standing positions in single shots, three-round bursts, and on fully automatic, using thirty-round magazines at a rate of 800 rounds per minute (rpm). They were also trained in the MP5K, a shorter version of the MP5, utilising a fifteen-round magazine and used as a semi-automatic replacement for the pistol; and in the MP5SD, also a short-barrelled model, but including a visual sight with a 'tell-tale' red dot indicating the mean point of impact, or MPI.

More ominous was the instructors' insistence that they endlessly practise the various methods of firing their standard-issue Browning High Power handguns. The fact that this insistence was combined with the sudden appearance of the Heckler & Koch MP5 range of SMGs – which were, in effect, automatic pistols – only made them realise that more than ordinarily close contact with the enemy (possibly CQB or hand-to-hand fighting) was anticipated by their superiors. Certainly, they were retrained in the one-handed, two-handed and alert positions for the Nine-Milly: standing, kneeling and prone. They also practised breathing and precise release-trigger hand pressure while adjusting their aim in the midst of firing.

As usual, these lessons were carried out in the blazing sun, when the heat was at its worst and the air filled with dust. The fact that a couple of the men collapsed in the heat during this retraining did nothing to deter their instructors, who pointed out that they would have to endure similar, and possibly worse, conditions during the assault on the Jebel.

Indeed, for this very reason, even while the remaining men were boiling in the heat and choking in the dust, they were severely restricted in their use of water, this being their instructors' way of teaching them to discipline themselves against chronic thirst for long periods of time. Also, as they sat there 'resting' between firing lessons or drills – which in fact meant being tortured further in the heat and dust – they were forced to listen to lectures on ways of combating dehydration, sunstroke, sunburn and, of course, lack of water. Naturally, while listening to such lectures, some of the men started suffering from dehydration, others came close to sunstroke and sunburn, and all of them nearly went mad with the need for a drink.

While in Arzat, they slept at nights on the ground, shocked by how cold it was after the day's scorching heat. Yet even in the cold they had to shake out their kit, invariably finding scorpions, centipedes or camel spiders in the canvas sheets.

Also, though it was cold, the night was still filled with whining mosquitoes, dive-bombing hornets, flying beetles and fat flies, none of which ever seemed to sleep, all of which were ravenous for human sweat and blood. The nights were therefore filled with the sounds of soft cursing and hands slapping bare skin.

Finally returned in the Bedfords to the base at Um al Gwarif, suntanned, covered in filth, badly bitten, sleepless, with eyes sore from constantly squinting into the sun, they were given time for only a quick shower and meal, then ordered to the 'Hotel' for a briefing about the assault on the Jebel, due to take place the following day.

Once in the big marquee, they were split into teams and sat around a couple of standard British Army six-foot tables with their individual maps of Dhofar spread out in front of them. The Intelligence Corps officer arrived shortly after, shook the hand of B Squadron's commander, Lieutenant Barkwell, and was then introduced as Captain Pearson. A larger map of Dhofar was pinned to a board behind the table.

'Tomorrow's operation,' Pearson began, 'codenamed Jaguar, has been designed to secure us our first firm base on the enemy-held Jebel around the village of Jibjat. The starting point is a former Sultan's Air Force base on the plain known as Lympne. The mixed assault force, consisting of SAS, SAF and *firqat*, will be split into two. The majority of B Squadron and G Squadron SAS, with the *Firqat Al Asifat*, the *Firqat Salahadeen*, and the Baluch *Askars*, will assault the airfield at Lympne on foot. The remainder of the force will be choppered in after a firm base has been established.'

Using a pointer to show the various locations, Pearson continued: 'At first light we leave the SAF staging post of Midway, located north of the Negd plain. From there, we drive south-east until we reach the foothills of the Jebel and the entrance to this major wadi.' He pointed to the beginning of the Jebel. 'We follow the wadi bottom until we run out of motorable track. We then debus and move on foot to the Mahazair Pools, where already we have a small base camp. As the monsoon's just finished, there should be plenty of water there, which is why we're making it our rest area.'

As if to remind them all that the *adoo* were still up there on the Jebel, waiting for them, the 25-pounders boomed from just outside the perimeter. A lot of the men glanced at one another, some grinning nervously.

'The actual operation against the airfield will be mounted the following night,' Pearson continued. 'The climb into the hills will almost certainly involve a running battle with the *adoo*. No matter the difficulties, we have to keep advancing until we reach the airstrips and water holes on the high plain, where most of the *adoo* are entrenched. Our task is to get them out for good and take command of the area. Are there any questions?'

'Yes, boss,' Marty said. 'What kind of resistance is expected?'

'We're anticipating that a diversionary attack to the south will draw the *adoo* away long enough for our main assault force to encircle Lympne without resistance. Once the *adoo* return, however, a battle lasting weeks, or even months, is expected. It won't be an easy fight. The *adoo* have state-of-the-art Soviet and Chinese automatic weapons, including Kalashnikov AK forty-sevens, Simonev semi-automatics, RPG sevens, RPD light machine-guns, GPMGs, and eighty-two-millimetre mortars. The battle will, however, be followed by the surrender of the *adoo* before the next monsoon season, beginning in June. Nobody's ever stayed on the Jebel through the monsoon, so it should be over by then. Any more questions?'

With no more questions to ask, the men left the 'Hotel' to prepare their kit, a task that took up most of the remainder of the evening. Late that night, still feeling exhilarated that he had a real war to wage, Marty shook out the sheets on his camp bed, checked for scorpions and centipedes, then tried to catch the last remotely decent sleep he would have for a long time.

CHAPTER TWENTY-NINE

They were up at first light, but did not leave immediately. Instead, after they had dressed in olive-green fatigues and jungle hats, they had a long morning of personal kit and weapons inspection, conducted personally by Marty. Though moaning and groaning, they did as he told them, bolting down their food and hurrying out of the mess tent to gather by the Bedfords parked outside the armoury. Though already heavily burdened with their standard issue US 5.56-millimetre M16 rifle, packed Bergen and personal kit, they were burdened even more at the armoury with Lee-Enfield sniper rifles, two types of Heckler & Koch submachine-gun, general-purpose machine-guns (or GPMGs), light anti-tank weapons, mortars and portable radio systems, with generators and rechargeable batteries.

'If the mountain doesn't kill us, all this crap will,' Tommy Taylor said.

'It will if you let it,' Marty replied, 'but you're not going to let it, are you, Corporal?'

'Absolutely not, boss!'

It took a good half-hour to hump the kit up into the trucks, but eventually the job was done and the men were driven out of Um al Gwarif for the short, rough journey to RAF Salalah. After being waved through the main gates by an armed SAF soldier, under the watchful eyes of two RAF guards in sangars, the Bedfords parked by the dispersal bays for the Skyvan cargo planes. Corporal Wellman from 55 Air Despatch Squadron of the RCT was there with other pilots and RAF loadmasters, most of them stripped to the waist, gleaming with sweat, and covered in the dust that billowed up from the ground every time they moved a crate of supplies to slide it into the cargo bay in the rear of a Skyvan.

The hundred-odd SAS men were divvied up and ordered on board the half-dozen Skyvans. Even with that number, the pilots would have to make quite a few trips to get the whole complement of men and equipment to the SAF staging post of Midway. Therefore, when they were in groups of suitable size, the RSM, Sergeant-Major Mike Patterson, allocated certain of the groups to individual Skyvans and told the rest to wait in the minimal shade offered by the walls of forty-gallon drums. These let out melodramatic groans of misery, but the CO solved the problem by arranging for the waiting men to be flown out in the RAF's three Hueys and the Sikorsky Whirlwind.

Suddenly, the whole area turned into a hive of activity, with restraining blocks being pulled away from wheels, Skyvan cargo-hold doors being closed, spinning helicopter rotors creating clouds of swirling dust, the Bedfords whining noisily as they reversed and turned away empty, and line men, or marshallers, with ear-defenders driving out in jeeps to guide the aircraft with hand signals to the holding point on the runway.

Knowing that the LZ was not far away, Marty was content to sit back and relax, despite the already suffocating heat, as the Skyvan's STOL twin engines roared into life, the props started spinning, and the aircraft shuddered violently, moving out of its dispersal bay and heading for the airfield. Within minutes it was racing along the runway and lifting off, following the other aircraft and choppers into the dazzling sky above the vast, dust-wreathed Salalah plain.

In less than half an hour, they landed at the SAF staging post of Midway. A disused oil exploration camp located about 55 miles north of the Jebel, it consisted of a number of Twynam huts scattered around an old airstrip in the desolate wasteland of the Negd plain and guarded by SAF troops with 7.62-millimetre FN rifles. A lot of Bedfords had been brought in already and were lined up along the runway near some of the huts. The troops just lifted in by the choppers were milling about the same huts, stretching their legs, smoking and drinking water. As the aircraft were taking off, creating a hell of swirling dust and sand, the men picked up what kit they didn't have on them and hurried away from the slipstream, stopping by the Bedfords at the edge of the runway.

The CO and RSM Patterson were near the old huts, shaking hands with the SAF commander who, like the rest of his men, was wearing a dark green *shemagh*. Looking in the other direction, Marty watched one Skyvan after another take off and disappear into the darkening late afternoon sky. Eventually, the CO left the SAF commander and gathered his men around him near the Bedford trucks.

'Since it's going to take all day for the Skyvans and choppers to bring in the remainder of the assault force,' he told them, 'we'll spend the rest of the afternoon and all night here, then move out at first light. In the meantime, you can basha down on that strip of waste ground near the SAF barracks' – he pointed to the dusty old huts – 'and boil up a brew. Don't plan on a rest as you'll be needed to help with the unloading, which should take half the night. All right, men, that's it.'

'That's enough,' Tommy muttered.

When the CO and Patterson walked off with the SAF commander, the troopers scattered to find a place on the waste ground to the right of the SAF barracks. After carefully checking their chosen basha space for scorpions, centipedes, spiders and snakes, they rolled out their sleeping bags and brewed up, boiling water in mess tins heated on lightweight hexamine stoves. It was a short, welcome break, but it didn't last long since the first of the Skyvans arrived back an hour later when the evening light was turning to darkness, bringing with it the cold. That first Skyvan was soon followed by another, then another, all disgorging more supplies and SAF soldiers and *firqats*, who looked as fierce as ever.

'A bunch of fucking Omani brigands,' Tommy whispered. 'They'd cut your throat as soon as look at you.'

'Good men,' Taff said dreamily.

Luckily, the *firqats* were marched off to bed down for the night in another strip of waste ground at the far side of the runway, while the SAF soldiers, despised by the *firqats*, were given beds or floor space in their own barracks. Meanwhile, the extra supplies kept coming in on plane after plane, to be unloaded by the exhausted SAS troopers and transported to the Bedfords lined up by the runway. Though the unloading did not take all night as some had thought, it was certainly well after midnight before the last of the Skyvans had been and gone, letting a merciful silence descend with the settling dust.

Reprieved at last, most of the men left the airstrip, leaving an unlucky few to stand guard on the loaded-up Bedfords. With the lucky majority, Marty made his way back to the waste ground, where he shook everything out and, still wearing his OGs, wriggled gratefully into his sleeping bag. Every bone in his body was aching and he felt like an old man.

For a few minutes, as he lay there, eyes closed, he visualised Diane in bed beside him and felt flickering tendrils of sexual heat, but they didn't last long. Like the flames in a fire that's been burning too long, they burned down and died away, leaving a smoky darkness. Marty sank into that darkness and was soon sound asleep.

At first light the following morning, the 250 men, including SAS, SAF and *firqats*, were driven out of the staging post in Bedfords, following a Saladin armoured car, which had taken the lead position to give them some protection from mines. For added insurance, the lengthy convoy drove parallel to the road.

The journey took them across a sun-scorched moonscape interlaced with dried-up stream beds, each of which caused the trucks to lurch wildly, nearly toppling over in some cases. In the rear of his Bedford, squashed between Taff and Tommy, Marty was repeatedly thrown into the others, their weapons and water bottles noisily banging against each other. The Bedfords were open-topped, which at least meant they had air, but as the sun rose in the sky, casting a silvery light on the desert, Marty began to feel the heat and knew, without a shadow of doubt, that it was going to get much worse.

Surprisingly, even in the wind created by the movement of the truck, flies and mosquitoes were still present in abundance, buzzing and diving ever more frantically as the men sweated more. Also, as the journey progressed, the gravel plain became rougher, filling up with patches of sand, and the bucking of the trucks increased, adding to the general torture of the passengers.

By noon, the convoy was still on the move, with the Arabian sun blazing relentlessly on the desert and turning it into a featureless white haze. Heat waves rose from the dusty plain, making the land beyond shimmer, and the trucks front and rear, when visible through the swirling sand, appeared to contract and expand as if only a mirage.

Marty felt just as unreal, consumed by heat, suffocating, assailed by flies and mosquitoes, sometimes by stinging hornets, while being forced repeatedly to wipe sweat from his face or sand from his parched lips and stinging eyes, his OGs soaked with his sweat, his weapons almost too hot to touch. With the sand came the dust, drifting everywhere, rising from the floorboards, blown in from the billowing clouds being churned up by the wheels of the Bedfords. The dust and sand, mixed with the sweat, made the other men look a mess. Marty knew that he must look the same and he grinned at the thought.

Even worse was the heat, now a veritable furnace, making even the slipstream of the trucks suffocatingly warm. Though men continued being ill along the whole length of the column, the drivers kept going without a break, reaching the wadi by late afternoon. By that time the fierce white sun had cooled to a more mellow golden light that brought detail back to the landscape and made it look real again.

Glancing along the wadi, with its sheer granite slopes casting stark black shadows on the sun-bleached gravel of the valley floor – a barren, silent, almost eerie terrain – Marty thought of the dark side of the moon. Entering the wadi, heading straight for the towering Jebel, the lengthy column of trucks soon left the sand-filled Negd behind and drove over a smoother surface of tightly packed gravel and small stones. Blessedly, the shadows cast over the convoy by the high rock faces on either side brought the men further protection from the sun and wind. Eventually the sun sank in the west, cooling them even more.

Now protected from the wind and dust by the sloping sides of the wadi, the men were removing the magazines from their weapons to clean them again, working the cocking handles to ensure that they were back in good order. Some were still hurrying to finish this task when the convoy ground to a halt where the wadi had narrowed so much that they would have to go the rest of the way by foot.

Standing on the gravel floor of the wadi as the other SAS, SAF and *firqat* troops also jumped down, rapidly filling up the formerly empty, silent area, Marty saw Taff staring at them, obviously admiring their deadly nature, the bright blue of his eyes emphasised by the moonlight, probably unaware that, with his bandoliers, weapons and knives, and with his fluttering *shemagh* covering his face, he looked as fearsome as they did.

The equipment was unloaded and divided among the men. As number two of the GPMG sustained-fire team, Marty would be carrying a steel tripod, weighing over thirty pounds, plus heavy ammunition belts, both wrapped around his body and in the Bergen, and four twenty-round SLR magazines. He also had his Browning High Power, belt kit with smoke and fragmentation grenades, rations, first-aid kit and three full water bottles. Also in his team were Tommy as gun controller, Taff as observer and a new man, Trooper Larry Purvis as number one, or trigger man. Between them, apart from personal gear, they had to hump the tripod, two spare barrels weighing six pounds each, a tripod sighting bracket, the spare-parts wallet, and the gun itself, weighing 24 pounds. Burdened with all this, they would have to climb out of the wadi, up onto the flat open area of the Mahazair Pools, which was their night basha spot, or staging post.

In preparation for the climb, Marty, already exhausted and trying not to show it, unlocked the front leg-clamp levers of the GPMG tripod, swung them forward into the high-mount position and relocked them. Then, with Purvis's help, he humped the tripod up onto on his shoulders with the front legs resting on his chest and the rear leg trailing backwards over his Bergen. His total burden now weighed a crippling 130 pounds and he was carrying his SLR with his free hand. He was sweating profusely.

All along the wadi, in the dimming afternoon light, the other men were also preparing, making a hell of a racket – 250 in all, spread out over about a quarter of a mile, between and around the parked Bedfords. Eventually they moved out, falling instinctively into a long, irregular file formation, spreading ever farther apart until the line was a good half mile long, snaking back from the slopes of the wadi to the Bedfords below.

Within minutes, the metal of the tripod cradle was digging viciously into the back of Marty's neck, letting him know that it was going to hurt. He tried to solve the problem by turning his head left and right, but this only rubbed the skin of his neck against the steel leg, causing it to hurt even more. In less than an hour the pain was worse, shooting down through his shoulder-blades, and the sweat was popping out of his forehead to drip into his eyes.

Glancing at those nearest to him, he saw that they were suffering the same – if not with a tripod, certainly with other gear – and sweating every bit as much as he was. No one spoke. They were trying to save their breath. To make the hike more tortuous, they were assailed, as usual, by flies, mosquitoes and the occasional hornet, but this time they couldn't slap them away, as their hands were otherwise engaged. Now it was hurting more than ever, sending darting pains through his shoulders – and those pains, combined with his increasing exhaustion, made him wonder if he could actually withstand the stress.

His fears were in no way eased when some troopers, one after the other, vomited from the strain and were pulled out of the column and ordered, in the RSM's words, to 'rest up, then catch up'. This brought no respite to the others, since the column continued moving. However, it stopped shortly afterwards, the men banging into one another, as voices called down the line for the medics. When those voices faded away, a series of hand signals came down the line, indicating that the men were to rest up until further notice. Gratefully, the men around Marty all sank to the ground.

'What's up?' Marty asked.

'I don't know,' Sergeant Crowley replied, 'but I'm going to find out.'

They fell silent after that, trying to get their breath back, not wanting Crowley to return and make them get up again. Unfortunately, he did so five minutes later.

'Someone collapsed,' he said. 'A radio corporal. His radio got stuck between some rocks and he almost had a seizure trying to free himself. He's conscious again, but he's going to have to be carried on a stretcher to the RV, then casevacked back to base.'

'Poor sod,' someone said.

After a few minutes, the arduous hike began again. Luckily, they were near the end of their journey. They had been marching for two hours and the sun was going down. After another three-quarters of an hour the slopes became less steep, indicating that they were nearly out of the wadi. Eventually, as the sun sank, a breeze blowing down from level ground cooled the sweat on their foreheads.

Marty was just beginning to believe that he was on his last legs – stabbing pains in his shoulder-blades, his neck aching, his lungs on fire – when they emerged from the wadi and headed across an open area, where, in the shadow of the mighty Jebel Dhofar, pale moonlight was reflected off the water in the Mahazair Pools. They could rest up at last.

The rest, however, lasted only a few minutes. At last light, with the eerie wailing of the mullah rending the silence, the *firqat* fighters, faces half hidden by *shemaghs*, knelt in circles and bowed their heads to pray while holding their rifles between their knees. Knowing that the *firqats* were not allowed to fight during the holy month of Ramadan, due to begin later in the month, Marty wondered how they could be depended upon. Right now, he knew, their praying was an indication that Operation Jaguar was about to begin.

'We'll be moving off soon,' he said to Taff. 'When those buggers stop praying.'

Glancing at the *firqats* kneeling in prayer, their rounded shoulders bathed in the moonlight when they bowed their covered heads, Tommy sighed and said, 'We're making the climb under cover of darkness? Is that what you're telling me?'

'Yes,' Marty replied.

'God help us,' Tommy said.

Realising that they were going to have to get up and go, the men drank more mugs of tea, cleaned and oiled their weapons, filled magazines and water bottles, and stared curiously at the still-praying *firqats*. Beyond them, near one of the pools, was the collection of tents and lean-tos of the SAS base camp that had been established here a few weeks before. Some of the troopers were outside their tents, having a supper of cold rations, not allowed to light their portable hexamine stoves.

Glancing up at the vast, imposing Jebel plateau, now almost jet black and ringed by stars in the gathering darkness, Marty was reminded of his last night on the Pen-y-fan in Wales, during Sickener 2, and had a good idea of the tortures awaiting him. The thought was disturbing, but also undeniably exciting, a contradiction of emotions that he had long since learned to live with. He was a soldier and proud to be so. That was all there was to it.

It was now completely dark, with no sign of the moon, and the sudden sound of equipment being moved in the *firqats*' area indicated that the operation was commencing.

Clambering to his feet with the others, Marty checked his kit and weapons, then let Taff help him hump the heavy GPMG tripod onto his shoulders. Instantly the rear leg bit into his neck, reminding him of what he was going to suffer, though he was absolutely determined to endure it, no matter the cost.

The *firqat* guides led off in the darkness, heading south-east, and the rest of the assault force, including the SAF, now all wearing *shemaghs* instead of berets, followed in a single file that gradually stretched out to form an immense human chain, snaking up the lower slopes of the Jebel. At first the slopes were gentle, presenting no real challenge, but soon they rose more steeply, sometimes almost vertically, turning the hike into a mountain climb that tortured body and mind. The steeper gradients were often smooth, making the men slip and slide, and often, where the gradients were less steep, loose gravel led to the same problem. A lot of cursing passed along the line. Men fell and rolled downhill. The climb was made no easier by the moonless darkness, which hid dangerous outcroppings and crevices. Nevertheless, the column continued snaking upwards, making slow, painful progress.

'Take five' were the words passed down the line an hour later when most of the men were sweating, out of breath and aching all over.

Removing the tripod, Marty slumped to the ground with the others and, like them, gratefully gulped water from one of his three rapidly emptying bottles. Five minutes later, they were on the move again, killing themselves as they slogged up the ever steeper gradients of the Jebel, slipping and sliding in loose gravel or smooth stones, getting their feet caught in fissures, banging their heads or elbows against outcroppings hidden in darkness, always sweating and gasping.

For the next five hours, they halted every hour to take five and wet their parched throats with more water. They soon began to run short. An hour later, after six hours of climbing, they halted again – unfortunately not for the well, but because another of the men, this one carrying *three* radios and marching right in front of Marty, suddenly choked, vomited and collapsed.

Tommy, who had special medical training, dropped immediately to his knees beside the unconscious man, loosened his webbing, removed the radios and other heavy kit, then hammered on his chest in an attempt to revive him. When this didn't work, he applied mouth-to-mouth resuscitation, but this also failed. Without thinking about his own diminishing supply, he opened the only one of his three bottles still containing water and poured some down the unconscious trooper's throat. The man coughed and spluttered back to dazed consciousness just as RSM Patterson appeared on the scene, having walked back from the front of the column.

Seeing the condition of the sick man, Patterson ordered four of the troopers to carry him all the way back down the mountain to the waiting Bedfords. The troopers would carry the stretcher two men at a time while the other two protected them, one out on point, the other as Tail-end Charlie. The men selected for this task were bitterly disappointed at being pulled out of the operation, but after the expected moans and groans they rolled the sick man onto a stretcher and commenced the long hike back down the mountainside. Then the column moved on again.

Knowing that first light would be at 0530 hours, the CO marched his men mercilessly, following the hardy *firqats* uphill through the darkness, still with no sign of the promised well and its life-giving water. Even at this time of the morning, in that total, moonless darkness, the heat was clammy and suffocating, rendered worse by the dust kicked up by those hundreds of marching feet. More men choked and were sick.

Marty began to suffer from heat exhaustion and dehydration: dry mouth and throat, swollen tongue, cracked lips. He also began to hear lurking *adoo* with every sound and to see them in the silhouetted outlines of rocks and outcroppings. Recalling that the *adoo* were superb marksmen, able to pick off enemy troops at distances so great they had been dubbed the 'phantom enemy', his imaginings along these lines became ever more vivid.

As they pressed on, the *firqats* up front decided to lighten their heavy loads by discarding valuable items of kit such as ration cans, portable hexamine cookers and blocks of hexamine. These littered the upward trail and made the going even more difficult for the SAS troops behind them. When reprimanded by RSM Patterson, the *firqats* started screaming angrily, threw their weapons to the ground, and threatened to return to the base camp. Appeased by Taff, who was able to relate to them, they picked up what they had just thrown down and continued the march.

Nevertheless, as the climb continued, more men collapsed and either had to be revived or compelled to keep going; or, if they were in serious condition, sent back to the base camp.

Eventually, about thirty minutes before first light, the men ahead began disappearing one by one over the skyline, filling Marty with the hope that this must be the top of the plateau. In fact, it was a false crest, only leading down into another wadi. Marty's GPMG team reached the bottom of that wadi just as dawn's light appeared in the east.

At the head of his hundred men, but behind the SAF and *firqats*, the CO consulted with RSM Patterson, both of them studying their maps by torchlight, neither looking pleased. Eventually, word came back down the line that the *firqat* guides, who should have known the way, had led the column in the wrong direction. Though exhausted and exasperated, the men did as they were ordered by the RSM, which was to turn back down the slope, circle around the mountainside until they came to the correct path, then commence the arduous climb again.

An hour later, just after the sun had risen, they arrived, with churning stomachs and aching muscles, on the plateau of the mighty Jebel Dhofar.

Marty sank gratefully to the ground, breathing harshly, exhausted. He felt oddly fearful.

As expected, the scrub ground being used as a makeshift *adoo* airstrip was deserted. This was confirmation that the other SAS troop's diversionary attack to the south had been successful in drawing the *adoo* away – hopefully long enough for the assault force to get entrenched above and around the airstrip, where they would wait for the enemy to return.

Nevertheless, receiving instructions from a combination of radio communication and hand signals, the 250 men sank into the ground in a line that snaked in an enormous arc around the airstrip. The CO then moved the assault group, team by team, across the open ground, receiving no resistance whatsoever.

Lying belly down on the ground, watching the mass of men advance towards the airstrip in small groups, jumping up and darting forward under cover of the others, then dropping down and jumping up again, Marty had the chance to study the terrain in the brightening dawn light. There were rocky, parched hills around the makeshift airstrip, but on the flatlands, on high elevations, he could see other makeshift runways and water gleaming in the area's few water holes. It was the watering holes, he knew, that made this area so valuable to the *adoo* and they would certainly fight fiercely to defend it. The airfields were little more than strips of level ground, levelled carefully by hand, surrounded by defensive trenches and the occasional hut of wood or corrugated iron. There were no control towers or even watchtowers. As for this particular airfield, Lympne, the *adoo*, in their zeal to defeat the SAS's diversionary attack to the south, had failed to leave even one man on guard. The airfield was completely deserted.

Gathering his men around him, the CO ordered Marty's GPMG team to take up a position on the eastern flank of the airstrip, halfway up the hill overlooking it. The rest were to stay more or less where they were, taking up positions lower down the slope. Before they did so, however, they were reminded that the SAF and *firqats* would be leading the advance against the adoo and that the *SAS* would give covering fire only.

With practically no rest, the very thought of climbing to his feet so soon filled Marty with weariness. Nevertheless, he did so, once more shouldering the machine-gun's tripod, then leading Taff, Tommy and the new man, Larry Purvis, towards the hills rising east of the airstrip. The hike took longer than anticipated, nearly an hour, and when finally they arrived at their position they were sweaty and breathless.

From here they had a panoramic view of the nearby hills and the valleys far below. The SAF and *firqats* had completely surrounded the airstrip. SAS troops were marking the runway with coloured smoke grenades for the reinforcements being flown in. It was 0815 hours and the sun was getting brighter, creating a jigsaw of shadow and light over parched hills and plains.

Having divested themselves of their kit, Marty and his team proceeded to build a sangar by wrenching boulders out of the ground with their bare hands and stacking them in a rough circle. While they were doing so, Taff kept watch and also listened for incoming calls on the radio. The sangar took the shape of a semicircular dry-stone wall three feet high and eight feet in diameter. When it was completed, they laid their

Bergens, kit and personal weapons around the inner wall, then mounted the machine-gun on the tripod and prepared it for action.

'Right, boss,' Purvis said to Marty, sitting back against the wall of the sangar, 'she's all set to go.'

Glancing over the wall of the sangar, down the hillside, Marty saw that many other SAS teams had constructed similar sangars on the slopes overlooking three sides of the airstrip and were covering it with GPMGs, light anti-aircraft weapons and mortars. Below him, a couple of thousand yards down the hill, Crowley was sharing a sangar with Troopers Welsh and Raglan, as well as a two-man mortar team. Not far to the right, all on his own, Sergeant Alan Hershey, a loner, was smoking a cigarette, studying the landscape, and resting his free hand on the sniper rifle lying on the wall of his small, one-man sangar. At the very bottom of the hill, on the level ground around the airstrip, SAF, *firqats* and Baluchi troops had taken over the unprotected *adoo* defensive trenches and appeared to be eating and drinking contentedly.

Looking over the wall of the sangar, Marty saw the first of the Skyvans appearing in the sky to the south. Soon the air was filled with them as lift after lift came in, followed by Huey and Sikorsky helicopters. One after the other, they landed on the makeshift airstrip belonging to the absent *adoo*, their propellers and rotors whipping up enormous, billowing clouds of dust that obscured the men pouring out of the aircraft and across the runway, carrying artillery pieces, mortars, ammunition, rations and, most important of all, water. Having inserted 800 men on the LZ, the aircraft took off again, creating more immense clouds of boiling dust.

While Marty was watching this spectacle and still fighting for breath, still feeling oddly fearful, an SAS trooper, Sam Greaves, laboriously climbed the hill, bringing with him two five-gallon jerrycans of water and the news that the diversionary attack to the south had indeed been a success, drawing the *adoo* away from this airfield and resulting in no SAS casualties.

'The attack's over now, though,' Greaves told them, 'and

the *adoo* are believed to be on their way back here. Expect fireworks real soon.'

After finishing his tea, Trooper Greaves waved goodbye and headed back down the hill to his own position.

He hadn't got as far as Crowley's sangar when the whole hill erupted.

The first explosions tore up the ground near Trooper Greaves, first showering him in soil, then picking him up and hurling him sideways. He hit the ground like a rag doll, bouncing off it, limbs flapping, then was lost in swirling smoke and more raining soil when the ground erupted again.

More explosions tore up the hillside, making a catastrophic din, as Marty glanced at the others, all of whom were staring back, then tentatively raised his head above the wall of the sangar to look out again. A stream of green tracer, surprisingly luminous in the morning light, snaked out of the boiling smoke, first appearing to be almost floating, then snapping overhead at fantastic speed to spend itself a good distance away. Another series of explosions erupted across the hillside, spewing earth and more smoke.

'The *adoo*!' Tommy exclaimed, huddled up beside Marty with his M16 rifle propped up between his knees.

'Right,' Marty said. Holding his SLR, he hugged the sangar wall as the western perimeter exploded with the stuttered snapping of incoming small-arms fire. Raising his head again, he saw that the tracer was coming from the rim of the western hillside. The *adoo* machine-guns, he reasoned, were just beyond the rim of the hill, as were their mortars. Even as he deduced this, a series of explosions erupted in a line that ran from the airstrip to the base of the eastern hill, tearing through the SAF trenches. More soil spewed upwards and rained down through the billowing black smoke.

Taff radioed base, located by the airstrip, asking for a medic to be sent up. The reply was affirmative. Taff put the phone down as another series of mortar explosions tore up the hill below. The *adoo* foot soldiers, Marty realised, were grouped beyond the rim of the western hill, staying put while their mortars and machine-guns softened up the SAS. Right now, there was nothing the SAS could do except sit tight. Which is just what they did.

The attack continued for another twenty minutes, with the mortar explosions erupting all over the western hill, between the trenches by the airstrip, and on the lower slopes of the hill itself, where SF troops were also entrenched and returning the fire with their own machine-guns and mortars. Soon the whole area was covered in a grey pall of smoke webbed by criss-crossing lines of green tracer from the *adoo* and purple tracer from SF troops, including the SAS.

'Might as well finish our tea,' Tommy said. 'Not much else we can do.'

All four of them sipped hot tea as the green tracers continued to streak over the sangar and more explosions erupted lower down the slope. Occasionally, through the drifting smoke on the western perimeter, they saw SAF troops, including the *firqats*, making their way uphill, trying to get closer to the *adoo* hidden beyond the rim. However, long before they reached it, the *adoo*'s attack slackened until only sporadic firing could be heard. Gradually even this died away and silence descended.

Glancing down the slope, Marty saw a couple of SAS troopers loping across the makeshift airstrip, from the western side, then up the hill to the sangar. It took them a long time to complete the journey and when finally they arrived they were breathless.

'So what's happening?' he asked.

'Twenty or thirty *adoo* hit the positions over on the west with Kalashnikovs and light machine-guns as back-up. The SF took no casualties, but had two hits, which makes us one up,' one of the men told him.

'Why has the attack tapered off?'

'We think the *adoo* were just testing our strength. Some of the SAF got over the rim of the hill and found the bastards already gone. The generally received wisdom is that they've retired to their stronghold at Jibjat, about six kilometres west. That's where we're going tomorrow.'

'Why?' Marty asked.

'Because the CO thinks that makeshift airstrip down there,

on Lympne, is fucking useless. Apparently it's already breaking up from this morning's resup landings. So tomorrow, at first light, we're going to march on Jibjat.'

'That's only seven thousand, five hundred yards away.'

'Right. A short hike to the enemy.'

'Who dares wins,' Marty said, wiping sweat from his fevered brow.

Just before first light, after a night in the sangar, during which they had taken one-hour turns on watch, or 'stag', they packed their Bergens and prepared the GPMG and tripod for carriage. Still before first light, they destroyed the sangar, dismantling it stone by stone, then moved down the hill to join Sergeant Crowley and the others. The ground around Crowley's sangar was pockmarked with shell holes and the sangar itself had been partially damaged by the blast of an explosion. Troopers Welsh and Raglan were still cleaning the weapons that had been clogged up with falling soil and dust. They both looked exhausted.

'We're marching to Jibjat,' Crowley told them. 'Six kilometres west with all our gear in the heat of the noonday sun. Talk about mad dogs and Englishmen . . .'

Amused by Crowley's laconic wit, Marty and the others helped to destroy the sangar, taking it apart stone by stone as they had just done with their own; then they picked up their heavy loads and took their position in the spectacular gathering of 800 men, broken up into dozens of extended, snakelike lines, stretching down the eastern hill, across the airstrip, then up the lower slopes of the western hill. All of them were wearing camouflaged clothing, with the *firqats* half hiding their faces in their windblown *shemaghs* and looking more fearsome by so doing. When everything was in order, a series of hand signals came down the line and the men moved out.

There was no talking. The various lines stretched out a long way, snaking over the western hill, but the only noise was the jangling of kit and weapons hanging from webbing. At first the air was cool, but the sun was rising fast, and before long, as the last men crossed the hill, the heat made its presence felt. Marty wiped sweat from his face, swatted flies and mosquitoes. Though almost blinded by the light, feeling weak and disorientated, he saw the line of men ahead snaking down the hillside, towards the flatland where the Jibjat airstrip lay. The *adoo* would be there, waiting for them, ready to fight, and they would fight to the bitter end. Marty felt his heart quickening.

The march didn't take long and soon the airstrip came into view in the distance, enclosed in a great horseshoe of high, rocky terrain, where the *adoo* were almost certainly entrenched.

Immediately, as if they were communicating with body language, a subtle change came over the hundreds of marching men as they instinctively became more tense and watchful. Moving slightly away from one another, they spread out across the desert plain, until they were covering the broad area leading up to the rocky bottleneck leading on to the airstrip.

All of this was accomplished without a word being spoken, with only their kit and weapons jangling to fill the vast silence.

Then the first shots rang out.

Surprisingly, they were single shots from Kalashnikov rifles, fired by the *adoo* with unerring accuracy to pick off some of the SAF troops up front and hopefully demoralise the others. Some men fell, but the others kept marching, first walking as before, picking up speed, then gradually breaking into a run as they raced for the bottleneck. More single shots rang out and some more SAF troops fell, then came the distant thudding sound of mortars.

The first explosions erupted on a wide arc where the troops were advancing, tearing up the ground between them and causing a screen of boiling sand and smoke. The men at the head of the column disappeared into it as the *adoo* opened up with their machine-guns. Green tracer illuminated the murk, exploded in silvery flashes, and tore up the sand in jagged, spitting lines that made some of the advancing troops go into convulsions and jerk violently backwards. The other troops continued to race into the murk as the medics ran to and fro, crouched low, bravely tending to the wounded and the dead.

'What the fuck are those bastards firing,' Tommy asked, 'that can reach us from the far side of that airstrip?'

'Twelve-point-seven-millimetre Shpagin heavy machine-guns,' Marty said as he gradually broke into a trot. 'They can out-range anything we have, so we'll have to get a lot closer before returning their fire. Come on, lads, pick your feet up.'

He and the others ran as well as they could while carrying the separate parts of the dismantled GPMG. For Marty it was hell, with the legs of the tripod biting into his neck and chest, but eventually he found himself in the thick of the smoke-filled, spewing sand, where the mortar shells and heavy machine-gun fire were causing most havoc. Here the other men advancing through the murk were no more than shadows.

'Christ!' Tommy said, running beside him, 'I can't see a damned thing.'

'Just keep running,' Taff told him.

Marty almost fell, one foot slipping into a shell hole, but Taff grabbed him by the shoulder and tugged him upright, then pushed him ahead. Tommy was there beside him, his face streaked with sand and sweat, running beside Welsh and Raglan – a trio of ghosts. The mortar shells were still exploding, causing the sand to roar and swirl about them, and green tracer stabbed through the murk with a vicious spitting sound.

Suddenly, from the gloom of the swirling sand, they plunged back into daylight.

For a moment it was dazzling, seeming brighter than it really was, but then, when Marty managed to adjust to it, he saw that the bottleneck leading to the airstrip had been blocked with a barricade of trees and barbed wire. Then he saw the *adoo* – they looked just like the *firqats* – retreating across the airstrip, firing on the move, and gradually scattering up the rocky slopes beyond, where they could hide behind boulders.

'We should be in range!' Crowley shouted. 'Set up the machine-gun!'

Relieved to be unburdened, Marty and Taff dropped to their knees and hurriedly set up the GPMG. Once it was on its heavy tripod, Marty closed the top cover on a belt of 200 rounds and Taff hammered out a test burst of fifty. After replacing the hinge-clip, he again took up his firing position and started pouring fire into the hills beyond the airstrip where the *adoo* were sheltering.

By now the other SF machine-gunners were also peppering the hill and the mortar crews were laying down a barrage that soon covered the whole area in smoke. The *adoo* were in retreat, moving back up the hill, allowing the SAS demolitions team, led by Corporal Alf Lisners, to race across to the bottleneck and begin the task of blowing away the trees and barbed wire that were blocking the way to the airstrip. They were given covering fire not only by the many machine-guns but by a fusillade of fire from the rifles of the SAF, *firqat* and Baluchi troops massed on both sides of the barricade.

With Marty feeding in the belts and Tommy acting as observer, Taff kept hammering away with his GPMG, helping to force the *adoo* back up the slopes of the western hill. Minutes later, a call came in over the radio, informing Marty's team that the barricade was about to be blown. By this time most of the *adoo* were well up the western hill, retreating over the rim, out of range of the SF guns, so the machine-gun fire gradually tapered off and Taff also stopped firing. Finally, the SF rifles fell silent and the troops at the barricade hastily left it to crouch on the ground near the SAS.

Marty saw the *adoo* clearly through his binoculars. Wearing *djellabas*, *shemaghs* and sandals, heavily burdened with webbing, ponchos, bandoliers of ammunition and *kunjias*, they looked just like the fearsome *firqats*. Most of them had stopped firing and were retreating back up the hill, holding their Kalashnikovs in the cradle of their arms. Marty lowered his binoculars as the last of them were about to disappear over the rim of the hill.

The demolition men had completed their work and were retreating backwards, crouched low, uncoiling the detonator cord as they went. From where he was kneeling, Marty could clearly see the plastic explosives taped to the upended trees.

The det cord, with one end fixed to blasting caps embedded in the explosive charges, was running out from the explosives to the roll being uncoiled by Corporal Lisners. When he and his assistant had reached the detonator, Lisners cut through the det cord with scissors, expertly bared the wires with a pocket knife, fixed them to the electrical connectors on the detonator, then rested his hands lightly on the plunger.

He eyeballed the barricade to ensure that no one was near it, then glanced at Lieutenant Barkwell, who was kneeling about ten yards to his right, beside Patterson and a radio crew. When Barkwell raised and lowered his right hand, Lisners pressed on the plunger with both hands.

The noise emerged from what seemed like the bowels of the earth to explode with a deafening roar and erupt in a mighty mushroom of spewing soil, sand, dust and loose gravel. The trees were blown apart and burst into flames, raining back down through the angry dark smoke as a fountain of fire, falling into the murk well to each side of the bottleneck, caused more dust to billow upwards.

The fading noise of the explosion was followed by another: the spine-chilling, macabre wailing of the excited *firqats*, rising eerily above the cheering and shouting of the SAF and Baluchi troops.

As one man, they jumped to their feet and raced through the smoke in the bottleneck, between the exploded, flaming trees, then spread out across the deserted airstrip, firing their weapons repeatedly in the air to announce their triumph.

The SAS, bemused by the furore, followed them in.

Marty was right there with them, between Taff and Tommy, running as fast as he could, exhilarated beyond measure and feeling his heart racing with excitement.

Suddenly, unexpectedly, he felt a stabbing pain in his chest, became dizzy, lost his balance. His weapon slipped from his hands as he plunged towards the ground and the pain clenched like a fist around his heart and seemed to squeeze the life out of him.

Oh, no! he thought. Now now!

When he hit the ground, darkness swooped in to claim him and release him from agony.

BOOK FOUR

CONSPIRATORS

31 JANUARY 1991

Feeling the unsteady beating of his own heart, the old man was reminded of his friend's heart attack and surmised that it had all started then. It would actually have started before, of course, with those deaths in the Malayan jungle, when he realised that war was not a game and that its horrors were manifold. He had certainly changed after that, becoming less naive, even cynical, forced to battle to hold onto his faith and youth's optimism. First that and then the women, those premature deaths, one an accident and the other self-inflicted, both damaging to him.

The second involvement was the bad one, the old man thought, feeling the handgun in the holster in the cross-draw position, waiting for that final double tap.

(*You let yourself be sucked into her paranoia and you never escaped. If you'd kept a reasonable distance, stayed aloof, you wouldn't have turned the wrong way. What she wrought, you sewed.*)

The early-morning street was quiet. It was usually quiet here. Cars constantly moved along the leaf-strewn road, but few people were out and about, and many windows were shuttered. The rich were always fearful, protected by bars and cameras, their gardens patrolled by armed security men and well-trained, savage dogs. His friend had come a long way for this, turning onto crooked highways, and now, with his new, embittered view of the world, he lived like a rich and powerful man who had placed himself above the law. He had become judge and jury and executioner in a valley of death. His trail was bloody and clear to see.

Plessey and Marconi and the Royal Military College of Science, the old man speculated, still sitting in the gleaming Mercedes Benz, looking across at his friend's house. They were all involved in top-secret defence projects and they may have been linked. They may have sold their deadly wares to corrupt, repressive regimes, though no solid proof for that has been found and probably never will be.

(*Nevertheless, whether or not this is true, it is what you believed and acted upon, my friend. You became the Grim Reaper.*)

Having targeted Plessey and the Royal Military College of Science, he followed the links he found in hearsay or imagination and moved against Marconi. The fifth victim, a former Marconi scientist reportedly working on radar, sonar and guided missile systems, died in his fume-filled garage, supposedly while servicing his car.

Just like the metallurgist in Oxfordshire, the old man thought. It couldn't have been an accident.

The sixth victim, a former Army brigadier working on secret defence projects for Marconi near Camberley in Surrey, was found dead by electrocution at the cottage in the grounds of the Marconi factory, his teeth wired to the mains supply.

Just like the scientist from the Plessey Naval Systems at Addlestone, the old man thought. That was no accident either.

The seventh victim, engaged in testing computer-based defence systems for one of Marconi's sister companies, died when, on his way to work, he inexplicably U-turned into a slip road on a dual carriageway and crashed into a disused building at 80 miles an hour.

This was supposedly after he'd been visited by unnamed members of the Special Branch, the old man thought. The Special Branch denied any such visit, so just who were those men? The same two who had visited all the others? The two he know so well?

The eighth victim, a 24-year-old computer expert working

on the world's most advanced electronic defence system for Marconi Underwater Systems, was found on a footpath 245 feet below Clifton's suspension bridge with his trousers pulled down and a puncture mark on his left buttock, reportedly en route by car to Bristol.

It was thought to be a suicide jump, the old man thought, until they found that puncture mark on his buttock. Now they weren't so sure.

(*But I am – I'm* very *sure. That victim was knocked out with an injection before being thrown off the bridge. You couldn't have done that, my friend, but it would have come naturally to your partner. There was little* he *wouldn't do.*)

After that, as the evidence clearly indicated, his friend, that man in the guarded house across the road, took a step back, perhaps shocked by what was happening, while his partner, the one who rarely blinked, went out of control and neutralised the rest in cruelly novel ways.

The ninth victim, also a computer expert at Marconi Underwater Systems and engaged in sensitive defence technology, apparently committed suicide by tying together four lengths of nylon rope, securing one end to a tree, the other to his neck, and driving away from the tree at high speed. He, too, was reportedly en route to Bristol when it happened.

The tenth victim, a 44-year-old defence engineer, also working at Marconi Underwater Systems, was found drowned in a partially frozen canal, weighed down by a painter's trestle, a few days after he had received a call from Marconi, saying they wanted to discuss his work.

The eleventh victim, a 46-year-old design engineer at Marconi Space and Defence Systems, Portsmouth, reportedly working on top secret weapons and satellite development projects for the government and NATO, died of a drugs overdose.

Almost a baker's dozen, the old man thought.

(*But it didn't go any farther. It didn't and won't.*)

He checked his wristwatch and glanced across the road, noting that the front door was still closed and that the guards seemed lethargic. His friend was running late. Usually he was punctual. This was the day that the Association met and he always came out at the same time to be driven to town. That time had now passed.

(*You did what you thought was right, but then it all went too far and, when you realised just how wrong you'd been, you started withdrawing. You're almost a recluse now, my friend, hiding in your own shadow, and you know that your friend has been neutralised and you're thinking about that. Almost certainly you've guessed who was responsible and know it won't end there. When you come out, which you will in the end, you won't be too surprised. You may even welcome it.*)

Sliding his right hand around his waist, the old man checked that his handgun was still in the cross-draw position in its Len Dixon holster. His fingers caressed the holster, which was worn smooth with age, and the touch of it took him back through the years to the very beginning. They had both been young then, filled with faith and optimism, secure in the knowledge that what they were fighting for was worthwhile, which it was at that time. Then it gradually changed, became more complex, less clean, and as they aged and the British Empire crumbled it became a lot dirtier. He was out of it then – the young man that he had been – but his friend, the one in hiding across the road, was still serving his country right or wrong, and in time he became disillusioned and let bitterness blind him.

He saw what he wanted to see, heard only what he needed to hear, and, impelled by self-righteousness and the pain of broken faith, he took all that he had learned and perverted it for his own kind of justice. He became the judge, jury and executioner for all those who had wronged him by betraying the regiment, his country, his faith, and he embarked on a cleansing operation of unparalleled ruthlessness. That man over there, that loving husband and decent father, that good citizen and courageous fighter, had travelled from the light to the darkness in search of redemption. He would find that in death.

The old man in the gleaming Mercedes Benz straightened up in his seat, removing his hand from the holster at his waist and staring across the quiet road. The security guards in the driveway of the big house had just listened to their handsets and were now taking up protective positions by the front door and main gate. They were preparing for someone to come out and they were taking no chances.

The end begins now. Let it be quick and clean.

It was quick, but it seemed a lot longer as the past rushed back in. He lived a life in mere moments.

CHAPTER THIRTY

Marty saw the first of the men emerging from the mist that clung like grey gauze to the snow-covered, rocky slopes of the mountain, with the landscape spread out eerily far below them. They looked like ghosts in the mist, though hardly human, misshapen as they were by overweighted Bergen rucksacks and rolled groundsheets, all carrying M16 rifles at the ready. They were still a very long way down the slope and were advancing upwards in irregular file formation, spaced well apart, with some hanging well behind, obviously close to exhaustion. The only sound, apart from the distant jangling of their equipment, was the low moaning of the wind that swept the snow off the rocks and blew it across the bleak mountainside.

Though covered in a blanket and protected by the stone walls of the small sangar he had built for himself, Marty was still numb with cold and feeling his age. Three years older than he had been when he'd had his heart attack during the murderous assault on the Jebel Dhofar in Oman, he was proud to be still unusually fit for his age and could hold his own against the men now advancing uphill. Nevertheless, he was pushing his luck by being here and knew that, if his superiors discovered that he had come against their orders, they would strongly disapprove.

Not that he gave a damn. He had done it out of boredom,

defying the gods. While he waited for the marching men to reach his hidden position, he thought back on the past three years and realised that, although his work since the heart attack had not been without its interesting side, it had slowly started to grind him down with its sheer repetition.

At the time of the incident, he thought that he had been shot in the heart and was dying. Only when he regained consciousness in the hospital did he realise that he was still alive. He was then informed by an RAMC surgeon that he had suffered a mild heart attack owing to the strain of humping the heavy GPMG up the sheer face of the Jebel. Mild though it was, it caused him deep humiliation, making him face the fact that he was ageing and that his days of truly challenging active service might well be over.

Certainly, mild or not, the heart attack was enough to ensure that he would not be sent back to Oman. Instead, he had been assigned as a member of the directing staff of 22 SAS training wing, where he recuperated while lecturing new candidates on the theoretical aspects of the ever-broadening programmes for basic training, continuation training and cross-training, both in Hereford and abroad.

By now the organisation of 22 SAS, totalling 750 men, had evolved into four 'Sabre' (fighting) squadrons: A, B, D and G; a reserve Squadron, R; and the Rhodesian SAS, C Squadron, which in the late 1960s had been involved in operations against black nationalists, including cross-border raids into Mozambique, Botswana and Zambia. There was also the 264 SAS Signals Squadron, detached from the Royal Corps of Signals.

During his subsequent three years at Bradbury Lines, while the war in Oman was still being engaged, he had been privileged to take part in the broadening of the regiment's scope with, in addition to the training wing, an operations research wing, a demolitions wing, a relatively new counter-revolutionary warfare wing, and an operations planning and intelligence wing, fondly known as the Kremlin and manned by the green slime.

Though he was nominally a DS with the training wing, Marty's past experience with the regiment had encouraged his superiors to involve him in the development of various counter-revolutionary warfare techniques and let him be privy to the inner workings of the Kremlin which, since the 1972 Munich Olympics massacre, had become increasingly concerned about the widening of terrorist activities worldwide and now envisaged the need for special training to combat them. Already, the construction of a 'Killing House', or close-quarter battle (CQB) building of the kind discussed frequently between Paddy Kearney and Bulldog Bellamy was nearing completion. Other techniques for combating terrorism had led to consultations and exchange programmes with friendly special forces groups such as the US Delta Force and similar in Germany, Holland, France and Italy. For this reason, though not involved in active duty, Marty had spent much of the past three years overseas, which had compensated somewhat for not being on active service.

Gradually, however, as links with other special forces groups were firmly established and the new programmes clearly defined, he had found himself spending ever lengthier periods in Hereford, lecturing the new candidates in map-reading, navigation, weapons maintenance, CQB tactics and field exercises. He had not been in the field himself and the loss had been deeply felt, gradually building up a well of frustration that had finally led him to defy his superiors and make his lonely hike up the mountain to build himself a sangar and keep watch in the early-morning hours as the new candidates made their painful way towards the snow-covered summit.

Now, as he shivered under his blanket and watched the hopefuls advancing up the misty, snow-covered hill, every man clearly frozen and none looking too bright in his state of physical and mental exhaustion, he recalled his own climb up the equally formidable, baking hot slopes of the Jebel Dhofar. In fact, the war in Oman was continuing this very moment and Marty understood that, while he missed being there, he was probably lucky to have got out while he could, no matter how painful his exit. Otherwise, he would have been in for years of particularly gruelling, dangerous work and, if not struck down by the *adoo*, probably killed by an even worse heart attack.

Though the assault on the Jebel Dhofar had finally been

successful, the fatalities had been high. According to what Taff and Tommy had told him upon their return to Hereford, the rest of the fight for the jebel had been hell, culminating in a march along the Wadi Dharbat with the *adoo* sniping at them and shelling them with mortars from fortified sangars high on the hills. To make matters worse, just as the combined SAS and SAF forces were about to capture the plateau, the unpredictable *firqats* decided to lay down their arms, insisting that it was the beginning of Ramadan, when they could not eat, drink or fight. Naturally, the minute they saw that, the *adoo* poured down the hills in their hundreds to annihilate the SAF forces with AK 47 Kalashnikovs, FN rifles and RPD light machine-guns, eventually coming so close that hand-to-hand fighting was engaged. Luckily, the SAS troopers were saved at the last minute by the arrival of RAF Skyvans, which devastated the *adoo* still on the hills with a load of Burmail bombs. So the battle was won eventually, but the cost was certainly high.

Wounded during the fight, Taff was flown back with other wounded to RAF Salalah and saw that the dead, including *adoo*, had been placed in body bags and just heaped on the Skyvan's floor, then lashed down with web straps, with the weight of the bodies squeezing out body fluids and blood to create a dreadful stench. Though normally imperturbable, Taff had later told Marty that all he could remember about that flight was recovering consciousness, seeing the body fluids and blood seeping out of the body bags, and smelling the stench. He had then passed out again, not recovering until the aircraft touched down in RAF Salalah.

By that time, Marty had already had his own operation and was recovering in a hospital in Hereford. However, as he was recuperating and trying to deal with the humiliation his heart attack had caused him, he was kept up to date on the events in Oman by a steady stream of visitors, including Taff, when he had recovered, and Tommy Taylor. From those conversations he learned that after he had been flown out on a casevac the SF advanced fifteen miles into communist-held territory and built three defensive positions on the Jebel Khaftawt. This was called the Leopard Line. From there, they moved out to surround the area with an aggressive patrol programme, clearing the *adoo* out of the wadis. Eventually, after ten days of fierce fighting, Operation Jaguar established the Sultan's forces on the Jebel Dhofar, which was a major setback for the *adoo*. Their attack on Mirbat the following year was their final, desperate bid to win back their prestige. But they lost that as well.

Glancing down the slope to where the early-morning sun was starting to burn through the mist, making the snow glint and letting the spectacular landscape far below emerge more clearly, Marty saw that the men in OGo were still clambering up towards him and would soon be within firing range. Moving carefully, making no noise whatsoever, he tugged the blanket off his shoulders, uncovering his SLR, then rested the barrel of the weapon on the wall of the sangar, squinted through the sights, and captured the leading trooper in the cross-hairs. He adjusted the sights, satisfied himself that the men were still slightly out of range, and relaxed while holding his position, letting the soldiers advance higher up the slope.

'Mirbat,' he whispered, thinking of the town where the last great battle of the war in Oman had been fought. 'God, I wish I'd been there!'

The battle begun with Operation Jaguar had been completed with the Battle for Mirbat, which became a turning point in the war, ultimately leading to defeat for the *adoo*. Thinking about it, Marty realised that even now, as he gazed down the misty slopes of this snow-swept mountain in Wales, the remaining *adoo* were being pushed back to the Yemeni border by other SAS troops. Marty wished he could be there instead of here, but he had to accept his lot.

Squinting through the sights of his SLR, he had to remind himself that the young men advancing laboriously up the hill were in fact new candidates engaged in one of the many gruelling exercises thought up by himself and other members of the DS. Selection training had been diabolically refined to weed out all but the *crème de la crème* of the candidates. It now consisted of a three-week build-up period commencing with a standard army battle-fitness test and followed by a daunting diet of road marches and timed route marches across the Brecon Beacons in South Wales, by day and by night, in all kinds of weather, carrying Bergens that were made progressively heavier until they weighed 25 kilos. Map-reading and cross-country navigation were included in the tasks. Stress was deliberately introduced by pulling the candidates out of bed unexpectedly, by not telling them the nature of the march they were about to embark upon, and by having RV points along the route, manned by ruthless training wing DS. Basic training climaxed with Sickener 1, the longest, most brutal march of this phase of training, which included the dreaded entrail pit.

Those who did not drop out during selection training – and many did – went on to Test Week, when the distances were increased, the times required to complete the march decreased, and the DS used every kind of brutal psychological ploy, known as 'beasting', to break the already exhausted candidate's spirit. Test Week culminated in the sixty-kilometre endurance march known as the 'fan dance' because it involved reaching the summit of Pen-y-Fan, the highest mountain in the Brecon Beacons, in twenty hours, even in gale-force winds, rain and snow, and 'cross-graining the bukets', or going from one trig point, or summit, to another, rather than taking the easy way around them, all the time being harassed by the relentless DS.

The few who survived this final march, or Sickener 2, would go on to continuation training, followed by jungle and parachute training, but the troops now advancing towards the hidden Marty had yet to make that final, dreaded march and were simply being put through an unexpected hike up the mountain, after being pulled out of their beds in the dead of the night. Two of them, already exhausted by the rigours of the previous day, had angrily refused and been RTU'd. The remainder, those advancing up the sheer, snow-covered slope towards Marty, were still in the running.

Their task in this particular instance was to hike up to the summit of the towering Pen-y-fan, reaching it before dawn and without being 'captured' or 'neutralised' by the DS scattered along the route. That they had managed to get this far was a tribute to their skill and tenacity, and Marty almost hated himself for what he was about to do to them. They would not, in this instance, be RTU'd, but they would certainly be shocked and bitterly disappointed to find themselves blocked off from the summit after coming so far to get so close, being too tired to notice the sangar blending in with the rocks just above them.

Squinting along the sights of his weapon, breathing evenly, aiming at the ground directly in front of the feet of the first man in the ragged column, Marty squeezed the trigger.

The roaring of the weapon split the silence, shocking the men below, some freezing instantly, others automatically throwing themselves sideways, even as the hail of bullets made the snow spit up in a long jagged line that cut from left to right across the front of the column. The first man, showered by the flying snow and doubtless imagining that he had been shot in the feet, was one of those who froze, hardly able to believe his eyes; but a second burst from Marty's SLR was aimed even closer to him and he suddenly jumped back, then flung himself sideways, behind the protective covering of a rock.

As the others did the same, all hiding behind rocks, Marty stopped firing, put the safety catch back on, then stood up to let the candidates see him.

'You stupid bastards!' he bawled, looking down as those startled, camouflaged faces peered out from behind the rocks, their eyes raised in disbelief to find their 52-year old Squadron Sergeant-Major standing there on the very summit of the highest mountain in the Brecon Beacons, before first light, in the dead of the winter. 'You've all been neutralised. You should have kept your eyes open and seen me and taken cover immediately, in which case I'd have passed you. But you've failed. You didn't make it. You let tiredness make you careless. Lucky for you, this isn't one for the record. Now get back down that hill.'

Either cursing in anger or hanging their heads in shame, the candidates made their way back down the mountain with Marty behind them. He sympathised with them, knew their suffering, but did not let it move him. Their shame and rage at this moment, if they could bear it, would give them strength in the future. This was the SAS way.

CHAPTER THIRTY-ONE

Marty woke late in the morning to the sound of Diane typing downstairs. Still half asleep, but with the grey light of Notting Hill Gate beaming in through the window, he kept his eyes closed and thought of how much more pleasant it was here than in the SAS base in Hereford. For a start, there were no women in the Sports and Social. Indeed, even in the town of Hereford the women were not exactly like Diane. Marty smiled. His body was limned with sensual heat. Diane liked making love a lot, but she preferred it in the mornings and she had woken him to have her way with him before starting her work. As usual, their lovemaking had been uninhibited, moving from desire to consummation with ruthless abandonment. Marty credited this to Diane, who had no qualms about sex, was often greedy for it, and blessedly had no pretences about it. Certainly, he was aware of just how lucky he was to have such a woman at his age. Many men would have envied him.

Awakening fully, he glanced at his wristwatch and saw that it was already ten in the morning. He must have dozed off again after making love to Diane. Though he often did this, she didn't seem to mind, doubtless because it enabled her to start her freelance work, which she liked to do first thing in the morning. Now, listening to her typing away downstairs, he had to concede that he was involved with a woman who was unusual in more ways than one. Independent as a person and ruthless as a journalist, she satisfied her sexual appetite to keep it from distracting her and leave her free to think about her work. As an investigative journalist, she was clearly at the top of her league, displaying a passion for the truth that was deeply impressive. It was also a passion that made her slightly neurotic and, at times, hard to handle. Certainly she was highly strung, but he felt that he could deal with that by keeping his distance.

Yawning, realising that he had a full day in front of him, he rolled out of bed, attended to his ablutions in the apartment's cramped bathroom, dressed in grey slacks, shirt and tie and went downstairs to have breakfast. Diane worked in a small, book-stacked study just off the main room, at a desk piled high with books, so he stuck his head around the doorframe, saw her from the back as she punched her old Remington typewriter, and jokingly asked, 'What about the workers, then? Can I get you a coffee?'

She glanced over her shoulder with a smile and nodded affirmatively. 'Yes. I could do with one.'

'Will I bring it in to you?'

'No, I'll come out and get it. Just give me a shout.'

'Right. I'll do that.'

She had already gone back to punching the keys when he made his way into the kitchen to put on the kettle. When he had made the coffee and toast, he called out to her, telling her it was ready, and the sound of the typewriter stopped as she came in to join him. She was wearing her customary work outfit of open-necked shirt tucked into blue jeans, emphasising her thin, undernourished figure. Though she was now in her middle forties, her face was still attractive, if rather severe, with her green eyes framed by short-cropped blonde hair, her face almost gaunt, the lips full and sensual. Her general lack of weight was, he knew, caused by too much tension, too many cigarettes and too little to eat.

After kissing him on the top of the head, she lit a cigarette, blew a cloud of smoke, then took the chair facing him across the big round table.

'Had a good sleep, did you,' she asked him, 'after your base desires were satisfied?'

'Bloody right. Not that it was *my* desires that were an issue, since you woke me up to have your way with me.'

'If you have an itch, scratch it, I always say. Then your head will be clear.'

She sipped at her coffee and blew another cloud of smoke while Marty spread marmalade on his buttered toast.

'So why do you need a clear head today?' he asked her. 'What are you working on?'

'An article about all those revenge killings in Ulster. Eleven people dead, six of them Catholics, plus four militant unionists killed in a car-bomb explosion. That place is a bloody nightmare now. Are your people in there?'

'No,' Marty said.

'Is that the truth or a diplomatic lie?'

'It's the truth,' he insisted.

'The SAS were there in sixty-nine – openly, wearing uniform, complete with beige berets and winged-dagger badges – and I'll bet they're still there.'

'D Squadron went there in sixty-nine to search the bandit country for Protestant weapons. That was a futile endeavour, so we haven't been called back since.'

'I'll bet,' Diane said sardonically, blowing a cloud of smoke at him.

In fact, her intuition was correct and he was being disingenuous. While the 'secret' war in Oman had prevented the SAS from having a sizeable presence in Northern Ireland, individual officers and NCOs were posted there regularly, covertly, to conduct intelligence tasks. Though he had not been so privileged, he was hoping that he would be compensated for not being in Oman with a tour of duty in the province in the near future. In fact, word on the grapevine had it that an SAS squadron was to be deployed there openly very shortly, probably in the new year, mainly for intelligence-gathering operations. If that happened, he was going to make sure that he was one of those sent – though naturally he was careful not to mention this plan to Diane.

'Christ, it's unbelievable,' she said, 'to have what amounts to a civil war on British soil. They're slaughtering each other over there and the British troops are caught in the middle. It's a pretty dirty business.'

'I certainly don't envy the greens,' he said, 'having to do *that* particular job.'

'The *what*?'

'Sorry, the greens – the British Army. That's what we call them in the SAS.'

'For a moment there I thought you meant the IRA.'

Marty smiled. 'No. Anyway, I don't envy the greens their job, being attacked by women and children, never knowing who's the enemy and who's a friend. It's pretty rotten for them. Maybe we should just get out and wipe our hands of the whole bloody business.'

'We should never have gone in in the first place, but now that we're there I don't suppose we can pull out. The Yanks would never forgive us, for a start. They're so romantic about it. Them and a lot of other stupid bastards who view the mess as a noble fight for liberty.'

'That's what it is from the Irish point of view.'

'Bullshit!' She exclaimed the word with passion, her pale cheeks slightly flushed, indicating that she was working herself up into a lather, which she tended to do far too easily. 'The IRA,' she continued, 'are a bunch of bloody Marxists, almost certainly aided by similar groups elsewhere – getting money, weapons and training from them. Believe me, the so-called fight for Ireland's freedom is only the first step in a link-up with terrorists worldwide. And God knows, there's enough of the bastards. Nationalists, separatists, anarchists, Trotskyites, Maoists, Leninists, communist proletariats and radical left-wing Marxists. Christ, they're springing up every day: that anarchist Baader-Meinhof lot in West Germany; Italy's ultra-left Red Brigade; the Red Army Faction and the June Second Movement; the PLO, the Spanish Marxist Basques of ETA; French Breton and Corsican separatists; the Japanese United Red Army; Argentine Montoneros, Uruguayan Tupamaros, and other South American groups being aided by Cuba.'

She stopped briefly and looked at Marty, but he said nothing, so she continued. 'The IRA's right in there, believe me, sharing their ideology. Now they and the others are coming closer together, Marty. They've been united by their mutual need for the theft of shipments of arms, stolen and forged documents, hot-money laundering centres, military training camps, safe houses, and so-called summit meetings between rival groups. It's a fucking nasty business and the Irish are right in the thick of it, trading and learning.'

'I gather you're not a fan of the Republicans,' Marty said drily.

'No, I'm not. Are you?'

'No, of course not.'

'You're a working-class lad and you can't help sympathising, but believe me, those bastards don't deserve it. They don't know what freedom means. Kangaroo courts, knee-capping, murder, extortion and money-laundering – that's their idea of freedom. Freedom's doing what *they* tell you to do. It's the law of the jungle.'

When she talked like this, her cheeks became flushed, her green eyes turned brighter, and she took on a messianic quality that he found disturbing. On the other hand, he agreed with her, at least most of the way, and was often swayed by the strength of her convictions. She had, of course, picked up some of it from her father, the socially committed lawyer, but Marty suspected, perhaps chauvinistically, that it also sprang from her inability to have children and her compensatory need to channel her energies in other directions. Certainly she was very single-minded and could not be ignored.

'I may be working-class,' he said, 'but I don't believe in Marxism and never have. I don't admire the IRA any more than you do. You can take that as read.'

Diane grinned and puffed another cloud of smoke, though this time turning her head to the side, letting it blow away from him.

'You'd say anything to avoid an argument,' she told him.

'Not true.'

'It is. You're so polite, Marty. I rant and rave, but you stay cool and keep your thoughts to yourself. Did you learn that in the SAS?'

'Maybe. I don't know. I have convictions, but I can't express them like you do. Your passion sometimes unnerves me.'

Diane chuckled. 'You should talk to my husband. David agrees with the man I lived with before I married him. They both thoght I was too opinionated, impossible to talk to, and absolutely stubborn. I'm amazed you've stuck with me.'

'You're not so bad, Diane.'

'I found a patient man in you. I'm grateful. You've no idea, Marty. You're the rock in my stormy sea.'

'We're good for each other.'

'What a sweet thing to say. You know, you're really a rare kind of man, Marty. Maybe one of a dying breed.'

'What kind of breed is that?'

'You have innate decency. It's so natural, you don't think about it. You have principles that you can't even define, but they've guided your whole life.'

'Shucks, you're embarrassing me.'

'You joke about it, but it's the truth. Paddy Kearney believed the same – he told me so – and that's why you and him have stayed friends for so many years. He's a born aristocrat, you're a working-class lad, and you're friends because you share the same values and respect each other for them. That's pretty rare, don't you think?'

'We're friends because of the SAS,' Marty said. 'That's what drew us together.'

'It's more than that, Marty, and you know it. You're friends because you're both men of principle and such men are rare.'

'What about women?' he asked. 'I think you're a woman of strong principles. Aren't you rare as well?'

She smiled and shook her head. 'No, it means I'm slightly crazy. I don't even trust myself. I believe in what I'm writing as I write it, but when I'm finished I start doubting what I wrote and wonder why I bothered. Women are always incomplete: they always need that other half. I picked up my father's sword, but it's still *his* and I feel like an imposter. I'm too emotional for my own good, too impulsive for constancy. That's why you're the rock in my stormy sea – you always think before you leap.'

'I certainly learned *that* in the SAS. It's probably all I'm good for.'

'For me, that's enough.' She stubbed her cigarette out.

'Anyway, I don't think you got it from the SAS. I think you got it from your parents and your children. Even though you and your first wife were divorced, you remained a loyal, supportive father. Then, of course, there was Ann Lim and . . .' She hesitated, embarrassed. 'You were a good husband and father then as well, until . . . Jesus! I'm sorry.'

Marty reached across the table to take hold of her hand and gently squeeze it. 'It's okay. It was years ago, Diane. It's not something I'll ever forget, but I've learned to live with it. These things happen in life.'

'Me and my big mouth.'

'It doesn't help to pretend it didn't happen and skirt around the subject. They were killed in a car accident. I know that. I don't pretend otherwise. It doesn't hurt any more.'

But it did, of course. It still hurt like hell. He still had bad dreams about it and felt gutted because of it. He would never forget it.

'You don't love me, do you?'

'I'm not a young man, Diane. I love you in my fashion. But it's not the kind of love that you feel when you're twenty or thirty. You shouldn't worry about it.'

'I worry, Marty. I think I'm too hard for you. I don't have any children and I live for my work and I sometimes forget to be a woman in the way that I should be. Oh, I know I'm good in bed, I make you happy that way, but I sense that that's not enough for a man like you and so we'll never be close – or not as close as we should be. It's in *me*, Marty. I *know* it! I'm too intense for my own good. I've no children and I'm into my forties and that's made me too self-obsessed. I can't help myself any more. It's just what I've become. I lost my father and I'll never have a child and so the work's all I have – that and the sex. That isn't love, Marty. It's a way to exist. It's a way to keep fear outside the door, but it doesn't let too much warmth in. I want you in my life. I think I need you, but I know you don't love me. You want me – you might need me as well – but you can't really love me because you sense I'm never quite here. I hate that in myself, but I can't help it; it's just what I am. Do you love me even a little?'

'More than that,' he said meaning it, but disturbed by

her outburst, knowing just how troubled she could be and wondering what it might lead to. 'I feel deeply for you, Diane, but I'm not that young any more. It's just different, that's all.'

She stared steadily at him, her eyes as bright as diamonds, then they softened as she smiled and leaned back, letting her hand slip from his. 'Well, then,' she said, sounding calmer, back in control. 'That's all I needed to hear. A woman needs to know certain things.'

'Are you all right?'

'I'm fine.' She smiled contentedly, brushed the blonde hair from her green eyes, glanced distractedly around the kitchen, then returned her gaze to him. 'You know, for a working-class lad, you're really a very sophisticated man. How did you manage it?'

'I didn't know that I had.'

'You're a man who's never known his own virtues and that can be dangerous. I sometimes worry about you.'

'It's nice to know that you do.'

She smiled again and nodded. 'It's nice to have a man who knows how to be nice all the time. Aren't I the lucky one?' It was a rhetorical question, requiring no answer. 'So what are you planning for today while I get on with my worthless work?'

Relieved that the conversation had lightened, he said, 'As a matter of fact, I'll be seeing my admirer, Paddy Kearney. Him and a bunch of other old friends. We're meeting in the West End.'

'Again?'

'Pardon?'

'You seem to be having a lot of those meetings these days.'

'Every two months. We decided that it might be a good idea to get together on a regular basis – a kind of old boys' club. Just to shoot the breeze, as it were, keeping in touch with each other.'

'I didn't think you were the kind to have regular nights out with the boys.'

'It's not a night out: it's a lunch. A get-together with

old friends from the regiment, to share a few reminiscences.'

'Invite a belly-dancer along, do you?'

Marty smiled. 'No. And no strippers either. Apart from the booze and the bullshit, it's a fairly pure lunch.'

'I'm sure there's a lot of bullshit flying around.'

'It's a regimental tradition.' He glanced at his wristwatch. 'Anyway, I'm dropping into John's office first, for a cup of tea and a chat, so I'd better get going.'

'Yes, you do that,' Diane said sardonically, then added with a good American accent: 'Y'all have a good day, now.'

Marty put on his jacket, threw his raincoat over his right arm, kissed Diane full on the lips, then left the apartment.

The lunch had already started when he entered the pub in Soho and took the stairs up to the lounge bar hired for the occasion. Entering the room, which was already filled with cigarette and cigar smoke, he found his friends seated at a table that ran almost from wall to wall, under two antique chandeliers, surrounded by fading paintings and a few modern lithographs. There was an L-shaped bar in one corner of the room, now covered with empty glasses – Marty had missed the welcoming drinks – but wine was being poured as two ladies in black dresses and white aprons served the starters.

So deep were some of the men in conversation that they hardly noticed Marty's late arrival; others waved at him and called out rude greetings. Waving back, he took his seat beside Paddy, at the place of honour at the end of the table, facing Taff and beside Tommy Taylor, now nicknamed 'TT' by his mates.

'You made it,' Taff said as Marty took his seat. 'I thought you'd got lost in the Big Smoke.'

'I'm amazed you two made it here at all,' Marty replied. 'You both being country boys and not used to big city ways.'

'London's a pleasant change after Oman, I can tell you,' TT responded, his dark eyes flashing admiringly at the waitresses, both of whom were quite young. 'It does my heart good.'

'You're a married man,' Taff reminded him, speaking

softly, his gaze still oddly distracted. 'So keep your eye off those ladies.'

'So sorry,' TT said, in mock contrition.

Though now in his early forties and filling out slightly, Taff, a sergeant, had remained youthful, his baby-blue gaze still distracted, his blond hair still plentiful. Despite his age, he was still a bachelor and loving son who lived at home in Wales with his parents when he wasn't on the base. The mystery of his ice-cold killer's instincts remained unresolved.

TT had been a corporal for some time now, and was the youngest at this meeting, still only in his late thirties, with his dark hair showing no change, matching the brown of his restless eyes. Though he had been quiet and nervous when he first joined the squadrons in Borneo, he had soon gained in confidence and proved himself to be a calm, courageous soldier. He was married with two children, both boys, but even though he talked constantly, affectionately about his wife, he was a bit of a playboy when off the base, always in trouble with some woman and living a complicated private life. Taff, on the other hand, though as far as any one knew not a homosexual, had never spoken about, nor been seen with, a girlfriend. That was a mystery as well.

As for Paddy Kearney, a little older than Marty and still extremely handsome and debonair in his pinstripe suit, his auburn hair was streaked with grey and his flushed face was becoming a little jowly from too much good living. Nevertheless, he was still an attractive man and remained Marty's best friend.

'You're late,' he said, grinning, after Marty had greeted Taff and TT. 'You missed the boozing session beforehand, but we drank your share. Hence the flushed, happy faces.'

'Then I guess I don't have to apologise. I did you a favour.'

'True enough, but it isn't like you to be late. Anything special?'

'No, not really. I just dropped in to see Johnny and forgot the time.'

'So how is your only son? For that matter, how are Lesley and Kay? I trust they're all doing swimmingly.'

'No problems, touch wood,' Marty replied, after sipping his wine and sampling his avocado vinaigrette. 'They're all doing fine.'

In fact, though his family was okay, he was having problems in believing how old they were. His son, John, a professional architect, had recently moved from Surrey to London to be a partner in a West End business specialising in the renovation of houses into flats. Now married with a wife and two children, both girls, he seemed particularly stable, satisfied and good-humoured. On the other hand, Marty's daughter, Kay, had studied to be a schoolteacher – her ambition since childhood – but married impulsively, at eighteen to a fellow student, Stanley Turrell from Leicester. A decent but weak young man, he had taken her off to Leicester as soon as he'd obtained his degree, which was one year before she was due to obtain her own, thus putting paid to her dream of being a teacher. Now he taught at a school in Leicester, took too many days off sick, was often in hot water with his superiors, and backed the horses too often with the housekeeping money while Kay looked after their three children, two girls and a boy. Though loving the kids, she was bitter about her lot and losing her glow. As for Lesley, the same age as Marty, she was healthily plump, grey-haired and maternal, older than her age. Still living in their old house in Weybridge, she led a busy social life, filled with charitable activities, including lots of socialising. She always insisted to Marty when they met, which they did about once a month, that she was happier living alone, in charge of her own life. He was inclined to believe her.

Nevertheless, he found it hard to accept that the years had flown so fast and his world changed so much. Even Ian, if he had lived, would have been almost sixteen years old. This was a frightening thought.

'And Diane?' Paddy asked with a teasing grin, always having had his doubts about her emotional stability and so expecting to hear the worst each time he and Marty met.

'Fine as well,' Marty replied blandly, though in truth this morning's outburst had made him wonder.

'Still trying to dig out political corruption wherever she sniffs it?'

'You bet,' Marty said.

'She has a particularly jaundiced view of politicians and politics, as I recall.'

'She has good reason for it,' Marty said. 'In the past few years she's covered Bloody Sunday, the bombing of the Para headquarters at Aldershot by the IRA, the so-called *inhumane* interrogation techniques of the greens in Ulster, the Munich Olympics massacre and the Watergate scandal. She also went on the election trail with Harold Wilson, which made her even more cynical. She investigated the murder of Lord Lucan's nanny, the attack on his wife and Lucan's subsequent disappearance which she reckons was aided and abetted by his highly placed friends, most of whom she despised. Last but not least, she recently flew to Vietnam to cover the fall of Saigon and the evacuation of the American Embassy. What she has to say about US involvement in that affair is best not described.'

Paddy laughed. 'She's some lady,' he acknowledged, then shook his head as if bemused. 'That's a very unusual relationship you have there, Marty. I must say, it intrigues me.'

'It may intrigue you, but it satisfies me, so I'm happy enough to be involved. How are things with you?'

'Angela sends her love. The kids are no longer children. Life runs on rails as smooth as a skating rink and my fingers are crossed that it stays that way.'

'How's the film production business?'

'Excellent. The dramatic increase in worldwide terrorism has only made our customers more keen to have counter-propaganda documentary films, which is what we supply them with. Since most terrorist groups are Marxist-based, I have no qualms at all.'

'Diane was talking about that very subject this morning,' Marty said as the used plates were removed, the main courses were placed on the table and the wineglasses were topped up. 'She said Marxist terrorist groups are proliferating worldwide and the IRA are probably involved with them.'

'She's right on both counts,' Paddy replied. 'Have you ever heard of Terrorist International?'

'I don't think so.'

'It's supposed to be an umbrella group for international terrorists, with strong roots in Colonel Gaddafi's Libya and the Soviet Union. I think Gaddafi supports the IRA and has trained some of its men. I'd like to make a documentary about that relationship, but unfortunately the British government doesn't approve of me and won't give permission.'

'Why not?'

Paddy grinned. 'They think I'm sticking my nose in where I shouldn't. Trading with heads of state who'd normally be the sole province of their ambassadors. But, given how inept our ambassadors usually are, I've no qualms about the British government either.' He tucked into the main course, roast beef, talking as he did so. 'Well, Marty, I hope you're pleased that you managed to get your informal association off the ground. This is quite a turnout.'

'Yes, I'm pleased,' Marty said. These lunches, which had begun eighteen months ago, were not, as he had told Diane, just casual get-togethers between old SAS friends. Though arranged as social events, their specific purpose was to enable this carefully selected group of individuals to discuss matters of concern relating to the regiment. Marty had personally arranged this about a year after returning from Oman. Most of those approached by him were NCOs who had openly complained about certain directions the regiment was taking or, in particular instances, had been forced to take by the mandarins of Whitehall or the Head Sheds in the Ministry of Defence. The function of the organisation was to have those grievances aired, decide if they were justified and, if they were, find a means of dealing with them. This was done by a variety of methods, including private conversations with SAS officers in a position to deal with the matter; passive resistance to unpopular directives by NCOs with a great deal of clout; and the leaking of information to friendly officers in highly placed positions or, when that didn't work, to the media.

'I have to tell you,' Paddy said, resting his knife and fork on his plate, 'that while I'm proud to be a part of this, and think we're doing good work, I *do* worry that we're too close to the edge. For the NCOs to bring pressure to bear on officers is, I believe, pretty reasonable. But when you do it with a group of NCOs who're actually part of what is, to all intents and purposes, a *secret* association, then obviously you're bordering on the unethical. Indeed, it might even run counter to the very principles that we're trying to uphold. And this association *is*, if I may say so, a secret one.'

This was true enough. Though the Association existed neither on paper nor in any official way, those who joined it had to vow that they would not discuss it with anyone not a member. To make the security even tighter, only those deemed almost certain to join were approached and, even then, cautiously – during informal conversations with the recruiting NCO, sometimes over a period of months, until he was certain that if the subject was raised the possibility of a rejection would be minimal. So far, this careful recruiting technique had ensured that no one finally asked to join had refused, which meant that only those in the organisation knew of its existence. In other words, it *was* a secret association and Marty could not deny the fact.

'I think you'd agree,' he said instead, 'that secrecy is unavoidable under certain circumstances – the defence of the realm, for instance.'

'I agree,' Paddy said.

'Well, since what we're doing is for the good of the regiment, which in turn is for the defence of the realm, the secrecy of this informal association is justified. Without the secrecy, we simply can't operate and that's all there is to it.'

'I'll accept that,' Paddy said, 'but what worries me more is the leaking of information to the media when we feel they'll have more sway than we have. Whether or not we approve of them, regimental policies are the regiment's business and shouldn't be leaked to the media just because we personally disapprove of them and want to bring outside pressure to bear.'

'I disagree,' Marty said. 'Even as long-serving NCOs, we can only bring a certain amount of pressure to bear. The media, on the other hand, can embarrass those in power and cause them to change their tune where we can't. So if we find that our attempts to correct a harmful policy are ignored, I think we're justified in leaking the details to the media in the hope that those hacks can do what we can't. We've done it more than once in the past few months and it worked every time.'

'The end justifies the means.'

'Exactly.'

Paddy sighed. 'I'm not sure that I agree, but I'm willing to go along with it for now, in the absence of anything more constructive. But please be careful, Marty, that you don't make a big mistake. You have a strong moral streak and are easily outraged, but don't let it make you overstep the mark with this association. In the end, all secret organisations are dangerous, open to corruption. Don't let that happen here.'

'I won't,' Marty promised.

Paddy grinned and nodded. 'So what's the main item on the agenda today?'

'The subject we first raised at the last meeting: a way to help men who've left the regiment, can't find work elsewhere, and are being shamelessly ignored by the government. I think I have an idea.'

'I can't wait to hear it.'

Over brandy and cigars, Marty read out the complaints he had received in the past two months. Most of them had common ground: the increasing tendency of those in power to use the regiment for dubious or unsavoury purposes, such as tasks more suitable to policemen or anti-riot police; special training of the armed forces of foreign powers with dubious political aims; and surveillance that increasingly came close to infringing the rights of the individual in a democratic society.

This led to a heated debate on the very subject that Paddy had just been discussing: how far the Association could go in combating such tendencies and whether leaks to the press were justified. In the end, after more heated discussion, the vote was that in this particular instance the end justified the means and that the leaks should continue.

This matter was followed by complaints about the fascistic, self-serving or otherwise damaging attitudes of certain SAS officers, NCOs and troopers, with discussions about how best they could be dealt with. In most cases, this involved little more than deciding which two or three of those present would approach the individuals in question to demand that they mend their ways and, if they refused, devise ways of bringing pressure to bear.

Finally, Marty raised the subject of retired SAS members who could not find decent work and were being ignored by those in a position to help officially. To counteract this, he proposed starting a company that would supply the growing demand for men highly trained in commercial security. Such a company, he explained, could also work for the heads of state in troubled countries, as personal bodyguards, as military advisors or as intelligence agents who could detect and then prevent a *coup d'état* before it took place.

This proposal generated a great deal of contentious debate over the brandy and cigars. In Paddy's view, it was tantamount to the creation of a private police force and, in the case of foreign heads of state, smacked of mercenary activities. Though Marty argued loudly against this, insisting that his proposed company would not seek to exert political influence and would work only for those whose politics were democratic, Paddy insisted that the matter be looked into more carefully and that the subject be raised again at the next meeting. When this was put to the vote, the vote came down on Paddy's side and Marty, though frustrated that he couldn't get going immediately, was pleased that it had at least come this far.

With the business of the day completed, the men around the table were able to relax and enjoy another couple of hours of drinking and talking, this time about less important, more cheerful matters.

That evening, when Marty returned to Bradbury Lines, he learned that the SAS was to be deployed in Northern Ireland and that he was one of those who would be going. This news made his day.

CHAPTER THIRTY-TWO

The SAS men selected for duty in Northern Ireland were shipped into Belfast from Liverpool, arriving in the early hours of the morning when dense mist still clung to the harbour. All were wearing civilian clothing – rollneck sweaters, bomber jackets, blue jeans, scuffed shoes – and carrying their personal belongings in deliberately battered, dirtied shoulder bags. Every one of them, however, though looking like a normal passenger, had a Browning High Power handgun holstered in the cross-draw position under his jacket.

After waiting in the lounge bar until the other passengers had disembarked and disappeared from the bleak quayside, Marty and his friends marched down the gangplank to the quayside. There they were surrounded by a protective cordon of RUC (Royal Ulster Constabulary) guards wearing flak jackets and armed with 5.56-millimetre Ruger Mini-14 assault rifles. As the new arrivals waited there, cold and windblown, seeing rain-drenched warehouses, huts, tanks and ugly prefabricated buildings emerging spectrally from the thinning mist, with the walls of the harbour rising out of filthy black water and stained a dirty brown by the elements, their Bergen rucksacks were unloaded and heaped up on the quayside. When the unloading had been completed, the RUC sergeant in charge of the guards waved his right hand and a green minibus emerged from the car park to stop right beside them. It was driven by a man wearing civilian clothing. Without introducing himself, he indicated that the newcomers should pile into the back of the minibus. When they had done so, one of the RUC guards slammed the door shut and the minibus moved off, heading into the mean streets of Belfast.

It was a once attractive city devastated by the Troubles, with bricked-up terraced houses, streets blocked off with barricades manned by heavily armed British Army soldiers in DPM clothing, crude paintings on the walls showing the customary propaganda of civil war – clenched fists, hooded men holding weapons, the various insignia of the opposing paramilitary groups – and defiant phrases such as NO SURRENDER! and SMASH SINN FEIN! scrawled in white-painted large letters on rusting corrugated-iron fences stretched across strips of waste ground to divide one warring side from the other.

Luckily, the minibus was soon out of the city and racing along the M1, surrounded by a more soothing landscape of gently rolling green hills. It soon became apparent, however, that those hills were not as safe as they looked. In fact, they were dotted with British Army observation posts and the sky was, at this time in the morning, being criss-crossed with the AH-7 Lynx helicopters that were inserting replacements and lifting out the soldiers already there. Those OPs, Marty knew, never received their resups by road, only by air – an indication of just how dangerous that peaceful-looking terrain actually was.

Eventually the minibus left the motorway and made its way along a narrow, winding lane to the picturesque village of Bessbrook where, in the old mill, the British Army had taken up residence. Located only four miles from the border, in an area of south Armagh where Catholic and Protestant death squads were killing people wholesale, the camp was hidden behind high stone-and-corrugated-iron walls topped with barbed wire and broken up by a series of concrete sentry boxes under sandbagged roofs and camouflaged netting. When, after passing through eerily whining, electronically controlled gates, the minibus stopped inside, the SAS men clambered out and found themselves in a bleak compound filled with Portakabins, Saracen armoured cars, tanks, Bedford trucks, RUC policemen with flak jackets and Ruger assault rifles, members of the British Army Sapper unit, and regular British Army soldiers with stun and smoke grenades on their webbing, most in DPM clothing and carrying M16 or SA-80 assault rifles.

'I feel like I'm in prison,' TT said. 'Look how high those walls are.'

'They're that high,' an unfamiliar voice said, 'because the IRA's flavour of the month is the Russian-made RPG Seven short-range anti-tank weapon.' Glancing to the side, Marty and the others saw a broad-shouldered British Army sergeant-major grinning at them, his thick legs outspread, a clipboard under his right arm. 'The RPG Seven,' he continued, 'can hurl a rocket-propelled grenade in an arc with an effective range of five hundred metres. But with walls so high, the IRA would have to come dangerously close to the base to get the elevation required for such an attack. Those walls keep 'em at bay.'

'I'm glad to hear that,' Taff said, offering his slight, distant smile. 'Now I feel right at home.'

'Are you Staff-Sergeant Butler?' the sergeant-major asked.

'Yes,' Marty replied.

'I'm Sergeant-Major Ben Wallace of Fourteen Intelligence Group, the unit you'll be working under. Can I just check your names, please?'

As the men shouted out their names, Sergeant-Major Wallace ticked them off on his clipboard. Satisfied that all were present and correct, he led them into the Portakabin they had been allocated as their basha. Containing no more than rows of steel-framed camp beds and metal cupboards on dusty wooden floors, it was as bleak inside as it was out. Before the men could even begin their ritualistic complaining, Wallace told them to dump their Bergens on their selected beds and then follow him out to the briefing room. This they did, marching to another Portakabin as Wessex Mark 3 and Army Westland Scout helicopters took off noisily from the nearby landing pads. Once inside the Portakabin, they were shown to the briefing room, which was small and packed with folding chairs. A British Army lieutenant was seated at a desk at one end of the room before a large blackboard covered with a map of Belfast and southern Armagh.

When the men were seated, Sergeant-Major Wallace said, 'You lot are on attachment to Fourteen Intelligence Company, which replaced Brigadier Kitson's Military Reconnaissance Force, the MRF, when it was disbanded in nineteen seventy-three after a couple of politically embarrassing incidents. The Fourteen Military Intelligence Company has been given the cover title of Fourteen Field Survey Troop, Royal Engineers, but it's also known as the Northern Ireland Training Advisory Team – NITAT – and the Intelligence and Security Group, or Int and Sy Group. The prime function of the group is intelligence-gathering. We operate out of unmarked Q cars – mainly Morris Marinas equipped with a covert radio and modified to hide a wide variety of non-standard weapons and Japanese photographic equipment. We also operate from static OPs in southern Armagh. Now let me introduce you to Lieutenant-Colonel Raymond LeBlanc, our present CO, who'll explain the set-up to you.'

Wallace stepped aside to let LeBlanc take his place before the blackboard. Surprisingly young, with auburn hair, warm brown eyes and a deceptively frail physique, LeBlanc did not look like a commanding officer, though he had to be one of more than average experience to be in charge of this particular, politically sensitive unit. Marty realised just how experienced the young lieutenant-colonel was when he explained at great length, in considerable detail, exactly what was happening in this troubled country.

At present, LeBlanc explained, there were fourteen British Army battalions in Northern Ireland, each with approximately 650 men, and each deployed in its own TAOR (tactical area of responsibility) or 'patch'. Because the RUC's B Special Reserve were highly suspect in the eyes of the Republicans, their responsibilities had been handed over to the Ulster Defence Regiment (UDR) who were already deeply unpopular with the Catholics, who viewed them as hardline loyalists. For this reason, the UDR were felt by many British Army commanders to be a liability, rather than a help, in hard Republican areas.

The regular Army and the UDR battalions were divided between three brigade HQs – one in Belfast, one in Londonderry and one in Portadown – and came under the command of HQNI (Headquarters, Northern Ireland) in Lisburn. Fourteen Intelligence Company was formed by volunteers from other regular Army units and had one detachment with each of the three Ulster brigades. It operated under a variety of names and, like the original MRF, devoted most of its time to setting up static OPs and observing known or suspected terrorists from unmarked Q cars.

Most of the static OPs were manned by members of 14 Intelligence Company and located in both Republican and Loyalist areas, such as Shankhill, the Falls Road, and West Belfast's Turf Lodge and the Creggan. The SAS would be used mainly for OPs in rural areas, notably the so-called 'bandit country' of southern Armagh, as well as observation and other tasks in Q cars in Belfast, armed with concealed Browning High Power handguns and small submachine-guns, such as the 7.62-millimetre Ingram, which could be silenced if necessary.

'Initially,' LeBlanc continued, 'you men will work under the supervision of Fourteen Intelligence Company NCOs, but when you're familiar with the territory, you'll be allowed to operate on your own. This work will commence this afternoon, once you've settled into your bashas and had your scran. Before that, however, immediately after this briefing, you're to sort yourselves into three-man teams, with at least one NCO to each team. Each of those teams will then be put in the charge of one of our NCOs and allocated a Q car. Are there any questions?'

Marty put his hand up. 'Yes, boss.'

'Yes, Staff-Sergeant?'

'What's the situation regarding the use of weapons?'

'When I step down, Sergeant-Major Wallace will give you general advice about what you can and cannot do in the streets of Belfast. That question will be covered. Are there any more questions?' He glanced left and right, scanning the room, but heard not a word. 'No? Then welcome to Fourteen Intelligence Company, gentlemen. Good Luck. *And be careful*.'

Lieutenant-Colonel LeBlanc sauntered out of the briefing

room as Sergeant-Major Wallace took his place on the stand and studied the men with piercing grey eyes, his pale face like granite. After a suitably dramatic silence, he said, 'Your main task in the Q cars will be observation, not engagement, so you'll only engage the enemy if it can't be avoided. In other words, when your life is obviously in danger and there's no time to make your escape. Does that answer your question, Staff-Sergeant Butler?'

'Part of it, boss.'

'So what's the other part?' Wallace asked in a tone of voice that suggested he already knew what the question was going to be.

'If we have to shoot, do we shoot to kill?'

This was a roundabout way of asking if there was a shoot-to-kill policy and Wallace answered it carefully by saying, 'We all know that shooting to wound rarely stops a potential assassin, so, if you shoot at the man coming at you, you can't take any chances.'

'You mean we aim for the heart?' Taff said.

'Yes, Sergeant, that's what I mean.' Having cleared the deck of that delicate subject, Wallace went on, 'So with regard to reconnaissance out of the Q cars, please bear the following rules in mind. One: as you haven't a hope in hell of passing yourselves off as locals, please don't try it by eavesdropping in Republican pubs or clubs. Two: beware of friendly teenagers, especially the boys, because if they speak to you, no matter how innocent they look, they're almost certain to be in the IRA youth wing and they'll be as ruthless as their elders. Three: never leave your Q car unless absolutely necessary. Four: if you're challenged, don't bother trying to use an Irish accent as you won't fool a soul. Instead, just say "Fuck off!" with conviction. If that doesn't work, get the hell out of there. Those are the main things to remember; the rest you'll pick up once you're out there. Now please gather outside, divide yourselves into groups of three, with at least one NCO to each group, then make your way to the motor pool where I'll assign each group to a particular driver. After that, you can make up your bashas, go for some scran, then meet back at the motor pool for your first tour of exotic Belfast. Okay? Dismissed.'

When the men had gathered outside the Portakabin, milling about in the windy compound filled with Saracen armoured cars, Bedford trucks and tanks, they divided themselves into groups of three as requested. Teaming up with his trusted mates, Taff and TT, Marty walked with them across the busy compound to the motor pool, skirting around groups of flak-jacketed RUC policemen and heavily armed greens. Once in the motor pool, which was filled with civilian cars, they were allocated a red Morris Marina and told to wait beside it. Not allowed to smoke, they stood there fidgeting until Sergeant-Major Wallace walked up to them and stared at them with flinty eyes.

'You're in my charge,' he said. 'After a couple of days touring the streets, when I'm convinced that you all know the area and exactly how to get around it without trouble, you'll be allowed to go out on your own – just the three of you. Once you've learned the business at street level, you, Staff-Sergeant Butler, will be taken out of the Q cars and brought back in to work here in Intelligence. I trust that's satisfactory.'

'I'd rather be in the streets,' Marty replied, shocked at the very thought of being pulled out.

'Tough shit,' Wallace said. 'They want you in Intelligence, so that's where you're going to be. Right now, though, you can have a two-hour break, to make up your bashas and have a bit of scran. Have a shower if you feel like it, but make sure you're still wearing civilian clothes when you return and that you have your Nine-Millies with you. We meet back here at thirteen hundred hours precisely. Enjoy it while it lasts. I'll see you all then.'

When Wallace had walked off, a disgusted Marty and amused Taff and TT went back to their Portakabin to make up their bashas and transfer their personal belongings from their Bergens to the metal cabinets beside the steel-framed beds. They then went to the NAAFI canteen for lunch, enjoyed their scran, followed it with a cup of tea and a smoko, then returned to the motor pool where they found Sergeant-Major Wallace waiting for them, looking rather different, though every bit as rough, in an open-necked shirt, leather jacket, blue jeans and badly scuffed suede shoes. After showing them the contents of the Ford Marina, he took the driver's seat, told them all to get in, then drove them out of the camp, through the high, electronically controlled, corrugated-iron gates, between two heavily reinforced sangars manned by greens with GPMGs and M16 rifles, past the operations room with its closed-circuit TV camera, and out onto the narrow country lane that led from the village to the M1. Their first day had begun.

For the next five days Marty and the others were driven around Belfast by the granite-faced, laconic Sergeant-Major Wallace of the Queen's Royal Lancers, all of them wearing civilian clothes, but with their handguns in the cross-draw position in a holster placed over the ribcage, each with four thirteen-round magazines. Though the Morris Marina looked perfectly normal from the outside, it was actually well equipped for surveillance work.

A Pace Communications Landmaster III hand-held transceiver with a webbing harness, miniature microphone, earphone and encoder, was located near the floor between the two front seats. Also, hidden under the Ordnance Survey map of Belfast that was always spread across Marty's lap, where he sat in the front beside Wallace, was a 35-millimetre Nikon F-801 camera with a matrix metering system, sophisticated auto-focus, electronic rangefinder and long exposure.

Finally, the Q car had been specially adapted to carry a variety of concealed non-standard-issue weapons, including the short, compact Ingram nine-millimetre submachine-gun with detachable suppressor and pull-out shoulder-and-hip stock, ideal for anti-terrorist work. All in all, then, Marty was impressed.

But he was quietly horrified by what he found in Belfast, which he still viewed as being a British city.

'It's about as British as Kenya during the Mau Mau terrors,' Wallace said laconically. 'Here, they'd cut your throat as soon as look at you – and don't ever forget it.'

In fact, Belfast didn't look like a British city at all, but like some Third World country during a *coup d'état*. Though placed in rolling green countryside and surrounded by the Divis Mountain, also known as the Black Mountain, the city was filled with bombed-out, bricked-up houses, police and Army barricades, barbed-wire fences and stretches of waste ground filled with rubble where houses had once stood. Invariably, Wallace drove them along Grosvenor Road, past the Royal Victoria Hospital where, so he informed them, most of those kneecapped or otherwise wounded were treated. Nearing the hospital, they had to pass a police station and regular Army checkpoint, surrounded by high sandbagged walls and manned by heavily armed soldiers, all wearing DPM clothing, helmets with chin straps, and standard-issue boots. Apart from the private manning a light machine-gun, the soldiers were carrying M16 rifles and had stun-and-smoke grenades on their webbing.

Frequently Marty saw soldiers with SA-80 assault rifles keeping a sapper covered while he carefully checked the contents of a rubbish bin. This, Wallace explained, was because of the Provos' Russian anti-tank weapons with their 500-metre range. The Provos used them mainly against police stations, army barracks and Saracen armoured cars, known to the locals as 'pigs'. They also command-detonated dustbins filled with explosives, which is why the sappers had to check all the rubbish bins near police stations and checkpoints.

The hospital itself was an enormous Victorian building guarded by RUC officers wearing flak jackets and carrying the ubiquitous Ruger assault rifles. After being checked by security and parking the Q car, Wallace took Marty and the others inside the building where they found the victims of kneecapping, mostly scruffy teenagers, either sitting in chairs or lying on stretchers, depending upon how bad their punishment had been. The kneecapping, Wallace explained, was a punishment administered not only to touts, or informers, but also to car thieves, burglars, sex offenders and so-called traitors to the cause. Reportedly, the people in the Catholic ghettoes were so terrified of the IRA that when they received a visit from them, saying they had to report for punishment, they actually went to the place selected for punishment of their own accord. Knowing what was going to happen to them, they sometimes tried to anaesthetise themselves beforehand by getting drunk or stoned on Valium.

According to Wallace, you could tell what kind of Catholic you were dealing with by checking just how he had been kneecapped. Pointing out the various kinds of ugly wounds on the knees, ankles and even elbows of those sitting forlornly on chairs or lying groaning on stretchers in the grim hospital corridor, Wallace informed them that if the wound was from a small calibre weapon, such as a .22, which does not shatter bone, and if it was either in a fleshy bit of the thigh or in the ankle, then the victim was only a minor thief or police informer. For something more serious he would be shot in the back of the knee with a high-velocity rifle or pistol, which would sever the artery and blow the kneecap right off. Worst of all was the 'six pack', which meant a bullet in each elbow, knee and ankle, thus putting the victim on crutches for a long time and letting everyone see that the paramilitaries had been particularly displeased with him.

Indeed, the kneecappings had become so commonplace that the victims were even allowed to remove their pants or other clothing so save them from being damaged by the bullets. Turning the punishment into another form of illegal commerce, the paramilitaries, when they had administered their punishment, would call for an ambulance to take the victim to hospital. If subsequently the victim was given compensation from the British government, the very men who kneecapped him would then pay him another visit, demanding part of his compensation. It was a lucrative business.

'So if that's what they can do to their own,' Taff asked, studying the shattered bone and bloody bullet holes of the wounded youths in the corridor, 'what are they likely to do to us if they capture us?'

'Don't ask,' Wallace responded grimly.

They visited the hospital every day to enable Wallace to check the details of the wounded and ascertain whether any of them were his touts or, even better, active IRA or PIRA members who could be interrogated. Leaving the hospital, they drove along the Falls Road to check out the activity on the pavements. The rules for this kind of reconnaissance were simple and undeviating. All journeys had to be planned carefully to avoid enemy territory wherever possible. The Q car was never to be left alone in the streets. If it was, it would be vandalised by the kids, stolen for joyriding – to be sold, or to be used by one of the paramilitary groups – or blown up by the Army on the grounds that it might contain a bomb. Even if left in a secured location, when they returned to it, they were to approach it from behind and bounce it on its springs, to trigger the bomb that might have been planted under the driver's seat.

When driving, they had to keep the windows locked at all times. If parked at a red light and approached by anyone, they were to go through the red light and keep going until out of sight. If approached by someone before they could move off, they were to snap, 'Fuck off!' and, if the stranger didn't do so immediately, drive away as quickly as possible. Finally, if they knocked someone down when in paramilitary territory, they were not to stop. If they did, Sergeant-Major Wallace explained grimly, they would almost certainly be killed.

Following these rules, they drove all over the city, familiarising themselves with it, adopting to its grim, threatening nature. Invariably, they would drive around Turf Lodge to Andersonstown, then back to the Falls Road. Looking like parts of London after the Blitz, those two areas contained rows of terraced houses with their doors and windows bricked up and gardens piled high with rubble. The pavements outside the pubs and certain shops were barricaded with large concrete blocks and sandbags. The windows were caged in heavy-duty wire netting as protection against car bombs and petrol bombers. Men and youths loitered on street corners, heavy housewives trudging wearily in and out of shops, and grubby children swarmed over burnt-out cars like flies over turds, smashing the remaining windows with sticks and screaming like banshees.

Even worse was the Falls Road, the Provo heartland and one of the deadliest killing grounds in Northern Ireland. In 'the Falls', everyone looked poor and suspicious, particularly the gangs of aggressively menacing, scruffy young men – the so-called 'dickers' – who stood on street corners, keeping their eyes out for the SF patrols or suspicious strangers. Invariably, with the gangs, there were young people on crutches or with arms in slings, having been kneecapped or shot in the elbows for some infraction or other.

The 'war zone', as the Falls was known to the SF, was always clogged with armoured Land Rovers. British Army barricades, topped with barbed wire and protected by machine-gun crews on Saracen armoured cars, or 'pigs', blocked off the entrance to many streets, with the foot soldiers heavily armed and looking like extraterrestrials in their DPM uniforms, boots, webbing, camouflaged helmets and chin-protectors. It was their job to check everyone entering the barricaded areas and, in many instances, take them aside to be searched. This they did with brisk, ruthless efficiency, making no friends with anyone.

The traffic in the Falls headed up towards the distant Cave Hill, the black taxis packed with passengers too frightened to use public transport or walk. When the grey-painted RUC mobiles or British Army Saracens passed by, Marty noticed that the officers were carefully scanning the upper windows and roofs on either side of the road, looking for possible sniper positions.

Even after five days of relentless driving around the city, Marty still found it hard to believe that what he was seeing was taking place on British soil. His feeling of disbelief was in no way eased by the many glimpses he had of static OPs with high-powered cameras on the roofs of tall buildings, recording every movement in these streets. The OPs were manned by soldiers of the 14 Intelligence Company armed with GPMGs and M16 rifles, the barrels always resting lightly on the sandbagged walls. They were equipped with a high-power telescope, state-of-the-art surveillance cameras and computers linked to vehicle registration and suspect-information centres. Each OP was backed up with another consisting of two to four soldiers and located near enough to offer immediate firearms support. Both OPs were in turn backed up by a QRF, or quick-reaction force, of soldiers or police, sometimes both, located at the nearest convenient SF base, which would respond immediately to a radio call for help.

Rather than being hidden from the people they were spying on, the OPs were deliberately given high visibility to remind the locals of their presence. This placed certain constraints on those being watched and, at the same time, allowed those doing the watching to check the movements of suspected terrorists and their friends. This in turn allowed the collators of intelligence at Lisburn and brigade headquarters – including SAS green slime – to investigate links between meetings of particular individuals and subsequent terrorist activities.

Marty also learned from Wallace that there were miniature spy cameras in the ceilings of suspected IRA buildings and bugs on the telephones.

Most times, when Wallace stopped the Q car, he would ask Marty to hand him the Nikon camera, then he would take photographs of specific persons or locations. Sometimes, just to show Marty and the others how dangerous the place was, he would deliberately let those he was photographing see him doing so. Invariably his subjects were groups of youths standing outside bookies', shops or pubs – some with long hair, some with heads closely shaven, all wearing an assortment of casual jackets with trousers rolled up high enough to reveal big, unpolished boots. Usually, when seeing the camera, the youths would start across the road towards the car, looking aggressive and threatening. At such times, Wallace always handed the camera back to Marty and raced the car away just before the youths managed to reach it and do some damage.

'They'd kick the shite out of us,' Wallace said, 'if they got their hands on us. They might even kill us. Those dickers are on their own killing ground and damned well they know it. They'd have good protection.'

In many ways, however, the Protestant heartland of Sandy Row was just as bad as the Falls. It was a busy road, lined on both sides with shops and pubs, the pavements bustling with shabby-looking pedestrians and the same kind of loiterers who had been so prevalent in the Catholic ghettoes. Wallace often stopped the Q car there, to take pictures of the men entering and leaving certain pubs which were, as he explained, UDR watering holes serving hardline loyalists who did as much damage as the IRA and so had to be watched.

One of those groups, Wallace explained, had a 'collection day' twice a week, when they demanded so-called 'protection money' for a loyalist splinter group. Indeed, the whole city, according to Wallace, thrived on protection rackets not much different from those of Al Capone or the present-day Mafia. Anyone in business in the ghettoes had to contribute, whether or not they liked it. Falls Road cabbies made weekly payments to the IRA. Protestants in Shankill – the owners of pubs, shops, betting shops, and those in the building trade – paid similar to the UFF or UDA.

Though Marty did not have to defend himself that week with his handgun, he and the others were given a good example of the violence of the city and how it was dealt with when, during the evening of the fifth day, they learned that some Catholic youths, approaching a Morris Marina parked near the Divis flats, had been shot by men wearing civilian clothes and armed with handguns. Though the identity of the men had not yet been ascertained, it was widely believed in the Catholic community that they were British Army soldiers. Subsequently, riots had broken out in the area.

'I think you better see this,' Wallace told the others.

Driving out of Sandy Row, he took the Donegall Road, then cut through the Broadway until they were back in the Falls. In a darkness illuminated by streetlamps, it looked even more dangerous than it had during the day, with gangs of youths and older men standing on street corners, many drinking from cans or bottles, all clearly aggressive. The bricked-up doorways and boarded-over windows were only rendered more ominous by the light-streaked darkness. Children smashing parked cars without reprimand from frightened passers-by seemed like scavenging animals. The flak-jacketed RUC officers and heavily armed soldiers at the sandbagged barracks and barricaded streets, all watchful, never smiling, seemed like faceless men in a bad dream.

Even before the tower block came into view, the crimson glow of flames was illuminating the dark, cloudy sky and the sound of sporadic gunfire could be heard. When Wallace finally turned off the Falls and reached the wasteground where the Catholic youths had been shot, they saw mobiles and foot patrols trawling flats that were being swept eerily by spotlights. The red glow in the sky came from a series of bonfires deliberately set ablaze to block the paths of the mobiles and Saracens, as well as frustrate the charges of the soldiers in flak jackets, Perspex-visored riot helmets and reinforced leg and arm shields.

Other fires were caused by the Molotov cocktails being thrown by gangs of teenage dickers. People were screaming when struck by rubber bullets. Others were racing out of clouds of CS gas with eyes streaming. Housewives were drumming bin lids on the concrete floors and balconies, children and youths were throwing stones and dropping bricks on the mobiles stopped by the bonfires, and unseen men were sniping on the soldiers keeping watch while their mates smashed in doors with sledgehammers and dragged out kicking, punching youths for transportation in RUC vans to the detention block at Castlereagh. Before being thrown into the paddy wagons, the youths' ankles were chained together to prevent them from kicking out or running away, but they still managed to scream a lot of abuse.

'What happens when they get taken in?' Marty asked.

'Let's go see,' Wallace replied.

He turned the car around and drove away from the hellish scene, out of the Falls, back through the city centre, across the Albert Bridge, then along the A23 to Castlereagh. Arriving at the detention barracks just before eight they were directed to the rear of the building by an armed RUC guard. Wallace parked the car in what looked like an enormous yard, like an empty car park, with a high brick wall running along one end. He turned the ignition and headlights off, leaving them in darkness.

'Any minute now,' he said, checking his wristwatch. 'This happens every single night, riots or no riots. It happens to all those picked up.'

Suddenly, a series of arc lights flared into life along the top of the wall the car was facing, bathing the wall and the ground in front in a dazzling light. Less than a minute later, a couple of armed RUC officers emerged from a door at one end of the wall to take up positions at both ends of it, about twenty feet away, covering it with their Rugers. When they were in position, first one, then two, then finally a whole group of dishevelled youths were coaxed out through the door and along the base of the wall by another RUC officer. When some of the youths, either blinded by the light or frightened, took a step back, the RUC officer prodded them forward with his baton. If this failed, he gave them a light blow with it, and this always worked. Eventually, the youths, nearly a dozen, were standing along the whole length of the wall, equidistant apart, in an eerily dreamlike chiaroscuro.

As the youths were standing there, squinting into the light, another, blue-painted Morris Marina inched forward out of the darkness beside Wallace's car, its headlights turned out, its motor turning over quietly, and stopped just out of range of the arc lights. At barked commands from one of the RUC officers, the youths were made to step forward one by one, stand there for about a minute, then step back against the wall again. Occasionally, the horn of the blue Morris Marina would toot when a youth stepped forward, and he would be marched away from the line-up and taken back inside the building.

'The men in that blue Morris Marina,' Wallace explained quietly, 'will be the ones who shot those Catholic kids earlier on. They probably did it when their parked car was surrounded and the kids were becoming aggressive or maybe even attacked them. Each time that horn's tooted, it means that one of the men in the car has recognised one of those kids as being at the scene of the incident. Those particular ones will be interrogated and possibly put on trial. The others will be set free later tonight.'

The process continued until the last youth in the line-up had stepped forward and been ordered back. Then the remaining youths were marched back in through the doorway for release and return to Belfast. When the last of the RUC officers had followed the young men through the door, the arc lights blinked out and the wall disappeared in the darkness.

Staring at the wall, trying to adjust to that total darkness, Marty had the eerie feeling that he was in a foreign country where the laws of civilised society no longer applied, where the normal rules of war had changed, and where honourable men had to do dishonourable things in order to win. He was one of those men and he didn't like the thought, but he believed that the end justified the means and that belief would sustain him. He was here to fight a very dirty war and that was what he would do. This was just the beginning.

'So that's it,' Wallace said, turning on the ignition of the Q car. 'Your breaking-in week is over. From tomorrow, you two in the back will be on your own.' He turned on the car's headlights, illuminating that grim wall, then turned his head slightly to grin at Marty. 'As for you, Staff-Sergeant Butler, tomorrow morning you'll report to the HQ at Bessbrook to commence your work with the green slime. No more street life for you.'

'Shit!' Marty exclaimed.

'That's exactly what it is,' Wallace replied, 'and unfortunately you're going to have to eat it. They have a special job for you.'

He turned the car away from the dark wall and drove back through the stormy night.

CHAPTER THIRTY-THREE

Already immersed in the esoteric language of the SAS with its bashas, bukits, casevacs, crap-hats, Head Sheds, percentage players, Ruperts, spiders, scran and wads and mixed-fruit puddings, Marty soon found himself having to adapt to another language altogether. Here, where the green slime of the Kremlin worked hand-in-glove with the spooks of 14 Intelligence company, Marty was plunged into the murky world of MIOs and Milos and Fincos and COPS, as well as MI5, MI6, the RUC CID, and touts and turncoats and dickers. He soon learned that this new language covered a multitude of sins, most caused by the constant, bitter conflicts between Army Intelligence, MI5, MI6, the RUC and even the green slime. He also soon learned that the nature of war was changing and that this war in Northern Ireland was dirtier than he could ever have imagined. It was war in a cesspit.

The two main non-military intelligence agencies were MI6, the secret intelligence service run by the Foreign and Commonwealth Office, never publicly acknowledged, and MI5, the security service openly charged with counter-espionage. Neither of these agencies trusted the other and each was always trying to block the other's plans, even where valuable. Likewise, the RUC, which had an almost tribal secretiveness, was running its Special Branch agents with scant regard for the needs or requirements of British Army security. At the same time, the RUC Special Branch was running its own, secret cross-border contacts with the Irish Republic's Gardai Special Branch, which effectively left the other organisations floundering in the dark.

Generally, then, as Marty sound found out, because of this complex web of mutually suspicious and secretive organisations, the few SAS intelligence men in the province, occupying key positions at the Army HQ in Lisburn and elsewhere, were often exposed to internecine rivalries when trying to coordinate operations against the terrorists. This was made even more difficult because the SAS were not trusted either and certainly their presence here was resented.

Every regular Army unit in the province hàd close-observation platoons, or COPs, specially trained for undercover operations; but the SAS had been brought in, among other reasons, because regular Army soldiers had often got into trouble when trying to pass themselves off as Irishmen in the pubs and clubs of the hard men. As the SAS were specially trained for covert operations, it was felt that they could act as watchers more efficiently. Nevertheless, their presence was resented and they often came up against strong resistance when offering proposals.

Indeed, while those few SAS officers struggled repeatedly, usually in vain, to create trusting relationships between allies who did not even trust each other, let alone the SAS, soldiers from other areas were acting as Military Intelligence Officers (MIOs) or Field Intelligence NCOs (Fincos) in liaison with the RUC. Such men and women came from the Intelligence Corps, Royal Military Police and many other sources. The link with each RUC police division was a Special Military Intelligence Unit containing MIOs, Fincos and Milos (Military Intelligence Liaison Officers). Therefore, a MIO or Finco working as part of such a unit could find himself torn by conflicting duties to the RUC, Army Intelligence and MI6.

It was the death of such a Finco that had started the whole bloody mess.

Marty's CO in Intelligence, Lieutenant-Colonel LeBlanc, explained to him that a Finco called Corporal Partridge had been one of the best of 14 Intelligence Company's undercover agents, infiltrating the most dangerous Republican ghettoes of Belfast and collecting invaluable intelligence. Unfortunately, though formally answerable to Military Intelligence, he had been pressured by members of the security service into routing his information to his own superiors via MI5. In doing so, he had innocently sealed his own fate, as well as the fate of six informants. A few weeks ago, he had handed over six first-class sources of information to MI5 and within a week they had all been assassinated, one after the other, by the IRA. Filled with guilt and traumatised, Corporal Partridge committed suicide.

Apart from the shocking loss of so many watchers, including Partridge, the assassinations proved that MI5 had a leak in its system. After investigating the case, LeBlanc discovered that the leak was 14 Intelligence Company's own source, Seamus O'Sullivan, who had always been viewed by the company spooks, or intelligence officers, as a hardline Republican not to be trusted. In fact, as LeBlanc found out upon examination of the facts, O'Sullivan was an active IRA member merely masquerading as a tout in order to pass on intelligence in two directions: valuable intelligence to the IRA, damaging intelligence to MI5. However, having ignored the advice of '14' and used O'Sullivan without its knowledge, MI5, instead of punishing him, had tried to avoid embarrassment by simply dropping him and trying to cover his tracks.

Outraged by this, a young officer with '14', Captain Peter Marsden, who had the reputation of a big-timer – someone working out on the edge and possessed of extreme braggadocio – determined to avenge the deaths of Corporal Partridge and his six unfortunate touts. He did so by driving without permission to O'Sullivan's farmhouse in the 'bandit country' of South Armagh and killing him with a Browning High Power handgun while he was seated at his own kitchen table

'According to one of my touts,' LeBlanc told Marty, 'Captain Marsden has a reputation with the IRA as a percentage player who's willing to take big chances and even bend the law of the land to gain a victory. For instance, he has an exceptional record of capturing IRA commanders in South Armagh and handing them over to the RUC. Most of those captured have insisted that Marsden crossed the border illegally to pick them up and deposit them back in Northern Ireland, where they could legally be arrested. Though Marsden has always denied this, we know it to be true, but naturally we accept his denials and let him get on with it. Nevertheless, such actions have gained him a high profile with the IRA and now, given the style of the O'Sullivan assassination as well as the weapon used – nine-millimetre bullets from a Browning High Power handgun were found embedded in the walls of the victim's kitchen – they're convinced that Marsden is the killer, which I don't doubt for a second.'

'So what's the sting in this tale, boss?'

LeBlanc sighed wearily. 'This war is a filthy business, Staff-Sergeant, and we have to do a lot of filthy things to win it. We close our eyes to the illegal activities of men like Captain Marsden, we use whores to seduce Catholics into turning and becoming our touts, then, when the touts feel they've done too much and are under suspicion, we blackmail them into continuing until they *are* caught. We spy on people. We set up illegal ambushes and say we shot in self-defence. We do all that and an awful lot more and now we want you to help us.'

Though morally outraged by what he was hearing, Marty said, 'I'm all ears, boss.'

Pleased, LeBlanc continued: 'Marsden's high profile is beginning to cause us embarrassment and could lead to serious trouble. We have it from one of our touts that because of the killing of Seamus O'Sullivan, a particularly troublesome PIRA ASU—'

'Pardon?'

'Provisional IRA active service unit.'

'Got it.'

'This particular PIRA ASU of four men, led by Jack Flagherty, has earmarked Marsden for a revenge assassination. We want Flagherty. We've wanted him for years. He's a leading hard man responsible for many deaths, including the six dead sources of Corporal Partridge. Flagherty also rules his own turf in the Falls with an iron fist, spying on his neighbours, holding summary trials in back rooms, and personally supervising the PIRA punishments. We can't afford to let Flagherty damage

Captain Marsden. Apart from personal considerations, it would be a great boost to the flagging morale of the IRA and we can't afford that. So we have to neutralise Flagherty before he gets to Marsden.'

'Which is where I come in.'

'Correct. One of my touts, Finn Riley, lives directly opposite Flagherty's house. Riley's the bookkeeper for his local IRA wing and started raiding the till to finance the high-flown tastes of his mistress. That woman was actually set up to seduce him on behalf of MI5. When the time came for Riley's books to be examined, he needed to replenish the money and tearfully confided in the woman. Naturally, she directed him to a member of MI5 who gave him the money required on the condition that he become a Fred, or a tout, for them – which he did. Now he's growing nervous that his IRA mates will eventually tumble him and he wants out before they do so. We've agreed to set him up in Australia with new indentification in return for the use of his loft for the next couple of weeks. I want you and a couple of your best men to set up an OP in that loft. We'll also put a bug in Flagherty's house, so you can overhear and record everything said there. Flagherty's PIRA unit meets three times a week in that house and I'm hoping that your surveillance will produce the information we need to move against him and either put him in Long Kesh or in his coffin.'

'How do we get into the loft?' Marty asked as professionally as possible, concealing the fact that he was disturbed to be involved in such a murky, immoral business.

'I'll call for a cordon-and-search sweep of the lower Falls Road, with particular emphasis on that street. This will be a big sweep, using hundreds of troops. We'll make a show of searching every house, throwing the occupants out into the street until the job's completed. While the houses are empty, we'll insert you and your men into Riley's loft, directly facing Flagherty's place. At the same time, we'll bug Flagherty's house with a miniaturised microphone probe turned to the STG surveillance equipment in your OP.'

'Sounds good, boss,' Marty said, though he still had his doubts about the morality of this kind of operation, which seemed a long way from honourable warfare.

'I'm not finished yet,' LeBlanc responded. 'Flagherty also has a country cottage in South Amargh, close to the border. He holds some of his PIRA meetings there and, we believe, sometimes uses it to store ammunition. While you men are keeping tabs on his house in Belfast, another two surveillance teams will be setting up rural OPs overlooking his cottage, one on the road that leads to Belfast, the other on the road leading to Dublin. Based on information we receive from the three OPs, we'll decide just where and when to move against him. The attack will have to be lawful as well as highly public, so the situation has to be just right. So do you want to be in on this?'

Still filled with doubts, but willing to try anything to get out of this office, Marty said, 'I'm your man.'

He saw the full and awesome might of the state operating against its own citizens when, in the early hours of the following morning, Saracen armoured cars, armoured troop-carriers, or 'pigs', and RUC paddy-wagons rumbled into the lower Falls with their headlights beaming into the darkness. The many vehicles moved ominously past police stations and army barricades along the Falls Road without interference, then broke up into separate columns that turned into three parallel side-streets to begin the early-morning cordon-and-search sweep. Within minutes the area was surrounded and the streets were blocked off.

When the roaring of an approaching helicopter was joined to the rumble of the advancing Saracens and pigs, a youthful 'dicker' looked up, saw what was happening, and shouted a warning, his voice echoing eerily in the silence. Instantly, his mates materialised out of dark doorways and narrow, littered alleys to add their bellowed warnings to his own.

Even as sleepy citizens started opening their front doors, many still wearing pyjamas or dressing gowns, British Army and the 'maroon machine' – Parachute Regiment troops – poured out of the pigs, into dark streets streaked with morning light. Wearing DPM clothing and helmets, but bulked out even more with ArmourShield General Purpose Vests, or GPVs, including ceramic contoured plates, fragmentation vests, and groin panels, they looked like invaders from space. Even more frightening, they were armed with sledgehammers, SA-80 assault rifles and Heckler & Koch MP5 submachine-guns – the last of these being particularly effective in confined spaces. Others, the 'snatch' teams, there to take in the prisoners, looked just as fearsome in full riot gear, with shields and truncheons.

RUC officers wearing flak jackets and armed either with Rugers or batons jumped out of the back of the paddy-wagons and surrounded their vehicles as the soldiers and paratroopers raced in opposite directions along the street, hammering on doors with the butts of their weapons and bawling for the people to come out. Meanwhile, regular Army snipers were clambering onto the sloping, slated roofs of the houses from lightweight aluminium assault ladders to give covering fire, if necessary, with Lee-Enfield sniper rifles. Wearing earphones, they would be warned of any likely trouble spots either by officers on the street or by the Royal Marine Gazelle observation helicopter that was now hovering right above the rooftops, its spinning rotors creating a fierce wind that blew the rubbish along the gutters.

'Get out, you Fenian bastards!' a paratrooper bawled. 'On the bloody pavement!'

Sitting in the claustrophobic interior of a Saracen, beside Taff, TT and Corporal Alan Pearson, their new signals specialist, Marty looked out through the partially open doors and saw the soldiers pushing angry women and dazed children aside to grab their menfolk and haul them out onto the pavement. Other soldiers were forcing their way inside the houses to begin deliberately noisy, destructive searches of the premises.

Shocked to see such a sight on British soil, Marty was even more shocked when, upon the refusal of certain tenants to open their doors, soldiers with sledgehammers smashed them open and then rushed inside, either pushing the tenants back in ahead of them or hauling them out onto the pavement. As the older male residents of the street, most still in pyjamas, were pushed face first against the front walls of their houses and made to spread their hands and legs for rough frisking, women screamed abuse, children did the same or burst into tears, and the youthful dickers further along the street hurled stones, lumps of concrete, and obscene abuse.

Still looking out of the Saracen, Marty saw two of the soldiers grab a suspect wearing pyjamas, haul him away from the wall where he had been frisked, and push him roughly into the centre of the road, where an RUC guard thumped him with a truncheon and forced him up into a paddy-wagon. A single pistol shot was followed immediately by the sound of breaking glass.

'Mick bastard!' a soldier bawled as he cracked a teenager's head with the butt of his SA-80, making him topple back and drop the pistol that he'd just fired wildly in the air. The teenager straightened up, removed his hand from his temple and looked in a dazed way at the blood on his fingers; he was then practically jerked off his feet by the soldier and kicked brutally towards an RUC officer who prodded him up into the paddy-wagon like someone using an electric sting on a cow. 'Get in there, you murderous Fenian bastard!' the RUC man exploded, giving the youth a last blow with the truncheon as he stumbled into the paddy-wagon. Elsewhere, soldiers with riot shields were herding groups of men against the wall and using truncheons to force their legs apart.

'Hands against the wall!' another soldier was bawling, either genuinely enraged or behaving as instructed by his superiors to cause maximum distraction. 'Spread your legs and don't make a fucking move!'

As other soldiers poured in and out of houses, often smashing their way in with sledgehammers, housewives continued to scream abuse and attacked them with their fists, children ran about like wild animals, some laughing, others crying, and the dickers further along the street kept throwing stones and lumps of concrete at the line of soldiers forming a cordon of riot shields across the brightening street.

Suddenly, as Marty was watching another couple of Catholic men being prodded up into the paddy-wagon visible outside the Saracen, the half-open doors were jerked open and Sergeant-Major Wallace appeared with a group of heavily armed paratroopers bunched up behind him.

'Right,' he said to Marty with an urgent wave of his free hand, the other clasping a Sterling submachine-gun. 'Let's go. Your kit's already been taken in, so let's get over there as quickly as possible. Don't stop for anything.'

The four SAS men climbed out of the Saracen. Like most of the army troops, they were wearing DPM clothing, but with camouflaged soft combat caps instead of helmets, and leather-and-Gore-tex Danner boots instead of standard-issue British Army boots. They did not have their Bergens, as these would have been spotted instantly; instead, they were carrying only what kit they could manage on their belts, in their pockets and in their hands. This included fourteen days' high-calorie rations, mostly candy, chocolate and sweets. It also included bivvy bags on the belt, containing changes of underwear and first-aid kit; flashlights and binoculars, also on the belt; and extra ammunition for the only weapons they were allowed on this operation: their Browning handguns and the short Sterling Mark 5 submachine-gun with retractable butt and 34-round magazines, which they were now carrying openly. However, as these alone would not have been enough for this lengthy urban OP, the rest of their kit was being carried to the OP location by an escort patrol from the maroon machine. Some of the paratroopers had already entered the house opposite and were 'mouse-holing' along the single loft space of the terrace to Riley's loft, located directly opposite Flagherty's house. The kit taken in by them included water in plastic bottles; spare radio batteries; medical packs; extra ammunition; cameras and rolls of 35mm film; tape recorders; thermal imagers and night-vision scopes; an advanced laser audio surveillance transceiver; brown, plastic-backed notebooks and ballpens; sleeping bags; packs of moisturised cloths for cleaning their faces and hands; towels, toilet paper, and sealable plastic bags for excrement and urine.

'Let's go!' Wallace snapped.

Protected by the ring of heavily armed paratroopers, temporarily deafened by the roaring of the helicopter hovering right above them, and increasingly shocked by the sheer brutality of the phoney cordon-and-search sweep, Marty ran with the other three across the road, through bawling RUC officers and watchful soldiers, past Saracens and armoured pigs, up onto the pavement on the opposite side. There, as soldiers were dragging reluctant men and women out of their homes, the paratroopers pushed their way into one of the houses. Once inside, a couple of them proceeded to 'search' the place by noisily sweeping ornaments and bric-a-brac off tables and cupboards, removing drawers and tipping their contents onto the floor, and generally smashing the place up, causing maximum distraction, while the others led the four SAS men upstairs to the trapdoor already opened in the floor of the loft. There, one of the hefty paratroopers formed his hands into a stirrup and the four SAS men, led by Wallace, took turns at letting themselves be hoisted up into the dark loft. Once all five were in, the big paratrooper below the trapdoor handed up the rest of their kit. When it was all in the loft, the men divided it between them and then mouse-holed their way along the terrace, practically the whole length of the street, until they reached the space above Riley's house, where the kit already brought in by the paratroopers was stacked around the solid, wooden edges of the dusty floor.

'This is it,' Wallace said, indicating the piled-up kit. 'And there's your OP window.' He pointed to where a slate pin in the roof had been removed and replaced with a rubber band that allowed the slate to be raised and lowered, providing a peephole for the naked eye, binoculars, cameras and thermal imagers. 'One of our signals specialists is putting a miniature microphone probe near the ceiling of the adjoining wall in the house next to Flagherty's without the occupants knowing about it. It'll be tuned to your laser system, and it'll enable you to hear, see and record most of what goes on in that bastard's place. Any last-minute questions?'

'No,' Marty said.

'Right. I'll take my leave now. The best of luck, lads.'

Wallace patted Marty on the shoulder, then made his careful way back along the terrace to the open trapdoor. Marty followed him. After Wallace had dropped through the small, square hole, back onto the landing, Marty replaced the trapdoor, checked that it was secured, then returned to join the others above Riley's house, where he found Taff squinting through the peephole.

'What's happening down there?' Marty asked.

'The greens have got Flagherty out on the pavement and he's going mad. They've just left the house next door, so the probe must be planted. I think the greens'll start pulling out now, taking some prisoners with them just for show. Yes, they've just taken Flagherty.'

'Clever,' Marty said. 'They'll pretend they came here just for him. They'll take him to Castlereagh, interrogate him at length, then release him and let him come home, thinking he's fooled them again. I don't think he'll check his own loft. He'll think this is genuine. And that they're also arresting the tout who owns this place will make the raid seem even more genuine.'

Taff turned away from the peephole and motioned Marty over. 'Here, take a look.'

Before going to the peephole, Marty told TT and Corporal Pearson to start unpacking the kit and equipment. 'And be quiet about it,' he added. 'From this moment on we'll have to be as quiet as mice and make damned sure that we're not heard from below. Loud noises will still be heard in adjoining houses, so keep it down.' Glancing at the adjoining loft, he added, 'That's going to be your bog, so be particularly quiet there. It belongs to the house next door.'

Catching TT's sardonic grin, he went to the peephole, raised the slate and looked down on the street. The hard man he recognised from the intelligence photo as Jack Flagherty was struggling violently and bawling abuse as two soldiers with truncheons dragged him off the pavement and manhandled him up into a paddy-wagon. Another man, who Marty suspected was the tout, Finn Riley, was being half-dragged from the pavement directly below the loft – obviously hauled out of his own house – to be thrown into the same RUC vehicle.

'I think they've got Riley,' Marty said. 'That's good. Flagherty'll now think Riley's also on our wanted list. It'll make Riley look good in the eyes of his mates and they'll be less likely to suspect he's part of this.'

'If they do, he's fucking doomed,' TT said.

'It's a rotten business,' Marty said.

When the doors of the paddy-wagon had been slammed shut on Flagherty and the tout, the people on the pavements bawled even more abuse at the soldiers and RUC officers. But the RUC men were already getting back into their vehicles and the engines were roaring into life.

As the first of the Saracens and armoured pigs moved off along the street, an even louder roaring came from directly above the house. Looking as high as he could through the narrow peephole, Marty saw the Gazelle helicopter flying directly overhead, heading back to Armagh. By the time it had disappeared beyond the parallel rows of rooftops, the last of the Saracens, armoured pigs and RUC paddy-wagons had also disappeared from below, leaving the street to the irate or shocked inhabitants. Some of the women hurried into their houses, only to rush out again, complaining tearfully about the devastation inside.

Disturbed by that sight, Marty dropped the slate back over the peephole and turned back to face the other three in the loft. Taff and TT had already unpacked a lot of the kit and were balefully examining the plastic bags provided for their own shit and piss. Meanwhile, Corporal Pearson was opening the tripod for the audio surveillance transceiver, which would be in his charge. Marty told them to take off their boots, which would cut down on the noise, and not put them on again until it was time to leave the OP.

'I've stayed in better places,' Marty murmured, gazing around the dark, dreadfully cold, cobwebbed loft.

'It's rent-free,' Taff said.

It did not take them long to realise just how uncomfortable their rent-free accommodation was going to be. By the end of the first day and night they felt tired, dirty and cramped, with nerves already stretched to breaking point. When the second day and night had passed, they felt grubby, exhausted, claustrophobic and increasingly tense. Also, the loft was freezing cold, with the snow falling outside, frost on the pavements, and the winter winds howling bitterly. In the loft, minus their boots, they could only wear extra layers of socks, but their feet still froze and their bodies, likewise wrapped in extra clothing, were cold more often than not.

The main problems, however, were domestic. As no food

could be cooked, they had to subsist on dry, high-calorie rations, such as biscuits, cheese, chocolate and sweets. Although they had a couple of thermos flasks of hot tea and coffee, this did not stay hot for long and after that then they could drink only tepid water from plastic bottles. With nowhere to wash, they could only clean themselves with moisturised cloths and clean their teeth, or freshen their mouths, with chewing gum. Even worse, the loft space of the adjoining house was designated as a toilet, with the men shitting and pissing into plastic bags, which they had to seal and store carefully after use. The newcomer, Corporal Pearson, found this business particularly humiliating and never got used to it.

'I promise not to look,' TT whispered the first time Pearson was going for a piss, 'on the grounds that it's probably not worth seeing anyway.'

'Go fuck yourself,' Pearson whispered back, scrabbling carefully over the wooden joists to the next loft, carrying a sealable plastic bag in one hand. 'I don't need your aggro.'

Worst of all, however, was the fact that they could rarely rest properly, being compelled to sleep sitting upright against the brick walls of the loft, wrapped in a blanket for warmth, a cushion under the backside. They rested two at a time, with one sleeping while the other, though nominally resting, kept his eye on the first in case he talked or cried out in his sleep, which would have alerted the neighbours on either side of the house directly below. For these reasons, they were all soon exhausted.

'That friggin' tout down below sleeps more soundly than we do,' Taff whispered to Marty. 'At least he has his own bed.'

Spying through the peephole, they had observed Flagherty and Riley returning together from their brief incarceration in Castlereagh detention barracks. Also, they could hear Riley moving about the house below and could more or less tell what he was doing from the various noises he made: the flushing of his toilet, the voices from his radio and TV, the opening and shutting of doors, drawers and cupboards, even conversations with visitors to the house or on the telephone. From some of these conversations they learned that Riley was becoming increasingly concerned for his personal safety and kept phoning that big-timer Captain Marsden to check when he was going to be lifted out for his promised new life in Australia. They also learned that Marsden, ignoring Riley's fears, was promising to arrange everything only when the SAS men in his loft had finished their work. For this reason, each time Riley phoned Marsden, he sounded increasingly nervous.

'A big-timer and a percentage player in one,' Taff whispered to Marty. 'That Captain Marsden is trouble.'

'I think you're right,' Marty whispered back.

In fact, for Marty the surveillance was a welcome distraction from the more oppressive aspects of the loft, where their movements were severely restricted and they were forced to be unnaturally quiet, talking only in whispers. Unable to release his building tension through the customary bullshit, he concentrated on the surveillance and found himself gradually drawn into the dangerous, murky world of Jack Flagherty and his PIRA cohorts. The surveillance was conducted with a variety of advanced audio-visual aids, including a Thorn EMI hand-held thermal imager, weighing only five kilos, which Marty carried on a string around his neck; a 35-millimetre Nikon F3HP with a heavy-duty titanium body, telescopic lens, and Davin Minimodulux image-intensifier, also used as a night-vision scope; and a miniature fibre-optic probe camera inserted near the ceiling of the wall in the house next door. This interacted with an advanced laser system that picked up the minute vibrations created by conversations in Flagherty's house and transmitted them to the tape recorder in Riley's loft.

When Marty used such instruments, he realised just how advanced technologically the SAS had become and how different this kind of war was from anything he had known before. The kind of war he had fought in the North African desert with the LRDG – an honourable war fought by men who respected the enemy – was now far behind him. That war had been fought out in the open, against a visible enemy; in contrast the war in Northern Ireland was much darker, less human, fought with torture, dirty tricks and advanced technology in back rooms, dark alleyways and dusty lofts. He wasn't at all sure that he approved, but he knew that nothing would stop it. The SAS was heading into the future and that future looked less honourable than the past. Marty was chilled by the thought of it.

Taking numerous photos of Flagherty as he entered and left his house, seeing him magnified through the viewfinder, his every blemish exposed, his every expression exaggerated, and listening in on the many conversations that took place in his house and were picked up by the miniature probe, Marty gradually built up an invaluable, increasingly hair-raising picture of the world of the terrorists and their hunters.

Released from Castlereagh with Riley, Flagherty had returned to his home and called an immediate meeting with the other three members of his PIRA murder squad. During that meeting, every word of which was picked up by the fibre-optic probe, Flagherty confirmed that Captain Marsden, sometimes alone, occasionally with other officers from 14 Intelligence Company, had made numerous illegal trips across the border to snatch wanted IRA men and bring them back to Northern Ireland, where they could be 'captured' by the RUC and imprisoned. Flagherty also had strong reason to believe that Marsden had personally shot Seamus O'Sullivan as retaliation for the deaths of Corporal Partridge and his six Freds, or turncoats. Intending to retaliate in kind, Flagherty was going to assassinate Marsden and seriously damage British morale into the bargain.

Picking up this information, but still needing to know when and where the hit would take place, Marty relayed his intelligence in short-burst transmissions to Lieutenant-Colonel LeBlanc, then resigned himself to more days in Riley's oppressive loft.

Temporary escape from the tension and claustrophobia of the loft came through communication with the outer world by means of the transceiver, operating in the VHF/UHF frequency range, or through the UHG band on the portable radio. Marty and the others were able to do this even when manning the surveillance equipment because they were personally equipped with Davis M135b covert microphones with standard safety-pin attachment and ear-worn receivers, positioned on the collars of their jackets, with the on/off switches taped to their wrists. One of these was tuned into the military command network at Lisburn, where LeBlanc was now stationed; the other to the surveillance network that included the QRFs, or quick-reaction forces, waiting to bail him and the others out of the OP should trouble arise.

Hoping to find out just when and where Flagherty was planning to ambush the troublesome Captain Marsden, Marty continued studying the street in general and Flagherty's house in particular, by day and by night, with the aid of his hand-held thermal imager, the image-intensifier on the camera and, most importantly, the fibre-optic probe camera inserted in the wall of the adjoining house and transmitting back to the STG laser system in the loft. He was able to build up an even more complete picture of exactly what they were doing and how they lived. In the course of this surveillance he learned that although the 'Troubles' may have sprung out of genuine grievances, Belfast was now a city increasingly ruled by graft, blackmail and mercenary violence, with protection rackets proliferating and gangs competing to rule their own patch, rewarding those who pleased them, punishing those who did not, and in general using the political conflict as a route to personal power. In this unsavoury stew, therefore, it was difficult to tell if a man was a sincere 'freedom fighter' or just another gangster.

This difficulty presented itself when Marty and the others observed Flagherty. Certainly, it was evident that he ruled his own street, was given due respect from his neighbours, and received a constant stream of visitors to his terraced two-up, two-down house. Most of the visitors were men, either seasoned PIRA co-workers or adolescent dickers who came to Flagherty for discussion or instruction. It was clear from the conversations that weapons were being handed over and taken back, usually accompanied by murmurs about 'single shot', 'both knees', 'six pack', 'house call', 'post office' or 'bookies', suggesting a combination of PIRA punishments, doorstep assassinations and armed robberies of local establishments. It also appeared, from the conversations, that Flagherty doled out the weapons and that they had to be returned when the job was done.

Money also changed hands. It was usually brought in by the

older men, who would hand it over while mentioning the names of various pubs, fish-and-chip shops, general stores or bookies, occasionally saying things like, 'We fired-bombed some sense into the stupid fucker and now he's really agreeable.'

Finn Riley had visited Flagherty's house once since getting out of Castlereagh, attending a PIRA meeting. During a conversation about 'funds' and 'more money for weapons', the 'books' were mentioned by Flagherty and Riley said he would have them ready soon. When Marty observed that Riley sounded nervous, Taff, sitting beside him at the tape recorder, responded, 'I can understand that – what with us being up in his loft and all. How would *you* feel?'

'I guess you're right,' Marty said.

At least once each day, Flagherty drove with some of the others to his house in Armagh. Judging from some of his bugged conversations, he went there to receive daily supplies of weapons, ammunition and explosives being brought in from across the border, probably in hidden compartments in the vehicles. As it would have been too dangerous for him to use his country house as an ammunition dump, Marty could only assume that the increasing number of trips he was making for those supplies indicated that he was planning some outrage, apart from the assassination of Marsden.

'With that amount of weapons and munitions,' Taff whispered to Marty, 'he could only be planning a major attack on a British Army barracks or RUC police station.'

'That's what I think,' Marty replied. 'And since he keeps mentioning Captain Marsden, it may be against Bessbrook itself. I'm going to talk to LeBlanc.'

But before he could do so Taff, who had been at the peephole, let out a gasp, then glanced back over his shoulder and said, 'Shit! Flagherty and some of his men have just stormed out of his house and are heading for here. They're all carrying weapons.'

'Damn!' said Marty. 'We must have been rumbled. We'll have to fight our way out.'

The first noise they heard from below was the urgent hammering of fists on Riley's front door. They didn't hear Riley opening the door, but the sound of angry shouting from the hallway indicated that Flagherty and his PIRA ASU group had entered and were accosting Riley. Riley screamed, 'No!' and then a pistol shot was heard, followed by the sounds of running feet and the banging of doors. The PIRA team, having shot Riley, were on their way up the stairs.

A woman down below screamed hysterically.

Instantly, Marty ordered everyone to put his boots back on. When they had done so, he told Pearson to get on the radio and call up a QRF. He then told Taff to keep the trapdoor in the adjoining loft covered with his Browning High Power.

'While you hold those bastards at bay,' he said, 'TT and I will pack up this equipment and have it ready for transportation with the QRF. Okay, men, shake out!'

Pearson was already on the radio, calling for back-up from a QRF, when Taff clambered over the joists to press his back against the bricks, raise his knees, and aim his Browning two-handed at the trapdoor of the adjoining loft, his blue eyes bright with the murderous light that Marty had seen so often. Turning away, Marty helped TT to dismantle and repack the valuable audio-visual surveillance equipment. As he did so, he heard footsteps coming up the stairs, then the whispering of men on the landing directly below the trapdoor. Something clattered and then squeaked – obviously a stepladder. Taff released the safety catch of his Browning and held the handgun steady, waiting for the first man to appear.

As Marty and TT continued dismantling the surveillance equipment, placing the separate pieces in reinforced canvas carriers, Pearson finished relaying his message to the RUC station where the QRF was located, then switched the set off and slithered sideways to glance down through the peephole.

'A lot of neighbours coming out of their houses to see what's happening,' he said, speaking over his shoulder. 'Apart from that, nothing.' He withdraw his Browning from its cross-draw position and aimed it at the trapdoor in the adjoining loft, preparing not only to give cover to Taff, but to stay near the peephole and keep alert for the arrival of the badly needed QRF.

Something banged against the wall just below the trapdoor

– obviously a stepladder being placed in position – then it made a muffled drumming sound as someone clambered up it. The trapdoor squeaked and shook a little, then it was pushed open, slamming back onto the floor with dust curling over the outspread fingers of the hand that had pushed it. A man's face appeared, his green eyes too wide as they adjusted to the sudden gloom, then his second hand appeared, holding a Webley Mark 6 handgun, its barrel wavering uncertainly as he tried to take aim.

'Halt!' Taff bawled, obeying the letter of the law by giving a formal warning before he opened fire. 'Security forces!'

The man took no notice. A single shot from his pistol reverberated through the loft and the bullet ricocheted off the wall high above Taff's blond head. The man was firing wild and blind, but that made him no less dangerous, so Marty returned the fire with a double tap. It resounded like a deafening thunderclap in the loft's confined space. The man's hand turned into a mess of spurting blood, torn flesh and shattered bones. He screamed, dropped his weapon, then fell back through the trapdoor, knocking the stepladder over as he crashed to the floor below. The other men down there cursed and bellowed instructions at one another, then a fusillade of pistol fire shot straight up through the ceiling, turning the floor of the loft into a convulsion of flying wood splinters, smashed asbestos and spitting white dust.

After pressing himself into the wall and inching his way around it until he was closer to the open trapdoor, Taff leaned forward and emptied the rest of his thirteen-round magazine, aiming down through the trapdoor. There were more shouts and screams. Satisfied, he pressed himself back against the wall and reloaded with a full magazine as the anticipated volley of return fire came from below, with the bullets smashing up through the floor in more spewing dust, asbestos and wood splinters to ricochet off the roof above his head.

Even as Taff leaned forward to shoot down through the trapdoor hole again, TT was inching forward with his Browning in one hand and a Royal Ordnance G60 stun grenade in the other. When he reached the trapdoor, he pulled the pin, dropped the grenade down through the hole, then threw himself back just as more shots were fired up through the ceiling. Dust and wood splinters were still spitting upward from the floor of the loft when the stun grenade exploded below with a loud bang and a blinding flash. This put an immediate stop to the gunfire, causing the temporarily blinded PIRA team to groan and curse volubly. Before the shocked terrorists could recover from the shock, TT had shuffled forward again, even closer to the trapdoor, with another grenade in his hand.

'Smoke grenade,' he whispered.

Taff glanced at Marty and Corporal Pearson as TT pulled the pin of the smoke grenade and dropped it through the hole. Exploding a second later, the grenade filled the landing below with smoke, making everyone choke and cough, even before it drifted up into the loft. Seeing what was happening and catching Taff's urgent glance, Marty, who had just packed the last item of surveillance equipment, nodded and reached down to another canvas bag, withdrawing four SF10 respirators. When he and the others had put them on to protect themselves from the smoke, which contained elements of burning CS gas, Marty went to the peephole, looked down on the street below, then stuck his thumb up in the air – indicating that the QRF force had arrived.

Wearing his respirator, and with his Browning ready to be fired single-handed, Marty moved forward to the trapdoor hole and looked down onto the smoke-filled landing. The steel ladder was lying on its side where it had fallen, but otherwise the landing was empty. From the ground floor, he could hear the hysterical babble of a woman – obviously the dead tout's wife – and more cursing and coughing from the PIRA men.

Going first as PC, Marty dropped through the hole, landing on his feet on the lino-covered floor just as gunshots were fired out in the street. He moved quickly along the landing, holding the High Power two-handed, kicking the two bedroom doors open, one after the other, and turning into the rooms ready to fire.

Both bedrooms were empty.

As Taff dropped down onto the landing behind him, also wearing his respirator and holding his Browning High Power two-handed, Marty hurried on down the stairs to the short hallway with the front door at one end, a living room to the side. Finn Riley was lying flat on his back on the floor of the hallway, his shattered head pouring blood from a gaping bullet hole. Ignoring him, getting ready to fire, Marty tentatively entered the living room to his right. The room was empty, though filled with smoke and CS gas. He then checked the kitchen and back door. The back door was locked. Satisfied that the whole house was empty, he hurried out to the hallway, just as the fearless Taff was pressing himself against the wall, his High Power still held two-handed, to stick his head tentatively around the doorframe and look into the street where more gunshots were being fired.

Taff disappeared outside. Stepping over Riley's dead body, Marty followed Taff out, dropping low as he did so, swinging the High Power from left to right, covering a wide arc. Women screamed and men shouted as the onlookers scattered. One woman was coughing and wiping her streaming eyes with a handkerchief, a man was squatting on the pavement with blood soaking his head and shoulders – the results, so Marty surmised, of Taff's blind shots down through the trapdoor hole – and a QRF team composed of British soldiers and RUC officers, all wearing flak jackets and carrying assault rifles and truncheons, were pouring out of Saracen armoured cars to take command of the street.

Two other QRF teams had also arrived. One, consisting entirely of British Army troops, was rushing into Riley's house to help TT and Pearson carry out their kit and equipment as quickly, as securely, as possible. The other, composed of flak-jacketed RUC officers, was returning the gunfire of two PIRA men who were covering Jack Flagherty as he dived into the back of his car. One of the PIRA gunmen managed to get into the car, also, but the second was cut down as the car roared off along the street and disappeared around the far corner.

As the dead PIRA gunman was picked off the road by two flak-jacketed RUC officers, some watching women screamed abuse and the men – mostly youths, including some known dickers – started throwing stones, empty bottles and Molotov cocktails, which exploded into yellow flames and black smoke.

Seconds later, an armoured pig came along the street to disgorge special Army riot-control troops. Wearing flak jackets, Perspex-visored helmets and reinforced leg and arm pads, they charged the crowd while holding up black shields and swinging their truncheons.

Again shocked by what he was seeing, scarcely able to believe that it was happening on British soil, Marty tugged the respirator off his face, letting it hang loose below his chin. Standing beside him, Taff did the same, then patted his dust-filled blond hair with fingers equally dirty.

'They found out about Riley,' he said. 'That's what led them to us.'

'I reckon,' Marty replied, shocked and outraged by what was happening. 'Now let's hold the doorway of his house until the others come down.'

Together they backed up to the door of Riley's house. There they stood guard, their Brownings at the ready, while angry youths threw stones and empty bottles at the shields of the riot-control troops, who were breaking up to swarm through the crowd and attack individuals. Minutes later, even as the street battle continued to rage, the QRF troops who had rushed into Riley's house came out again, this time forming a protective circle around TT and Corporal Pearson, both carrying packed-up surveillance equipment, as were some of the soldiers.

When TT and Pearson had been rushed to a waiting Saracen, Marty and Taff left the doorway, rushed across the street, ducking the flying debris, and clambered up into the same vehicle. The doors were slammed shut by one of the soldiers, then the armoured car moved off, leaving the QRF teams and riot-control soldiers to contain the continuing street violence. The Saracen was stoned as it turned out of the street and headed back to Bessbrook.

'What a bloody nightmare!' Marty exclaimed, releasing his anger. 'What the hell are we doing here?'

No one bothered to answer.

CHAPTER THIRTY-FOUR

It was close to midnight when Marty, Taff, TT and Alan Pearson were driven out of Bessbrook in a dark-blue Hiace van to set up a second covert OP overlooking Jack Flagherty's country cottage in the 'bandit country' of South Armagh. Though normally the overt OPs were manned and resupped by helicopter, this one would be left alone during its existence and was being set up in strict secrecy. The Hiace van was, therefore, being driven by a British Army REME corporal in civilian clothing, guarded by a crack marksman of the maroon machine, a hefty man, also wearing normal clothes. The OP's SAS team, on the other hand, were wearing DPM windproof clothing, Danner boots with Gore-tex lining, and soft, peaked, camouflaged combat caps. The exposed parts of their faces, necks and hands were smeared with stick camouflage, suitable for blending in with local foliage.

Stopped repeatedly by army road blocks, the men in the van had to show their IDs, which in this case were genuine. They were always then allowed to proceed. Nevertheless, the many stops slowed them down considerably and it was just after two in the morning when finally they reached their destination.

Flagherty's converted farmhouse was in rolling farmlands surrounded by hills, high enough to afford a glimpse of Carlingford Lough and the Irish Sea. The REME corporal parked the van and killed his headlights in a pitch-black winding lane, then the men hurriedly climbed out and unloaded the equipment guarded by the big paratrooper. No one said a word.

When the unloading was completed, the four SAS men strapped on their heavily laden Bergens, distributed the rest of the equipment between them, then clambered over a fence to commence the long march up a dark, windblown hill. As they did so, the REME driver, still protected by the paratrooper, turned the van around and headed back to Bessbrook.

The men marching up the grassy slopes were heavily burdened indeed, with packed Bergens weighing over fifty pounds and the rest of their weapons, ammunition, equipment, water and rations, either fixed to their webbing or carried by hand to form an even greater burden. The weapons included a GPMG, a couple of L42A1 Lee-Enfield bolt-action sniper rifles with starlight scopes, M16 assault rifles with M203 grenade-launchers, and two 5.56-millimetre Colt Commando semi-automatics with thirty-round box magazines. As the equipment included various surveillance systems and recording machines, as well as a PRC 319 radio, it was a daunting load to carry for any distance.

Following Marty's hand signals, the men advanced up the hill in a well-spaced line. Marty was out front as point man, TT and Corporal Pearson were in the middle to cover both flanks, and Taff was bringing up the rear as Tail-end Charlie.

Marching silently across the dark fields, keeping his eyes peeled for any unnatural movement, Marty could not help thinking about what had led to the rumbling of the urban OP and the dreadful consequences of its discovery by the IRA. Unfortunately, though the British Army in the shape of 14 Intelligence Group had been largely responsible for it, the SAS had not come out of it well either.

The whole damned mess had obviously been started by that big-timer, Captain Marsden, when he assassinated Seamus O'Sullivan, arousing the wrath of the IRA. A sentence of death had been placed upon Marsden and Jack Flagherty's PIRA wing was ordered to carry it out. This matter was only made worse when Colonel LeBlanc of 14 Intelligence Company, though angry with Marsden, encouraged him to virtually blackmail his tout, Finn Riley, into letting the company use his loft for an SAS OP, even knowing that to do so would put Riley, and possibly others, in great danger. That was not, to Marty's way of thinking, an honourable way to operate and in the event what he had feared came to pass.

Grandstanding as always, Captain Marsden had determined to neutralise Jack Flagherty before Flagherty could get to him. Breaking every rule in the book, Marsden donned civilian clothing, armed himself with a hidden Browning handgun, and drove to a pub in South Armagh, known to be frequented by Flagherty. Trying to pass himself off as an Irishman, Marsden did not fool anyone and was captured by Jack Flagherty and his PIRA team who, alerted by some of the customers, were waiting for him when he left the pub. According to LeBlanc's tout, he was beaten badly, then driven to an empty country cottage where he was tortured for hours, including getting a six pack: bullets through the knees, ankles and elbows.

Though it was to his credit that he did not talk, he had compounded his initial stupidity by embarking on his search for Flagherty while still carrying his real identification and, even more damaging, a small notebook containing the names and telephone numbers of his tout, Finn Riley, and the woman he had thought was his girlfriend. When Flagherty and his gang then visited the girlfriend, she *did* talk under torture, confessing that Riley had let the SAS set up an OP in his loft in return for protection, a false identity and a new life in Australia. When she had talked, she was shot. A notebook found in her possession then led Flagherty and his gang on an orgy of revenge killings against all those connected to her and Riley. Finally, Flagherty and his gang went back to their own street, reloaded their weapons in Flagherty's place, then crossed the road to Riley's house, where they shot him and attacked the OP.

Fleeing when the QRF arrived to give back-up to the OP, Flagherty was now on the run. Though eventually he would head across the border, it was believed by Lieutenant-Colonel LeBlanc that he was hiding in the vicinity of his country cottage and would return there, at least temporarily, to rescue valuable PIRA documentation and also ensure that the weapons and ammunition being stored there were moved on to another safe place.

Marty's job, LeBlanc had said, was to recce the farmhouse from a rural OP and neutralise Flagherty or his cohorts when he or they materialised. When Marty queried the word 'neutralise' in this context, he was informed that he was dealing with dangerous men and that while a shoot-to-kill policy was not actually in force, to shoot to wound would be, in this instance, counterproductive and could lead to tragedy for his own men.

Knowing that he was being asked to assassinate Flagherty and, if they showed up, his men, Marty was outraged and said, 'That isn't the way we do things in the SAS.'

'You may be in the SAS,' LeBlanc replied, 'but right now you're attached to Fourteen Intelligence Company and under my personal command. So you'll do as you're bloody well told – and that means neutralising them. You understand, Staff-Sergeant?'

'I think so,' Marty said.

Now, feeling disgusted by the sordid machinations of LeBlanc but still determined to do his job the way he saw fit, which may yet mean capturing Flagherty instead of neutralising him, Marty led his team to the OP by a zigzagging route that took in a series of predesignated RVs, or rendevouz points: the gate of a fence, a copse of trees, a certain hill. Though this took up more time, it was a vital part of their anti-ambush tactics. Eventually, however, after a final rendezvous, or FRV, during which they checked the map with the aid of a pencil-torch, they arrived at the location chosen for the OP. This was the windblown summit of a hill with a glimpse of the lough and sea on one side and, on the other, an unobstructed view of Flagherty's house – necessary not only for eyeball recces, but for the line-of-sight path required for the STG laser surveillance system. The location had also been chosen because it was on the direct line of a hedgerow that snaked over the crest of the hill and could be used as the protective wall of the OP.

'Right,' Marty said, speaking for the first time as he lowered his heavy loads to the ground. 'This is the place.'

The clouds were low and patchy, showing stars between, and moonlight made strips of sea glitter in the distance. The wind was cold and strong, howling eerily across the fields, and frost glinted here and there on the grassy ground.

While the other men sorted out their kit, Corporal Pearson used the radio to establish communications with the base at Bessbrook, using short-burst transmissions. Having confirmed that the OP had comms, or communications, from this location, Marty took guard and radio watch, leaving the experienced Taff and TT, with the help of Pearson, to prepare the OP.

While it was unlikely that they would be seen by enemy aircraft, of which there were none, it was possible that a British Army helicopter crew, not knowing of their mission, would mistake them for a PIRA murder squad. For this reason, the first thing they did was put up a hessian screen, with a poncho and camouflage net for overhead cover, supported on wooden stakes, looped at one end over the hedgerow, and held down with iron pickets and rope.

Once this basic form of protection had been raised, the three men used spades and pickaxes to dig out a large rectangular area suitable for a long-term, top-to-tail OP, with one end running under the hedgerow. Four shallow scrapes were then dug in the main scrape: one for the observer, one for the sentry, and two as 'rest bays'. One of these was for the man having a proper sleep in a sleeping bag; the other was for the man resting from guard or observation duties while taking care of his personal administration matters – such as jotting down his observations or perhaps just having a snack and a rest while remaining awake. A fifth shallow scrape was dug out of the middle of the triangular OP as a kit well for water, high-calorie foods, weapons, spare ammunition, batteries, toiletries and other equipment. The soil from the scrapes was scattered around the ground a good distance away from the OP. The hessian-and-net covering of the OP was then covered in grass, gorse and vegetation torn from the hedgerow.

A camouflaged entry/exit hole was shaped in the hessian hanging to the ground at the rear end of the OP. Last, but most important, a camouflaged, rectangular viewing hole was shaped from the hedgerow and hessian covering the side of the

OP overlooking the target – in this case Flagherty's house and the road passing it, about 150 metres away, across the road at the bottom of the hill.

With the OP completed, the rest of the equipment was unpacked and prepared for use.

'Now you can come into your own,' Taff whispered to Alan Pearson. 'You can play with your toys.'

'About time,' Alan whispered back. A former electrical research engineer with Marconi, then with the Pilatus Britten-Norman experimental aircraft production company in the Isle of Wight, Alan had joined the army specifically to get into the Royal Corp of Signals and through that regiment into the Special Air Service. Immediately after being badged, he had spent six weeks each at the Hereford and Royal Signals establishments at Catterick and Blandford, where he had learned about the special surveillance requirements of the SAS, with particular regard to counter-terrorist (CT) operations in Northern Ireland. 'I thought I'd never get the chance to use this stuff properly,' he said, as he started unpacking. 'Just sit back and watch me.'

The tripod set up by him in front of the viewing hole overlooking Flagherty's house was not for the GPMG, which would be used only in dire emergency, but for the cumbersome Thorn EMI multi-role thermal imager, including infrared, or IR. Looking like an exceptionally large video camera, it could scan outside walls, track body heat, and reveal the position of those inside the building, by day or by night, in smoke or in fog.

'If that bastard even goes to the bog,' Alan informed Taff and TT when he had set the imager up, 'we're all going to know it.'

Complementing the large, tripod-mounted thermal imager were two other items of highly advanced equipment. The first was a Davin Optical Modulux image-intensifier connected to a Nikon 35-millimetre SLR camera with interchangeable long-distance and binocular viewer lenses. Combined, these would enable them to take photos of those entering or leaving Flagherty's house, whether by day or night. The second tripod-mounted instrument was a Hawkeye Systems

Model HT10 thermal imaging camera capable of detecting men and vehicles at long distances, either in low light or in total darkness, while producing high-quality video pictures with up to seven times magnification. While the thermal picture was displayed automatically on an integral video monitor for direct viewing, it could also be displayed on a separate monitor for remote applications, such as recording for later visual analysis.

Satisfied, Alan set up two more tripods and fixed what looked like complicated transmitters, or recording devices, to them. Camouflaged in hessian, the end of one camera-shaped object was poking through the viewing hole. The other object, which looked like a radio receiver, was joined to the first by a complex combination of electric cables. It was, in fact, the same STG laser surveillance system he had used in Riley's loft.

'We'll use it to record conversations in Flagherty's farmhouse and transmit them back here,' he said, explaining to the others what they already knew, perhaps just needing to talk. 'I'm setting the transmitter on what's known as a line-of-sight path to the house, to direct an invisible beam onto the front window.' Seeing TT's confusion, he added, 'Try to imagine the window as the diaphragm of a microphone with oscillating sound waves. The invisible beam bounces off the window, back to the optical receiver in our OP. The optical receiver then converts the modulated beam into audio signals that are filtered, amplified and then converted into clear conversation. The conversation can then be monitored through headphones and simultaneously recorded on a tape recorder. Pretty damned good, eh?'

'Not bad,' Taff said. 'But what happens if those PIRA bastards try sneaking up in the dark?'

'No problem. I've got a hand-held thermal imager operating on SWIR – that's short-wavelength infrared. Also, an item called Iris, which is an infra-red intruder detection system, remote-controlled and effective up to five kilometres distance. Each of the two men on guard will have one or the other of those to give them an extra set of eyes and ears.'

'You win,' Taff told him. 'My ears are ringing with all that technical know-how. I'm sure we're in safe hands.'

'We fucking better be,' TT said.

As the surveillance equipment was being set up, Marty, still on watch, took a couple of brown, plastic-backed 'bingo' books out of his Bergen and laid them on the ground below the viewing hole, beside the legs of the tripods. Already containing the names of wanted men, missing vehicles and suspected addresses, the bingo books would soon also include details of everything seen and heard during this lengthy recce.

'Can we go now?' he asked Alan, turning away from the viewing hole.

'Yes, boss,' Alan said.

'Good.' Marty turned his attention on Taff and TT. 'We only have coverage of the front of Flagherty's house, so Corporal Pearson's going to plant miniaturised bugs at the side and rear of the building. We're going down together and we'll be back in an hour or so. You two stay here. If any of these instruments indicate that someone's coming, check whether it's us before you open fire.'

When Taff nodded, indicating that he understood, Marty picked up a Colt Commando semi-automatic and a couple of thirty-round box magazines, then crawled out through the entrance/exit hole of the OP. Seeing him go, Alan hurriedly took an olive-green canvas shoulder bag from the kit well, slung it over his right shoulder, picked up an M16 assault rifle, then followed him out.

It was still dark and cold outside, with the wind howling across the fields, but they made their way rapidly, carefully, down the hill until they reached the road running past the farmhouse. After glancing left and right to check that no vehicles were coming, they crossed the road, opened the garden gate, closed it carefully behind them, then hurried up the path to the house, stopping near the front door.

Marty glanced left and right, then cocked his head as if listening. 'No dogs,' he whispered, then led Alan around the side of the house, stopping about halfway down the drive, by the kitchen window. There, while Marty kept watch with the Colt Commando crooked in his left forearm, in what is known as the Belfast Cradle, Alan found a ladder in the back garden, placed it against the wall by the window, climbed it, then used a small hand-drill to bore a hole silently through the top of the wooden window frame. When this was done, he pushed a fibre-optic probe camera, less than an eighth of an inch thick, through the hole, fixed its wired end to the outside of the window frame, then attached a miniaturised transmitter to the frame, right beside the probe, and wired the probe to it. Though visible to a watchful eye, it was unlikely that anyone not deliberately looking would see either the tiny probe or the small transmitter.

'One more,' Alan said. Removing the stepladder from the wall and carrying it around to the back of the house, he placed it over the window of the rear living room and proceeded to fix another probe and transmitter to the top of the wooden frame. When the job was completed, he placed the ladder back where he had found it and carefully checked that nothing else had been disturbed. Satisfied, he glanced once more at his handiwork, then said, 'The laser surveillance system in the OP will pick up from the front room, the probe in the side will pick up from the kitchen, and the probe out back will pick up from the second living room. Okay?'

'You're a sweetheart,' Marty replied. 'Now let's get the hell out of here.'

Still holding his Colt Commando in the Belfast Cradle, he led Pearson back across the road and up the dark, windblown hill. A good distance away from the OP, but within speaking range, they stopped and identified themselves, each personally announcing his own presence for voice identification. Given Taff's permission to continue, they made their up to the summit, slipped through a space in the hedgerow, dropped onto hands and knees, then crawled breathlessly back into the OP.

'All done,' Marty said. 'Now all we have to do is wait for Flagherty to come calling, which he will soon enough.'

Coins were tossed to see who would take first watch. Marty and TT lost the toss, allowing Taff and Alan to crawl gratefully into the scrapes and catch up on lost sleep.

It was Marty who first saw the shadowy figure in the field to the side of Flagherty's house. On watch at the viewing hole shaped out of the hedgerow and camouflaged in hessian, scanning the area around Flagherty's house with a pair of binoculars instead of the tripod-mounted thermal imager, he was really just trying to distract himself until it was time to waken Alan and let him take over the watch.

In fact, he had been thinking about Diane, her general political commitment, and how she was particularly passionate about the need to get the Brits out of Northern Ireland and leave the country to solve its own problems. Unfortunately, her convictions in this department had become even more concrete ever since she had learned that political prisoners in Northern Ireland were being tortured, or at least seriously mistreated, in order to make them confess or pass on information about the IRA. In the weeks just before Marty had left for Northern Ireland, Diane had become almost obsessive about this subject, begging him to get out of the posting and not lend himself to what she termed a 'debased and degrading war'. At that time, however, Marty had been desperate to get out of the training wing at Hereford and back into active service, so he had lied and said he couldn't refuse the posting. That Diane didn't believe him was evidenced by the fact that they had more than one fight over the issue until, feeling very relieved, he had boarded the boat to Belfast.

Now, when he thought back on Diane's accusations of British dirty tricks in the province, he was forced to accept that she'd been right and that he was now involved in a war that often made him want to throw up. Nevertheless, when he saw that shadow moving in the field beside Flagherty's house, he instantly tensed and became a professional soldier again, putting that before all else.

'Hey, you lot, wake up!'

Taff jerked out of sleep first and sat up to learn what was happening. As TT and Alan also awoke, Taff scrambled across the OP to glance out of the viewing hole.

'What is it?'

'Something moving down in that field by Flagherty's house, heading towards the fence.' Even before the excited Pearson could reach him, Marty was using the camera with its attached image-intensifier to check that shadowy figure. In the infrared binocular viewing lens, he saw immediately that it was indeed the figure of a man, now clambering over the fence and into Flagherty's garden.

'It's got to be Flagherty,' Marty said, unable to hide his excitement. 'He's about to enter the house.'

Immediately, Alan Pearson went to the second tripod-mounted instrument, the Hawkeye Systems thermal imaging camera, and adjusted it to take in the man making his way at the crouch across the garden. As the man reached the side wall, just below where a fibre-optic probe camera and transmitter had been installed in the window frame, Alan worked the Hawkeye Systems imaging camera and the man's form, magnified, appeared on the thermal picture that was displayed automatically on the integral video monitor for direct viewing. This magnified picture clearly showed the man moving stealthily along the wall until he reached the back of the house. Once there, he disappeared around the corner.

'He's going to let himself in by the back door,' Marty said. 'We should hear every move he makes when he's inside. Isn't that right, Corporal Pearson?'

'It sure is,' Alan replied, looking pleased with himself as he first glanced at the video monitor, then turned on a separate monitor and a highly advanced tape recorder. 'That thermal picture's going to be displayed on a separate monitor,' he said, 'which will record it. Then it can be analysed later.' He switched on the STG laser surveillance system. 'Once he's inside, the laser system will pick up and amplify most noises and pick up any conversation. I'll be recording all that on this tape recorder, but if you pick up those headphones, boss, you can hear what he's saying.'

Marty put the earphones on in time to hear what seemed to be a mechanical clicking sound, repeated two or three times, followed by the amplified creaking of wood and the squeaking of hinges. Confused at first, he soon realised that he was listening to the intruder, presumably Flagherty, turning his key in the lock of the back door and then pushing the door open. This was confirmed when he heard the door closing, then footsteps moving through the rear living room. The footsteps stopped at the living-room door, as if the intruder was hesitating, then they moved out of range of the fibre-optic camera and transmitter at the back of the house, faded out almost completely, then became louder again as the intruder passed through the kitchen and was picked up again. Once through the kitchen, the footsteps faded away again and this time there was silence for a long time, other than what sounded like distant creaking and squeaking.

'I think he's casing his own house,' Marty said, 'to see if anyone's hiding in there. He's a hard man all right.'

'Judging by the sound of it, he's upstairs,' Pearson said. Though wearing earphones as well, he was able to hear those speaking nearby. He was also keeping his keen gaze on the video monitor, which right now showed nothing. 'That muffled sound – it's still the sound of footsteps. Now he's coming down again.'

Marty listened intently through the earphones and heard the muffled thump-thumping sounds growing louder until they became very distinct.

'He's entering the front room,' Alan said, growing more excited. 'Now he's *in* the front room.' He turned and glanced at the video monitor attached to the combined Thorn EMI multi-role thermal imager and STG laser surveillance system. At first it was blank, but then, as the intruder's body heat revealed his position inside the front room, they saw that he was at the window, raising his right hand. When Marty then glanced through the binocular viewer lens of the Nikon with its image-intensifier, he saw the curtains move in the front window and caught a glimpse of a pale, shadowed human face before the curtains were dropped back.

'He was checking if anyone's out front,' Marty said. He glanced at the body-heat image on the video screen of the multi-role thermal imager and saw that the intruder was sitting down, picking something up and holding it to his head. Through the earphones, Marty heard a repeated clicking sound, followed by a pause, a muffled electronic sound, then a man's voice.

'Yes, it's me.'

There was another silence filled only with that odd, muffled electronic sound.

'He's speaking to someone on the telephone,' Alan explained. 'We won't be able to hear the other voice, but might pick it up when this recording's electronically analysed.'

'The grocery man,' the voice said, sounding agitated. 'Sure who the fuck do ya think it is?' A pause while the other person replied, then: 'You know where I am. I have the groceries for collection. I want you to come in a car and take the groceries away. Sure you can give me a lift while yer at it. Save me takin' a train.' A pause while the other person spoke, then: 'Sure, don't I know that? But what else can we do? Sure we've got t'get these groceries out of here an' I have t'go with 'em. We've got t'do it tonight. We've got to do it right now. So you get yerselves out here right now and let's get the job done.'

There was a sudden bang as the receiver was slammed down. Marty glanced at the video monitor and saw the body-heat image standing up and going to the other side of the room. The man bent down. A cupboard door opened and closed. There was the rattling of glass, a splashing sound, a brief silence, then the sound of walking feet as the body-heat image returned to the window and took a chair by it.

Studying the same sight through the binocular viewer lens of the camera with image intensifier, Marty saw the curtains move in the front window again and caught a glimpse of the same pale, shadowed face before the curtains were dropped back.

'He poured himself a drink,' Alan Pearson explained, studying the body-heat image on the other video monitor, 'and now he's sitting at a chair by the window in the darkened room, just watching and waiting.'

'What did you make out of that one-sided conversation?' Taff asked of Marty. 'Did it make any sense to you?'

'Yes. The groceries are the weapons and ammunition. The grocery man's the man delivering them – and that's Flagherty. That man down there is Flagherty. He wants them to come in a car and take the groceries away, but he also wants them to give him a lift to save him taking a train. That means they're to come and help him clear out the house, delivering the weapons and ammunition to someone across the border and taking Flagherty with them when they go.'

'What about: "Sure, don't I know that? But what else can we do?"' Taff asked him.

'The other party must have mentioned the fact that Flagherty's house might be under surveillance. He responded by saying they have to take that chance, hopefully getting out under cover of darkness.' Marty grinned and patted the multi-role thermal imager. 'But he doesn't know about little toys like this. One up for you, Alan.'

Pearson grinned, but said nothing.

'So what now?' TT asked. 'We could go down there and surround the house and he's almost bound to surrender. We could have him before his PIRA mates get here.'

'And if LeBlanc threw a cordon-and-search sweep of the lower Falls within the hour,' Taff said, 'he could pick up all the rest of those bastards before they left Belfast.'

'Get on to LeBlanc for me,' Marty told Pearson. 'I want to sort this out with him. No need to worry about being intercepted. Flagherty's got nothing down there. Get LeBlanc on the PRC three-one-nine. I want to talk to him personally.'

When Pearson contacted Army HQ in Lisburn, he handed the phone to Marty, who explained the situation to Lieutenant-Colonel LeBlanc and requested that Flagherty's PIRA ASU be picked up in a cordon-and-search sweep of the lower Falls while he and his men surrounded Flagherty's country house and tried to force his surrender.

'I don't think that's desirable,' LeBlanc replied blandly.

'Pardon?' Marty responded, shocked.

'If you try to make Flagherty surrender, you could lose him completely.'

'Excuse me, boss, but I don't believe that's possible. There are four of us here and we're going to surround the whole house. That's one man to each side. There's no way he can get out.'

'He might slip through,' LeBlanc said.

'He can't slip through,' Marty insisted, knowing that LeBlanc wanted Flagherty neutralised, once and for all, and would stoop to any kind of dirty trick to ensure that it happened. 'You know that damned well, boss.'

'I told you what I wanted in this, Staff-Sergeant.'

'And I can't oblige, boss. I have to try to make him surrender. And if he knows that his PIRA mates won't be coming, I think he'll do that.'

Trapped, LeBlanc was silent for a moment; then finally, practically grinding his teeth, he said, 'All right, Staff-Sergeant, have it your way. I'll call up a cordon-and-search sweep of the lower Falls and get back to you as soon as it's over.'

'When will that be, boss?'

'Approximately one hour to commencement, another hour for the sweep, and another to confirm that we have our fish in the net. Is that satisfactory?'

'Yes, boss,' Marty said, ignoring LeBlanc's icy sarcasm. 'As soon as we hear that the fish are in the net, I'll go down there with my men, inform Flagherty of what's happened, and persuade him to come out with his hands up.'

'You do that, Staff-Sergeant. Over and out.'

The line went dead. When Marty put the phone down and turned to look at his men, he saw that all three of them were grinning at him.

'You've got him hopping mad,' Taff said.

'Serves the bastard right,' Marty said.

But when the telephone rang thirty minutes later, it was his turn to be hopping mad.

Handing the receiver of the PRC 319 back to Pearson, Marty felt his heart racing and had trouble in accepting what LeBlanc had just told him.

'What was it?' Taff asked.

'That fucker!' Marty exploded. 'He said he's not calling up the cordon-and-search sweep because it'd be a waste of time. He said that he'd just talked to his tout, to confirm that the PIRA ASU was in the area before calling up the sweep, and was told that they'd already left town and were heading right here, armed to the teeth.'

'Why the fuck would they do that?' TT asked. 'I mean, they're supposed to be coming to help clear out that house and spirit their boss away. They're not coming here for a firefight. They don't even know that we're here.'

'They do now,' Marty grimly informed him. 'Someone told

the bastards about this OP. At least that's what LeBlanc's tout told him. He told LeBlanc that an unknown source had informed the PIRA ASU that the SAS were in an OP above their boss's house and were working on a shoot-to-kill policy. He told LeBlanc that it was straight-out execution and that Flagherty had to be rescued. Now, apparently, Flagherty's PIRA hit squad is on its way here from the Falls to take out the OP, leaving no one alive, while another PIRA group is coming from Dublin to remove the groceries from Flagherty's house and spirit the grocery man across the border. And they're coming with an RPG seven rocket-launcher, so they must mean business.'

'Shit!' TT exclaimed.

'I like a good firefight,' Taff said with soft-voiced pleasure, 'and that's what's coming our way.'

'Exactly,' Marty said. 'There won't be any surrender now. This is going to be a fight to the finish – either them or us. And what I'd like to know, what I'd *really* like to know, is who the hell told those bastards we were here? And, even worse, here to work by a shoot-to-kill policy. Who the fuck told them that?'

There was silence for quite a while, then Taff said, speaking with calm certainly, 'Lieutenant-Colonel LeBlanc.'

There was another long silence, during which time Marty felt himself turning cold. The cold melted and turned to burning fury, but he fought to contain himself.

'Right,' he said. 'That bastard, LeBlanc. His tout didn't tell him anything. He wants Flagherty out of the picture – all the way out, *kaput* – and he also wants his whole ASU put down as well. Not only as clear retaliation for the murder of Captain Marsden, but also to smash the morale of the IRA once and for all. So his tout told him nothing. It was *him* who informed his tout. He told him to pass on the word about this OP and our supposed shoot-to-kill policy, knowing that it would ensure no surrender on Flagherty's part. That bastard, LeBlanc, has us boxed us. We'll have to fight for our lives now.'

'He must have a lot of faith in us,' Taff said, smiling with barely concealed admiration. 'He must be convinced we'll survive.'

'And we'll only do that if we kill the men he wants dead. Yes, he's one clever bastard. Clever and ruthless.'

'If we do it, we have to do it now,' TT reminded them. 'Otherwise, they'll be onto us.'

'That's right,' Taff responded, obviously keen on his firefight. 'We've no time to waste getting mad at LeBlanc. We have to take the initiative.'

'An ambush.'

'Correct.' Marty choked back his rage and concentrated on the job at hand. Finally, he took a deep breath and let it out slowly. 'They have an RPG Seven rocket-launcher, so my bet is they'll stop partway up the hill to lob one into the OP, thinking we're in it. Given the elevation requirements of the rocket-launcher, they'll have to fire it from near the bottom of the hill, not much higher than the lower slopes, so that's where we'll locate – to take them out before they can fire the missile.'

'Sounds good,' Taff said.

'There's a hedgerow running down the side of the hill, about fifty yards west of the OP. Three of us will dig in there, near to where it levels out, and wait for the bastards to arrive. The fourth man will remain here on the GPMG to give us cover when the firefight starts.'

'If we're down that low,' TT reminded him, 'we'll be close to the road, which puts us within range of the firepower of the ASU team clearing out Flagherty's house.'

'Exactly,' Marty replied. 'Which gives as a legitimate excuse to attack them as well and get our hands on the incriminating evidence – the weapons and explosives.'

'One of LeBlanc's little dodges.'

'Pretty damned good,' Taff said. 'He's a bigger percentage player than the late Captain Marsden – but you've got to admit, he knows the game better.'

'A Keeni-Meeni operator,' TT said. 'A real snake in the grass. So who stays in the OP?'

'You,' Marty told him. 'Apart from me, you're the most experienced, so you shouldn't need supervision. I trust you to use your initiative and not make mistakes.'

'Such as shooting us instead of the ASU team,' Alan said with a wide grin.

'If I shoot you,' TT said, 'it'll be intentional. I don't make mistakes, kiddo.'

'You two,' Marty said to Alan and Taff, 'will come with me. We'll need short-handled pickaxes and spades for the scrapes. Attach the grenade-launchers to your M sixteens. At my signal, you'll lay two grenades down on the ASU. When they explode, TT'll take that as the signal to open up with the GPMG. What damage not inflicted by TT will be inflicted by us. So let's let's get the fuck down that hill and make sure we're ready.'

'Hey, kiddo,' TT said to Alan. 'Whatever way it goes, the surveillance is finished, so take that thermal imager away and let me put the machine-gun in its place.'

Pearson did as he was told, but insisted on leaving the Nikon SLR with the image-intensifier to enable TT to take photos of the PIRA members when they arrived.

'They'll be helpful as evidence,' he explained.

'What a bright boy you are,' TT said, though he grinned and nodded agreement.

Marty and Taff checked their weapons, ensured that they had a plentiful supply of thirty-round magazines, then clipped short-handled spades and pickaxes to their belts. As they were doing so, TT set up the tripod for the GPMG. Meanwhile, Alan dismantled the bulky thermal imager, then removed it from in front of the viewing hole. Alan placed the thermal imager back in its canvas carrier while TT set the GPMG up on its tripod, with the barrel poking out through the viewing hole, angled down the hill, beside the Nikon SLR camera and Davin Modulux image-intensifier. As TT was feeding the ammunition belt into the GPMG, which normally required a two-man team, Marty slid a short-handled spade and pickaxe towards Pearson, saying, 'Here, clip these to your belt and take as many magazines as you can reasonably carry. Plus fragmentation and buckshot grenades for the M203s. Let's give them a sore arse.' Pearson grinned and did as he was told.

'Are you okay, sport?' Marty asked TT.

Now sitting on a wooden box behind the GPMG, TT stuck his thumb up in the air. 'Straight line-of-sight between here and the house. I can't possibly miss, boss.'

'You fire when the pineapples go off,' Marty reminded him. 'One belt's all you need.'

'We all get what we ask for,' TT said. 'God told me that.'

'Faith moves mountains,' Marty rejoindered, then turned to the others. 'Let's get the fuck down that hill. See you later, TT.'

'Right, boss,' TT said.

Holding his Colt Commando in the Belfast cradle, Marty crawled out of the exit hole, followed by Taff and Alan. Once outside, they headed downhill at the half crouch, zigzagging automatically over the boulder-strewn grass and turf, heading obliquely towards the fuchsia hedges that bordered the western side of the field and praying that Jack Flagherty was not watching at that moment or, if he was, would fail to see them in the gradually brightening early morning. When they reached the hedges, Marty led them farther down until they were about fifty metres from the fence separating the hill from the road running across the front of Flagherty's house, one way to Belfast, the other to Dublin.

'Our patch,' Marty whispered, relieved to know that if Jack Flagherty had seen them he would certainly have fired at them.

Wearing DPM clothing, and with their weapons wrapped in tape of a similar colouring, they blended into the hedges even before digging out their scrapes. Nevertheless, using their short-handled pickaxes and spades, they made themselves shallow scrapes that extended into the foliage, letting it fall back over them when they crawled in and lay on their bellies. Though not comfortable, they were practically invisible and ready to fire.

Glancing downhill to his right, Marty could see the road beyond the fence and, behind that, Michael Flagherty's house, now emerging from fading darkness to the dawn's misty grey light. It was a modest building, two stories high, with brick walls and slate roof, set well back from the road and surrounded by high, rolling fields in which no other houses could be seen. That, at least, was a blessing.

Lying belly down in his shallow scrape, half buried in the foliage, cradling his Colt Commando in his arms, with Taff on one side of him, Alan on the other, both nursing M16s with M203 grenade-launchers attached, Marty saw the rising sun, its light smothered by dense clouds, and shivered, suddenly feeling very cold.

Fifteen minutes later, hearing nothing but the birdsong and the occasional car passing on the road below, just in front of Flagherty's house, Marty glanced up the hill at the OP, barely visible in the mist, then sideways at Taff and Alan Pearson. He had placed them about fifteen metres apart, with himself closest to the road, Taff in the middle, and Alan farther up the hill. This, he had calculated, would give them a triangular field of fire homing in on where the ASU would be compelled to set up the RPG 7 for the elevation required to hit the OP. He prayed to God he was right.

Still waiting, he distracted himself by studying the scenery: the tree-lined green fields; sunlight glinting off a stretch of sea glimpsed beyond the distant hills; birds winging through a jigsaw of brightening blue sky and patchy, dark clouds. When you looked at this scenery it was hard to imagine that it was known as 'bandit country', notorious for the torture and murder that took place all over it. In fact, it was hard to imagine what was happening here in general, with the British fighting a mean war on British soil. Of course, the Irish didn't think it was British soil, which explained the whole damned war.

Marty was still lost in this bitter reverie when a blue Ford came along the road from the direction of Belfast and pulled into a layby just around a slow bend. Although he could see the car clearly from his vantage point halfway up the hill, he realised that it would be out of sight of the OP. Knowing that this must have been deliberate, he instinctively tensed, preparing himself for action.

Eventually, three men got out of the car, leaving the driver behind the wheel, presumably to do the talking should an Army or RUC patrol come along. The men were wearing corduroy trousers or denims, jackets and open-necked shirts. One of them lay on his belly, groped under the car, and eventually withdrew a long object wrapped in some kind of covering – the RPG 7, Marty surmised. Another leaned back into the rear of the vehicle, as if groping around beneath the seats, and eventually withdrew two more long parcels – probably wrapped rifles or submachine guns. Meanwhile, the third man was leaning into the rear door at the other side and eventually straightened up, holding a canvas bag, which Marty assumed was filled with magazines for the weapons.

After leaning down to the front window to converse briefly with the driver, the man holding the wrapped RPG 7 led the other two through a gateway in the high fuchsia hedges and wooden fence bordering the road, into the field at a location approximately 45 degrees east of the line of vision of the OP. The men then made their way alongside the road, though they were shielded from it by the high hedge. They were also hidden from the OP by a dip in the ground where the field ran down steeply before levelling out near the fence. They were able to clamber a good twenty metres up the steep, lower stretch of the hill while remaining out of view of the OP and without being seen by the few cars passing by. When eventually they chose the spot from which to launch their attack, they were just below Marty, positioned obliquely to the right of Taff and Alan.

Hidden in the hedge, Taff and Alan set their M203 grenade-launchers to fire, judged the angle of elevation required, then held their M16s steady.

The blue Ford remained parked in the same position: just around the bend in the road, out of sight of the OP.

The man with the wrapped RPG 7 checked his wristwatch, then said something to the other two. Immediately they began unwrapping their parcels. The large parcel was, indeed, a wrapped RPG 7 rocket-launcher and the other two were Russian 7.62-millimetre AK-47 automatic rifles, beloved of terrorists everywhere and instantly recognisable, even from this distance, because of the unusually curved thirty-round box magazine. When the weapons were unwrapped, the man with the canvas bag opened it and started handing out ammunition, including magazines for the AK-47s and a 2.25-kilogram missile for the RPG 7.

Marty thrust his left hand out of the hedge and raised it in the air, preparing to give the signal to fire.

The man with the RPG 7 checked his wristwatch again,

then glanced back over his shoulder, down the hill and across the road to Jack Flagherty's house. Shaking his head as if exasperated, he loaded the missile into the launcher, then glanced back over his shoulder again.

A grey removal truck came along the road from the direction of the nearby border. It pulled into the driveway. Four men got out, glanced up the hill in the general direction of the covert OP, and waved.

Obviously knowing that his comrades would be seen by the OP, the man knelt in the firing position and aimed the RPG 7.

Glancing back over his shoulder at Taff and Alan, Marty dropped his hand, signalling, 'open fire.' Leaning forward into the stock of their M16s, they simultaneously fired their M203 grenade-launchers and were violently rocked by the backblast. The two grenades exploded at the same time, one on either side of the three men, with soil and buckshot spewing up and outwards through boiling columns of black smoke. Even as the smoke was still obscuring the men, the shocking roar of the GPMG firing from the OP joined the harsh chatter of Marty's Colt Commando and the M16s, now switched to automatic and firing rapidly repeated three-round bursts into the swirling smoke from the buckshot grenades. One of the men was already down, bowled sideways by the blast. The other two were dancing wildly in a convulsion of spitting earth created by the combined firepower of the GPMG and three assault rifles. Taken by surprise, and confused as to where the firing was coming from, the remaining two did not even have time to fire their weapons before they were cut to shreds and collapsed.

Even as the two men fell, the blue Ford screeched into life, reversed out of the layby, and raced back around the bend, returning to Belfast. Seeing what had happened, the men at Flagherty's house raced across the driveway to get back into the relative safety of the removal van. As they did so, a front window of the house was smashed, obviously by Flagherty, and gunshots were fired at the SAS from what sounded like another Soviet AK-47.

When TT's GPMG trailed off into silence, Marty leapt out

of the hedge and raced across the field, weaving left and right to avoid the bullets from Flagherty's assault rifle, his Colt Commando in one hand, a Landmaster III transceiver in the other. He went down on one knee to examine the bloody ASU team – all of whom were dead – and spoke into the transceiver at the same time. The removal van, meanwhile, was lumbering out of Flagherty's driveway and one of the men left behind, obviously senseless with anger, bellowed a string of abuse in a broad Ulster accent, then raced across the road and clambered over the fence. He dropped down the other side, took aim with his Webley pistol and fired at Marty.

Stepping out from the hedge, Taff adopted the kneeling position, took aim with his M16 and coolly fired a couple of three-round bursts. The man was punched backwards so hard, he smashed through the fence before landing on his back in the tall grass.

'Stop that van!' Marty bellowed, pointing down the hill, then speaking again into the transceiver.

While Alan Pearson poured a fusillade into the smashed window of the cottage, keeping Flagherty pinned down, Taff switched back to the M203 and loaded a grenade while running a few more yards down the hill. The removal van had just driven out through the gates of Flagherty's house and was turning into the road, in the direction of the border, when Taff calculated the angle of elevation and fired a fragmentation grenade. The backblast socked his shoulder and his head rang from the noise. Then the grenade exploded just in front of the truck, practically under the left wheel, shattering the windscreen and lifting the whole vehicle up onto two wheels. It slammed back down again, but careened across the road, bouncing over a ditch, then smashed through the fence and embedded itself deep in the hedgerow.

Alan Pearson was racing past Taff when first one, then two of the men in the crashed van jumped to the ground, then straightened up, firing their handguns. Alan fired on the run and Taff fired a second later. One of the men jerked spasmodically, dropped his handgun, fell back and shuddered violently against the side of the van as more bullets stitched him. He was sliding to the ground, leaving a trail of blood on the side of the van, as the other man backed across the road, firing as he retreated. He had almost reached the fence of Flagherty's house when a combined burst from Alan and Taff nearly cut him in two, then picked him up and slammed him back into the fence, which immediately buckled under his falling body. Pouring blood from his chest and stomach, the man rocked like a seesaw on the fence for a couple of seconds, then fell backwards into the driveway.

Even as Marty was continuing to pour a hail of bullets into the cottage, something exploded inside with a mighty roar and a side wall blew out in clouds of pulverised mortar, red dust and black smoke. As more of the wall collapsed, part of the roof fell in and more black smoke billowed up to the grey sky. Yellow fingers of flame started flickering through the smoke as, presumably, curtains and other items inside caught fire. When Marty stopped firing, there was no retaliatory fire from within.

Aware of that deadly silence, Taff and Alan raced down the hill to check the dead and the wounded.

The only wounded was the driver of the van, his eyes bloodied and blinded by shards of glass from the shattered windscreen, his forehead split open, his nose broken upon impact with the steering wheel. He was unconscious, but groaning. The other men, including the one across the road, had been torn to shreds by the high velocity 5.56-millimetre bullets of the M16s. Soaked in blood, with bone gleaming through gristle, they were certainly dead.

'Let's check the house,' Pearson said.

'I wouldn't do that if I were you,' Marty replied coming up to stand beside him and Taff. 'My bullets must have set off some explosives and there must be a lot more of those in there. They could all start detonating each other, so I'd keep well out of there.'

Even as he spoke, more explosions did indeed reverberate inside the house, this time blowing out part of the front wall, including the window from which Flagherty had been firing. The three SAS men crouched low behind the PIRA truck until the repeated explosions had stopped and the flying debris had subsided. Only then did they advance on the remains of the smouldering house, choking in swirling dust and smoke, eventually reaching where the front wall had been. Gazing down into what was now no more than smouldering rubble, they saw the scorched, crushed remains of Jack Flagherty.

'Good riddance,' Taff said.

Removing his Radio Systems walkie-talkie from his webbing, Marty called TT in the OP, told him that the area had been cleared, and asked him to call HQ on the PRC 319 and give them the details of the man making his escape in the blue Ford. He also told him to call up a team of sappers to check the remains of the house for unexploded munition, a REME team to remove the crashed, badly damaged van, and an ambulance to attend to the wounded and remove the dead.

'Hear you loud and clear,' TT came back. 'Over and out.'

Marty switched the walkie-talkie off and said to Taff and Alan, 'They should be here pretty soon. Meanwhile, I want each of you to take up a blocking position on the road, about a thousand yards north and south of here – you Taff, on the road from Belfast; you, Alan, on the road to Dublin. Stop any traffic coming through. Check the drivers and passengers carefully. Then, no matter who they are, make them turn back and take another route. The only people you let in are our own. Is that understood?'

'Right,' Taff said.

'You bet,' Alan said.

When the two men had walked off in opposite directions, Marty glanced automatically at the bloody body lying face up by the fence, then crossed the road to the crashed removal van. The driver was still unconscious, but had mercifully stopped groaning and was now lying with his forehead resting on the steering wheel, which was covered in a mess of congealed blood, some of which had dripped from his blinded eyes. Since there was little he could do for him, Marty left him as he was and went around to stand guard by the side of the van, facing the road coming from Belfast.

From where he was standing, he could see that TT was removing the kit from the OP and piling it up beside it. Marty waved to him. TT waved back. Taff and Alan Pearson repeatedly stopped the early-morning traffic, checked the drivers' credentials and then made them turn back. Thirty minutes later, a team of sappers, a couple of medics, and a REME team in two Bedford trucks arrived to inspect the debris, remove the wounded man and the many dead, board up the remains of the house and fence off the area. They were all hard at work when Marty led his SAS team back up the hill to the dismantled OP.

Forcing himself to suppress his anger and bitterness at how he had been tricked, Marty called Lieutenant-Colonel LeBlanc on the PRC 319, told him that the area had been cleared and asked if he had any news about the man in the blue Ford. Sounding as deadpan as ever, certainly not trying to gloat, LeBlanc told him that on receipt of the car's details, Bessbrook had set up a roadblock and helicopter recce to bring him in. The man had just been caught.

'Congratulations on doing a good job,' LeBlanc said. 'You may now demolish the OP. Prepare to be extracted by chopper at fifteen hundred hours precisely. Over and out.'

The OP was demolished, the chopper arrived on time, and fifteen minutes later the men were back in Bessbrook, relaxing over a beer in the NAAFI canteen.

The following day, Marty was called to Lieutenant-Colonel LeBlanc's office at 14 Intelligence Company, Bessbrook, and informed that his participation in this operation could have him marked as a wanted man by the IRA and that he was therefore being flown back to Hereford. Knowing full well that he was being pushed out by LeBlanc simply because he knew too much about what had, in the end, been a filthy, immoral job, Marty bowed to the inevitable and flew back without argument.

CHAPTER THIRTY-FIVE

'Northern Ireland disgusted me,' Marty confessed to Paddy as they lit up cigars in the old English ambience of Rules in Covent Garden, which he could not have afforded on his own. Luckily, though he had arranged the lunch, he was here as Paddy's guest. 'As long as I live I'm not going to forget that I was used by that smooth green bastard LeBlanc in a campaign of dirty tricks – the kind that go against every moral credo of the SAS. Now, more than ever, I'm convinced that the regiment's starting to be used in shitty ways by bastards like LeBlanc and others higher up. The regiment could be degraded by this kind of activity and I'm determined to put a bloody stop to it.'

'Through the organisation.'

'Right,' Marty said. If nothing else, his tour of Northern Ireland had encouraged him, when he returned to Hereford to his less exacting work as a DI in 22 SAS Training Wing, to pick up where he had left off with his informal, secret organisation of like-minded souls. 'I'm trying to make it more effective with a formal code of practice and much broader aims, but I need your support.'

'You mean the support of Vigilance International,' Paddy said, referring to his TV franchise business, now highly successful at producing anti-communist propaganda films and selling them to the Third World and the Middle East.

'Yes, Paddy, that's what I mean. Apart from making your propaganda movies, you're also exploiting the growing demand in the domestic security market by offering advice and tangible assistance on security measures to a growing number of commercial companies.'

'True enough,' Paddy said, exhaling a cloud of cigar smoke. 'More and more companies, particularly the multinationals, are concerned with high-technology-based industrial sabotage and with the growing threat of international terrorism. This includes the danger of assassination of key executives by left-wing individuals or groups. Those are the kind of companies I'm now dealing with. But so far we've offered only advice, instruction and practical training in the installation and handling of high-tech surveillance devices. The actual provision of bodyguards isn't included in the service – and that's what you're going to ask me to do. I can tell just to look at you.'

As Marty had arranged the lunch to discuss this very matter, he could only grin at Paddy's perception. 'Well, it *is* an opportunity to give gainful employment to former SAS members who've been shamefully neglected by the mandarins of Whitehall and the Head Sheds of the War Office. We have to do what those bastards *won't* do.'

'I think it's dodgy,' Paddy said. 'If you use former SAS soldiers as professional bodyguards, you're inviting comparisons with mercenaries – and that could rebound on us.'

'Bullshit,' Marty said. 'If men who've served their country so well are left on the dung heap, I say that finding them work as bodyguards is perfectly justified. Besides, as you said yourself, your organisation only deals with commercial companies, not governments, and certainly not those mixed up in military or political activities. So where's the harm, I say?'

Paddy blew a stream of smoke from his cigar and speculatively sniffed at his brandy. He sampled it, seemed satisfied and put the glass down again to squint through the smoke. Though no longer young – he was 56 this year – many judged him to be younger than he was and the ladies still loved him. His hair had turned grey, but he didn't have a bald patch, and his green gaze was clear, almost sparkling, above the slightly sardonic smile that women found so enchanting. He'd had the odd affair, Marty knew, though nothing too serious, and was still married to the seemingly contented Angela and close to their children. He had, however, softened slightly in appearance since leaving the regiment and now seemed so urbane, so comfortable in pinstripe suit and old-school tie, that it was difficult to imagine him as a soldier who had fought some of the toughest campaigns on record and performed heroically.

'The harm,' he said, 'is that finding them work as bodyguards could be the first step down the slippery slope that leads to mercenary activities.'

'They'd be bodyguards – not mercenaries – and, just as your company's doing now, we'd only hire them out to commercial enterprises. Nothing political.'

'It's hard to avoid politics, Marty. Even commercial companies are tied to politics. This is an aspect of my own business that I'm always aware of.'

'So how do you deal with it?'

'By carefully checking the backgrounds of those who approach us – or those we think worth approaching – and only becoming involved with them if I personally approve of the nature of their business.'

'Or politics.'

Paddy shrugged. 'Or politics.'

'What about the franchise TV company? Don't you make those propaganda documentaries for the governments of the countries you deal with?'

'Of course. And I know that propaganda is politics. But again, I have to personally approve of their political aims before I agree to work for them.'

'In other words we can't avoid politics, no matter what we do. We simply have to ensure that what we do is in line with our beliefs – and we can do that even if we farm out former SAS men as bodyguards to commercial companies that aren't overtly political and are part of the democratic community.'

'Well . . .' Clearly still doubtful, Paddy didn't finish his sentence, though he offered a slight, sardonic smile and a steady, questioning gaze.

'Tell me,' Marty said, enjoying himself but serious for all that and determined to have his way. 'What would you say is the basic principle behind your propaganda films?'

'To combat the growing communist influence in the Third World and the Middle East.'

'So you're doing what you believe in, are you not?'

Paddy grinned again, his head slightly tilted to the side as he squinted through the cloud of purple smoke spiralling up from his fat cigar. 'Yes, Marty, I am.'

'So let's use that as our *modus operandi* – not only when choosing who retired SAS men can work for as bodyguards, but also for the more formal organisation we've decided upon.'

He was talking about the decision to turn their informal gatherings of concerned SAS men into a registered organisation, with a listed membership and offices in the West End of London. Where the former gatherings had consisted only of serving members of the regiment, the new organisation would be open to former members of all ranks. In fact, it would openly solicit former members, since one of its primary functions would be to aid them either financially or by seeking work for them. The second function, of course, at least in Marty's view, would be covert protection of the regiment from those who would attempt to use it wrongly or, as was often the case, seek to have it disbanded altogether as being no longer relevant.

'What, exactly, is the *modus operadi*?' Paddy asked.

'The overt purpose is to find work for SAS personnel either retired from, or nearing retirement from, the regiment. The covert purpose is to combat antidemocratic, mainly communist, activities throughout the world and, of course, to protect the regiment from our enemies, such as civil servants, politicians and high-ranking military officers who disapprove of us.'

'I agree with the sentiments,' Paddy said, 'but I still have doubts about the way you're going about it.'

'Why?'

'Helping old mates is one thing; hiring them out as bodyguards or security specialists is another. As for the covert purpose, I'm not sure that we – by which I mean the proposed organisation – should be secretive about anything. After all, if our purpose is to combat anti-democratic activities, why, since we live in a democracy, should we have to be covert?'

'You know damned well,' Marty said, feeling more passionate by the minute, 'that our democratic values aren't shared by everyone, least of all our superiors. In fact, the regiment and everything it stands for is constantly under pressure from above – the Head Sheds, politicians, civil servants, you name them – to act against its own principles and, in many cases, against its own best interests. That, my friend, I saw in spades in Northern Ireland and I haven't forgotten it.'

'A dirty war,' Paddy agreed.

'Not dirty: filthy – and getting more so all the time, with the SAS being used for purposes that can only degrade it. Also, as you well know, we've come close more than once to being disbanded entirely by bastards who have their own interests at heart – and those bastards aren't going to stop unless we put a stop to them. We have a lot to do, Paddy.'

His good friend sighed, exhaling more cigar smoke, looking simultaneously amused and sad. 'Marty, Marty . . .' He shook his head. 'I've said it before and I'll say it again: you're a born idealist, a man of passionate beliefs, but in many ways that could be your downfall. You're too romantic, Marty. Too moral for your own good. You can't accept imperfection on any level – and that, in itself, is a deadly trap. If you take this too seriously – if you take it to its limits, which is what I think you're doing – you'll end up creating the very thing you despise: a secret organisation that answers to no one but itself. That's the danger here, Marty.'

'That's melodramatic,' Marty said.

'I'm not the melodramatic type. I'm simply telling you that, although your motives are honourable, your methods are unsound – and possibly dangerous. The regiment isn't as pure as you make it sound; it has its vices as well, its good and bad, its strengths and its weaknesses. Don't make too much of it, Marty.'

Much as Marty admired Paddy, he felt more frustrated every minute, wondering why his friend, the most principled man he had known, did not share his passionate concern to protect what both of them believed in.

'What's dangerous about it?' he asked, trying to suppress his frustration, though barely able to do so and realising that this was the first time he had ever felt annoyed with his friend.

'The secrecy,' Paddy replied. 'The very idea that we can have an organisation that protects the regiment and its principles by covert actions against those who don't agree with us. And, even more dangerous, by covertly taking action even against supposed enemies *outside* the regiment – individuals in the War Office, Whitehall, perhaps even the media. That's very dangerous indeed.'

'Who dares wins,' Marty said.

'That motto has its limitations. It's the regimental motto – no more than that – and certainly we can only act upon it in the context of war. Don't try to take that motto out of context. It will do you no good.'

'I believe in that motto. I've lived my life by it. Without it, I wouldn't be where I am and you bloody well know it.'

'Don't I know it?' Paddy grinned and Marty laughed, though he didn't feel that merry. In fact, he felt deep resentment at Paddy's reluctance to go all the way.

'Anyway,' he said, trying to lighten the conversation, 'let's put this bullshit aside for the moment and concentrate on the main function of the organisation: to aid retired members, or those about to retire, by finding them gainful employment. You'd agree, wouldn't you, that it isn't always easy for former SAS men to find decent work in Civvy Street?'

Paddy nodded. 'It's a sad fact of life that the specialist skills picked up in the SAS aren't in great demand there. In fact, their SAS skills often render them virtually unemployable. It's not easy to get a routine job when you've been in the SAS.'

'Right,' Marty said. 'The prospective employer tends to imagine you're some kind of wild animal just let out of his cage.'

'Not quite, but he certainly thinks you're not likely to settle down to some commonplace task. I think that's the main problem.'

'So we have to find work suitable for our own kind – and that means security and bodyguard work. If that's the only kind of work we can get for them, then we should go out and get it.'

'God, you're inexhaustible,' Paddy said, but he was smiling again. 'All right, I'll help you with the organisation, but only if we make certain ground rules. We can form the organisation under the umbrella of Vigilance International and use some of our empty offices for its headquarters. Our services will include advice on security aimed at anticipating and preventing the violent overthrow of democratic governments, but the company will not otherwise seek to exert political influence. Indeed, so long as we remain a strictly commercial operation, we won't be able to become involved in politics, which should keep our hands clean.'

'And the services of former SAS men as bodyguards?' Marty asked eagerly.

Paddy sighed in mock defeat. 'All right, Marty. Vigilance International will also supply instructional training and actual security men or bodyguards where required, on the strict condition that they only be used for defensive purposes and on behalf of friendly, anti-communist heads of state. Should the situation change at any time, those men will be withdrawn without any notice given. These qualifications will be incorporated in the company rules and included in any contracts drawn up with clients. Agreed?'

'Agreed,' Marty said.

'You're grinning like a Cheshire cat,' Paddy said, stubbing his cigar out in the ashtray and indicating with a wave of his hand that he wanted the bill. 'Stop looking so satisfied with yourself.'

'I'm a kid with a new toy,' Marty replied. 'I just can't help myself.'

'I'm sure I'm going to regret this,' Paddy said.

'You won't,' Marty told him.

When the bill had been paid, they left the busy restaurant and stepped out into Maiden Lane. It was a bright summer's day and the girls passing by were exposing as much skin as possible in provocative clothing. Provocative at least to Marty who, though no womaniser, was at that age when every pretty girl reminded him of lost opportunities.

He and Paddy turned down Bedford Street and stopped in the Strand, where Paddy waved down a black cab.

'So what are your plans for the rest of the day?' he asked. 'Are you seeing Diane?'

'Yes. I'm staying there for the weekend.'

'I never fail to be surprised that your relationship's continued,' Paddy said. 'You seem like such an odd couple.'

'Don't we all?' Marty asked him.

Paddy grinned and nodded as he slipped into the rear of the black cab. Before it moved off, he rolled the window down and looked out. 'We'll formally set up the organisation at the next meeting,' he said. 'By that time I'll have everything in order regarding the paperwork and the offices. You'll soon be part of Vigilance International, so I hope you're pleased now.'

'I am. And thanks, Paddy.'

Paddy grinned and waved as the cab pulled away from the pavement and inched into the dense traffic of the Strand, heading for Fleet Street. Satisfied, Marty walked to the Embankment to catch a tube train to Notting Hill Gate, where Diane still lived in the same flat. His visits to Diane were now so common that he kept everything he needed in her place and never had to bring anything to London. It was pleasant to travel light.

The world's certainly changing, Marty thought as he emerged from Notting Hill Gate station and passed a large poster showing the legendary Russian ballet star, Rudolf Nureyev, kneeling on a tigerskin rug, stark naked except for the Arab turban around his head, with an equally naked girl crouched between his outspread thighs, her bare breasts covered only by her long hair and Nureyev's hands. An advertisement for the new Ken Russell biographical movie about Rudolph Valentino, it was a symbol to Marty of how far values in the country were slipping. Nor was he overwhelmed with pleasure at the sight of the many theatrically wan young men, many wearing make-up, including lipstick and eyeshadow, who hung around the station entrance, looking suspiciously like the androgynous rock star, David Bowie. Marty tried to be liberal in his thoughts about this changing world, but couldn't do it. He felt very old-fashioned.

As he turned down Kensington Church Street, he consoled himself with the thought that his refined organisation, to be called the Association, was going to be placed on a proper footing and could, perhaps, protect some of the values represented by the regiment. Those values were his, also, and he felt a burning passion to protect them, no matter the cost.

Letting himself into Diane's flat with his own key, he found her stretched out on the settee, wearing blue jeans and a loose shirt, drinking a gin and tonic, watching a TV news item about the hijacking of a Lufthansa airliner by four Palestinian terrorists at Mogadishu airport in Samolia. As he had been one of those who had secretly advised the crack German anti-terrorist unit, GSG-9, with regard to a rescue attempt, he was thrilled to see that the 86 passengers had been rescued just before the terrorists' deadline for blowing up the plane. The daring rescue had been led by two British SAS soldiers, Major Alastair Morrison and Sergeant Barry Davis.

When the news flash ended, Diane turned the TV off and said, 'Christ, these terrorists are spreading like fungus. It's a whole new world out there.' She rolled off the settee and stood up to smile at him. 'I see that some of your mates were involved. I bet you're burning with envy.'

'Bloody right.' Walking up to her, he slid his arms around her, pressed her into him and kissed her full on the lips. She was skin and bone these days, too much smoking, too little eating, and even in his embrace she was like a coiled spring, too tense for her own good. She was obsessed with her work, with conspiracies, and it was eating her up.

'You're becoming too old for that kind of thing,' she said, slipping out of his arms and picking up a packet of cigarettes. 'It's all planning for you these days.'

This was a truth that Marty had to face constantly, but it still hurt to hear it.

'Well,' he said, 'they did a bloody good job. Not one passenger hurt.'

'Those passengers were just lucky, Marty. One mistake and

they would have copped it, too – from the terrorists or from the men trying to rescue them. It was a hell of a gamble.'

'In a situation like that, there's no choice. Can I pour you another?'

She flicked her lighter on, lit her cigarette, exhaled a stream of smoke. 'Why not?' As Marty was pouring the drinks, she sat back on the settee and asked, 'So how did your lunch go?'

'An enjoyable feast. Particularly since I wasn't paying. That place is beyond my means.'

'Paddy did the right thing, getting out of the service. Financial security's guaranteed if you stay in, but the money's modest. If you want to live the way Paddy lives, you have to get out and do something else.'

'I don't want to live that way. I just enjoy it occasionally. My lunches with Paddy are my treats. I'm content with that.' He handed her the gin and tonic, then raised his own in the air. 'Cheers.'

'Cheers.' They both drank. Diane rested the glass on her lap and puffed a couple of smoke rings. 'So is he going to buy this idea of yours?'

'Yes. The Association will be a subsidiary of Vigilance International and we'll staff it with former SAS men. The company already offers advice and training on security matters, so Paddy will use that side of the business to put our own men forward as security guards or personal bodyguards.'

'Dodgy.'

'Don't you start. Paddy and I have argued it through and think we can handle it.'

'Just don't let it obsess you, Marty. That's in your nature. You're basically a moral puritan and becoming more so as you get older. Stick to helping your former mates get work and don't do anything else.'

'Such as?'

'I know you. You've talked enough when you've been in your cups. You and that crowd you've been meeting every month in the West End. You do more than just talk about old times.'

'Oh, do we now?' Marty wasn't pleased to hear that he let his tongue slip when drinking, particularly as he'd been drinking more in the past few years, trying to deaden the pain of loss and what he felt was the general shrinking of his horizons. That was bad enough, but to learn that he had talked about the meetings was truly disturbing. 'So what do we talk about?'

'You're a kind of pressure group,' she said. 'You swop stories about men who do things you don't approve of – fellow SAS men, high-ranking officers, civil servants in Whitehall and elsewhere – and you devise ways to stop what they're doing or make them fall into line.'

'We're just trying to uphold the values of the regiment,' he insisted, 'and protect it from anyone who threatens it. I think that's worth doing.'

'It may be worth doing, but if you go about it the way you do – covertly – you're becoming a law unto yourselves and that can't be a good thing. It makes you conspirators. You're also judge and jury. Situations like that can get out of hand, becoming corrupt and destructive.'

Marty sipped his gin and tonic, trying to contain his anger. 'You're paranoid, Diane. You see conspiracies in everything. Ever since you've involved yourself in investigative journalism – particularly regarding Northern Ireland – you've started seeing spooks in every corner. I'm not the one who's obsessed. *You're* the one who's like that. If you're not careful, your work's going to drive you bonkers. Even now, you can hardly sleep at nights. You have too many bad dreams.'

Still drinking, she looked flushed and agitated, which was not a good sign. 'I'm obsessed because I know what's going on,' she said. 'I know what governments get up to behind closed doors, what they hide behind their bland words, how they say they're doing one thing while they're doing another. I also know that I've been marked in certain quarters as a troublemaker and I'm certain my phone's been tapped. You think this is a free country, Marty? If you do, you're deluded.'

'Why would they have you down as a troublemaker? Why would they tap your phone?'

'Because of Northern Ireland – my constant exposure of their dirty tricks there. They bugged my phone when I started publishing articles about the inhuman treatment and torture of political prisoners in Long Kesh and Castlereagh. Those articles led to complaints from the European Community and the complaints are getting louder every day. Those bastards are worried about that.'

Whether what she said was true or not, Marty knew that she meant it. Certainly, for the past year, she had been convinced that she was being watched and that dirty tricks were being used against her: smear stories in rival papers, anonymous complaints to the Press Council, valuable mail going missing, her telephone being tapped, and so on. Marty believed that all of these things were possible, but he didn't like to admit it. At least, he didn't want to increase her fears by agreeing with her. She was already close to being a nervous wreck and getting worse every day.

'How do you know your phone's been bugged?'

'Because they found out things about me that could only have been learned from my telephone conversations. Damn it, Marty, they've bugged me!'

'I don't think the British government is in the habit of bugging the phones of honest citizens.'

'Don't bullshit me, Marty. They've bugged the fucking phones of half of Northern Ireland. They've bugged plenty here, too – criminals, political activists, politicians, other journalists – and the more they do it, the more widespread it becomes. The more *routine* it becomes, the easier it becomes to get permission to do it. Christ, even your precious SAS taps people's phones. Isn't that true, Marty? Don't you have to do that for your surveillance? Come on, sweetheart, admit it!'

'No,' he lied. 'We don't do that.'

'Bullshit!' she said.

Of course, she was right. He was giving her bullshit. Though initially he had been shocked by what he and others had been forced to do in Northern Ireland, the more he thought about it, the more he accepted that some methods of surveillance were unavoidable. He was even coming to accept that certain dirty tricks could only be fought with the same methods. His informal association had, after all, been forced to use some dirty tricks in order to stop the actions of certain individuals who were acting against the interests of the regiment: confidential regimental policy decisions had been leaked to the press; certain individuals had been pressured by members of the association into retracting published opinions; SAS officers who tried to introduce unpopular measures had been harassed in numerous ways until they backed down; even ordinary NCOs and troopers with unhealthy attitudes had found themselves coming under fire . . . He had his doubts about such measures, but increasingly he had come to accept the necessity for them. In certain cases, the end justified the means. This was a hard fact of life.

He finished his drink, placed his glass on the mantelpiece, then went over to sit on the edge of the sofa, beside Diane's outstretched body. Her face was gaunt. Her eyes under the fringe of blonde hair held an unnatural brightness. They were also bloodshot with drink – she drank too much these days – and he knew, when she gazed up at him and smiled, that she was close to the edge.

'You look lovely,' he said.

'You're a very sweet liar. I look like hell on earth and you know it, but you'd never dare say it.'

The butt of her cigarette was smouldering between nicotine-stained fingers, so he removed it and stubbed it out in the ashtray, then turned back to lean over her.

'You need a break,' he said. 'Get away from all this. You work all the time – you don't *do* anything else – and the things you write are starting to take you over, blocking everything else out. You've become obsessed with politics, with the filth of it all, and your obsession's becoming unnatural and eating you up. Let's go on a holiday, Diane, and forget this shit for a while.'

Her smile was slightly mocking and oddly sensual; her green gaze was steady. 'I hate holidays,' she said. 'They're so boring. Dawn to dusk with not a fucking thing to do. I just need work and sex.'

The open neck shirt was hanging loose over her denims, so he slid his hand up under it, felt the bones of her ribcage, then cupped one of her small breasts in his fingers and lightly rubbed the nipple. When the nipple stiffened, she closed her eyes and sighed. 'Yes, Marty, that's all I need.'

'It's not enough,' he replied, though the feel of her aroused him, making him feel younger than he was, lost in sensual reverie. She was going mad, he was convinced, but he needed what she could give him and he knew, when she turned her body towards him, that she would hold him by that. He squeezed her breast with one hand, unbuttoned her shirt with the other, let it fall away, rustling, on both sides and pressed his lips to her bare skin. She sighed and arched her spine. He ran his tongue down to her belly. She unzipped herself and tugged her denims lower to let him kiss her down there. Yes, he felt younger. The self-deception was necessary. He licked her stomach, her pubic hair, her inner thighs, and was briefly renewed. Too many years had gone by, too many loved ones had died, too many friends had been lost in the wars that had helped shape the century. He was losing himself as well. He sensed it even as he stroked her. This man and this woman, together, were losing track of themselves. He and Diane. Two idealists turning bitter. He knew that what he was doing was wrong, but he could no longer stop himself.

He put his tongue inside her. She gasped and then groaned. He licked and sucked to consume her and in turn be consumed. He wanted to lose himself, to forget what he most feared: his ageing, his disillusionment, his shrinking horizons, his growing feeling of isolation in a rapidly changing world.

She was wearing no shoes. He tugged her jeans down over her feet. When she spread her legs, groaning, whispering, 'Fuck me!' he rolled over on top of her. 'Yes!' she whispered. 'Fuck it, do it!' He fell between her legs and did it. He was harder than he had been for a long time and the feeling was good. Inside her, he became her, almost sensing her thoughts, and knew that she had somehow taken him over and made him believe in her.

She saw corruption everywhere. He had started seeing that as well. As they made love, as their bodies became as one, he sensed the madness in both of them.

'Fuck me!' she gasped. 'Fuck me senseless! Fuck you, *fuck* me! Just do it!'

He came on those words, obliterating her, finding oblivion, and remained there, when his spasms had subsided, for a very long time, breathing harshly, despairing.

He was not the young man he had been and felt destroyed by the knowledge. He felt used up and abused and betrayed and that filled him with rage. He would take the rage and use it to give him strength and the hope of renewal. He would right what was wrong.

It was the SAS way.

CHAPTER THIRTY-SIX

'Those bastards!' TT said, switching off the TV, flicking his dark hair off his brown eyes and looking in a stunned way at the others. 'Those IRA cunts!'

Earlier that morning the 79-year-old Earl Mountbatten, former supreme Allied Commander in South-East Asia and Viceroy of India, had driven with members of his family from their Irish home, Classiebawn Castle, to the harbour of Mullaghmore in Country Sligo, and set out for a day's fishing in his thirty-foot boat, *Shadow V*. The boat had scarcely left the harbour when an explosion blew it high in the air, smashing it to smithereens, killing Earl Mountbatten, his grandson Nicholas, aged fourteen, and a seventeen-year old boatman. Earl Mountbatten's daughter, Lady Brabourne, his son Timothy and her mother-in-law, the Dowager Lady Brabourne, were all in critical condition in an intensive care ward. Already, the IRA had claimed responsibility for the 'execution' of Lord Mountbatten and said that the boat had been blown up by a remote-controlled bomb containing fifty pounds of explosive.

'I don't believe it,' Marty heard himself saying. 'I just don't believe it. Him, of all people. That man was respected and loved by everyone, even the Irish. How the fuck could they do that?'

'Probably that's *why* they did it,' Taff said quietly, stroking his nose and staring at Marty with his steady, unnerving gaze. 'Because he *was* loved by so many. They wanted to cause maximum outrage, so they picked someone popular – someone even popular with the Irish. What they're saying is, *no one* is safe. It's a clear message, right?'

'Right,' Alan Pearson said, sharing the table with them because his work in Northern Ireland had bought him his sergeant's stripes. 'He was popular and important. Cousin of the Queen, wasn't he? Prince Phillip's uncle. Even acted as a mentor to the Prince of Wales. You can't get closer to royalty than that. I'd say that's why they picked him.'

'I agree,' Taff said quietly, showing none of the anger Marty was feeling. 'Good tactics, that.'

After all these years of knowing the mild-mannered blond Welshman, Marty still couldn't get used to his almost inhuman distance from everything that normally moved people. On the one hand, he had never known Taff to behave indecently or with cruelty; on the other, he had never known anyone who could face danger or kill his fellow man in such a calm, detached fashion. You could neither love nor loathe Taff – he was someone out of reach – but for a second, looking into his fathomless blue gaze, Marty wanted to strangle him.

'That's your only reaction to what's happened?' he asked. 'To call it *good tactics*?'

Taff shrugged. 'We all agree why they picked on him, Marty, and in their terms it makes sense. I'd call that good tactics.'

'He's right,' TT said. 'We may think that what they did is disgusting, but it wasn't without point. Those bastards knew exactly what they were doing when they choose that particular target. That's a real showcase killing.'

'Jesus Christ!' Marty exclaimed. But of course they were right, disgusting though that truth was. 'So who's next?' he asked rhetorically. 'Prince Phillip? The Queen? And meanwhile, the bastards who did this will get off scot free. There'll be a lot of public condemnation from politicians and that's as far as those arseholes will go. It's all politics and bullshit in the end. It's all fucking diplomacy. We should go back to Northern Ireland and have a range war and not stop until all of those rats are flushed out of their holes. We should, but we won't.'

'Politics,' Alan Pearson said. 'You used the right word there. They play politics while the IRA keeps killing and we get egg on our faces.'

'The IRA and others,' Marty said. 'What about Mogadishu airport? If we hadn't advised the Krauts otherwise, that bloody Baader-Meinhof gang would probably have won their gamble. The bleeding-heart liberals would have refused to let GSG-Nine risk the passengers' lives and another bunch of terrorists would have got exactly what they demanded.'

'But they didn't,' Taff reminded him.

'No, they didn't,' Marty retorted, not to be appeased. 'Because we sent a couple of our best men to Germany to give the Krauts some sound advice. They listened and did what they had to do and that put an end to it.'

'That Mountbatten killing,' TT said. 'I mean, I think that's really bad. If nothing else, they should send a couple of us in there under cover to find out just who did it and put paid to the bastards. Not Long Kesh and not a fucking soapbox trial – just a clean double tap. I know that's what *I'd* do.'

'Damned right,' Alan Pearson said.

Agitated, Marty went to the bar to buy another round. Returning to the table with the four glasses, expertly balanced, he was surprised to see that his hands were shaking a little – a sign of his anger.

'It's not just the IRA,' he said, taking his place at the table and distributing the pint glasses. 'It's all these other terrorists groups, like that Baader-Meinhof gang – a bunch of middle-class kids, for Christ's sake – and others springing up all over the place. The Western governments can't seem to do a thing about it – but you're right, TT, *we* could. We could find out just who those bastards are and do it all on our own. If not the terrorists, then the bastards who supply the weapons.'

'At least we all know who *they* are,' TT said, now growing almost as excited as Marty. 'I mean, they're *legal*, right? Those bastards get knighthoods. They're either going to fancy dinners at Ten Downing Street or being photographed surrounded by blonde bints in night clubs in Marbella. They're grandstanders, most of them – they like the publicity. They make money for the country, so they're fêted instead of condemned, and they drive around in big fancy cars while the weapons and bombs they sell to the terrorists are turned against their own citizens. A right shower of wankers, they are, and they should all have their lights put out.'

'I agree,' Marty said. 'They're even worse than the terrorists. Without them, the terrorists couldn't exist, but they're the ones who not only get off scot free – as TT says, they're actually given fucking knighthoods or the equivalent in their own bloody countries. I mean, I wouldn't be surprised if the explosives that killed Lord Mountbatten were sold to the IRA by some fat cat who moves in the best of circles and gets his dick sucked by the aristocracy. And as TT pointed out – you're being bright today, TT – at least we know, or can find out, who those bastards are. We should do something about them.'

'Then why don't we?' Taff asked, speaking in his usual quiet, deadly serious manner. 'Why not use the Association to track them down and then neutralise them? That's something we could certainly do and its something *worth* doing.'

Everyone went silent and stared nervously at Taff, as if he had touched upon something that all had been thinking about. Certainly, when he glanced at Taff's steady blue gaze, at his youthful, unreadable face, Marty realised that *he* had been thinking about it ever since the Association had been formed and, in particular, been fronted by Vigilance International.

In the past couple of years, working out of offices in Paddy's company, the Association had spread its wings and done many good things, most importantly in the obtaining of jobs for former SAS men: as military advisers, security officers and personal bodyguards to commercial companies and highly placed individuals in foreign countries. It had also kept an eye on what was happening to the regiment and corrected what they felt was going wrong. Paddy had organised most of the former through his connections in the City, where security requirements were increasing every day, and through his video production company, which had introduced him to many influential friends overseas. While he had been thus engaged, Marty had headed the Association and monitored its activities in his spare time, organising the meetings, acting as chairman and otherwise doing all he could to assist, given the limitations on his time imposed by his normal duties for the regiment. Naturally, this particular part of his life was known only to other members of the Association – not to anyone else in the regiment. The administration of the Association itself was carried out by former SAS members who were formally working for Paddy's Vigilance International.

The three men gathered around this table, Taff, TT and Alan Pearson, were active members of the Association and had been highly efficient at correcting what was wrong as decided at the 'Chinese parliaments' of the monthly meetings. They and other members of the Association had persuaded NCOs to resist certain changes in direction suggested by unloved Ruperts, recommended RTUs for undisciplined troopers, brought pressure to bear on NCOs who were deemed to be behaving in a manner detrimental to the values of the regiment, and passed on to Marty any information they received about policy proposals or orders that could be harmful to the regiment in the long term. Where such proposals could not be blocked or amended by pressure from Marty and his fellow NCOs, the information was passed on to Paddy, who would leak it to the media as a means of embarrassing those responsible. In this way, the Association had, among other successes, been able to prevent the regiment from being used for undesirable purposes, such as acting as strike-breakers or thinly disguised policemen. What the Association had *not* been able to do, however, was exert a positive influence on decisions regarding the neutralising of enemies of the state, such as the IRA or other terrorist groups – and that, Marty realised, was exactly what they were talking about now.

'Track them down?' Alan Pearson asked softly to break the long silence. 'Neutralise them?'

'Why not?' Taff replied calmly. 'That's what we've been trained to do. We can do it, but we rarely get the chance because everyone's playing at politics and nothing gets done. Let's do it ourselves, I say. We now have the means at hand. We have the Association, so let's use it to do something worth doing – something more than just getting jobs for old mates and correcting wrongs in the regiment.'

'I'm not sure,' TT said. 'I mean, that's taking things a bit far. I think—'

'Take this Lord Mountbatten business,' Taff interjected with calm conviction. 'We all revered the man and we're all mad at what's happened, but we know we can't do a thing about it, which makes us feel even worse. And what about the regiment? It's rarely used any more. We get the odd terrorist outrage, one or two of us get called in, but most times we're just sitting on the shelf with nothing to do. We're the best-trained men in the whole damned country and we're sitting here, rotting. Even worse, we're burning up with frustration because while we're forced to sit here, twiddling our thumbs, every activist and terrorist in the country's having a field day. So let's initiate a few things ourselves and get some self-satisfaction.'

He had been speaking to TT, but now he turned his head to stare straight at Marty, smiling in a way that Marty sensed was almost a challenge. A little shaken by what he had heard, yet knowing that Taff was deadly serious, he was pleased to realise that the Welshman was only articulating what he had often considered doing himself. In principle he agreed – he was frustrated enough, God knows – but the proposal would definitely be the first decisive step down what Paddy had called a 'slippery slope'. Though Marty's anger had often made him contemplate what Taff was now suggesting, he wasn't quite ready for it yet. Indeed, the fact that he had even contemplated it was frightening enough.

'Would you actually be prepared to do that?' he asked.

Taff shrugged casually. 'Sure. Why not?'

Marty glanced at the other two. TT looked embarrassed, then shook his head. 'I don't think . . . *Maybe* . . . under extreme circumstances, but I'd have to be convinced.'

'It'd have to be official,' Alan said. 'I don't think I'd do it for the Association. Well, *maybe*, if . . .'

'What?' Taff asked, gazing levelly at him.

Confused, Alan glanced around the bar as if to distract himself.

'If what?' Taff asked, not letting him off the hook.

'Maybe if . . .' Alan shrugged as TT had done. 'If someone else started it. Someone senior to me. You, Marty – or maybe even Paddy Kearney . . . Someone I trust. Maybe after the first one.'

Taff smiled and turned back to Marty. 'There you go,' he said. 'You just have to give the pebble a little kick and let it roll down the hill. All the others will follow in its wake. It's a natural thing, like.'

Defeated by Taff's steady gaze, disturbed by the knowledge that in essence he agreed with him, Marty finished off his beer, then kicked his chair back and stood up.

'I don't think so,' he said, though he didn't think he sounded too convincing, not even to himself. 'I can understand the sentiments behind it, but it's going too far. I think we're doing all we can do and I'm happy with that. I'll see you all on Monday.'

He walked out of the bar, sensing Taff's steady gaze boring through his back, feeling relieved to get out. When he reached the car park and was putting his key in the lock of his car, he saw that his hands were still shaking. He certainly wasn't himself these days.

Neither was Diane. He was reminded of this when, late that afternoon, he met her in the French pub in Soho, grateful to be stepping in from the pouring rain, though not particularly keen on this particular rendezvous. Famous as a watering hole for hard-drinking literary types such as Dylan Thomas, it was often packed, though now with journalists and those from other fields of the media. Marty never felt quite comfortable in the place and now, as he hurried in from the rain and saw the usual sea of flushed faces in a cloud of cigarette and cigar smoke, most talking animatedly, he felt self-conscious and out of place again.

Those not standing were sitting on stools along the bar, by the windows overlooking Dean Street, and at tables in the alcove to the left of the bar. The walls were covered in photos of all the famous who had drunk there previously and, in some cases, still did so. Marty was glad to see that Diane was on a stool at the bar, drinking a large glass of white wine and having a heated conversation with someone on the next stool. The man's thick white hair appeared to be electrified and his black gaberdine was draped like a cape over the shoulders of a shabby grey suit. He was wearing a polka-dot bow-tie and his ageing face was flushed with drink. Unfortunately, Diane, who was deadly pale when sober, was just as flushed as the man, which was not a good sign.

As he pushed his way through those standing between the doorway and the bar, Marty was glad that he had followed his lunchtime pints in the Sports and Social with a couple of large whiskies on the train coming in to London. More fortified than he normally was when entering this watering hole, he came up behind Diane and planted a kiss on her head, cutting her off in mid-sentence. Glancing sideways, she stared at him with bloodshot eyes, then smiled and said, 'Ah! Here's my man! You actually made it.'

'Why wouldn't I?'

'I thought a few drinks in the Sports and Social might lead to a few more and make you forget me.'

'That's never happened.' He glanced at her nearly empty glass. 'Can I get you another?'

'Yes. Make it a large one.'

'And the same for me, old chap,' the man with the electrified white hair said. 'We're both drinking the same, dear.'

Diane giggled drunkenly, then introduced the man beside her. 'This is Angus. Don't ask me his other name. We just met today.'

Angus stuck his hand out. 'Angus Lazenby. And you are . . .?'

'Marty Butler.' He shook the man's hand, which was as frail as a bird's body. 'Was it whisky?'

'Both whiskies,' Diane said. 'I decided to make a day of it. Couldn't bloody well work.'

Diane had been working less and less lately, complaining that she couldn't get as many commissions as before because she was being slandered by her unknown enemies. In his view, this was due to the fact that she was falling into a state of paranoia not helped by her heavy drinking. He therefore ignored the remark and ordered three large whiskies. While he was waiting for the drinks to come, Diane and Angus continued their conversation, which seemed to be a heated debate about the increasing constraints being placed upon investigative journalists. The debate ended only when the barman brought the drinks. Angus hastily finished the one he already had and picked up the fresh one.

'Cheers!' he said. He had a sip of his fresh drink, then asked of Marty, 'So what do you do?'

'What?'

'You're clearly not a journalist or a writer, so what do you *do*? Are you in sports, or what? I heard your charming lady here make mention of the Sports and Social – sounds absolutely ghastly – and you *do* look rather fit, if I may say so. Naturally, therefore, I assumed—'

'No, I'm not in sports. I'm in the—'

'Angus,' Diane said, cutting Marty short, 'why don't you have a talk with that nice friend on your right? The one you were talking to when I came in. He's been dying of loneliness since you cruelly turned your back on him.'

'Oh, I see,' Angus said, looking affronted. 'Suddenly I'm superfluous to requirements. I *do* beg your pardon, dears.'

When Angus huffily turned away to engage his friend in conversation, Marty slipped in in front of Diane, carefully positioning his back to Angus, whom he didn't much care for. Another *poseur*, he thought, then leaned close to Diane and whispered, 'Thanks.'

She grinned, lit a cigarette and puffed a cloud of smoke. 'I don't think this is the place to announce that you're a soldier,' she said. 'You're not a breed they would understand.'

'They're not a breed *I* understand,' he replied, 'so I think you were wise.'

'I'm the rock in your stormy sea.'

Marty smiled. 'Your own seas are too stormy for me, Diane. Have you been here long?'

'Don't lecture me, Marty. I knew this morning, when you phoned to say you were coming, that I couldn't sit at home and wait for you. It was a dog-day morning, believe me. I just had to get out.'

'You could have gone for a walk in Hyde Park.'

'I can't stand fucking parks. Anyway, that's why I told you to meet me here. My own place gets me down these days.'

'I've noticed.'

'What does that mean?'

'You're working a lot less than you used to and you drink a lot more. That's enough to make anyone depressed and I think it's your problem.'

'Wise man.' Her sarcasm was patent. 'I'm working less these days because I'm not *getting* the work and you and I know the reason why. Ever since I started accusing the government of dirty tricks in Northern Ireland I've had nothing but problems. Now my editors are growing wary of me; they don't want the hassle.'

'You think they're being harassed?'

'If you mean are they being put under pressure from above – then, yes, I'd say that's the case. Every story I write has to be vetted by Whitehall and those bastards aren't letting too much through. Then, when I *do* manage to slip a few home truths through, someone somewhere writes a letter of complaint and I'm back in the shit. But you think I'm imagining this, don't you?'

'No, I don't,' he said. Indeed, he was painfully aware of the fact that the constrictions placed upon press reporting had increased dramatically in recent years and seemed to be increasing even more. Even Paddy, who had close ties with Fleet Street, had told him that many of his journalist friends had been complaining about the difficulties they were having in doing their job. A Watergate scandal could not happen in England because English journalists did not have the freedom of the *Washington Post*. The Official Secrets Act was a mighty weapon, being used, or abused, with more abandon every year. And Margaret Thatcher, as Marty saw it, was not about to be more liberal than her predecessors. Nevertheless, the extent to which Diane was being harassed was still problematical. With her, you could never tell where reality ended and fantasy began. All Marty knew for sure is that she was growing paranoid and drinking more heavily. He was very disturbed by it. On the other hand, he shared many of her concerns and was inclined to believe most of what she told him. This brought him no comfort.

'So how are things between you and Paddy?' she asked him while indicating to the barman that she wanted the glasses filled up.

'Fine,' Marty said. 'Why shouldn't they be?'

'I'm not implying anything, Marty. I just thought that being involved in that organisation that's finding work for your old mates might lead to complications in your formerly perfect friendship.'

'Why should it?'

'You're questioning everything I say.'

'Well, why should it?' In fact, having followed his lunchtime beers with the whiskies on the train and now having more, he was feeling the effects and they weren't good. It was ironic that he should worry about Diane's drinking when he was drinking more himself these days – not nearly as much as she was, but probably still too much – and he had noticed that increasingly the drink was making him more tired than drunk, which in turn made him easily irritated. Realising that her remark had made him just that, he silently vowed to be careful.

'I'm not saying it should,' Diane replied, sounding weary. 'I'm just asking if working through Paddy's company has led to any complications.'

'No,' he said. 'None. I don't know why it should.'

'Well, I know from what you've told me – in your cups, of course, darling – that you and he have disagreed about certain small matters, such as exactly what your Association should and should not be doing.'

'Routine disagreements,' he corrected her, though he felt uneasy that the subject had been raised. 'We have what the SAS call "Chinese parliaments", in which everyone can say what they think. Naturally, there are bound to be disagreements, but they're always ironed out.'

'You used never to have disagreements at all,' she insisted. 'Certainly not with your hero and mentor, Paddy Kearney. You hung on his every word. The disagreements only started when you got involved with Vigilance International. I know that. You've told me so.'

Pouting like an aggressive schoolgirl, she reached out for the fresh drink that had just been placed on the counter by the barman. After having a good slug of it, she banged the glass back down on the counter and inhaled on her cigarette. When she exhaled the smoke, she didn't bother turning her head aside, deliberately letting it blow over him. He pretended not to notice, though he felt angry.

'It's a democratic organisation,' he insisted, 'so we agree to disagree. I think that's normal and healthy. But I don't want to discuss this any more. Can't we change the subject? You know that Paddy's coming to join us for a drink, so please let's have no bloody nonsense.'

'Pardon *me*!' Diane exclaimed, then she smiled and reached out to stroke his cheek. 'Sorry, sweetheart. I'm just playing my wicked games. Blame it all on the drink.'

'I do,' Marty said, though she had touched a raw nerve, since what she had said was essentially true. He and Paddy *had* had differences over the extent to which the Association should be used and they *were* the first disagreements they had ever had. It hurt Marty to accept that this was true, but he could not deny it. He sighed. 'What the hell!'

Diane picked up her glass and drank most of the whisky, then put the glass down again, inhaling and exhaling more smoke, squinting through it to see him. 'Talk of the devil,' she said, sounding perfectly pleasant now. 'Paddy's just walked in.' She waved and cried out, 'Over here!'

Paddy pushed his way through the crowd blocking the way from the door to the bar. Reaching them, he kissed Diane on the cheek and affectionately squeezed Marty's shoulder. 'So how goes it, my loves?'

'Fine,' Marty said, pleased as always to see him. 'What would you like?'

'Is that whisky?'

'Yes.'

'Fine.'

Marty ordered three more whiskies while Paddy, looking distinguished in his customary pinstripe suit with shirt and old school tie, glanced curiously around the crowded bar. 'I always imagine I'll see some old school chums here,' he said, 'but most of them never make it up from Fleet Street, which is their little ghetto. Have you two been here long?'

'Not long enough,' Diane said.

Paddy grinned. 'You look flushed and red-eyed,' he said, 'so I assume you've been here a while. A lively spot, I'll confess. I've been in it a few times before, but not for some time now. They're mostly writers and media types here, I gather; not your hard-bitten journalist. Present company excluded, of course.'

He bowed his head in Diane's direction and she smiled and said, 'A lot of journalists come here as well, so if you stay long enough, Paddy, you're bound to see someone you know.'

'I hope not,' Paddy said. When their drinks came, he had a sip of his whisky, then said, 'Christ, did you hear the news about Lord Mountbatten? Bloody dreadful, yes?'

'Yes,' Marty said.

'Unforgivable,' Paddy said with feeling. 'Those bastards are beyond the pale in my book. Even for them, that was too much.'

'That's what the lads were saying in the Sports and Social,' Marty told him, feeling slightly drunk and relieved to be letting it out. 'I had a few beers with them and they were all spitting mad. They were talking about using some of *our* lads to take action where the authorities either can't or won't. They were talking about neutralising some of the bastards responsible – and I think they half meant it.'

Paddy frowned in consternation. 'What do you mean, some of *our* lads?'

'The ones working for Vigilance International,' Marty told him, not wanting to mention the Association in front of Diane.

'To *neutralise* some of those responsible?'

Marty nodded. 'Yep.'

'You mean the IRA?'

Marty shook his head. 'Nope. On the assumption that they probably couldn't get at the terrorists without official sanction and help, they thought it might be better to start with the arms dealers, who have a much higher public profile. So, you know, they'd be much easier to find. That's what the lads were talking about doing.'

'And when they find them?' Paddy asked, still frowning.

Marty shrugged. 'Put out their lights.'

Paddy glanced at Diane. She just grinned and raised her hands in the air, as if offering a prayer.

'I take it this *was* a drunken conversation?' Paddy said.

'Not *that* drunken, Paddy. We just had a couple of quick pints.'

'I trust you quenched their enthusiasm,' Paddy said, sounding very serious.

'I did,' Marty said. 'But I have to confess that, the more I thought about it on the train, the more I was convinced it's a sound idea. I mean, what the hell? *Someone* has to do something about it and who better than our men? A few covert hits here and there and the world would soon be a better place.'

'I take it that *you're* drunk,' Paddy said, 'and just making a poor joke.'

'Not necessarily. I may be a little bit drunk, but I know what I feel. And after what those bastards did this morning I wouldn't mind taking out the other bastards who supplied them with weapons.'

'Damned right,' Diane said, exhaling another cloud of smoke. 'The worst bastards of all are the arms dealers who trade with all sides. The government condemns the terrorists even while fêting the men who sell them weapons. So if you put a stop to *that* filthy trade, you'll put a stop to the terrorists.'

'Right,' Marty said, feeling exultant and nervous at once, aware that his friend Paddy was glaring at him.

'I hold no truck with the arms dealers,' Paddy said, clearly trying to contain his anger, 'but the very suggestion that our men should covertly do something about them is not one I'll agree with. And that you, Marty, drunk or sober, should say you approve of the idea absolutely disgusts me. Let's hear no more of it.'

'It was just a thought,' Marty said, resenting the way Paddy was talking to him.

'You've had thoughts like that before, Marty, and I don't care to know about them. They're unhealthy and possibly based on paranoia, so let's please drop the subject.'

'Everyone's dropping subjects today,' Diane said in a droll

manner, then raised her glass to her lips and had another sip of her whisky.

'I'm leaving,' Paddy said. 'I've had enough of this. It isn't even a joke.'

'It was just a thought,' Marty repeated.

'You think too much, Marty. Particularly when you've been drinking. I trust that when we next meet you'll be more sober in thought and deed. I'll call you next week.' He nodded at Diane, not smiling, then he turned and walked out.

Marty watched him leave, pushing his way through the packed drinkers, disappearing through the doorway as if dissolving in the clouds of smoke that hung above the bobbing heads in the crowded bar. When he had gone, Marty turned back to Diane and said, 'Well, you were right. We disagree a lot more these days.'

'He was really angry this time.'

'Yes, I guess so.'

At that moment, the white-haired Angus lurched away from the bar, leaving his whisky-stained copy of the *Evening Standard* lying on the counter. Staring down at the headline on the front page, Marty was shocked for the second time that day. Picking up the paper to read the lead story, he learned that the British Army had just had its worst day in living memory at the hands of the IRA. Following the bombing of Lord Mountbatten's boat, an IRA bomb containing more than half a ton of explosives hidden in a hay cart had exploded at Warrenpoint in Country Down as an army convoy drove past, killing fifteen soldiers and seriously injuring eight others. A helicopter trying to casevac the wounded was damaged in another explosion and a gun battle had ensued between troops and IRA men across a nearby loch. The death toll was the worst suffered by the Army in any single incident.

'Jesus Christ!' Marty exclaimed, disgustedly throwing the paper down in front of Diane. 'I don't give a damn what Paddy says. We should take those bastards out. And if we can't get at them personally, we should go for the people who sell them arms. Damned right, we should.'

'Think about it when you're sober,' Diane replied.

'I will,' Marty said.

CHAPTER THIRTY-SEVEN

Marty had spent most of the past few years dividing his time between theoretical planning with the green slime of the Kremlin – the intelligence section of Regimental HQ – and leading his SAS troopers in CRW exercises that often took place in the CQB House, or 'killing house', of the Counter Revolutionary Warfare Wing in Bradbury Lines in Hereford. There, wearing their all-black CRW overalls and respirator masks, the men were compelled to make their way through the six 'killing rooms' of the mock-up house, firing double taps from the Browning High Power handgun and short bursts from their Ingram submachine-guns, at various pop-up 'figure eleven' targets. They were also armed with real Brocks Pyrotechnics MX5 stun grenades and had to use these, even more dangerously, in certain unexpected situations recreated in one of the six rooms.

The CQB house was dubbed the 'killing house' for two good reasons. First, its purpose was to train men to kill at close quarters. Second, real ammunition was always used and at least one SAS man had been killed accidentally while training with it. Prior to exercises in the killing house, the men were trained to enter captured buildings by a variety of means, including abseiling with ropes from the roof, sometimes firing their handguns as they clung to the rope with the other. The killing-house training was, however, essentially to prepare them for what they would meet in a hostage-rescue operation and make them skilled in distinguishing between terrorist and hostage. This was done with the aid of pictures on the walls and dummies – the figure-eleven targets – that were moved from place to place or popped out suddenly from behind artificial walls or up from the lower frame of windows.

As an indication of the changing times, the figure eleven targets had once been made to look like Soviet troops; now they were dummy men wearing anoraks and balaclava helmets.

While hitting the terrorist quickly and accurately was one of the main points of the exercises, the more important one was teaching the men how to avoid hitting a hostage when they had only mere seconds to distinguish between the two. They also had to be careful to avoid the worst possibility of all: an own goal, or shooting one of their own comrades by accident.

Training in the killing house was claustrophobic and nerve-racking, with a high fallout rate for those who applied. Those who managed to survive the course went on to spend many months overseas, learning an even wider variety of hostage-rescue skills from West Germany's GSG-9 border police and France's Groupement d'Intervention de la Gendarmerie Nationale (GIGN) paramilitary units, the Bizondere Bystand Eenheid (BBE) counter-terrorist arm of the Royal Netherlands Marine Corps, Italy's Nucleo Operativo Centrale di Sicurezza (NOCS), Spain's Grupo Especial de Operaciones (GEO), and the US 1st Special Forces Operational Detachment, created specially for CRW operations. The overseas training placed a special emphasis on physical stamina, endurance and marksmanship, including practice at indoor firing with live ammunition in other kinds of 'killing houses' such as mock-up aircraft, ships and public streets; abseiling and parachuting onto rooftops, parked aircraft and boats; hostage rescue in a variety of circumstances (with cross-over training in mountaineering, skiing and scuba diving); and the handling of CS gas canisters, and stun (flash-bang), fire and smoke grenades. By the end of all this, if they managed to survive it, they were as well trained as any soldiers could possibly be for counter-terrorist (CT) work.

Marty was well pleased with the work he was doing in the CRW Wing, though dissatisfied at the lack of opportunities he'd had to put it into practice – even the Spaghetti House restaurant siege of 1975 and the Balcombe Street siege, two months later, which the SAS could have tackled superbly, had been dealt with by the Metropolitan Police.

He was therefore both shocked and excited when, on the afternoon of 30 April 1980, he received an urgent phone call from his CO, Lieutenant-Colonel William Osborne, informing him that earlier that morning a group of six armed terrorists, members of the Revolutionary Movement for the Liberation of Arabistan, had taken over the Iranian Embassy at 16 Princes Gate in London, and were holding captive nineteen Iranian nationals and four British citizens.

'We might be called in for this,' Osborne told Marty, 'so I think you'd better get over here.'

During the subsequent briefing, which took place in a room filled with members of the green slime and regimental NCOs, Marty learned that the six terrorists holding the embassy had already been identified and were known to have been trained in Iraq, to have entered the country with Iraqi passports, and to have been supplied with weapons brought in by diplomatic bag from Baghdad. Those weapons included two Skorpion W263 Polish submachine-guns, three Browning self-loading pistols, one .38 Astra revolver, five Russian RGD5 hand grenades and, as far as could be ascertained, lots of ammunition.

The stated purpose of their mission was to publicise the plight of Arabs in Iran and to demand the freedom of 92 political prisoners held there. The hostages included the Embassy's British caretaker and chauffeur, Ron Morris; a Diplomatic Protection Group constable, PC Trevor Lock; and five visitors to the Embassy, four of whom were journalists, including Chris Cramer, a BBC news organiser, and Sim Harris, a BBC sound recordist. PC Lock was known to have had a standard police-issue .38 Smith and Wesson pistol concealed on his person when captured, which could prove to be dangerous.

So far no one had been seriously harmed, though Lock's face had been cut by flying glass and Dr Ali Afrouz, the Embassy's chargé d'affaires, had badly bruised his face and sprained his wrist while attempting unsuccessfully to make his escape. Ninety minutes after the seizure of the embassy, the terrorists had asked for a woman doctor to be sent in. Though at first it was assumed that she was needed to attend to PC Lock, she was in fact required to attend to the embassy press officer, Mrs Frieda Mozafarian, who had suffered a series of fainting fits combined with muscular spasms.

An hour before, at approximately 1500 hours in a basement office in Whitehall, a top-level management team known as COBR, representing the Cabinet Office Briefing Room but including the police, MI5 and the SAS, had discussed the issue and decided on a preliminary course of action. First, the Metropolitan Police would call in specially trained police psychologists to negotiate with the terrorists, using their undoubted desire for media coverage as a bargaining chip. Having met them halfway with this demand, the police negotiators would then try to talk them out of the building, letting the affair stretch out as long as necessary. During that period, they would soften the terrorists up with food, medical attention, communications, more access to the media, and the involvement of their own ambassadors and those with other friendly Middle Eastern states. The negotiators would then ask for the release of certain hostages, particularly those ill or wounded. This would not only reduce the number of hostages to be dealt with, but also encourage the terrorists to feel that they were contributing to a positive dialogue.

In fact, all of this was simply a way of buying enough time for the police and MI5 to plant miniature microphone probes inside the building by drilling quietly through the walls. It would also enable them to scan it with parabolic direction microphones and thermal imagers, which would show just where the hostages were being held.

Should negotiations fail, or if the terrorists should kill a hostage, clearance would be given for the SAS to attack the building.

Codenamed 'Pagoda', the SAS operation would use the

entire CT squadron: a command group of four officers plus a fully equipped support team consisting of one officer and 25 other ranks. A second team, replicating the first, would remain on a three-hour standby until the first team had left the base. A third team, if required, would be composed of experienced SAS soldiers. The close-quarters support teams would be backed up by sniper groups, who would pick off targets from inside the embassy, and specially trained medical teams to rescue and resuscitate the hostages.

As Marty had discussed many times with Diane and Paddy, London had gradually become a battleground for numerous Middle East terrorist groups; so, given Paddy's disapproval of covert action against them, he was delighted to be tackling them on home ground with official approval.

Convinced that this particular group would not come out voluntarily, he left the briefing room in a state of exhilaration, then went immediately to the spider in Bradbury Lines, to put together his two CT teams. After selecting his most experienced men, including Taff, TT and Alan Pearson, he briefed them on what was known to be happening and what was required of them in the event of an assault. The assault, if it came, would have a single objective: to rescue the hostages from the embassy. The assault force would be divided into three teams: Red Team, tasked with clearing the top half of the building, from the second to the forth floor; Blue Team, tasked with clearing the lower half from the basement and garden, upwards to the first floor, and also to handle evacuation procedures; and the perimeter containment group, or snipers, to be codenamed Zero Delta and placed in position along the front and sides of the building.

The assault teams were to be insinuated into the Royal College of Medical Practitioners at 14 Princes Gate, next door to the embassy. To avoid the press, they would be transported from Bradbury Lines to the Regents Park Barracks of the Household Cavalry, in Albany Street. When required, they would be smuggled into the grounds of the college in the same Avis vans. From there, they would make their way to the Forward Holding Area (FHA) in the college by clambering unseen over the walls and rear gardens. Once in the FHA, they would have to be ready for an assault on the embassy at ten minutes' notice. If the terrorists started killing, the SAS would launch the Immediate-Action Plan, which would involve breaking in through the windows to clear the building room by room with CS gas and firearms, trusting that they could reach the hostages before the terrorists started killing them. Their second task was the Deliberate Assault Plan, which was to be put into motion at a time chosen by the CO, which would not be until the location of the hostages was known and the terrorists were believed to be exhausted.

Once briefed, the men were transported from Hereford to London in hired vans, all wearing civilian clothing like that of factory workers, none of them armed. Their weapons and equipment were transported separately in crates stacked high in furniture vans. Arriving at the Household Cavalry Barracks in Albany Street, Regents Park, they were given camp beds in a cold and dusty unused barracks, then made to unpack the crates of weapons and equipment that arrived shortly after.

When the crates had been unpacked, the men stripped off their civilian clothing and put on their gear: black CRW assault suits with felt pads in knees and elbows; flame-resistant underwear; GPV 25 wraparound soft body armour with hard ceramic composite plates front and back; NBC hoods for protection against heat, dust and smoke (they would not be wearing helmets); and the 800-gram S6 respirator with nosecup filter for protection against gases, aerosols and smoke; scratch-resistant, polycarbonate eyepieces resistant to chemical or solvent attack; tinted lenses for protection against the flash from stun grenades; and microphones mounted in front of the mouthpiece, to be linked by means of a communication harness to the assault team's radio transmitter.

Leaving their temporary bashas, they proceeded to the lecture hall where they were divided into three teams – Red, Blue and the perimeter containment group – then allocated their weapons. Though previous hostage-rescue operations had favoured the Ingram submachine-gun, this time they would be given the Heckler & Koch MP5, which was small and compact, could fire 800 rounds per minute with uncommon accuracy, and had an effective range of 200 yards. More importantly, though firing rapidly and precisely, it did so at low velocity; this meant that the bullets would hit the intended target without going through it and striking one of the hostages. Each man would also have a Browning High Power handgun and some would be armed with Remington 870 pump-action shotguns, which would be used to blast the locks from the doors of locked rooms.

The two assault teams would also carry flash-bangs (ISFE and MX5 stun grenades) for their shock effect during the first few seconds of the assault, CS gas grenades to choke and blind the terrorists temporarily, and a variety of explosive devices, including frame charges for the blowing out of windows and the skylight. The perimeter containment group, led by Sergeant Tommy Taylor, would be given the L42A1 bolt-action sniper rifle with tripod. Finally, the equipment was distributed according to each man's assigned role in the operation. This included W.J. Crow lightweight aluminium assault ladders; sledgehammers, axes, wrecking bars, glass-cutters and grappling hooks.

Lieutenant-Colonel Osborne personally gave them another briefing in the Regents Park Barracks, where diagrams of the embassy, including the layout of each room, were pinned to blackboards. When the men had been informed in detail about the tasks of each team, they packed their kit, piled back into the Avis vans, and were driven to the Royal College of Medical Practitioners, adjoining the embassy, where they moved into the rooms designated as the Forward Holding Area.

Once settled into the FHA, the men of Red Team clambered up onto the roof in full CRW gear, made their way stealthily across to the adjoining roof of the embassy, and quietly tied abseiling ropes to the chimneys, leaving the rest of the rope coiled up beside each chimney. When this job was completed, they crossed back to the college and made their way back down to the FHA.

They were now officially on standby and ready to go.

Marty was bitterly disappointed that his age precluded him from taking part in the actual assault, but at least he was part of the command group led by the CO and a special controller liaising between the SAS and the Metropolitan Police, operating from a sixth-floor apartment overlooking the rear of the embassy, out of sight of the journalists at the front. However, they could view the embassy building from all sides with the aid of their highly advanced audio-visual surveillance equipment, including multi-role IR (infrared) thermal imagers, which could scan outside walls, track body heat, and reveal the position of those inside the building, by day or by night; image-intensifiers connected to cameras with interchangeable binocular lenses; and thermal imaging cameras that produced high-quality video pictures that could be displayed automatically on an integral video monitor for direct viewing while also being recorded on another monitor for retrospective visual analysis.

The building had, furthermore, been subjected to the implantation of SGT laser surveillance systems, including miniature audio surveillance probes coupled to a combination of tape recorders, 35-millimetre cameras and CCTV (closed-circuit television). Thus, while Marty and the rest of the command group were at one side of the building, they could not only see what was happening on all sides, but also hear some of what was going on inside.

Being out of sight of the media, Marty thought, was all to the good. Certainly, when earlier that evening he had gone for a walk round to the front of the building, he had been shocked to see the floodlit metal scaffolding and canvas marquee of the press enclosure hastily constructed in Hyde Park, near Exhibition Road, as well as the numerous vans, cars and trailers of the police and broadcast media, with TV and communications cables snaking across the road. It looked like a circus – and Marty realised, with a sinking heart, that, if his men had to go in, they would be doing so, for the first time, in full view of the media, which meant not only the local populace, but virtually the whole world. If that happened, the anonymity of the SAS would end overnight. The thought of this shocked him.

Trying to adjust to this new kind of warfare, this very public form of combat being treated as a media spectacle, he spent the next five days flitting between the command centre at the side of the building and the Forward Holding Area in the Royal College of Medical Practitioners. By now, the Metropolitan Police were communicating directly with the terrorists either by phone or through the embassy windows, in English and Arabic, using their skilled negotiators to buy more time. This was valuable to the police, but to the SAS men waiting on standby it was extremely frustrating.

If Marty at least found some distraction in his daily high-technology surveillance of the outside and inside of the captured embassy, his assault teams in the FHA were not so lucky. For the next five days, as the negotiations continued, they were forced to endure a non-stop learning process in the frustrating periods between false alerts ('Hyde Park' alerts) and being stood down again. This happened many times. Each time they were stood down, they had to strip off their heavy CRW outfits, put on casual clothing, and go back to familiarising themselves with both the Immediate Action Plan and the Deliberate Assault Plan, as well as studying repeatedly every photograph, drawing and report that the SAS green slime and Metropolitan Police had dredged up on the terrorists and their hostages.

Then, as yet another terrorist deadline approached and they received the alert message 'Hyde Park', they had to get back into their CRW outfits and clamber back up to the roof, prepared to go into action on the more important radio message, 'London Bridge', at four minutes' notice. When that terrorist deadline also passed without incident, the frustrated assault teams were stood down again – and so it went on and on.

It was a cat-and-mouse game of gradually mounting tension and, inevitably, of horror.

At 1630 hours on the first day, the terrorists released a female Iranian hostage, wrongly thinking, because she had fainted, that she was pregnant.

At 1800 hours the terrorists stated that, if their demands for the release of the prisoners in Arabistan were not met by noon the following day, the embassy and all inside it would be blown up.

At 2315 hours one of the hostages, the BBC news organiser

Chris Cramer, suffering from virulent dysentery, was released, was seen to by a doctor, and then gave the police invaluable information about what was going on inside.

In the early hours of the second day the terrorists announced that the British hostages and other non-Iranian hostages would not be harmed, though the deadline for the safety of the others was still valid. Shortly after, the audio-surveillance devices picked up the sound of a terrorist firing a threatening burst into the ceiling of Room 9A, second floor, where the hostages were all being held, causing some of the women to scream.

Ten minutes after the noon deadline, the terrorist leader phoned to say in broken English that he was giving the Iranian government until two that afternoon to meet his demands, but when that deadline also passed, with no response from the Iranian government, the expected explosion did not occur.

That afternoon, the terrorists again insisted that, if the Iranian government acceded to their demands, the siege would end peacefully. When the Iranians again failed to respond, the terrorists changed their tune and asked for three Arab ambassadors – from Jordan, Iraq and Algeria – to arrange for a plane to take them out of Britain when they were ready to go.

That evening, while the terrorists were waiting for a response to their latest demand, the police were drilling holes in the walls of the embassy to insert more audio-surveillance probes. Even as they were doing this, two of the hostages appeared at a window, both covered by a terrorist gunman, to ask what the noise was. The police claimed not to know and another night passed without incident.

During the third day, shortly after the audio-surveillance team had confirmed that the hostages were being held in Room 9A, the terrorist leader appeared at the window, pointing a pistol at the head of the embassy's cultural attaché, Dr Abul Fazi Ezzatti, and threatened to kill him unless he was allowed to talk to the media by telephone or telex. When the police negotiator smoothly insisted that he could not do that just yet, the terrorist screamed abuse at him, though again he did not kill the hostage.

This incident, merciful as it seemed, was an indication to

Marty that the terrorist leader was starting to crack and that the killing would start soon.

The leader then set another deadline, this time demanding a talk with someone from the BBC, which he would conduct through his BBC hostage, Sim Harris. The police negotiator tried refusing this demand as well, but acceded to it when more death threats were made.

Later that afternoon, a BBC TV news editor conducted a conversation with Sim Harris, who was standing at a first-floor window with a gun aimed at his head from behind the curtain. The demand this time, made through Harris, was for a coach to take the terrorists and their hostages, plus at least one unnamed Arab ambassador, to Heathrow. The non-Iranian hostages would be released there. The aircraft would then take the terrorists, their hostages and the unnamed ambassador to an unspecified Arab country, where they, also, would be released. The terrorist leader also wanted a communiqué about his aims and grievances to be broadcast by the BBC that evening.

The authorities met the demand only halfway. That evening the BBC gave the terrorists' demands as brief a mention as possible, and again, though the terrorist leader expressed his outrage, no harm came to the hostages.

Later that evening, however, another hostage was released: the embassy secretary, Mrs Hiyech Sanei Kanji. Any hope that this was a sign of capitulation on the part of the terrorists was dashed when Mrs Kanji informed the police that she had been released only so that she could give them another message: if the terrorists' demands were not broadcast in full, they would kill a hostage.

Learning of this, Red Team again clambered up onto the roof of the Royal College of Medical Practitioners and then made their way across to the roof of the embassy, where the abseiling ropes were still tied to the chimneys. Their hopes for action were then dashed once more when they were informed that Prime Minister Margaret Thatcher had just endorsed the agreed strategy of 'maximum patience'. Frustrated again, the men of Red Team picked up their weapons and equipment, crossed back to the Royal College of Medical Practitioners, and made their way back down to the FHA to continue their interminable, repetitive learning process and training, including abseiling from the roof of Pearl House, a police residence in Pimlico.

Day Four commenced with the terrorist leader announcing that because of 'British deceit' the British hostages would now be the last to be freed. He also demanded another talk with the BBC. When this request was refused, he said that a hostage would have to die.

Relenting, the police brought another BBC news-desk deputy editor, Tony Crabb, to talk to the terrorist leader through Sim Harris, who was again exposed at an upstairs window with a gun to his head. When the BBC representative explained the BBC's minimalist broadcasting of the terrorist demands as a 'misunderstanding', the terrorist leader said that if they did not broadcast his statement every hostage in the building would be killed.

Two other hostages were brought to the window to confirm that the terrorists were deadly serious. The terrorist leader gave his statement while pointing his gun at the head of one of the hostages. Crabb wrote the statement down in his notebook, but the police then used his promise to broadcast it in full as a bargaining point to obtain the release of two more hostages. The terrorist leader agreed, but insisted that if his statement was not read out on the nine o'clock news that evening, he would send out a dead hostage.

By now it was clear to Marty, from the increasing violence of the terrorist leader's outbursts, that he was reaching the end of his tether and might indeed soon start killing.

Three hours before the due broadcast, the terrorist leader released one of the two promised hostages as a gesture of good faith. The broadcast was made as promised. Minutes after it ended, the second hostage was released.

Nevertheless, the deadly game continued. By the evening of the fifth day, when it was clear that no Arab ambassadors were willing to involve themselves in the matter, the terrorists reduced their demands to a request for one Arab ambassador to act as mediator and a guarantee of safe passage for the terrorists. The police, however, kept playing for time, fearful that an assault on the embassy could lead to the deaths of some, or all, of the hostages.

Marty, on the other hand, given what he had learned from a combination of his audio-visual surveillance and the reports of the released hostages, was aware that both the terrorists and the hostages were becoming more volatile – indeed, earlier that evening one of the terrorists had lost his temper and almost shot a hostage during an argument. Because of this Marty was convinced that the attack should begin before crisis point was reached. The Police Commissioner, however, remained adamant that the talking should continue.

Later that evening, another hostage, the journalist Mustafa Karkouti, was released, suffering from severe diarrhoea and fever. Interrogated by the police, he gave them a wealth of information, including the names of the terrorists, the weapons they were holding, the exact whereabouts of the hostages, and the psychological state of the terrorists, which was, he said, now one of mounting despair, tension and irritability. All of the terrorists, he said, now wanted out. For this reason, their leader had given Karkouti a message to give to the police: if they did not get in touch with the Arab ambassadors 'something bad' would happen.

Hearing those words, Marty hurriedly made his way to the SAS Forward Holding Area and told his men to prepare for action.

On the morning of the sixth day, still calling the terrorists' bluff, the Home Secretary let it be known that the 'ambassadorial phase' had passed and that the only concession they would get was a visit from an imam from the Regent's Park Mosque, who would attempt to act as a mediator. However, while the imam was being brought to the embassy, the terrorist leader, discovering that the police were inserting more bugs in the building, flew into a violent rage. When, shortly after, Iran's foreign minister sent the *hostages* a telegram, praising them for their forbearance in the face of the 'criminal actions' of Ba'athist Iraq, the terrorist leader flew into an even worse rage and said that, if the Arab ambassadors did not enter negotiations, a hostage would be shot in half an hour.

The male hostages were then moved out of Room 9A, on the second floor, overlooking the rear garden, and put into Room 10, overlooking Princes Gate.

According to messages received from PC Lock and Sim Harris, the terrorists had since put on their anoraks and wound their *keffias* around their heads, indicating that they were ready to fight or kill.

At approximately 1330 hours, when no Arab ambassador had yet shown up at the embassy, the terrorist commander trussed the hands of a hostage, the 28-year old Abbas Lavasani, behind his back and then tied him to the bottom of the bannisters. Handing PC Lock the phone, he told him to tell the police that he was about to shoot one of the hostages. Lock duly conveyed this information to them.

Still playing for time, the negotiators informed the terrorists that the Arab ambassadors would be meeting at 1700 hours to discuss the matter. Shortly afterwards, they received another call from the embassy and, when the phone was picked up, they heard Abbas Lavasani identifying himself.

Three shots were then fired in quick succession, followed by groaning, a choking sound, then silence. The terrorist leader then informed the police that he had just shot a hostage.

There was, however, no proof that a hostage had actually been shot. The terrorists could still be bluffing. Indeed, they had accepted the five o'clock deadline for the appearance of the Arab ambassadors. COBR therefore decided that if the ambassadors did not show up – and it was generally believed that they would not – control of the situation would be passed from the police to the SAS.

When Marty was informed of this through Lieutenant-Colonel Osborne, he confirmed that his preparations for the Deliberate Assault Plan would be completed by that time and that from 1700 hours the assault could be launched without delay.

By 1700 hours, none of the Arab ambassadors had shown up.

Mercifully, there was no response from the terrorists.

Thirty minutes later, however, the Police Commissioner received a call from the terrorist leader, saying that, if the

Arab ambassadors did not show in another thirty minutes, another hostage would be killed and his or her body thrown out onto the pavement.

By this time, the imam being offered as mediator had been collected from the Regent's Park Mosque, taken to Hyde Park Police Station, made to languish there for an hour and a half, then taken on to Princes Gate where he was escorted into the police negotiating room of Alpha Control, located in the nearby nursery school, from where he talked to the terrorist leader by radio phone. Told not to negotiate or bargain at all, but simply to convey the police terms for surrender, the imam did so. The terrorist leader responded by stating that, if the Arab ambassadors did not turn up in thirty minutes, the terrorists would kill not one but two hostages.

Even as the imam was putting down the phone and telling the police that the terrorist leader had sounded 'very disturbed', Marty was placing his Red and Blue teams on a ten-minute standby.

In Alpha Control the telephone rang again. Picking it up, a negotiator was informed that the terrorists were not going to wait for another thirty minutes. Instead, they were going to kill a hostage in two minutes.

When the imam urgently rang the terrorist leader back and quoted the prophet Muhammad to him, the terrorist slammed the phone down. Mere seconds later, when the phone rang again and the imam picked it up, he heard only the sound of heavy breathing. This was followed by the sound of three shots. Then the line went dead.

Shortly after, the front door of the embassy opened and a dead body was pushed out onto the pavement.

The embassy door was slammed shut again.

A few minutes later, at 1907 hours, the SAS formally took control of the situation and the assault began.

'Shake out!' Marty snapped.

CHAPTER THIRTY-EIGHT

Even as a police pathologist was discovering that the body dumped on the pavement outside the embassy was that of Abbas Lavasani, who had been dead for hours and could not have been killed by the three bullets just fired – which meant either that there was another dead body inside or that the second 'killing' had just been a bluff – the SAS were springing into action.

By 1905 hours the members of the two assault teams and the perimeter containment group were all dressed in their black CRW assault suits with GPV wraparound soft body armour, S6 respirators, anti-flash hoods and goggles, and armed with the requisite weapons and assault gear, ready to go. Sitting on their beds in the FHA at the Royal College of Medical Practitioners, looking like extraterrestrials, they were briefed once more by Marty, then told to synchronise their wristwatches at 1915 hours.

At precisely 1919 hours, they left the FHA and went in their separate directions, with Red Team taking the stairs to the top of the building, Blue Team heading for the basement area of the rear garden, and the perimeter containment group, or Zero Delta sniper team, divided into two smaller groups, one to be located in a block of flats at the rear of the embassy, the other at a camouflaged position in Hyde Park. Both sniper groups, when the attack commenced, would fire CS gas canisters through the windows of the embassy and then give the assault groups covering fire if and when the terrorists emerged from inside the building.

Though prevented by his age from taking part in the assault, Marty was able to follow most of it with the aid of the audio-visual surveillance equipment in his sixth-floor command centre overlooking the rear of the embassy. Even as the CCTV monitor was showing the members of Red Team crossing from the Royal College of Medical Practitioners to the roof of the embassy, codenamed 'Hyde Park', the police negotiator at ground level was talking to the terrorists, keeping them distracted with the false promise of a bus to the airport with PC Lock driving. As the men of Red Team reached the abseiling ropes on the roof of the embassy, the men of Blue Team were taking another route, emerging quietly onto the adjoining balcony that led from number 14 to 16. There they stopped and waited.

The time was precisely 1920 hours.

On the roof of the embassy, the men of Red Team divided into two groups, Call Sign 1 and Call Sign 2. The four men of Call Sign 2, led by TT, went immediately to kneel around the well around the fourth-floor skylight and prepare the explosive frame to be lowered by rope. As they were doing so, the men of Call Sign 1 went to the rear of the building, overlooking the lawns eighty feet below. There they found the abseiling ropes still tied to the chimneys and coiled beneath them, as they had been from the first day of the siege. With their Heckler & Koch MP5 submachine-guns slung over their shoulders, they put together the three components of the abseiling equipment, first clipping the metal descendeur to the harness, then slipping the nylon rope through the descendeur. Standing on the edge of the roof, each member of the abseil team covered his face with his respirator, hood and goggles, checked that the integral microphones and radio receivers were working, and prepared to go over the side.

By now the four men of Call Sign 2 had fixed ropes to the sides of the large frame explosive and were lowering it down the well to the fourth-floor skylight. When the frame was dangling just above the skylight, they manoeuvred it into position by tugging gently on the ropes, then dropped it carefully over the frame of the skylight until both frames were matching. This delicate task completed, they laid the ends of the four ropes gently on the roof, set the explosive charge with a timer and electronic detonator, then covered their faces with their respirators and joined the other abseilers on the edge of the roof overlooking the rear of the building.

Meanwhile, on the balcony behind protective walls at ground floor and garden level, the Blue Team soldiers, who had already covered their faces with their respirators and goggles, waited with explosives and ladders, each man tuned into the radio frequency that would enable him to strike the moment the attack signal, 'London Bridge', was given.

At that very moment, the attention of the terrorists was still being distracted by the false promises of the police negotiators. Each time the negotiators stalled, which they were now doing constantly, first making a promise, then trying to wriggle out of it, the terrorists would become more agitated and distracted.

The male hostages in the telex room, Room 10, overlooking Princes Gate, and the female hostages in Room 9A on the second floor, were becoming increasingly fearful as the protracted negotiations continued and the terrorist leader started showing visible signs of cracking.

Finally, under orders from the terrorists, PC Lock phoned the negotiators, asking them to get the bus to the embassy as soon as possible because the terrorists were expecting an attack any minute. When the negotiators smoothly denied that such was on the agenda, the terrorist leader wrenched the phone from PC Lock and screamed that he could hear suspicious noises all around the building.

At that very moment an explosive charge blew away the reinforced skylight roof and the attack commenced.

At the sound of the explosion, which came within seconds of the radio signal 'London Bridge', Alan Pearson, with Red Team, slipped on the harness and resolutely stepped backwards off the embassy roof to begin his dangerous drop down the wall. Hanging out from the wall, with an eighty-foot drop below him, did not make for a comforting sensation, but Pearson gamely lowered himself, using the descendeur to control the speed of his drop.

'First man over,' a voice reverberated eerily in his electronic ear defence headset. 'Second man over.'

Glancing upwards, Pearson saw the second abseiler, Trooper Jock McGregor, only a few feet above him, stepping backwards off the edge of the roof, using his booted feet for leverage as his body arched out over that eighty-foot drop to begin the descent. Satisfied, Pearson glanced down and saw the third-floor window about a dozen feet below him. Growing more optimistic and excited, he continued his descent, first passing the attic floor, then approaching the balcony window below it. However, he had travelled only about fifteen feet when his rope snagged, leaving him dangling just below the attic floor, above the third-floor window.

Cursing, he told Trooper McGregor what had happened, his voice being channelled through his throat mike. McGregor dropped lower, but stopped just above Pearson's head, waiting to see if he could untangle his harness. Pearson attempted to do just that, but the harness was so hot that he almost burned his fingers. Realising that the rope had overheated because of the friction caused by his weight and then ravelled into a knot, he cursed into his throat mike again (all of this being recorded on the audio-surveillance equipment in the command centre where Marty was located) then started wriggling frantically 65 feet above the rear terrace and lawns, turning frantically this way and that, his feet pressed to the wall as he used them for leverage.

'Damn it, I can't do it!' he bawled.

Inching lower in his own harness to stop right above him, McGregor tried to set him free. For a moment he felt dizzy, looking down that dreadful drop, but he took a deep breath, opened and closed his eyes, then tried a second time to set Pearson free. Instead, he jerked too hard, made his harness go into a spin, and had to swing his feet out to prevent himself from crashing into the wall. There was the sound of breaking glass. Glancing down, he saw, with despair, that his booted foot had gone through the third-floor window and the glass was breaking noisily, with some shards raining into the room, others falling all the way down to the terrace where they smashed to smithereens, making even more noise.

Knowing that the operation was compromised, shocked and angry that it had happened so quickly, Sergeant Pearson bawled into his throat mike: '*Go! Go! Go!*'

He was still bawling when the frame charge placed over the well skylight exploded with a deafening roar, blowing the glass to pieces, making the whole building shake, and causing part of the roof to collapse. Debris showered down on the stairs that joined the front and rear second floor.

Simultaneously, the Zero Delta sniper team, located behind a high wall at the front of the building, began firing CS gas canisters through the broken windows. Likewise, from ground positions in front of the embassy, other members of Zero Delta fired CS gas canisters into the second floor, smashing those windows as well. The noise was appalling.

While Alan Pearson and Trooper McGregor continued struggling in their harness just above the broken third-floor window, the second pair of abseilers, TT and Trooper Dennis 'Geordie' Webb, dropped past them, not stopping until they reached the ground-floor terrace. Another pair, Lance-Corporal Wilson and Trooper Art Penrose, dropped rapidly to the first-floor balcony window.

Once on the terrace, TT and Geordie shucked off their harnesses. Without a word, Geordie swung his Remington 870 pump-action shotgun into the firing position and blasted the lock off the doors, causing wood splinters and dust to fly away in all directions. Kicking the doors open as Geordie dropped to one knee, holding the Remington in one hand and withdrawing his Browning High Power handgun with the other, TT hurled a couple of MX5 stun grenades into the library and rushed in even as they were exploding. Geordie followed him, turning repeatedly left and right, preparing to fire a double-tap if he saw any movement. Though their eyes were protected from the blinding flash by the tinted lenses in their respirators, a combination of condensation on the lenses, natural adjustment to the half-light, and the swirling smoke from the flash-bang made them view the thousands of books on the walls through what seemed like fog.

'Fucking empty,' Geordie said in frustration to TT as the condensation on his lenses cleared, though the smoke continued swirling about them.

'Right,' TT replied, equally frustrated. 'So let's head for the stairs.'

When Geordie had slung the Remington over his left shoulder and removed his submachine-gun from his right, they hurried out of the library, leaving the smoke behind them, and carefully made their way to the cellar stairs. There they were joined by a couple of soldiers from Red Team, emerging from another cloud of smoke, looking inhuman and unreal in their black CRW outfits, NBC masks and hoods. Using a silent hand signal, TT indicated that they had to investigate the cellar. Though aware that terrorists might be hiding down there and that the entrance could be booby-trapped, they wrenched away the ladders covering the door, tugged the door open, and made their way carefully down the stairs, into the gloom below. The sounds of battle were raging in the embassy above them, but the cellar was deadly quiet.

As they could see little in the gloom, Geordie, when only halfway down, hurled a stun grenade. It bounced rattling off the stone floor, then exploded with a thunderous crack that ricocheted eerily around the basement. Getting a brief look at the cellar in the dazzling, fluctuating illumination of the flash-bang, TT saw no signs of movement and decided that it was safe to descend all the way.

Reaching the corridor at the bottom, he carefully tried the door of the first room but could not get it open. Assuming that all of the rooms would likewise be locked, he took aim with his handgun and 'drilled' the lock with a couple of nine-millimetre bullets, causing more wood splinters and dust to fly away. When the lock was blown off, he dropped to one knee and gave cover with his Nine-Milly as Geordie threw in a flash-bang and rushed in with the others, aiming left and right, preparing to fire as the grenade exploded and illuminated the room with its brilliant, phosphorescent light.

The room was empty.

Without a word, still using hand signals, TT led them quickly to the next room where they applied the same procedure. Finding that room empty as well, they tried the next one along, but that too was empty. They repeated this SOP all the way along the corridor, clearing one room after another, but finding all of them empty.

However, when entering the last room, TT thought he saw something moving in the brilliant, fluctuating illumination from the stun grenade. Without hesitation, he fired a burst of twenty rounds from his submachine-gun. This produced an incredibly noisy, metallic drumming sound and he caught a glimpse of something rolling away from him. When the bullets stopped hitting the rolling target, he saw that it was only a dustbin. There were no terrorists here.

Frustrated again, TT led his team back up the cellar stairs and into the reception area. Once there, they crossed a hallway filled with the smoke from stun grenades and burning curtains. It was also filled with the noise of other members of the assault teams who had burst into the building from the front and rear and were now clearing the rooms on all floors with a combination of flash-bangs and CS gas grenades. The walls and carpets in the hallway and along the landings were singed black and shredded by a combination of grenade explosions and bullets.

Separating from the other two men, TT and Geordie headed for the smoke-wreathed stairs, where they could hear the hysterical voices of female hostages. When they reached the source of the bedlam, they found soldiers forming a line and passing the women down with a speed that left little time for kindness. Some of the women were in shock and the eyes of all were streaming from the CS gas. They were guided down the stairs and through the library, then out onto the lawn, where some wept with joy.

Though the embassy seemed crowded with soldiers, some were still outside. Indeed, on the first-floor balcony, the plan to blast a way through the rear french windows had to be abandoned because of the risk of injuring or killing Alan Pearson, still struggling with Trooper McGregor to break free of his harness and now in danger of being burned alive by the flames pouring out of the third-floor window.

As both of them twisted in their harnesses, swinging in and out, getting scorched by the flames and choking in the smoke, vainly trying to release the jammed descendeur, Pearson bawled angrily at McGregor to do something. But McGregor, now also entangled, couldn't do a damned thing and the two men continued to struggle in their harnesses about seventy feet above the ground, hearing the sounds of battle raging from within, which just frustrated them more.

Meanwhile, far below them, on the first-floor balcony, Wilson and Penrose smashed through the windows with sledgehammers and threw in flash-bangs. Shucking off their harnesses, they clambered into the office of the Chargé d'Affaires even as the brilliant flashing from the grenades was illuminating the gloomy room.

At the front of the embassy, Blue Team, caught in the golden light of the early evening, in full view of the stunned reporters and TV cameras in Hyde Park, clambered from the adjoining balcony and along the ornate ledge until they reached the heavily reinforced windows of the minister's office. From the press enclosure, and even on TV, the distant, black-clad, hooded men looked very sinister indeed.

Glancing sideways as he made his way along the narrow ledge, Taff saw the police cordon in the street below and the press enclosure across the road, where the many TV cameras raised on gantries were focused on the embassy and, it seemed, on him. Startled, he looked away and continued his careful advance until he came up behind the first two men.

Lance-Corporal Dave Roberts and Trooper Barry Samson, being the first at the window, saw Sim Harris staring at them in disbelief from the other side of the glass. Roberts bawled through his respirator for Harris to stand back from the window and get down on the floor. Though clearly stunned to see the hooded, masked men on the balcony, Harris did as he was told, stepping away from the window and lowering himself to the floor as Roberts and Samson, covered by Taff and Corporal Jerry Manson, placed the frame charge over the window.

While they were still putting their plastic strip charges in place, a terrorist armed with a Skorpion W263 Polish submachine-gun appeared at the second-floor window of the telex room immediately above them. The man flung the window open and hurled down a hand grenade. However, the grenade bounced harmlessly away – either it was a dud or the terrorist had forgotten to draw the detonating pin.

Before the terrorist could throw another or fire his submachine-gun, a Delta Zero sniper, hiding across the road in Hyde Park, aimed along the telescopic sight of his bipod-mounted bolt-action sniper rifle and hit him with a single, deadly round. Staggering backwards, the terrorist dropped his weapon, then disappeared from view.

As the frame charge blew in the first-floor window, filling the air with showering glass, Taff hurled in a stun grenade. The exploding flash-bang ignited the curtains and filled the room with smoke.

Almost immediately, Sim Harris reappeared, emerging ghostlike from the smoke, looking gaunt but alert. Carefully approaching the window, he leaned out to stare disbelievingly at the SAS men in their black CRW suits, body armour, respirator masks and balaclava helmets. However, before he could ask any questions, Taff and Corporal Manson, ignoring the crackling, scorching flames, grabbed him by the shoulders and roughly hauled him out through the smashed window. Once they had him on the balcony, they pressed him down onto his hands and knees and told him to remain there and keep his head down until someone came for him. Harris nodded and lay there, but as Taff and the other three members of Blue Team scrambled through the window, he sat up on his haunches and shouted excitedly at their departing backs, 'Go on, lads! Get the bastards!'

Blue Team, having clambered in through the broken window, disappeared in the thickening smoke.

By now, Red Team's Lance-Corporal Wilson and Trooper Art Penrose had made their way across the smoke-wreathed stairs of the first floor. There they heard shouts from the nearby office of the minister's secretary. Rushing in, they found a uniformed policeman struggling violently with a bearded Iranian who was holding an RGD5 Russian-made hand grenade in one hand and a Skorpion W263 Polish submachine-gun in the other. Though clearly in pain, the hostage policeman, PC Lock, was wrestling gamely with the bearded terrorist, trying to stop him from throwing the grenade by holding his right wrist and falling with him over the furniture, making lots of noise. Lock had drawn his formerly hidden revolver with his free hand and was trying to put it to his opponent's head, but either he just couldn't manage it or he was reluctant to kill at close quarters.

As the two men wrestled furiously, Lance Corporal Wilson grabbed Lock with his free hand and jerked him away from the terrorist, whom he recognised from photographs as the leader, Salim. Wilson turned away from Lock as Salim, who had almost fallen over, was trying to regain his balance. Before he could do so, Wilson fired a burst of automatic fire at his head and chest. Trooper Penrose did the same. Hit by fifteen bullets, Salim was thrown backwards and smashed down through the furniture to lie face up in the debris on the floor, dying instantly.

After checking that the terrorist leader was dead, Wilson and Penrose left the room and made their way across the first-floor landing towards the rear of the building, past burning curtains, through pockets of smoke, brushing against other hurrying, bawling SAS soldiers, to try the door to the ambassador's office. Finding it locked, Wilson was just about to blow it open with his MP5 when it was opened from inside and a youthful terrorist appeared before him, armed with a Browning High Power handgun. Before Wilson could open fire, Penrose, just behind him and to his right, fired a short, decisive burst from his MP5, causing the terrorist to scream in pain and stagger, shuddering violently, back into the room. Wilson threw a stun grenade after him. The blast threw the terrorist even farther back and he stumbled blindly for another second or so in the dazzling flash. Penrose fired a second time, making the terrorist scream out again. Instead of falling, however, he gained the strength of the desperate and staggered deeper into the depths of the smoke-filled room, eventually disappearing.

Knowing that the terrorist was wounded, desperate and still armed, Penrose and Wilson felt compelled to go after him. Squinting to see through the condensation on their respirators, as well as through the smoke, they advanced carefully into the room. Unfortunately, when the smoke was swirling about them, Wilson felt himself choking and realised that the CS gas had penetrated his respirator. Coughing harshly, he staggered outside, ripped his respirator off, breathed in lungfuls of air – which itself was filled with the smoke from burning curtains – then placed his respirator back over his face and took deep, even breaths. As he was doing so, Penrose, now trapped in the dense smoke in the room and not able to see a thing, was bawling into his throat mike for someone to come in with a light.

Taff, on his way up from the ground floor, met TT on the stairs and both of them heard Penrose's cry for help. Hurrying on up, they found Lance-Corporal Wilson about to advance back into the smoke-filled room. However, Taff had a flashlight bolted to his MP5, so he turned it on, held the weapon as if about to fire from the hip, and advanced into the room with TT and Wilson beside him. When Taff moved the submachine-gun left and right, up and down, the thin beam of light from the torch bolted to the weapon illuminated the smoke-filled darkness and, eventually, Trooper Penrose.

Not wishing to speak, Penrose used a hand signal to indicate that he thought the terrorist was hiding in the far left corner of the room. Nodding, Taff advanced on Penrose, waited until he had fallen in beside him, TT and Wilson, then advanced carefully through the dense smoke, aiming the barrel of the MP5 left and right, up and down, illuminating the darkness and, more dangerously, pinpointing his own position to the hidden enemy.

No shots were fired at him and eventually, in that thin beam of light, he and the others saw a hand, then a face . . . and, finally, a Browning High Power handgun.

Covered in blood, the wounded terrorist was sprawled on a large sofa near the bay window overlooking the garden. Seeing them, he weakly took aim with his pistol, but his hand shook and wavered uncertainly from left to right, letting Taff and the other three SAS men fire their MP5s simultaneously, stitching the terrorist repeatedly, throwing him into convulsions and making him writhe dementedly as pieces of torn upholstery, foam filling and feathers exploded from the sofa, eventually drifting back down like snowflakes on his bloody remains.

On the outside wall at the rear of the building, level with the third floor, just below the dangling Trooper McGregor, Alan Pearson remained trapped in his abseil harness, kicking and twisting ever more frantically 75 feet above the terrace. Even worse, flames from the fire in the general office were now roaring out of the window and starting to burn up his legs. To avoid being burnt badly or choked to death in the billowing smoke, he had been kicking himself away from the wall as if on a swing, but, each time he swung back to the wall, he found himself in the smoke and flames again. Finally, in desperation, he ordered Trooper McGregor to cut him loose.

Aware that if he cut the nylon rope, Pearson could plunge 75 feet to a brutal death, McGregor was reluctant to do it; however, with the fire in the third-floor room growing stronger and the flames licking out ever closer to Pearson, he realised that this was Pearson's only option. With a great deal of effort, being himself trapped in mid-air and scorched by the flames, he withdrew his Sykes Fairburn commando dagger from its sheath and hacked through the nylon cord snagged in the descendeur. As the last threads were shredded, he bellowed a warning to Pearson, who fell through the flames onto the balcony. Burnt and blistered, but free at last, he smashed the third-floor window with his small, belt-held sledgehammer, hurled in some stun grenades, then swung himself into the smoke-filled interior of the general office where, according to the briefing, most of the hostages were held.

The room was empty. It was also locked, barricaded and piled high with flammable material that had just been ignited by the flash-bangs. Nevertheless, when Trooper McGregor had followed him into the room, Pearson, though badly burned and in pain, advanced blindly through the dense smoke and flames until he reached the locked door, which he recognised only after tracing it with his fingertips. Already in a temper because of his bad start, he blew the locks apart with a couple of shots from his Nine-Milly. The locks exploded in flying dust and wood splinters, but the doors, barricaded from the other side, remained firmly locked.

Determined to try another route, Pearson retreated to the balcony and clambered across to an adjoining window ledge. From there he could see inside the room, where a terrorist was striking matches to set fire to paper piled up against the wall, obviously intending to burn valuable documents. Before the terrorist could look up and see him, Pearson smashed the window and hurled a stun grenade. The loud, brilliant explosion temporarily blinded and shocked the terrorist; so, although he had raised his pistol to fire, he fled from the room instead.

Still perched on the window ledge, Pearson aimed his MP5 submachine-gun and fired from the hip. The gun jammed. Cursing, he drew his Nine-Milly, clambered off the ledge and into the room, then went after the terrorist, whom he had recognised as Shakir Sultan Said. Losing the terrorist temporarily in the smoke, he then saw him racing into what he knew was the telex room, where most of the male hostages were held, located off to the right across the landing, which was covered in smoke.

Unseen by Pearson, another terrorist, Feisal, the group's second-in-command, had just run into the room with two other terrorists, Ali and Makki when Said, fleeing from Trooper McGregor, who had been following Pearson, also reached it. Seeing the unarmed male hostages huddling fearfully together in the corner of the room, Feisal brutally raked them with a burst of automatic fire from his Skorpion submachine-gun, killing some and wounding others. Inspired by this gross act, Ali emptied his Astra revolver into them as well.

Checking for wounds as he huddled with the other frightened hostages, some of whom were now drenched with blood, the embassy doorman, Abbas Fallahi, discovered that he had been saved from death because a 50-pence coin in the pocket of his jacket had diverted the bullet. Even as he was whispering his thanks for his salvation, a smoke canister fired by Zero Delta from the other side of Princes Gate smashed through the window of the telex room, hitting him and knocking him to the ground.

The room filled up with smoke.

Having helped in the slaughter, Ali dropped his pistol in panic and wriggled his way in among the surviving, coughing, blood-soaked hostages. As he was doing so, his friend Feisal was throwing his submachine-gun through the window and emptying his pockets of ammunition. Said, being the last to enter, could think of nothing to do but stand in the smoke-filled room with his finger crooked inside the pin of a grenade.

Hearing the shots and screams of the victims, Pearson raced towards the telex room with McGregor close behind him. Even as the two men were coming to the rescue, some of the surviving hostages were wriggling out of the blood-soaked group on the floor, grabbing the discarded weapons and ammunition of the terrorists, and throwing them out of the window, into the street below. With his MP5 held in his left hand and his Nine-Milly in his right, Pearson reached the telex room, kicked the door open and immediately turned the corner, crouching, handgun raised in a classic CQB stance. When he saw the figure to his left, grenade in hand, he quickly fired a single round aimed at the head. Having entered Said's skull just below the left ear, the bullet exited through his right temple, killing him instantly.

Still in a foul temper and in agony from his burned legs, Pearson checked the group on the floor and found one dead terrorist, one dead hostage, and two badly wounded men. Demanding to know if any of the survivors were terrorists, he received no response, so he grabbed the first English-looking person he could find and jerked him roughly to his feet. Before Ron Morris, the embassy's caretaker and chauffeur, could identify himself, Pearson threw him roughly across the room towards the door. From there he was manhandled, just as roughly, by other SAS men, down the stairs, wreathed in smoke, through the smoke-filled library, and out onto the rear lawn where, like all the others, terrorist and hostage alike, he was given an 'undiplomatic reception', which meant being laid face down on the ground and trussed up like a chicken.

Still in the telex room, Pearson was again attempting to separate the terrorists from the hostages. Taff and TT burst in as an Iranian on the floor, being bawled at by Pearson, pointed tentatively at two men sitting with their backs to the room and their hands on the wall. Before Pearson could stop them, Taff and TT fired a sustained burst at the two men, hitting one in the head, the other in the neck and pelvis, punching both of them forward, face first, into the wall, where they slid, shuddering, down to the floor, smearing the wall with their blood.

After commanding the huddled survivors to remain where they were and not speak unless spoken to, Taff began the task of checking for terrorists by separating the wounded and the dead from those still untouched. Among the hostages attacked by the terrorists, Dr Ali Afrouz, the embassy Chargé d'Affaires, had been hit by two bullets, one of which passed through his right thigh; Ahmed Dagdar, the embassy's medical adviser, had been savagely wounded by six bullets; and another member of staff, Ali Samad-Zadeh, had been killed outright.

As little could be done for the dead, Lance-Corporal Wilson, a medical specialist, temporarily staunched the wounds of the two hostages with field dressings. Satisfied that he had done all he could here, Taff left Alan Pearson to cover Lance-Corporal Wilson and continue questioning the group still huddled on the floor while he and TT went downstairs to take part in the evacuation of the building.

Even before the survivors were moved out of the smoke-filled telex room, Alan Pearson, now cooled down, and Trooper McGregor, still level-headed, tried identifying the 'worms' who had wriggled their way into the huddled mass on the floor. The hostages, some with eyes streaming from CS gas, others covered in the blood of those killed or wounded, all dishevelled, most in shock, were bundled out one by one, then passed by the chain of Red Team soldiers along the corridor with its smouldering curtains, bullet-peppered walls and blackened carpets, down the smoke-wreathed stairs, across a hallway reeking of CS gas, all the way out through the relatively untouched library and onto the rear lawn, where darkness was falling.

The first 'worms' were easily identified because, when wriggling into the other hostages, they had forgotten to remove their green combat jackets. Others, however, had had the sense to do so and were marched with the genuine hostages down the stairs to the lawn, where the female hostages were already face down on the grass, their hands and feet tethered.

One of the terrorists did not make it that far. As the last of the hostages was being moved out of the telex room, the Red Team searched the suspects and were put on their guard by two who seemed too wary and alert to be hostages. Leaving both men to the last, they waited until the other hostages had left, then ordered the smaller, more nervous of the two suspects to lie face down on the floor. When the man did so, he turned his face to the side and stretched his arms above his head without being asked, like someone experienced in this kind of thing. When Pearson, standing over him and aiming his MP5 at his spine, asked him who he was, the man simply described himself as a student. Not believing him, Pearson stepped away, kept him covered, and ordered Trooper McGregor to search him. McGregor did so, running his hands over the suspect's body, then pushing his legs open and squinting into his crotch. There he saw the glint of metal – something that resembled a pistol magazine – and then a holster tangled up in the trousers.

Suddenly drawing his arms in towards his body, the suspect started rolling over onto his back. Just as he was turning, Pearson fired a short burst into his back, killing him instantly and punching his body, belly down again, onto the floor. When McGregor turned the body over, he found a hand grenade as well as the magazine for a .38 Astra revolver. Frisking the body, he came up with an Iraqi identity card, naming the dead man as 25-year-old Makki Hounoun Ali, a Baghdad mechanic.

McGregor was about to hand the identity card to Pearson, but Pearson started to see double. Realising that the burns on his legs were hurting dreadfully and that the pain was causing him double vision, he ordered McGregor to stay in the telex room while he went out to find a medic before he collapsed. Turning away to leave the room, he suddenly felt nauseous, saw double again, then did indeed collapse. Shocked, McGregor leaned over him, checked that he was still breathing and realised that he'd passed out from a combination of pain and exhaustion. Using the throat mike on his S6 respirator, McGregor called up the special medical team, asking for a stretcher.

As McGregor was thus engaged, the second suspect, Feisal, who had an Afro hairstyle and was second-in-command of the terrorist group, slipped away into the smoke and gathering darkness to mingle with the last of the freed hostages on their way down the stairs.

The members of the Blue Team who had cleared the basement and ground floor had met up with the rest of Blue and Red from the upper storeys to form the chain along which the hostages were now passed or – as some would later have it – thrown from hand to hand down the stairs and out through the library, then onto the lawn to be trussed up like chickens for more intensive body searches and interrogation. Brutal though this would have appeared to the uninitiated, it sprang from the soldiers' fear that the terrorists might have hidden an explosive charge on one of their own or on a hostage as their final response to this attack.

Taff was standing in the chain, next to TT, about halfway down the smokelogged main staircase linking the first floor to the ground, when he heard the sounds of what he thought was a scuffle above him and shouted a warning to the members of Red Team up on the landing. In fact, it was only the last of the hostages who were stumbling down the stairs, most either frightened or shocked, their eyes streaming from CS gas. Then Taff, with many years of hard experience behind him, saw a face that was calculating rather than scared, which is all he needed to know.

'*That one's a terrorist!*' he bawled.

The sound of his voice cut through the fearful atmosphere

like a knife as those dark eyes under an Afro haircut stared down in panic. Instantly recognised as a terrorist by his green combat jacket – Taff's outburst having merely confirmed it for the doubtful – he was struck on the back of the head by the butt of a trooper's MP5. Crying out and stumbling forward a few steps, he then advanced down the broad stairs almost at the crouch, his hands over his head as he was punched and kicked down by the chain of soldiers. When he drew level with Taff, the Welshman saw that he was holding a Russian fragmentation grenade with the detonator cap protruding from his hand. Without thinking twice, Taff removed the MP5 from his shoulder and slipped the safety catch to automatic. Unable to shoot because his fellow SAS men were in the line of fire, he raised the weapon above his head and brought the stock down on the back of the terrorist's neck, hitting him as hard as he could. The man's head snapped backward.

At that moment, the four Red Team members at the top of the rubble-strewn stairs opened fire simultaneously, emptying their magazines into the terrorist even as he was falling. First convulsing wildly in the murderous hail of bullets, then rolling down the stairs and coming to rest on the floor, the terrorist spasmed and vomited blood. He then opened his hand to release the RGD5 grenade, which rolled a short distance across the floor and then came to a stop, making a light drumming noise on the tiles. Luckily its pin was still in its housing.

After hurrying down the stairs to frisk the dead man, Taff withdrew a wallet containing an identity card and some other papers, naming the dead man as Shakir Abdullah Fadhil, also known as Feisal. Pocketing the identity card and papers, which he would pass on to the green slime, Taff leaned over the body to make a rough count of the bloody wounds, which totalled, as far as he could see, forty. Satisfied, Taff made his way through the library and out onto the rear lawn.

For some time after that incident more shots echoed throughout the building as Red and Blue teams blasted away locks to check other rooms. The fires started with the burning curtains had now engulfed the top of the building and the smoke was forming black clouds that drifted all the way down.

The integral UHF radio headsets in the S6 respirators crackled into life as the controller informed his men that the building was ablaze and must be abandoned.

'The embassy is clear. I repeat: the embassy is clear.'

Outside on the rear lawn, most of the hostages were lying face down on the grass, their feet and hands bound. Those remaining were being processed the same way.

The BBC sound recordist, Sim Harris, also bound hand and foot, was asked to identify any surviving terrorists. There was only one left. Identified by PC Lock and Harris, as well as the other survivors, he was Nejad, also known as Ali Abdullah. Dragged roughly to his feet by Taff and TT, he was handed over to the police and driven away with all dispatch.

Taff, TT and Alan Pearson were still standing on the lawn when Marty, having hurried down from the command centre, arrived in their midst. Gazing at the hostages still lying on the ground, then at the burning, smoking embassy building, he grinned with a great deal of pleasure and said, 'Who dares wins.'

'Damned right,' Taff retorted.

BOOK FIVE

OLD COMRADES

31 JANUARY 1991

Eleven men dead, the 70-year-old man thought as he sat in his rented Mercedes Benz and gazed at the house across the road. Eleven men good and true. Dead by electrocution, by carbon monoxide poisoning, by injection and fatal car crash, garroted, blown up, lost at sea.

(*Eleven innocent men.* You *did all that and more, much more. It doesn't seem possible, but it's true and you're over there right now.*)

Waiting for his friend to emerge from the house and meet his fate, the old man thought of the wives and children of those dead scientists and winced at what they had suffered. He knew what pain was – he now lived with it every day – and understood that no kind of physical suffering could match the anguish of grief. This knowledge was based on personal experience, his past year of hell on earth, caused by the knowledge that he was dying and that his family would suffer. A growing tumour in the brain. The physical pain was bad enough. But even worse, more unbearable, was the pain that he had caused his wife and children when he gave them the doctor's diagnosis and said they must be prepared. His wife and daughter had wept. His son had hidden his shock in silence. He had devastated their lives with the news and that felt worse than his own pain. Now he knew just how the families of the eleven unfortunate dead were suffering. He had to make his friend pay for that.

(*I'm responsible. I taught you all you know. I did it for good reasons, my motives were honourable, the cause just. But then the world changed and you took what I had taught you and perverted it totally. We both came a long way to get to here, but we could not have imagined it.*)

His skull contracted and filled with pain, reminding him of his mortality. He swallowed a tablet, waited for the pain to pass and then sighed with relief. Not moving from where he sat, feeling secure in the expensive car, he removed the newspaper from his lap, placing it on the seat beside him, then again slid his hand around his waist to feel the leather of his Len Dixon holster, now worn smooth with age. It took him back through all the years, to the very beginning, not quite as far as Oxford, when his faith had been intact, but to those early days in the North African desert where he had fought a just war. That's where he had met his friend, gauged his potential and nurtured it, determined to make him a good soldier and succeeding in doing so. His friend had been young then, unsophisticated, lacking discipline, but he had shaped up to become an excellent trooper and a fine human being. They had stayed friends for years.

(*We're still friends. Surely that's why I'm here. It's the respect and the love I still have for you that has brought me to this. I have come here to save you.*)

He needed to be saved, to be redeemed by death, to make amends for the wrongs he had done and die as he had lived. It had begun a long time ago, with his apprenticeship in the desert, and since then he had learned the deadly skills that had led him to carnage. Eleven scientists had died, mostly innocent men, and the man who had killed them had done so with uncommon skill. His talents were wide and varied, perfected in many wars, wrought in steel and iron, forged in fire and fury, finely honed in dark jungles and blazing deserts, on icy mountain peaks and in stormy seas, in mean streets and booby-trapped houses where death held dominion.

The killer, now a victim, had learned how to fire weapons, handle explosives, track his quarry, kill by stealth; he knew all about surveillance and the covering up of trails; he could neutralise, terminate or cleanse without leaving a trace behind. He had learned those skills over the years, as the world spun and changed, even as he had changed with the changing world to become someone else: an angel of vengeance.

Almost certainly, if not solely responsible, he had done his fair share.

(*How many out of the eleven were yours?*)

The old man removed his shaking hand from his worn holster as his heart beat too quickly.

(*You surely started on your own, but your friend eventually helped you and together you were even more deadly, one supporting the other. Well, no matter how many you did alone, it now makes little difference. Your friend is dead and soon you will come out of hiding to face the same fate. There's no point in counting.*)

Yet it pained the old man. He felt responsible for what had happened. As he looked across the road and saw the guards behind those gates, he could only think of the good in the man he was going to kill. He had once been a young man, impetuous but decent, honest and courageous. He had fought in North Africa, in Malaya and Borneo, in Oman and Aden, in Belfast and the Falklands, for what he strongly believed in. Alas, the world had changed, eroding all he had valued, and faithless, his soul shrivelled by disappointment, he had gone out for vengeance. Not alone, but certainly leading the way, he had set out to right all the wrongs that he felt had destroyed his world. In so doing, he had become more corrupt than those he thought were his enemies.

(*It's my fault. I was your mentor and friend. I took you into the desert, made you live in the jungle, taught you how to stalk and kill, how to cover up your tracks, and then I filled you with the kind of idealism that always turns on itself when disillusionment sets in. You believed in just wars, in the defence of the realm, and you took your pride from being with a regiment that stood for all you believed in. Then the world changed and the nature of war changed with it, becoming dirtier, more brutal, forcing you to lend your support to all you despised. When that happened, you took what I had taught you and used it to other ends. I am as guilty as you are.*)

Sighing, wiping tears from his rheumy eyes, the old man studied the guards in the driveway of that big house and saw that they had taken up positions by the front door and main gate. That meant his friend was coming out. He was late, but he was coming out at last and this had to mean something. His partner was dead. Almost certainly, he had heard about it. If he had done so, he would know who was responsible and would be thinking about that as well. He would not be frightened – this was not in his nature – but certainly he would have contemplated the matter, wondering what he should do. He would know his own time was coming, but would not know where or when, though perhaps he didn't care any more and was in secret agreement. If this was so, he would deliberately make it easy for his own executioner.

Please do that, the old man thought as he straightened up in his seat in the gleaming Mercedes Benz, blinking against the brightening morning light and preparing himself.

(*Do the honourable thing, my friend.*)

He saw the guard at the front door raising the handset to his lips and speaking into it. He saw the second guard, at the main gate, listening in on his handset, then slipping it back into his pocket and becoming alert. He saw the chauffeur emerging from the garage and heading for the Rolls Royce. He saw that someone was coming out.

In the few minutes left to him before the end came, the old man saw two lives fusing together as one to engage the same fate. He wanted it quick and clean, without fuss, with courage, and he prayed that his victim, his friend, would be wanting that also. Almost certainly he would. Indeed, why would he not? He was a man who had lived a life of violence and would die the same way. There was justice in that.

The lost years unravelled in the old man's mind and resolved all his doubts. He saw himself as a gay, naive young student in his room at Oxford College; as a drunken, rebellious 8 Commando officer in the MPs' cells in Bab el Hadid; as an exuberant SAS lieutenant in the vast white plains of the North African desert; as a patriotic, determined escaper in Colditz Castle; as an emaciated, exhausted captain in the steaming jungles of Malaya, as a contented husband and father in his family home in Hereford; as a well-fed, successful businessman in London and the Middle East; as a welcomed guest in pinstripe suit in the Paludrine Club in Bradbury Lines; as a loneller, much older person in his small apartment in Highgate; and, finally, as this broken old man in this rented Mercedes Benz, dying from a brain tumour and waiting to kill his best friend before taking his own life. He saw himself with old school chums, with university pals and girlfriends, with his wife and his children, with his doctors and nurses, with his parents and a host of other relatives – and, of course, with his best friend. He saw exactly what had happened to his best friend and why it had to end here.

Let his will be done, he thought. He knew.

(*We all knew.*)

CHAPTER THIRTY-NINE

Taff knew. He had always known. These days, when Marty gazed into Taff's baby-blue eyes under the healthy head of blond hair, at that schoolboy face with its slight, distracted smile, he did so in the full awareness that Taff understood what they must do and was willing to do it. There was no fear in Taff, no hesitation or doubt; he was a man without ego or malice or cruelty, but he had been born with the instincts of a killer and now they were finely honed.

Being a professional soldier, Marty, like Taff, had killed a lot of men and understood that, brutal though it might seem to outsiders, it was an unavoidable evil in a violent world. All democracies needed protection, needed men like him and Taff, the ones who could do their dirty work while they kept their hands clean. Taff knew this and had always known it, hiding the knowledge behind his smile, but since joining the Association, since talking through its possibilities, he had made it clear that he believed that his skills were not being used nearly enough, nor for the right reasons.

Marty wanted to use the Association to more ambitious ends – right a few wrongs, clean up some of the scum, remove those who aided the terrorists who were turning London into a battleground – and he knew that Taff, for one, would not hesitate to do what needed doing.

The problem was Paddy.

Ever since the embassy siege, Marty's burgeoning frustrations had turned into an outrage that kept him constantly on the boil. The sight of Abbas Lavasani's dead body being dumped on the pavement outside the embassy had convinced him that what was needed was prophylactic action against terrorists or those who aided them, even if indirectly – this included arms dealers. He was convinced that the regiment's role was now strictly limited and would be more so in the future, to be used, in the absence of a major war, only for the odd counter-terrorist operation or the usual surveillance work in Northern Ireland. Meanwhile, while the regiment languished ineffectually in Hereford, arms dealers and fellow travellers were helping to turn the streets of London – and the whole of Europe – into a battleground and were being rewarded for their sins. The Association could do something either to reduce this or to stop it altogether, but he had yet to persuade Paddy of the need for it.

Unfortunately, their differences of opinion on the matter had caused friction between them for the first time in their long relationship. That friction had been noticeable ever since Paddy's angry outburst in the French pub nearly a year ago, on the day of Lord Mountbatten's assassination. Though he and Marty had not fought since then, there was a distance between them that had not been there before. Marty deeply regretted this, but he was not put off by it. He still hoped to persuade Paddy that the use of the Association for the neutralisation of undesirables was the justifiable means to a worthy end.

The opportunity came when he had a lunch with Paddy in their favourite pub in Hereford and the subject of the embassy siege came up.

'I have to hand it to you,' Paddy said. 'That was a hell of a job and you men did it well. You should be proud of yourselves.'

'The shortest battle we ever fought,' Marty responded.

'Yes. It must surely be some kind of record.'

'I think so. Fifteen minutes to clear the building, thirty-five minutes to check the premises and conduct an undiplomatic reception for the rescued hostages, then another fifteen minutes to pack up our kit and move out of the Forward Holding

Area. Sixty-five minutes from start to finish, then back to Hereford. Not bad at all, Paddy.'

'Pretty damned exceptional, I'd say.'

Pleased, Marty continued: 'About two and a half hours after the siege ended, the CO handed control of the cleared embassy back to the Deputy Assistant Commissioner of the Metropolitan Police, and that officially ended our involvement in the matter.'

'Received a congratulatory visit from the Home Secretary, I believe.'

Marty grinned. 'He came to the Regents Park Barracks just before we were driven back to Hereford in the same Avis vans that brought us to London. An emotional man. He even had tears in his eyes as he thanked us for what we'd done.'

'Well, you deserved that. Five hostages released before the assault, nineteen rescued, and only two dead, neither killed by the SAS. On top of that, there were no SAS casualties. I'd say that was superlative.'

'Not everyone thinks so. Though five of our men were personally decorated by the Queen, certain segments of the media still criticised us for using unnecessary force and practically destroying the building. I mean, there we were, tasked with the rescue of hostages in a building reportedly wired for a Doomsday explosion and defended by a bunch of fucking terrorists who'd already killed two of their hostages – and *we're* the ones who used unnecessary force! You just can't please some of 'em.'

'They should have kept the press out of there altogether,' Paddy said. 'The SAS is supposed to work in secrecy and that means they should never be seen on TV, discussed on the radio, or even read about in the papers. All that's gone since the Princes Gate siege and I think it's a bad thing.'

'I agree,' Marty said. 'I'm proud of the way our lads handled themselves, but I certainly don't like the way the operation's been blown up by the papers. We've always tried to stay in the background, but the siege of the Iranian Embassy's destroyed our anonymity and possibly even made us notorious. Personally, I hate the thought of that.'

'Your disapproval comes too late, Marty. Because of that

one operation, the regiment's become the most well known in the world – it *has* gained notoriety. You're now going to become the focus of relentless public and media scrutiny. That won't be helpful to future operations. It won't be easy to deal with that.'

'We're trying,' Marty told him. 'In the absence of a major military task, we're now concentrating on intelligence-gathering and security while we try to sink back into our former anonymity.'

'You'll never get that back,' Paddy said. 'Once you've lost it, it's gone for good. From now on, you'll always be working in the spotlight and that won't help at all.'

'All the more reason,' Marty responded, seeing his golden opportunity, 'to use the Association for jobs that can only be done covertly. Because we're virtually anonymous – or at least seen as an agency whose sole purpose is to find legitimate work for former members – we can be covert in a way that the regiment can't. We can do things it can't do.'

Paddy stared carefully at him, considering his reply, clearly annoyed that Marty had returned to a subject that had become a sore point between them.

'Marty—'

'I know you don't like me talking about this, Paddy, but I can't let it go. I'm not the only one in the Association to believe that we're in a good position to do more than simply find jobs for the boys.'

'It's not just jobs for the boys, as you put it,' Paddy responded testily. 'I've aready caved in to you on finding them work as bodyguards and it's given me a lot of headaches – reports in the press about former SAS men becoming mercenaries for foreign governments; complaints from Whitehall about Vigilance International meddling in military affairs – so I'm not about to cave in to you again, particularly regarding what I feel would be, in essence, the creation of an assassination squad. No way, Marty.'

'That's a melodramatic way of putting it,' Marty said. 'It wouldn't be that at all. We'd simply be doing without permission what we've often done under orders in Northern Ireland and elsewhere: neutralising enemies of the country for the general good. We'd simply be taking matters into our own hands where others with more authority have failed to do so.'

'You'd be breaking the law.'

'For a bloody good reason.'

'Neutralising means killing, my friend, and that's assassination. You'd be no more than a bunch of hit men practising lynch law.'

'We wouldn't be lynching the innocent,' Marty said. 'No one would be touched who wasn't known to be a villain. We have superlative intelligence to back us up and we'd all vote before decisions are made. There's no way in the world that someone undeserving would be neutralised. We're only thinking of going after the big fish and they're easy to recognise.'

'What kind of big fish?'

'Arms dealers, munitions manufacturers, known terrorists who can't be touched because of some arcane legality. You know the villains as well as I do and there's no doubt about what they're getting up to. The world will be a better place without them, so I think it's a good cause.'

'It's not a good cause; it's taking the law into your own hands.'

'Only where the law's ineffectual.'

'That's exactly what lynchers always say.'

'People don't get lynched any more.'

'No, Marty, they get shot and blown up instead, but it's still the same thing.'

'Paddy—'

'I don't want to hear any more about this, Marty. I don't mind heading Vigilance International as a production company for anti-communist videos, as a commercial company offering advice and training and supplying bodyguards for security purposes. I don't even mind it as an unofficial regulating body that keeps its eye on what goes on within the regiment. But I refuse – I *categorically* refuse – to let it be used as a regulating body for the country as a whole, much less one that will act as jury and hanging judge when it comes to certain undesirable elements. Suggest it once more and I'll cut the Association out of Vigilance International and you'll be on your own again.'

Startled by Paddy's vehemence, Marty waved his hands in the air as if beating him off. 'Okay, Paddy, all right, calm down. I promise I won't mention the subject again.'

'Good. But I have one more thing to say.' Paddy finished off his pint and started pushing his chair back, still annoyed and obviously preparing to leave the pub. 'If I get the slightest hint, the merest whisper, that something in that line has been going on behind my back, I'll dissociate myself and the company from you completely. Is that understood?'

'Yes,' Marty said.

'Good. Now I have to be off.'

'So do I,' Marty said, hiding his growing annoyance and resentful that Paddy could talk to him so. Together they pushed their chairs back, stood up and crossed the pub to the front door. 'I'm going to London straight from here,' Marty said. 'That's why I suggesting meeting here, instead of picking you up as usual. I have to get to the station.'

'Staying with Diane?' Paddy asked, obviously trying to cool down and be his good-humoured self again.

'Of course. Where else?'

They left the pub and walked to the car park. The June sun was bright, falling on the green fields and trees of the Hereford countryside. Marty welcomed the heat on his face as he squinted against the light. He saw the spire of the Norman cathedral soaring above the slate rooftops of the nearby town. It was a sight that gave him a feeling of permanence in a rapidly changing world.

Paddy opened the door of his Honda Accord, then turned around.

'So how's Diane these days?' he asked. 'The last time I saw her, in that pub in Soho, she seemed rather strung out.'

'She was drunk,' Marty replied too quickly, uneasily.

'I think it was more than that. I've always thought she was much too intense and she seemed to get worse over the years. How is she really?'

Marty decided to tell the truth. 'Not too good. She drinks

too much during the day and takes sedatives to put her to sleep at night.'

'Why?'

'Well, as you rightly said, she's been that way for a long time – from when she lost her father, I suspect. She worshipped him and based her whole life around him, so when he died something broke inside her and she was never the same again. Nowadays, though, it's her work. You know how obsessed she'd become with it. Couldn't bloody live without it! Then she started concentrating on corruption in politics, various abuses of power, causing a lot of controversy and landing herself in hot water too many times. Finally, when her reporting on Northern Ireland helped sway the European Court of Human Rights into finding the British government guilty of inhumane treatment and torture over there, she became the victim of a dirty-tricks campaign. It was, so she said, designed to slander her and make editors too scared to print her articles. Certainly, the commissions gradually dried up and now they've practically stopped altogether. So she's broke and desperate and paranoid, which makes her hard to live with.'

'Why don't you get out?'

'I can't leave her when she's in this state, Paddy. That isn't my style. Besides, I'm genuinely fond of her. I also happen to be sympathetic because I tend to believe most of what she tells me. Almost certainly, she's the victim of a dirty-tricks campaign and we both agree on who we think started it.'

'Who?'

'Sir Charles Alfred Seagrove.'

'The arms dealer?'

Marty nodded. 'Exactly. Diane's been after him for years, tormenting him in the papers with one sordid revelation after the other, and he's threatened her with legal action many times. But a few months ago she published an article pointing out that Seagrove had been selling arms to Gaddafi, that Gaddafi had been training and arming the IRA, and that the IRA were then returning to Northern Ireland to kill British soldiers with those same weapons. She emphasised in the article that this was the work of a man recently knighted for his services to the realm.'

'Fair comment,' Paddy said.

'I believe so. Anyway, when Seagrove read the article he went bloody mad and personally phoned Diane to tell her that her writing days were over. He didn't specify what he meant by that, but Diane was in no doubt that he was going to use friends in high places to put pressure on her editors and get her squeezed out of journalism altogether. As certain highly placed people in Whitehall had already made it clear to her *and* her editors that they were incensed with her reporting on Northern Ireland, she didn't think that Seagrove would have too much trouble in raising a few allies when it came to a dirty-tricks campaign against her. And true enough, from that point on, her troubles began and neither of us has any doubts that the man behind them is Seagrove.'

'You're probably right.'

'I *know* we are,' Marty said.

Paddy was silent for a moment, then eventually he said, 'Listen to me, Marty. It's my belief that a lot of your recent thinking, of which I strongly disapprove, has been caused by your relationship with Diane. I'm not disputing for one second that a dirty-tricks campaign has been used against her – it isn't the first, God knows, and certainly it won't be the last – but I *am* saying that you can't take it too personally or let it turn your head to thoughts of personal vengeance. More importantly, you mustn't let it motivate you into going ahead with your idea of turning the Association into a private, covert vigilante force. I said it before and I say it one last time: if I pick up the slightest hint that you've done so, I'll dissociate Vigilance International from the Association. Do you understand that?'

'Yes,' Marty said.

'And will you take heed?'

'Yes,' Marty repeated.

Paddy stared searchingly at him, then smiled slightly. 'So do we still part as friends?'

Marty held his hand out. 'Yes, Paddy, we still part as friends.'

They shook hands, both smiling, then climbed into their separate cars, Paddy heading back to his home in nearby

Peterchurch as Marty drove on to London for another weekend with Diane.

Coming off the Westway and inching into the dense traffic heading east, Marty was in a state of deep depression. The sun was still shining, reflecting off the windows of the elegant Georgian houses, and people were out enjoying the summer's weather, walking instead of taking buses, many on bicycles or motorbikes, weaving expertly between the honking cars, roaring trucks, black taxis and red double decker buses, commuting between Shepherd's Bush, Holland Park, Earl's Court and Notting Hill Gate in a festive atmosphere that had doubtless been encouraged by the good weather. Nevertheless, as he crawled along in the traffic, feeling hot and sweaty, his spirits were not uplifted by the sight of the many young girls in miniskirts, hotpants, skin-tight blue jeans and low-cut or halter tops, many of them beautifully suntanned. Instead, he was still gloomily considering what Paddy had said – as he had been since beginning the long journey – and also wondering what state Diane would be in this particular weekend.

As he crawled on in second gear, inching past Ladbroke Grove Station, where the newsvendor was waving his edition of the London *Evening Standard* and bawling about English soccer fans rioting in Turin – news that was receiving more coverage than the ten million people facing starvation in East Africa – he realised that, though he had told Paddy about Diane's fraught condition, he hadn't told him the half of it. In fact, Diane's condition was so bad that he could hardly admit it to himself, though every weekend he saw her was worse than the one before and he was certain that she was coming close to the edge. Between the drinking, which she did all day, and the sedatives, devoured each evening, she was almost catatonic and came alive, temporarily revitalised, only when some news item on TV reminded her of her work and of all the wrongs, real or imagined, that had been done against her.

Over the past few months, her tension had developed into full-blown paranoia mixed with chronic fear and despair, making her drink even more and rail at him about the world's iniquities. Marty sympathised with her, believing most of what she told him, but for all that he was finding it more difficult to deal with her outbursts. Smoking like a train, cursing like a trooper, often sobbing hysterically, she would pace the lounge of her flat like a caged tiger, trying to talk it out of her system, and exploding into rages at even the slightest hint of disagreement. She was like a wild, wounded animal.

'You don't believe me,' she would say. 'You think I'm fucking mad. You pretend to believe me, but you just don't want a fight. You're fed up and you want to go back to Hereford and play fucking soldiers.'

'No, Diane, that's not true.'

'I can't get fucking work. Every door's been closed to me. That bastard, that knighted shithead Seagrove, has trampled all over me, pulled every plug, and now you're telling me that I shouldn't drink too much. So what do I *do*, Marty? Where do I go from here? I sit here on my own, day in and day out, and I wait for the fucking phone to ring and it never rings any more. I try ringing out sometimes – oh, yes, I *do* try – but now my old friends are always at a meeting when I happen to call. Do they ever call back? Not any more, they don't. So I sit here from dawn to dusk, in interminable silence, and I drink – damn it, Marty, yes, I drink – to deaden that silence. What else can I do?'

It was pointless arguing with her – she was too far gone for that. Being well into her forties and deprived of her work, she had not the slightest glimmer of a future that would be worth the having. Marty had said he would stick with her, even marry her if she wanted, put her into a safe harbour where she wouldn't need to work, but that only added insult to injury and made her even more angry.

'That's so fucking magnanimous! Make a decent woman out of me! Leave me sitting there at home, in a house with a garden, pruning hedges while you run off to the Sports and Social to have fun with your mates. And what about *my* work? My journalism was my fucking *life*! I'm not about to be dependent on an SAS pension. I'm not going to sit at home like the good little wife while bastards like *Sir* Charles fucking Alfred fucking Seagrove not only arm terrorists but get rewarded with knighthoods and then dig graves for those who try exposing them. Why the fuck don't you do something about it instead of offering to marry me?'

'Do what, Diane?'

He often wondered about that question, haunted by feelings of impotence, and found himself thinking increasingly about the Association and its potential as a corrective, cleansing force against people like Seagrove. That bastard had armed the terrorists who were killing British soldiers in Northern Ireland, planting bombs in British streets, holding British citizens hostage, and he was willing and able to destroy the journalists who tried to expose him. More than that, he had been knighted, had friends in high places, and was therefore very well shielded from the law and the media. In short, he was exactly the kind of person that Marty, Taff and others in the Association believed should be neutralised. He was a shining example.

Shocked that even now, after his confrontation with Paddy, he was still thinking of defying him, Marty turned right at the lights at Notting Hill Gate Station and drove down Kensington Church Street, which he thought had retained the charm that was disappearing from so much of London. Turning right again, he drove along Diane's street, glancing appreciatively at the elegant Georgian houses, most of which had been turned into flats. His appreciation of these architectural splendours was obliterated when he could not find a parking space and had to explore the surrounding streets for another ten minutes before he managed to do so. Ending up at a parking meter a good twenty minutes' walk from Diane's place, he made his way back to her flat boiling over with nervous tension and anger. These dangerous emotions, he realised, had become more common of late and could clearly be attributed to a variety of causes, including the impotence he felt over Diane's burgeoning condition and the realisation that he was fighting with his best friend, Paddy, even as he was suffering grave doubts about his own proposals for the Association.

You're in a state of deep confusion, he thought. Get a grip on yourself.

If only he could.

Using his own key to open the front door of the converted Georgian house, he took the lift to the third floor, now feeling even more tense and nervous. As he opened the door to Diane's flat with the other key, he wondered what mood she was in and felt a wave of dread passing through him. Much as he had wanted her and possibly even loved her, he didn't think that he could take much more of her tantrums, let alone the guilt he felt at the thought that he could do nothing for her.

Closing the door quietly behind him, he walked into the living room and saw that the TV was on, showing haunting images of starving men, women and children in the refugee camps of East Africa. Diane was not there. Assuming that she was in bed – since she often went to bed in a drunken stupor at this hour of the day, leaving the television set on – he went into the bedroom and saw that the bed, though dishevelled, was empty, with an almost empty gin bottle on the bedside cabinet beside an overflowing ashtray. The room, he noticed, smelled awful: a combination of alcohol, stale cigarette smoke and a general lack of fresh air.

Having long since adjusted to Diane's slovenly ways, he ignored all of this and walked straight to the bathroom, expecting to find her soaking in the bath, probably smoking and drinking at the same time. In this he was not wrong.

She was in the bath all right, naked, her eyes closed. There was an ashtray on one side of the bath and a bottle of gin on the other. The cigarette stub in the ashtray had smouldered out a long time ago. The bottle of gin was nearly as empty as the one in the bedroom. A razor blade covered in blood lay on the floor by the bath. The water in the bath, while covered in soap bubbles, was also red with blood.

Feeling himself slipping into a nightmarish unreality, he bent over the bath, heard himself shouting, 'Diane!', then grabbed her under the armpits and tugged her out of the water. Her head flopped to the side, falling over his right forearm, and as he pulled her up higher, unable to stop his choked sobbing, he saw the ugly slashes across her wrists and, in the bath, just beneath her right hand, the dull gleam of the bloody breadknife.

He sobbed uncontrollably, holding Diane close to him, trying to bring her back to life with his warmth, receiving only her coldness. He fell to his knees, leaned over the side of the bath, and held her the best he could in his soaked arms, whispering, 'No! Oh, God, no!' He stayed there until his grief turned into rage and he could reach a decision. He made that decision even as his tears continued falling. His tears fell a long time.

CHAPTER FORTY

There was no turning back now. Deciding to be the first, to ask no one for help, he drove to the house after midnight, continued driving past it, then parked about a thousand yards from it. It was a large house in Surrey, backed by a golf course, with burglar alarms and spy cameras on the walls, an armed guard in the front drive. Having already checked this, knowing just what he would do, he emerged from his car, wearing a black rollneck pullover, black trousers and black shoes, carrying a travelling bag over his shoulder. After glancing left and right to check that the street was clear, he slipped into the narrow lane near the end of the street, emerged to the golf course, and made his way to the rear of the house. Moving forward at the half crouch, avoiding the range of the spy cameras, he knelt by the back wall, removed the bag from his shoulder and withdrew a small home-made bomb. It consisted of RDX plastic explosive with a time-fuse connected to a non-electric firing cap. After taping it to the high brick wall, which was, he knew, wired to the audio-visual surveillance systems, he set the time-fuse for five minutes, then made his way back to the narrow lane and emerged once more to the street.

Slipping back into his car, he checked his wristwatch, waiting until it showed zero minus one, then turned the ignition on, made a three-point turn and drove back to within a few yards of the big house. He went into neutral, applied the handbrake, kept the engine purring over as he opened his door. When he heard the explosion out back, he jumped from the car.

He had only a few minutes now. The bomb out back would have blown down part of the wall and knocked out the audio-visual surveillance systems long enough for him to do what he had to do. By the time he reached the front gate, the uniformed guard had already raced around to the rear of the house to check on the nature of the explosion. With the burglar systems knocked out, he, the intruder, had enough time to race into the garage, crawl beneath the parked Rolls Royce, and attach a more powerful bomb, this one consisting of C3/C4 high explosive with an electrical firing system to be detonated by remote control. Once the bomb was connected to the bottom of the vehicle, well hidden in the exhaust system, just beneath the rear seat, he scrambled back out, climbed to his feet, and raced unseen across the driveway and back to his own car, still parked a few yards from the house's main gate with its engine ticking over quietly.

Less than five minutes after the bomb had exploded out back, acting purely as a distraction for the guard, he was driving away from the house, unseen by anyone. He parked the car a few streets away, on a stretch of his intended victim's normal route to work. After placing the remote-control initiator on the seat beside him, he covered it with a newspaper, then sat back and began his long wait. He had all the time in the world.

The following morning, two weeks after Diane's funeral, Marty sat in her apartment, drinking neat whisky and watching the news on TV. The main item was the assassination of Sir Charles Alfred Seagrove, arms salesman, who had died that morning when a bomb exploded under his Rolls Royce as he was being driven to his office in the City.

According to the news report, another, much smaller bomb had destroyed part of the back wall of Seagrove's house, knocking out his sophisticated audio-visual burglar-alarm system and drawing his personal bodyguard away from the front of the house. Deducing that the bomb was the instrument of a botched assassination attempt, the police had not thought to check the rest of the house, let alone the Rolls Royce parked in the garage. Assuming that he had survived the attempt on his life, Seagrove had then used his normal vehicle to get him to work. The second bomb, obviously planted under Seagrove's car while his security system was out of order and his bodyguard was at the back of the house, had been detonated by remote control shortly after the car passed through the police cordon that had been placed there to keep people away from the scene of the first incident. The car had exploded in an empty stretch of road, killing the knighted arms dealer and his chauffeur.

Though initially the assassination was believed to be the work of the IRA, it had denied responsibility and the identity of the perpetrator was still unknown.

The news broadcast had barely ended when the telephone beside Marty started ringing. He knew that the caller could only be Paddy, but he didn't pick up the phone to check. It rang for a long time and continued ringing all day, but Marty just sat there, drinking whisky, not picking it up. He was still sitting there when night came, bringing darkness and silence. The phone did not ring again.

CHAPTER FORTY-ONE

It was Marty's last war and, from the organisational point of view, the most complicated. It began when, on 2 April 1982, Argentina invaded and captured the Falkland Islands, overwhelming the single company of Royal Marines guarding the islands' capital, Port Stanley. The British response was to assemble a Royal Navy Task Force including frigates, destroyers, troop carriers, landing ships, supply ships, submarines, and the aircraft carriers, HMS *Invincible* and HMS *Hermes*. These were packed with Harrier jump-jets and Sea King HC4 helicopters of the 846 Naval Air Squadron. Being shipped out with the fleet were over 1,000 troops, including Royal Marines, Paratroopers and Special Forces. At the same time, other ships were leaving Plymouth to link up with more forces from Gibraltar.

All in all, it was Britain's greatest display of naval strength since Suez and its purpose was to let the Argentinians know that Great Britain was serious about the fate of the Malvinas. For this reason, the Royal Navy Task Force sailed to a jingoistic waving of flags and playing of brass bands, with television and the press well represented. The Union Jacks were waving in the wind and the whole world could see them.

Behind the scenes, however, the green slime of the SAS had been boning up on all the information they could find about the islands in the MOD map room, most of it from the British Antarctic Survey's headquarters in Cambridge and other, more confidential sources. From this wealth of information they had ascertained that the nearest feasible base from which to launch an amphibious assault against the Falklands was Ascension Island, nearly 7,000 kilometres from the UK ports and airfields. Therefore, on 5 April, the day after the Royal Naval Task Force sailed off in the limelight, a small advance party from D Squadron, 22 SAS, including Marty, Taff, TT and Alan Pearson, under the command of Lieutenant-Colonel Osborne, was flown out to Ascension Island to take part in the highly secret Task Force 317.9, specially formed to recapture South Georgia.

They flew out on C-130 Hercules transport aircraft specially converted to flight-refuelling tankers. With their passenger and carrier holds containing long-range fuel tanks, the aircraft were claustrophobic, horribly noisy and relentlessly bumpy, making for a long, dreadfully uncomfortable flight that put no one in good mood.

'My arse feels like it's made of stone,' said the big, black trooper, Will Simpson, when the Hercules finally touched down and they were getting off their seats for the first time. Simpson was from Fiji, but his father was an English engineer. 'It's been hammered so much, it's as solid as a bloody rock. I don't like these long flights, man.'

After disembarking on Ascension Island, the eighty troops were driven in Bedfords from Wideawake airfield, located in featureless, windblown terrain and filled with Vulcan bombers, Victor tankers, Starlifters, Nimrod recce planes, and other Hercules transports, to be billeted in an equally desolate, disused school surrounded by flatlands of volcanic rock.

'About as welcoming as a morgue,' TT said. 'If we don't freeze to death in this fucking place, we'll choke to death in the dust. I think it's warmer outside.'

'It's the cold I don't like, man,' Will Simpson responded, choosing one of the steel-framed beds for his basha and throwing his Bergen rucksack onto it. 'Me, I can breathe dust with no problem, but this cold, man, it kills me.'

'Stop whining, the pair of you,' Marty told them, 'and

get your arses outside with the others. We've no time to waste.'

'We're on the way, boss,' Trooper Simpson responded. 'We can't wait to get out there in the fresh air and see what the place is like.'

'I'll bet,' Marty said.

In fact, it was as dismal outside as it was inside the school. The island was no more than a volcanic dust heap, nine miles across at its widest. With a total population of little over one thousand souls, it had a BBC relay station, a 10,000-foot runway built by NASA, a satellite tracking station and a firing range. However, now being used as a staging post for the Task Force, it was receiving an average of six Hercules flights a day, as well as a constant stream of men: M Company of 42 Commando, RM (Royal Marines), the RAF, the Royal Naval Aircraft Servicing Unit, Royal Engineers, and other members of the British Forces Support Unit. Their equipment was ferried in from the fleet anchored out at sea.

As the RSM, Marty was placed in charge of the special training, which began that first day and covered a wide variety of situations. The Falklands are notable for cold weather and wind so severe that combined they can lead to windchill, which freezes exposed flesh in minutes. For this reason, the men had to get used to operating in windproof and waterproof clothing that covered the whole body and was based on the so-called 'layer system', whereby layers of clothing are added or taken away depending on the temperature and level of activity. Most of the arctic battle gear was therefore made from Gore-tex, which keeps air but allows moisture to escape before it freezes on the body. Other items of kit distributed to them that first morning included mittens, face masks, ski boots, snow shoes and skis.

'I take this as an ominous sign,' Trooper Simpson, who loathed the cold, said. 'I hate the Falklands already.'

Nevertheless, even kitted out like this, the kind of training the regiment could do was fairly limited. Wearing their bulky Gore-tex weatherproof jackets, woolly-pully sweaters, Royal Marine DPM trousers and heavy boots was a distinctly uncomfortable way of undergoing Marty's special training. It was, however, vitally necessary as the main key to survival in the arctic environments of their ultimate destination was to get out of the wind and defeat the cold; thus, apart from wearing their thick, weather-resistant clothing, they were given training in the construction of shelters such as snow holes, snow caves and igloos, as well as instruction in ski techniques and navigation in arctic conditions. They were also shown how to keep their weapons in working order in the wet, freezing weather of the Falklands, which could make lubricants thicken, leading to sluggish actions or even the complete jamming of moving parts. To this end, all unnecessary lubricants had to be removed and even ammunition had to be cleaned of all oil and condensation.

Finally, they tested their weapons on the firing range, rehearsed in canoes and Gemini inflatables in the shallow waters just off the beach, and practised abseiling from noisily hovering Wessex helicopters. Meanwhile, out in the bay, Navy helicopters, known as 'helos', were cross-decking troops to let them be shipped onto the Falklands – a sight that sorely frustrated the SAS troops.

'They're flying hundreds of those bastards out every day,' TT said, 'while we sit here twiddling our fucking thumbs.'

'Our time will come,' Taff said quietly, reasonably, always willing to wait for what he wanted. 'Just be patient, TT.'

'I can't stand all this bloody retraining. It's all shit we've done before.'

'And you'll do it again and again,' Marty said, having walked up to join them. 'Just as long as I tell you to.'

'Aye, aye, boss,' Alan Pearson said.

Mercifully, just as they were becoming too restless for their own good, they were given orders to sail in the 22,890-ton Royal Fleet Auxiliary, *Fort Austin*, for a proper assignment. About twelve hours later, in the pearly light of dawn, they were driven away from Wideawake airfield, past planes, helicopters, fork-lifts, supply trucks, advance-communications equipment and stockpiles of fuel, rations and medical supplies, to the nearby beach, where Gemini inflatable boats were waiting to take them out to the fleet of battle ships that would carry them on to the South Atlantic.

Fort Austin sailed under the Blue Ensign in company with the large destroyer HMS *Antrim* (6,200 tons), the frigate *Plymouth* (2,800 tons), and the large fleet tanker *Tidespring* (27,400 tons). Maintaining radio silence, the fleet soon left Ascension Island far behind to become surrounded by the deep swells and ominous waves of the heaving, forbidding sea.

Although normally unarmed, the RFA *Fort Austin* was carrying improvised weaponry including GPMGs. It had also embarked four Lynx helicopters specially fitted for firing the Sea Skua missile and it was loaded with 3,500 tons of ammunition, stores and spares. With a length of 183.0 metres, a beam of 24.1 metres and a draught of 14.9 metres, she was an impressive sight to behold and, to the uninitiated, overwhelming inside.

Spending most of their time in the dimly lit, sweltering hold in tightly packed tiers of bunk beds and hammocks, surrounded by dangling equipment and clothes hanging from stanchions, in a tangle of bags, packs, Bergens and weapons, with little to do except be patient, the SAS troopers passed the time by studying as much intelligence about the islands as they had been given by the green slime, playing cards, writing letters in which they could not state their whereabouts, visiting the latrines out of boredom as well as need, and exchanging the usual banter and bullshit. When feeling trapped or claustrophobic in the crowded, noisy hold, a man could make his escape by touring the immense ship and observing the constant activity that went on in its holds and on the flight deck. Most of this revolved around the transfer of stores and equipment, either to smaller ships alongside or by Jackstay rigs or helicopters to HM ships. The noise both above and below decks was therefore considerable and usually didn't stop even during the night.

While most of the men found this part of the voyage a torment, mainly because of the deadly boredom and lack of exercise, Marty found it to be so only because it gave him too much time to think – and what he mostly thought about was what had happened in the past two years, since Diane's suicide, his own subsequent neutralising of Sir Charles Alfred Seagrove and Paddy's response to that particular cleansing operation. Naturally, Marty had always denied any personal involvement in the matter, but Paddy, though unable to prove anything, had refused to believe him and their friendship had suffered accordingly. Marty was proud of what he had done, but even now, after so many subsequent cleansing operations by the Association – which had also incensed Paddy, though again he could prove nothing – he was deeply hurt by the damage done to their friendship and found himself trying to put that, as well as the other agonies of the past years, out of his mind. Alas, this was not easy.

He was, for instance, still tormented by Diane's suicide (why hadn't she talked to him, picked up the phone, left a note?) and undeniably guilty at what he thought was the necessary evil of the Association's activities. Though the end justified the means, he could not deny what he felt – and what he felt was great guilt. How relieved he was, therefore, to be engaged once more in a war that was far removed from home. He didn't care how bad this war might be: he just needed escape.

On the fifth day of the voyage *Antrim*'s fleet linked up with the ice patrol ship, *Endurance*, 1,600 kilometres north of South Georgia, and, escorted by it, began closing in on the island. However, to the immense frustration of the already bored men, it had to drop anchor and remain where it was until permission was received to commence the assault, codenamed Operation Paraquat.

For the purposes of Operation Corporate (the overall operation to recapture the Falklands), the work of the special forces, including the SAS and the Special Boat Squadron, was being coordinated through a command cell on HMS *Hermes*, the flagship of the Royal Navy Task Force. SAS officers were already aboard the flagship and Marty would end up there eventually, but right now, because of his advancing years and the heart attack he had suffered long ago in Oman, which officially prevented him from taking part in the fighting, he was with Lieutenant-Colonel Osborne in the command cell of the *Antrim*, helping to orchestrate the planned assault on South Georgia.

Given the hostile nature of the Falklands, the SAS men on *Fort Austin* were divided into the two groups most suitable for this kind of operation: the Mountain Troop, which would be used for land-based reconnaissance and engagements; and the Boat Troop, to be used for any required amphibious landings. While the ship sat at anchor, the men of the Mountain Troop were kept as busy as possible with interminable lessons on the geography and topography of the Falklands, while the Boat Troop had similar lessons on the tides and waterways of the islands and with the constant checking of their Gemini inflatable assault boats and Klepper canoes.

Nevertheless, as one day drifted into the next with no word from HQ, life aboard ship became increasingly boring, leading to general restlessness and even an occasional angry confrontation between SAS troopers and the ship's crew. Marty was therefore very relieved when, ten days later, word was received that Operation Paraquat could commence.

Lying 1,300 kilometres east-south-east of the Falklands and, as the main base of the British Antarctic Survey (BAS) teams, South Georgia was particularly important to Great Britain. The capture of the island, it was assumed, would be a clear indication to the world in general and Argentina in particular that if necessary the British would fight to recapture any territory stolen from them.

The assault, however, was not, strictly speaking, an SAS operation. In fact, the commander of the landing forces would be Major Guy Sheridan, the second-in-command of M Company, 42 Commando RM, who would work with the SAS Commanding Officer aboard *Antrim* in planning the assault on the island. Marty was part of their strategy team. In addition to D Squadron, 22 SAS, Sheridan had 120 men of M Company, 42 Commando, and about 25 swimmer-canoeists of 2 SBS, Royal Marines. He also had a small detachment of marines aboard *Antrim* with M Company's Recce Troop, a mortar section and the company OC. In all, about 235 men against an enemy of unknown quantity.

Marty was in the command cell aboard *Antrim* when a signal was dropped from a maritime reconnaissance aircraft, authorising the SAS to carry out covert recces on South Georgia. Immediately, working under Lieutenant-Colonel Osborne, he drew up plans for the Mountain Troop to land north of Leith, where reportedly the Argentinians had been collecting scrap from an old whaling station. At about the same time, 2 SBS would land in Hounds Bay, south-east of the island's main settlement of Grytviken, and move up the coast in inflatable boats to establish observation posts, which could observe the settlement from across five kilometres of open water.

Because South Georgia was out of range of land-based aircraft, D squadron transshipped by Wessex helicopter from *Fort Austin* to the ice patrol ship *Endurance*, which would sail closer to the shore, enabling them to fly in to their LZ. Though smaller than *Fort Austin*, *Endurance* was equipped with two Wasp helicopters. To facilitate their landing, a large hangar had been built aft of the ship's funnel, extending her poop deck to create a helicopter landing pad – and it was onto this that the Wessex helo landed, rocking unsteadily above the treacherous, surging waves, before settling at last on the swaying, creaking deck.

Once the SAS were aboard the new ship, Osborne held a briefing for the sixteen members of his Mountain Troop. Marty was standing beside him throughout the briefing, which took place in a large cabin above the flight decks, with drenched portholes giving a distorted view of the featureless grey sea and sky outside. While the SBS had been given the task of reconnoitring Grytviken and King Edward Point, the SAS Mountain Troop under the command of Captain Michael Peters, a former mountaineer, were to be landed on Fortuna Glacier, South Georgia, to establish observation posts for the gathering of intelligence on the Argentinian forces. This would not be as easy at it seemed as the glacier was a potential death trap with its five arms, flowing down into the South Atlantic, veined with hundreds of deep fissures and pressure ridges. Even though it was comparatively level at the top of the glacier, where the weight of the ice pressured downwards, there were hundreds of crevasses, most nearly a mile wide, which could swallow a man up to his waist. Finally, the men would almost certainly face sub-zero temperatures and gale-force winds.

Nevertheless, the importance of that high point overlooking Grytviken and Leith Harbour was enough reason to take a chance and attempt a landing. The buildings on King Edward Point had housed the British Antarctic Survey settlement before the Royal Marines were forced to surrender to the Argentinians. The same buildings now housed the Argentinian HQ. They were at the mouth of a cove a thousand metres from Grytviken, which is what the green slime hoped the men would be able to observe from the OP on the Fortuna Glacier.

Still feeling bitter than he had not been allowed to take part in the Princes Gate siege, Marty was almost heartbroken at the thought of missing this assault on the glacier, particularly given his abiding love and experience of mountaineering. Knowing that he would soon be retiring anyway, so hardly concerned about any disciplinary measures that might be taken against him, he approached Captain Peters when the CO had departed and begged to be allowed to come along, emphasising his previous mountain-climbing experience and carefully omitting any mention of his heart attack in Oman. Not aware that Marty had been restricted to tactical planning and intelligence, Peters, grateful to have a man so experienced, gave his consent.

Elated, Marty hurried down to the lower deck, where he found the rest of the men preparing themselves with their usual thoroughness. Arctic cold-weather kit was drawn from *Endurance*'s stores, including Swedish civilian mountaineering boots, which they used instead of their normal DMS boots. Weapons were signed for and carefully checked, including SLRs with twenty-round steel magazines; 7.62-millimetre GPMGs; a couple of Armalites with single-shot, breech-loaded, pump-action grenade-launchers; M202s with 66-millimetre, trigger-mechanism incendiary rockets; Browning High Power handguns, and fragmentation, white phosphorous, CS and smoke grenades. The weapons were thoroughly checked, then the machine-guns, rifles and pistols were cleansed of unnecessary lubricants, to prevent them from seizing up in the freezing temperatures of the glacier.

Other equipment, apart from food and drink, included a couple of PRC 319 HF/VHF radio systems and an older Clansman High-Frequency set, which could also be used as a Morse or CW transmitter. Also loaded onto the troop-carrying

A/SW Wessex helicopters were four long, lightweight sleds, or *pulks*, which could be hauled by hand and would be used to transport the weapons and other equipment from the LZ to the summit of the glacier.

When these necessary tasks were completed, the men gathered on the landing pads of the ship and took their places in the two Royal Marine Wessex Mark 5 helicopters and the smaller Wessex Mark 3, from the RFA *Antrim*, to be flown by Lieutenant-Commander Randolph Paterson.

Taking off at midday, the helos headed for South Georgia, flying above a sludge-coloured sea, through a sky filled with black clouds. Looking out past Lieutenant-Commander Paterson's head, Marty saw a charcoal-coloured, snow-streaked stretch of mountainous land on a grey-smudged horizon, growing larger each second: the coast of South Georgia. Paterson was hoping to reach the LZ 500 metres above sea level, but within minutes the mountains of the approaching island could be seen and clearly they were covered with falling snow, which would make the landing dangerous. True enough, as the helo neared the LZ, it was met by wind-driven snow that created a white-out by making earth and sky indistinguishable. Nevertheless, with the aid of the helo's computerised navigational system, Paterson was able to lead the other two helos on through the dangerous gorges until the sheer face of the Fortuna Glacier emerged eerily from a curtain of falling snow. There the helos hovered, ascending and descending, trying to find a place to land, being buffeted constantly, dangerously, by the fierce, howling wind.

'This LZ is a nightmare,' TT said. 'I see us being smashed to hell down there.'

'Let us pray,' Alan Pearson said.

The first attempt to land was indeed unsuccessful, so eventually Paterson and the others flew away to circle the glacier and hopefully find a clear area. In fact, they weren't able to land until the third attempt, later that afternoon, when the wind was blowing at fifty miles on hour.

When the sixteen troopers disembarked from the helos, the fierce wind was driving fine particles of ice before it. These stung the men's eyes if they were not wearing goggles and, more dangerously, choked the mechanisms of their weapons. As they unloaded their equipment and *pulks*, they were sheltered from the worst of the weather; also, the hot exhaust fumes of the helos gave them a deceptive feeling of warmth. But when the helos lifted off, the troopers were suddenly hit by the full force of those winds and realised just what they were up against.

Wiping snow from their arctic hoods, they examined their weapons and found that they were covered in ice. After thawing the weapons out and wiping them dry, they split up into four groups, each roped together, and prepared to go down the glacier in arrow formation. In this way, it was felt, they would be less likely to lose each other and could also help each other out if there was trouble. Attaching themselves to the *pulks* loaded with food and ammunition, they began their advance down the glacier, looking inhuman in their bulky arctic suits and hoods, ghostlike in the mist and swirling snow.

One patrol had orders to watch Leith, one Stromness and one Husvik, seven kilometres from the LZ. The fourth, led by Taff, had intended going down the opposite west slope to recce Fortuna Bay for boat and helicopter landing zones. But this did not come to pass. As the men moved slowly forward, the storm grew worse, with the wind howling louder and the snow thickening around them, reducing visibility to almost zero.

The ice surface of the glacier was covered with snow, which was gathering in the crevasses. The men could not always see the indentations in the snow and within a few metres they came to a halt when a new trooper, Sammy McCulloch, became the first to cry out as he plunged through the snow-covered ice. Luckily, his fall was stopped by his Bergen straddling the fissure, leaving him buried from the waist down, still holding onto the rope. When he had been rescued by the others, who dug him out with pickaxes and then pulled him up by tugging on the rope, they all stepped over the crevasse, leaned into the wind, and continued their advance down the white gleaming side of the glacier. Then a second trooper fell into another crevasse, compelling them to stop and start the rescue procedure all over again. This occurred repeatedly and it was also happening to the other groups, visible as shadowy, inhuman shapes in the snowstorm, clearly struggling but also making little headway.

As the storm grew worse, their advance was reduced to a snail's pace. By nightfall, when already they were frozen and exhausted, they had managed to cover only one kilometre and Marty suspected that they were wasting their time.

'This weather's too dreadful,' he confided in Taff. 'We'll just get blown away by it.'

'Blown away and blinded,' Taff replied. 'There's no way we can work in this.'

Unable to do more in the relentless snowstorm, the four patrols regrouped in the gathering gloom of the evening and attempted to make camp for the night. Seeking protection from the piercing cold, they found the least exposed part of the glacier, under a rock outcrop, and there tried to put up three-man tents. When these were violently whipped away by the gale, snapping noisily as they disappeared in the darkness, the men dug snow holes and attempted to sleep in bivvy bags with their boots on. By midnight, however, hurricane-force-eleven winds were howling over the mountains, which not only prevented sleep, but also offered the real possibility of hypothermia and frostbite. At this point, Captain Peters decided to give up.

'The frostbite can be so bad,' Peters reminded Marty, 'that a man can even lose a limb. So get on that radio, RSM, and ask them to lift us out.'

Marty did as he was told. After explaining the situation to HMS *Endurance*, he was informed that three Wessex helos would be dispatched at first light, one from *Antrim*, the other two from HMS *Tidespring*, and that he was to send up a flare when he saw them. Marty promised to do so.

The ensuing night was hellish with the force-eleven wind not abating at all, the snow and ice beating at them every second, instantly flaying them if they made the mistake of exposing a patch of skin to the elements. Sleep was impossible, or at least came in fits and starts, and by dawn, when a pale sun shone through, they were exhausted and numb.

The Navy pilots, however, were as good as their word. Even

before he heard them – since the wind was still roaring, the sweeping snow still hissing – Marty saw the three helos coming in to attempt a landing on the glacier. Wriggling quickly out of his bivvy bag, he sent up a chemical flare as the rest of the group came back to life, looking up to see the green smoke spreading through the still-dark, snow-filled sky. Sitting upright, they smacked the snow off their hoods and gloves, then slapped themselves to get their circulation going.

Contacting the lead helo through the PRC 319, Marty learned that the pilot was again Lieutenant Commander Paterson and that he had spotted them and was coming in for a landing. The Mark 3 duly descended through the still-raging blizzard, its rotors causing a more violent snowstorm as it nervously touched down. It was followed immediately by the other two helos.

As quickly as possible, given the appalling conditions, the men distributed their equipment to the three helicopters, then took their own places, with Marty and Alan Pearson taking seats in Paterson's Mark 3, which lifted off first. It was followed by the two Mark 5s, one of which was carrying Captain Peters, Taff Hughes and TT.

'Thank God for that,' Alan Pearson murmured, shivering with cold where he sat beside Marty in the Mark 3, both staring up through the swirling snow as the helo ascended. 'I thought I was going to lose my fucking balls, I was so fucking—'

He stopped in mid-sentence when he saw one of the Mark 5s flying into a particularly fierce gust of snow, a virtual white-out, then shuddering violently and turning off its true course. Tilting downwards, it headed nose first for the ground, through the sweeping snow of the howling blizzard.

'Shit!' Marty exclaimed as the helo wobbled widely, screeching, fighting to right itself, then went down even more quickly, obviously out of control, to crash into the glacier in a mess of buckling skis, breaking rotors and flying glass, throwing up a great fountain of snow.

Even as the helo was shuddering like a dying elephant, half buried in snow, Marty heard the other Mark 5 pilot, Captain

Ranleigh, speaking on Paterson's radio, saying that he was going to land again in a rescue mission.

'We're coming down after you,' Paterson said. 'Over and out.'

Marty saw the Mark 5 turning around and descending, heading straight back into the blizzard until it had practically disappeared in the swirling snow. Paterson's Mark 3 followed suit and soon it too was enveloped in a thick curtain of snow, virtually another white-out, in which the glacier and sky merged as one. Then the snow thinned a little and Marty saw the Mark 5 landing, its spinning rotors sweeping up more snow and hurling it in great white waves over the crashed, wrecked helo as shadowy figures hurried out of it.

The wall of the glacier was now directly outside the window of the Mark 3, appearing to rise rapidly as the helo descended, then the rotors whipped up more snow as the chopper settled down on its skis, bounced a little and stopped.

'All out!' Lieutenant-Commander Paterson barked.

Marty and his men jumped out of the helo, intent on a rescue operation. But when they had disembarked and crossed to the Mark 5, positioned beside its crashed counterpart, they found Captain Peters's group already helping the survivors into their own helo, all of them swept by the snow and ghostlike in the blizzard.

An SAS corporal, a new man, was the only person injured from the seven aboard. Even though the pilot's cabin had been smashed to hell, the pilot was okay. On the grounds that his Mark 5 could hold more men than Paterson's Mark 3, Captain Ranleigh insisted that Paterson take three of the men, including Captain Peters and the injured man, while he lifted off the remaining four. Paterson saw the sense in that, but still recommended that the passengers ditch everything but their weapons and belt equipment. He also suggested lightening the Mark 3 by leaving some of its special equipment on the ground. When the men had done as they were told, discarding everything but weapons and belt equipment, and the Mark 3 had been stripped of some of its special equipment, which was buried carefully, deeply, under the ice and snow, the men were distributed between the two operational helos and they took off again.

The Mark 3 had barely lifted off the ground when it flew into a white-out, was buffeted by a fierce wind, and, with its heavy load, became the second to crash. Marty felt the helo shaking like a car with punctured tyres, then it tilted to one side, showing the ground directly below, and Paterson called out a warning just before it went down. The rotor blades made contact first, snapping off and spinning away, then the skis buckled beneath the crashing fuselage, making the helo tilt further. The men inside were scattered like skittles, thrown into each other, and scrambled about on the floor of the passenger cabin, cursing loudly as their weapons and other equipment were scattered and clattered about them. The helo shuddered and shrieked, its metal buckling, glass breaking, then it shuddered in the exploding, swirling snow and sank into impacted ice.

'All out!' Captain Peters bawled, as he and Paterson unbuckled their safety belts and turned back into the disordered passenger cabin. Surprisingly, no one had been hurt and all of the men were able to make their escape from the wreckage, dropping down onto the ice and snow, back into the raging storm and its fiercely swirling snow.

Even before the last man had emerged, the remaining Mark 5 helicopter became visible in the stormy sky as Captain Ranleigh courageously returned to the glacier, checking out their location. Managing to find them, he contacted them by radio and informed Captain Peters that he was too short of fuel to be able to land again, but was going to fly back to the *Antrim* to top up his tanks, after which he would return and pick them up.

Captain Peters turned off his radio as the helo turned away and headed back out to sea, eventually disappearing beyond a broad bank of dense clouds and dark, snow-streaked sky.

'What a fucking disaster!' TT said. 'Two choppers down and here we are still trapped on this glacier. Who would have believed it?'

'All I know, man,' said Trooper Will Simpson, wiping snowflakes from his black face, 'is that I don't want hypothermia or frostbite, so I'm belting in and wrapping up.'

'Fucking good idea,' TT said.

This, Marty knew, would be the worst time for all of them: the time when the strongest man could break. First the failure of the mission, then a night of hellish cold, then two helicopter crashes in a row, now being trapped here. The physical enemy was the cold, but the loss of morale could be more dangerous, particularly if it led to self-pity or a sense of despair. It was also, however, the kind of situation that the SAS were specially trained for. He was therefore pleased to see his remaining men rising to the challenge by making themselves as comfortable as possible with hardly any kit and sharing only one survival tent between them. It was a long, hellish day with the blizzard unrelenting and the men, taking turns to keep warm in the single tent, gradually becoming covered in snow and merging into the landscape. The snow, continuing to fall without respite, eventually buried them.

'I'm fucking dying,' Simpson complained, blowing repeatedly into his hands to try to warm them. 'I can't take this cold, man.'

'Hang in there,' Alan Pearson said.

As promised, Ranleigh returned a few hours later, trying to find a landing place. But, defeated by the increasing ferocity of the storm, he had to go back once more to the ship, thus filling those on the glacier with despair. Later that day, however, he courageously returned, this time managing to land, and picked up the frozen, exhausted men.

Dangerously overloaded, the Mark 5 limped back to the *Antrim*, a red streak in the vast greyness, and dropped onto the swaying deck like a bloated fly too heavy to stay aloft. It was not a graceful touchdown, given the weight of the helo, but eventually the men tumbled out onto the deck, most of them exhausted and shivering with cold, none warmed by the knowledge that the mission had been a disaster.

The wind continued howling across the deck, bringing with it the snow. The men went below decks again.

CHAPTER FORTY-TWO

The Boat Troop succeeded where the Mountain Troop had failed. To make up for the Fortuna Glacier disaster, the men of the Boat Troop were tasked with establishing a couple of OPs on Leith and Stromness, using Grass Island on the north-west of the island as their LZ and inserting by sea instead of air. Once the OPs had been set up and the surrounding area recced, the full-scale invasion of South Georgia would commence.

They left at last light from the docking area at the stern of the ship, which had been opened and was already being flooded when the men of the Boat Troop gathered near the launching bay. Kitted out with waterproof clothing and the usual array of weapons, the Boat Troop also carried special survival suits, lifejackets and SARBEs, (search-and-rescue beacons) to facilitate the pick-ups and, if necessary, aid rescue from the sea.

The five Geminis, two large and three small, already inflated and roped to the docking bay, were being lifted towards the men on the rising sea as it poured into the open stern to flood the bay area, roaring and spewing spray in every direction. Viewed from that vantage point, the sea appeared to slope up to the distant, stormy horizon, soaring and rolling dramatically in immense, shadowed waves that appeared to be about to swamp the ship, thought they actually just made it rise and fall as if it were made of cork. The sky was just as threatening, hanging low, filled with black clouds, and the wind that came rushing in to smack the men was icy and vicious. Nevertheless, they embarked in the five Geminis, three to each boat, with Captain John Banville in charge of the lead craft. The two large Geminis were powered by forty-horsepower outboard motors, the three smaller ones powered by eighteen-horsepower motors. The small boats were roped to the larger ones: two to one and one to the other. When the docking ropes had been untied and the outboard motors turned on, the inflatables cruised out of the docking area to be carried away on the giant swells of the fierce, windswept sea.

The immense waves picked the boats up, carried them through shrieking wind, above ravines of light-flecked darkness, then swept them back down into roaring, spinning tunnels formed by waves curling practically above them, threatening to swamp them. When the inflatables were low in the water, the waves pounded against them and washed over the men, pummelling them mercilessly and making a dreadful drumming sound against the rubber hulls. When they were raised on high, barrelling along the crest of the waves with the men glancing down what appeared to be dizzying depths of light and darkness, their outboard engines, coming clear of the water, shrieked and shook dementedly.

Within minutes, the *Antrim*, which had been towering above them like a brightly lit skyscraper, receded beyond the stormy ocean, blending in with the grey haze where sea and sky merged, until little of it remained within view. Then it disappeared completely, leaving only the sea and sky, while the inflatables, rising and falling, plunging in and out of the water, shrieked and vibrated like wild things that could not be controlled.

In the smaller inflatables, roped to the large boats, the men on the rudders had to fight to keep close to the one ahead in case the rope snapped. This required great physical strength, since the howling wind and raging, roaring water between them threatened to tear the rudders away. Meanwhile, the men seated up front were leaning forward, heads bowed, stretched out over the strapped-down weapons and equipment in the hope of keeping them as dry as possible. In the middle of each small inflatable, the signallers with the waterproof PRC 319 radios were keeping in contact with Captain Banville's larger Gemini, which, a good distance ahead of them, repeatedly disappeared in immense fountains of spray and then reappeared, often on the crest of giant waves that seemed to float on high, almost touching the black, tumultuous clouds, as if about to take wing.

In many ways it was a miracle that they made it at all, but long before they reached the island the eighteen-horsepower outboard motor of one of the small Geminis cut out and the rope connecting it to the larger Gemini was stretched as taut as it could go. Within minutes, the outboard motor of a second small boat cut out as well and then its rudder was smashed loose by the pounding waves and it went out of control, its rope snapping and sending it adrift. Finally, the rope of a third small inflatable actually snapped in two and the craft, set free, its outboard motor not working, went spinning away out of control. It disappeared beyond a series of high waves and did not reappear.

As the lost craft was swept westward, towards Antarctica, Captain Banville, in the large Gemini, was left with only one dinghy in tow, while the other large Gemini had none. He had just lost two boats and six good men, with little hope of getting them back. Luckily, while the remaining inflatables were still intact, the jagged hills of Grass Island emerged out of the storm. The beach was only half a mile away and the boats were heading straight for it.

The storm abated a little as they headed for the shore, but about 400 metres out, when the white, frozen hills were visible through the mist, snow started falling upon them to make up for the lessening wind. The men huddled up in their waterproof outfits and prepared for the landing.

Luckily, the closer they came to shore, the less the wind blew and the more settled the formerly raging sea became. Slowing down their outboard motors, the pilots of the two large Geminis inched carefully into shallow waters, then stopped and anchored, enabling the men to clamber out and wade to the shore, carrying their light M16 rifles above their heads.

Leaving his exhausted men on the beach, within sight of the inflatables bobbing out in shallow water, Banville held his M16 at the ready and hurried up the snow-covered hill directly ahead. Reaching the summit, he was able to look across the small island to Leith Harbour, only three kilometres away. Blocks of ice were floating in the water, but the storm had abated. Glancing around him, Banville saw nothing but other snow- and ice-covered hills; no sign of Argentinian troops. Looking out to sea, he could not even see the British fleet, nor was there any sign of the two missing dinghies – only what now looked like calmer sea under a dark, stormy sky, from which snow was falling.

Satisfied that they would no longer be bothered by the storm, he returned to the men resting on the snow-covered shore and they took the inflatables out again, first cruising around the small, bleak island, then starting across the three kilometres of ice-filled water, heading straight for South Georgia. The sky was low and ominous, but the storm did not return, and the darkness, which had fallen with great speed, offered protection from Argentinian observation posts. Cruising slowly, quietly, between drifting blocks of ice, they managed to reach Stromness Bay without seeing, or even hearing, Argentinian patrol boats. However, just as Banville was beginning to feel more confident, thinking his troubles were behind him, the blocks of ice gave way to drifting packs of gleaming, sharp ice splinters that punctured the inflatables, one after the other in rapid succession, letting the air hiss out and forcing them to abandon the boats.

They were only about thirty metres from shore, in ice-filled, shallow water, which allowed them to clamber out of the hissing, sinking inflatables, form a chain from the boats to the shore, and pass the equipment along the chain before the inflatables crumpled completely and sank for good.

Now, no matter what happened, they had no means of returning to the fleet, hidden beyond the horizon.

Encircled by mountains that hid them from the Argentinians in Grytviken, they hid under an outcropping of rocks until they had dried all of the equipment, shucked off their lifebelts, and were ready to march on in pursuit of locations suitable for observation posts.

After checking his map for two areas of high ground overlooking Leith Harbour and Stromness Bay, Banville broke his remaining group into two separate units, one to establish an OP in the hills above Leith, the other, his own, to establish the same above Stromness. He then marched his own team up to his selected vantage point overlooking both areas, where they settled down to building an OP. Because he had no idea when the assault from the fleet would take place, he anticipated a long stay here and therefore had the men dig a rectangular OP layout, rather than the short-term star shape.

The spoil, or earth, from the digging was removed in Bergens and sprinkled unobtrusively over the ground a good distance away. Once this had been done, the hole was lined with plastic sheets and the men put up a hessian screen, with a poncho and overhead camouflage net, supported by wooden stakes, iron pickets, and chicken wire, and including a camouflaged entry/exit hole. When this business was completed, the troopers, wearing face veils and thick leather gloves, settled down in the OP, taking turns as telescope observer and sentry, as well as alternating in the rest bays, with their kit, including the weapons, piled up in the middle.

From the completed OP the group signaller was able to establish communications with *Antrim*, enabling Banville to inform the CO of what had happened to him and the others. In return, he was informed that one of the missing boats had been found by helicopter and the crew returned safely to the fleet. The other boat was still missing and its occupants presumed drowned.

Disturbed by that news, Banville tried not to show it and instead encouraged his men to settle down to the business of observing Argentinian movements from their OP.

Thirty years earlier both areas had been whaling stations, boasting hundreds of workers, but now they were virtually deserted and, as viewed from the wind-whipped, moaning hills, they revealed themselves only as a few scattered lights in the night's chilling, occasionally moonlit, darkness.

The wind howled eerily all night long. The snow covered them like a blanket. Before very long, they were cramped, cold and uncomfortable, boots wet, limbs numbed by constricted blood.

For many it would have been a night of hell, but Banville and his men had been trained for this and stoically endured.

In their private cabin aboard the *Antrim*, now anchored with the other ships far north of South Georgia, Marty and other members of the joint Royal Marine–SAS planning team were informed by Lieutenant-Colonel Osborne that an Argentinian submarine had been observed reconnoitring the coastline of the island, almost certainly looking for signs of British landings. It was not believed that they had witnessed the insertion of Captain Banville's Boat Troop, which had since been in radio contact to confirm that two OPs had been set up overlooking Leith and Stromness. In the event, Randolph Paterson was out searching for the Argentinian submarine when he spotted one of the two missing SAS inflatables and lifted its three men to safety. The crew of that inflatable had the foresight to sink it before letting themselves be lifted up. Lieutenant-Commander Paterson had confirmed in his report that the inflatable sank before he left the area. To date, there had been no sign of the second missing inflatable and it was believed to have either sunk or been blown clear of the island, into the southern ocean.

According to Argentinian radio signals monitored by *Endurance* while she was anchored in Hound Bay, the enemy submarine had recently landed reinforcements on the island, bringing the Argentinian garrison strength up to about 140 men. However, just before first light, Lieutenant-Commander Paterson, busy as always in his helo, had spotted the submarine on the surface as she sailed over the shallows of Cumberland Bay, heading out to look for the British fleet. After reporting her location to the fleet, he straddled her with two depth-charges. Soon afterwards, she was attacked by *Endurance*'s Wasp and the Lynx from the destroyer, HMS *Brilliant*. Those helicopters forced the submarine to run for King Edward Point, her conning tower damaged and listing after being hit by missiles. It was assumed, and hoped, that it would either sink before reaching its base at King Edward Point or at least be incapacitated when it reached there.

Finally, with the enemy submarine out of action and the two SAS OPs sending back invaluable intelligence about Leith Harbour and Stromness Bay, Major Sheridan had given clearance for an immediate landing to seize those two areas. This would be accomplished by a quick-reaction force of the three composite troops aboard the *Antrim*. The first QRF would be composed of the Mountain and remaining Boat groups of the SAS. The second would include 2 SBS and the commando recce sections of '42'; and the third would be made up from commando mortar-men and the ship's marines. Though that made up a total of only 75 men, scarcely more than half the strength of the Argentinian garrison, it was believed that the superior quality of the British troops would help win the day.

'Who dares wins,' Marty said.

After three days in his OP overlooking Stromness, Captain Banville was virtually buried in snow, feeling as miserable as his SAS troop looked, but resolutely sending back to the fleet every scrap of information he had picked up on the movements of the Argentinians, both on land and out at sea, including the frequent submarine patrols out of Leith Harbour. This information had come from a combination of radio interception and visual observation, the latter either from foot patrols which went dangerously close to the Argentinian bases, to spy on them at close quarters, or by using binoculars to scan the sea from the hills. Either way, it was meticulously recorded and radioed back to the British fleet under the most uncomfortable, dangerous circumstances.

The men, though now buried in snow, smelling their own shit and piss, increasingly frozen and exhausted, would hold out to the bitter end.

Like his men, Banville was able and willing to hold out as long as necessary, but during that early afternoon of the third hellish day, with the snow still falling upon him, he was finding it difficult because of his concern for the three men still missing in the lost inflatable, almost certainly drowned at sea because of the weather. Nevertheless, determined not to give in to morbid thoughts and to uphold the precepts of the SAS by sticking here as long as possible, Banville gazed over the piled-up snow of his OP to observe Grass Island and, beyond it, the vast, grey, empty sea, now dimly, eerily lit by early afternoon's pale sun.

Suddenly, a fiery flickering illuminated the horizon and the distant roar of the fleet's big guns made the whole OP shake. The first shells exploded far below, sending smoke billowing up from the lower slopes of Leith Harbour and Stromness Bay.

The assault had begun.

With the thunder of *Antrim*'s two 114-millimetre guns pounding in their ears, Captain Peters and his SAS troop, all with full battle kit, filed into the helicopters clamped to the ship's landing pads. As Peters still didn't know about the restrictions placed upon Marty because of his health, he was still using his RSM as his second-in-command and Marty gladly took a seat between Taff and TT, strapped himself in, then glanced out through the rain-streaked window as the ship slowly tilted to one side. The sea, which was filled with deep swells, seemed very far below him. When he looked in the other direction, back towards the ship, he saw the big guns jolting each time they fired, wreathing the whole deck in smoke.

The combined bedlam of the RN helos and the guns was like the end of the world and became even worse when, with more noise and much shuddering, the holding clamps were released and the helos lifted off the deck. They ascended vertically, hovered above the landing pad, moved sideways to hover right above the sea, then headed for shore.

The big guns of *Antrim* and *Plymouth* were continuing to roar in a relentless barrage, which would ensure that the landing area and Brown Mountain, dominating it, were clear of Argentinian troops. Looking across that short stretch of mottled grey sea, Marty saw the billowing columns of smoke where the shells were exploding. The shore was now rushing forward, pebbled, streaked with snow, with the shells exploding further inland, on the hills of Brown Mountain. Marty glanced westward, beyond the other two helicopters, to where sea and sky met, thinking glumly of the men who had been lost in their Gemini inflatable. Either they had drowned or were still drifting helplessly towards the Antarctic, in which case they would almost certainly freeze to death, after suffering hypothermia and frostbite. It was not a comforting thought.

When he looked down again, he saw the shore whipping out of view, to give way to the inland hills and valleys, mostly barren and brown, though brightened here and there with snow and frost. The ground was rushing up at him.

'Prepare to disembark!' the RN loadmaster shouted from up front.

After unclipping their safety belts, the men stood awkwardly in a metallic jangle of sniper rifles, submachine-guns, hand grenades, bayonets, ammunition belts and water bottles. Burdened with Bergen rucksacks and bulky in their Gore-tex jackets, they held onto the safety straps above their heads. The helo shuddered as it slowed down, hovering right above the ground. The loadmaster opened the door as the helo descended, letting the freezing air come howling in.

Captain Peters was at the opening, standing beside the RN loadmaster, a radio telephone held up to his ear, his free hand firmly gripping a support as the wind beat wildly at him, threatening to suck him out and spin him away like a twig. As they neared the LZ, the rotors whipped up dirt and snow, made foliage dance and bend, creating a minor hurricane that shook the whole helo.

'Go!' Peters bawled – and the first man disappeared through the opening before the helo had touched down. It did so as the second man went out and the queue inched towards the door. The helo was still bouncing lightly on its landing skis as Marty followed the man ahead out, slapped brutally by the slipstream but landing safely on the snow-covered ground.

The men fanned out as they marched away from the helo, leaning forward to escape the drag of its swirling slipstream. Though all of them had their weapons at the ready, there was no sign of enemy troops; only that desolate, rolling landscape, covered in snow and frost, viewed hazily through the curtain of loose snow that was being whipped up around them.

'Move out!' Peters bellowed, using his raised right hand to give the signal meaning 'advance'.

The DZ was on the lower slopes of Hestesletten, a high valley located two kilometres south-east of the former British Survey buildings on King Edward's Point, but separated from it by Brown Mountain. The sea surrounded them on all sides, flat and featureless from the heights, but the fleet was now clearly visible, with its aircraft carriers, destroyers, frigates, tankers and supply ships spread out as far back as the horizon.

The guns of *Antrim* and *Plymouth* were still firing, laying down a barrage that would methodically move forward to within 800 metres of the enemy position, the aim being to demoralise them rather than cause physical damage – a further ploy in the diplomatic war to recapture the Falklands. Plumes of smoke were still billowing up from the other side of Brown Mountain as the shells fell relentlessly around King Edward's Point. As the men marched away from the LZ, the helos took off again, whipping up more soil, stones and loose snow, and soon were mere specks in the distance, heading back to the fleet.

Fanning out even more and starting uphill, the men were heavily burdened under their packed Bergens and their usually wide assortment of firepower, including Heckler & Kosh MPA3 submachine-guns, M16A2 assault rifles, 7.62-millimetre SLRs, Browning Nine-Millies, 81-millimetre mortars, and fragmentation, white-phosphorous and smoke grenades, plus all the ammunition required for them. For this particular operation they had also brought with them laser rangefinders, thermal imagers for night viewing, a couple of PRC 319 tactical radios and, in the heavily loaded Bergens, food, drink, toiletries and survival kits. As the guns roared out at sea and shells exploded at the far side of Brown Mountain, filling the air beyond the summit with billowing clouds of smoke that dispersed under sullen clouds, the men marched uphill with weapons at the ready.

Glancing back over his shoulder, down the slopes of the

mountain, Marty saw half a dozen landing craft assault (LCA) boats cutting a swathe through the sea as they surged away from the fleet, heading for shore under the protection of Sea King helicopters. Those LCAs were bringing the other two composite troops to shore. The three troops would advance on King Edward's Point from different directions and meet up at the British Survey buildings.

Glancing left and right, to where his men had fanned out along the frosty, brown-grass-and-stone slopes, he saw Taff marching behind Will Simpson. Behind the big Fijian, Taff seemed very slight indeed, though that appearance belied his killer's instincts and skills, which Marty had since witnessed in Civvy Street during certain, highly illegal, covert actions, the nature of which was still haunting him. Not wanting even to think, at this particular time, of the activities of the Association, nor of Paddy Kearney's reaction to them, Marty concentrated on the task at hand. The surrounding hills could be filled with Argentinian troops, so this was no time for bleak thoughts.

Out at sea, the big guns of *Antrim* and *Plymouth* were continuing to pound. More smoke was billowing up from beyond the summit of Brown Mountain, obviously rising from the explosions in the area of King Edward's Point and Grytviken at the opposite side of the bay. Knowing that there could be mines in the area, Captain Peters ordered the men to spread out even more as they advanced across open ground in diamond formation. They marched for another hour in a tense, watchful silence, relieved only by the pounding of the guns out at sea and the explosions from the far side of the mountain. The hills over which they marched seemed devoid of all life, though the wind was constantly moving the sparse foliage, keeping them on edge and aiming their weapons at anything that moved, ever ready to open fire.

In fact, the men quite often opened fire after mistaking the movements of elephant seals through the grass for the rise and fall of the balaclava helmets of enemy snipers. Automatically calling out a warning, these men would drop to their knees and let rip with bursts of gunfire from their M16A2s, the roaring of their weapons reverberating around the hills as they blew the tussocks of grass apart and killed only the unfortunate seals. Surprisingly, though many seals bought it by making a sudden movement and going down in a hail of bullets before the men finally reached their destination, no Argentinian troops were seen throughout the long march.

From the mountain's summit, through a curtain of smoke created by the exploding shells of the fleet, the troop could see only what looked like a deserted settlement with white flags flying from several buildings. The Argentinian flag, however, still flew from its mast near the headquarters, formerly the British Antarctic Survey settlement, on King Edward's Point. Most of the barrage had been laid down with air-burst shells, but other shells from the fleet's guns had torn up the hills above the rocky cove, covering them with ugly black holes. The barrage had deliberately been stopped before reaching the cove itself, leaving the white-walled, red-roofed buildings on King Edward's Point intact, as was the old whaling station of Grytviken on the opposite shore.

The Argentinian submarine damaged by AS 12 missiles had indeed managed to limp into harbour and was beached there, right in front of the untouched settlement.

'It doesn't look very threatening from here,' Captain Peters said to Marty.

'The naval barrage might have done the trick,' Marty replied, 'but it might be wise to check with the fleet first.'

'My very thought,' Peters said.

Making radio contact with the operations room on the *Antrim*, he learned that Major Sheridan had already been in contact with the Argentinian headquarters in the Antarctic Survey buildings and learned that they were ready to surrender. Keen to accept their surrender, but aware from his intelligence briefings that there were minefields strewn around the Argentinian weapon pits, Peters decided to go in by the shore.

'But please warn the men,' he said to Marty, 'to keep their fingers off their triggers. If the Argies come out with their hands up, as promised, I don't want them harmed.'

'I'll see to it,' Marty said.

Once the men had been duly warned, Captain Peters and

Marty led them across hills pock-marked by scorched shell holes, high above the settlement, then carefully downhill towards the shore, keeping their eyes peeled for buried mines. No mines went off and no shots were fired. As they reached the shore and were advancing on the tall radio towers in front of the settlement, Argentinian soldiers emerged from the buildings, a few waving white flags, the others raising their hands in the air. While some of the SAS troop fanned out to surround the Argentinians and keep them covered, others entered the buildings to check for snipers and booby traps.

'These don't look like the kind of bastards who could make Royal Marines lie face down on the ground,' TT observed, keeping his SLR aimed at the unshaven, frightened men who were coming out of the buildings with their hands raised.

'They're mostly conscripts,' Marty explained. 'Practically schoolkids. Not professional soldiers. Most of them didn't even want to fight this war. The poor sods were forced into it.'

'I'd still like to waste them for what their mates did to those Royal Marines in Port Stanley,' Taff said.

'You keep your finger off that trigger,' Marty replied, 'and don't start any nonsense.'

'Yes, boss,' Taff said, smiling tightly.

Carefully covered by Alan Pearson and TT, Captain Peters and Marty advanced to meet the Argentinian captain walking cautiously towards them, beside a corporal holding a make-shift white flag. The officer wasn't young and he carried himself with dignity. When he reached Peters, he saluted, introduced himself as Captain Bicain, and formally offered his surrender. Peters accepted the surrender on a temporary basis, pointing out that the formal acceptance would take place tomorrow when more British troops, including his superiors, flew into Leith. In the meantime, he would ensure that his prisoners-of-war were treated with respect. Relieved, the Argentinian commander let himself be marched back to his quarters, where he and his men would be kept under guard until they were shipped out in a day or two.

The enemy weapons were collected and piled up in front of the HQ. The rest of the captured Argentinians were searched, locked up and kept under guard in the settlement buildings, and then the SAS settled down to wait for the arrival of the men from the LCA boats.

When the replacements finally arrived, they brought good news with them. The three SAS men lost at sea had not been drowned or frozen to death. In fact, after being blown westward for a bit, they had managed to wade ashore on the north coast of Stromness Bay, about four kilometres from their intended LZ. Building themselves an OP, they had remained there for the past three days, maintaining radio silence to avoid endangering the operation. Only when they learned through their radio that the SAS had captured South Georgia did they send out a SARBE signal, asking to be lifted out by a helo. Right now they were all back on the *Antrim*, having a well-earned sleep.

When Marty called his men together and relayed this story to them, they cheered wildly, threw their berets in the air, and excitedly slapped each other on the back.

The following morning, SAS and SBS teams flew into Leith and formally accepted the surrender of its garrison. The Argentinian flag was lowered and the White Ensign and Union Jack were raised once more, to flutter together over Grytviken. South Georgia had been recaptured. Their next stop was the Falklands.

CHAPTER FORTY-THREE

Marching over the snow-covered hills towards Port Stanley, past dead Argentinian soldiers and the burned-out remains of their OPs and slit trenches, with the acrid smell of cordite and smoke in his nostrils and British aircraft roaring constantly overhead, Marty realised that, contrary to liberal thinking about the horrors of war, the past three weeks had been, for him at least, his final fling, the last of the days when he was likely to feel really alive and filled with excitement.

Now, when he looked back on it, he could scarcely believe that so much had been crammed into so little time and that the SAS had managed to cover so much ground in so many areas. It was hard to accept that it was only three weeks ago that he had been in the SAS HQ – actually the unused ladies' toilet, which caused much amusement – aboard the 22,890-ton Royal Fleet Auxiliary *Resource*, with Lieutenant-Colonel Osborne and Captain Peters, planning the insertion of deep-penetration SAS reconnaissance patrols into East Falkland and West Falkland. Given the absence of aerial or satellite pictures, it was the task of the patrols to obtain as much eyeball intelligence as possible of those two areas and try to ascertain the exact deposition of the Argentinian garrison's defences prior to the British invasion of the islands. The raids would cover not only the two main islands, but also some of the smaller islands around the 15,000-kilometre coastline.

This, Marty knew, would not be an easy task. East and West Falkland between them covered a total area nearly equivalent to that of Wales, with a terrain like Dartmoor: rough, windswept, barren pasture, with not even trees to offer protection from the elements or enemy surveillance. To make the hikes even more difficult, the hills along the northern side of East Falkland, though rising only to 450 metres on Mount Kent, had a climate similar to that of English hills twice that height. Also, there were many bogs and rock runs of slippery, moss-covered boulders, which were difficult and dangerous to traverse.

Nevertheless, plans were drawn up for the insertion of four-man SAS patrols to recce both islands. Once inserted, the groups would disperse in all directions, marching by night to predetermined RVs for their individual OPs, where they would stay as long as necessary. Radio silence was to be maintained until they had done as much as humanly possible and required lifting out. Operation Corporate, the main assault on the Falklands, would commence only when the SAS intelligence had been gathered and fully assessed.

With Captain Peters now assuming that Marty was allowed to take part in patrols and, indeed, relying on him as an experienced sounding board, Marty was able to recommend himself as the PC of a four-man patrol that also included Taff Hughes, Will Simpson and the recently badged Trooper Sammy McCulloch. When the men had been kitted out and supplied with a variety of weapons, a PC 319 tactical radio, SARBE rescue beacons and passive night-vision goggles (PNGs), they and the others patrols were flown in on two 845 Squadron Wessex Mark 5 helicopters and inserted 125 miles away near the centre of East Falkland.

Using an illuminated compass and aligning landmarks and roads with the map to follow their preset route, they yomped throughout the night, along the frosty valley, over the snow-covered hills, on constant lookout for mines and enemy snipers, the wind moaning about them. They marched in single file formation with Taff out on point, Marty second in line as PC, Sammy McCulloch in the middle, carrying the PRC 319 radio, and Alan Pearson bringing up the rear as Tail-end

Charlie. So difficult was the terrain, however, that by dawn the next day, though they had neither seen nor been in contact with the enemy, they had covered only ten miles.

Under orders to travel only by night, they used their short-handled spades to dig shallow scrapes and raise temporary LUPs with camouflaged roofs of wire strewn with local vegetation and turf. They slept and kept watch in two-hour shifts throughout the wet, freezing cold day. They were made no more comfortable by the fact that they could not light a fire or use their hexamine stoves – instead sustaining themselves with cold rations of cheese, biscuits and chocolate. By nightfall, they were on the march again across the dark, windblown hills.

During that second night, as they neared Port Stanley, they began to see the Argentinian troop positions, their campfires glowing eerily in the distance. Each time they saw such fires, they recced that area and kept a record of the information gathered. Also, they began to see an increasing number of foot patrols moving past them through the misty, moonlit darkness. As their task was not to engage the enemy but only to gather intelligence, they did not open fire on these patrols and instead lay low until they had passed.

During the second day, they rested up again in camouflaged shallow scrapes, enduring the rain and freezing wind, eating cold rations, and moving on again only when dawn light penetrated the mist wreathing the distant brooding hills and the sea beyond. During that third night, they passed through areas patrolled constantly by Argentinian troops and, again not firing upon them, took note of their movements, numbers and weapons. They also took note on the movements, now more frequent, of Argentinian helicopters and aircraft.

Eventually, just before dawn on the third night, they reached the high ground overlooking Port Stanley and located the ridge chosen for their OP. Being high and exposed, the ridge offered little natural cover from the elements, enemy patrols or aircraft. Marty therefore made sure that the rectangular OP was camouflaged with a roof and turf which, if nothing else, would hide their presence from the thermal imagers of Argentinian reconnaissance helicopters.

The OP had a narrow aperture, which offered a good view of Stanley airport and the Argentinian positions in the surrounding hills, so for the next three days they gathered invaluable intelligence with the use of black-painted, camouflaged binoculars, telescopes and night-vision aids. Visual information was also photographed and the details overdrawn on maps and aerial photos taken from previous recces. However, even more vital intelligence was gathered by making foot recces down the hill, near to the enemy positions in Port Stanley.

As Argentinian helicopters made frequent reconnaissance sweeps over the hills and enemy patrols constantly eyeballed them from the ground, the SAS foot recces were particularly dangerous. Nevertheless, they were undertaken, usually in darkness, the men guided to the enemy positions by the glow of their fires or the lights shining from occupied buildings. Sometimes Argentinian soldiers marched past mere feet away from where the SAS men were lying, pressed tight to the earth.

Although the foot recces were dangerous, they were at least preferable to the boredom of spending all day and night in the OP. When forced to do that, their only distraction was either entering notes in the logbook by candlelight or listening to the BBC World Service through muffled headphones. Through this they learned that the Falklands situation was reaching crisis point. A day after Marty's patrol had been inserted on East Falkland, the British submarine HMS *Conqueror* sank the Argentinian heavy cruiser the *Belgrano*. Two days later, an Exocet missile fired from an Argentinian Super Extendard warplane sank HMS *Sheffield*, resulting in many British dead and wounded. During the same period, three British Harrier jets were lost, one shot down, two colliding over the sea. The war with Argentina was thus truly engaged with Port Stanley's airport being bombed from the air and bombarded from the sea every night. In fact, the bombings and bombardments eventually became another form of distraction for the SAS men who, through the narrow aperture of the OP, were offered nightly the spectacle of dazzling, silvery explosions and blazing buildings in the dark port, with clouds of crimson sparks and black smoke boiling up to blot out the stars.

When, after five days in the OP, Marty was convinced that they could learn no more by staying there, he told Trooper McCulloch to radio back to base and ask for a chopper to come and lift them out. As Marty collated his intelligence, McCulloch and Simpson dismantled and filled in the OP. Taking point as sentry, Taff was lower down the hill behind an outcropping of rock, overlooking the lights of the otherwise darkened port. Fifteen minutes before the helo was due to descend for the pick-up, a three-man Argentinian foot patrol made its way up the hill, the soldiers in triangular formation, weapons at the ready.

Realising that the Argentinians had located the approximate area of the OP from the radio call made by Sammy McCullogh to the fleet, Marty indicated that McCulloch and Simpson should lie low and let Taff deal with the enemy patrol. This Taff did with his customary, cool-headed efficiency. As the Argentinian scout, far ahead of the other two men, passed Taff's position, Taff rose silently behind him, a mere shadow against the skyline, and applied the silent killing technique by covering his victim's mouth with one hand and swiftly slashing his jugular vein with his dagger. He held the body tightly, ensuring that it could not go into spasm or start thrashing noisily, then lowered it gently to the ground. He then moved, crouched over, towards his next victim, circling around to come up behind him. The second death occurred in darkness, out of view, but a brief thrashing sound, a falling body crushing bracken, made the last Argentinian look around him in panic. Before he could see anything a white hand covered his mouth and jerked his head back, then the blade of a dagger gleamed in the moonlight as it slashed his throat. He shuddered, dropped his rifle and then started to collapse, but was held up by Taff, who then lowered him slowly to the ground, keeping the noise down.

Eventually, Taff straightened up again and extended his right hand, waving it in towards his body, silently indicating, 'As you were.' Marty and the others heaved sighs of relief, then completed the filling in of the OP, gathered their kit together, and awaited the arrival of the RN helo. Ten minutes later, they had been lifted off and were being flown back to the RFA

Resource to hand over the intelligence which, along with that of the other SAS patrols from both islands, would enable the plans for the invasion of the Falklands to be finalised.

The first step on the road to Port Stanley was the landing beaches at San Carlos Water, on the west coast of East Falkland, but before those landings could take place the Argentinian aircraft located within range of the beaches had to be destroyed. This task was given to the SAS. According to intelligence picked up by the advance patrols, the aircraft were based on a grass strip near the only settlement on Pebble Island. They included 1A-58 Pucara ground-attack planes with twenty-millimetre cannons, four 7.62-millimetre machine-guns and bombs or rockets, all of which could be used to strafe British ground troops. As it was not known exactly how many Pucaras were on the airstrip, a four-man SAS patrol, formed from the boat group and commanded by Captain Mick Clarke, was inserted by two Klepper canoes, tasked with conducting an eyeball recce and bringing the required information back.

Taking his bearings from the moon and stars, Clarke guided both canoes away from the immense, flooded docking bay of the *Resource* and across the gently heaving, dark sea until the beach of Pebble Island came into view, leading gently up to low, frost-covered hills. After checking the length of the shore for campfires or other signs of the enemy's presence, and seeing none, Clarke jotted down useful notes on the tides, beach gradients and general topographical details that would help in selecting the best areas for amphibious landings. Both canoes were then paddled in to shallow water, where the men waded to shore and then hauled the canoes in and carried them carefully across the beach to hide them under chicken-wire covers, camouflaged with turf and local foliage.

Still not speaking, the men strapped their packed Bergens onto their backs, hurried off the exposed beach and commenced the march up the moonlit slopes of wind-blown grass, then along a narrow waist of land – completely exposed with the sea on both sides – to the Argentinian airstrip. Once there, they viewed the enemy aircraft, eleven Pucaras, through binoculars, from behind a hedgerow on a slight rise about two miles from the grass airfield, and noted that they were being guarded by heavily armed Argentinian troops. Many other troops were positioned all around the airfield – about a hundred in all – and others were positioned along the waist of land running parallel to the airstrip, as protection against attacks from the sea.

After constructing a short-term, diamond-shaped OP, which they camouflaged with ponchos covered in turf and local shrubbery, they spent the night and following day taking turns at sleeping and watching the airport through binoculars, jotting down notes on everything they saw. By the evening of the first day, they had all the information they needed and Captain Clarke decided to move out.

This was not as easy as he had thought it would be. He had been shocked the first day to note that the ground on which the Pucaras were parked was on the top of another rise that put it on the same level as the OP. This, he realised, was going to make it difficult for the patrol to get away, even in darkness, without being silhouetted by the sky. Now, however, as the other men dismantled and filled in the OP, Clarke noticed that there was a slight depression running back towards the sea in the general direction of the LZ. He decided that they should try to crawl along it until they were out of sight of the enemy.

They moved out under cover of darkness, running at the crouch to the slight depression that snaked around the top of the hill and ran back towards the sea. Unfortunately, it also took them dangerously close to the Argentinian sentries. To make matters worse, when they started crawling along the depression, they saw that their Bergens were jutting above the top of it. Given no other option, they ditched the Bergens, then moved off again, wriggling along on their bellies, holding their M16 rifles out ahead of them. This agonisingly slow, physically draining form of locomotion had to be continued for about half a mile, which took them three hours to cover, and, by the time they were out of sight of the Argentinians, they were sweating profusely even in the freezing cold. Nevertheless, now out of sight of the enemy, they were able to climb to their feet and march the six miles back to the beach, stopping only once, about two and a half miles from the airstrip, to lay down a base-plate for the L16 ML 81-millimetre mortar that would be used during the subsequent assault.

Once back at the beach, they uncovered the hidden Klepper canoes, carried them down to the water, anchored and loaded them, then rowed themselves back out to sea. About forty minutes later, the two Kleppers were gliding back into the brightly lit, cavernous holding bay of the *Resource*.

A few days later, after the SAS had been cross-decked to HMS *Hermes*, the assault on Pebble Beach commenced. Tasked with destroying the Argentinian aircraft in a hit-and-run night raid lasting only thirty minutes, thus ensuring that the Sea King helos were back aboard the *Hermes* before first light, the raiding party consisted of the Mountain Troop led by Captain Peters and armed, in addition to personal weapons, with 66-millimetre light anti-tank weapons (LAWs); and the Boat Troop led by Captain Clarke, which would lead the assault group to the airstrip, then give them covering fire with mortars.

At 1130 hours on 15 May, the three Sea King helos lifted off the immense, floodlit flight deck of the *Hermes* and headed for shore. Inside the helos, the SAS men were crushed together with an extraordinary variety of weapons, including L1A1 SLRs; L7A2 7.62-millimetre GPMGs; M72 LAWs; M16 and M203 grenade-launchers with cartridge-launched grenades; L16 ML 81-millimetre mortars with calibrated dial sights; white phosphorous, smoke and fragmentation grenades; and, of course, the standard-issue Browning High Power handgun. Though they did not have to carry rucksacks or sleeping bags (as the plan was to get in and out within thirty minutes) their Bergens weighed up to 140 pounds because of the additional heavy weaponry, including the mortars, extra 200-round belts for the GPMGs, radio systems, batteries, binoculars and personal first-aid kits. Even heavier equipment was being carried as underslung loads on the helos.

Thirty minutes later the helos were at the LZ and hovering mere feet above the ground to let the men jump out one by one. The first men down formed protective rings around the helos, their weapons at the ready, while others released the underslung loads containing the heavy equipment. When the men were on the ground, the helos ascended vertically, then flew back towards the fleet, leaving the men to get on with their work.

The LZ previously marked by the Boat Troop was located approximately six miles from the airstrip. Before setting off on the march, Captain Peters called his Mountain Troop together and divided them into three smaller groups: one would seal off all approaches to the airstrip, the second would blow up the Argentinian aircraft, and the third would be held in reserve.

The Mountain Troop fell in behind the Boat Troop and were led by them to the airstrip, stopping only at the previously laid base-plate to set up the mortar. Each member of the squadron was carrying two bombs for the mortar, which they now left with the selected mortar team – Corporal Garth Thomas and Trooper Phillip Reid of the Boat Troop – who would fire indirectly at a target identified by a forward observer placed with the assault group at the airstrip and using a PRC 319 tactical radio system for communication with the mortar crew.

With the mortar crew in position, the rest of the men moved off again, into the windblown, freezing darkness. Two and a half miles on, having met no opposition from the enemy, Captain Clarke, who had commanded the original reconnaissance patrol, led them to positions that gave a clear, moonlit view of the eleven Pucaras. The lights of campfires burned all around the airstrip, along that narrow waist of land thrusting into the sea, and in front of the ammunition and supply dumps, helpfully giving away the Argentinian positions.

While one of the Mountain Troop units disappeared into the darkness to seal off all approaches to the airstrip and another took up their reserve positions, looking none too happy about this, the third such unit, led by Captain Peters and Marty, advanced on the airstrip, crouched low with their weapons at the ready. When they were less than 300 yards away, Peters signalled for them to prepare for the engagement, then he made radio contact with the fleet and, using the designated code, told them to commence the covering barrage. As he was doing so, Marty was on the other radio, giving the distant mortar crew compass bearings and telling them to start firing immediately.

Even as Captain Peters was raising his right hand to give the 'open fire' signal, each of the troopers with a 66-millimetre LAW, having already extended the 90-centimetre tubes and removed the protective cap from each end of the launcher, thus making the folding sights pop up, was holding the LAW to his shoulder and preparing to press the trigger switch.

Hearing a high-pitched wail from the direction of the sea, Marty glanced up at the sky and saw the para-flares fired from the *Glamorgan*'s guns exploding spectacularly in the sky to illuminate the airstrip below. Simultaneously, the first of the bombs from the mortar exploded between the aircraft in fountains of fire, showering sparks, boiling smoke and erupting soil. Finally, when Captain Peters dropped his hand, the LAWs and GPMGs roared into action, the former sending rockets racing like tracers into the airstrip, the later peppering the same area with 200 rounds per minute.

Explosions were erupting between the Pucaras as the Argentinian sentries, taken by surprise, either ran for cover or fired back with rifles and automatic weapons. Hit by a LAW shell, one of the Pucaras exploded, with pieces of metal flying in all directions and the cockpit engulfed in crackling, vivid, yellow flames; at the time same, air-burst shells were exploding overhead and mortar explosions were erupting between the aircraft to crater the runway.

Forced to take cover, the Argentinians ran back to their slit trenches at the edge of the airstrip, aiming occasional bursts of inaccurate rifle fire at their attackers. Observing that retreat, Captain Peters jumped up, gave the 'advance' hand signal, and led his men at the run to the dispersal area. There, even as he was being fired upon by the Argentinians in the slit trenches, with bullets tearing up concrete in jagged lines all around him, Marty was one of those who ran from one Pucara to the other, rigging explosives to those not already being destroyed by LAW rounds and lengthy bursts from the GPMGs. When the charges exploded, the aircrafts' nose-cones were blown off and their undercarriages demolished, causing them to tilt forward with their smashed noses deep in the earth and smoke belching out of them.

At that moment, the shells from the fleet's guns reached the enemy's defensive positions, hitting the petrol store and ammunition dump. They exploded spectacularly, with searing yellow, red and blue flames stabbing through oily black smoke that was carried back on the wind to choke the Argentinian troops in the slit trenches. While those men were temporarily blinded, the last of the charges rigged to the Pucaras exploded, causing more flames, smoke and flying debris as the SAS men backed away.

One Pucara, however, remained untouched. Seeing it, Taff ran back to it, ignoring the Argentinian troops who had clambered out of their smoke-wreathed trenches and were firing at him as they spread across the airstrip. Given covering fire by Marty and TT, both firing their SLRs as they retreated, and as mortar shells continued to explode all around him, Taff clambered boldly onto the untouched Pucara, rigged the explosive charge, then dropped back to the ground as some Argentinians rushed at him. Dropping to one knee, ignoring the bullets whistling around him and thudding into the Pucara, he fired his SLR with cool, murderous accuracy, downing the men advancing upon him. He then jumped up and fled from the aircraft, which exploded behind him with a mighty roar. Punched forward by the blast, falling face down on the runway, he jumped up immediately and raced back to Marty and TT, who were keeping up a relentless barrage of fire as they backed away from the airstrip.

'That made number eleven,' Marty told him. 'Now let's get the hell out of here.'

Firing on the move, they backed away from the Argentinians advancing across the runway, weaving between the blazing aircraft and the many explosions from the mortars. Just as they had cut most of those down, a truck filled with more enemy troops raced at them. Dropping to one knee, Will Simpson raised a LAW to his shoulder and prepared to fire. Before he could do so, however, a mortar shell exploded right beside him, bowling him over and obscuring him in smoke. Scrambling back to the firing position almost instantly, shaking his head to clear it and ignoring the blood seeping from many shrapnel wounds, he took aim with the LAW again, pressed the trigger switch, and was rocked by the backblast as the rocket shot straight into the advancing truck, now practically on top of him. The shell exploded inside the driver's cabin, blowing it to smithereens and making the truck careen sideways to crash into the blazing Pucara, which also exploded. Wiping blood from his eyes, Simpson jumped to his feet, threw the LAW across his right shoulder, and raced back to join the other men.

Withdrawing alongside the rest of the assault group, still under cover of mortar fire and naval support from the *Glamorgan*, Marty saw some Argentinians emerging from the smoke swirling darkly across the airstrip. Even before he could fire his SLR, he heard the savage roar of a GPMG right beside him and turned his head to see Alan Pearson shaking spasmodically to the pulsing of the machine-gun as he fired a 200-round burst that cut some of the Argentinians down and forced others to beat a hasty retreat.

When the surviving Argentinians had disappeared back into the smoke, Alan jumped up, slung the heavy weapon over his shoulder, grinned at Marty, then raced with him back towards the sea. On their way, they passed a wounded SAS trooper who had been thrown into the air by an exploding land-mine and suffered a smashed kneecap, lacerated legs and concussion; he was being rolled onto a stretcher by two medics while other troopers gave them covering fire. Marty and Alan joined in, keeping the enemy pinned down until the medics had carried the stretcher away, then they headed once more for the beach.

Looking back from the hill that overlooked the airstrip, Marty saw that all of the Pucaras were either still burning or smouldering in the flickering, eerie light of the air-burst shells from the fleet. Craters pock-marked the runway and the ground between the burning planes. Dead bodies were scattered all over the area, though many were obscured in the languidly drifting smoke.

As Marty and the others made their way back to the beach, they heard the roaring of GPMGs and the snapping of small arms from one side of the airstrip where the SAS troopers sent to seal off the approaches were stopping the advance, or flight, of Argentinian soldiers trying to get along the sea road. Even as Marty stared in that direction, a series of explosions sent smoke billowing into the sky in the vicinity of the gunfire, indicating that the group had called in for support from *Glamorgan*'s big guns. Not long after this, the sound of battle died away, which meant that the second group had stopped the advance of the Argentinians and was now also heading back to the LZ.

When they were about halfway back, the assault party stopped to pick up the two-man mortar crew, then they all proceeded on to the LZ. Exactly as planned, the Sea Kings returned just before first light and the squadron was lifted off and returned to the *Hermes*.

With that particular batch of Argentinian aircraft out of action, the invasion of the Falklands could commence.

Now, as he neared Port Stanley, marching beside Taff, also exhausted but still quietly resolute, Marty was recalling the eighteen replacements who had drifted down from the night sky to replace the eighteen who had died.

It was a memory that would never leave him and it haunted him even now as he made his way over the brow of a hill cratered with shell holes to look down upon the recaptured Port Stanley, amazed that he'd made it.

The eighteen men, who had survived so much in battle, had died in the least expected manner: when they were being cross-decked from the *Hermes* to the *Intrepid*, prior to being inserted by sea at Darwin on East Falkland, for a diversionary raid against the enemy. Though the *Intrepid* was cruising a mere half-mile away, the Sea King used for the cross-decking, which took place two hours after last light, crashed into the sea, either because of a birdstrike or because of overloading, and the eighteen men, from D Squadron, died as a result.

Though the news of the crash and the gradual mounting of the death toll as the SAR helos brought back the survivors sent shock waves rippling through the rest of the squadron, as well as many others on both the *Hermes* and the *Intrepid*, it was decided that the raid must go on. Subsequently, eighteen replacements were flown in from Hereford. When they parachuted down from the Hercules transport in the middle of the night, many friends of the dead, including Marty, were standing on the flight deck of the *Hermes*, watching them splash into the sea, their parachutes billowing out on the black water like eighteen white flowers, one for each of the dead. It was a singularly moving moment for Marty and he would never forget it.

Nevertheless, with the arrival of the eighteen replacements, the diversionary raid against Darwin went ahead as planned, as did similar raids being created that night to distract the enemy's attention from the main landings on the opposite coast, far to the north of Darwin. That evening, Marty was one of the sixty men of D Squadron to be inserted by Sea King helo near Goose Green, not far from Darwin. For this particular operation, the men were armed with GPMGs, a MILAN anti-tank weapon with SACLOS semi-automatic guidance system, an American Stinger surface-to-air (SAM) missile system, L16 ML 81-millimetre mortars, and the usual collection of automatic and semi-automatic rifles, favouring the Heckler & Koch G3, the L1A1 SLR and the always popular M16. This time their task was to let the Argentinians know, quite deliberately, that they were there and create the impression that a battalion ten times their number had landed.

Once inserted, the squadron embarked on a 24-hour forced march south, across rolling fields of marshy peat and tussock grass whipped relentlessly by freezing wind and sleet. They yomped throughout the night, rested up before first light, gulped down a cold breakfast of high-calorie rations and water, then moved on again, into the day's equally filthy weather. Twenty-four hours later, most of them exhausted but still prepared for the fight, they arrived at the Argentinian garrison, which was, to their surprise, brightly illuminated, its defensive slit trenches clearly visible in the lights beaming out of the many huts raised behind them.

The diversionary raid was deliberately mounted in a manner that drew as much attention to the SAS as possible while making them appear to be much greater in numbers than they were. This was accomplished by dividing the men into three groups, spreading the first group out over as wide an arc as possible, and then having the men attack the unwary Argentinians with everything at their disposal. Even as the Argentinians were being pummelled by the combined might of the SAS weaponry, including the GPMGs and the MILAN anti-tank weapon, the 4.5-inch guns of the *Ardent*, out at sea, were laying down a devastating support barrage and turning the Argentinian slit trenches into hell on earth. Finally, when the battle was fully engaged, the squadron commander, Major Piers Hudson, contacted the other two groups by radio and ordered them to change positions repeatedly, moving even farther apart, to convince the enemy that the line of attack was much wider and involved at least a full battalion.

Between the barrage from the *Ardent*'s 4.5-inch guns, the 88-millimetre shells from the mortars, the anti-tank missiles from the MILAN, the 200-rounds per minute being fired by the GPMGs and the increasingly broad arc of fire from the personal weapons of the SAS, the Argentinians were indeed convinced that they were being attacked by a full battalion and refused to be drawn out of their trenches.

Pleased, Major Hudson made radio contact with HQ on HMS *Hermes* and was informed that the invasion of the Falklands had commenced. At that very moment *Fearless* and *Intrepid* were anchored off Jersey point on West Falkland, with the troops already disembarking from the LCUs and advancing inland; *Brilliant*, *Canberra*, *Norland*, *Fort Austin* and *Plymouth* were anchored in the Falkland Straits; the *Antrim*'s guns were shelling Fanning Head in support of the landings there; more ships were steaming into San Carlos Water; and Port Stanley was under constant air attack.

Exultant, Major Hudson passed the word down through Captain Peters and Marty that the men were to spread out even more and continue the mock assault on the Goose Green defences. When they did so, the arc of fire seemed at least a mile long.

The attack continued, with the three groups advancing and spreading out until they were forming an immense semicircle around the burning, smoking enemy defences. About an hour before first light, Hudson learned from radio communication with the fleet that twelve British ships were now in the Falkland Straits, another five warships were patrolling just outside the Straits, and the landing troops, including 40 Commando and 2 Para, were occupying Port San Carlos and Ajax Bay. Hearing this, Hudson told his men to keep firing until dawn, then circle around the Argentinian positions, advance under cover of the morning's remaining darkness, and meet up at the RV north of Darwin. When they did so, they learned that the diversionary raids had worked, the landings on the opposite coast had been a great success, and the battle for the Falklands was well under way.

Approximately two weeks later, looking down on Port Stanley from the crest of the hill, Marty saw that it was covered in smoke from the exploding shells of the naval gunline bombarding the airport, the racecourse and Sapper Hill. The port had not yet been taken, so the sky was filled with British and Argentinian aircraft, the former bombing Port Stanley and inland, the latter attacking the fleet anchored out at sea. Helicopters, all British, were landing and taking off in a race to transport the growing numbers of wounded to the Forward Dressing Stations of Teal and Fitzroy or the Main Dressing Station at Ajax, farther away on San Carlos Water.

Gazing down at that awesome picture of modern warfare, knowing that it would soon result in defeat for the Argentinians, Marty realised that, although he had personally enjoyed the fight, the cost of getting this far had been high.

Following the success at Goose Green and knowing that the invasion had commenced, Major Hudson broke his men up into sixteen groups of five and ordered them to head north, but with each covering a different area, and gradually make their way to Port Stanley, harassing the enemy in whatever way they could until they reached the port. He wanted hit-and-run raids, disorientation and confusion, outside the normal chain of command, all the way to Port Stanley.

As usual, Marty made sure that he was in a group with Taff, TT and Alan Pearson, under the command of Captain Peters, who was relatively young but had proved himself to be trustworthy. Once they had received their individual grid reference, they moved off, heading north, and soon lost sight of the other groups in the wide, mist-wreathed fields and hills. Alone in that vast, frozen landscape, whipped constantly by the wind and rain, they marched in single file formation, with Marty out on point, Captain Peters second in line as PC, Alan Pearson third as signaller, TT fourth in line and heavily burdened with his GPMG and packed Bergen, and Taff bringing up the rear as Tail-end Charlie, though with a formidable American Stinger SAM system strapped across his Bergen.

By nine in the morning they learned through Pearson's radio that the landing at San Carlos Water had been successful, with the loss of only three Royal Marines air crew, forced down when fired upon. They also learned that Port Stanley and the enemy positions around it were being attacked relentlessly by Sea Harriers dropping air-burst shells and 1,000-pound bombs, as well as by Vulcans firing American Shrike radiation-homing missiles. Indeed, the sound of distant bombing was clear even from where they were marching, smoke was darkening the horizon in the direction of Port Stanley, and the sky directly above them was filled with Argentinian aircraft, including Skyhawks, Daggers and Pucaras, flying from the mainland and Port Stanley, towards the sea and back, obviously attacking the fleet and landing force.

Four hours later, when they had stopped for a cold lunch of high-calorie rations and water, they took turns at studying the southern landscape through binoculars and saw the troops of 2 Para advancing across the high ground south of San Carlos Water, on the road to capture Darwin. Seeing this, they knew that the advance would not be stopped now. This was confirmed when, much farther north, where the flights of enemy aircraft to and from the sea had increased dramatically, they heard over the radio that in San Carlos Water, dubbed 'Bomb Alley', the British force – having gained a foothold on the Falklands – was poised to break out and advance on Port Stanley.

Their first contact with the enemy came when they arrived at an isolated farmhouse in a windblown valley between Bluff Cove and Fitzroy, with the sea of Port Pleasant Bay visible beyond the edge of the distant cliff. Lying belly down on the ground and examining the house through binoculars, they saw that smoke was rising from its chimney and an enemy troop truck was parked in front of it. Armed Argentinian soldiers were wandering casually in and out by the front door, some drinking from mugs. About halfway between the farmhouse and the SAS group, though certainly well away from the farmhouse, an Argie soldier was on guard, though in a distinctly careless manner: sitting on a bucket, smoking a cigarette and distractedly studying his own feet.

Noticing that an antenna had been attached to the roof of the farmhouse, Captain Peters assumed that the Argie soldiers comprised a mobile radio patrol and were using the place as an OP, making daily trips around the area and reporting back what they learned about British troop movements. Deciding to put a stop to their activities, he sent his best 'silent killing' man, Taff, forward to dispatch the sentry.

Lowering his Bergen and American Stinger SAM system to the ground, holding his commando dagger firmly in his right hand, Taff advanced crouched low, with the stealth of a cat, dropping down and rising and running crouched low again, until he was coming around, then behind, the unsuspecting guard. As silent as a ghost, he rose up behind the guard, pressed one hand over his mouth, blocking off all sound, and slashed his jugular vein with the dagger. The guard quivered like a bowstring and kicked one leg spasmodically, but Taff dragged him off the bucket and lowered him to the ground until both of them had disappeared in the tall grass. Within seconds, Taff came back into view and waved the other men forward.

When the patrol had taken up positions by the dead Argie guard, TT fixed his GPMG to its tripod and Alan Pearson clipped his M203 grenade-launcher to the barrel of his M16 rifle.

One of the Argentinian soldiers looked across the field, directly at Alan, just as he took the firing position, squinted along the pop-up sight of the M203, braced himself by spreading his legs, and fired. The Argentinian shouted a warning just before the M203 roared, the backblast rocked Alan, and the grenade smashed through a window of the house, sending glass flying out in all directions. Exploding, it blew the other windows out, producing screams of pain and shouting from within. At the same time, TT's GPMG roared into action, peppering the house at the rate of 200 rounds per minute, smashing more glass, causing stone and dust to explode from the front walls, and cutting down some of the Argentinian soldiers before they could manage to dive for cover. Other soldiers were picked off by the combined firepower of the SLRs fired by Marty, Taff and Captain Peters.

When Alan fired his M203 again, the grenade exploded inside the house, igniting some form of gas, and searing yellow flames curled out through the windows. The front door burst open and some soldiers rushed out, screaming and slapping at their burning uniforms, then either collapsed of their own accord, rendered unconscious by pain, or were cut down by the semi-automatic fire of the SLRs and M16s. As those unfortunates were dying, TT was continuing to rake the house and the ground in front of it with his GPMG, making the walls spit lumps of stone and cement dust while the men out front tried to crawl back indoors, writhing and shuddering in clouds of exploding soil, their screams drowned out by the roaring of many guns.

Eventually, Captain Peters signalled the advance and the men did so carefully, stepping over the dead and the dying to enter the farmhouse cautiously. It was a mess. The fragmentation grenades from Alan's M203 had torn the place to shreds – walls scorched, floorboards splintered, furniture smashed to pieces – and the Argentinians, all dead, were peppered with shrapnel. Their radio equipment, also damaged in the explosions, was spitting sparks and smoking.

Searching through the debris of the ruined building, Captain Peters found official documents giving precise details of the Argentinian defences. Excited, he made radio contact with HQ on HMS *Hermes* and relayed the information he had found. Pleased with himself, he then decided to use the Argentinian truck to take him and his troopers to Port Stanley. Piling into it, with Marty at the wheel and Peters beside him, they soon left the smouldering farmhouse and dead Argentinians far behind and found themselves rolling across open country, heading towards that thickening pall of smoke on the distant horizon.

By dawn the next day they were well on the road to Port Stanley. Stopping for another cold breakfast, they heard over the radio that the enemy garrisons at Goose Green and Darwin, psychologically destroyed by the SAS diversionary raid, had fallen to 2 Para, with 1,300 Argentinians taken prisoner. Since then, 42 Commando had yomped eastward, from Ajax Bay on San Carlos Water to Teal Inlet, about ten miles north-west of Port Stanley, which they had secured with the aid of SBS teams inserted the previous night.

Exhilarated, they drove on, now more keen to reach Port Stanley, but were attacked soon after by a British Sea Harrier flying in from the west. Momentarily forgetting that he was driving an Argentinian Army truck, Marty accelerated automatically, then slammed on the brakes as the Harrier swept in low to rake the 'enemy' truck with his guns. Careening across the road, the truck ploughed into soft earth, letting the men jump out and run as far away as possible before the Harrier, completing a great circle above the Atlantic, returned for another attack. It swept in with all guns roaring, their bullets creating lines of spitting soil that raced across the field, peppered the truck, then punctured the petrol tank and made it explode.

Marty was just throwing himself to the ground beside the others when the truck's doors were blown off, its tyres burst into flames and started melting, and its canvas top became a great bonfire under an umbrella of oily smoke. The Harrier had already ascended and disappeared in the distance when the truck, already a blackened shell wreathed in flame and smoke, hiccuped from internal convulsions and collapsed onto wheels devoid of tyres, the melted rubber still smouldering.

'Our own bloody fault,' Marty observed pragmatically. 'We should have remembered we were in an enemy truck.'

'No point crying over spilt milk,' Captain Peters told him. 'Okay, men, let's yomp it.'

Marching in single file, eventually they reached the broad, rolling fields between Sapper Hill and Bluff Cove, where the sounds of battle from Port Stanley were much louder and the sky was filled with British and Argentinian aircraft. Later that afternoon, they were attacked by an Argentinian Pucara that appeared out of nowhere and roared down upon them, guns firing. Even as the bullets were stitching the ground near his feet, Taff unslung the Stinger SAM system from his Bergen, inserted a missile canister armed with a three-kilogram high-explosive fragmentation warhead, and fired it at the Pucara. Armed with an infrared seeker and sensors that could track its target by the heat of its exhausts, the Stinger's surface-to-air missile streaked upwards and hit the Pucara as it was levelling out to ascend again. The plane exploded into a spectacular ball of searing flame and boiling smoke, with its debris thrown far and wide, raining down on the field a good distance away.

'Nice one,' TT said, slapping Taff between the shoulder blades as the rest of them picked themselves off the ground and continued the march.

Just before last light, realising that, the closer they came to Port Stanley, the more exposed they would be to Argentinian patrols, Captain Peters decided that they should hole up in an OP and spend the next few days roaming the surrounding country and engaging in hit-and-run raids against the enemy. Before dusk, a camouflaged rectangular OP had been constructed and the men had settled in for the duration. The wind blew. The snow fell.

The snow was falling even now as Marty stood beside Taff on the hillside and looked down on Port Stanley. Though the port itself had not yet been taken, the British forces were moving in on all sides, fighting their way down the hills, clearing out the Argentinian bunkers en route and gradually closing in on the smoke-wreathed town. Feeling guilty because he had actually enjoyed this war, helplessly viewing it as his last fling, a farewell to his days of active service, Marty glanced sideways at Taff, whose blond hair was filthy, whose blue eyes were weary, and realised that he and Paddy were now virtually the only friends he had left.

It was hard to accept that the others were gone, but they

surely were. They were gone and they would not be returning and their graves would be unmarked. They had, in SAS vernacular, failed to beat the clock. And, like most events in war, their dying had come unexpectedly.

After spending ten days in the OP, roaming out under cover of darkness to engage in hit-and-run raids, they had heard over the radio that the attack on Port Stanley was about to begin, with night attacks against the major mountains of East Falkland, Longdon, Two Sisters and Harriet. Realising from this that they had done all they could from the OP, Captain Peters decided that it was time to pack up and move on, hopefully to help in the forthcoming liberation of Port Stanley.

After dismantling and filling in the OP, they moved out again, yomping throughout the night, sticking close to the coastline, whipped constantly by sleet, snow and freezing winds, intending to come in south of Port Stanley. It was not a dull night. Only a couple of miles to the north, the attacks on Mount Harriet, Tumbledown and Mount William were being undertaken by 4 and 7 Infantry Regiments, supported by 5 Marine Battalion, so the night sky was criss-crossed with dazzling white phosphorous tracers, coloured crimson, blue and yellow by fire, stained black by smoke. Also, for most of the march they could hear 105-millimetre and 115-millimetre Argentinian artillery, the return fire of the 4.5-inch guns of the fleet, 105-millimetre howitzers, 66-millimetre anti-tank rockets, exploding 81-millimetre mortar shells, chattering machine-guns and whining, growling aircraft, most of them British. All in all, it was a night of sound and spectacle.

The breaking dawn, however, revealed a landscape devastated by war, with streams of mist drifting over blackened shell holes and enemy sangars filled with corpses buried in debris. Luckier, though hardly happy, were the hundreds of weary Argentinian prisoners who were being marched at gunpoint to makeshift camps of barbed wire and canvas, where they would be held until the reconquest of Port Stanley, then almost certainly shipped back to Argentina.

Yomping over the rocky, frost-covered hills around Port Stanley, still out front on point, Marty saw battle-weary but jubilant Royal Marines, Commandos, Paratroopers, Scots Guardsmen, Welsh Guards, Gurkhas, REMFs, and even forward observers from 148 Commando Battery, Royal Artillery. Port Stanley was now visible from the heights, though covered in a pall of smoke from the naval bombardment and being criss-crossed by the casevac helos that were picking up the wounded and flying them to the various Forward Dressing Stations.

The end for Marty's friends came abruptly. Making their way downhill towards Port Stanley, circling around a rocky hillock, they emerged unexpectedly to another farmhouse. Even before they saw the radio antenna on its roof and the Argentinian truck parked outside it, a machine-gun roared from one of its windows and bullets ricocheted off the rocks around them.

TT cried out and was punched backwards to the ground. Marty and the others had already dived for cover and were opening fire from behind rock outcroppings as TT quivered spasmodically on the ground, was peppered by another burst from the Argentinian machine-gun, shuddered violently, screaming in agony, then coughed blood and was still.

Cursing, not thinking, Alan Pearson dived out from behind his rock, dropped belly down on the ground, and reached out to grab TT and drag him, dead or alive, away from the line of fire. Even as Marty and Captain Peters gave covering fire with their SLRs, and as the cool-headed Taff was unslinging his SAM system from his Bergen, the Argentinian machine-gunner fired another sustained burst that made the ground spit around TT and Alan, turning the latter into a convulsion of flapping limbs and shredded clothing soaked in blood, until he fell face first over TT, groaning and twitching.

Shocked and enraged by that sight, Marty kept firing his SLR at the windows of the farmhouse while Taff, seemingly unmoved, took aim with his SAM system, then fired a fragmentation warhead with deadly accuracy through the window where the machine-gun was firing. The explosion blew out the window frame and part of the wall, with pieces of the machine-gun sailing out of billowing smoke and the gunner disappearing into the yellow flames filling the room.

When the front door burst open and some Argentinians ran out, trying to escape from the flames and firing from the hip, Marty and Peters cut them down with their SLRs. Taff, meanwhile, had reloaded the Stinger SAM system and now fired another fragmentation warhead into the building. This time, the explosion blew out most of the front wall and made the roof collapse, with those not killed instantly buried in the rubble, screaming or groaning as clouds of white dust billowed skywards.

'*Advance*!' Peters bawled.

They did so cautiously, crouched low, weaving left and right, stepping over the dead Argentinians on the ground to enter the ruined house. The rubble was piled high, still smouldering, wreathed in drifting dust, and the men who had been screaming were now moaning and gradually dying, practically buried alive.

Marty was just about to bend down and push the rubble off one of the groaning men when he heard the sound of running feet and looked up to see an Argentinian soldier racing around the side of the house and back towards the rocks where Alan Pearson was sprawled over TT, still groaning and twitching. Reaching them, the Argentinian fired a short burst from his submachine-gun into the back of Alan's head, making it burst open like a pomegranate, then he hurried around the side of the hillock and disappeared.

'Bastard!' Captain Peters screamed.

Suddenly, the harsh snapping of small arms came from lower down the hill and bullets ricocheted off the ruined walls of the farmhouse. Glancing down the hill, Marty saw a troop of Argentinian soldiers making their way up uphill, firing on the move.

'More Argies!' Marty bawled. 'Let's get out of here!'

Without a second's hesitation, he and Taff jumped over the broken wall to their right and started racing down the hill at the other side, out of sight of the advancing Argentinians. Captain Peters followed them, but then he hesitated, glanced over his shoulder, and called out, 'What about TT? He might still be alive!'

Marty and Taff stopped running and turned to look back

up the hill, where Peters was framed by the ruined house and the snow falling out of a cloudy sky.

'He's dead!' Taff shouted back. 'If he's not, he soon will be. And so will we if we go back up that hill. Come on, Captain, let's go!'

'No!' Peters shouted, trying to make himself heard above the harsh chatter of the Argentinian small arms and the ricocheting of their bullets. 'I've got to go back and check!'

Ignoring their protestations, he turned away and clambered back up the hill, cutting across at an angle to reach the hillock fifty yards from the farmhouse. Shocked, Marty hurried after him and saw, as he clambered up the hill, Argentinian soldiers bursting into the ruined farmhouse to see Captain Peters near the hillock. Even as Taff, who had remained lower down the hill, opened fire with his SLR, giving cover to Marty, the Argentinians opened up on Peters. Their combined firepower tore him to shreds, making him jerk wildly, then punched him back to the ground where he shuddered spasmodically, bloodily, in a convulsion of spitting snow and soil.

'Shit!' Marty exclaimed, turning automatically to fire a short burst at the Argentinians, making them dive for cover, before he bolted back down the hill to join Taff. Together, they ran farther down the hill, weaving left and right, dodging the bullets of the Argentinians, not stopping until they were out of range and, finally, out of sight. They slowed down at that point, but kept marching, not speaking, and eventually came to one of the hills that loomed over Port Stanley.

Still not speaking, they hiked up the hill until they reached the summit, where they were offered a panoramic view of the town and its port. The town was wreathed in smoke, as were the port and surrounding hills. The ships of the British fleet were spread out across the sea and British aircraft were now controlling the wintry skies, flying this way and that.

Shocked by the death of his friends, Marty marched down the hill beside Taff until they reached the recaptured port. Side by side, they made their way past damaged British ships still smouldering in the docks, 42 Commando Marines, the Red Berets of 2 Para, and dejected Argentinian prisoners huddled around fires beside discarded weapons and helmets. They also marched past traffic jams of troop trucks, Land Rovers, Mercedes jeeps and Panhard armoured cars, under a dark sky filled with Chinook, Lynx, Scout, Sea King and Wessex helicopters, as well as Sea Harrier jets and Vulcan bombers. Eventually they passed wooden-framed houses, miraculously untouched, and finally entered the Upland Goose pub. Though the pub was filled with journalists and celebrating soldiers, sailors, pilots and Red Cross workers, Marty and Taff fought their way to the counter and stared straight at the barman.

'A pint of best bitter,' Taff ordered.

'The same for me,' Marty said.

They drank to old comrades.

CHAPTER FORTY-FOUR

Marty became a wealthy man within months of his retirement from the regiment. He bid his comrades farewell during a party at Bradbury Lines, five months after the war in the Falklands had ended, and then went on to a new life as a civilian, making more money than he had ever imagined possible.

It had happened so quickly that he still couldn't quite grasp it, but he knew exactly when it had all started, which was when his SAS career had reached its natural conclusion and he was faced with the retirement he had dreaded.

The war in the Falklands was his last and when it ended, on 14 June 1982, it ended a lot of other things for him. With the deaths of Captain Peters, Alan Pearson and, in particular, TT Taylor, he realised that the only real friends still alive were Taff and Paddy, though both friendships were based on shared experiences going back a long way, rather than on affection or lasting trust.

In Taff's case, given his nature, his unbreakable reticence and oddly inhuman remove, this seemed perfectly natural and did not bother Marty one way or the other. He had long since accepted that any friendship with the quiet killer was bound to be strictly limited and could not run too deeply. Paddy, on the other hand, was a very special case whose friendship he had valued above all others, so the breaking of that relationship was something that still hurt him profoundly.

Nevertheless, given the limitations of those two remaining friendships, he understood that those men were the only real friends he had left. Most of his past was now gone and buried, and his future was narrowing.

He realised this, in particular, during the party he threw on the day of his retirement from the regiment. It took place during an open day to which family, selected friends and serving SAS members were invited. Also invited were Lesley, John and Kay. Lesley was now plump, grey-haired and heavily lined, while John and Kay were mature adults whom Marty could scarcely recall as children. Indeed, his pleasure at seeing them was uneasily balanced by how old their maturity made him feel. Even Ian, his son by Ann Lim, had he not died in that car crash, would have been twenty-two years old this year. It was hard to believe.

'You look wonderful,' he said to Lesley.

'Still the charmer,' she replied. 'The word "wonderful" hardly applies, but I could have been worse. So how are you, Marty?'

'How do I look?'

'As fit as someone your age can be. There are certain things to be said in favour of being a soldier and you sum them up. You look surprisingly good, in fact.'

'I'm not as good as I look. I don't think I'm suited to retirement. I'm already starting to feel old.'

'That's unavoidable, Marty.'

'Well, it's nice to see you and the kids here. It makes me feel less guilty.'

'About what?'

'About not always being a good husband and attentive father.'

Lesley smiled. 'You weren't good, that's for sure. Even when you were home, you weren't there – you always had that glazed look. You weren't *that* bad, though. Always good with the kids. You didn't see them that much, they never quite got your attention, but at least you had a good sense of humour and always managed to make them smile. Kids will forgive an awful lot for that and John and Kay think you're okay. In fact, they think you've been a pretty good dad and I can't argue with that. You were just a soldier, that's all.'

'A *good* soldier,' Marty corrected her, grinning.

'I wouldn't know,' she replied.

Paddy also attended. He had lost a fair bit of weight since Marty had last seen him, only a few months ago, just before the start of the Falklands war, and he was losing his good looks at last. His skin was lined and slack on a surprisingly gaunt face, his eyes had lost their radiance and his formerly thick, dark hair was grey and thinning with bald patches showing. Marty knew that, though he was younger than Paddy, he would soon look the same. It was not a comforting thought.

Clearly, given his coolness when he and Marty talked, he had turned up only out of loyalty or for appearances' sake. Though this hurt Marty, it did not unduly surprise him. He had gone off to the Falklands war already knowing that the friendship, if not entirely over, would certainly never be the same again. It had changed for the worse when Paddy confronted him about the assassination of the arms dealer, Sir Charles Alfred Seagrove, demanding to know if he was responsible for it. Though Marty had resolutely denied that he'd had anything to do with it, Paddy had not believed him and insisted that if he had any reason to suspect him in the future – or any other member of the Association – regarding similar incidents, he would cut them out of Vigilance International and his personal friendship with Marty would end.

'This isn't an idle threat,' he had insisted. 'I mean just what I say. I believe that you or someone known to you – another member of the Association – put paid to Seagrove. If I'm right – and I happen to think I am – then you're a bloody disgrace to the regiment and I don't want to know you. I hope and pray that I'm wrong, but my instincts say otherwise. I'll be watching you, Marty.'

Though shocked by the vehemence of Paddy's response, Marty still felt no guilt. While it was true that he had personally undertaken the assassination when in a state of shock and rage at Diane's suicide – for which he'd held Seagrove personally responsible – he surprised himself after the event with the gradual realisation that he felt little remorse for what he had done.

Quite the opposite, indeed. Pleased with the relative simplicity of the operation, even more gratified with its success, he had confided in Taff, who had responded, in his typically cool manner, that the Association could now undertake similar 'cleansing operations' as discussed so frequently between them. Thus encouraged, Marty decided to raise the motion at the next meeting of the Association, but the Falklands war then intervened. When it was over, TT and Alan Pearson were dead and Marty's retirement came onto the agenda. Marty decided to put the matter aside until a more appropriate time.

'There's too much euphoria over the victory,' he told Taff. 'I think it's best to wait until all that's died away and the boredom of peacetime has returned. Our kind are the kind who can't stand too much inactivity, so that's when we should talk to the other men. We can offer them a new form of excitement and I think they'll go for it.'

'*I* will,' Taff replied. 'Believe me, I'll be there. You just point me in the direction you want and I'll squeeze the trigger. You can count on it, mate.'

'I already do,' Marty said.

For days after the retirement party, when he had moved into his new apartment in Belsize Park in London and was trying to adjust to the fact that he would never again wear his beige beret and badge or fight a war overseas, he suffered bouts of severe depression and found himself endlessly poring over old memories, from his early, relatively innocent days with the LRDG to the disillusioning dirty-tricks campaigns of Northern Ireland. In particular, he found himself repeatedly recalling the few days he had spent in Port Stanley after the British flag was raised again over Government House. Even though he had just lost all but two of his remaining friends, he was convinced that those few days may well have been the last exciting days of his life.

On the other hand, though undeniably exciting, that war had caused him to feel deeply disillusioned about where his world was heading. He had long been convinced that the old values were being destroyed and that even the British government, of which he had once been so proud, was becoming more immoral and oppressive. Many of these beliefs had developed over the years as his SAS work, particularly in Northern Ireland, had shown him just how pragmatic those in power could be when it came to the use of dirty tricks to gain what they wanted. Any doubts he had about this had been cancelled out by the gradual breakdown and eventual suicide of Diane. Now, more than ever, he was convinced that Diane had been right all along and that there were those in the government who would stop at nothing to protect their own interests.

In a more general sense, the unprecedented 'blanket' censorship imposed by Margaret Thatcher over the reporting of the Falklands conflict had reminded him that even his own government was becoming ever more secretive. This in turn had convinced him that his Association must keep a close watch on what the British and other governments were doing behind closed doors, particularly when it came to the increasingly widespread suppression of individual freedoms, the growing sale of arms to repressive regimes for purely mercenary reasons, the broadening military support for 'secret science' to be used mostly to aid oppression, and, more personally, the enforced use of the SAS for tasks that were, to say the least, unsavoury, including thinly disguised police work and the training of security forces in communist or anti-democratic countries. Finally, when he heard on the grapevine that a few specially selected SAS officers and NCOs had been sent to Cambodia to 'advise' the disgraced Khmer Rouge, he decided that enough was enough and that something had to be done.

'We can't let the regiment be degraded that way,' he told Taff, 'and we can't stand by while scum like weapons manufacturers and arms dealers, or like those IRA bastards who pretend to be politicians, turn the streets of our cities into battlegrounds. So, if we have to neutralise a few of the swine, then I say let's do it.'

'Damned right,' Taff said.

With Taff's encouragement, he called together certain members of the Association – those who had previously expressed sympathy with his cause – to confess that he had been personally responsible for the assassination of Seagrove and felt that the Association should now engage in similar 'cleansing' exercises. Though most of the men present had previously agreed with him in principle while expressing doubts about the morality of taking the law into their own hands, the knowledge that he had committed the first cleansing operation finally swayed them in his favour. They were also swayed by his use of the euphemism 'cleansing' instead of 'assassination' or 'murder'. Indeed, the last word had never been mentioned in any conversation relating to the subject. The word 'cleansing', with its positive connotations, would leave them with clean hands.

As soon as he had received their backing, his deep depression, which he had often felt was rooted in feelings of impotence, lifted dramatically and he plunged into his work for the Association, which he could now do full-time, with renewed enthusiasm and vigour.

As the covert purpose of the Association, under the umbrella of Paddy's Vigilance International, was to find work for unemployed former SAS members, and as Paddy himself appeared to have lost his initial enthusiasm for it and, indeed, seemed in general much less energetic than he had been, Marty advanced on this side of the operation with all the energy and commitment that formerly he had given to the regiment. He did, however, also take it much farther than Paddy had done and, while Paddy increasingly withdrew from the business, turning up less and less, he quietly started finding work for members as military advisers and personal bodyguards for any government or individual with anti-communist and pro-democratic policies.

'To hell with the accusation that we're supplying mercenaries,' he told Taff who, also recently retired from the service, was keen to be used in any capacity in which his singular skills could be exploited. 'Without this particular kind of so-called mercenary, a lot of people would have no security at all. I don't care *what* Paddy says to the contrary. What we're doing is justified.'

'Paddy's out of it, anyway,' Taff responded. 'He hardly ever comes into the office any more – and when he *does* come in, he's usually depressed. He's also losing weight and seems lethargic. I think he may have problems.'

'What kind of problems? His health?'

'Either that or domestic.'

'Just keep your eye on him.'

Paddy, however, though not regaining his lost weight, came back to life when the media began writing about the recent series of assassinations of certain highly placed men, particularly weapons manufacturers, arms dealers and certain individuals either known or suspected to be involved in terrorist activities, both at home and abroad. As some of those assassinations had been carried out with the bombing of cars – as was the case with the assassination of Seagrove – and others with weapons firing nine-millimetre bullets, Paddy was convinced that they were being carried out by members of the Association. At first he kept quiet about it, merely passing the odd comment, but finally, after a particular assassination, he stormed into the office, looking surprisingly old and gaunt, but temporarily energised with rage.

'It's you, isn't it?' he said, waving a newspaper under Marty's nose, letting him see the lead story about the most recent assassination. A former IRA leader, widely believed by the authorities to be responsible for the purchase of arms from Colonel Gaddafi, had been found the day before lying beside the open door of his car in the long-term car park of Heathrow Airport, shot twice through the heart with nine-millimetre bullets, apparently just as he was about to get into his car after arriving on a shuttle flight from Belfast. 'If not you personally, then one of your damned Association members. Isn't that the truth, Marty?'

'No,' Marty lied, knowing that the latest cleansing operation had been carried out with cold efficiency by Taff. 'I know nothing about it.'

'I don't believe you, Marty. You wanted to do this kind of thing, you suggested it to me, and now you're actually doing it, using Vigilance International as a cover.'

'That's bullshit, Paddy. If you came into the office more, took a bit more interest, you'd know more about what's going on and stop getting these crazy ideas. The Association's finding work for its members and protecting the interests of the regiment, as originally agreed. That's all it does, believe me. Nothing else. The rest is all in your head.'

In fact, while some members of the Association did that and only that – work at administration and finding employment for retired comrades – others, such as Taff, were jumping at the chance to put their specialist skills to good use. These were men specially trained in demolitions, high-technology surveillance and, not to put too fine a point on it, the killing of their fellow man, and some of them had been at it so long that they could no longer imagine life without it. Though Taff was one of them, the most obvious example, he was certainly not alone and had plenty of back-up when it came to doing the dirty work. They had been doing it for some months, had neutralised half a dozen, when Paddy finally exploded in Marty's office – but Marty still denied it. He persisted with those denials for months, but Paddy never accepted them.

'I know it's you,' he insisted one day, sitting behind the desk in his own office, looking ravaged, clearly in failing health, though he refused to discuss this. 'I don't give a damn what you say. I know that you and the members of your Association are behind all those killings. Don't talk about *cleansing*, Marty. Don't cover it with euphemisms. You're running a private vigilante army and neutralising – murdering – a lot of people. An unsavoury lot, certainly, and few will weep for their loss, but you can't act as jury and hanging judge and expect me to support you.'

'It's not what—'

'Don't bullshit me, Marty. I'm not listening any more. I know what's going on and I think it's the very opposite to the highly moral crusade you clearly believe it to be. I'm not blind, Marty. Nor am I dumb. Though I haven't been coming in much lately – I've been too disgusted to do so – I've come in enough to check what's been going on and I happen to know that, apart from your so-called cleansing operations, you've been using the Association, under the umbrella of my company, to sell the services of SAS men to any despot who wants a private army. I think that's disgusting.'

'I don't do that,' Marty said. 'That isn't true at all. I only sell security advice and military training to any organisation or government that I deem worthy. I don't sell to communists, fascists or despots. That's absolute bullshit. I'm only doing what you taught me to do and I apply the same principles. I sell to the same kind of people you were making propaganda videos for. I sell to those whose political aims we share and I'm bloody careful about it.'

'No, you're not,' Paddy insisted. 'You were at first, but now you're being corrupted by the necessity to finance the Association – that and your blinkered puritanism. You're blind to your own faults.'

'What does that mean?'

'You *began* by selling our services only to those who shared our values, but recently, as I've given less attention to Vigilance International, with a subsequent fall in income, you've been forced, in order to keep the Association financially sound, to turn a blind eye to the true, long-term motives of those you're dealing with. They're no longer the people who share our political aims: they're just the people who're most keen to buy our services – *your* services – and who'll pay you to have them. You're now selling to the highest bidder, Marty, and that's all there is to it.'

'That's not true.'

'I'm afraid it is, Marty. It's reflected in your present lifestyle, which has, if I may say so, improved immeasurably these past few months. The Mercedes Benz, the fancy restaurants, now the search for a larger house . . . Why the hell do you need a larger house when you live all alone? You're living high on the hog, old friend.'

This could not be denied. The clients of the Association paid handsomely and promptly. Indeed, Marty had been surprised by just how much he was offered and, although he had poured a lot of the income into the Association, in the end there was more money than the Association could use and so he started to keep more for himself . . . then more . . . and more still. Now he was a man of considerable means and he saw nothing wrong with it. He was earning it, after all, by doing good, so he had no need for guilt.

'You've lived very nicely all your life,' he retorted, justifying himself, 'being blessed with a privileged background, a good education and inherited wealth. You were having a very good time, Paddy, with a nice home and fancy cars, when I was laying bricks for a living and didn't know champagne from white wine. Given that, I'm surprised that you should resent the recent improvement in *my* lifestyle. I work bloody hard for what I get and I take my few pleasures where I find them. You've had them all your damned life.'

'There's nothing more pitiful than working-class resentment of the middle classes – and I'm surprised that you, of all people, should suddenly display it. That, in itself, is a sign of how you've been corrupted. You didn't resent me before.'

'You probably just didn't notice.'

'If the resentment had been there, I'd have noticed, and it just wasn't there. You resent me now because I criticise what you're doing and you can't stand that. You think you're a man of principle – and indeed you once were – and the very suggestion that you may no longer be so makes your blood boil. This isn't an issue of class, Marty. It's a question of morals.'

'My blinkered puritanism.'

'Yes.'

'So where does that come into it?'

'Your so-called cleansing operations.' Paddy raised his right hand, begging Marty to be silent, cutting him short before he could issue another denial. 'In other words, your assassinations. You always had that moral streak, the need to separate good from evil, but somewhere along the line, probably when you were with Diane, you let it blind you to the possibility that you might sometimes be wrong. You became unyielding, perhaps even fanatical, and you started looking neither right nor left, but only to the front, following the rigid lines of your own reasoning and brooking no argument. You saw enemies everywhere, saw them getting away with murder, and so, in order to bring them to what you felt was justice, you turned into the very kind you most despised: those who believe that the end justifies the means, no matter what those means are. In other words, you became a common criminal –

and that's just what you are. The end *doesn't* always justify the means – and *your* means are criminal. I wash my hands of you, Marty.'

'You're wrong,' Marty said, feeling rage and fear at once, understanding, even as he denied it, that Paddy was right. 'But even if you were right – which you're not – how would you wash your hands of me?'

'By closing down Vigilance International and going into retirement. Which is just what I'm going to do.'

Though shocked to hear this, Marty tried not to show it. 'You're retiring?' he asked.

'Yes.'

'Because of the Association?'

'That amongst other things. I'm also tired. I have a few health problems. Angela complains that the business keeps me travelling all the time, that I'm rarely at home, that we never do anything together, that it's time for a change. She wants to move back to London – it's where she was born – and so we're selling the house in Hereford and moving into a smaller flat in Highgate. We'll live more modestly there.'

'Those reasons seem sound enough to me.'

'They're reason enough in themselves, but in the end it's you, Marty. I don't believe a word you say. I know damned well what you're up to. You and Taff, the born soldiers, the ones who can't live without war, have created your own little war to keep yourselves sane. You can't live in retirement, can't stand normal life, and so you've found a way to continue being soldiers and come up with a justification for it: the cleansing of corruption where you see it and bugger how you do it.

'Well, you go ahead, Marty, but do it without my help. I'm packing it in, closing Vigilance International, and, whatever you decide to do in the future, you'll have to do it without me. I won't be part of a vigilante group and that's all there is to it. I'm folding the company next month. After that, the Association is on its own. I won't wish you good luck.'

That's how their friendship ended, bringing joy to neither party, but when Paddy closed his company, sold his house, moved back to London, Marty used the connections he'd made over the past months to build up the business of the Association and rake in even more money. This did not take very long – the need for exceptional military skills was growing quickly, dramatically – and he buried in the rich soil of success any doubts that still nagged at him.

Within a year, he was dealing with anyone who would pay and justifying what he was doing by continuing his cleansing operations through the Association. A lot of those whom he deemed corrupt, or who threatened the regiment, or who were, in his view, politically dangerous, were neutralised with all the skill that the men of the Association had developed over the years fighting for their country. They were men who thrived on danger and needed excitement; men who said 'neutralise' instead of 'kill' and viewed the deed as a normal task. They were men who did what they had to do if they believed it was right. Marty knew that and used it. He became wealthy doing it.

Nevertheless, he was lonely. About eighteen months after Vigilance International was closed down and the Association took over the company premises, he moved out of Belsize Park and into St John's Wood, into a house that was too big for a single man. He was even lonelier there. Most of the rooms remained unused. The few that were used were occupied only by guests, most from the Middle East or the Third World, visiting him solely to discuss business before flying elsewhere. They expected bodyguards and Marty obliged, first hiring them temporarily for individual jobs. But eventually, deciding that he needed bodyguards for himself, he put a couple full-time on his payroll. Though he felt more secure with them, he also felt more like a prisoner. In the silence, he heard the creaking of his bones and understood what old age meant.

He was lonely and knew it. Most of his friends were dead and buried. His best friend, Paddy, was now an enemy; and Taff, who was neither friend nor enemy, could glide across the face of the sun and not cast a shadow. Of course, he had his children, but in truth he rarely saw them; he had loved them in his own, distracted way, but they had not been his life. The regiment was his life. His way of life was not normal

He was a man who had lived his life for war and now had no war to fight.

Yes, Paddy was right. He had created his own war. He had used the Association to fight a battle that could never be won. Now, he was tired. He felt neglected and lost. He was haunted by Paddy's accusations, wondering if they were true.

Were they true?

Yes, they were.

Marty knew this when his intelligence produced a list of names of people who were working on top-secret high-tech warfare systems that were being sold to various Third World countries and, in one reported instance, to the Khmer Rouge. Marty knew it when he decided to neutralise all those people – eleven in all – and personally helped Taff and other members of the Association to carry out the task. He knew it, too, when he found himself suggesting that since the numbers were so large and the victims so widespread, a wider variety of methods of neutralising them should be employed. This would encourage misinformation about the deaths and obscure the fact that one group was responsible for them. Some of the deaths had to look like assassinations – this would be a warning to the authorities – but others should look like suicides, thus causing confusion in the minds of the media and, ultimately, the public.

When the Association had voted in favour of this, the project had commenced.

The first victim was a former SAS signals expert, now working for Plessey on the System X digital communications project which was known to have defence connections. Marty and Taff took care of him by arranging a fatal car crash.

The second victim, a senior metallurgist working on an electronic warfare system for the Royal Military College of Science at Shrivenham in Oxfordshire, was found dead under his car in his closed garage, his mouth aligned with the car's exhaust pipe, after Marty and Taff had paid him a visit.

The third victim, also at the Royal Military College of Science, was blown up in his yacht when Marty and Taff, who had escorted him there at gunpoint, activated a button job and then fled the scene in a stolen SBS inflatable.

The fourth victim, employed by the Plessey Naval Systems at Addlestone, was electrocuted in a shed at his home, his teeth wrapped in electric wires plugged into the mains socket. As Marty and Taff knew, this was originally a form of torture, often leading to death, practised by the guerrillas of Malaya and Borneo. In using it to neutralise this scientist, he and Taff made the murder look like suicide.

The rest of the victims had all worked for Marconi on a wide variety of top-secret, defence-related projects that Marty believed would end up in the wrong hands. They therefore had to die and did so by a wide variety of methods, some of them deliberately bizarre. This confused those investigating the deaths and led to much speculation. No one knew if the deaths were suicide or murder, but the cases were closed.

Then Taff was killed.

Eleven scientists had died when Taff was found dead, shot cleanly through the heart with two nine-millimetre bullets as he was stepping out of his car to enter his bachelor apartment in Holland Park in London. No motive for the murder was ascertained, but Marty knew who had killed him.

A nine-Milly, he thought. Two bullets straight to the heart. A double tap by an expert.

When Taff was assassinated, Marty's world blew apart and he realised, in grief and despair, that he had been given a message. He took it to heart, let it tear away the veils, and accepted that he had let the Association take things too far. He decided to stop. He *wanted* to stop. He would stop when the most recent, the most important job of all, the final cleansing operation, was completed and he could call it a day. He would stop at that point and call Paddy and say, 'It's all over.' He would shake Paddy's hand and then embrace him and beg his forgiveness. They would be friends again.

Marty left his big house. He wanted to go out for a walk. He was feeling tired these days and he couldn't walk far, but he would walk along the pavement for a bit and then turn back again. He would breathe the fresh air.

He walked past his limousine, past his bodyguards, to the gate, and saw a grey-haired old man in a pinstripe suit, staring at him as he hurriedly advanced upon him. Marty recognised that face. It took him back through all the years. The old man, who had once been a wickedly charming young man, had green eyes that were losing their lustre but not their intelligence. He smiled tightly as he approached and that smile said it all. Marty recognised his friend and stepped forward and then he saw the gun.

It was a Browning nine-millimetre High Power handgun and it was pointing straight at him.

Marty knew, on the instant, that it was over, and it seemed right and fitting. He went back through all the years, seeing them flash before his eyes: his honeymoon night with Lesley in the Savoy hotel, making love as the bombs fell on London; the exotic streets of Cairo, the cherry brandy bints, Tiger Lil's and a night in the Union Jack and then out to the desert. Those innocent early years in the clean sands of North Africa, first with the LRDG, then with L Detachment, learning how to survive and fight an enemy that deserved your respect. Then the POW camps, escape and recapture, then back to Britain and the Territorial Army, and finally the SAS. Malaya and Borneo and Oman, taking pride in the work; then marrying Ann Lim, losing her and young Ian, learning what it was to suffer pain and cracking up for the first time.

After that, it could not be better. It could only be not so bad. Losing Ann Lim and the boy, he lost himself and never quite found his way back. Then Aden and the Yemen, where national pride was replaced with shame, then Northern Ireland and a final disillusionment with those in authority. It had all changed then. It was not what it had been. Innocent enthusiasm became soured professionalism and then rage and despair. The old order was crumbling. The world he wanted was disappearing. The values he had fought for had been lost and would never come back. Diane had taught him that. What she had feared had come to pass. The clean wars had been replaced with counter-revolutionary warfare and the dirty tricks of counter-terrorist work – the moral lines were all blurred there. Terrorists and hostages: who could tell the difference these days? The undiplomatic receptions on back lawns were a sign of the times: the victims trussed up like chickens.

Diane saw the changes coming. What she saw then changed her. She went mad, as he, Marty, had gone mad – and, like him, she paid the price. He went to the Falklands, broke the rules in order to fight, fought his piece and felt the brief resurrection of the pride he had lost. After that, it was all over. His life ended with retirement. He had tried to get it back through moral outrage and vengeance, the cleansing operations conducted by the Association, but that was no more than an escape from his feelings of loss. The loss of his childhood, his parents, his first wife; the lost of faith and pride; the loss of friends like Tone Williams and Bulldog Bellamy and TT; and, last but not least, the loss of the affection of Paddy Kearney, his hero and mentor, the best friend of all.

Paddy . . . Now standing right there in front of him, his face gaunt and wrinkled, his hair grey and thinning, his hands shaking as he raised the Nine-Milly in a single, quick movement to do what he had to do.

Marty knew, on the instant, that it was over, and it seemed right and fitting. He stepped forward, smiling, knowing what real friends were for, and automatically raised his right hand to shake Paddy's hand.

'Why not?' he said.

There were worse ways to die.

CHAPTER FORTY-FIVE

Paddy understood death. He knew all about it in its many manifestations and now that it was coming to himself he decided to help it along. He had known that it was coming, felt it growing in his soul, though in truth the tumour was growing in his head and gradually taking command of him. You always thought you could beat it, but in the end you never could. Even pain, which he had endured with such pride in the past, when he had been with the SAS, in the desert and in the jungle, finally became too much and overwhelmed you. When it did that, when you knew that it wouldn't stop, it was time to get out.

Paddy was going to join the Exit Club, taking his own life, making sure it didn't drag out, thus saving himself misery and increasing humiliation, preventing his family from having to watch him suffer, making it better for everyone. He was dying and nothing would stop the process and that was enough to know.

He would take his own life in the cleanest way he knew, but not before he had completed his final task by putting a stop to the rot. There was no turning back from this any more – and there was no going forward. It had to end right here and now.

He had begun the process with the shooting of Taff and even now he was struck by the realisation that Taff had died as he had always lived: without fear or doubt. He had seen Paddy coming at him, the Nine-Milly raised, and he had smiled and reached under his coat for his own hidden handgun, though he did it too late. When Paddy shot him, when the bullets pierced his heart, he died on the instant, his blue eyes, beneath the shock of blond hair, wide open and blind. He appeared to be still smiling, perhaps in mockery, when Paddy walked away from him. He lived and died as a mystery.

Don't we all? Paddy wondered.

Sitting in his rented Mercedes, in a street in St John's Wood, he studied that big house across the road, a wealthy man's house, secured with armed guards and surveillance cameras, marvelling that his pupil, that impulsive young man, had come so far only to lose his way and end up in the wrong place. He did not belong in that house, even though he could afford it; that house was not the place for a working-class lad who had lived his life by a code that placed honour above material success, achievement above its rewards, courage above all else.

The road to wisdom was rocky and not without suffering, but that young man, gaining wisdom through suffering, had then thrown it away. He had done so because everything he valued had been taken from him. The world had changed and he could not accept the changes and that had destroyed him. In retirement, faced with long, lonely days, bitter about the past and fearful for the future, he had turned his own values inside out to become someone else. The old Marty, that honourable young man, was still there inside him, but fearful, retreating. The new Marty, the puritanical avenger, had taken command.

Paddy had to stop him. He could not let this continue. Though Marty had denied everything, Paddy knew that the assassinations of the past year had all been his doing – if not personally, then certainly through his Association, using old friends like Taff.

It was truly bizarre, Paddy thought. Marty had his sense of honour, his unshakeable belief in justice, but he was too puritanical for his own good and in the end it had poisoned him. He thought he was doing right, cutting down those who were wrong, but in taking the law into his own hands he had placed himself beyond the pale, reinterpreting what he had learned through the regiment and perverting its truths. There was a thin borderline between the soldier and the criminal. Marty had stepped over that line and could never turn back. Now he could only go forward and so he had to be stopped. Paddy, who had taught Marty most of what he knew, who had been his friend and mentor, now felt obliged to stop him once and for all, just as he had recently stopped his friend, Taff, with two bullets through the heart.

A final double tap, he thought. It seems right and fitting.

He knew that Marty was planning something really big and he thought he knew what it was.

'She's the worst of all,' Marty had told him just before their disagreement. 'She presides over the most repressive government in British history and she's getting worse every bloody month. The Falklands war's a good example. It was practically blanket censorship. Only one or two journalists were given access – the ones toeing the party line. She also backed that bastard, Seagrove, had him knighted, sang his praises, ensured that him and other swine like him had a nice, easy ride. She won't tolerate criticism, surrounds herself with yes-men, and grows more arrogant with every passing year, more like a despot. Even worse, she's had the SAS training the Khmer Rouge, so God knows what she'll dream up for us next. Of all the people I'd really love to neutralise, she's first on my list. I just wish I could do it.'

'You can't, Marty. Forget it.'

'Some day . . .' Marty had said.

That was a long time ago, before the cleansings had begun, and although the Iron Lady hadn't been the first in line, she was almost certainly still on his hit list. Sooner or later, if not this year, then the next, he might even go for it. Paddy thought this was possible.

Glancing across the leafy streets at that grand mansion house with its spy cameras and armed guards, its long gleaming limousine with tinted-glass windows, he tried to imagine Marty inside, all alone, planning retribution for all the world's wrongs, either real or imagined. He had never once admitted his involvement, but Paddy knew it was he.

Sighing, checking his wristwatch, he wondered when Marty might appear and help him put an end to it.

Glancing down at the newspaper, he studied the front page again, not reading it in detail this time, merely scanning the long list of scientists who had been working on secret defence projects and died in mysterious circumstances. His gaze was drawn irresistibly to the article about the signals expert and former SAS man who had been picked up by two unknown men, left home with them, then died when his vehicle crashed through the central reservation of a bypass.

Marty and Taff, Paddy thought. But now Taff is no more.

When he studied the separate article about the British government's embarrassment over widespread revelations that it had been using the SAS to train the Khmer Rouge in Cambodia, he knew that Marty would be setting his sights high when he chose his next targets. He would go straight to the top.

Shaking his head in disgust, or possibly despair, Paddy put the newspaper down, then slid his right hand around his waist, automatically checking that his Browning nine-millimetre High Power handgun was still in the cross-draw position in its old Len Dixon holster. Satisfied, he gazed across the road, studying the front door of the house, realising with grim amusement that the Browning High Power was the most apt weapon to use for this job – for more reasons than one.

He also brooded on the fact that he was about to assassinate his best friend. This thought gave him pause.

Not for long, though. At that moment, Marty emerged from the house across the road and stepped into the driveway. He spoke to his armed guard. The man nodded and went inside. Obviously deciding that he could do without the guard, Marty walked past his gleaming limousine and headed for the front gate.

Paddy climbed out of his car. His bones ached and his head was hurting. He felt almost as old as Marty looked when he reached the front gate. Paddy hurried across the road. He had no time to waste. He stepped up onto the pavement as

Marty walked out through the gate and then turned towards him. Marty looked directly at him, recognised him, showed surprise, and Paddy felt himself smiling automatically until he remembered his purpose here. Marty, also smiling, kept walking towards him, raising his hand in welcome, and Paddy was washed in a great wave of love and grief that almost rendered him senseless.

Marty stopped and stared at him. He glanced down at Paddy's waist. Paddy whipped the Nine-Milly out, spread his legs in the classic stance, held the pistol in the two-handed grip and took aim all at once.

Marty saw what he was doing. He looked surprised, then he smiled again. He raised his hands in the air, as if releasing a white dove, then he shrugged and seemed to relax, perhaps even welcoming it.

'Why not?' he said.

Paddy fired a double tap, aiming at Marty's heart, and Marty crashed backwards into the railing and slumped to the pavement. Paddy didn't have to check: he knew that Marty was dead. Turning away, he hurried back to his rented car and climbed in and slammed the door. He glanced once across the road and saw that Marty hadn't moved. Reaching down for the button job in the glove compartment, he curled his fingers around it. His thumb rested on the button. He looked at Marty's slumped body. The light seemed to shimmer and expand around Marty as Paddy saw the real world for the last time, brilliantly illuminated and magically magnified, caught in an unforgettable instant that stretched out for ever.

He smiled and pressed his finger on the button job, thinking, *Who dares—*

GLOSSARY

agal	small Arab cap or band for holding a head-dress in place
ARU	Air Reconnaissance Unit
atap	a kind of jungle palm
BBE	Bizondere Bystand Eenheid
beasting	psychological trick of pleasantness followed by abuse, used by trainers
Bofors guns	light anti-aircraft guns
casevac	casualty evacuation (a casevac helicopter)
CCO	Clandestine Communist Organisation
changkol	a kind of hoe
chappal	Indian sandal
COBR	Cabinet Office Briefing Team
COMMCEN	communications centre
COPS	close-observation platoons
CQB	close-quarter battle
CT	communist terrorists (note: two CTs – see next)
CT	counter-terrorist
DPG	Diplomatic Protection Group
DPM	disruptive-pattern material
DS	directing staff (in exercises)
DZ	drop zone, a landing zone for parachutists
E and E	escape and evasion

exfiltration	surreptitious withdrawal of troops, spies etc., esp. from danger
Fincos	field-intelligence NCOs
FOB	forward operating base
Fred (a Fred)	a tout for MI5
futah	long-sleeved Arab robe
GEO	Spain's Grupo Especial de Operaciones
Gharries	horse-drawn carriages
Ghibili	a hot, dust-carrying wind
GIGN	Groupement d'Intervention de la Gendarmerie
GPMG	general-purpose machine-gun
green slime	nickname for members of the SAS Intelligence Corps
GSG-9	German border police anti-terrorist unit
HALO	high-altitude, low-opening, said of a certain kind of dangerous parachute jump
Int and Sy Group	Intelligence and Security Group
jarit	a meal of raw pork, rice and salt, left to putrefy buried in the ground in a bamboo shoot, favoured by the Dyaks of Borneo
Ju Stukas	German fighter planes
Keeni-Meeni	Swahili term used to describe movement of a snake in the grass, adopted by soldiers as a description of undercover work
kijang	a barking deer found in the jungle
Kremlin, the	nickname for the intelligence section of Regimental HQ
kukri	a machete
kunjia	Omani knife
LMG	light machine-gun
LRDG	Long Range Desert Group
LUPs	laying-up positions, dug out of the desert floor or earth, usually for sleeping in
LZ	landing zone
maroon machine	Parachute Regiment troops in Northern Ireland
Milos	military intelligence liaison officers
MIOs	military intelligence officers

MPI	mean point of impact, a term used by marksmen
MSR	main supply route
NITAT	Northern Ireland Training Advisory Team
NOCS	Italian Nucleo Operativo Centrale di Sicurezza
OP	observation post
padi	Malayan paddy-field
parang	large, heavy, Malayan knife also used as a weapon
PC	patrol commander
PIRA ASU	Provisional IRA active-service unit
PNGs	passive night-vision goggles
R and I	resistance to interrogation
RAOC	Royal Army Ordnance Corps
rattan	Malaysian climbing palm
REME	Royal Electrical and Mechanical Engineers
RTU	return to (original) unit, a form of punishment for failure or misdemeanour
RV	rendezvous point
samsu	a strong spirit made from rice
SARBEs	surface-to-air rescue beacons
SBS	Special Boat Section
seladang	wild ox or bison of Malaya
Senussi	Muslim fraternity founded in 1837
SF	security forces
shemagh	a type of shawl worn around the head by Arab peoples
souk	Arab market-place
tab	route march
TAOR	tactical area of responsibility
tapai	a rice wine favoured by the Dyaks of Borneo
ulu	Malayan jungle as known to the natives
yomping	a colloquial word for marching